"In *Elusive Dawn*, anything but elusive well-drawn character until the very last pa{

at is d by et go

MW00904133

"*The Summer Before the Storm* by Gabriele Wills is a beautifully written story that shows humanity from all walks of life - from the very wealthy to the poorest." – *Writer's Digest Magazine*

"Gabriele Wills is as enterprising in the book world as she is adept in story-telling. A tribute to both these qualities is the fact that Muskoka Chautauqua selected *The Summer Before the Storm*... for its esteemed 2010 Reading Circle List." – *J. Patrick Boyer, Q.C., Muskoka Magazine*

"*The Summer Before the Storm* is a richly detailed, complex novel - one that will stay with you long after you've turned the last page." - *The Book Chick – Jonita Fex*

"Just like *The Summer Before the Storm, Elusive Dawn* had me riveted from the beginning. Once again Gabriele Wills has done an almost superhuman amount of research and has managed to combine her knowledge into an incredibly readable book about the horrors of war." - *The Book Chick – Jonita Fex*

"*The Summer Before the Storm* and *Elusive Dawn* are not only well written, suspenseful, and enjoyable, but also historically accurate." - *Arthur Bishop, WWII pilot and author, son of Billy Bishop, VC, Britain's top WWI Ace*

"Gabriele Wills' novels... all share one thing: they provide one of the best portraits of a particular era and the region in which they are set.... Small wonder that her many readers have exclaimed about each novel by this wonderful writer, 'I just couldn't put it down.'" - *Dr. R.B. Fleming, historian and biographer*

"Both Muskoka Novels... are historical fiction at its best." - *Focus on Books – Gisela Kretzschmar*

"If you are a fan of *Downton Abbey*, you will love [the Muskoka Novels] series!" - *Teddy Rose, So Many Precious Books, So Little Time*

"The [*Summer Before the Storm*] is sweeping and epic in scale and feel with a marvelous grandeur of times past." -*BookNAround*

"There was never a moment in reading *Elusive Dawn* that I wasn't completely captivated with the story. I absolutely adore Gabriele Wills!" - *Peaceful Wishing*

"Ms. Wills is one of the most talented writers I have read in a long time." - *A Book Lover's Library*

"It has EVERYTHING I adore. Ms. Wills is such a great author that she has created characters that I cannot wait to continue with in the next volume." - *Bags, Books, & Bon Jovi*

"Gabriele Wills has once again combined impeccable research, actual events, and real people with a finely embroidered story, poignant and vividly detailed." - *The Eclectic Reader*

"When I came up for air, I was actually surprised to find myself in 2012 instead of 1914." – *Popcorn Reads*

"[Ms. Wills] truly brings history alive through her descriptions and her characters. I didn't want the story to end." - *Broken Teepee*

"Wills writes her characters in such a way that you literally feel like you're on this journey with them. The second book in this series is fantastic." - *To Read, or Not to Read*

"If you liked Downtown Abbey, you would love [*Under the Moon*].... Wills has become one of my very favourite writers and I am looking forward to reading her other books... I LOVED IT." – *Maria Duncalf-Barber, Counsellor, Educator and Writer*

"I enjoyed [*Under the Moon*] immensely.... Can't wait to see what happens next." – *M. Denise Costello*

"An exceptionally well-told story.... *A Place to Call Home* offers a delightful glimpse into Canada's past, told through characters who come to life and jump off the page." – *Writer's Digest Magazine*

"Once in a while a novel grabs the reader's attention from the opening pages to long after the final words have been savoured. Such is *A Place to Call Home*." - *Anne Forrest, NUACHT*

Lighting the Stars

Book 4 of "The Muskoka Novels"
by

Gabriele Wills

MIND
SHADOWS

Cover photos by Melanie Wills (except original Spitfire image, which is from a stock shot)
Cover design and photo composites by dubs & dash (www.D2-Group.com)

Library and Archives Canada Cataloguing in Publication

Title: Lighting the stars / by Gabriele Wills.
Names: Wills, Gabriele, 1951- author.
Description: First edition. | Series statement: Book 4 of "The Muskoka novels"
Identifiers: Canadiana 20200363050 | ISBN 9781775035411 (softcover)
Subjects: LCSH: World War, 1939-1945—Fiction.
Classification: LCC PS8595.I576 L54 2020 | DDC C813/.6—dc23

Comments are always appreciated at info@mindshadows.com

First Edition
Published by Mindshadows
Mindshadows.com
Printed and bound in Canada

Foreword

Many thanks to the following generous people for research and other help: (Alphabetically)

Anselmann Winery, Germany; Al Bacon (re: Little Norway and Lost Airmen in Muskoka); Andrea Baston (re: Little Norway); J. Patrick Boyer, Q.C.; Julie Borden Bullen and Chris Bullen; Sandra Bradley; Canadian Warplane Heritage Museum; Muriel Cluett; Marion and Cyril Fry (Gravenhurst Library Archives); Jeannette Gropp; Sandra Howes (re: Little Norway); Judy Humphries (Gravenhurst Library Archives); Gina Heinbockel-Bolik (National Air Force Museum of Canada); Dr. W. Allan King; Katherine Kurck; Jessica Lamirande (National Defence); Helen (née Stephen) Langevin; Laura Langevin; Marilas McInnis; Jane Naisbitt and others at the Military History Research Centre, Canadian War Museum; Emily Naish (Archivist, Salisbury Cathedral, U.K.); Jean Ogilvie (re: Irene Ogilvie, RCAF,WD photographer); Arthur Patterson (memoirs as a POW); The Rev. Fay Patterson; Isla Patterson (RCAF,WD); Cecil Porter (re: POW Camp 20, Gravenhurst); Captain Randy Potts (Sunset Cruises); Marjorie Reid (RCAF,WD); Cassandra Rodgers (5 Otter Literary); St. Ives Archives, U.K.; Munroe Scott; Mark Stirling (Muskoka Airport); Jan-Terje Studsvik Storaas (Royal Norwegian Embassy); Mary Storey (Muskoka Discovery Centre Archives); Vic and Laurie Tavaszi; Andrew Wagner-Chazalon.

Thanks once again to my friend Amitav Dash of "dubs & dash" for generously creating the stunning cover design, and for ongoing marketing ideas.

My deepest love and gratitude to my family for their unfailing support and encouragement. This book would not be as rich without the thoughtful, creative input from my daughter and editor, Melanie Wills. Once again, I'm delighted that her evocative photos grace the cover. My husband, John, as well as helping to edit, is my innovative e-guru - responsible for e-books, e-commerce, and e-marketing advice. Fur-baby Felix inspired a "character" in the novel. Thanks, team!

In loving memory of my German-Hungarian parents, Katie and Paul Tavaszi, and my American and British in-laws, Kay and Michael Wills, who lived through these life-changing times on different continents and sides of the battlelines.

Cast of Characters

(ages in 1940 or when we first encounter them, if relevant)

Sutcliffe Family: Hope Cottage: Gravenhurst:
Claire (Wyndham) Sutcliffe
Captain Colin Sutcliffe – her husband
Merilee Wyndham Sutcliffe – 16 - their daughter

Wilding Family: Gravenhurst:
Lois & Lorne Wilding – neighbours of the Sutcliffes
Peggy Wilding – 17 – their daughter
Ned Wilding – 18 – their son
Barry & Ken Wilding - their sons

Thornton Family:
Wyndwood Island:
Ria (Wyndham) Thornton – cousin of Claire, Jack, etc.
Air Marshal Chas Thornton – her husband
Drew Thornton –17 - their son
Charlie Thornton – 25 - their adopted son
Blackthorn Island:
Rafe Thornton – Chas's younger brother
Elyse Thornton – 20 - his daughter
London, England:
Lady Sidonie (Sid) Thornton – Rafe's ex-wife, Elyse's mother
Priory Manor, England:
Sophie (Thornton) Chadwick – 30 – Chas & Ria's adopted daughter
Philip Chadwick – her husband
Jason Chadwick – 5 - their son
Alayna Chadwick – 3- their daughter

Wyndham Family:
Thorncliff Island:
Jack Wyndham – Claire's brother
Fliss (Thornton) Wyndham – his wife, Chas & Rafe's sister
Sandy Wyndham – 20 – their son
Kate Wyndham – 18 - their daughter
Joe Wyndham – 14 – their son
Wyndwood Island:
Max Wyndham – cousin of Ria, Claire, Jack, etc.
Maxine Wyndham - 17 - his daughter
Gus and Dick Wyndham – his sons
Richard and Olivia – his parents

Cousin Phoebe (Wyndham) – Ria, Max, & Jack's cousin

Grayson Family: Wyndwood Island:
Grayson – Ria's butler/ estate manager
Mrs. Grayson – his wife – cook & housekeeper
Alastair Grayson – 20 - their son

Spencer Family: Wyndwood Island:
Zoë (Wyndham) Spencer – Max's twin sister
Freddie Spencer – Zoë's husband - architect

Seaford Family: Port Darling:
Esme (Wyndham) Seaford – Max & Zoë's sister, Claire's cousin
Stephen Seaford – her husband – boat builder
Adam Seaford – 14 – their son
Amy Seaford – 14 - Adam's twin
Jean – Stephen's sister – runs Pineridge Inn

Carrington Family: Red Rock Island:
Hugh Carrington – 21
Bryce Carrington – 18
Anthea Carrington – 17
Lady Antonia Carrington – their mother, Ria's friend

Roland Family: Ouhu Island:
Dr. Ellie Roland – friend of the Wyndhams & Thorntons
Professor Troy Roland – her husband
Ginnie Roland – 17 - eldest of their 3 daughters

British Evacuees: Wyndwood Island:
Vera Carmichael – 11
Bertie Carmichael – 9
William Baxter - 13
Jane Baxter -10
George Baxter – 8

Other friends and relatives in Canada:
Lieutenant Ross Tremayne – with the Royal Canadian Engineers
Deanna Tremayne – 13 - his sister
Gail Dennison – friend of Merilee & Peggy
Gord McLaughlin – friend of Merilee & Peggy
Rosemary Whitaker – Sandy Wyndham's girlfriend
Stella Talbot – RCAF WD – Merilee's colleague & friend

James and Helena Wyndham – Ria's father & stepmother
Lizzie (Wyndham) Delacourt – Jack & Claire's sister
Alain de Sauveterre – Lizzie's eldest son from her first marriage

POW Camp 20: Gravenhurst:
Oberleutnant Erich Leitner – 20 – Luftwaffe pilot
Leutnant Axel Fuchs – his roommate - pilot
Hauptmann Christoph von Altenberg – his roommate - pilot
Oberleutnant Wolf Sturm– his roommate – pilot
Oberleutnant Rudi Bachmeier – his roommate – pilot
Major Gerhardt Drechsler – his roommate – pilot
Helmut Geisler – Nazi leader in camp
Korvettenkapitän Hofmeister - 1st German Commandant (Lagerführer)
Oberstleutnant Benedikt Richter – 2nd German Lagerführer
Major Falkenrath – German Adjutant - 2nd in command
Colonel Winterbourne – Canadian Commandant of the camp

Erich Leitner's Family and Friends: Germany:
Gustav Leitner – Erich's brother – 24
Klara Leitner - Erich's sister – 15
Trudi Leitner– Erich's sister – 12
Karl Leitner – Erich's brother - 10
Angelika – Erich's girlfriend
Simona Forst – Erich's girlfriend in Karlsruhe

Little Norway: Gravenhurst:
Lars Pedersen – Norwegian pilot
Gunnar Svensen – Norwegian pilot
Ole Knutsen – Norwegian pilot
Karina – Ole's girlfriend in Norway

Stoneridge Farm: Ottawa Valley
Lloyd McKellar – farmer
Winnie McKellar – his wife
Scamp (Sally) McKellar – their daughter - 12 in 1943
Aileen McKellar – Sally's older sister

Britain:
Elyse and Sidonie Thornton's Friends:
Roz Fenwick – 21 – Elyse's ATA colleague & housemate
Flight Lieutenant Theo Beauchamp – 24
Lady Marguerite Beauchamp – Theo's mother & Sid's friend

Sir Algernon Beauchamp – Theo's father
Sara Beauchamp – 20 - Theo's sister
Jim – Theo's cousin
Alexandra, the Countess of Evesham – Bryce's aunt

Merilee Sutcliffe's Friends:
Eva Nilsson – 21 in 1944 – RCAF, WD - Merilee's flatmate
Mathias Nilsson - her eldest brother
Oskar Nilsson – 23 in 1944 - her older brother
Connie Fulton – 22 in 1944 – RCAF, WD - Merilee's flatmate
Irene Larkin – RCAF, WD - Merilee's colleague in London
Sam Oldershaw – RCAF pilot friend of Ned
Mrs. Travers– caretaker at Merilee's London flat

Real People: Alphabetically:
Diana Barnato – British socialite & ATA pilot
Woolf Barnato – her father
Lord Beaverbrook – press baron & friend of Winston Churchill
Air Marshal Billy Bishop – Canada & Britain's top Ace pilot in WWI
Margaret Bishop – his wife – granddaughter of Timothy Eaton
Arthur Bishop – their son
"Jackie" Bishop – their daughter
Winston Churchill – Prime Minister of Britain
Crown Prince Olav of Norway
Crown Princess Juliana of the Netherlands
Daphne du Maurier – British author
Lady Eaton – widow of Sir John Eaton (son of Timothy Eaton)
Margot Gore – Commanding Officer of the ATA Hamble ferry pool
Reichsmarschall Hermann Göring – Luftwaffe Commander
Pauline Gower – aviatrix, established the women's branch of the ATA
Matthew Halton – CBC war correspondent
Adolf Hitler – Nazi dictator of Germany
Snakehips Johnson – popular jazz band leader in the 1930s and '40s
Alison King – Ops Officer of the ATA Hamble ferry pool
Vincent Massey – Canadian High Commissioner to Britain
Alice Massey – his wife
William Lyon Mackenzie King – Prime Minister of Canada
Anna Neagle – British actress, wife of producer/director Herbert Wilcox

Arthur Patterson – father of the author's friend, Fay, whose Muskoka cottage inspired the novels

Beatrix Potter – British children's author

Colonel Ole Reistad – commander of Royal Norwegian Air Force in Canada

Field Marshall Rommel - Commander of the German Afrika Korps

Jack Stephen – bomber pilot officer, killed in action 1944

Andy Stephen – brother – Hurricane pilot - killed 1941

Helen Stephen (Langevin) – younger sister of Jack & Andy

Wing Officer Kathleen Walker – head of RCAF Women's Division in Britain

High Flight

By Pilot Officer John Gillespie Magee Jr.
Killed in Action Dec. 11, 1941, aged 19

Oh! I have slipped the surly bonds of Earth
And danced the skies on laughter-silvered wings;
Sunward I've climbed, and joined the tumbling mirth
of sun-split clouds - and done a hundred things
You have not dreamed of - wheeled and soared and swung
High in the sunlit silence. Hov'ring there,
I've chased the shouting wind along, and flung
My eager craft through footless halls of air....

Up, up the long, delirious, burning blue
I've topped the wind-swept heights with easy grace.
Where never lark, or even eagle flew -
And, while with silent, lifting mind I've trod
The high untrespassed sanctity of space,
Put out my hand and touched the face of God."

Muskoka: June 1940

Chapter 1

Merilee's eyes were drawn to the abandoned Sanatorium, scanning the many windowed bays for the ghosts that still lingered. Hundreds had died there, so how could the place not be haunted? Although she had grown up in its shadow, Merilee never ventured too close on her own, for she was sure she had glimpsed spectral faces or a passing wraith.

It had been different when the tuberculosis patients had shuffled about the extensive grounds, although then she hadn't been allowed near the place for fear of contagion. Her parents, who had both been ill and met here, knew how difficult it was to fight and win the battle to breathe.

But five years ago, this private San had closed, and the Muskoka Hospital for Consumptives just north of here had expanded. So the woods and cliffs had become her domain.

Merilee scrambled over the massive rock that undulated along the lakeshore, preferring to take the scenic route to her friend Peggy's house, which lay just beyond the San. She loved the sunbaked, pink-swirled granite with its frosting of green lichen. Shrubs and grasses and a few tenacious trees flourished in the pockets of soil; pines and slender, white-stemmed birches clung to the cracks in the sides of the cliffs.

From one of the lower ledges of the bluff, about thirty feet above the lake, she and Peggy relished launching themselves into the water – unbeknownst to their parents, of course. But it was early June, the lake still cool for swimming despite the heat. Only a distant, solitary canoe silently cleaved the calm water.

Merilee tucked herself into a rocky and shady alcove that was invisible except from the lake. She'd been amused when she discovered that her parents had met here secretly when they were patients.

"Romances were discouraged," her mother, Claire, had told her. "But it was one of the incentives that kept us sane and alive during our three years here." In fact, Colin had relapsed after Claire had been discharged, so she had married him and taken him home to Hope Cottage to nurse him herself.

A canary-yellow airplane precipitated out of the thin clouds with an almighty roar and swooped low over the lake. Merilee watched it climb into a steep loop and held her breath as it plummeted back towards earth. One of the boys training at Camp

Borden, no doubt. The Royal Canadian Air Force used the nearby Muskoka Airport to refuel. She breathed a sigh of relief when he leveled out just over the treetops, and stormed up the lake.

That was one of the few reminders that they were at war. She crinkled her brow with concern about her cousin Charlie Thornton, who'd been in England with the Royal Air Force since '34. And it worried her that his younger brother, Drew, was planning to join up as soon as he was old enough. He already had his private pilot's licence, and had taken Merilee and other cousins up for thrilling flights over the lakes.

But she shouldn't dawdle, since she'd promised Peggy that she would help her study for their French exam. Merilee's grandmother was French-Canadian, so Merilee was effortlessly fluent. She had also visited France, which was just another one of the things that made her different from the other kids in town. Some hadn't even been outside of Gravenhurst.

It was partly because they both felt like outcasts that Merilee and Peggy had become such close friends.

Merilee brushed dried pine needles from her skirt and headed toward the long, curved three-storey building that showed signs of neglect in the broken windows and sagging steps. She wouldn't go any closer than the overgrown gardens before veering off to the dirt road.

But she froze as she heard the creak of an unoiled door. Terrified yet mesmerized, she stared, afraid to look away from the building as if compelled to confront whatever monstrosity emerged from it. She bit her lips to stifle a scream as the front door opened.

Something growled behind her. Merilee shrieked and would have run if her legs hadn't turned to jelly.

A supportive hand took her by the elbow, and a kind voice said, "Sorry, Miss. Didn't mean to startle you."

On reflection, she realized that the "growl" had been "Pardon me".

The young officer regarded her with amused hazel eyes. Embarrassment burned her face.

"I expect there aren't many people who come here, except a few locals out to make mischief," he said astutely.

"Yes, although most are afraid of it," she stammered. "I live next door." She pointed south, toward the base of the bluff. "I rather think of this as my backyard."

"How delightful! But I'm afraid it won't be for much longer." In response to her quizzical look he added, "The military's taking it over. I'm with the Royal Engineers, and we're making preparations."

"Will it be a training camp?"

"Unfortunately not. I'm not at liberty to discuss this at the moment, but you'll find out soon enough." He looked at her sympathetically as he added, "Sorry to ruin your backyard."

An older, obviously high-ranking officer had stepped out of the building with a couple of Engineers, and stared expectantly at them.

Merilee's companion said, "Do excuse me, Miss."

"Sutcliffe," she added before realizing that he wasn't seeking her name. She flushed crimson again.

"Lieutenant Tremayne," he responded gallantly, giving her a warm smile. "A pleasure to meet you, Miss Sutcliffe. The Colonel appears anxious to hear my report about the grounds."

"Yes, of course. I expect I'm a trespasser now."

"Not yet. Enjoy your domain while you can."

The Colonel seemed to be glaring at her, so she moved briskly away, no longer scared, but excited to tell Peggy of her encounter with the deevie Lieutenant. She was surprised to see a convoy of military vehicles dusting along the normally deserted road and pulling up behind the old San. One of the men on the back of a truck wolf-whistled while another waved his cap gaily at her. She giggled and ran the short distance to the Wildings'.

Peggy's great-grandfather had cleared and tried to farm the free land granted to him in the 1860s, but amidst all the rock there was little soil that could sustain agriculture. So the old farmhouse was hemmed in by a small orchard, a large market garden, a patch of meadow for the cow, and a jumble of outbuildings, including a chicken coop and a workshop for Mr. Wilding's carpentry. The forest behind provided wood and maple syrup, which they boiled down and bottled each spring, selling most of it to tourists. The Wildings had long ago sold off the rocky waterfront acres to what had first been a hotel and during the last war had become the Sanatorium. Mr. Wilding had been employed there as the handyman, but when it closed during the Depression, he'd struggled to make ends meet with his woodworking skills. The Wildings were grateful when Merilee's extensive network of family and friends needed his services at their cottages, and indeed, kept him and his sons busy most summers.

Chipper, the golden Labrador retriever, greeted Merilee with wagging tail and expectant affection. When she had ruffled his head and scratched behind his ears, telling him what a lovely lad he was, he bounded off happily to the workshop behind the house. He trusted people, so he wasn't much of a watchdog, but he did keep the chickens safe from animal marauders, and enjoyed hunting with his masters.

Merilee was a welcome visitor at the Wildings' – a second daughter, Mrs. Wilding insisted - so she merely tapped on the side door and walked into the kitchen. Lois Wilding was baking something scrumptious; tangy nutmeg and cloves and mouthwatering cinnamon scented the warm air.

"Spice cake," Merilee ventured. "Yum!"

Lois smiled. She was a slim, energetic woman, always happiest when she was busy, especially in the kitchen. With three tall, hard-working sons, she maintained she spent most of her time keeping them fed. She had been one of the nurses at the San in its early days, which is how she'd met Mr. Wilding. "With rum-and-maple custard. Barry's favourite. You know he's leaving next week."

"So soon?" Merilee was sad to think that Barry was already the second son to enlist.

"Don't know how long I can keep Ned from joining up," Lois admitted. "He never liked being left behind."

Ned had just turned eighteen, and was the brother that sixteen-year-old Peggy was closest to. "How would Peggy manage without him?" Merilee asked with some alarm. Ned was like a big brother to her as well. He still took the girls fishing and boating, although Peggy could no longer go blueberry picking. She'd been crippled by polio during the epidemic in '37.

To avoid contagion, Merilee hadn't even been allowed to see Peggy then, and had spent that entire summer at various relatives' island cottages on Lake Rosseau.

"She'll manage, like we all will, if it comes to that," Lois said firmly. She didn't pamper or indulge Peggy, because she wanted her to be strong and independent, not consider herself a helpless invalid.

Ned was the one who helped Peggy struggle up the stairs and pushed her wheelchair down to the small sandy beach at the end of the road, where he and Merilee made sure that Peggy didn't drown. The aquatic exercises did help her regain the use of her right leg, although the left defied that as well massage, electro and physiotherapy, and was still encased in a brace. But Peggy swore that she would walk properly, even run again one day.

Merilee heard the piano stop, and said with a grin, "She senses I'm here. Wait until I tell her what I just found out!"

"Anything to do with the cars I heard driving down to the Sanatorium?"

"Yes, it's the army!"

Lois Wilding obviously hadn't expected that answer. She stopped stirring and looked up at Merilee. "What in God's name do *they* want here?"

"I don't know, but an officer told me that I should enjoy the grounds as long as I can. Not a camp, he said."

"Maybe a convalescent hospital," Lois speculated with interest. She had time to do some nursing again, especially now that two of her boys would be away from home. "Might give me some useful war work, not just rolling bandages for the Red Cross."

"I can hear everything you're saying, so stop jabbering with Mum and come in here!" Peggy called from the adjoining parlour. Merilee grinned and bounced from the room.

Peggy hobbled away from the piano. She was a talented player who readily got lost in her music. Merilee played the flute, and Ned, the fiddle, so they sometimes practiced together and gave small concerts to family and friends.

"So spill!" Peggy ordered.

When Merilee had finished, Peggy said, "Hm. Merilee Tremayne has a nice ring to it."

"Do stop!" Merilee giggled. It was an old game between them, because surely your husband's name needed to sound good with yours. But she was fifteen and wasn't even supposed to be thinking about boys yet, let alone a dashing officer who must be in his early twenties. "He probably considers me a little kid."

"I bet he gave you admiring glances." Peggy wondered how any man could not be enchanted by Merilee. With her sapphire eyes and pale complexion contrasted by glossy mahogany hair, she had a delicate beauty.

"It could be fun if soldiers are stationed here," Merilee admitted. She was concerned by Peggy's pallor and the purple crescents under her usually expressive amber-green eyes. It meant that she was in a lot of pain again. Peggy often pushed herself too hard to attempt to overcome her paralysis.

"You mean we might get invited to dances in the Mess?" Peggy snorted.

"On second thought, Mum would probably make me take the long way along Louise Street to get here, so that I don't see any soldiers," Merilee admitted.

There was a peremptory knock on the front door, which was unusual as most people came to the side door. "Merilee, could you? I have my hands full," Lois yelled from the kitchen.

Merilee opened the front door, which led onto a screened-in veranda where the Colonel and a couple of other officers were waiting.

"I'd like to speak with your father, young lady," the Colonel announced.

"Do come in, gentlemen," Merilee replied graciously, "and I will fetch Mr. Wilding. I'm just a guest here." She hesitated for a moment, but thought it best to show them into the parlour, even though Peggy was there. She would have to leave if necessary.

But Peggy was intrigued and made no move to go anywhere. "I'll entertain our guests until you fetch Father," she said. "I'm afraid Mother's tied up in the kitchen, but may I offer you some tea?"

"No thank you, Miss," the Colonel said, looking slightly uncomfortable as he noticed Peggy's withered, braced leg and the crutches propped beside her.

Merilee scampered out to the workshop, where Mr. Wilding, Barry, and Ned were building an oak refectory table. They followed her back to the house.

Merilee decided that she'd better wait in the kitchen, but edged her way out into the hallway so that she could eavesdrop when she heard Mr. Wilding say heatedly, "No, I will not consider renting you my home for the duration!"

She didn't catch the muffled response. Lorne Wilding grew even more indignant as he said, "I'm as patriotic as the next fella. One son's in the army and another's leaving this week. I was wounded in the last war, at Ypres, Colonel. "And still limped, Merilee thought. "We make our livelihood from this land, and I have my workshop here. Nope! It's impossible for us to move elsewhere."

Wiping her hands on her apron, Lois tiptoed up behind Merilee, who had sidled even closer to the parlour entrance. They heard someone say, "That's most unfortunate, Mr. Wilding, since that will put your family inside the boundaries of the camp. We have secured permission from the owner to all the property of the former Sanatorium, including the Director's house."

So they were evicting Matron Morrow, who had rented and turned the lavish lakeside house into a luxury tourist home when the San had closed. Even during the Depression there were people who could afford the time and money for a pampered vacation.

The Colonel stated, "You might change your mind when you find yourselves surrounded by Germans."

Merilee was thunderstruck. After a moment of shocked silence, Barry exploded. "Hell and damnation! Whose fool idea is it to send prisoners here? How will you keep them from escaping into the woods and the lake, and threatening the townspeople? You're putting our women at risk from those rapists! Jesus Christ!"

"The prisoners will be well guarded, Mr. Wilding. The citizens will have nothing to fear, and no contact with the POWs. Except for your family perhaps."

There was an expectant silence, but then Lorne Wilding said, "We'll just have to take that risk. No goddamn German's going to chase me off the land that my grandfather laboured to clear! What the hell did we fight for last time, and now again? Freedom, Colonel. Democratic rights. So I'll not allow the government to force me off my land either."

"I doubt it would come to that, Mr. Wilding," one of the other officers reassured him.

"Just be aware of what you're letting yourselves in for," the Colonel cautioned. "Louise St. will be the outer perimeter on the east side. You'll be behind the main gates as well."

Zowie! Merilee thought. She could hardly believe that her treasured "backyard" would be taken over by bloodthirsty Nazis. No wonder the Lieutenant had regarded her sympathetically. And Peggy would virtually be imprisoned with them!

An officer said, "I see by the sign on your truck that you're a master carpenter, Mr. Wilding. We have troops coming to erect fences and auxiliary buildings, but we could use some local tradesmen to begin repairs on the old Sanatorium. Are you interested?"

"I will do what I can to help, other than move, Major."

"Then perhaps you could come with me, and I'll show you what is required most urgently."

Merilee was ready to scarper back into the kitchen, but Lois Wilding stood her ground and put her hands firmly on Merilee's shoulders. The soldiers gave them only a cursory glance as they left, although the Major from the Royal Engineers nodded as he said, "Good day, ladies. And good luck."

When they had gone, Ned went to the cupboard under the stairs. Among the rubber boots and warm jackets were several hunting rifles. Pulling out a .22, he said, "I'm going to teach you girls to defend yourselves."

"I couldn't shoot someone!" Merilee protested.

"Oh, I think you could if you or your family were threatened."

•   •   •

Like giant mushrooms, tents sprouted between Hope Cottage and the San overnight. A cacophony of hammering and drilling and trucks rumbling to-and-fro violated the tranquility. Merilee was amazed at how quickly extra buildings, lofty guard towers, and tall chain-link fences topped with barbed wire sprang up.

She was most disturbed to see the prickly boom fence carving out a large swath of the bay, encompassing the rocky bluff right to the edge of her family's property as well as the beach on the north side where she and Peggy swam. Peggy would be livid.

Merilee watched as the Royal Engineers, by way of boats and barges, created the wicked-looking barrier.

She photographed this mutilation of her beloved domain and lake for posterity. Her mother's eldest sister, a renowned photographer, had recognized and encouraged her talent to capture a moment with a unique eye.

Despite the noise, Merilee heard the approaching footsteps this time before Lieutenant Tremayne spoke.

"I'm afraid we're spoiling your view as well, Miss Sutcliffe," he apologized.

"It looks rather terrifying," she admitted, the barbed wire rising several feet above the water. "But can't they swim underneath it?"

"The fence is anchored to the lake-bottom, so no. Besides, they'd have to break out of the main enclosure first." Which was the old San and some grounds surrounded by two rows of formidable fences with a guards' catwalk between, and a cascading mesh of barbed wire beyond.

"Oh good, so they won't be swimming then." She imagined paddling from her dock and seeing the hated Germans just a few feet away.

"That will depend upon the camp commandant, but I expect he'll allow them out on parole."

"Parole?"

"When officers give their word that they won't try to escape, they can be allowed out for walks or swims or whatever."

"But that's crazy! I mean…," she stammered, blushing.

He chuckled. "I know it sounds illogical, but the men need to exercise and be kept busy. We've laid out a tennis court and games field inside the prison enclosure, but that may not provide enough recreation space if the place is filled to capacity."

"But will they really not try to escape?" She was incredulous.

"Honour is a serious obligation."

"Even to the evil Nazis?"

"Let's hope so." He smiled warmly, "But please don't worry, Miss Sutcliffe. I think you will be quite safe here, even if any of them do escape. They'll be heading for the train station as quickly as possible."

"And go where?"

He chortled. "Precisely! It's a long and difficult journey back to Germany. Impossible if the Americans join the war."

"Will you be stationed here?" she asked hopefully. Although she had initially dismissed Peggy's teasing, the Lieutenant did set her heart aflutter. He surely wasn't all *that* old.

"A small core of Engineers will stay once we've finished constructing the guards' barracks and outbuildings, but I have no idea where I will be. Probably sent overseas," he added, looking wistfully at the lake.

"That's too unfair that you have to risk your life while the enemy will be enjoying a lakeside holiday!"

He smiled at her indignation. "Yes, it does rather seem that way. But I expect you have family and friends already involved in the war. None of us will escape duty, I'm afraid."

"I should like to do something useful, too. My mother's cousin drove an ambulance in France during the last war and won a couple of medals for bravery." That was just one of the things that Merilee admired about Drew's mother, Ria Thornton.

"Plucky lady! But hopefully the war will be over by the time you're old enough."

Merilee felt deflated. He did think of her as a child after all.

Looking at her astutely, he said, "There are lots of things you young ladies can do to help, other than put yourselves in danger."

"Like bake cookies for the troops?" she quipped.

He chuckled. "Well, we wouldn't turn them down. I have to admit that there are delectable smells wafting from that civilian house in the compound that you visit."

So he had noticed her going to Peggy's.

"The Engineers' barracks and Mess are being built next door, so we'll be constantly tantalized, I expect."

"Mrs. Wilding is the best baker around. She taught me and Peggy – that's her daughter."

"Is she the one who plays the piano so beautifully? Peggy, I mean."

"Oh yes. And we often play duets - me on the flute."

"So you could entertain homesick chaps with cakes and concerts."

Merilee laughed. "It would be our pleasure. Do drop by some time, Lieutenant Tremayne," she added saucily.

"I certainly will." His smile made her wilt just a little.

Eager to catch Peggy up on the latest news, Merilee rode her bicycle over. It was disturbing to see the gate that was being constructed across Peggy's road at the junction of Louise St. – a gate that she and the Wildings would have to pass through every time they came or went. The men grinned at Merilee and paused in their work while she passed, making her feel suddenly self-conscious. How would Peggy feel having the Engineers almost next door to the east, and the officers in the old Director's house to the west, beyond the large garden that had provided fresh vegetables for the San and then the tourist home? Perhaps more importantly, were the trees behind the San tall and dense enough to shield Peggy's house from view by the enemy within?

"They're taking over our beach?" Peggy fumed.

"It's not technically ours, dear," her mother reminded her, pummeling the bread dough more vigorously, nonetheless.

"More ours than the Germans'," Peggy grumbled. The San had allowed them to use the beach, as only the healthiest patients ever swam there. "Where will we swim now?"

"At my place," Merilee offered. Hope Cottage was perched at the base of the granite bluff, which sloped into the water, but there was also a small crescent of sandy beach beside the dock.

"And how will I get there? Ride my bicycle?"

"Sarcasm is unbecoming, dear. Merilee is trying to be helpful."

"And will be even more so when I teach her how to ride my motorcycle," Ned said, having come into the kitchen at the tail end of the conversation. He had built a cleverly engineered sidecar onto his bike so that he could easily transport Peggy to school and outings.

"What?" Merilee asked in shock. "Me, drive a motorcycle?"

Even his mother had stopped kneading to await the reply.

"Your father's been teaching you to drive the car. It's not that different."

"Baloney!"

"Are you telling me that you can't because you're a girl?" Ned challenged, his eyes sparkling mischievously.

Merilee's heroine, Ria, had not only driven ambulances in France, but had also flown those flimsy old matchstick airplanes when she was only nineteen. "Of course not! But... why don't you just drive Peggy over when she wants a swim?"

"Because I have *important* work to do. And besides, when I go off, someone has to be able to take Peggy places."

'Off' meaning to war, they all knew, and although Lois clenched her teeth, she said nothing.

"Come along, Private Sutcliffe. We might as well start lessons now."

"Who are *you*? The Sergeant?"

"That's right! And when you've mastered the bike, you'll be promoted to Corporal in charge of transport."

"I'm not missing this!" Peggy said, following them outside.

Merilee knew how much Ned treasured his ruby-red 1928 Indian Big Chief motorcycle. He had stumbled upon it, shrouded and neglected in an old shed while doing some work for a wealthy American cottager further up the lake. He hadn't dared hope that he could afford it, but it had belonged to the only son of the family, who had crashed his floatplane on the island in Port Darling in the '30s. His mourning parents hadn't had the heart to dispose of the bike until Ned had inquired about it. "Take it as payment if you want," the father had said dismissively. So it had become Ned's for just a week's work fixing the docks. Hardly used, the Indian had polished up beautifully, and Ned had babied it ever since. "Big Red", he called it.

He sensed her trepidation and said, "Don't worry. You can handle it, Merilee. And I won't kill you if you get a scratch or two on it."

"Thanks for the reassurance!" she shot back.

"First of all, get comfortable sitting on it. It's just a big bicycle."

"Baloney!"

He chuckled and helped her get a feel for the bike. "You have to be the boss, just like you are with that .22, Annie Oakley," he teased. Merilee had been as surprised as Ned and Peggy at how consistently she hit the bull's-eye in target practice.

Nervously, she tried to absorb everything he was telling her. But he was a patient teacher, and she was soon relaxed enough to go slowly down the laneway, with Ned jogging alongside, guiding and encouraging her.

After a couple of forays, applauded by Peggy, Ned declared that was enough for the first lesson. "Shorts aren't the best clothes for riding, so sturdy trousers. Once you have your licence, you can take Peggy further than your house. Although I have to warn you that you're not allowed to take this out of town or go faster than 30." He eyed her sternly.

"Yes, Sergeant, Sir!" Merilee replied, giving him a mock salute.

Watching them spar and laugh, Peggy dearly wished that Ned would marry Merilee, and then they could be real sisters. But Ned, even if he was enthralled with Merilee – which he wouldn't admit - felt she was too good for him. She was, after all, a Wyndham. Grandfather Wilding had laboured in one of the Wyndham lumber mills that once dominated Muskoka Bay, and Merilee's Uncle Jack was one of the most prominent and successful businessmen in Canada.

Peggy could never believe that Merilee's mother and her siblings, including Jack - disinherited by the powerful Wyndhams -

had actually grown up often hungry and cold in the slums of Toronto.

The third day of lessons had them travelling up and down the quiet and mostly unpopulated perimeter roads, Ned on his bicycle, and by the fourth day, Peggy was riding in the sidecar, which significantly changed the balance and dynamics of the vehicle. But Merilee felt mostly in control.

They were a cheerful crew as they returned to the farm. Merilee was pleasantly surprised to see Lieutenant Tremayne walking up the laneway carrying a couple of bags. "Well driven, Miss Sutcliffe!"

Ned seemed a bit surprised and then sullen when Merilee introduced the Engineer to her friends.

"I've heard that your mother is an excellent baker, so I have a request to make," Tremayne said.

They ushered him into the kitchen.

"Mrs. Wilding, I have a couple of pounds of butter, some cocoa, sugar, and flour here, and wondered if I could hire you to bake a large birthday cake for one of our chaps. He's turning twenty-one tomorrow and is far from home."

"I could bake a dozen cakes with this!" Lois said.

"One will do," Tremayne replied with a grin.

"As you wish. But there'll be no more talk of payment, Lieutenant," she said firmly, leaving no room for argument. "Will you take a cup of tea?"

"I'd be delighted."

Lois insisted they move into the parlour, but Tremayne said, "I find kitchens cheerful."

"You're missing home," Lois said shrewdly. "Which is where?"

"Kingston."

Merilee wondered if she was the only one to notice the dark shadow flit across his face.

"I've been enjoying your music, what I can hear of it between the sawing and hammering," he said to Peggy as the late afternoon sun streamed into the fragrant kitchen. "My mother tried to teach me piano, but I was a mediocre student. You have a great talent, I think."

Peggy was taken aback, but managed to say sardonically, "I play more because I walk less."

"So, you've aced the hand that you've been dealt. My little sister barely survived polio, but I'm afraid she hasn't found her way back. She's not even practicing her violin anymore, although she was exceptionally good." He looked at Peggy almost beseechingly.

She was suddenly alive to his interest and need. "If I can be of any help…"

"Perhaps. Yes. A pen pal might be helpful. Someone who understands."

"Of course! What's her name?"

"Deanna. She's thirteen. She was in an iron lung for three months, and can't walk at all. She was an accomplished equestrian as well, and had dreams of competing in the Olympics."

"She shouldn't give up on her dreams yet," Peggy stated unequivocally.

Tremayne smiled gratefully. "I'm Ross, by the way."

"What did you do before signing up, Ross?" Lois wanted to know, offering him another slice of spice cake, which was too delicious to refuse.

"I just finished my engineering degree."

"Do you have other siblings?"

Peggy shot her mother a don't-be-so-nosey look, which Lois ignored.

He hesitated, and then slowly said, "We had a sister who was halfway between Deanna and me. She died of meningitis when she was nine."

"Oh, how tragic," Lois said, placing her hand sympathetically over his. "Be optimistic, for Deanna's sake. It does helps."

"I do try," he said with a forced smile.

"We can never predict where life will take us. Merilee's parents were both incarcerated at this Sanatorium for years. I was a nurse, and it was heartbreaking that a third of our patients never went home again. But Merilee's mother is now a famous artist, and her father, a renowned writer."

Tremayne looked at Merilee quizzically. "Sutcliffe – good Lord, the 'Enchanted Waterfall' series?" When Merilee nodded, he continued, "We grew up with those books. And your mother did the fabulous illustrations?"

Merilee flushed with both pride and slight embarrassment at having the attention now focussed on her. Peggy tried not to look put out, since she also loved the classic children's books that Merilee's parents had created.

"Dad also writes history books," Merilee explained. But it was the continuous sales of the popular children's series that provided the comfortable income for the Sutcliffes. They had long ceased to rely on Uncle Jack's generosity.

"I took inspiration from Drusilla," Peggy admitted, referring to a character in the novels who was crippled by polio, but transformed into a nimble dragonfly as she and her friends solved mysteries.

"Which is what I reminded Deanna of," Tremayne said. "She'll be amazed when I tell her!"

He had visibly relaxed in their company, so when he seemed reluctant to depart, Lois said, "You must stop in whenever you need a break, Ross. The kitchen door is always open."

"Thank you, Mrs. Wilding. I would be delighted. But I would suggest that you start locking the doors when our *guests* move in. Just in case."

•   •   •

It was all very secretive, so no one knew when the POWs were supposed to arrive, but Merilee and her father, Colin, were downtown at the end of June when they did.

Hundreds of prisoners were being marched from the main train station, flanked by guards shouldering bayonet-tipped rifles. Locals going about their business lined the street, gawping in astonishment, many hissing and booing, a couple shouting out obscenities. Most of the Germans ignored the crowd; some chatted amongst themselves as if they were out for a pleasant stroll, others stared arrogantly ahead, and a few glared menacingly at the citizens. Someone started singing and soon they all joined in.

"Denn wir fahren gegen Engeland, Engeland!" The foreign words belted out lustily and accompanied by the rhythmic pounding of their marching seemed like an assault, although the threat against England was now just bravado.

Merilee reached for her father's hand, and he gave her a reassuring squeeze.

The prisoners walked tall and proud. She felt guilty for thinking that some of the young officers in their smart uniforms were rather handsome. She didn't want to admire the enemy.

When they had passed, she said to her father, "Most of them don't look like baby-killers." That was what the *Toronto Telegram* had called them.

"And most aren't. I know from the last war how propaganda misleads and plays on fears. But you also know that you can never judge people by their looks. I don't trust the Nazis – I mean the ones who are actually party members. They've been annihilating opposition and freedom of speech for years, killing their own people, which is truly frightening. Not all Germans are Nazis, as I've mentioned before. Some are just doing their duty the way our boys do, although I think they also have no choice. Try not to worry, sweetheart. I doubt that the prisoners will have much impact on us."

He couldn't have been more wrong.

Muskoka: Summer 1940
Chapter 2

Merilee was caught up in the holidaymakers' excitement at the Gravenhurst Wharf. Porters and harried husbands were hauling trunks and crates of supplies between the train, just arrived from Toronto, and the steamship. Mothers were wrangling boisterous children who were dashing about the bustling throng. One family, obviously staying for the summer, was anxious that their piano survive the journey intact. The steamer belched sooty smoke and her engines thrummed as if eager to race off.

Merilee was happy, as always, to be going to the ancestral island on the upper lake to spend time with her cousins. Since most of them lived in the city the rest of the year, Merilee tried to see them as much as possible in the summer. Now she scanned the crowd for Elyse Thornton, who would travel with her.

She wasn't surprised to finally spot Elyse strolling along languidly, chatting and laughing with a distinguished young man in a pilot's uniform. Elyse always turned heads, but there was something beyond her stunning beauty - the soulful green eyes and raven hair that curved voluptuously about her shoulders – that captivated people. Merilee thought she had star quality, and was surprised that twenty-year-old Elyse had not opted to put her formidable acting talents to use. She'd once aspired to be the next Greta Garbo, and take Hollywood by storm.

"Ah, here is Merilee." She introduced the Flight Lieutenant, saying, "He's from the RAF, here to train our flyboys." Turning back to him, she said, "Do enjoy your stay in Beaumaris, Lieutenant." She smiled and shook his hand.

"It's been a tremendous pleasure, Miss Thornton! Might I take the liberty of calling upon you?"

"Of course. Although you might find me difficult to track down."

"Wyndwood Island is etched into my memory. And should you prove elusive, I will ask your uncle. In fact, I should be delighted to meet Air Marshal Thornton. I greatly admired his legendary exploits in the last war." Chas Thornton had been Britain's top Ace for a while, and had a chest-full of medals, including a Victoria Cross. His younger brother, Rafe, was Elyse's father.

Although they all boarded the steamship, the Flight Lieutenant took the hint that he had been dismissed and reluctantly left them, but stayed within gawking range.

"You could keep talking to the bewitched pilot, and I'll amuse myself," Merilee offered.

"Hell no! He chatted me up for almost three hours on the train. One must leave men wanting more. Anyway, I haven't seen you in ages. You have to catch me up on all your news."

Although not blood relations, Merilee and Elyse shared an aunt and uncle, several cousins, and a lifetime of summer memories. Merilee's Uncle Jack was married to Chas and Rafe's sister.

The ship hooted throatily and pulled away from the wharf. Once it had rounded the rocky peninsula that sheltered the steamship harbour from the rest of Muskoka Bay, Merilee could see Hope Cottage, and waved enthusiastically in case her mother was watching from the veranda.

She was suddenly gripped with apprehension as her beloved home appeared to be overshadowed by the looming presence of the POW camp - a perspective more dramatic and sinister from the ship's deck than from a canoe, and hardly visible from the house itself. For a panicked moment she felt as if she were deserting her parents.

Her father, Colin, a lawyer by training and a lieutenant in the previous war, could read and speak some German, so he'd managed to secure an administrative job at the POW camp headquarters, thereby freeing up an able-bodied officer to more active duty. He'd jested that his job mostly consisted of making sure the Geneva Convention was followed, and dealing with complaints by the prisoners that it wasn't.

Now her mother would be alone at home all day, and vulnerable if any of the prisoners escaped. Was it really that difficult for them to evade detection when they were swimming, even if they were behind the menacing boom fence? Couldn't they clamber up one of the crevices on the rocky bluff, sneak into the woods, and slide between the two simple barbed wire strands of the perimeter fence that bordered her family's property? She wasn't convinced that Lieutenant Tremayne was right about the prisoners not trying to escape while out of the main enclosure on parole.

There were Germans diving from the rocks, while others played water polo. Armed guards wearing sun helmets stood about on the shore, looking hot and envious of their charges frolicking in the water.

"Some of those Germans are quite dishy," Elyse purred provocatively, leaning on the railing as if trying to get a closer look. "Lovely muscles. Skimpy swimsuits."

"Elyse!"

She laughed. "If they weren't the enemy, you'd agree with me. Anyway, they've been defanged and are quite harmless now."

"They make me nervous, being next door, even though there's a sentry post at the end of our lane and another almost in our back garden." There were tall guard towers on the cliff as well, and one across from Peggy's laneway, with machine guns mounted on top. Merilee did actually feel safer knowing how to use a rifle, but her mother had never handled one.

"You might catch an escapee some time. Wouldn't that be thrilling!"

Merilee had always been fascinated by Elyse. She seemed not to care what people thought of her, and was brazen and often unconventional - probably because of her unusual upbringing. Her mother, a British society beauty, had abandoned her family when Elyse was just six, and lived extravagantly on the Riviera, "with plenty of lovers", Uncle Jack's daughter, Kate, once confided to Merilee with malicious satisfaction.

Since Elyse's father, Rafe, had been preoccupied with his racehorses and subsequent wives, and had moved his equestrian enterprise to a farm thirty miles north of Toronto, Elyse lived primarily with his elder brother Chas's family. Merilee couldn't believe that Elyse's mother had not once written to her or cared to see her, so she felt terribly sorry for her.

Merilee began to relax as the camp slid away and they sailed toward a headland crowned by the Muskoka Hospital for Consumptives. The steamer tooted in greeting to patients waving from the distinctive gazebo, and also in warning as it approached The Narrows.

Once out in the broad expanse of Lake Muskoka, the girls went into the oak-panelled dining room for lunch.

"Mum told me that you flew Uncle Jack to Ottawa," Merilee said between bites of her chicken sandwich. Uncle Jack – who had also been an ace fighter pilot in the last war – owned a floatplane in order to get to business meetings more quickly from the cottage. So that Elyse could build up her hours and he could work en route, she would often fly him about.

"I had a ball in the capital! There are plenty of servicemen up there. I do so like men in uniform, don't you?" She grinned. "Uncle Jack is now a 'dollar-a-year' 'man, which means that the government is taking advantage of his formidable financial skills and paying him nothing. That's his contribution to the war effort."

When they were back on the promenade deck after their meal, Elyse offered Merilee a cigarette. Her parents didn't approve of smoking, so Merilee hesitated, but then boldly took it.

Gazing out at the expanse of shimmering lake, they watched water-skiers carving arcs across the frothy wake of powerful launches, canoes slipping effortlessly along the calm shore, sailboats catching a breeze – all the delightful and fleeting summer activities on the lake.

Elyse breathed out a long stream of smoke and admitted, "I'm going to miss this."

"Why? Where are you going?"

"To England. I was going to join the WAAFs," she said of the Women's Auxiliary Air Force, "but discovered that women pilots are being recruited by the Air Transport Auxiliary." She gave Merilee a conspiratorial smile. "As you know, Uncle Jack is an old friend of Lord Beaverbrook, who's in charge of aircraft production and is in Churchill's Cabinet. I still have to pass a flying test, but that will be a piece of cake. I've logged more than the 500 hours they require."

"You'll be flying airplanes? In the war?" Merilee gasped and choked on the unaccustomed smoke she had inadvertently inhaled.

"Just ferrying them from factories to bases. Not particularly dangerous, I should think."

"But how exciting!"

"I'll be happy to be close to Charlie and Sophie again." They were the French orphans that Ria and Chas Thornton had adopted during the last war, and the family that Elyse had grown up with. "And Drew threatens to enlist when he turns eighteen next year, so I can't be left behind!"

And feeling responsible that Charlie ran off to join the Air Force, Elyse had a mystery to solve. When she had pointed out a photo of a young Charlie looking remarkably like Drew at the same age, Charlie had gone livid and confronted Chas, and then stormed away. He never told her why, but there was obviously something secretive and possibly scandalous about his parentage.

"I'm also planning to see my mother," Elyse confided, looking out at the lake so that Merilee couldn't read her expression. "Uncle Jack convinced her to leave the Riviera in case the Germans invaded, so she's living in her London townhouse."

"Gosh!"

"I'm curious about her. I remember her being glamorous, but distant. Never a warm and cuddly mother like Aunt Ria's always been. I wonder if Milady is as shallow and empty as I've imagined." Confronting her mother was an old movie that had long played in Elyse's head.

Merilee didn't know what to say.

Elyse regained her vivacity as she turned to Merilee and said, "Will you write and catch me up on the latest news and gossip from the home front? We're cousins in spirit if not blood, don't you think?"

"Of course," Merilee replied, delighted that she would be privy to the details of Elyse's adventures.

"Smashing!"

The steamship dropped vacationers at cottages and resorts en route, gliding past picturesque islands with whimsical names and cozy cabins or astonishing mansions. As they were nearing Beaumaris, an area known as "Millionaires' Row", largely populated by Americans, Elyse took pity on the Flight Lieutenant, who was visiting distant and unknown relatives, by wishing him well before he disembarked at the government wharf.

He stood there beaming at Elyse as the ship departed.

"Seriously smitten," Merilee proclaimed.

"Poor chap," Elyse commiserated. "I'll be such a disappointment to him. Even if I weren't leaving next week."

Port Darling straddled the narrowest loop of the Indian River where it cascaded from the upper lake. The ships locked through here, but Merilee and Elyse disembarked, since one of the relatives would fetch them by launch for the fifteen-minute boat ride to the island.

Today it was the twins, Amy and Adam Seaford, in a Seawind runabout crafted by their father's boatworks here in Port Darling.

Merilee wasn't sure when she'd realized that their mother, Esme, had defied convention by marrying outside the Wyndhams' social class. Stephen Seaford had been a Thornton boatman – a servant, really - before Chas had bought into the Seaford brothers' boatworks and helped it to succeed with his championship race boats.

"Let's get ice cream before we head back," Amy said.

Busy shops lined the wharves above the locks on Chippewa Bay, including Mercer's Drugstore and Ice Cream Parlour, a favourite haunt. They sat in the mahogany launch as they licked their double cones.

The twins' lovely house was perched on a rocky cliff on the far sweep of the Bay, but they and their younger sister stayed with their grandparents on Wyndwood Island in the summers, sometimes overnight when their mother had busy days.

Esme was the administrative force behind the Spirit Bay Children's Retreat, which Chas and Ria had started twenty years ago. Funded by the Thornton Foundation, it had begun as a convalescent summer home for disadvantaged children, but during the past few years had become more of a rehabilitation facility for polio victims. It was run by Dr. Eleanor Roland – "Aunt" Ellie – who was not happy with the archaic methods of dealing with paralyzed children. Peggy had spent three weeks there in '38 and '39, and was booked in again next week.

But now that the twins were fourteen, things were changing. After this week with their Wyndham grandparents, Adam was to spend the rest of the summer working with his father, and Amy would be helping out at Pineridge Inn. Like so many of the hardscrabble settlers in Muskoka, the Seaford family had long ago turned their expanded farmhouse into a successful resort.

"I'm going to enjoy scooping ice cream at the Inn," she declared.

"You'll probably eat as much as you sell," Adam razzed. "And then you'll get as fat as a pig."

Amy stuck her tongue out at him. "You're lucky you don't have any horrid brothers," she said to Merilee and Elyse.

Adam kept glancing over at the boatworks along the quay as if he expected his father to come out and chastise him for idling his time away. He gobbled down his cone, and then zoomed toward the narrows into the lake.

They dropped Elyse at the south end of Wyndwood Island. The massive cottage at "The Point" had been the original Wyndham summer home, built by Merilee's great-grandfather over sixty years ago. Ria had inherited it from her grandmother, while her uncles and cousins had built their own cottages around the sixty-acre island.

The twins' grandparents owned the largest of the four cottages in Silver Bay, just a few minutes up the west side of the island. The others belonged to their children, so there were always plenty of people in the bay.

The twins were closest to Merilee, not only because they lived in Port Darling - and spent plenty of time visiting back and forth - but also because their mothers were best friends as well as first cousins. Merilee was not happy that Amy and Adam would be living with their grandparents in Toronto this year so they could attend private schools. The small school in Port Darling was deemed inadequate by the Wyndhams. When all her relatives returned to the city in September, Merilee would now be the only one left in Muskoka. Everything was suddenly changing.

While Adam went to a neighbouring cottage to find his cousins, Merilee and Amy swam and then bronzed themselves on the dock.

"A bunch of us are playing tennis at the Club tomorrow with the Carringtons," Amy said, giving Merilee a sly glance. "In case you need an excuse to see Bryce."

Merilee blushed and Amy giggled.

The Carringtons from nearby Red Rock Island were old and dear friends of the Wyndhams and Thorntons. Eighteen-year-old Bryce, as well as being swooningly handsome, was fun loving and adventuresome. Being so much younger, Merilee didn't think that he paid her any special attention. But she liked to daydream about him.

A German shepherd came bounding toward them, giving Merilee a quick sniff in greeting, and then running excitedly to the end of the dock, tail wagging. It was Drew's faithful companion, Zorro. He barked as Drew and Elyse canoed within hailing distance.

"Welcome back, Merilee," Drew said. "Can't come any closer, or Zorro will leap in." The dog did indeed seem to be gauging the distance in preparation to jumping into the canoe. "We're going to Thorncliff to see Granny.... Zorro, go home to Mum!" Drew commanded, but the dog yelped back in protest.

"Not very obedient, is he?" Amy chuckled.

"He was trained to look after Drew, and does his job too well," Elyse said.

"He'll go right to the north end of the island and wait there until he sees us heading back," Drew explained. Thorncliff Island was just a quarter mile north of Wyndwood.

"You'll have to rethink the idea of going off to war, Drew. It would break Zorro's heart if you left," Elyse said melodramatically.

"You've been conniving with Mum!" Drew accused, splashing her with his paddle. She splashed him back, and a furious battle began.

"You've ruined my hairdo, brute!" Elyse complained.

"You've soaked my trousers," Drew retorted.

"It's too hot anyway. How about a swim?"

They laughed as they deliberately tipped the canoe. Zorro leapt into the water and paddled up to them. Merilee and Amy dove in as well.

"We can't visit Granny like this," Elyse said after more watery hijinks. "I think my blouse is see-through now."

Amy brought towels from the change house and deposited them at the edge of the dock where the water was shoulder deep. Elyse grabbed one and draped it around herself.

She and Drew looked sorely bedraggled as they sloshed their way along the shoreline path back to The Point. They returned just a short while later, smartly dressed and ready to get back into their canoe. Elyse had wrapped her wet hair in a turban, pinned with an exquisite butterfly brooch, its gold-laced wings studded with sapphires and diamonds. It was one of the many magnificent pieces of jewellery that her mother had left behind, not wanting anything that Rafe had given her – except a sizable chunk of his fortune.

"Do you want to come to Thorncliff, Merilee? I should have asked you earlier," Drew said.

Their mutual cousin, Jack's daughter Kate, who was eighteen, felt she was *so* much older and more sophisticated than Merilee, and they had little in common. "Not today, thanks. Kate probably has lots of city friends up anyway."

Elyse raised a sardonic eyebrow, a la Garbo. Merilee knew she got on even less well with Kate, who had never wanted to share her toys or parents. Now that Elyse was flying Uncle Jack around, Kate was jealous that her father spent time alone with Elyse when he had so little for his own children.

"We'll give everyone your regards," Elyse offered.

"Yes, please!" Merilee replied with a grin.

"Damn! Zorro got away from Mum again," Drew said, seeing the dog tearing down the path. "Paddle like hell, Elyse."

Kate hated dogs, which was why Zorro was never allowed to visit Thorncliff.

Merilee was surprised when Peggy telephoned her at teatime and said, "Could you ask your Aunt Esme if I can give up my place at the Retreat to Deanna Tremayne? She sounds terribly dejected, so I think she really needs to be somewhere where she won't feel so isolated, and where she'll get proper help."

"Are you sure, Peggy? What about you?"

"I know the routine. Mum gives me daily massages. I can manage."

"That's awfully nice of you!"

"Baloney! I need to remind myself that others are worse off, so that I don't wallow in self-pity," she said sardonically.

The twins' mother, Esme, arrived at her parents' cottage tired and grateful for dinner that she didn't have to prepare. Her husband, Stephen, showed up just in time to partake.

When the maid had deposited the roast lamb on the table and left the dining room, Adam said, "A bunch of the guys are going on a canoe trip down the Moon River to Georgian Bay next week. Drew says it's a rite-of-passage for us Wyndhams, and he'll lead the expedition. So I won't be able to start working next week," he added, looking down at the minted peas he was chasing around his plate.

"There will be excursions going on all summer that I expect you'd like to take part in, but you have obligations," Stephen said firmly.

Esme looked sympathetically at her pouting son.

"I don't see why I have to work while everyone else just gets to have fun!" Adam exploded.

"We're doing important war work." The Seafords had secured a good contract with the Navy to build lifeboats and 26-foot minesweepers and had to ramp up production. "Grant and Roy have been working summers for years," Stephen said, referring to his brother's sons.

"They *want* to! And they're not Wyndhams!"

"We've already discussed this," Stephen warned.

"No we haven't! You just declared that I had to work. I don't want to build boats, not now or ever!" But Merilee remembered how much he'd enjoyed tinkering with the engines and helping out in the wood-scented shop when he was younger. When it had been novel, and a matter of pride to be allowed into the adult male sanctum.

"What *do* you want to do?" Grandmother Olivia asked gently, trying to defuse the building tension.

"Fly airplanes."

"Then it will be good to have more familiarity with engines," Stephen said.

"I already know enough about them!"

"There's merit in boys participating in these rites. Much like a job, it gives them experience in being self-reliant as well as co-operative, with comrades in arms, so to speak. That Moon River trip was certainly one I will never forget," Grandfather Richard said. Ignoring his daughter's pleading *stay out of this* look, he went on. "Social skills and sportsmanship are every bit as important in building character and preparing children for the future as are hands-on skills. Why not let Adam ease into working? He's only fourteen."

Stephen clenched his teeth, and Esme said, with an air of finality, "It's something that we can certainly consider."

"Well, I'm looking forward to working at Pineridge," Amy bragged.

"You'll just be playing there, as usual," Adam said dismissively.

"No, I won't! Aunt Jean is going to teach me how to run the place, so that I can take over from her someday. And she's going to pay me!"

Merilee had recently overheard Esme tell Claire that Stephen wasn't at all happy about the twins attending private schools in the city. "He thinks they're already becoming spoiled. Of course, he doesn't have more than his grade 8, so I suspect he's afraid that the children will look down on him from their lofty private school perches. But we all went there, and I don't consider myself a snob."

Sensing it was a good time to change the subject, Merilee mentioned Peggy's request.

"Is Deanna a charity case?" Esme asked.

"No. Her father's a university professor. But because she lives in Kingston, she's too far away to become one of Aunt Ellie's private patients. Peggy said that she's in a very bad state, and not getting the help she needs. Surely that's just as critical. I expect the Tremaynes would be happy to pay."

Esme was thoughtful. "Leave it with me."

When Esme and Stephen had departed in their separate boats, Amy said to Adam, "They're going to have an argument when they get home, and it's all your fault!"

"Well, I hope Mum wins!" Adam snapped, and then stomped off to visit his cousins.

"I hate it when my parents argue about what's best for us," Amy confided to Merilee. They were wading in the warm, shallow water of Silver Bay, the pale sand hard-packed and ridged. They weren't allowed to wear shorts to dinner, so they hiked their cotton dresses up over their knees.

"Do they often?"

"More so these days. Of course, they don't in front of us, but sometimes we can't help overhearing. And we can tell when they're mad at each other."

Merilee loved them both dearly, so she was distressed to hear this.

"It doesn't help that Adam no longer wants anything to do with the boatworks, as if it's beneath him," Amy said astutely.

"But Uncle Chas owns half."

"I know! But he's a 'silent' partner. Doesn't get his hands greasy. And Drew has never worked there. He gets to do whatever he wants, including fly airplanes. Adam just wants to be a Wyndham."

"I can understand that."

"So can I. But it hurts Dad."

Merilee wondered if there was a solution that would satisfy everyone.

While they were having their bedtime cocoa, Esme called to say goodnight to her children, and then asked for Merilee.

"We'll take Deanna. But I've spoken with Ria, and she said that you and Peggy can stay at The Point, and you may use one of the runabouts to chauffeur her to the Retreat every day for treatments. How does that sound?"

"Oh, that's wonderful! Thank you, Aunt Esme!"

When Merilee was off the phone, Amy asked a pensive Adam, "Well, what did Mum say?"

"That I have to earn my time off this summer by working hard from 6:30 to 1:00 Monday to Saturday. But I can go on the trip next week and will have all my afternoons off to play tennis and golf and stuff!" He grinned widely.

"While I slave away every day at the Inn," Amy said.

"Play, you mean."

She stuck her tongue out at him.

Things were back to normal.

•   •   •

The Summer Residents' Association – SRA - Golf and Country Club sprawled between Pineridge Inn and The Spirit Bay Children's Retreat on the mainland. The Wyndhams had been founding members of the SRA in the last century, and Chas had been Commodore through the 1920s. Uncle Jack was the current President.

Taking a break from tennis, Merilee and the others were savouring iced lemonade on the flagstone terrace overlooking the small harbour and docks lined with gleaming mahogany launches. A bright yellow airplane roared overhead, interrupting their conversation.

"A Harvard!" Drew exclaimed, his eyes gleaming. "That's what I want to be doing!" Zorro barked, either protesting the noise or Drew's sentiment.

"Why are they always flying over?" Amy asked petulantly.

"They're from the advanced training school at Camp Borden," Drew informed her. "It's not that far south."

"Why can't they just fly over the bush and stop disturbing us?"

"I expect they enjoy seeing what lazy people are doing. Maybe thumbing their noses at us a bit," Elyse said. The plane skimmed over distant Wyndwood and then regained altitude.

"Pretending they're dropping bombs on the boaters," Adam joked. "That's what I want to do!"

"Drop bombs on boaters?" Elyse teased.

"On Germans!"

Anthea Carrington said, "I told my parents that you're going to fly airplanes for the war effort, Elyse, and Mum absolutely forbade me to think about flying, or driving ambulances, or whatever when I'm old enough. So it was OK for her and Aunt Ria, but not for me? We'll see about that! You know Hugh's leaving soon, joining the Air Force," she added, throwing her eldest brother a regretful look.

"Why are you interrupting your law studies?" Elyse asked him. "I'm sure guys are flocking to enlist so they can learn to fly. You could wait and see if you're needed."

"I have no desire to fly," Hugh admitted. "But Uncle Chas said they need plenty of ground crews, like wireless operators." The older generation amongst the family and friends were honorary "Aunts" and "Uncles" - which caused plenty of confusion for newcomers - but Chas and Ria were Hugh's Godparents.

"I could do that! And if they won't let me, then I'll chauffeur Generals or make bombs," sixteen-year-old Anthea announced.

"You'd probably blow up the factory," Bryce teased his sister.

"And what will you do?" she challenged.

"Dad says I have to get my Senior Matriculation first, so that I can get right into university when the war's over. So next summer I'm joining the RCAF to be a pilot. It's swankier than the other forces."

"You mean that the Air Force uniform attracts more girls," his brother, Hugh, jested.

"If it has wings. Being a knight of the skies surely sets one apart from mere grounded mortals like you," Bryce countered with a grin.

"I hope the war isn't over before I'm old enough to join," Adam said.

"That's selfish!" Amy reproached. "We don't want the war dragging on for four more years!"

Looking abashed, he stammered, "I didn't mean it like that. Just that Dad will probably never let me fly otherwise."

"It took me ages to persuade my Dad," Drew said. "Luckily for me, Elyse wore him down, too."

"But flying is only fun when others aren't trying to shoot you out of the sky," Elyse pointed out.

Amy cried, "Oh my God, that plane is coming right at us!" as the yellow Harvard seemed to be rocketing toward them.

"Just someone being a daredevil or an idiot," Drew said dismissively. "Dad says that chaps can be court-martialed for low flying." But there was no engine noise as the plane descended ever lower and closer. "Bloody hell! He's going to crash!"

They were awed as it whooshed uncannily silently overhead, just clearing the hydro lines that stretched from the access road to the clubhouse. They jumped up to watch it spiral toward the golf course, obviously looking for a spot to land. There were shrieks from people on the tennis courts, while golfers scattered on the greens. The friends ran toward the Harvard as it smacked down on the second hole, bounced, and swerved sharply to avoid a line of trees and rocks.

After a moment, the pilot slid back the canopy and scrambled out.

"Well flown!" Drew said as they reached him.

Zorro jumped excitedly up on the pilot, who rubbed the dog's head affectionately. He removed his goggles and helmet, and grinned at them. "Hi all! Just thought I'd drop in for a visit."

"Alastair! Bloody hell!" Drew exclaimed. "Glad to see you in one piece. I thought you were done for!"

"So did I! The engine conked out over Mortimer's Island. There's not a lot of flat terrain around here, as you know. Thought about ditching her in the lake, but I wasn't high enough to bail out."

Alastair Grayson was the son of Ria's butler – now "Estate Manager". Even when she a child, Ria had been closer to Grayson than her own bitter father, so she had taken Alastair under her wing. She and Chas were his Godparents and treated him as part of the family.

"That was a superb forced landing," Elyse said. Alastair was a few months older than she, and easy to get along with. There was a quiet dignity about him, and maturity beyond his years. "Uncle Chas will be proud of you. But I bet you could use a drink now."

"Damn right! I'd better call in to the base first, so they can come and fetch me and this traitorous machine."

"We'll take you to Wyndwood in the meantime," Drew said. "It'll be hours before they get here."

"I look forward to climbing out of this suffocating gear and having a swim!" Already he was stripping off his parachute pack.

First, he went into the Country Club office to apologize for the new hazard on the course.

Alastair's parents were surprised and delighted to see him, but alarmed at the circumstances, although Alastair downplayed the danger.

After a refreshing swim, he was sipping cocktails on the veranda with the others.

"You should have seen him land on the golf course," Adam told Ria and Chas. "It was wizard!"

"I'm relieved to hear that," Ria said. "But it shouldn't have been necessary in the first place."

"We need more mechanics," Chas said. "Hell, we have too few of everything except students at this point – airfields, planes, instructors, ground crews, even cooks."

When war had seemed imminent, Chas had offered his services to the RCAF and been made an Air Marshal, along with his old friend, Billy Bishop, who was in charge of recruiting. Chas was helping to organize the British Commonwealth Air Training Plan throughout Canada.

"Then you should consider forming a women's auxiliary, like Britain's WAAFs," Ria suggested.

"You're quite right, my darling. I expect we will."

"I could help."

"I doubt you'll have the time once your evacuees arrive." Turning to Alastair before Ria could protest, Chas said, "I will be there to pin on your wings when you graduate. There should be no issue about you getting a commission, since you have your engineering degree. And you kept your head today. That will stand you in good stead as well."

"Doesn't every pilot become an officer?" Adam asked.

"They would if it were up to me," Chas replied. "But Britain sees things differently. Officers should be brilliant leaders, gentlemen of good character..."

"You mean with important connections or blue blood," Ria intervened.

Chas smirked. "We're more generous and grant the top third a commission. But it bothers me that the rest become sergeants when they end up doing exactly the same job. Imagine how awkward it is for a sergeant-pilot if his observer is an officer who must be saluted and called 'Sir'. Bad for morale, in my opinion, especially when the officers get fifty percent more pay as well."

To Drew he said, "So if you're not going to attend university, you'd better ace your courses when you enlist. And I don't mean flying, but things like navigation, wireless, meteorology, and so on."

"You mean Drew won't be a shoo-in because he's a Thornton?" Elyse quipped.

"I expect he'll have to prove himself even more, so that it doesn't seem like nepotism."

"Point taken, Dad," Drew said. To Alastair he drawled, "Did you *have* to do quite so well? You're making my life difficult."

"I'll give you pointers." Alastair grinned.

"You're on!"

Grayson, who had been hovering on the fringe, found the opportunity to say to his son, "Your mother's prepared an early supper for you."

"Wonderful! I've missed Mum's cooking, although Air Force food isn't bad. Our British instructors think they're in heaven after experiencing the rationing over there."

"Sophie looks forward to the care packages we send," Ria said of her adopted daughter. "But I do wish she would see reason and come home for the duration." Sophie and her British husband had two young children.

Chas gave her hand a reassuring squeeze. "Priory Manor is not close to any military targets, as you know, my darling. Which is why Sophie has a houseful of friends and their kids."

"But if the Germans invade…"

"We'll ensure they won't, even if it means my getting back into a plane." He winked. "We know Charlie appreciates having Sophie there, and I'm sure Elyse and Alastair and other family and friends will as well."

"Certainly!" Elyse said. "And I'm not averse to shooting down Germans if necessary."

"Dear God!" Ria said. "Now I have to worry about you as well."

"Admit you want to come along, Aunt Ria," Elyse teased.

Ria laughed. "Of course I do!"

Merilee took her camera along when they returned to the Country Club. She photographed Alastair in front of the Harvard, and then with Elyse and Drew, who perched on the wings, hamming it up. Elyse climbed into the cockpit and spread her arms out triumphantly. Merilee snapped away until an RCAF mechanic arrived and said, "Down you get, Amelia Earhart. No joyrides today."

"So I noticed," Elyse replied drolly. "I wanted to get a sense of it so that I could tell LAC Grayson how it compares with the Spitfires I'll be flying in England." She raised an eyebrow mischievously to the others, while the mechanic exploded in laughter.

"Pardon me, Miss, but you do have a wicked sense of humour!" He shook his head as he tried to stop chortling.

As they bade farewell to Alastair, he said to Elyse, "Take care flying those Spitfires."

She grinned and gave him a quick hug. "I'll see you in England."

"I'll look forward to that."

As they walked away, Elyse started singing the popular tune "Wish Me Luck as You Wave Me Goodbye".

"They'll never let you fly Spitfires," Drew said dismissively.

"We'll see about that!"

"Well they *shouldn't* let you fly them. You'd probably get deliberately 'lost' and end up in France battling Messerschmitts."

Elyse grinned. "You're just jealous that I get to fly in this war before you do."

"Damn right!"

Merilee was amused to see that the British Flight Lieutenant did indeed find his way to Wyndwood and became even more besotted by Elyse during the week. She agreed to stay in touch, and he vowed he would see her in England as soon as he could get sent home.

To Merilee, she said, "War is not a good time to forge long-term relationships. Too much potential for heartbreak. And guard yourself well from those cocky young men who just want a fling before going off to pursue heroics." She smirked, adding, "And thus ends my big sister lecture."

Muskoka: Summer 1940
Chapter 3

"Sometimes I'm convinced that you're just an imaginary friend," Peggy said to Merilee as they sat on the deck of the boathouse at The Point that was all theirs for three weeks. "Who else but you has famous parents *and* a cousin who's a composer of music I learned in piano lessons?"

"You might be interested to know who once slept in this boathouse," Merilee said with a grin. "The Prince of Wales before he became Edward VIII and gave up his crown for the woman he loved."

"Holy cow! You're not kidding, are you."

"Uncle Chas knew him at Oxford, and bragged about Muskoka. The Prince came to Canada incognito sometimes to visit his ranch in Alberta, so he stopped here once, and there was a big ball in his honour at Thorncliff. People still talk about it. I can show you pictures when we go up to the Old Cottage."

"You see, I *have* gone through the looking glass with Alice."

Merilee laughed.

Peggy shook her head in disbelief. "And are you serious that THE Max Wyndham wants to hear me play? I've been haunted by his music since I first heard it."

"And you play it exceptionally well. Not many do."

"That's because I can feel and understand the pain behind it."

Merilee was surprised. "Mum did say that Uncle Max was severely shell-shocked in the last war."

"That explains it. Jeepers, I can't tell you how excited I am!" Peggy felt as if she had indeed entered a magical world where all things were possible. She loved this fabulous boathouse, which had two spacious bedrooms, a bathroom with a walk-in shower that she could easily access, a sitting room with windows wrapped around two sides and French doors opening onto a deck large enough for a party. There was even a slide from this second level into shoulder-deep water. It was all framed by stunning views of rocky islands and lapped with serenity they didn't have at home in Muskoka Bay, with its constant boat and whistle-blasting steamship traffic. "Dare I say that this is even better than staying at the Retreat?"

"Aunt Ellie calls it Karma – when something you do reflects consequences back on you."

"Well I'm so glad that Deanna was able to take up my offer."

Deanna had arrived earlier in the day with her mother, who had managed to get a room at the Pineridge Inn, just a ten-minute walk from the Retreat on the other side of the Country Club.

They were both so grateful to Peggy, who instantly bonded with Deanna. "She seems so frail, don't you think, Merilee? Like she's had the stuffing knocked out of her."

Of course, Peggy understood the excruciating pain, the fear when creeping paralysis took command of your body, the humiliation of being as helpless as an infant, the anxiety about whether you would ever walk or be "normal" again. But at least she had never lost the ability to breathe and been kept alive by an iron lung, as Deanna had. The kids in her hospital ward had been terrified of being entombed in those metal monsters.

"I expect she has! But you and Aunt Ellie will soon put her to rights."

"Dr. Ellie says I'm a good role model," Peggy admitted with a grin. "So, tell me who I'm going to meet this evening, other than your Uncle Max. And why did I never realize that he was your Aunt Esme's brother?"

Because they lived nearby, Peggy had met Amy and Adam and their family several times.

Merilee shrugged. "Anyway, you're only going to meet the rest of the Silver Bay relatives this evening, so there'll be about twenty of us."

"Jeepers!"

"Are you nervous?"

"As hell!"

"They're all really nice, so don't worry."

"Of course they are. But such a lot of nice people can scare the daylights out of me."

Merilee laughed. "Let's go up before they arrive, and I'll give you a tour of the house."

She guided Peggy down the steps to the dock, where an inclinator - an enclosed platform that crawled up rails - took them up the slope to the house. "This is so cool! Was it put in for your Uncle Chas?" Peggy was impressed that Chas, whose shattered knee from a war injury, managed so well with his disability, still playing tennis and even driving a car once again, now that he had one without a clutch.

"He hardly uses it. It's mostly for taking luggage and supplies up."

"How many miles long is this veranda?" Peggy asked when they reached the top. They were at the spot where the broad veranda, which encircled the house, segregated the kitchen wing. With servants' quarters above, that alone was nearly as big as her house, which would fit at least four times into the rest of the cottage.

"Are there ghosts?" she asked as they wandered down the dim hallway. The walls and ceilings were panelled with pale basswood, and the fragrance of the old wood somehow suggested spirits lingering.

"Oh yes. Cousin Phoebe sees my great-grandmother, who was quite a character, I've been told. An old tyrant." Who had disowned Merilee's grandfather, Alex, because he had married beneath him - a 'showgirl'. Merilee couldn't associate that word with her respectable grandmother, now married to a doctor. Alex, an aspiring but unsuccessful artist, had died of TB when Claire was just a child, and the family had been destitute. It was all because of Jack's shrewdness and hard work that they had come so far.

"Be careful she doesn't hear you say that!"

Merilee laughed. "I've never felt afraid here."

But Peggy was glad they were staying in the boathouse. Maybe you had to grow up in big spaces to feel comfortable in them. Her own bedroom was probably the size of a closet here, but safely cozy.

They glanced into the billiard room, dining room, and library, everything gleaming with rich wood, plush furniture, sparkling glass, and polished silver. Walls of French doors opened onto the veranda from each room.

The entire front of the cottage was a ballroom-sized sitting room anchored by two massive granite fireplaces, the mantelpieces bristling with trophies won in various Regatta races. Like a hotel lounge, there were groupings of deep armchairs and comfy sofas, glossy tables ready for cards and other games, and a grand piano almost lost in one corner.

"Holy cow, it's a Steinway!" Peggy exclaimed.

Paintings on the walls included several by Claire and Jack, who, as well as being an Ace, had been a renowned war artist commissioned by Lord Beaverbrook.

"Here's a photo of Uncle Chas and Aunt Ria with the Prince," Merilee pointed out. "Sophie's dancing with him in this one. She was only thirteen, but allowed to go to the ball. And here he is on the deck of the boathouse." Cocktail glass in hand, the Prince eyed the photographer with a satisfied smirk.

"Wow!" *Pinch yourself, Peggy Wilding*, she kept saying silently.

Peggy was wearing her very best summer dress, but felt shabby as they joined Ria and Chas, who were having drinks on the front veranda. Ria was one of the most beautiful and elegant women Peggy had every seen. Fit and with the fresh, sun-kissed complexion of someone who relished time outdoors, Ria looked younger than her forty-four years.

Although Merilee had warned her, Peggy was still slightly shocked by Chas. He must have been devastatingly handsome before the left side of his face had been scarred by flames when his plane was shot down in the last war.

"Have you settled into your digs?" Ria asked.

"Oh, yes. They're splendid!" Peggy enthused. "Thank you for your kind hospitality, Mrs. Thornton."

"Not at all. But I insist you call me Aunt Ria. Mrs. Thornton is my mother-in-law," she added with a captivating smile. She and Chas weren't Merilee's real aunt and uncle either, since Ria and Claire were first cousins. "There's a telephone connection to the house, so you must call up to Grayson if you want anything. Guests seem to prefer being right on the water, and they make it sound so delightful that I think Chas and I might have to move in there."

Peggy was momentarily speechless when Drew joined them. She hoped that her jaw hadn't dropped at his astonishing looks. He had his mother's mesmerizing turquoise eyes and the blonde beauty of both his parents.

"Merilee has told us so much about you that I think I have the advantage," he said with a disarming smile. Zorro, at his side, gave Peggy a sniff of approval.

She was saved from conjuring a witty rejoinder as they heard the chatter and clatter of guests coming along the veranda well before they appeared. Introductions were made, Peggy wide-eyed with awe at meeting Max.

But he didn't turn out to be at all what she'd expected. Instead of a serious, tortured soul, he was witty and lighthearted. She wondered if all his war-born demons were channeled into his compelling music.

Drew and the boys were leaving on their Moon River jaunt in the morning, so they were discussing final preparations over dinner.

"Remember when you took us much younger chaps on that trip, Chas?" Max asked.

"*Much* younger? You make me sound ancient," Chas riposted.

"You were nineteen, and just back from your first snobby year at Oxford." To the others Max said, "We had to bring him down a few pegs, so we hid his trousers one night, and when Chas discovered they were gone, he didn't even bat an eyelash. He just packed up his gear and was prepared to start out on the day's journey in just his underwear and a shirt that barely covered his derriere."

They laughed, although many had heard the story before.

"Don't get any ideas!" Drew warned his cousins.

"How long will you be away?" Merilee asked. Adam had told her that the trip was over seventy miles long, with challenging rapids and twenty-odd portages – some involved carrying the canoes a mile or more.

"Five days, maybe six. Depends on what interesting things we encounter en route," Drew replied.

"Capsizing and soaking your matches and sleeping bags, which will never dry out, bears stealing your food…" Max said.

"You do have to be careful of bears," Ria advised. "Keep all your food supplies in one canoe and well away from your tents."

"Yes, Mum. Dad's already drilled us on that," Drew said with a reassuring smile. "I'm sure this trip won't be any more dangerous than driving ambulances during air raids," he reminded her.

She grinned. "As my son, you're supposed to do as I say, not as I do."

"Yes, Mummy dear. Anyway, Zorro will look after us."

Ria hid the sudden sharp fear that gripped her and then clawed through her veins leaving her limp and shaken. How long would it be before these children, fearless and eager for adventure, would be risking their lives in the war? If this one lasted as long as the last one, most of them would be old enough. Dear God!

Max's eldest son, Dick, said, "Wish I could go with you guys, but I'm heading off this week to join the Signals."

"Not the Air Force, like just about everyone else?" Chas asked.

"Drew took me up for a flight once, and that was enough for me!" Dick replied.

"Hey! I was easy on you," Drew countered with a grin.

"I'm amazed at how many boys think flying's the greatest thing on earth," Chas said. "But then they find that the reality is far from the dream. Some lose their lunch and others lose their nerve. I heard about one chap recently who was up for his first solo flight, after doing well in dual training, and just couldn't land the plane. He kept circling around the aerodrome, making at least thirty attempts to bring her down, but always pulling up at the last minute. He finally flew up to 3,000 feet and bailed out with his parachute, leaving the plane to crash in a farm field."

"Good God!" Max said. "I would have thought jumping was worse than landing the damn thing."

"It was a waste of a fine Tiger Moth." Chas said.

"So, is this chap a complete washout?" Drew asked.

"He'll be reassigned to gunnery or navigation, since he at least has the stomach for flying."

"Now that the army's been pushed out of France, do you think this war will be won in the air? Churchill alluded to that," Max said.

The Allies' devastating defeat and massive retreat from Dunkirk was still fresh in everyone's mind. Hitler had consumed much of Europe, and now seemed poised to conquer Britain.

"It's what our Prime Minister's been thinking all along," Chas said. "Nobody wants to sacrifice the manpower we did in the last war. That's why Mackenzie King is such a staunch supporter of the Air Training Plan, and Britain agreed that it could be our major contribution to the war. Right now, we're keeping most of our graduates as teachers, not sending them overseas to fight just yet."

"That's not fair, Dad!" Drew complained. "That's why we sign up!"

"Idealistically. Realistically, it's greatly to your benefit to log many more hours of non-combat flying time. That gives you a much better chance of survival. Grayson will be happy to know that Alastair shows such leadership ability and calmness under pressure that he will make an excellent and valuable instructor."

Grayson, who was serving wine, allowed himself a relieved smile.

"I'll make sure I do neither," Drew grumbled.

"Then you may well end up just flying students about for gunnery and navigation practice. Tedious as hell. Don't try to outsmart the system. We know all the tricks."

"No one should go eagerly or naively off to war," Max said seriously, his face suddenly grey. "Having to kill someone and watching your pals dying haunts you forever."

"At the Wings ceremonies, I tell the boys that they're making a vital contribution whatever job they're assigned to, whether here or overseas. And joining up should never be a quest for personal glory."

"Says the man who has every medal possible," Drew pointed out.

"Only because I did my job well while trying to stay alive. I'm not exactly a poster boy for war, am I?"

"Which is why Bishop does the recruiting, and you bring the boys back down to earth from their dreams of glory," Ria said.

"Quite right, my darling," Chas replied with a chuckle. "So remember, chaps, we have plenty of important non-flying jobs that need smart and capable boys like you."

"You need smart and capable women as well," Ria reminded him.

"We might well be forced to go that route," Chas jested.

Peggy felt awkward being served by a butler and maid, and nervous that she would somehow make a faux pas. The dining table had room for them all, and was laid with dishes bearing the Wyndham crest, engraved silverware, cut crystal glasses, and tall candelabra.

Overwhelmed by being in the company of this illustrious family, she barely tasted the delectable roast beef dinner. She appreciated that they tried to make her feel like one of them. Her bad leg was cramping more than usual, probably because she was so tense, so she needed to breathe deeply and relax, or she would never be able to play.

"The kids irreverently call me Uncle Adagio, so they obviously don't take me seriously. You mustn't either, Peggy. Just enjoy playing for us, if you will," Max encouraged as she sat stiffly at the piano.

And she did. One of his compositions - a poignant, sometimes turbulent, and technically challenging piece in a minor chord.

There was a moment of silence when she finished, and then tremendous applause.

"Bravo!" Max said. "Well done, indeed."

"You are very talented, dear," Great-Aunt Olivia agreed.

Peggy glowed.

"I hope you're planning a music career," Max said. "You must certainly attend the Conservatory in Toronto."

"I would love to! But I don't know if I can..." She almost said "afford it", which she realized at the last second would be gauche in this company.

But Merilee anticipated that, and saved Peggy embarrassment by saying, "Yes, of course you can. We'll go to the city together, and I'll be at the university, so we can support each other."

Olivia said, "Richard and I have established a scholarship to the Conservatory. I think you have an excellent chance of winning it, Peggy, when you're ready to go."

"Absolutely!" Max agreed.

"Wow!"

"And if you have time while you're here, would you like me to give you a few pointers?" Max asked.

"That would be wonderful!"

"Now it's time for *you* to play for your supper," Ria teased Max.

Peggy was spellbound and humbled by his command of the instrument. She could never play like that. But she would sure try!

After exhibiting his formidable prowess with one of his own pieces, Max slipped into a jazzy and brilliant rendition of Cole Porter's "Let's Misbehave".

"Now you have to play our Wyndwood song for Peggy, and we'll all sing it," Maxine said to her father.

There were a few good-natured groans from some of the others, but everyone joined in.

Oh, Wyndwood, fairest isle,
You everyone beguile,
With ancient rocks and stately trees,
Silv'ry sand and balmy breeze,
Fiery sunset, misty morn,
Moonlit water, heaven-born,
Stars a-sparkling and a-shooting,
Steamships passing and a-tooting,
Secret hideouts in the glade,
Laughing loons that serenade,
Lapping water, distant isles,
Spiffing views for miles and miles,
Charming homes, perhaps with ghosts,
And the world's most welcome hosts!
Our souls' delight, dear Wyndwood,
You make us feel SO good!

Max finished with a dramatic flourish, and Zorro howled on cue to laughter and Peggy's applause.

"We kids wrote that a few years ago at one of our cousins' parties," Merilee explained to Peggy. "And Uncle Max obliged us by composing the tune."

"It's super!" Peggy had heard about the annual party at The Point when dozens of young cousins got together. She suddenly envied Merilee this large and enchanting family.

"Time for Racing Demons," Drew declared. "I hope that Merilee has taught you, Peggy. It's a Wyndham tradition."

"Oh, yes!" She was glad to fit in by knowing the lively card game that soon had the young people engaged in hilarious battle.

The maid brought in hot cocoa and buttered tea biscuits with jam as the evening wound down, and Peggy, suddenly hungry, ate appreciatively.

"Why do you kids call him Uncle Adagio?" Peggy asked when she and Merilee were back in the boathouse.

"Because he talks to us like we're notes on a staff. When he wants to hurry us along, he'll say briskly 'presto' or 'vivace', and if we're too noisy we get a very soft 'pianissimo'."

Peggy laughed. "Your relatives are wonderful! But I never realized how hoity-toity you are."

"I am not!"

"OK, privileged then."

"Get over it, Peggy. I'm the same person you knew yesterday."

But not in Peggy's mind.

• • •

Besides the massage, heat treatments, exercise, and physiotherapy Peggy and the others received at the Spirit Bay Children's Retreat, there were plenty of things to keep them happily occupied. Crafts, board games, art and music lessons, evening bonfires, and boat trips around the lake were interspersed with time to rest on a chaise lounge on the veranda. But Peggy felt she didn't need the latter when she could spend time at Wyndwood instead, where she could continue her own water exercises, and practice on the grand piano. She was thrilled that Max spent time with her every few days, honing her talent. She had long surpassed the skills of her own music teacher.

So while Peggy was having her morning treatments, Merilee played tennis with cousins and friends at the Country Club next door, and lent a hand at the Retreat by reading to the younger patients and helping them write letters home. She also tried to spend time with Deanna Tremayne.

They and Peggy were talking on the veranda when Ross suddenly appeared at the end of the first week. Deanna's elfin features lit with a tremendous smile.

"I managed to wrangle a car and a couple of hours off," he said as he pulled her up into a big hug. "How's my Deedee?"

"Oh, Ross, it's so wonderful here! Just look at the lake and the islands! And Mummy comes over in the afternoons and plays piano for our singsongs."

"It really is spectacular here," he agreed.

"And isn't it just like the books, Ross? I've heard a loon. I'm sure it's Lewis! And I've got a copy of *The Mystery of Spirit Bay*, signed by Merilee's parents!"

Ever since Colin and Claire had published the first of the "Enchanted Waterfall" series, Ria had arranged for every child at the Retreat to have a signed copy of that book to take home. Although the stories were obviously inspired by the Children's Retreat, few people knew that the stream that trickled down the rocky hillside was where it all started.

"I'm going to let you in on a secret," Merilee said. "But you mustn't tell anyone else, or it will lose its magic."

"Of course!" Deanna said happily.

"We're going to go for a little walk."

Ross pushed Deanna's chair as far as he could along a dirt path that led into a shady glade, but then had to carry her up a short slope to the where the brook tumbled over a shelf of rock. He sat her down on a granite outcropping.

Ferns fringed the shore, and the clear, shallow water invited you to throw off your shoes and wade in.

"Mum painted this when she was eighteen," Merilee explained. "See what looks like a little cave behind the waterfall? When Mum spent long months forced to lie quietly in bed at the TB Sanatorium, she sometimes wasn't even allowed to read. So she conjured up imaginary worlds, and painted them when she was better. This is where Faith, the fairy, was born." The four heroes were endowed by Faith with the power to transform into their animal soul mates - like Lewis into a loon.

The others were impressed. "Look! There's Drusilla!" Deanna exclaimed excitedly as an iridescent dragonfly hovered nearby.

"So it is!" Ross agreed, delighted to see his sister so animated.

Back at the Retreat, Deanna had so much to show and tell him that Merilee and Peggy left them alone until Deanna was scheduled to go for physiotherapy. Ross promised to visit whenever he could.

"Thank you for that gift, Merilee," he said when she had gone. "You and Peggy have been an inspiration to Deanna. And we can't tell you how grateful we are to you for arranging this, Peggy."

"Thanks to Merilee's connections, it's worked out perfectly," Peggy replied.

"Well, I can already see a positive change in Deanna. She even taken up the violin again."

"So now you can worry a little less," Peggy said astutely.

He chuckled and looked at her appreciatively.

"Karma," Merilee said to Peggy when he had excused himself to go and lunch with his mother at the Pineridge Inn.

"What do you mean?"

"You'll see."

•   •   •

Life on Wyndwood was even more fun when the boys returned from their camping expedition. In the evenings, cousins and island friends gravitated to The Point for raucous games and card tournaments, singsongs around the bonfire, and impromptu dances – which Peggy watched enviously – and they taught her how to play pool. In the afternoons, there were outings and practices for the annual SRA Regatta.

Peggy – and Zorro - enjoyed riding in the Wyndhams' aptly named speedboat, *Miss Behavin'*, as a spotter when the others were waterskiing. It wasn't a trophy competition at the Regatta, but they were eager to put on a show.

Peggy admired their beautiful, straight, and strong limbs, cursing her own withered one. She was impressed by their expertise, and surprised that Merilee was so accomplished that she made cutting elegantly in and out of the wake seem effortless.

For one stunt, Drew and Merilee skied side by side, each on one ski. He looped the towrope handle around his ankle and stuck his leg out in front while she raised a leg gracefully behind, like a ballerina.

That looked difficult enough, but Peggy thought their newest trick dangerous, especially since they didn't wear life jackets.

Merilee and Drew sat side-by-side on the dock, skis dangling from their feet, towropes in hand. "Remember to fall backwards if you have to," he reminded her. So that she wouldn't be hit by his skis.

When they had practiced the basic acrobatics in the bay it had been easy, but it would be different when skimming across the lake.

Drew gave the thumbs-up signal to Max's son, Gus, who was driving the boat.

Merilee dropped her first ski as they closely approached Silver Bay, and then stepped onto Drew's bent knee, dropping her other ski. He crouched down so that she could throw a leg over his shoulder, but they suddenly overbalanced and collapsed backwards.

Zorro barked excitedly and Peggy held her breath until they resurfaced and signalled that they were fine.

They got it right on the next attempt. Once she sat safely on his shoulders, she tucked her feet around his back, passed him her rope, and stretched her arms out in triumph. As they passed the Stepping Stone islands, Merilee waved gaily to the Carringtons, who were sunning themselves on the dock.

"Does your mother know what you get up to?" Peggy asked as they quaffed lemonade afterwards.

Merilee giggled. "We've been skiing since we were little. It's not that dangerous."

"Baloney!"

"Merilee doesn't know her own strengths, Peggy," Drew said. "And she's a jolly good sport."

Merilee was delighted when the Carringtons arrived. "That trick looked like fun!" Anthea declared, accepting Drew's hand to climb out of the boat. "Could I have a go?"

"Sure!" he replied enthusiastically.

Merilee gave Anthea pointers as she practiced climbing onto Drew's shoulders in the bay, and when they actually tried it on skis, they managed it the third time.

"What if Merilee and I try it as well?" Bryce suggested. "Then we might be able to do it in tandem at the waterski exhibition. Are you game?" he asked her.

"Of course!" She tried to hide her excitement.

He was a strong skier, and they managed it first time. As they neared The Point, Merilee slid down into his arms. It was such a powerfully intimate and romantic moment that she wished she could just stay in his embrace as they sank into the shallows.

She blushed furiously as he set her down and said, "Well done! But I think we need lots of practice so that we work flawlessly as a team, don't you agree?" His hazel eyes held hers for a long moment, as if he had just realized that she was a blossoming young woman, alive with interest in him.

"Oh yes!"

"You're still glowing," Peggy said later when they were taking the inclinator up to the house. "Merilee Carrington does have a nice ring to it."

"Do stop!" But Merilee was exhilarated.

At dinner that evening, Ria said to Drew, "I've been thinking about your friends who are coming to visit next week. How would you all like to stay at Westwynd?"

"That's a super idea, Mum!"

"Houses have to be lived in and loved or they'll wither. I'm hoping that Charlie or Sophie and her family will use it after the war, but we have to look after it in the meantime."

Westwynd was the elegant cottage north of Silver Bay, built by Ria's father, James, for his new bride, Helena, in 1915. James had died there the previous summer, dropping dead of a heart attack. The cottage already belonged to Ria, who had bought it from her father when he lost most of his fortune in the stock market crash. Helena had resented that she was living there on Ria's charity, as they had never got on, so she abandoned the cottage, claiming she couldn't bear to be there without her beloved James. When war broke out, Helena decided to leave Toronto as well, and move back to the neutral United States to be near her influential friends. After all, she had yet to find a suitably rich husband for her haughty and pampered daughter, Ria's half-sister. And another one for herself, Ria figured.

"The catch is you have to clean it first," Ria said with a grin. "The servants already have too much to do here. Mrs. Grayson will advise you."

"We can manage that," Drew replied. "In fact, we'll have a 'working' picnic and invite all our island friends."

"Clever boy!"

"I take after you, Mum," he teased.

Westwynd was only a twenty-minute walk along the shore from The Point, but Merilee, Peggy, Drew, and Zorro arrived by boat the following afternoon, laden with picnic hampers. Peggy was awed by the opulent cottage, even larger and grander than The Point. A domed conservatory doubled as a ballroom, its many arched French doors opening onto a balustraded flagstone terrace that perched at the water's edge. It was a fairytale palace, which once again confirmed Merilee's exalted status as a Wyndham.

"It's a shame to see this place unused," Peggy said as she hobbled inside.

Everything had been left as if someone had just stepped out and was expected back momentarily. Except that cobwebs draped the corners and dead bugs littered the floors.

"You can entertain us on the piano, if you like, Peggy. Or take charge of the gramophone," Drew suggested as he and Merilee opened all the windows and French doors. "When the others arrive, tell them that there are brooms and buckets in the servants' wing," he added with a grin.

"Sure thing!" she shot back sarcastically.

Left alone as he and Merilee disappeared into a hallway, the sound of their distant footsteps ascending stairs, Peggy was suddenly spooked. She wished that at least Zorro had stayed with her.

Welcome though it was in the stuffy sitting room, the breeze must have whipped up that mysterious whirlwind of dust, but didn't account for the fact that she was sure she wasn't alone. Was it because she knew someone had died here? Probably that stern-looking fellow in the family photograph, who must be Ria's father, James. She tried to ignore his backstabbing eyes as she began playing the eerily out-of-tune piano.

"You can feel the sadness, can't you? Of emptiness."

Peggy jumped and stifled a shriek as she turned to see a middle-aged lady who looked as if she had just stepped out of the 1920s. Her bespangled diaphanous dress, once the height of elegance, was shabby, and her jewelled headband sported ragged plumes.

"Oh dear, I've rattled you. It's scary enough being in Uncle James's company, isn't it?" She ran her fingers absently through the dust on the piano as she looked around curiously. "We were hardly ever invited here. Helena's so hoity-toity. But *I* know her secret." She paused and raised an eyebrow at Peggy. "Although no one believed me."

She shrugged and then cocked her head as if listening to someone speaking to her. "Silas says I must be careful, since we all have secrets. I wonder if he knows mine now. And what was *his?*" She looked puzzled.

"Who's Silas?" Peggy managed to say.

"My husband. His canoe capsized in a storm not far from Wyndwood... A lifetime ago."

Peggy was struck by the heart-wrenching sorrow that seemed to emanate from the stranger in palpable waves.

But she was suddenly alert as she heard Drew and Merilee descending the stairs. "Must dash. My brother doesn't like me being seen in these old clothes. But they envelope me in happy times."

She seemed to glide silently, almost wraith-like from the room, disappearing as the others walked in.

"Peggy? You look like you've seen a ghost," Merilee said.

"I think I have. She was dressed like a flapper, and said the strangest things."

"Oh, that's Cousin Phoebe," Merilee explained. "She lives on the east side of the island."

"Mad as a hatter," Drew said casually. "I'll have to warn my chums that she flits about like a spectre."

The Carringtons arrived as the Silver Bay cousins and a few other island friends trooped in, including Amy and Adam and Dr. Ellie Roland's three daughters, who often helped out at the Retreat. So the place was soon a hive of activity.

When the cottage had been dusted and swept, the mattresses hauled out of the tin-lined cupboard and the beds made, they all had a swim and then gathered in a shady spot on the terrace for the picnic.

They were startled when a door slammed shut deep within the house. Zorro jumped up and stared intently at the screen doors that led into the conservatory.

"Must be Uncle James," fifteen-year-old Gus Wyndham teased.

"Don't be silly," his older sister, Maxine, chided.

"I'm not kidding! People see lights here at night sometimes," Gus explained in a creepy voice. "When no one's here."

"So, he's just one of the souls who doesn't want to leave the island," Drew said nonchalantly of his grandfather as Zorro settled down by his side again.

"Who else is there?" Peggy couldn't resist asking.

"Great-grandmother Augusta," Drew explained. "She fell off a cliff on the east side just as the last war started. Even a servant at The Point."

"Great-Uncle Albert died at his cottage some years ago," Gus added.

"Didn't his first wife as well?" Amy asked. "During the last war?"

"I'd forgotten about her."

"Peggy has to see our film!" Amy declared. "*Shadows*. Sooooo spooky!"

"Good idea," Drew said. "We'll have movie night when my chums arrive. I'll talk to Sandy about it."

"Cousin Sandy is crazy about filmmaking and Elyse loves acting, so they wrote and produced a couple of short films," Merilee explained to an intrigued Peggy, who knew that Sandy was Uncle Jack's son.

"Don't leave us out!" Anthea implored. "But now let's dance."

The younger boys groaned, and Adam complained, "Do you girls always have to dance? Let's waterski! Dad says that we'll probably have gas rationing if the war drags on, and won't be able to use our motorboats for pleasure."

"Why don't we see how many of us Gus can tow behind *Miss Behavin'*?" Drew suggested. "That could be pretty impressive for our show."

They thought that a terrific idea, and scooted home to fetch their gear, agreeing to meet at The Point. Because there were a dozen of them, they started out from the large steamer dock. Some of the younger children, who hadn't been at the picnic, begged to go along in the boat as spotters, so Peggy opted to stay behind and watch from the boathouse deck. Ria and Chas followed at a safe distance in their launch to scoop up any kids who fell.

After a few false starts, the line of skiers took off and made an impressive sight. It wasn't until their final approach, when they all raised their left arms to wave in triumph that a couple fell close to shore, while the others released their tow ropes and glided into the shallows below Peggy. There was plenty of laughter as some of the guys deliberately took down their neighbouring skiers.

"That was wizard!" Adam enthused. "Can we do this at the Regatta, Drew?"

"Why not? We'll have to practice lots."

"I only have weekends off," Amy lamented.

"Persuade your Aunt Jean to let you have the afternoons free next week," Merilee suggested. "Tell her you're an important part of the team."

Amy managed to do that, and the Wyndwood crowd had a busy week. The boys also practiced canoe tilting at the Spirit Bay Retreat to entertain the patients. This involved teams of two, one steadying the canoe with a paddle while the other stood, flourishing a long, padded pole and trying to knock his opponent into the water. Much hilarity ensued. The patients were also treated to a waterskiing spectacle.

Deanna Tremayne was enthralled. The next morning, she said to Merilee, "Golly, you're an amazing skier! It must feel like you're flying."

Noticing her wistful tone, Peggy said, "It rather feels like that in the boat as well." The small lift of her eyebrow communicated the thought instantly to Merilee.

"Especially when Drew is driving one of family's race boats. Would you like to come along for a ride, Deanna?"

"Oh, could I? Truly?" She beamed.

Drew was more than happy to oblige.

Windrunner IX was the first in the line *not* built to race internationally, but as a family launch that could haul at least half a dozen people comfortably at impossible speeds - and still win regattas. With help from one of the male university students working at the retreat, Drew managed to manoeuvre Deanna into the boat. Once they were all buckled into their life jackets, the engine rumbled impatiently as they glided out of Spirit Bay. But then Drew unleashed all the formidable horses. The long gleaming bow rose out of the water as if about to take to the skies, leveled out, and hissed over the surface of the lake as if barely touching it.

Hair flying like a flag, her laughter snatched by the wind, Deanna grabbed Peggy's hand in excitement and for reassurance. But it was Peggy whose heart caught in her throat as the shoreline whizzed by in a blur. While the others seemed exhilarated, she was nervous at this excessive speed, so much faster than *Miss Behavin'*. She tried to stifle shrieks when they bounced over waves. The fifteen minutes it took them to reach the top of the lake were terrifying for her, and she felt such a coward.

Drew slowed to a crawl and pointed out Kawandag. "That's Lady Eaton's cottage."

"THE Eatons?" Peggy asked. "Store? Catalogue?"

"Yes. They're family friends."

The massive mansion with a two-storey columned entrance hardly qualified as a cottage, she thought. It was even grander than those on Wyndwood. "I wonder if it's furnished with things from their store, like the rest of Canada," Peggy speculated wickedly.

They laughed.

Drew drove sedately along the eastern shoreline on the way back, taking them past cottages and resort waterfronts busy with happy, splashing children and mothers sunning themselves on docks or beaches.

As if to remind them where some of the men were, half a dozen Harvards flew over in formation. It was an impressive sight. The boaters waved in case Alastair was among them.

Drew drove at breakneck speed again for a few miles as they headed toward the western shore. Then he stopped and asked Deanna, "Would you like to try?"

"Golly! Could I?"

"Piece of cake," Drew reassured her. He showed her what to do, guiding her hand on the throttle. "Now let's fly!"

Let's not, Peggy thought, imagining them hitting a submerged rock and becoming projectiles. Living in lake land, she heard enough stories about tragic accidents and drownings. She just had to trust that Drew knew the lake well. But how could anyone when it was so huge? Even some of the big steamers were caught on shoals, and they plied the lakes constantly during the season.

She could finally breath again when they slowed down at the entrance to Spirit Bay.

"That was thrilling!" Deanna said. "I did feel like I was flying. Thank you so much!"

Her radiant smile made it all worthwhile, but Peggy decided that she would forego any future trips offered in a race boat. She was also impressed, but not surprised, to think that Ria had once driven the *Windrunners*, and won local races, as Drew did now.

Peggy had to admit that she was sorry her time at Wyndwood was winding down. She and Merilee would be going home after the upcoming August holiday weekend. With so many interesting people and adventures, it was little wonder that Merilee spent so much of her summers here.

With the arrival of Drew's schoolmates came the promised cinema evening. Merilee had refused to tell Peggy anything about the "spooky" short film, but had just said, with a smirk, "You'll see!"

A large screen was set up at one end of the sitting room in the Old Cottage. Chairs were rearranged and added to accommodate the dozen or more cousins and friends who would be joining them. Bowls of popcorn and jugs of lemonade, Coke, and beer awaited the guests.

The Carringtons, along with the three Roland girls, were the first to arrive, just as the sinking sun ignited the lake. Hugh, duly enlisted in the RCAF, was back for ten days before heading to the Manning Depot at the CNE Coliseum in Toronto.

"Have to learn how to march and salute before we start our real training," he told them. "Then it looks like I can go straight to the Wireless school in Guelph. The recruiters were pleased that I didn't want to be aircrew, but I'm even happier!"

Peggy was quick to realize that Hugh and Ginnie Roland were in love. They held hands and she leaned against him with a tinge of sadness at talk of his imminent departure.

"Ginnie can come to visit us on weekends, and then you can see each other," Maxine suggested slyly, her family having a country estate just south of the town. Her mother and Hugh's father were brother and sister.

"Excellent idea, coz!" Hugh agreed with a big grin.

"Kate sends her regrets," Sandy Wyndham said as he and his brother, Joe, arrived from Thorncliff.

"Her friend Rebecca brought her brother along for a visit, and Kate's head-over-heels in love. Again," fourteen-year-old Joe explained, rolling his eyes. "I think it's the pilot's uniform." The others chuckled.

Once the Silver Bay cousins arrived, along with Amy and Adam, who would be spending the night with their grandparents, Sandy took charge, saying, "Have a good look around while it's still light enough. The veil between the past and the present, between the living and the dead is often gossamer thin in old places like this. Reality inspires."

"He means that Cousin Phoebe sees ghosts here," Adam said.

Amy elbowed and shushed him.

"Maxine has generously offered to play for us, fulfilling her secret ambition to be a cinema pianist for silent movies," Sandy continued.

The assembly chuckled.

"So that you new chaps don't interrupt the showing with questions about the star, Elyse... Yes, she's our cousin, yes, she should be in Hollywood, and yes, she's even more glamorous now than when we shot the film in '36."

More laughs.

"But she's abandoned potential stardom, and is en route to Britain to ferry airplanes for the war effort."

"Damn, she sounds like my kind of gal!" one of Drew's friends announced eagerly.

"Not a snowball's chance, Alderson," Drew assured him. "She's much too classy for you.'"

Alderson pouted melodramatically.

At a nod from Sandy, Maxine went to the piano and began playing eerie tunes to set the mood.

"Drew has assured me that we're the only ones in the cottage this evening," Sandy murmured with a conjurer's voice. "Be aware. Of the shifts in light and shadow that make you question what you've seen. Of creaks. Is it the ancient building settling into the coolness of nighttime? Or footsteps from the past? Is that chilling breath on the back of your neck a breeze squeezing through the screen door? Or a ghostly touch?"

Peggy shivered as she was drawn in by Sandy's soothing voice and mesmerizing personality. How easily he had the audience in thrall. Surely a good sign for someone who wanted to make a career out of entertainment. Merilee had told her that he was at university, studying arts and literature, but always furthering his ambitions to write and produce movies.

But Merilee had also told her that Jack wasn't pleased that Sandy has no ambition to become involved with the family empire. Jack struggled to *not* alienate his son, since his own father had been disinherited by his parents for not bending to their will.

"Beware the *Shadows*," Sandy advised as he turned on the projector and Drew turned off the lights.

"And consider that Sandy and Elyse were only sixteen when they created this," Drew said.

Expecting a flickering home movie, Peggy was surprised at the quality of the film. It began with a bustling costume party set in the pavilion to the east of the house, decorated with fairy lights and flowers. She was sure she recognized Ria and Chas, a young Merilee and her parents, and others, despite their disguises. But Elyse, dressed in a scintillating Cleopatra costume, stole the scene. She went eagerly into the arms of her lover – played by Hugh Carrington, also sixteen at the time. As they waltzed, she laid her head seductively on his shoulder.

A moment later, Elyse opened her eyes to find herself alone amidst withered leaves blowing across the empty dance floor. She was puzzled and fearful - emotions conveyed so subtly and elegantly that there was no doubt she was a born actress.

In the next scene, Hugh appeared at the dock in his father's WW1 army uniform, ready to head off to war. The lovers kissed and released each other slowly, reluctantly. A tearful Elyse beckoned him back as he set off in a skiff, but he kept rowing away until he disappeared into the distant, rising mist.

Elyse drifted uneasily about the cottage, always alone, though shadows lingered around corners and elusive faces momentarily flashed in mirrors she was passing. Never long enough to be sure that they were real. Out of the corner of her eye, she glimpsed an old lady seated in a chair by the fire in the sitting room. When Elyse turned to look, there was no one, just the empty chair rocking gently.

She ran out onto the veranda, but there was no one in sight. Even the lake was deserted, with only the wake of a long-gone boat sending dying waves onto the shore. The camera slowly zoomed in to those ripples as they washed away footprints in the sand.

In the next scene, Elyse was holding a telegram, which the audience could read, informing her that her lover had been killed in action. Her anguish was painful to watch.

Peggy felt increasingly unsettled as the movie progressed, startling at any slight change of the camera's focus. From Elyse's frightened face to sinister shadows following her. Maxine played softly, with the occasional crash of a discordant chord at the perfect moment, heightening the suspense.

In the calm Back Bay, Elyse was floating on her back in a gossamer gown, her dark hair fanning around her like swaying seaweed. Her eyes were open and gazing at the emerging dawn, but sightless, as if she were dead. Then she began to sink without protest. A few bubbles broke the surface.

A moment later she woke in a panic in her bed. She jumped up and ran in and out of every empty room, down the stairs and throughout the cottage, searching. Emotionally exhausted and weeping, she staggered into the sitting room and leaned her head against the mantelpiece.

When she looked up, she noticed a newspaper clipping among the faded photographs of long-departed relatives. Her horror was almost palpable. The camera zoomed in showing a photo of Elyse and the headline "Tragic Drowning". She looked up at the mirror over the mantelpiece but saw no reflection of herself. She covered her scream as she turned around to find quivering lights in the room materialize into smiling people. An old lady draped in Edwardian lace rocked contentedly in her chair. Chas in his RAF uniform from the last war was sitting beside her smoking a pipe, a cane propped at his side. Merilee in a Victorian gown was cuddling a doll. And Hugh, unscathed, was holding out his arms to Elyse. She went gratefully into his tender embrace.

Maxine plunged into a lively rendition of "The Charleston" as the camera pulled away, showing people in 1920's garb throughout the room - the twins, Gus, Drew, Anthea, Bryce, and other relatives engrossed in a wild game of cards, Maxine at the piano, the older generation chatting while taking cocktails out to the veranda – all completely oblivious to the ghosts, who regarded them with benevolence.

The lights came on amid enthusiastic applause and cheers.

"Wow, that was... awesome," Peggy said. "One of the best scary movies I've ever seen!" She was once again grateful that she and Merilee were sleeping in the boathouse and not in the cottage.

"I think I'm in love. With a gorgeous ghost," Alderson jested.

"Did you recruit everyone on the island to play a part?" Peggy asked Merilee.

"And neighbouring islands. Sandy actually filmed the beginning scene at our annual Dominion Day costume ball."

"It looks like such fun to make a movie!"

"We all had a blast being part of it," Merilee agreed. "Even Chas's mother, who played the old lady, really enjoyed herself." In fact, Marjorie Thornton had become one of Sandy's biggest champions for his career goals, making it even harder for Jack to try to change his son's mind.

"We had interesting challenges, like filming a completely deserted lake," Drew said. He had helped to shoot scenes from other angles. "Which we did at dawn. And the eerie lighting and shadow effects weren't always easy to achieve."

"I think you're brilliant, Sandy, so I hope you keep making movies," Merilee said.

There was a united "Hear, hear!" from the guests.

He grinned. "That's my plan. But we'll see what the war demands of me."

"I'm sure you can put your cine-camera to better use than a gun," Drew said. "What about making those newsreels we see at the pictures?"

"Now there's a thought! I'll have to look into that."

"In the meantime, could we watch the film again?" Alderson asked. "I think I missed some of the subtle nuances. Like how all those dancers suddenly turned into dead leaves."

There were good-natured groans, but no one left their seats.

As the room dimmed again, Peggy suddenly caught a movement out of the corner of her eye and looked out at the veranda backlit by the lingering, indigo twilight. A woman turned and crept away.

Following Peggy's alarmed gaze, Merilee whispered, "Just Cousin Phoebe. She's attracted by the music."

Had she been watching from the shadows all along? That spooked Peggy even more than the film.

•   •   •

A large contingent of evacuee children was being brought in from British universities through the University of Toronto, where Dr. Ellie Roland's husband, Troy, was a professor. He had a friend at Cambridge who wanted his children safely out of England for the duration of the war, so Troy had promised to help. Not having enough room in his own busy household, Troy had asked Ria, who not only had plenty of space in her city estate, but also loved children.

"Troy called to say he and the kids will be here by teatime tomorrow," Ria informed them the following day. "And he asked if we had room for two more. It seems that our three evacuees have cousins who came along, and are reluctant to be parted from them. Of course, that's fine with me. We could easily take half a dozen more."

"Mum! Five brats running wild on Wyndwood?" Drew jested.

She laughed. "Perhaps we should ensure that they *do*. I expect they'll be very proper and perhaps even diffident."

"And snobbish, lording it over us Colonials."

"If so, it won't last long, I can assure you. I can be just as toffee-nosed. Don't forget that your great-grandmother was an Honorable, and you have aristocratic relatives in Britain," she said with mock haughtiness.

"Do you have to be so pleased about your new guests?"

"You're planning to go off to war as soon as you're old enough - which is too soon for my liking." For a moment there was a naked look of love and fear in her eyes, but that was quickly shuttered. "What's a mother to do but find other sprouts to raise?" she teased.

Drew shook his head. "So now it's all my fault that we're going to be overrun by kiddies? And I suppose you want me to look after them."

"Of course! You've been spoiled far too long, being the youngest."

"Well, I'm escaping while I can, and taking my chums golfing right now."

"We'll see you at dinner. And be prepared to do some entertaining tomorrow. I expect the children may already be feeling homesick, and possibly scared. Who knows how long this war will last and they'll be away from their families," she said seriously.

"I'll be an impeccable host," Drew assured her. "And I'll make sure my chums behave as well."

Troy and the children arrived on schedule the following afternoon. The evacuees seemed a sad lot, but Merilee could only imagine what they must be feeling after a long and dangerous journey to a strange place so far from home.

"These are my friend John Baxter's children - William, Jane, and George," Troy introduced them. "And their Carmichael cousins, Vera and Bertram."

"How do you do, Mrs. Thornton?" Bertram said, extending his hand. "I should prefer to be called Bertie, if you don't mind."

Ria stifled a chuckle at the nine-year-old's formality. "Yes, of course. And I prefer to be called Aunt Ria. What about you, William? Is it Will or Bill or Billy?"

"It's William, Ma'am," he said stiffly. At thirteen, he was the eldest.

"You've had the weighty responsibility of your siblings and cousins upon your shoulders, William."

"Yes, Ma'am."

"Well, everyone looks in fine form. But I expect you're all ready for some tea and cakes, and then perhaps you'd like a swim."

"We don't know how to swim," eleven-year-old Vera admitted as she gazed at the inviting lake.

"I've outfitted them with a cottage wardrobe, Ria, including swimsuits," Troy said. "The rest of their luggage is in the city."

"Then anyone who wants a lesson can start after tea. The water is warm but refreshing on such a hot day. Merilee will show you to your rooms."

Merilee grabbed the large bag from the youngest, eight-year-old George, and led the children into the house.

"You're so good to take them all, Ria," Troy said. "Vera and Bertie looked so forlorn when they were about to be parted from the Baxters. I think it makes a difference to the kids that I'm not a complete stranger, as they've heard John talk about me." They had known each other at Harvard before the last war. "We'll be sure to spend plenty of time with them, and have them over for weekends when you need a break. I have a feeling that you won't have it easy with William."

"He seems a bit resentful," Ria observed.

"He thinks it's his duty to be in England."

"And doesn't want to look after four younger kids."

"It annoys him when George gets weepy. William keeps telling him to buck up and be a man."

"Poor little mite! He's only eight."

"Jane stands up for George, but that causes problems between her and William. Vera bravely tries to mother them all. Bertie is the only one who seems to think this is a merry adventure... which may last for a few weeks until he realizes he can't go home."

"Don't worry, Troy, I can handle them. We'll keep them busy and interested."

"The girls will help," Troy said of his three daughters. "Ellie doesn't really need them at the Retreat."

"Super! They can also help teach the kids to swim. I'll feel better about them wandering the island or canoeing if they can save themselves from drowning. God, it just occurred to me what a responsibility it is to look after other people's children!"

At her panicked look, Troy laughed. "You know how resilient children are, Ria. And you will charm them and become their favourite aunt before the week is out."

"I would say so," Peggy added. "You've certainly made me feel like part of the family."

"And welcome back any time, my dear," Ria said sincerely.

Peggy was elated.

Upstairs, Merilee had shown the children to the spacious girls' and boys' dorms, which were separated by Drew's room. All three shared the west-facing balcony, which was partitioned with low walls.

Ria had left a copy of *The Mystery of Spirit Bay* on each of their beds, and the rest of the series on the dressers. The youngest ones enthused about them, but William said dismissively, "Why would Mrs. Thornton think *I* would be interested in children's books?"

"They're considered classics," Merilee explained. "My father wrote them and my mother illustrated them."

William was a bit taken aback. "Well, they're... attractive."

"You'll learn something about life in Canada if you read them."

"Hmm," he muttered disinterestedly.

He would learn some valuable life lessons as well if he deigned to read them, Merilee thought, trying to dismiss her annoyance at his arrogance.

She pointed out the bathroom at the end of the hall, and Chas and Ria's suite at the front.

"Who sleeps over there?" William asked of the four rooms on the east side.

"No one at the moment," Merilee replied. "But Uncle Chas is bringing a friend home for the weekend. Now, if you're all ready, I'll show you around downstairs."

In the dining room she said, "When you come down in the morning, you'll find breakfast laid out on the sideboard, so you can just help yourselves."

"May we really have as much butter and jam as we like?" Vera asked hopefully.

"You certainly may. I expect you're ready for some cakes now." Merilee led them back out to the veranda.

Their eyes gleamed when they saw the plates of small sandwiches on white bread, crusty scones, and moist fairy cakes accompanied by iced tea and lemonade, which Grayson deposited on the table beside Ria. They ate hungrily, and eagerly accepted seconds.

"We should get some rules straight right from the beginning so that there are no misunderstandings," Ria said. "We have staff to help us, but we all have to pull our weight. We make our own beds in the morning, put our clothes away – dirty ones into the laundry hamper - and keep our rooms tidy. There's always fruit and a pitcher of ice water on the sideboard in the dining room, but you may also go into the kitchen and ask Mrs. Grayson for a glass of milk or a cold drink, and if you're starving and can't wait for the next meal, she has yummy cakes and cookies that she'll hand out to polite children," she added with a grin. The little ones giggled.

"If you do your bit, there'll be a weekly allowance of $1 for those ten and under and $2 for the older ones," Ria said. "Anyone who does something beyond their chores – helps around the house or grounds in some way – will receive more. That way, you will have some of your own money to spend on yourselves and buy gifts to send to your family and friends at home."

"Like butter and jam?" Vera asked.

"Certainly. We'll put food baskets together, shall we? Mrs. Grayson makes delicious jam from our island blueberries. You can all help to gather them."

"Will that give us extra allowance?" William asked.

"I suppose that would count," Ria agreed.

Troy suppressed a grin.

Ria went on. "It's very important that you never leave the cottage without letting one of us know where you're going, whether that means down to the beach or the dock, in a boat, or anywhere on the island. And no one *ever* goes into the water alone, even when you can swim, is that understood?" She fixed them with a no-nonsense stare until each nodded.

"Good! If you're exploring the island and get lost, make your way to the shore and follow it back or stay there. We'll find you eventually."

"Are there bears?" little George wanted to know. "William said that there are wolves and bears and other nasty things in Canada that gobble you up."

"There are certainly wild animals on the mainland, and people do have to be careful. But we don't have bears or wolves on the island. Just deer and raccoons."

"Are there Loch Ness monsters or whales in the lake that can eat you?" George persisted.

"Nothing at all dangerous," Troy assured him. "In fact, we eat the fish. I'll show you how to catch them."

"And we all love swimming," Merilee added. "Is anyone ready to try yet?"

"Oh yes!" Vera said. The others, except William, agreed.

"If it's not required to swim, then I should prefer to write to my parents," he said.

"Swimming lessons needn't begin today, but will be mandatory," Ria replied firmly.

"I don't do sports," William countered.

"Think of this as a skill that everyone who summers on the lake requires for safety. Whether you choose to enjoy it as a sport is up to you."

"I expect to be back home before next summer, so it would be a waste of time."

"I hope you can be, too," Troy interjected. "But in the meantime, your parents will also be happy that you learn to swim. And you'll find that your hosts have an indoor pool in their city home, so you can swim all year. My daughters will teach you."

"If you insist, Professor."

Ria hoped that she wouldn't have to rely on Troy to constantly intercede with this truculent teenager.

"Mrs. Thornton, I noticed that there are empty bedrooms upstairs. Might I have one of those?" William asked. "I don't share with George at home, and he and Bertie are so much younger."

"Yes, I suppose you could, unless we have a houseful of guests, in which case you'll have to move back in with the boys. You may have the one beside the bathroom."

It was the smallest and the only one without a balcony.

When the kids, as well as Merilee and Peggy, left to change into their swimsuits, Ria said, "OK, Troy, I take back what I said about being able to handle them. Am I getting too old for this?"

He laughed. "Never! You've already won them over, except for William. I will help with him as much as I can."

"He certainly seems to respect you, *Professor*."

"John warned me that William is a bit of an intellectual snob. He's already studying theoretical physics on his own."

"Dear God, then I really am out of my depth!"

Troy chuckled. "Think Isaac Newton and Einstein, for example."

"At least I've heard of them," she said with a grin.

"William's mother, Mary, earned a first-class mathematics degree at Cambridge, so he comes by that naturally. One of the reasons John sent the children out is that Mary's been recruited by the government to work at a top-secret facility. I would suspect as a codebreaker. The children don't know this, of course. It's all quite hush-hush."

"Thank goodness! What a paragon that mother is."

"Don't underestimate yourself, Ria. Just do what you do best — offer love and stability and lots of fun adventures. That will allow the kids a chance to grow into themselves."

"You mean they've been pushed in directions they may not want to go?" she asked shrewdly.

"I would say so."

Drew and his high-spirited pals arrived, seeming to fill up the empty spaces of the airy veranda. Reminding Ria yet again what a void there would be in her life once he left.

"We've missed tea!" he lamented.

"Not quite," Grayson said, bringing out a tray. "Mrs. Grayson heard you arrive and thought you'd be ready for these."

"She's a treasure! We're going to have trouble getting rid of these chaps, since they've become accustomed to Mrs. Grayson's cooking."

"I'll say!" Alderson concurred as he lathered butter and heaped jam on a scone.

"So, Uncle Troy, I'm assuming you've delivered the British sprouts for Mum," Drew quipped.

"And you get to look after them while they cool off in the lake," Ria stated. "None of them can swim. Yet."

"We came prepared. Just need to strip off our shorts and shirts."

The children seemed excited when they came back down in their new swimsuits, clutching the colourful towels that had been laid out on their beds. William lagged behind but was prepared to obey Troy. While the others still had compact children's bodies, William was gangly and so skinny that his joints were rudely prominent. Ria wondered if he was self-conscious about his awkward, pubescent body, and hence unwilling to participate in sports or be seen in a swimsuit. Next to Drew and his athletic, tanned friends, he would surely feel even more ungainly.

After introductions were made, Ria said, "You can head down to the beach while I get into my own suit. I'm not going to miss out on a swim."

Merilee showed the kids how the bottom shelved slowly into deep water. "So, until you know how to swim, you shouldn't go any deeper than the middle of that dock," she warned.

Drew said to her, "Climb up and we'll show them how deep it gets by the end of the bay."

It was a trick they had done many times. Merilee stood on his shoulders, he, holding her ankles to steady her as he walked into deeper water. When his head disappeared, it looked as if Merilee were gliding on the water, until she, too, began to sink.

Even Peggy held her breath until Merilee began swimming and Drew popped up beside her.

"May I do that?" Vera asked eagerly.

"Me too!" Bertie and Jane shouted.

"As soon as you learn how to swim," Drew assured them. "Then you can go down the boathouse slide as well."

Clever boy, Ria thought as she joined them.

He hauled beach balls out of the boathouse, and several games of 'monkey-in-the-middle' in the shallows had the kids hilariously engaged.

Except for William.

Troy was sitting on the long dock that edged the main boathouse, and William, who had waded in, went over to stand beside him in the waist-deep water.

"I have to be off shortly, but my family and I will be back for dinner," Troy said to the boy. "That's our island, just over there. Ouhu." He pronounced it "Oh-you-who", which made William grin.

"Is that an Indian name?" he asked.

"No, it's just a joke because the islands are so close that you can shout over to your neighbours. We call them the Stepping Stone Islands."

"May I visit Ouhu?"

"Of course. You'll be back and forth lots. If you learn how to swim, you'll be able to row over by yourself. I think you'll be interested in talking to my father-in-law. He's a retired physics professor, and built the original cottage on the island."

"My father told me about Professor Emeritus Carlyle. I would be honoured to meet him!"

"But now, I suspect you're going to meet your host," Troy said, noticing a boat speeding toward them. On the train ride up from the city, he had apprised the children about the Thorntons, and about Chas's wartime injuries.

The launch pulled into one of the boathouse slips, and a few minutes later, Chas appeared with an RAF officer.

Ria swam over to the dock.

"Darling, you remember my best pilot and right-hand man..." Chas began.

"Good God! Bruce McPherson!" Ria exclaimed. "If I weren't wet I would hug you!"

Bruce had taken over Chas's squadron after his near-fatal crash, and had been a staunch support to Ria and Chas during his recovery. Troy, who had worked at the Harvard University base hospital in France, had met him before.

Bruce laughed. "I don't mind at all getting wet. In fact, I'm looking forward to ditching this uniform and joining you in the lake. It seems to be everything that you and Chas used to brag about."

"Why has it taken you twenty years to find out?" Ria asked.

"I came back after the war, but didn't stay in Canada," Bruce replied.

"He's had an adventuresome life, most recently as a British Airways pilot, but rejoined the RAF and is now in Trenton setting up the instructor training program," Chas explained. "He'll tell you more later, but first I have to meet all our new guests, and then I, too, will join you in the water."

He turned to William, and said, "You've arrived just in time to experience one of the highlights on the lake. The annual Regatta is tomorrow. See what you might enjoy, and then practice, so that you can participate next year."

Ria was only a bit surprised that William didn't respond with his "no sports" excuse, but said simply, if unenthusiastically, "Yes, Air Marshal Thornton." Titles obviously impressed him.

"At home, I'm Uncle Chas, OK? We don't need to be reminded of the war."

"Yes, Sir." He tried not to stare at Chas's scars.

The children seemed surprised that Chas was such a strong swimmer despite his gimpy leg. Vera and Jane were eager to learn, while Bertie and George were happily building elaborate sandcastles on the beach with Drew's friends.

When Troy announced he was leaving, William asked Ria if he might go up to his room now. Troy gave Ria a knowing glance as he said, "William, would you like to come to Ouhu with me? We'll be back here in a while for dinner."

The boy's eyes lit up. "Oh yes! I should like that indeed!"

When William ran up to his room to change, Troy said, "It's early days, but if William doesn't settle in, I expect we can find room in our house for him. Our two youngest could bunk together and free up a bedroom."

"I'm not ready to admit defeat yet. Ellie has enough to do running her practice and keeping up with the girls. You're always writing up your research and have even less time once classes are back in session. And Drew might be a good influence."

"True."

Before dinner that evening, Troy managed to tell Ria privately, "William is between Jackie and Blythe in age, but he wasn't really interested in anything they or Ginnie had to show him or talk about. But he did hit it off with Ellie's dad."

"Ah yes, the *Professor Emeritus.*"

"I think William's smart enough to get into the University of Toronto Schools, and since we and Ellie's folks live so close, William would be better off staying with one of us." Only the brightest boys were accepted into the challenging curriculum of the UTS. "The Carlyles have offered to take him in September. I'm sure John and Mary will be pleased with that arrangement as well. And I think the youngsters might benefit from not being bossed about by William."

"Giving them a chance to blossom," Ria agreed. "And in the meantime, we might just be able to un-starch William a little during the rest of the summer."

William certainly seemed more amenable and less surly, although he chastised George and Bertie for their boisterous exuberance when they watched the Regatta events the following day. They were particularly impressed with the waterskiing exhibition, and even more eager to learn to swim when Drew promised to teach them to waterski after they mastered swimming.

Lessons began Sunday afternoon, with the Roland girls helping.

The adults were sipping cocktails on the upper deck of the boathouse and watching the antics.

"This is a delightful piece of paradise," Bruce McPherson said wistfully. "It's hard to imagine that there's a war on. It will be difficult to leave tomorrow."

"You'll have to come and visit often," Ria suggested.

"Gladly! And I'll let the other chaps know about Muskoka, when they need a break. There seem to be plenty of resorts."

"Actually... We have an entire cottage that's sitting empty most of the time," Ria said, an exciting idea dawning. Looking at Chas, she added, "What if we turned Westwynd into a refuge for aircrew who need a rest or are recuperating from illness or accidents?"

"That's a terrific idea!" Chas agreed.

"Could it be staffed by the RCAF? It's so hard to find help these days."

"I'll look into it, my brilliant darling. Come along, Bruce. I'll take you over to see the place, and you can perhaps help me make this happen."

"Absolutely!"

They returned half an hour later in high spirits.

"The bedrooms are large enough to sleep four comfortably in each, and with the sitting room and the upper floor of the boathouse turned into dorms, we figure that Westwynd can accommodate about fifty, and there are fifteen small rooms in the servants' wing for staff," Chas said. "We can put extra tables into the conservatory for dining, and with the billiard room and library, there are plenty of public areas for lounging about. I'd forgotten that your father had a furnace installed, so it's feasible to run it from early May to the end of October. If the Air Force doesn't buy in, then we'll just go ahead ourselves, Ria, if you're willing to take the helm. Not all that different from the Club you set up in the last war."

"I thought that was far behind me, and never again necessary," she said. "But of course I will. And I'll have Grayson to advise me." He had pretty well run the Canadian soldiers' respite home that she had helped create in England before going off to drive ambulances in France.

Merilee's parents had spent the weekend at Uncle Jack's cottage on Thorncliff Island, so they and Jack's family arrived, followed by the Carringtons and the Silver Bay crowd. The Point bustled with chatter and activity.

Doing her water exercises while steadying herself beside the dock, Peggy was sad to be leaving this luxurious and fun place. Because Merilee's father couldn't get more than two days off, they would be setting out late this afternoon for home.

They had bidden a tearful farewell to Deanna Tremayne yesterday, and Peggy had promised to write weekly. Deanna had begun walking with braces and crutches, and was so much improved in spirit since she'd arrived. Ellie said that Deanna could return next summer if she wished.

A formation of Harvards flew low overhead, the shrill whine of the engines startling. Vera screamed as she grabbed her little brother and bolted, looking around frantically and then cowering with him under a pine tree. Drew and Merilee were already at their side when Ria, Ellie, and others came running.

"What is it, Vera?" Merilee asked anxiously.

Vera was sobbing and shaking. Bertie clung to her, equally terrified. "Bombs!" she managed to blubber. "Where's the shelter?"

"Those weren't enemy planes," Drew reassured her. "They're our pilots training to go to England."

"They live on the south coast and have witnessed bombings and air battles," William explained. "One of Vera's schoolmates was killed."

Ria embraced Vera and Bertie. "Oh, you poor dears! You don't have to be afraid here. The war is far away."

"What about Mummy and Daddy?" Vera asked through streaming tears.

"Your parents will be better able to look after themselves if they don't have to worry about you. Why don't we send them a telegram tomorrow just to let them know that you're OK? And we'll ask them to cable back."

Vera nodded. "I should like that very much."

"And I have a secret hideout where you can go whenever you feel afraid," Drew said. "Come and I'll show you. It needs a bit of cleaning up, but we'll do that right now."

All five kids went to see Drew's old playhouse – the former icehouse built into the rocky hill under the kitchen wing. Windows had been added on either side of the door.

"It's a Hobbit house!" William enthused for a moment, before re-engaging his aloofness.

"You like Tolkien's book?" Drew asked.

"I read it when I was a child," William said dismissively.

The book had only been published three years ago, so Drew said, "Well, I wasn't a kid, and still enjoyed it."

"Could we really use this?" Vera asked, brightening. "I should be ever so happy."

"Of course!" Drew said. "And you can decorate it however you wish."

He and his friends set to work sweeping out dead leaves and cobwebs, while Ria suggested Merilee take the kids to the storage rooms in the cottage to scout out stuff for their hideaway. Ellie's daughters went along to help.

"Dear God, Ellie, it's a stark reminder of how dire things are in Britain," Ria said as they went to rejoin the others.

"And how traumatizing it is for the children," Ellie said. "Of course, you had first-hand experience when you and Sophie went through raids in Calais." One of which had killed Sophie's mother.

"It scares the hell out of me that she and the kids are in England. And I'm so afraid for Charlie fighting air battles."

"How *are* things with Charlie?" Ellie was one of the few who had always known the truth about him.

"His letters are more heartfelt and more frequent. But I don't know whether he's forgiven us yet. It preys on Chas, although he hides it well." Her breath caught on a sob. "It's heartbreaking, Ellie, having seen and held him in my arms only a few times in the past six years."

Sophie and her family had spent at least six weeks at Wyndwood every summer before the war, but Charlie had refused to come home. So, Ria, Chas, Drew, and Elyse had gone to England several times to visit him. Initially he had been dutiful, but distant, especially with Chas, but his hugs had become warmer. Only his relationship with Drew and Elyse had never changed, and they spent plenty of time together. Charlie took them for flights over the English countryside, instilling a love of flying in them as well. Ria understood all too well that Chas, having witnessed and suffered so much, never wanted his sons to become pilots, especially during wartime.

Ellie put her hand reassuringly on Ria's shoulder. "Charlie's a grown man of twenty-four, and perhaps mature enough to realize that we all make mistakes. And that war affects us profoundly on so many levels."

Ria prayed that losing any of her children wasn't one of them this time.

Muskoka: August 1940
Chapter 4

"It makes me boil to think that they're enjoying our beach," Peggy snarled.

She and Merilee were cooling off in the lake outside Hope Cottage, and could hear prisoners splashing about nearby. Although the menacing barbed wire in the water was uncomfortably close, a large bulge of the rocky promontory blocked their view of the next bay to which, thankfully, the Germans were restricted.

"I thought it was just the heat making your face so red," Merilee teased. It was another blistering August day, the thick moisture blotting the blue out of the sky. Merilee hoped that a thunderstorm would wring out the air.

They watched a boat slowing down and edging close to the boom fence. Someone shouted, but Merilee caught only a few words: "Damn Nazis... should be strung up!" A man stood up and hurled something toward the unseen prisoners. A crack of gunfire startled the girls, and the boaters took off, veering away sharply to send a large wake across the barrier.

"What was that?" Peggy asked in alarm.

"Dad said the guards will fire a warning shot across the bow of any boat that comes too close. That's why he told me to stay well clear when I'm out in the canoe." He'd explained that the boom fence was as much to keep people out as the prisoners in. With daily reports of the Battle of Britain escalating, vindictive anger was rife.

"I have to tell you that I've been awfully tempted to try target practice at the camp," Peggy said. From their house, the Wildings could see the prisoners when they were playing soccer between the barbed wire and the San building, which was the German officers' quarters.

"Peggy! You wouldn't!"

"Of course not!" She paused and then admitted, "Dad says that some of them are quite pleasant, and grateful for the work he does there." He was still helping the Engineers fix and modify things, but the Germans also pitched in, so Mr. Wilding sometimes worked alongside them, albeit silently. The civilian contractors were not allowed to communicate with the prisoners, even if they could.

"I bet they're happy to be out of the fighting."

"If they have any sense, they should realize how lucky they are! It's all so stupid anyway!" Peggy added in frustration. "I'm fighting mad that Ned is joining up. Not at him, of course, but at the damned Germans for making it necessary!" She wouldn't voice her fear that none of her brothers would return, because that would make it too possible.

"I think it's cool that Ned opted to join the RCAF as a mechanic." Merilee had suggested that to him after hearing Chas say how desperate they were for ground crew. "That means he won't be flying, just making sure the planes work properly. At the airfield, where he'll be safe."

"Aren't the Huns bombing the air bases in England now? And knowing Ned, he'll *want* to fly."

"Well, he'll be training here for quite a while, and able to come home on leave. Uncle Chas says the RAF will soon put a stop to the air raids. And many eager chaps who've dreamed of flying don't have the stomach for it."

"Do you always have to be so positive? I *want* to be angry and miserable."

"No you don't!" Merilee grinned and Peggy laughed.

The girls were sitting waist-deep in the water on the rock next to the boathouse dock. Having just finished her swim, Merilee's mother, Claire, brought them icy lemonade and settled herself on the broad veranda of the house behind.

Merilee loved the rambling slate-grey bungalow that straddled a small stretch of lawn between sloping rocks, backed by woodland that circled around to the San. Over the years, the house had sprouted charming bays and wings, including a sunroom, which was glorious in winter, and a screened porch where they ate most of their meals in summer. The Sutcliffes had added a studio for Claire and an office for Colin. Flowers tucked into rocky crevices and artistically weaving the house into the landscape were thoughtfully designed to provide colour and variety from spring daffodils to fall asters, and softened the surrounding ruggedness, adding to the magic.

The boathouse sheltered a couple of canoes and their *Seawind* runabout, and provided an old-fashioned change room for swimmers. But in this oppressive heat, the girls just spent the day in swimsuits, topped with flowing beach robes when necessary.

"You must miss Wyndwood. I do," Peggy said wistfully. They had only been home for a week. "And I bet you're pining for Bryce Carrington."

"Peggy!"

"Well, I'd be spending as much time there as I could, if I were you."

"Mum and I are going to be there for the last week of August. She's staying with Uncle Jack, but I'll be at Wyndwood so that I can help Drew and Aunt Ria with the evacuees."

"And be closer to Drew's crowd. Good thinking."

"So, when was Ross Tremayne last over?" Merilee asked slyly.

"Yesterday. I think he's adopted Mum as his second mother."

"I'm sure he enjoys spending time with you as well."

"He likes listening to me playing while he's munching on Mum's cakes. That's all."

"Is it? I think he likes you, Peggy *Tremayne*."

"Don't be silly! Who wants to marry to a cripple?"

"A kind and sensible man who realizes that it's insignificant."

Peggy harrumphed.

Merilee had noticed how many people shunned those disabled by polio, including school friends. Even some teachers were impatient with Peggy, and overly demanding and critical of her work. It embarrassed and angered her to catch a look of disgust on someone's face when they watched Peggy's painful gait, so she felt deep sympathy for her friend. Never pity, however, because Peggy despised that. "You won't be doing yourself any favours if you're an old sourpuss!"

Peggy splashed her, and they dissolved into giggles.

So, it took a moment to register the shrill, distant blasts from the Rubberset factory whistle. It meant that a prisoner had escaped.

"Bloody hell!" Peggy swore.

They both turned to stare intently at the sharply rising rock and trees that blocked evidence of the camp, expecting to see someone dashing towards them.

Colin came down to the dock. Today was his day off, but he said, "I'd best go over to the office and see how I can help. Get into the house as quickly as you can. Lock up and have the rifle handy, Merilee."

She helped Peggy hobble up to the house, her mother looking pale as she hastened them inside. Claire locked the doors and windows, trapping the heat as well.

"I'll call your mother and let her know you're safe," Claire said to Peggy while Merilee went to fetch the .22.

It seemed absurd to be holding a rifle in preparation to shoot someone. Was this how the men felt when they went into battle? Scared, morally conflicted? "Shoot to kill only if necessary. A leg wound can effectively disable," her father had advised when she started practicing. But hitting a paper target had seemed like just a fun test of skill.

"Perhaps you could keep an eye on the boathouse, Peggy," Claire suggested. "I expect that an escapee would be looking for a means to get away quickly, and not interested in coming into our house."

That seemed reasonable, and Claire tried to sound reassuring, but then paced about the many rooms, monitoring the windows. There suddenly seemed too many of them.

Merilee hoped that Ned's motorcycle, parked behind the house, was safe, but checked to make sure she had brought in the key. She wandered about as well, but was never far from Peggy, who, of course, wouldn't be able to move quickly should someone come barging through the veranda door. The gun became heavy in her sweating hands as the temperature kept rising.

"Can we blame the Germans if we die from heat stroke?" Peggy asked.

Claire took a moment to bring them ice, and said, "Rub this on your wrists and forehead."

"I think I'll just climb into your Frigidaire," Peggy quipped.

Aside from the library, which had floor to ceiling bookcases, other rooms, including this sitting room, and every available nook in Hope Cottage contained books where wall space wasn't taken up by Claire's evocative paintings. Peggy always marvelled at the sheer quantity and diverse selection of reading material, which she often borrowed. She'd been amused that last year Merilee had decided to catalogue and organize the collection, a task that soon overwhelmed her, and still wasn't completed.

This main sitting room also held a baby grand piano, which Peggy loved playing – hers being merely an ancient upright – but she had no inclination to at the moment.

The swollen air seemed to muffle noise, so that even the grandfather clock ticked faintly as they listened intently for any unusual sounds. And gunfire.

They tensed as footsteps thudded along the veranda. Merilee gripped the rifle tightly and raised it to her shoulder, breathing a sigh of relief as Ned appeared and knocked on the French door.

"Good Lord, it's stifling in here!" he said as they let him in. "The authorities are on their way to search your boathouse and every other building in the area, so you can come out soon. But I expect he's long gone." He looked at Merilee approvingly and asked, "Were you prepared to use that?"

She relaxed her white-knuckled grip on the rifle and replied, "Not on you."

He laughed. "Glad you're not trigger-happy!"

"Do you know what's going on?" Peggy asked.

"One of the swimmers disappeared."

So much for German honour, Merilee thought.

"Maybe he drowned," Peggy said hopefully.

"They don't think so, but guards are searching the lake. The OPP and RCMP have also been called in. Come along, Peg. I'm taking you home and then I'm joining the posse."

"Like in the Westerns?"

"Deputy Wilding at your service!" He scooped Peggy up. Thin and petite compared to her robust brothers, she seemed almost weightless in his arms. It struck Merilee again how much Peggy would miss even just the physical help that Ned provided.

"Ned, dear, when you have time, would you kindly look at the car?" Claire asked. "It's being cranky about starting."

"Sure thing, Mrs. Sutcliffe. I expect it's the spark plugs again." He often did odd jobs for them, since Colin was not mechanically inclined, and Merilee marvelled that he could fix almost anything. "I'll be over first thing tomorrow."

Rifle still in hand, she walked with them to the motorcycle, thankful to be outside again. Although it wasn't much cooler, the breeze was somewhat refreshing.

A couple of RCAF planes flew low overhead, obviously joining the search.

"Stay safe," Ned advised her, but already the soldiers were arriving, one with a bloodhound.

"And you!"

Merilee was surprised that the guards searched the house as well, looking under beds and in closets. "Do they think we're hiding him?" Merilee asked her mother.

"They have to be thorough, and Dad said there could be Nazi sympathizers who would help them escape."

Merilee was shocked.

"But I expect the guards are concerned for our safety. The prisoner might have sneaked in while we were all outside. They don't know exactly when he went missing."

Merilee was chilled to think that her beloved home could so easily be invaded.

After the guards had left, she dared to go for a refreshing swim, her mother keeping vigil on the veranda. But she glanced nervously at the cordoned-off stretch of lake, wondering if she would suddenly see a body floating there. Or what if the clever chap used a piece of hose to breathe while staying underwater and working his way along the shoreline? If he waited until the search had moved well away, he could climb out at the base of the cliff where the boom fence ended. He could hide until dark and then invade Hope Cottage for supplies and weapons and steal a boat. Maybe even murder them, since they were enemies. How would she sleep tonight if he weren't caught soon?

It helped that a couple of soldiers in a canoe were scanning the water and shoreline of the enclosure, checking to see if the prisoner was tucked into one of the many crevices of the rugged bluff.

She was cheered when the *S. S. Sagamo,* the largest of the steamship fleet, slowed down as she sailed back to harbour, the orchestra tauntingly playing *There Will Always be an England* as they passed the camp, as had become customary these past weeks.

And she was relieved when her father arrived home. "The army and police have put roadblocks on all the highways in the district, and extra guards at the railway stations and at key points along the Moon and Severn Rivers," he told them over dinner on the screened porch.

"Should we be worried?" Merilee asked, trying not to jump at every snap of twigs or furtive scurrying of chipmunks and squirrels.

"I don't think so, sweetheart. We know that the prisoners are constantly plotting to escape. It's as much a game as an irritant to their hosts. The guards have already found the beginnings of a tunnel, which was abandoned when it ran into rock. Those who actually manage to get out will be nervous and keeping a low profile, blending in so they can get as far away as possible. They have nothing to gain and everything to lose by harming someone."

"You and I know what it's like to be 'imprisoned' at the San," Claire said. "I expect they're bored even though they're not confined to bed like we were. Weren't we always plotting our 'escapes' and trysts?"

Colin chuckled. "Indeed! And there are four or five men living in each of our old rooms, so I imagine they want to get away from each other as well."

"Heavens! That many!"

"We have over four hundred prisoners here, mostly officers. There are some enlisted men who do the cooking and cleaning and such, but they're housed in separate barracks."

"I expect they will get on each other's nerves."

"They're outside as much as possible, playing soccer and tennis, even just sunbathing. Winter will be a different story. Actually, I'm impressed that some of them are organizing classes, not only in English – which would help them if they do escape, of course – but also in sciences and law and history and so forth. They figure they might as well get further education, and some of the officers were professionals and teachers, even at the university level. The YMCA is supplying materials."

"You should donate your books to them," Claire suggested. "Then they can learn history properly once they can read English." She grinned at him.

Several of his books were about the last war, but none were dry tomes. He had a knack for elucidating events through personal stories that engaged people, and quirky facts that fascinated them.

"I might just do that," he replied with a smile.

"And they could learn English with the *Enchanted Waterfall* series," Merilee said dryly.

They laughed at the absurd image of German officers reading children's picture books, and the mood lightened.

Dark clouds tumbled in, obscuring the sunset. A wind suddenly tousled the leaves. The first rumble of thunder was deeply welcome.

"At last!" Claire sighed, fanning herself.

The lake turned black and forbidding, whitecaps breaking on what had not long ago been mirror-still water. Tortured treetops bent in trembling submission as lightning and thunder exploded overhead. Merilee loved watching storms, and stayed on the porch, enjoying the cooling spray of driving rain that blew through the screen. The powerful and annoying searchlights that beamed onto the bay from the camp every night came to life, eerily highlighting the needles of rain bouncing off the turbulent lake.

She hoped the escapee was getting a good drenching and scare if he was still nearby, and would turn himself in.

The storm grumbled southward, having sucked away most of the intense heat. The dripping flowers dared to raise their heads, but the leggy hollyhocks had been flattened and several tree branches had come down.

Back in the sitting room for the evening, Merilee couldn't settle down to anything. She had already processed, in her dark room, the hundred plus photos she'd taken at Wyndwood last month, and riffled through them yet again.

Sensing her agitation, Colin said, "You should keep a diary, sweetheart. This is a unique experience in unusual times. You can even add your photos to it. You never know how useful your thoughts and observations will be in the future, to you as well as historians."

He grinned at her. She knew how important memoirs and journals were to his research. Forestalling her skepticism, he added, "You might be a renowned and influential woman one day."

She giggled. But the idea did excite her. She fetched a blank notebook from his office, and began scribbling down the events of the day, which soon overflowed into weeks and her feelings about the camp, and people like Lieutenant Tremayne. She particularly liked writing about Wyndwood and Bryce Carrington. And there were Ria's evacuees and Elyse Thornton. The delightful group photos with Alastair Grayson's downed Harvard nicely illustrated that dramatic event. Peggy had even taken some pictures of her and Bryce waterskiing.

She was so absorbed that she hadn't realized how late it was. When the telephone rang at 11:20 – well past their usual bedtime - Claire said, "I hope it's good news."

Colin answered and soon gave them a thumbs-up. "Yes, Colonel.... I see.... We definitely will.... Thank you for informing us."

When he put the phone down, he said, "They've captured the prisoner, although maybe it's fair to say that he seemed happy to be back in custody, even if he now spends a month in solitary confinement. His story is that he went into the woods to relieve himself and got lost." Colin chuckled. "Hard to credit, but Colonel Winterbourne said that he was dressed only in his swimming trunks and thin shoes, with no identification papers or money, so he couldn't possibly have gotten very far. Seems the mosquitoes drove him back toward the lights of civilization, and they found him close to the camp."

Claire laughed. "Who would have thought that we would ever be grateful to mosquitoes?"

"Well, he won't be very popular with his comrades, since swimming will now be curtailed for a while."

"With this heat wave, he certainly won't be!"

Despite the relief, Merilee checked under her bed before climbing into it. But it was too hot to close the window, and, realizing how easily someone could knock out the screen and climb in, she slept little that night.

•   •   •

Merilee was drifting on her back, gazing dreamily into the rain-washed blue sky as she thought about Bryce. It was silly to wish the summer away, but she could hardly wait to see him again, to sit on his shoulders as they waterskied, her naked legs wrapped around his bare arms and back, sinking into his strong embrace. Maybe he would fall in love with her, and...

She was suddenly rocked by a disturbance in the water. Although she knew it was unlikely that it could be a prisoner, she was still skittish, and stood up quickly. She was backing up as she scanned the lake where ripples were spreading outward near the end of the dock, and shrieked when a head popped up yards away.

"Ned! You scared the living daylights out of me!"

"I said hello, but I guess you didn't hear me."

He swam towards her with powerful strokes. "I sure miss my morning swims."

"You know you're welcome here anytime."

"Much appreciated, but I don't like to intrude."

"You're not. And since you *are* here, I can swim out farther," Merilee added with a grin. When alone, she wasn't allowed to go deeper than where she could easily stand.

"If I'd known I could be your bodyguard, I'd have been here every morning," he said with a cheeky grin.

"I'll race you to the island!" she yelled as she set out for the tiny, uninhabitable isle in the middle of the bay.

"Hey! That's cheating!"

He dove in after her and quickly caught up, staying beside her until the last few yards when he easily outpaced her. They crawled onto the scrubby shore.

"Oh God! Did you tell my parents you were here? They'll think I've drowned!"

"I did, and your mom asked if I wanted to join you for breakfast."

"Will you?"

"Already had mine... Before I did my morning chores."

"I've been up since dawn!"

"Long swim, then," he teased.

"Reading a suspenseful book on the veranda with my coffee. Enjoying the morning tranquility before the tourists intrude."

The harbour to the south was lined with small factories, docks, and private boathouses, no longer so busy with the war on. But beyond the humpbacked peninsula to the west, the mighty *Sagamo* was getting up a head of steam before setting out for the daily "100 Mile Cruise" through the three large, interconnected lakes. The smaller *Segwun* was blasting her whistle as she pulled away from the wharf. They easily recognized the voices of the different steamships.

"You should come over every morning before the summer disappears," Merilee suggested.

"Would if I could. But I'm off to the RCAF Manning Depot in Toronto tomorrow."

"So soon! You didn't say."

He shrugged. "Just got my notification a few days ago."

"Peggy said you wanted to be a pilot."

"Sure. Just like everyone else."

"At least you have your Grade 12, so you qualify."

"They told us that there are too many would-be pilots and a heck of a lot of other jobs that need to be filled. We'd be assigned according to our skills. And I'd say, according to our families. The private school boys will get first dibs as pilots, of course. So, I took your advice and said upfront that I wanted to be a mechanic. The recruiting officers were happy."

"Are *you*?"

"Sure. I like messing around with engines. Maybe one day I'll get to fly," he said wistfully.

"Gosh, I wonder if you'll meet Hugh Carrington at the Manning Depot."

Ned snorted. "Aren't his grandparents bluebloods with a castle in England?"

"His mother is actually *Lady* Antonia, but she hardly uses her title. And Anthea said that only part of the castle is habitable. Roofs have collapsed and walls are crumbling. Trees are growing inside the ruins!"

"Well, who needs a hundred rooms anyway?" Ned quipped.

"Anthea said it was kind of creepy, but cool. She's only been there once, about five years ago, and was miffed that she missed half the summer at the cottage. But I'm sure it would be interesting to see it."

Ned harrumphed.

As the *Segwun* rounded the headland into the wider bay, they waved at the eager passengers lining the railings.

"Well, I should get back and look at your car."

"I want to watch, so will you wait while I wolf down some breakfast?"

Ned chuckled. "If you really want to."

He had coffee while she ate her scrambled eggs and toast.

The royal blue McLaughlin-Buick with its white-walled tires was a showpiece, which Ned treated reverently.

"OK, so tell me how engines work and what you're doing," Merilee said when he'd opened up the hood. She had her camera at the ready.

He laughed. "I haven't got all day! Why do you suddenly want to know, anyway?"

"Anthea Carrington talked about being a driver if we girls get to do something important, like her mother and Aunt Ria did in the last war. They also had to maintain their ambulances, so I should know something about engines."

"Trying to impress your boyfriend?"

"He's not!... I'm *not*! Anyway, with you abandoning us, we should become a little self-sufficient, don't you think?"

"This isn't a job for you," he said, removing a spark plug.

"Because I'm a girl?" she challenged.

"No. Because you'll muck up your lily-white hands and that pretty dress."

"Baloney! I'll clean up just as well as you."

He snorted. "OK, a five-minute lesson." He gave her a brief synopsis of the internal combustion engine, which had her head spinning.

"Eight cylinders, eight spark plugs," he said, cleaning and checking the gap on another one. "Want to take over now?"

She hesitated, but wasn't about to admit defeat. "Sure!"

"We work on one at a time so that we don't mix up the leads... the wires to the distributor cap. That could damage the engine.... Make sure you clean off all the carbon deposits."

He let her do two more and then said, "Good job! Now I'd better finish up and get home."

She scrubbed her hands on a rag, and then brushed back her hair. Ned looked at her and grinned. "Forgot to mention the inevitable smudge on the cheek."

"Blast! But I guess I'm a real mechanic now," she giggled.

The car started without hesitation.

"I think you'll manage just fine if Bessie acts up again. Just don't touch anything else under the hood!" he warned, eyeing her sternly.

"Yes, Sergeant, Sir!"

Claire joined them, opening her wallet.

"There's no need to pay me, Mrs. Sutcliffe. It wasn't a big job, and Merilee helped."

"You say that too often, Ned, but this is a gift. I know you'll be leaving soon." She handed him a bill.

"Fifty bucks! That's more than a month's pay! Much too generous."

"Nonsense! It's good to have something stashed away for a rainy day. Or just to have some fun," Claire added with a grin.

"If you get sent to England, I'll expect postcards from all kinds of places," Merilee said. "Especially Cornwall. I'm reading *Rebecca* by Daphne du Maurier. It begins, '*Last night I dreamt I went to Manderley again.*' Doesn't that intrigue you?"

"And you want to visit Manderley?" Ned chuckled.

"You bet! And Jamaica Inn on the brooding moors." Merilee shivered with delight at the thought.

"OK, I promise to send postcards. Thank you, Mrs. Sutcliffe. By the way, Merilee has now been deputized to take over cleaning spark plugs."

Ned returned after lunch with Peggy. She had a big grin and a small dog on her lap in the sidecar.

"It's adorable!" Merilee exclaimed as Peggy handed her the fuzzy black-and-tan bundle.

"Ned thought you would feel safer having a guard dog around, like Zorro, and I figured that you won't be going too far now, so you can have a pet."

"I asked your dad," Ned explained, "and he said it was a great idea. German Shepherds are very loyal and protective. A friend just happened to have some pups looking for a good home. Germans aren't very popular right now,'" he jested. "So, they're calling them Alsatians again, like in the last war."

"He's really mine?" Merilee was astonished. Peggy was right that because her family travelled so much, she was never able to have a pet, much as she had longed for one. She hugged the little dog, which sniffed her and then nuzzled her neck and licked her cheek, making her laugh.

"Peggy can help you train him."

"Oh, thank you! This is the best present I've ever had!" Merilee glowed with delight.

"He needs a name," Peggy said.

Merilee thought for a moment, holding the puppy out in front of her to examine him, eye to eye. "Saxon," she declared.

Ned chuckled. "Weren't the Saxons Germans who conquered Britain?"

"That was *ages* ago. We *Anglo*-Saxons are not going to allow the Germans to do that again," Merilee avowed. "Except by furry four-footed ones."

"I think it's a splendid name," Peggy said.

"I'll leave you girls to pamper Saxon. I have to go and pack."

"Good luck!" Merilee said. "I'll see you when you're on leave."

He looked at her for a long moment, as if expecting more. She hugged him warmly, with all the joy and thankfulness of their shared childhood. "Will you write to me if you have time?"

He grinned. "You bet!"

Leaving the motorcycle for Merilee, he walked off jauntily.

If only, Peggy thought wistfully. Ned surely *was* in love with Merilee, who was just as obviously oblivious.

Merilee found a shallow wooden box in the shed, and appropriated a cushion and blanket to make a bed for Saxon, which she put into a corner of the sitting room. Peggy had brought along some of Chipper's dog biscuits to start Merilee off, and showed her how to give a command and reward the puppy.

Claire called him "precious", but said, "I expect Mabel will complain of dog hair." The local woman came in once a week to clean.

"She complains of everything," Merilee replied dismissively.

She fell in love with her new pal and, although he was still little at six weeks old, she already felt safer having him around. Peggy assured her that he would grow quickly.

Which was a good thing, since it was only a week later that the alarm shrieked again – at 7:00 AM.

Merilee was lounging in bed, enjoying the morning light streaming in after another violent storm had awakened her and Saxon in the night. He liked sleeping in her room, and suddenly leapt onto her bed, excited by the strange wailing. Front paws on her chest, he stood alert, ears pricked, staring at the window.

She rubbed his head and said, "Good dog! Let's go see what's happening."

They met her parents in the hallway, Saxon giving them a whining howl and a yip as if telling them a story.

"Get dressed while I check in with the Colonel," her father said. Due for work soon, he was already in uniform. By the time she joined her parents in the kitchen, he'd been on the phone, and informed them that a prisoner was missing from morning roll call. "He could have escaped hours ago, and may no longer be in the area."

This time the uncertainty and tension and the fear of venturing outside were not as acute. She took Saxon for his morning toileting, but they stayed between the house and the lake, which seemed slightly protected.

"Is this our new way of life?" Merilee asked as she buttered her toast at breakfast.

"I expect so. But much less dangerous than being in Britain," Colin pointed out.

"And we can still slather our bread with butter," Claire added, reminding Merilee about Britain's rationing.

"OK, I'll stop complaining!"

Her parents smiled.

"But don't stop being vigilant," Colin informed her with a wink as he rose to leave.

Not expecting Merilee to fetch Peggy under the circumstances, and with Ned gone, Mr. Wilding drove her over to spend the day.

"He came up in our corn patch. The prisoner," Peggy informed her when they had settled on the screened veranda with Saxon, who was gnawing and shaking a stuffed teddy bear that Merilee had bought him. "From a tunnel. Probably during that storm last night, which is why Chipper didn't even bark."

"It's bizarre to think of someone rising out of your cornfield in the wee hours. Like some Halloween spectre."

They looked at each other and giggled.

The escaped naval officer was apprehended in Montreal two days later. After that, Merilee stopped being terrified every time the Rubberset factory whistle blew.

England: Autumn 1940
Chapter 5

Elyse was annoyed that she was nervous. Was it to make her feel unwelcome that her mother had left her waiting in the drawing room for twenty minutes already?

Elyse had been a bit surprised that she'd been invited into Lady Sidonie's Belgravia townhouse after telling the maid who she was. She'd been prepared to demand to see her mother if she'd been turned away, but the elderly French servant had simply said, "Milady will be with you shortly, Miss Thornton. May I offer you a cup of tea?"

Now she'd finished two cups and craved something stronger.

Elyse rose restlessly and wandered about the elegantly furnished room examining the eclectic collection of original art – Picasso, Dali, Renoir, Monet, Matisse. Surprisingly, there was a watercolour by Uncle Jack of her family's cottage on Blackthorn Island, which was just north of Jack's Thorncliff. Her father, Rafe, preoccupied with his stables and races, had little time for the cottage, which was why Elyse spent most of her summers on Wyndwood. Did her mother have some happy memories there after all?

Of course, there was no photo of Elyse among the several that stood about the polished side tables and on the marble mantle. She was interested to see one of Sidonie aboard a yacht with the Duke and Duchess of Windsor, who had a villa at Cap d'Antibes, not far from Sidonie's, and were part of her illustrious social circle.

There was one of a teenaged Sidonie with Chas and another chap, who must be her brother Quentin – Chas's best friend at Oxford - an uncle whom Elyse never had a chance to know.

The three sets of tall French doors and windows were strapped with tape to prevent flying glass in case a bomb exploded nearby. Blackout curtains hanging at the ready added to the gloom, so Elyse stepped out onto a wide balcony overlooking the park that was the center of the square. Potted plants screened the neighbours, and colourful flowers and vines cascaded over the wrought-iron railing.

Elyse was about to go back inside to fetch a cigarette when she noticed an officer emerging from the portico below her. He paused to glance up and down the street as if reconnoitering, lit a cigarette, and strolled away. She wondered if he was one of her mother's lovers.

Deciding not to be at a disadvantage by being seated, Elyse stood by an open door, one arm crossed under her breasts and supporting her other elbow as she puffed languidly on a cigarette.

Lady Sidonie walked in, and without a greeting or apology said, "You're even more beautiful than your photos. Do sit down, darling. Monique is bringing us champagne. You will stay for a glass?"

"Are we celebrating something?" Elyse asked, trying to keep sarcasm from her voice. She knew that the "darling" wasn't an endearment, but probably how her mother addressed everyone.

Sidonie chuckled softly. "I'm always ready to celebrate. So... Perhaps the fact that you've turned out to be an admirable young woman despite – or perhaps because - of my neglect."

Elyse was momentarily speechless, so Sidonie continued. "Jack and Ria keep me well informed."

Neither spoke as the maid poured them brimming glasses of Veuve Cliquot. When Monique had left the room, Elyse challenged, "Why did you marry my father?"

This time Sidonie was taken aback. She secured a cigarette in a long holder before replying, "There was no one left whom I liked or who had the wherewithal to keep me in luxury. Besides, all my best friends were returning to Canada, and I didn't want to stay behind with the ghosts in England." For a split second there was profound melancholy in her face, but it was quickly masked.

Elyse knew that her mother's first husband and both her brothers had died, and that her parents had been financially unable to keep the beloved ancestral estate going. They had sold it and moved to the French Riviera where everything was cheap after the war. Elyse steeled herself against sympathy for this woman who looked so much like her, and who must have been about the same age when the last war broke out.

But she couldn't help wondering how she would feel if she lost Charlie and Drew and a husband she hadn't even met yet. Damn Sidonie for arousing her compassion!

"I know you've joined the ATA. Max Beaverbrook told me even before Jack wrote. I'm impressed that you're a pilot, but not surprised, considering that you've had Ria and Chas as role models."

"Actually, Uncle Chas was very much against any of us flying. It was Charlie who inspired me."

"Ah yes, the French *orphan*."

"Why do you say it like that?" Elyse demanded.

Sidonie shrugged nonchalantly, "One isn't an orphan when one has a living parent." She took a deep swig of champagne and said, "Are you in London for long?"

"Just here for a few days to be fitted for my uniform." Elyse realized that Sidonie would tell her no more about Charlie. But it confirmed her suspicions.

"Where are you staying?"

"At the Ritz." Which wasn't far away. Chas and Jack both gave her generous allowances, since her father had nothing to spare.

"One of my favourite places."

Elyse wondered what she would do if she were invited to stay in this luxurious four-storey house that was absurdly large for one person. But the offer wasn't made, and she was slightly miffed as well as relieved. She didn't want to begin now to fit into her mother's life.

She was somewhat disconcerted by Sidonie's direct and assessing stare.

"That brooch looks very chic on you, although I wouldn't have thought to wear it on a suit."

Elyse had deliberately worn the extravagant, jewelled butterfly brooch, more suited to an evening gown, but definitely making a statement on her periwinkle blue jacket.

"I'm glad to see that your father didn't give it to one of his other wives or use it to pay off debts."

"He said you wanted me to have all your jewellery." Elyse was puzzled.

"That was unexpectedly thoughtful and generous of him. I suppose he didn't want you to hate me too much." Sidonie was constantly pulling the rug out from under her.

"Why did you leave us?"

"I needed my freedom, darling. I was slowly suffocating. You might as well know that I never wanted children. Rafe did, so it wasn't fair to either of us to be stuck in an arid relationship after the fun wore off."

It would be pathetic to bemoan the fact that her mother obviously didn't care about her or have any desire to be part of Elyse's life. Mustering all her dignity, Elyse said, "I appreciate your honesty. And I won't take any more of your time."

"I have nothing but time, darling. I don't mind in the least if you stay. Join me for my dinner party, if you wish. Max Beaverbrook is coming, and some other society people it might be useful for you to meet."

"I wouldn't want to steal your thunder."

Sidonie laughed. "Witty and feisty. I'm glad to see that. I'd be delighted to introduce you to my friends. Honestly, darling, I do want to see you make a good match and be happy. Just because I'm a failure as a mother, doesn't mean that I'm callous or heartless."

"Perhaps some other time."

"As you wish. And do feel free to kip here when in town. I usually have a few friends staying, but there's always a room free."

"I'll keep that in mind." *Never!*

They strolled side by side down the broad curved staircase to the black-and-white tiled entrance foyer.

"Elyse, I am here to help should you need or want it. I know all too well that it's pointless to remain angry and bitter about something you had no control over and can't change. It eats away at you until you're empty inside. For your own sake, forget or forgive me."

They stared at one another for a long moment, Elyse looking in vain for a sign of regret or remorse or tenderness.

"It's early days," Sidonie said. "Do come to visit again. And call me Sid, like all my friends do. It will give us a new beginning for a different kind of relationship."

Elyse was just walking out the door when a young man carrying a kit bag came bounding up the three shallow steps and nearly collided with her.

"I'm frightfully sorry, Miss," he said, doffing his cap. Bemused, he looked at her and then at Sidonie standing in the doorway. "I'm seeing double!"

Sid chuckled. "Theo, meet my daughter, Elyse. Theodore Beauchamp is the son of old friends, who likes to pop up to London when he's off duty, and knows that he can cadge a comfortable bed and good meals here."

"None better! I do hope you're joining us this evening, Miss Thornton."

His icy blue eyes held hers with interest and hope, and she was fully aware how handsome and refined he was. He wore the smart blue uniform of an RAF Flight Lieutenant, which was the equivalent rank of an army Captain. But was he one of Sidonie's lovers? He couldn't be more than twenty-five, so the thought revolted her.

"I have other plans this evening."

"Pity," he said, holding her gaze. Turning to Sidonie, he asked, "Is there room in the inn? I have forty-eight hours off, and right now I need a hot bath and a stiff drink. It's been a busy day. I managed to shoot down a bomber and a Messerschmitt."

"Well done, Theo! Yes, of course there's a room for you. And you'll be interested to know that Elyse has joined the ATA."

He was astonished. "Then we have plenty to talk about, Miss Thornton! I'll look forward to seeing you again." He gave her a chivalrous bow and seemed unable to tear his gaze away.

"By the way, darling, if you're still in town on Sunday, you could join me at the Officers' Sunday Club at the Dorchester," Sidonie said to Elyse. "Some friends and I have organized these weekly *thé dansants* because London is deadly dull on the Sabbath for unattached young men, especially those from overseas."

Elyse looked skeptical.

"It's quite respectable, darling. The Prime Minister's wife is a member of our committee." Sid's smile held a mocking challenge.

"I'll consider it, if I stay."

Elyse was unusually self-conscious as she bid them farewell and walked away. Surely she could feel his seductive eyes on her. She was intrigued, and wanted to know more about charming Theo.

When she arrived at the Ritz, she was handed a note that had been phoned in. It read, "May I join you for a quiet dinner at your hotel this evening? Theo."

It was unconventional for women, especially unmarried ones, to dine without friends or an escort, and Elyse suddenly didn't want to be alone. She telephoned to graciously accept the invitation, and then asked to speak to her mother.

"What should I know about Theo and his family?" Elyse could almost feel the satisfied smirk at the other end of the line.

"Beecham spelled Beauchamp, darling. Comes from a long line of comfortable gentry with a few minor aristocrats thrown in. His mother was one of my school chums. His father's a Knight and an MP. Theo has an economics degree from Cambridge and was in banking before the war. I told him your father lost his fortune, but he probably realizes that you are my heir, and I have done exceedingly well with Jack's sage advice. And of course, Jack and Chas would ensure that you had an ample dowry. So be aware that you may be seen as an heiress."

Elyse was stunned to think that her mother planned to leave her considerable fortune to her, and almost missed the next words.

"Theo is suave and something of a playboy, so do be careful, darling. But have fun. It's important to seize every moment of happiness, especially at times like these."

Elyse indulged in a scented bath, realizing how different her creature comforts would be once she started working. She loved the gilded opulence of the hotel's Louis XVI décor and her luxurious room with French doors opening onto a narrow balcony that overlooked the vibrant city. She could afford to have this as her London getaway. Her mother was right – why not enjoy herself while she could.

She had been in England for a month, staying with Sophie at Priory Manor while awaiting her interview and test flight with the

ATA. Of course she had aced that. Once she had her uniforms, she would be given some training before starting work.

She was happy that she had also seen Charlie Thornton, who had managed to spend two days with her at Priory Manor. But he had been upset that she was going to ferry planes.

"It's bloody dangerous, Elyse!" he had said. "I wonder if we're actually going to survive this 'Battle of Britain'. So many planes destroyed, pilots lost or worked to the point of exhaustion. Once the RAF is shattered, there won't be anything to stop Jerry from invading."

"Which is why you need to have male pilots operational, not ferrying planes," she had protested.

Glad that she had packed an evening gown, Elyse slipped into the midnight-blue silk dress embroidered with glittering swirls of silver encircling her like a sash from the padded right shoulder down to the left side of the cinched waist and up the back. The butterfly brooch looked stunning on the opposite breast.

Theo's face lit with admiration when they met in the lounge. "Father told me that Sid was considered the most beautiful debutante in England in her day. I think you've outdone her."

Elyse laughed, and said, "I have to warn you that I'm immune to flattery." But she was pleased, nonetheless. "Unless you care to praise my flying skills."

"I should very much like to." He offered her his arm, and they ambled down to the subterranean restaurant, the sumptuous main dining room with ceiling-high windows and mirrored walls being mothballed for the duration.

"This is rather a surprise," Elyse said as they were shown to their table. A panoramic mural of the Western Front animated the room. Sandbags shored the walls behind metal poles. Wax dripped from candles stuck in wine bottles on the tables.

"Welcome to the last war," Theo said with a chuckle.

"It's like a stage set. Except that the officers are real." Among the smart set dining here were many, like Theo, in uniform.

A waiter arrived with an ice bucket sprouting a bottle of champagne.

Theo raised his glass to her and said, "Here's to new friends."

"And to your victory today," she responded.

"With the Luftwaffe targeting our airfields, you'll be in danger when you're ferrying planes." He looked at her with touching concern.

"I'd feel safer in a Spitfire, but they won't allow women to fly operational aircraft. They think we can't handle powerful machines, so we're stuck with slow trainers like the Tiger Moth."

"I can vouch for Hurricanes, although I wouldn't mind getting my hands on a Spitfire as well." There was amusement in his eyes.

"It's ridiculous that only the men get to ferry the fighters and bombers, since a few of them have only one arm, or one eye, and are rightly known as Ancient and Tattered Airmen," she said indignantly. The ATA men were either not physically fit or too old to join the RAF, many having served in the last war.

He laughed. "I saw some of the outrageous remarks in the press about allowing women to join the ATA."

She grinned. "It's not that we 'lack the intelligence to scrub the floor', but that we'd far rather be doing something more important and challenging, like flying!"

"What you ladies certainly don't lack is spunk."

"Why thank you, kind sir."

"What inspired you to take up flying?"

"It's in my blood. My father was a pilot in the last war, although he was shot down and taken prisoner... by the Red Baron, no less. Then, of course, there's my Uncle Chas..."

"The legendary Ace and squadron commander. We were taught his battle tactics."

"Which he reminded me of before I left, in case I encounter any hostile aircraft."

Theo regaled her with stories of pre-war jaunts around Europe in his private plane, flying to Switzerland to ski, or Paris for lunch.

Their lavish dinner seemed unaffected by rationing, and included smoked salmon, roast pheasant, potatoes au gratin, and Poire Belle Hélène smothered in liqueur, chocolate sauce, and Devon cream.

Over the last of their wine, he said, "I'm glad I discovered you before the rest of London does, and all those RAF chaps you'll be meeting. I hope you don't go to Sid's tea dance on Sunday."

"I'd rather spend time with my cousin at Priory Manor."

"Your mother can be brutally honest. It's refreshing, and one of the things I like about her. She told me that she hasn't seen you in fourteen years, so I can understand completely why you wouldn't want to suddenly become part of her world. But I am glad that you allowed me to spend this delightful evening with you."

"As long as you're not a spy."

"Good God, no! In fact, Sid warned me to be on my best behaviour." He grinned.

"I expect you know her better than I do," Elyse suddenly realized.

"She's always spent the autumn *Season* in London, and my family sometimes stayed at her townhouse. So perhaps I do." He regarded her with compassion. "Shall we go on to a nightclub?"

"Yes, let's."

It was a cool September evening, so she fetched her mink coat.

"The Café de Paris, I think. It's only a ten-minute walk in daytime, but more challenging at night," Theo said as they stepped outside.

"I'm not yet used to the utter darkness of the city," Elyse confessed. How bright and vibrant it had been on her previous visits with Chas and Ria. With heavy cloud cover, there was not even a celestial glow tonight.

Because of petrol rationing, there were few vehicles on the roads other than taxis and buses, but with their dimmed lights barely visible, they presented a hazard. Other strollers carried weak flashlights, shining them down onto the sidewalk.

"I should have thought to bring a torch," Theo said as he nearly bumped into a lamppost.

The sumptuous Café de Paris was several stories underground. From the columned, second floor balcony, which swept around the room, ornate staircases curved down, bracketing the stage beneath.

"This is cool," Elyse said when they had secured a table abutting the dance floor and ordered pink gins.

"The Prince of Wales was a patron in the '20s, so it became the poshest club in London. Before the war you couldn't get a table down here unless you were in full evening dress. If you were in a soft collar, you were relegated to the balcony. Things have changed now, of course."

Talented 'Snakehips' Johnson and his West Indian Orchestra were on stage, and the dance floor was crowded with mostly officers in uniform and glamorous young women in evening gowns.

"Can you dance to Swing?" Theo asked.

"I taught my cousins."

"I think I can just about manage. Shall we try?"

They soon fell into step, Elyse obviously being an accomplished dancer. But they preferred the slower music that allowed them more intimate contact. Their drinks were mostly neglected. Neither of them wanted the evening to end, but Theo looked exhausted and Elyse insisted that she, too, needed her bed.

She was surprised that she felt such an instant connection with him, as if they had known and liked each other for years. Or were they just infected with the fevered frenzy among the patrons to revel in every moment? In case this might be their last.

So when they were back in the darkness of the shrouded city, Elyse responded to his passionate kisses.

"Let's spend the day together tomorrow," Theo suggested. "There's nothing I'd rather do."

"I have a fitting for my uniforms in the morning."

"I will sit there and wait patiently. I only have tomorrow and then it's back into weeks of unrelenting work."

And danger. She wanted to prolong their time together as well. "If you're sure, then yes, I would like that."

Despite the late night, Elyse woke early. She tried to temper her excitement about the day ahead by chastising herself for having allowed Theo to affect her so profoundly. Her fondness for previous boyfriends had been tame, and she had always been in control – and the one to break off when the relationship threatened to become serious. Now she fleetingly considered inviting Theo into her bed. She certainly didn't want to die a virgin. But she also didn't want to be seen as *fast* or *easy*. Like her mother. Better to step back a bit, and not be carried away by his charm and his ardent interest in her.

But when he arrived after breakfast with a fragrant posy of flowers, she forgot her resolve. They were young and momentarily carefree.

After her fitting at Austin Reed's on Regent Street, they went to Selfridge's, since Elyse needed to purchase a few items. She had come to Britain well stocked with clothes and precious silk stockings, but realized that she needed some practical things, like flashlights, and a more attractive box for the gas mask she was required to carry.

Theo insisted on buying her a gold necklace of a bird in flight, suspended on the chain by its wingtips - stunning in its elegant simplicity. "As a good luck charm," he said.

"Then I shall find something for you."

"Just give me photo of yourself. I would treasure that."

"Let's find a photo booth."

But as they passed the toy department, she saw the perfect gift. It was a pocket-sized teddy bear sporting a Union Jack vest.

Theo chuckled and said, "He'll be my new best pal. I'll christen him 'Thornton'. But I still want a picture of you."

They finally found a photo booth, and Elyse posed differently for the four shots - looking defiant, coquettish, wistful, cheerful.

"You've been captured perfectly," Theo said with a grin.

"Now you must join me," she said, drawing him into the little booth and closing the curtain.

"Hmm, this is cozy," he said suggestively, putting his arms about her. The first two snaps caught them kissing. In the third, they were gazing at each other, in the fourth, laughing.

"Those are mine!" Elyse objected when he tried to pocket the strip of small photos.

"Alright. Let's do it again so that I can have a set."

It wasn't hard to reproduce.

They had a leisurely lunch at Claridge's, and then strolled through Hyde Park. It was strange to see barrage balloons, some flying high over the park; others moored at treetop height until an air attack was expected.

"You'll have to be careful of those when you're flying," Theo told her. "It's deadly to get caught in the wires. And they're not just here in London."

The corpulent silver blobs were gleaming in the sunlight. "They're quite visible, and I won't be flying at night."

"My dear girl, you have yet to fully experience English weather! The worst thing is when you're suddenly enveloped in smothering cloud and wonder what's on the other side as you try to descend – a hill, a spire, another plane."

"You're scaring me."

"Good!" He smiled at her. "I want you to be cautious. Can you fly by instruments?"

"I can, actually, although it isn't a requirement for the ATA."

He snorted. "It bloody well should be!"

"We have strict rules about when a flight is washed out, and not flying over the top of the weather."

"Then you'll hardly get off the ground," he joked. "Where will you be stationed?"

"I'm reporting to HQ at White Waltham this week for some training, and then reconnaissance flying. I have to become acquainted with the airfields where I'll be delivering planes."

"I'm at Northolt, just a hop away. Close enough to drop in after work."

"Flying one of His Majesty's planes off duty?"

"It's a perk of the job." He smiled disarmingly. "But you might have difficulty finding *us*. The airfield's been disguised to look like homes and gardens from the air, with a painted stream flowing across the runway. Stymies even those who know where it's supposed to be."

They sat down on a bench overlooking the Serpentine. Theo lit cigarettes for them.

"I would love to go for a swim," Elyse said, watching swans glide across the expanse of water. "Of course, this doesn't qualify as a real lake," she added with a grin.

"Is that what you'd be doing if you were in Canada?"

"Yes, savouring the last chilly swims of the season. Canoeing in the early morning through mist rising from the mirror-still water. Hearing nothing but the soft dip of your paddle and the haunting calls of the loons. Sometimes they pop up beside you when you're sitting still in the canoe. They're such beautiful and rather mysterious birds. They fascinate me."

"Your summer life fascinates me."

She looked at him and said sincerely, "I hope you can experience it some time."

"As do I!"

When they arrived back at the Ritz, Elyse said, "You look tired. I know that you RAF chaps have borne the brunt of this 'Battle of Britain'. I saw the toll it's taken on my cousin Charlie, and Churchill was right to say that 'so much is owed by so many to so few'. You're all heroes. If you're back on ops tomorrow, perhaps we should call off dinner tonight."

"Not on your life! I will have a nap and pick you up at seven."

Elyse didn't think she could sleep, but dozed off and had to scramble to be ready on time. Instead of her mother's brooch, she wore Theo's necklace.

"The Savoy," Theo instructed the taxi driver. When they arrived at the hotel, situated along the Thames, they noticed billowing smoke in the distance. "Looks like factories in the East End have been bombed again."

They shared a delicious Chateaubriand and a decadently expensive bottle of wine.

"This is one of Churchill's haunts," Theo told her. "My father's in his Cabinet, and the PM likes to bring his Ministers here for lunch."

"Is your father in the city?"

"He has a suite at the Dorchester. Sid offered him a room, but he doesn't want to impose. Besides, my mother wouldn't be pleased. She knows Sid too well." He grinned.

"She is rather notorious, from what I've heard."

"Beautiful and unconventional women are often regarded that way. You'll have to watch yourself."

She laughed. "You'll hardly think me sexy in my trousers or flying overalls."

"On the contrary." He gazed deeply into her eyes. "It's always tantalizing to imagine what lies beneath. Certainly a shapely pair of legs, as I've noticed."

"And here I thought you meant my mind and soul," she chided with amusement.

"Oh, I already know those – the one, sharp; the other, soft."

Over the last of their chocolate mousse, Theo said, "The 400 Club is a popular spot. Shall we dance there tonight? It's not far."

"You're the tour guide."

"We'll take a slight detour along The Embankment, if you're game," Theo said when they stepped outside.

"Of course."

The sky to the east was aglow from distant fires still burning from the earlier raid. The waxing moon turned the Thames into a pewter swath through the deepening twilight, and Elyse could pick out the darkened towers of Big Ben and the Houses of Parliament against the emerging stars to the west.

Theo pulled her behind a tree, saying, "I can't wait any longer to do this," as he took her into his arms and kissed her deeply.

They jumped apart in shock as air raid sirens began wailing. Searchlights bloomed, frantically probing the encroaching darkness. Hearing distant bombardments in the east, they were horrified to see a menacing swarm of bombers heading toward them.

"What the hell!" Theo swore.

Elyse and Theo were so mesmerized that they didn't even consider their own safety at first. But when they saw deadly black specks spewing from the bellies of the planes, he said, "The Savoy's our best bet," as he grabbed her hand and pulled her into a run.

The belligerent whine of the engines grew louder and more ominous as they neared the hotel. A bomb screamed overhead. Elyse, in her high heels, tripped, but Theo had a firm grip on her and pulled her protectively into his arms as a deafening explosion nearby shook the ground beneath them.

"Welcome back, Sir, Miss," the doorman greeted them with forced calmness. "You'll find the ballroom in the basement a safe haven. There's an excellent orchestra playing tonight, which won't disappoint."

Heart still pounding, Elyse almost burst into laughter. "We're going to dance through an air raid?" she asked Theo as they made their way downstairs.

He grinned. "Why not? But first we both need a stiff drink."

Scaffolding and the ubiquitous sandbags reinforced the cavernous room, but the music was boisterous, as if the band were trying to drown out the percussion of explosions. Some, uncomfortably near, tinkled the chandeliers. But the dance floor was bustling, as people seemed determined not to allow the Luftwaffe to spoil their evening.

As Elyse sipped the welcome cognac, she marvelled at their nonchalance.

The band played until after midnight, but still there was no 'all clear'. Hotel guests in dressing gowns mingled with revelers in their finery as they were shown to adjacent dormitories, where mattresses and camp beds were covered in brightly coloured bedding. There were separate areas for single men and women and married couples.

"We'll find somewhere cozy to sit," Theo said.

"You need sleep," Elyse protested.

"I can sleep anywhere." He grinned. "Let's take a peek at the action."

Upstairs, the hotel was eerily empty save for a few anxious staff, who advised Elyse and Theo to return to the safety of the shelter below.

But like mischievous children, they held hands and sought a window where they could see the Thames.

"Bloody hell!" Theo exclaimed.

Beyond the lattice of tape, hell indeed seemed to be erupting from the bowels of the city. Thick clouds of scarlet smoke reflected the inferno beneath. The menacing pulsing of planes was counterpointed by the booming of anti-aircraft guns spitting brilliant sparks into the billowing canopy. Incendiary bombs plummeted into neighbourhoods south of the river, flashing with blinding intensity, some quickly extinguished while others burst into yet another conflagration. The ack-ack guns must have hit a bomber, which tumbled out of the smoke and spiralled into some hapless neighbourhood.

Theo looked grim as he muttered, "I think Hitler just upped the ante."

They sank into a deep leather sofa away from the windows, chandeliers, and other potential projectiles. Elyse snuggled into the crook of Theo's arm and drew her fur coat over them both like a blanket. It felt dangerously seductive to be held so intimately, despite the layers of clothing that separated them.

She didn't think she would actually fall asleep, but they were both awakened at 5:00 AM by the bustling sounds of people emerging from the basement as the 'all clear' sounded.

There was a crushing pall of smoke over the city, and fires still appeared to be raging along and across the Thames. There was less damage visible in the West End until Elyse and Theo began to wend their way toward The Ritz, sometimes around craters in the road and the twisted, skeletal remains of vehicles. Civil Defence Workers were digging frantically amid the dusty rubble of partially collapsed buildings, some still smouldering, others exposing walls, like a child's dollhouse, where photographs and mantelpieces clung precariously. Elyse looked away as a body was pulled from the wreckage. Shopkeepers were sweeping up debris from shattered showcase windows and blasted storefronts, doggedly putting up signs declaring they were 'Open for Business'.

Theo said, "I hope this was a one-off, and not a free-for-all savaging of London. Night attacks are much harder for us to defend."

Elyse squeezed his hand. "I expect I'll have to worry about you now."

He grinned. "You needn't fear, as I'll have my lucky teddy to look after me. But I am chuffed that you'll be thinking about me." He kissed her.

When he released her reluctantly, he looked longingly into her eyes and said, "Damn, I'm going to miss you!"

•   •   •

Periwinkle Cottage
October 17, 1940
Dear Merilee,

Don't you just adore the name of my new abode? Of course, it's not a cottage in the Canadian sense, but rather, a cute little house with an exuberant garden. There's no central heating and the boiler that heats the water is temperamental, so I expect we shall freeze once winter sets in. We're only allowed to run 4 inches of water for baths, but I have made do with less when it's lukewarm!

I'm renting this place along with my new friend and colleague, Rosalyn – Roz - Fenwick. Her family lives on the ocean south of Boston, but she's half Canadian, as her mother hails from Montreal. She has an older brother, who she claims is a quiet intellectual, forcing her to be the adventuresome one. She took up flying a few years ago and had enough hours to qualify for the ATA. It turns out that her aunt and uncle in Montreal know Billy Bishop, and he put in a word for her. She could hardly believe that we're friends of the Bishops, and that they summer on our lake.

Coincidences like that always make me wonder if there is some "bigger plan" in the universe for these connections. Like your friend Ned meeting Hugh at the Manning Depot in Toronto after Hugh had just met his sister Peggy at Wyndwood! You'd be accused of contriving the plot in books or movies.

Anyway... Roz is professional and serious about her flying, but also great fun. We've really hit it off, partly because we're the same age and both from "over the pond", with, I daresay, a similar irreverent sense of humour.

I've bought a small Vauxhall, but with the petrol restrictions, also have a bicycle to get me back and forth to the aerodrome. It's not far, but we have to haul our parachute packs, which weigh 40 pounds!

A real pain that is when we have to lug them with us on our train trips back from our deliveries, many to training schools in Scotland. Three or more hours flying there in an open cockpit is already freezing me, so I can't imagine how I'll survive winter. But the overcrowded trains aren't warm either, and if we don't manage to get bunks – which we often can't – we try to snatch some sleep perched on our packs. One of the girls stretches out in the luggage rack!

There's talk of instituting air taxis to pick us up from our various destinations, as it would save everyone time and discomfort. I'd relish being able to sleep in my own bed every night!

Roz and I are planning a short biking excursion in Dorset next week. We work 13 days and then have 2 off, so we try to cram in as much as we can when we're free. And really, who wants to chance London these days with the nightly bombings? Did you hear that Buckingham Palace was hit while the King and Queen were there? That has endeared the Royal couple even more to beleaguered Londoners. I've never considered myself a coward, but after having experienced the first of these Blitz attacks, I'd rather enjoy the relative tranquility and safety of the countryside.

So why Dorset? It seems that I am not good at heeding my own advice. Newly minted <u>Squadron Leader</u> Theo Beauchamp drops in to see me whenever he can steal a few minutes, and I must admit that his ardent wooing is breaking down my defences. His family estate is in the Purbeck Hills in Dorset, and I fancy seeing the area where he grew up. We won't be able to get too close, as the military has taken it over for the duration, and his mother is staying with her sister in Salisbury.

I've been told that Corfe Castle is worth a visit in any case. Roz and I have booked a room at an ancient inn with, we've been assured, a commanding view of the castle ruins looming above us. It sounds *so deliciously romantic that surely I should be staying there with Theo.*

You're right to say that he sounds too perfect, which is why I'm not ready to trust him. I expect he has plenty of women in his thrall, especially the WAAFs at his aerodrome, who have the benefit of daily contact. And he's certainly a hero, having already been awarded a DFC and a bar.

I just received a letter from Sandy and was thrilled to hear that he's now in Ottawa working for the National Film Board. How perfect! He says that he was hired as a screenwriter and editor, but hopes to eventually get into producing and directing as well. He's particularly chuffed to be working on a "documentary" film about the BCATP, and I suspect that having Air Marshal Chas as his uncle had something to do with that assignment. He did say that our little film, Shadows, impressed his boss, who wondered if I couldn't be of some use to the NFB. Sandy suggested I could star in a film about the ATA. Haha! It did make me laugh when you described movie night at The Point with Drew's chums. Encore indeed!

Not surprisingly, Uncle Jack wasn't pleased about his dropping out of university. But he wasn't happy about Sandy studying literature instead of economics either.

I suspect Sandy is also relieved to be living away from home. Kate always needles him about being too intellectual, and boring her friends, which I consider a blessing, none of them being worthy of him. We all need freedom to find our way and blossom into our talents. Naturally Sandy has been installed in the house that Uncle Jack bought in Rockcliffe Park for his business trips to Ottawa, but hopefully he won't be there all that often or long, and Sandy will mostly have it to himself.

Yes, Aunt Fliss told me that Kate is engaged to the brother of her school chum, Rebecca, who is too self-absorbed for my liking. Of course, Kate has to be the first of her circle to be married. But apparently the wedding won't be as elaborate as hoped, since the bridegroom, Gerard Jr., is finishing his RCAF training and expecting to be shipped out, so there is need for haste.

As the best pilots are kept at home to teach for the time being, I fear that our cousin may soon be a widow. But I'm sure she'd play that tragic role to simpering perfection as well. Oh, how spiteful of me to even think such a wicked thing.

I am, as always, your devoted and loving cousin-in-spirit. Elyse

Muskoka: Autumn 1940
Chapter 6

Much as Merilee loved summer, autumn was resplendent on the lake. With the tourists and cottagers mostly gone, there was quiet time to reflect and to absorb her surroundings, which glowed with vibrant colours.

"It isn't anything like as pretty in the city," Amy grumbled when she and Adam were home for the long Thanksgiving weekend in October. "I like visiting Toronto, but I don't want to live there."

"That's because you're just a country bumpkin," Adam retorted.

"Is that what they call *you* at school?" Amy shot back.

"Don't be stupid! Most of our cousins and friends are at my school."

"Mine too! I don't mind it too much... I guess... Mum says I have to uphold the Wyndham tradition and excel at something. Aunt Ria was the reigning tennis champ for four years, Aunt Zoë won all the academic awards," she said, referring to her mother's elder sister. "And can you believe that Mum was the debating champion of 1919? Her name's on a trophy."

"So she should win all the arguments with Dad," Adam declared.

"Doesn't she usually? Lucky for you," Amy snapped back. "Elyse was the star of the dramatic society, of course. So, what am I supposed to do?"

"Stop whining?" Adam suggested.

Amy stuck her tongue out at him.

Merilee giggled as she said, "Put that tongue to better use. Debating would probably stand you in good stead."

"Yeah, she never shuts up anyway," Adam complained. "I have homework to do."

When he'd slouched off, Merilee asked, "When did *he* become studious?"

"Ever since he figured that if he excels at school and gets into university, Dad can't make him join the boatworks."

"He still wants to enlist in the RCAF, even when the war's over?"

"Yup! He says if Alastair Grayson can become an officer, why shouldn't he."

"He'll have his work cut out for him then. I heard that Alastair did brilliantly at university."

They were sitting on the expansive veranda of the twin's home, which seemed to have been carved out of the granite and pine hillside overlooking Chippewa Bay and Port Darling. Aunt Zoë's husband, Freddie - a renowned architect - had designed the beautiful, rambling house. The delicious aroma of roasting turkey wafted out through the screen doors.

"That reminds me," Amy said. "You know that Anthea Carrington's at my school? Well, she told me that Bryce has a new girlfriend... a real dish, apparently... so now he's not as keen to join up. Boys!"

Merilee tried to hide her shock as she mumbled, "They're fibbers, aren't they."

She felt a stab of pain as she recalled the Summer's End Ball at Thorncliff. Bryce had been flatteringly attentive all evening and seemed completely absorbed in her when they'd danced. She'd had her first, sweet kiss under the stars, and become even more smitten by him.

As they'd strolled hand-in-hand along the shore, her heart took wing when he said, "You've always seemed like a summer girl to me. A bit magical - like that fairy in your parents' books - because I only see you here. I'm going to miss you, Merilee." He'd kissed her again. "A lot."

"We can write."

"Sure thing!"

She had thought him too busy, but now she knew why her letters hadn't been answered. It wasn't until she lay in bed that night that she allowed the tears to come.

"The rat!" Peggy snarled when Merilee told her a few days later. "He is rather full of himself though, isn't he? Probably thinks that girls are falling all over themselves to be with him."

She was still fuming from a nasty incident after school. One of the boys had lurched up beside her like Quasimodo in last year's chilling movie, *The Hunchback of Notre Dame,* and growled, "Hey Peg, wanna shake a leg at the dance on Saturday?"

There were amused chuckles from the other guys in the hallway, and titters from the girls watching expectantly.

Her eyes blazing, Peggy had turned to him and simpered deceptively, "Why Harvey, how nice of you to offer. And here I thought you didn't have a decent bone in your entire body. But since you still have less intelligence than a slug, I shall have to decline."

Amid the astonished guffaws, Harvey strode up to Peggy, pushing her against the lockers as he'd barked, "Stupid peg-leg bitch! No one wants to stick it in you, even if they could!"

"Shut up, you vulgar ignoramus!" Merilee yelled as she'd pulled him away from Peggy.

He shook her off. "Kiss my ass, Miss Hoity-Toity!"

One of the other boys had bellowed, "Maybe they're screwing the fuckin' Jerries. Practically live with them, don't they?"

"You and Harvey should go and fight the Germans instead of picking on girls. Or don't you have the guts?" Gail Dennison had accused as she'd come upon the altercation. She went to stand supportively beside Peggy.

"Bang on," Gord McLaughlin added as he'd joined them. He was the school's star athlete and a year older than the others. His parents and Gail's were good friends of Colin and Claire's. "Put your money where your mouth is, or are you just full of hot air?"

"I'll be fighting the fuckin' Krauts as soon as I'm old enough," Harvey had blustered.

Gord had looked at the miscreants challengingly. "Be sure you do."

With her friends beside her, Peggy had left with as much dignity as she could muster, considering her awkward gait. She was livid when cruel laughter followed them down the hall.

"Don't give them the satisfaction," Gord had advised, preventing the girls from turning around to protest.

"I'll be glad when I get out of this town," Peggy had said when they were outside and she felt able to breathe.

"Won't we all!" Gord had agreed. "I'm off to fly airplanes as soon as I can."

"Aren't you expected to go to university?" Gail had asked.

His father was a doctor at the Sanatorium, and he had an older brother and sister who were already studying medicine. "I told Dad that I'm not cut out to be a doc. Guess I'm the black sheep," he'd added with a disarming grin.

"Let's all be rebels," Gail had suggested devilishly.

"Hell yeah!"

Now Peggy and Merilee sat munching hot buttered scones lathered with homemade raspberry jam in Peggy's kitchen. Merilee had helped to gather the berries from the prickly canes that tumbled over the split-rail fence along one edge of the Wildings' property.

Lois was collecting the washing from the line that stretched across the back garden, so Merilee answered the knock on the kitchen door.

"Ross! How lovely to see you," she said, leading him in. "You're just in time for tea."

"That would be delightful," he said, sitting down across from Peggy as he greeted her. "I've had such reassuring letters from Mum and Deanna, who seems to be improving daily."

"Yes, so have I. It's really encouraging."

"She's already looking forward to coming back next summer. And seeing you again."

Peggy smiled happily, her anger at the juvenile boys chased away by his warmth and sincerity. This was how *real* men behaved, and she was grateful that he was a friend. Her nighttime fantasies about him were her treasured secret.

Tucking into his treats, Ross looked intently at Peggy as he said, "I'm certainly going to miss all this."

"They're not sending you overseas?" Lois asked, coming in with a heaping basket.

"Not yet, Mrs. Wilding. Just off to build more POW camps."

Peggy felt her joy deflate.

"You'll be missed," Lois stated.

"I doubt that anyone can make me feel as much at home as you all have. I'd like to stay in touch, if I may."

"Of course! We'd be sad if you didn't," Lois assured him with a motherly smile.

Merilee excused herself, pleased to see that Ross made no move to leave.

Military buildings sprawled along one side of this road that formed the eastern boundary of the camp, including the guards' centre and the lock-up for prisoners being punished for escaping or other infractions. The buildings that housed the Germans, and the grounds within their secure inner enclosure were too far away and hidden by trees, so there was nothing to see from here – the closest point that most civilians could reach. Some of the kids from school had daringly tried to sneak up to the outer gates to peek in and had been disappointed.

She passed one of the sentry posts, waving to the guard. They all knew her by now, and each had a friendly greeting. The Veterans Guard, in charge of camp security, were mostly ex-WW1 soldiers. It had made sense that when Mr. Wilding had finished his carpentry work on the old San building, he'd joined the Guards as well. "Nothing like working right next door," he'd quipped.

Merilee was hopscotching on the crunchy dead leaves that blanketed the dirt road, delighting in the rich, peaty fragrance that was released. So, she didn't notice them right away as they rounded the corner from the next sentry post at the top of her laneway.

A few dozen Germans were being marched toward the camp.

There was nowhere for her to go except to step off the road and shelter at the side of a thick oak. She was too curious to hide behind it.

They were a rag-tag group, most in the blue-grey uniforms of the Luftwaffe – the German Air Force. Many looked so young. In fact, there was one who somewhat resembled Drew. She stared at him in amazement, catching his eye. He smiled at her and winked.

Embarrassed, she looked away, but only until he'd passed. Then she watched him walking toward his imprisonment. Once again, she felt traitorous for thinking that the Germans were not much different from her family and friends caught up in the conflict.

Erich Leitner wanted to look back at the beautiful girl he was delighted to see enjoying a carefree moment playing in the leaves, and then watching him from the edge of woods like some mystical sylph.

"Do you think they even provide us with women here?" Axel Fuchs asked Erich. "Wouldn't mind that one in my bed." He whistled appreciatively.

During the long journey since his Messerschmitt had been shot down in England in August, Erich wondered what his fate would be. Arriving in Halifax, he had noticed that life was already better here in Canada, with plentiful good food aboard the warm train. Once away from the brightly lit cities, the train had brought them through increasingly wilder countryside - beautiful, to be sure, but what privation or hardship lay at the end?

So, he was hopeful when he entered the camp and saw the lovely building that looked like a hotel.

The new arrivals were greeted in a spacious common room by the senior officer and therefore the Lagerführer – German Commandant of the camp - as well as his Adjutant. They were given a lecture about the rules and expectations, learning that they were pretty well free to run their own show within the compound, and that the Canadians provided supplies and ensured that no one escaped. So, as well as thrice daily roll call, there were random checks by scouts, and no one was allowed outside after 10:00 PM.

The Lagerführer had commanded a U-boat and wore a smart Navy uniform. "Now I want to know what each of you brings to us. Careers, skills, languages, hobbies. You there, begin. Name!"

"Oberleutnant Erich Leitner, Korvettenkapitän Hofmeister. I was training in electrical engineering. I also play the flute and speak French. Only a little school English."

"And his family owns a winery, so he knows how to make booze," Axel Fuchs interjected amid muffled amusement.

"A skill worth exploring," the Adjutant, Luftwaffe Major Falkenrath, said, forestalling a reprimand from the obviously annoyed Hofmeister.

"Now you, the one so eager to talk!" the Lagerführer snapped at Axel.

"Leutnant Axel Fuchs, mechanic and shit-disturber, Sir, if you need one. I play a mean game of soccer. And I'm ready to dig tunnels or whatever it takes to escape from here."

"We are still at war, so we won't make it easy for our captors. But no one attempts to leave here without my permission. And if any of you break your Ehrenwort while on parole, I'll personally see that you're strung up for bringing disgrace to the Wehrmacht!" Hofmeister growled. "Fuchs, you can join the Escape Committee. Next!"

When the initiation was over, they were finally shown to their quarters. Erich and Axel were assigned to a room on the third floor already occupied by three other officers.

Erich thought it absurdly wonderful that the room had a large screened balcony, which overlooked a stunning vista of sparkling lake.

"Not so bad for a prison," one of the roommates said as if reading his mind. "Hauptmann Christoph von Altenberg. Welcome to our holiday camp. We can even swim here," he added, pointing out the fenced beach. The Captain looked to be in his late twenties, with the cultured ease of an aristocrat.

"Oberleutnant Wolfgang Sturm, career pilot," a lanky fellow said. "Dressing for dinner, as you can see," he added, donning his uniform jacket.

Erich and Axel had just been issued their prison garb – jeans with red stripes down the sides and denim shirts and jackets with a large red circle on the back – required when out on parole if not in uniform. But they could also order certain things through the canteen, Major Falkenrath had told them. And new uniforms would be shipped to them through the Red Cross, since theirs were now shabby.

"Major Gerhardt Drechsler," the third occupant said dismissively, as if being so senior in rank he owed them nothing. "Where the hell is that useless Finkle? He was supposed to polish my boots."

There was a knock on the door and a young man came in carrying shiny boots.

"What took you so long?" Gerhardt Drechsler demanded.

"Sorry, Sir. There was lots of mud."

"You mean you had too many cigarette breaks."

"No, Sir."

"There's a scuff mark here," Drechsler accused, examining his tall boots.

"I worked on it, Sir. But the leather is worn."

Drechsler harrumphed.

"Gentlemen, this is Finkel, our batman. He is most amenable, especially if you share some of your chocolate rations with him," Christoph von Altenberg said. "Finkel, meet your new charges. They look like they could use your services."

"It's been a long journey," Erich said. "What I want more than anything is a bath."

"No time for that now, as the highlight of the day awaits," Wolfgang Sturm said.

"Wolf is always thinking about his stomach," Christoph teased.

"What else is there in this God-forsaken place?"

"I suppose these bunk beds are ours," Axel said, throwing himself onto the lower unmade one. "Not bad. A bit crowded in here though. I hope you guys don't fart or snore too much."

"Christ, we've got ourselves a smart-ass," Gerhardt Drechsler snorted.

"Better than a dumb one. So, what happened to the guys who used to sleep here? Escaped, did they?"

"The Canadians are opening new camps, so they transfer people out. Then you lot have to get yourselves shot down and cramp the quarters again." Wolf Sturm said wryly.

"I shouldn't be billeted with you junior officers," Drechsler complained. "It's outrageous! I expect that the Geneva Convention is being violated."

"If Hofmeister can't do anything about it, have him take it up with the Canadian Commandant," Christoph von Altenberg suggested. "Perhaps they'll move you to one of the new camps."

Drechsler seemed to miss the implication that his removal would be most welcome by his roommates. "You should complain as well," he replied.

"I was an Oberleutnant until my promotion came in last week, so I think not," von Altenberg replied.

"How do you get a promotion in prison camp?" Axel was eager to know. "I was about due to become Oberleutnant."

"So you probably will."

"Hot diggety dog!" It was an English expression he'd heard aboard the ship and found amusing.

Erich stepped out onto the large balcony through the French door. The barbed wire enclosure allowed for a bit of lawn and tennis court, but the rugged landscape beyond was undulating rock and thickening woodlands. The boom fence seemed to give them a generous section of the lake as well. It was glorious. Too bad he would never swim there, since he expected the war to be over by next summer.

Dinner was plentiful and, since it was cooked by their own enlisted men, had delicious favourites like potato salad and pork schnitzel. There was the luxury of white bread and butter and real coffee. Erich and Axel dined with two of their roommates – pompous Gerhardt Drechsler sitting with senior naval officers – and learned that Wolf Sturm had won an Iron Cross. Christoph von Altenberg was from an old aristocratic family, and, having spent a few years at Oxford University, spoke perfect English. So, he was the official translator for the camp. They were introduced to others from the Luftwaffe, who were eager to hear news from home.

"I was shot down in late August, so all I can tell you is that when I was in hospital in London, there was nightly bombing close by," Erich said. It had scared the hell out of him, as the beds jumped and brilliant flashes lit up the ward. The guards had locked them in and retired to the safety of the bomb shelter.

"They didn't get me until September, so I can assure you that we're destroying the RAF and scaring the shit out of the British," Axel declared. "I'm sure it's only a matter of weeks until we invade."

"Good! Then there's no point in my learning English," Wolf Sturm said. "Papa Christoph has organized a class, but I've declined. It's defeatist anyway."

"Papa?" Axel asked.

"He's our room elder, so we have to do what he says," Wolf teased.

"And I say it won't hurt you to learn English, especially if you're planning to escape," Christoph stated. "That's not defeatist; that's preparation."

"Has anyone escaped?" Axel asked.

"A few have, but they're soon back. Do you realize the size of this country and how far we are from Germany?" Christoph asked.

"And all the action!" Wolf lamented. "That's why we have to ruffle feathers here. Not let the Canucks think it's easy to keep us locked up, or have our comrades back home think we're just sitting on our lazy asses."

"Do you always eat like this?" Erich asked, scooping up the last of his apple strudel.

"Damn yes!" Wolf said. "And we can buy things from the canteen, including chocolate and beer and cigarettes."

"With what?" Axel wanted to know.

"The Canucks have to give us monthly pay according to our rank. Oberleutnants get $21 a month, but only in credit tickets, not real money. Papa Christoph is going to be making $25 as Hauptmann, so I'm going to put in for promotion," Wolf added with a smirk.

"We can even order from this." One of the men showed them the thick Eaton's catalogue, which contained practically anything that anyone could ever want or need.

"Hot diggety dog!" Axel said, flipping through. "I'll order one of these!" He pointed to a pretty girl modeling a dress.

"I don't think that dress will look so attractive on you," Erich quipped.

"Ah but may be a good disguise for when you escape," Wolf jested.

Erich leafed through the enticing pages and was excited to see that there were flutes for sale. He would buy one as soon as he had enough money. But he also needed gym shoes, pyjamas, underwear, a warm sweater, hat, gloves, and God knows what else.

At evening roll call, the Canadian Sergeant hesitated a moment when he came to Axel's name. He cleared his throat and mumbled "Axel Fux".

"I'll bet he does," someone with a good command of English said, amid laughter.

Confused, Axel corrected him. "Fooks. English 'Fox'."

"That's a relief," the Sergeant said with a grin, and there were more chuckles.

"What's so funny about my name?" Axel asked Christoph afterwards.

When Christoph explained, Axel roared with laughter. "Axel fucks whenever he gets the chance!"

"Not much chance here," Wolf said.

"Don't remind me! That'll be the worst thing about being imprisoned," Axel said dejectedly.

Erich lay awake for a long time, thankful that he was alive, with a nice place to wait out the war, but wondering how long it would be until he was home again.

This new life began on a sunny day in August when his fighter squadron had been sent up from their French base near Calais to do a "free chase" over England's south coast. Their objective: to engage as many enemy fighters as possible and clear the air for the bombers that would soon follow to cripple the RAF airfields and factories.

With the advantage of height and the sun behind them, they dove down on oncoming Spitfires and Hurricanes south of London. Erich had one squarely in his sights and couldn't have missed. Astonishingly, both his guns failed. While his comrades were engaged in fierce battle, he had no choice but to head back. But he was now an easy target for several planes that took after him.

He flew aggressively to outmaneuver them, but his Messerschmitt was riddled with bullets, one ripping through his thigh. The engine stuttered and burst into flame. More than anything, he feared being roasted alive.

Erich had never been given practice in parachute jumping, but knew what he should do. He released the canopy, unfastened his seatbelt, and was suddenly sucked out of the cockpit and somersaulting though the insubstantial air at 10,000 feet.

There was another moment of panic until he found the ripcord and the parachute ballooned into life. He drifted serenely toward the pretty green fields of Kent below. Those were his last seven minutes of freedom.

He spotted his reception committee well before he had a hard landing that jolted his wounded leg and caused him to black out momentarily. Willing hands helped him up, someone put a cigarette in his mouth, and another hastily tied a bandage around his leg.

"Good morning. Welcome to England," one of the elderly Home Guard said pleasantly.

"Good morning," Erich replied, his high school English now rattling around in his head until he realized he should say nothing. But they were decent and considerate toward him, and it seemed only civilized to respond in kind. Besides, these Brits would soon be welcoming hordes of Germans to their shores, so he would try to be a good ambassador.

He was taken to a nearby defence unit headquarters, where an army doctor examined his wound, and declared him lucky that it was only a deep graze, which he stitched up. Badly sprained ankles from the landing would also heal soon. After a brief interrogation, he was transported to Woolwich Hospital in London. In his Luftwaffe ward, he was surprised and delighted to see old comrades, missing in action, even though some poor chaps were badly burned. His injuries paled in comparison, and he was released after a few weeks to the interrogation centre at Cockfosters No. 1 Camp, a stately mansion in the north of London. Here he happily met up with more old colleagues, including Axel Fuchs. He was questioned occasionally, but knew no vital or new information in any case, so it wasn't a hardship being there, although the food was meager and tasteless.

His twentieth birthday present was discovering that he was to be sent to Canada.

That had shocked and dismayed him. He would be even further from home and from the ensuing invasion of Britain, in which he wouldn't be able to participate now. He knew nothing about Canada other than that it was home to Indians and Eskimos and red-coated police called Mounties. It was a vast land, bitterly cold and snow-covered much of the year.

So, this was a pleasant surprise. He hoped his family knew where he was and didn't think him dead. He would write to them first thing in the morning. Erich wondered if his sweetheart, Angelika, would wait for him or fall in love with another. Their families had been friends for years, and everyone expected they would marry.

But as he drifted off to sleep, he was savouring the memory of the enchanting forest girl who somehow symbolized his new life.

Muskoka: Winter 1940
Chapter 7

Erich Leitner was helping to shovel the skating rink, which had been the tennis court in fine weather. A magnificent blizzard yesterday had whitewashed the landscape; fluffy snow still blossomed on every branch and twig – so beautiful that it lifted his spirits.

It was ridiculous to hope they could have been home by Christmas, especially after Operation Sea Lion – the invasion of Britain - seemed to have been abandoned.

In the darkening days of winter, there was a doleful atmosphere in the camp. But he and his fellow prisoners had to make the best of things. Horst Schiffer had been on Germany's Olympic hockey team, so he was giving lessons and forming teams. Erich was glad that he knew how to skate, since many didn't and would find little to do outdoors in winter. The War Prisoners' Aid had supplied them with equipment.

It was glorious to be out in the snow-muffled stillness and sunshine. The dry cold was not unpleasant, but Erich was glad that he'd bought sturdy "Moosehead" boots, long underwear, and a thick sweater from the Eaton's catalogue.

Axel came running out of the building, shouting, "The mail's here, and there's a parcel for you from home!"

Not having heard from his family yet, Erich had begun to worry about them.

"And we got our Christmas orders," Axel enthused as they went to the mailroom.

Reichsmarschall Göring, the Commander of the Luftwaffe, had offered each of his 'boys' a Christmas present worth up to $20, to be bought through a representative of the International Red Cross. Many of the men had selected from the Eaton's catalogue. Erich had chosen a flute, so he was thrilled that he would be able to play again.

But first he wanted to open his treasure trove from home. He would read the enclosed letters when he had a private moment, knowing that he'd be overwhelmed by emotion.

His twelve-year-old sister, Trudi, had knitted him warm socks and a cozy scarf – black with wide bands of red and gold at each end.

"Very chic," Christoph pronounced when Erich wrapped it around his neck. "And clever to use the colours of our homeland."

"Yes, much more dashing than this white one my mother sent," Axel said in mock disgruntlement. "I'll just blend into the landscape."

The friends were in their room, and all had a care package but Wolf. His mother was a widow, who didn't have a penny to spare.

They had a new roommate, Oberleutnant Rudi Bachmeier, having exchanged him for the stiff and prickly Prussian, Major Drechsler. Rudi was a law student from Bavaria, and since they all hailed from southern Germany, there was a more relaxed atmosphere in their confined space.

"My scarf is a sensible brown, which doesn't match anything," Rudi said with a chuckle.

"And Christoph's is cashmere, if I'm not mistaken," Wolf said.

"My wife has rather refined tastes," Christoph said with a grin. She had also sent his favourite pipe and plenty of tobacco. He had two young daughters, who had drawn a picture of themselves outside a large house – two little stick figures and mommy, waving to a sad daddy stuck on a tiny island in the far corner. Erich could see what effort it took for Christoph to keep control.

Erich handed Wolf a pair of socks saying, "I don't need three, so please take one."

Wolf hesitated, not wanting charity, but Erich was insistent.

"Very soft!" Wolf said, obviously pleased.

Erich threw him a pack of cigarettes as well. "I'll tell my brother not to bother sending me any, since I can get enough here."

He pulled out a fine wool jacket, a few books, various jams made from the fruits of their orchards, his old ski sweater, leather gloves, and winter cap. Ten-year-old Karl had sent him a delightful drawing of their dog, while fifteen-year-old Klara had painstakingly embroidered the Leitner family crest on a linen cloth. He would frame it and hang it above his bed.

"Another aristocrat!" Wolf snorted. He often teased Christoph, who did hail from noble lineage, which was no longer acknowledged in modern Germany. But his family still had a vast estate in Bavaria.

"There's never been a 'von' in our name," Erich replied. "But we've had this crest since the 16th century. We use it on our bottles."

"Wish they could have sent some of those," Axel lamented.

Erich looked curiously at a bottle of hair tonic that his older brother had enclosed. "I don't know why he would send this, since I've never used it." It was screwed tightly shut, but he managed to open it with some difficulty. He sniffed and laughed. "Trust Gustav! It's our best brandy! Get the glasses and we'll have a sip."

They toasted their families and each other.

Still unwrapping presents, Erich said, "My mother makes the best Stollen. Lots of booze in it!" He handed slices to his friends, so there was suddenly a party mood as they ate the brandy-soaked cake heavy with nuts, dried fruits, and marzipan.

They were impressed with Erich's photos – the Leitner family in front of their charming and substantial half-timbered home, the long vista of orchards and vineyards climbing up into the wooded hills behind.

"Your sister Klara is a knock-out!" Axel declared.

"Good thing you're locked up here," Erich jested.

He kept aside the parcel from his girlfriend, Angelika, not wanting to open it in front of the others. He finally took it and his letters to the expansive, open-sided sunroom atop the north wing of the building. Now that winter had closed in, few ventured out here.

Angelika had sent him an expensive watch and the stuffed bear that he had once bought her on an outing to the Black Forest. She wrote:

You must now look after my dearest friend, Kuschi, as he has been charged to take care of you in my stead. I am ecstatic that you are safe! We must endure this terrible war, but it's easier knowing that we'll be together again one day. How I long to be in your arms!

He hugged Kuschi tightly as he read on.

In the meantime, I've decided to help out your family. Gustav has successfully expanded the market garden – the food is so much needed - and everybody has been working long hours. Your father's rheumatism is acting up, and your mother collapsed from exhaustion – after the harvest, of course. Gustav can barely find time to sleep, which is aggravating his asthma. I'm so glad that Papa persuaded me to learn bookkeeping, as I've now taken over that task from Gustav, and have been told that I do an exceptional job. I help supervise the boys and girls from the Hitler Youth who are required to work on the land, as I'm also eager to get away from the desk for a while.

Erich felt guilty and useless, sitting here 6000 km from his family, who were struggling with their livelihood as well as wartime restrictions. He was comfortable, well fed, and frustratingly impotent.

I'm so much happier here than I would be working in Papa's factory, which had been the plan when I took my courses. You know I've never much liked Mannheim, although it was a good career move for Papa to manage the plant. I so much prefer to live on the land or in a village, so I hope that you won't be persuaded by Papa to work at the factory or in any big city when you're finished your engineering.

I'm sleeping in your room during the week, as it's too far to travel home every day, and I adore it – the view up the hillside, being surrounded by your books and the model airplanes and radio you built, and the photos of us. It makes me feel as if I'm with you, and actually expect you might walk into the room at any moment. Wouldn't that be heavenly!

He could almost not bear the seductive thought of her in his bed and not being with her.

She'd included a photo of herself against the wall of climbing roses in his family's garden. Now nineteen, she looked more sophisticated than when he had last seen her nearly a year ago.

He began to fantasize about their life together, trying to get beyond the arousing images of making love to her. She had let him once, when he signed up. "To prove that I am truly yours," she'd said.

They had lain in a meadow resplendent with wildflowers, basking in the sunshine and their lovemaking, the scent of freshly mown hay wafting to them from a neighbouring field. He had never felt so alive, so powerful, so intoxicated. He'd wanted to compose a symphony for her.

But she hadn't allowed him to make love to her again, saying, "You don't get pregnant the first time, but I might the next, so we mustn't do this again until we're married."

But how long would that be now? How would he deal with the strong urges that he couldn't satisfy, especially in this community where there was no privacy?

So, he needed to discipline his body and his mind. Exercise, study, and music would have to be his salvation.

He heard the drone of airplanes overhead, instantly wishing he could be up there with them. He leaned out over the railing to get a better view of a Nomad as it passed low overhead. Then he saw something that made his blood run cold. Another one suddenly appeared from the east, on a collision course. He held his breath, watching in helpless horror as they crashed, crumpled, and plummeted into the lake beyond the far headland. There was no chance that anyone could have survived that, as they were too low to bail out. His first thought was sadness for the poor buggers. He should be rejoicing that a couple of enemy pilots would never fly against Germany now, but he couldn't shake the feeling of fellowship with all airmen. No doubt those were traitorous thoughts, which he would keep to himself.

But he thought the Canadians should know about it, so he told the Adjutant, Falkenrath, suspecting that the Lagerführer would just ignore the information. They were, after all, still at war.

• • •

"The RCAF is looking for a couple of planes that went missing yesterday," Colin said to Claire and Merilee over dinner the next evening. "One of them was last seen refueling at our airport. They were on a search-and-rescue mission, trying to find a trainee pilot from Camp Borden who went missing during that sudden blizzard the day before. They eventually found that chap in his crashed plane just a few miles from base."

"Oh, how sad!" Claire said. "And now they've possibly lost two more men."

"Four. Two instructors and two pilots who had just earned their wings. One was scheduled to go home on leave yesterday, but volunteered to look for his colleague."

Merilee felt a shiver of fear, thinking about the dangers her cousins and friends could be in, even in training. And then remembered that Alastair Grayson had been assigned to teach at Camp Borden. "I'm assuming that Alastair wasn't one of them, Dad. Otherwise we would have heard, right?"

"Thankfully, no one we know. Apparently, someone witnessed a mid-air collision, and then one of the search planes discovered an oil slick on the lake not far north of here, so tomorrow they're sending out boats to drag that section of the lake. It'll be a race against the cold, as the water is rapidly freezing."

What Colin couldn't tell them was that Major Falkenrath had asked to see him, which was not unusual, as the German Commandant left all the administrative work to Falkenrath, and dealt with the Canadians only when necessary to establish his authority within the enclosure. The Major spoke passable English and with Colin's bit of German, they didn't require the Canadian camp interpreter, whose German wasn't all that good anyway. He was kept busy censoring the mail.

There were often complaints from the prisoners about exercise space or rations or anything that they felt contravened the Geneva Convention. Colin was also their liaison with the War Prisoners' Aid, run by the YMCA, and with Switzerland, which Germany had chosen as the Protecting Power for the prisoners, through its Consulate in Toronto.

Falkenrath had begun, "The piano is popular, but many play also other instruments. They wish to make orchestra. There is a man who was music teacher. Is it possible?" He handed Colin a list of instruments.

"These would indeed make an orchestra. I will certainly pass this along to the WPA." Colin's Commander, Colonel Winterbourne, stressed that they should do what they could to keep the prisoners happily occupied, and thus, out of mischief. "Perhaps you could have these by Christmas. Is there anything else?"

Falkenrath had hesitated, as if unsure of the wisdom of what he was about to say, but then plunged in. "I trust you as officer and gentleman, Captain Sutcliffe, so what I tell you must never go beyond us. You agree?"

"If it doesn't involve the safety of a guard or prisoner, then yes, I do."

"A man saw yesterday two air force planes crash over the lake. Today there are much planes out looking, yes? But you must not say we Germans told you. It would not be good for us to help our enemies, you understand?" he added with a nervous smile.

"I can appreciate your situation, Major. I will inform the RCAF only that someone witnessed a crash. Can you tell me approximately where it happened?"

"He was looking to the north, not far over the lake."

"Thank you, Major. You are an honourable man." And such a pity that they were enemies.

England: Winter 1940 - 1941
Chapter 8

"You and Roz seem to have hit it off," Elyse said to Charlie Thornton. They were savouring a nightcap in the sunroom at Priory Manor, Sophie and the others having just retired. Rosalyn had diplomatically, if perhaps somewhat reluctantly, left the two cousins to themselves.

"She's a refreshing change from the girls who want to land a pilot rather than a plane," Charlie replied with a chuckle.

"She's as eager to get her hands on a Spitfire as I am."

"I have no doubt! You girls are obviously doing a terrific job, since the ATA is recruiting more women." Charlie lifted his glass to her in a toast. "The Spit's a beautiful beast to fly, Elyse. Like an extension of oneself. Almost effortless."

Elyse was happy, as always, around him. He was like a dear and caring older brother.

She was relieved that he was out of the battle for a while at least. Having finished his first tour of duty in October, he was teaching at an Operational Training Unit, which provided the final instruction for new pilots on the planes they would actually fly in combat.

Already having received a Distinguished Flying Cross and promotion to Squadron Leader in the summer, during the Battle of Britain, he had recently been awarded the even more prestigious Distinguished Service Order for his courage and leadership.

She looked at him affectionately in the soft light cast by the Christmas tree and a few candles that burned low. Had they not needed to shut out the night with blackout curtains, the scene would have been even more enchanting with moonlight sparkling on the powdery snow that shrouded the Gothic ruins of an ancient priory in the garden. Roz and Charlie had left fresh footprints there earlier in the evening. "It's ridiculously romantic," Roz had confided to Elyse.

"Our fearless leader, Pauline Gower, is agitating for us to be allowed to ferry combat planes," Elyse said. "She's already managed to wrangle some of her first recruits into Harvards, so I know she'll succeed eventually. I was hoping to fly a Spitfire before Theo does, but his squadron is converting to Spits."

"Sweet on him, are you? I'll have to give that chap a good grilling tomorrow."

Sophie had invited Theo to Boxing Day luncheon.

"He has to pass muster, does he?" Elyse asked impishly.

"Damn right!"

"Well, he's looking forward to meeting you as well. He has great admiration for your father," she added carefully.

Charlie snorted derisively. "Yes, the great World War I hero. I deny any relationship whenever possible."

"That's terribly sad. I expect Uncle Chas would be hurt if he knew."

"I don't want favours or comparisons just because I'm his adopted son!"

Elyse didn't want to spoil the evening, so she hesitated before saying, "Charlie, I've guessed that Chas is your real father."

He stared hard at her before gulping down the rest of his cognac. "Is it so bloody obvious?"

"Not with your Errol Flynn moustache. And perhaps only to those who know you both well. I see some resemblance – your blue eyes, the curve of your lips. The way your hair curls onto your forehead." He was no longer as blonde as he'd been as a child, or like Chas and Drew were.

He turned away.

"Why does that hurt you so?" she asked gently.

"Because he made me a bastard, and then lied to me all those years! Why couldn't he have told me before?" He clenched his fists.

She poured him another cognac and went to sit next to him. "Did he and Aunt Ria really have a choice? You know what a scandal the truth would have caused, and how you would have been regarded by society. It's hard to keep secrets, especially for kids. They love you and did what they thought was best for you…. And you were lucky that they took you in. I've worked out that Ria and Chas were engaged when you were… conceived. It must have been difficult for her to adopt you."

Charlie stared morosely into his glass as he swirled the amber liquid about fiercely. "I was just a mistake."

"As was I, apparently. My bitch of a mother said that my resentment would eat away at me if I didn't forgive or forget her. I hate to admit it, but she's right."

Their eyes locked in mutual pain.

"I've already realized how war affects us profoundly in so many ways," Elyse went on. "Surely you see every day how desperate people are to live fully and exuberantly before it's too late. One more dance. One more kiss."

"The conquest of yet another girl's virtue to notch up on one's scorecard," Charlie added bitterly.

"Enough of them are willing. And why shouldn't we women enjoy ourselves as well? We could all die tomorrow... And if we don't, we'll have had a lark and be eager for some more dalliances," she jested to lighten the mood.

Elyse hooked her arm firmly in his as she said, "Do you know the most marvellous gift I've just been given? It's to know that you truly are my cousin. I would hate to think I was just related to people like Kate."

Charlie laughed and then hugged her tightly. "Thank God for you, Elyse."

•   •   •

"I've been longing to do this," Theo said as he pulled Elyse into his arms and kissed her.

Heart pounding, blood rising, that deep intimacy made her want to abandon her body and soul to him, but her rational thoughts always grasped the last threads of caution and hauled her back reluctantly.

When she pulled away from his roaming hands and insistent lips, he whispered, "What a convenient hideaway this is."

They were in the summerhouse at the edge of the small ice-rimmed lake, far enough from the house for complete privacy.

"But too cold now for seduction," she quipped as she sat down in a wicker chair.

Perching on the edge of one beside her, he said, "That was so kind of Sophie to invite me to share your *Canadian* feast today." He grinned and added, "So, have I passed the test?"

His charm seemed effortless, an integral part of him, and he had obviously made an impression. At one point during lunch, Sophie had glanced meaningfully at Elyse and smiled her approval. "Definitely with Sophie. Charlie is my champion and was undoubtedly skeptical... But I think you won him over as well."

"And what about you?" He leaned toward her and took her cool hands in his as he gazed deeply into her eyes.

"I enjoy your company, Squadron Leader Beauchamp."

He pulled a small silver box out of his pocket as he said, "Enough to want to spend the rest of your life with me?" He opened it to reveal an etched gold band studded with brilliant diamonds. "I didn't think you could wear a large stone when you're flying, so I thought this would make do for now."

She was stunned, but managed to say, "It's beautiful."

He watched her hopefully as she gathered her thoughts.

"Theo, I'm not considering marriage yet. I have a job to do..."

"And I would never expect you to give it up, Elyse. I have to admit to being rather chuffed that my girl is a heroine of the skies." He stroked her cheek. "I love you, Elyse. Madly, completely, intoxicatingly. I want to spend every moment I can with you, to make you happy, to plan a future together after this damn war is over. But I can't wait that long. We'll steal as much time together as we can."

And she wanted to be with him. No one had ever touched her heart and soul as he had.

"I would have suggested we marry next week. But I'm willing to wait a few months," he said with a grin. "Will you accept this ring as a token of my love and commitment you? If you decide you couldn't possibly marry me, then I won't hold you to anything."

"A tentative engagement?"

"A chance for me to win you over completely. Without other chaps trying to woo you."

"Sid warned me that you were a playboy."

"Ha! I have plenty of friends, but I can assure you that I haven't left a trail of broken hearts. Sid threatened to eviscerate me if I ever caused you any distress, so I don't make this proposal lightly."

Although surprised that her mother cared at all, Elyse laughed. And realized that she shouldn't jeopardize her own happiness to distance herself from Sidonie and her world.

She took the ring purposefully and slid it onto her finger. "Let's say that we're *going steady* for now, instead of engaged. The fact that you guessed my size is a good beginning."

"Thank you, my precious darling." He gathered her happily into his arms, kissing her passionately.

Elyse felt joy creeping in to replace the momentary panic at her impetuous decision. And then ecstasy at the realization that she had someone of her very own, someone who loved her and wanted to spend a lifetime with her.

•   •   •

"My parents are eager to meet you," Theo said to Elyse on the telephone a week later. "Will you come to Salisbury with me on your next day off?"

"Yes, of course. I have to inspect them as well before I commit to anything," she teased.

He laughed appreciatively. "I'm certain they will adore you." He hesitated. "I know a cozy inn where we could stay. It's not the Ritz, but it would give us a chance to get to know one another."

"A naughty tryst?"

"Separate rooms, if you insist."

"If I approve of your parents, then one will suffice."

"I'll ensure that they're on their best behaviour." Happily, he added, "I can hardly wait, my darling girl."

The ancient, converted mill straddling a millrace was impossibly quaint, and had a spectacular view of Salisbury Cathedral in the distance.

"This is just like Constable's painting!" Elyse enthused as they ambled along a deserted footpath that crossed two rivers and frosty meadows into the city, with the magnificent Cathedral as the focal point. "All that's missing is the grazing cattle. I feel like we've stepped into the past."

She gripped Theo's hand tightly. The promise of later intimacy hummed electrically between them.

It was a soft day with shafts of sunlight dissolving pewter clouds and coaxing mist off the dusting of snow. Ducks paddled carelessly in the shallow streams.

But the pastoral illusion was shattered as a squadron of Spitfires zoomed low overhead.

Once they entered the city, they were among many other people in uniform, Salisbury being central to plenty of military camps and aerodromes.

The finely tailored, navy ATA uniforms were flattering and invariably turned heads and opened doors, but Elyse was most excited by the embroidered gold wings above the left breast pocket of her tunic. The male ATA boss insisted the women wear their uniforms - with skirts, not their flying trousers – even when on leave, and Theo thought it a good idea. "So that Mother realizes you're dedicated to your job, and not yet ready to abandon everything to give her grandchildren. Besides, you look incredibly sexy in it. I can hardly wait to peel it off you."

She'd had to resist those attempts when they'd checked into their room. "I can't possibly face your parents with equanimity if we make love now."

"And we'd be late for lunch," he'd agreed as he trailed kisses down her neck. "Mmmm. Or forego it altogether." His hand had sought her breast.

"Do stop!" she'd implored, laughing.

From one of the narrow, medieval streets, they walked through a crenellated and battlemented stone gate into the walled Cathedral Close.

Puzzled, Elyse asked, "Are we sightseeing?"

"Not until later."

"But…"

He grinned. "My aunt lives here. Her husband's grandfather was Bishop of Salisbury, and his wife took a fancy to one of the houses in the Close. She bought it with her generous dowry when the opportunity arose."

"I can see why!" Elyse exclaimed as they turned into a circular drive and approached a stately house with a dozen tall windows facing the Cathedral.

"The front section is a Queen Anne addition, built onto a 15th century dwelling. King Charles II stayed here when he was trying to escape The Plague in London."

"Impressive. I expect there are secret rooms and ghosts," she jested.

"Definitely."

Felled by influenza, Aunt Hermione had reluctantly taken to her bed. Her husband was absorbed by war work in London.

Although the place was much smaller than the rambling Thornton and Wyndham mansions Elyse had grown up in, it had elegant rooms with beautifully detailed plasterwork, tasteful art, and a sense of comfortable intimacy.

Theo's parents were gracious and soon put Elyse at ease over pre-prandial sherry in the drawing room, which overlooked a surprisingly extensive and private garden. A small fire burned in the ornate hearth.

His mother, Marguerite, was petite, but exuded such cheerful self-confidence and energy that she seemed formidable as well as warmly compassionate. As Sid's contemporary, she was in her mid-forties, but clad in sensible, if elegant, woolens, she was nothing like the glamorous, seductive Sidonie. So, Elyse found it hard to believe that the two women were still friends.

"You remind me so much of your mother when we were young," Marguerite said. "I spent memorable school holidays at her family estate, Blackthorn. Have you seen it, dear? A splendid Elizabethan palace! Such a shame that it had to go out of the family. Sold to a war profiteer," Marguerite lamented with a decided sniff of disgust.

"I've only seen photographs, but I know that Sid cherished it. She named our summer home and island in Muskoka after it," Elyse said.

"Ah yes, Muskoka. I remember Chas Thornton talking fondly about it all those years ago. I met him and your father at Blackthorn over Christmas in 1913. I do believe that Sid had a pash for Chas then."

That surprised Elyse. Then she recalled Sid saying that she'd married Rafe because all her best friends were returning to Canada. Had Chas rejected Sid in favour of Ria? Was that the reason for Sid's outrageous and rebellious lifestyle?

"Of course, we girls were constantly falling in love. I was sweet on Sid's brother Quentin. Before I met Algernon, of course." She smiled at her husband.

Knowing that Elyse didn't want to discuss her mother, Theo said, "Speaking of Muskoka, you'll enjoy that blueberry jam from the family island berries, and collected by the British evacuees that Chas and his wife have taken in."

Elyse had presented the Beauchamps, as well as Theo, with a gift package of food, which also included smoked ham, a block of cheddar cheese, and a decadently rich, cognac-soaked Christmas cake baked by Mrs. Grayson.

"A treat indeed! So kind of you, dear Elyse. And so good of Chas to take in the children," Marguerite said. "I'm horrified every time I think of the poor mites on the ship that was torpedoed in September." She was referring to the over seventy children lost in the sinking of the *City of Benares*, headed for Canada. Ria had told Elyse how shocked her evacuees had been at the news, and then tearful to think that they were truly cut off from home now, since their parents would never let them travel until the war was over. *It didn't help that William told the younger kids that the first war had lasted over four years,* Ria had written. *I'm relieved that he's living with the Carlyles now.*

"We've taken in a couple of young sisters from Southampton," Marguerite continued. "They're still a bit diffident with us, and prefer to be in the kitchen with Mrs. Butterworth, who is rather grandmotherly. In any case, their mother has taken them out today, as it's her day off from her factory work."

An elderly woman – surely Mrs. Butterworth, Elyse thought – limped in and announced that luncheon was served, so they moved across the wide and welcoming entrance hall to the dining room.

The fine repast included leek and potato soup, poached salmon in a dill sauce, roasted herbed potatoes, honey-glazed carrots and turnips, and jam tart.

"This is delightful!" Elyse said.

"It certainly is, Mum. You must have been saving your rations for a week to produce this."

"We do some judicious bartering. Jars of beets and cucumbers that Hermione and I pickled in exchange for cream and honey. The cellar is stocked with cabbages and root vegetables because we plowed up most of the lawns and flowerbeds for our Victory Garden. It seems almost a sacrilege to have turned the Orangery into a hen house, but having a regular supply of eggs is divine. Our evacuees delight in looking after the chickens, almost as if they were pets."

"I'm impressed at how domesticated you've become, Mum," Theo teased.

She grinned as she replied, "You should see me making and serving tea at the Red Cross canteen."

"Indeed I should!"

"Your mother is the driving force behind the Women's Institute as well. She would make a splendid Major-General," Algernon said to Theo with a twinkle in his eye.

As if on cue, they burst into the Gilbert and Sullivan song, "She is… 'the Very Model of a Modern Major General'."

"Do stop, you fools!" Marguerite said, laughing. "Elyse will think us touched."

But Elyse relished this lighthearted moment, and the easy, enviable relationship between Theo and his parents. She suddenly wanted to be part of this family.

"Our chaps who travel to Canada are astounded by the abundance of the food, despite some rationing, and delighted by the brightness and safety of the cities. It's not only brave, but damned fine of you to give up all that comfort to come over here to do a dangerous job, young lady," Algernon said to Elyse as he topped up her wine.

"I'm happy to help by doing something I love, Sir Algernon."

"Even after Amy Johnson's tragic death?" Marguerite asked.

"We're all still shocked by that," Elyse admitted. She had admired the legendary aviatrix, who had accomplished many "firsts", and been thrilled to work with her in the ATA. Because Amy had been by far the most experienced pilot, it was sobering to realize how easily their jobs could become fatal.

Amy had died a couple of weeks ago while ferrying a twin-engine Airspeed Oxford. Against ATA regulations, she had taken off in bad weather. They speculated that she had also disobeyed the rules by flying over the blinding clouds, and not finding an opening to come back down. Far off course and out of fuel, she had wisely bailed out, but had plunged into the freezing Thames Estuary. A nearby ship had tried to rescue her, but had failed in the heaving seas, the commander losing his own life in the attempt. Amy's body had not been recovered.

"Weather is our biggest challenge, especially since our planes aren't equipped with radios," Elyse said. "But if we only flew on good days, then we wouldn't deliver enough aircraft. As you'd predicted, Theo."

"So, you all break the rules?" he asked.

"It's expected, within reason. We're our own captains, and make those decisions. Most of us didn't fly that day, but Amy had been stuck out for days in Prestwick and was probably bored and frustrated. Some of us fly when the men won't," Elyse added with a grin.

"Ha! Pride goes before the fall, doesn't it?"

"And women have to work harder to be accepted," Elyse shot back.

"But why don't you have radios?" Marguerite asked.

"Something to do with national security, I was told. And since we're supposed to fly 'contact', meaning within sight of the ground," Elyse explained to Theo's parents, "we shouldn't need them."

Theo frowned. "That's idiotic!"

"I'm thankful that Sara is in the WAAFs," Marguerite said of her youngest daughter.

"She's not any safer at Biggin Hill, Mum," Theo pointed out. "They've been bombed a dozen times already."

"I refuse to go up to the city until this Blitz stops," Marguerite declared. "Did you know that a bomb fell in the street behind Sidonie's? It blew out her rear windows. Fortunately, no one was injured. I don't know why she insists on staying in the thick of things. We've offered her a room here."

"Ah, I nearly forgot," Sir Algernon said as he drew an envelope from the inside pocket of his tweed jacket. "Sidonie asked me to give you this. She doesn't have your address."

Elyse took it reluctantly. "Thank you."

"I'm going to take Elyse on a tour of the Cathedral before we head back," Theo said.

Marguerite managed to draw Elyse aside as she was preparing to leave. "I think it's terribly sad that Sidonie missed out on so much of your life." Staring at Elyse as if reaching into her soul, she added, "But I do believe that it was best for you, my dear."

When she and Theo headed across the swath of green toward the Cathedral, Elyse said, "I do like your parents. But I have the distinct impression that if I were more like Sid, your mother wouldn't approve of me."

"She warned me of that."

"Why didn't you tell me!"

"Because I didn't want you to pretend to be anyone but yourself. I knew she'd like you." He grinned.

"You're very lucky, you know."

He put his arm about her shoulder and hugged her to him. "I know. I have you."

"That's not what I meant. But one room will suffice tonight."

Elyse was awed by the sheer size and splendour of the Gothic cathedral.

"My cousins were friends with the Dean's son, so we five chaps used to clamber about in the rafters and climb up the tower. There's a terrific view over the countryside from the base of the spire. When we played hide and seek, I found it eerie to be alone among the bones of the building."

"What fun!"

"We had plenty of that. You see that level of shorter arches above these tall ones?" he asked as they gazed up from the nave. "Once, when I was ten, we gutted a down pillow and tossed small feathers from there, just one at a time, which would flutter gently to the floor or onto someone's head. Looked like angels had lost bits of their wings. There was hell to pay when the Dean caught us, but the Bishop was there as well, and thought it rather amusing. 'I expect you've reassured a goodly number of people about the afterlife,' he told us. 'But let's leave that to God from now on, shall we?'"

Elyse laughed. "Tell me about your cousins."

"Mike's in the navy, on Atlantic convoy duty, Dr. Rob is a medic with the army, and Jim, who's my age and an aeronautical engineer, is working at the Royal Aircraft Establishment in Farnborough. This and The Close were our 'castle', which of course we had to defend against marauders."

As he fondly recounted childhood adventures, she glimpsed the boy inside the man, and fell even more in love with him. "It sounds as if you had a magical childhood."

"I suppose I did. But nothing as exotic as your summers on private islands in bewitching Muskoka."

"Perhaps not. I can hardly wait to show it to you."

They stepped out into the cloisters – wide, vaulted passageways with a continuous procession of arches within arches enclosing a large, grassy quadrangle. No one lingered out here on a cool winter's day, so they had this area all to themselves.

"It's so peaceful and secluded here. I can almost hear the echoes of hooded monks ambling along, chanting," Elyse said.

"You would have been interested to see one of the original copies of the Magna Carta, which was kept in the Chapter House. But it's being stored in some safe and secret government repository for the duration, along with other national treasures."

"I hope that the Luftwaffe spares Salisbury."

"Mum said that the night Coventry was bombed, hundreds of German planes flew overhead for hours. It seems that Jerry is using the Cathedral spire as a landmark. It's the tallest in England, so perhaps it will be safe… for the time being. Apparently, Coventry Cathedral is just a ruined shell now."

"It may seem wrong to bemoan the destruction of historic buildings when so many people are dying, but I do find that sad as well."

"As do I, dear girl. I marvel at the ingenuity and craftsmanship of the medieval architects and stonemasons who built this. And what took centuries to create could be ruthlessly destroyed in a matter of hours."

"Not with you to defend *your castle*, Squadron Leader Beauchamp."

"If only I could."

They ambled back to the inn under a dusky sky rent with rusty slashes of sunset. When they'd ensconced themselves in their room in the deepening darkness, their lovemaking seemed so natural, just a physical extension of the day, of the joys of being together — young, in tune, passionately in love.

Elyse woke early and tried not to disturb Theo as she slid out of bed. Wrapping her nakedness in the thin, discarded bedspread, she curled up in a chair by the window, its curtains left open as they had made love again by moonlight. Mist played above the stream and shrouded the distant cathedral in a mystical light, like a Monet painting.

Elyse finally read the letter from Sidonie.

Darling Elyse,

I've heard that Theo has really fallen for you, which hardly surprises me. I do hope that you are happy, and that he never breaks your heart. But one always takes risks in love.

Having witnessed your father's and my experiences with marriage, you may be reluctant to take that plunge. But if you do, I would be delighted to finance and arrange the wedding.

You may, of course, wish to organize everything yourself, but know that I am available to help in whatever capacity.

Unless you're happy to become pregnant, get yourself a Dutch cap, darling. We can't trust men with our bodies or their motives to control them.

Affectionately, Sid

Its terseness and cynicism didn't surprise Elyse, but did cement her intention not to invite Sid to the wedding – if that time ever came.

Elyse didn't realize that Theo had been awake and watching her. Seeing the flicker of pain across her face, he said tenderly, "Come back to bed and I'll keep you warm."

She went gratefully into his arms.

England: March 1941
Chapter 9

"Are you sure I can't persuade you and Charlie to come up to London for the evening?" Elyse asked Roz.

"No, and I'm glad you're staying there, because I have plans."

Elyse raised an eyebrow. "Should I be concerned about my cousin's honour?"

"He's the one getting serious because he told me about his parentage. He said that you had guessed, so he thought I should know that he was 'a bastard', before I became too involved with him."

"Hell's bells! What did you say?"

"That he was damned lucky his real father adopted him."

"Good for you! He still seems so angry at Uncle Chas."

"Has your uncle's knightly lustre dimmed for you?"

"I was surprised, of course, and a bit disappointed. But he's always been kind and loving to me. Often more involved in my life than my own father. I don't know the circumstances of Charlie's conception, so I won't judge Uncle Chas for something that happened in times we're only just beginning to understand. And I know that he cherishes Aunt Ria. She obviously forgave him."

"And generously took in his child. I'll work on Charlie. Starting with a romantic dinner tonight."

"And who knows where that will lead?"

"Precisely."

Elyse didn't particularly want to go to London, but Theo's sister Sara had turned twenty-one yesterday, and her boyfriend insisted they celebrate at the Café de Paris tonight. It seemed the perfect opportunity for Elyse to meet Sara.

Elyse had only been to London briefly since the Blitz began, and was astonished that there was so much damage in the West End. But the Ritz had not suffered, and she gratefully indulged in a luxuriously warm bath after a busy day. A tap on the bathroom door startled her.

"Is *Mrs. Beauchamp* presentable?" Theo's muffled voice asked.

"Not at all. But do come in." She floated her washcloth into a strategic position.

Elyse was constantly amazed at the rush of joy and excitement she felt at his presence.

"Such modesty," he jested as he leaned over to kiss her, swishing the washcloth away. He had already discarded his jacket and tie. "Is there room for me?"

"Always. Which means that we can surely add another four inches of water." She turned on the taps.

She admired his firm body as he stripped, titillated by his obvious desire as he entered the water. They soaped each other as they talked half-heartedly about their day, the conversation soon lapsing into sighs and moans of pleasure. Still damp, they made love on the sumptuous bed.

Both were on duty again in the morning, but they had these thirteen precious hours together.

"You look ravishing," Theo said when Elyse had slipped into a sleeveless lavender and black gown that draped tantalizing about her curves. A beaded black lace bolero jacket swooped down to her waist at the back and ended in embroidered points at her wrists.

"It's delicious to be out of uniform for a little while."

"I'm always happy to oblige with that."

"Cheeky!"

Fortunately, it was a quiet night, and it had been several days since the last bombing.

"Do you know Sara's boyfriend?" Elyse asked as they strolled to the Café de Paris.

"I've bested him on a few tennis courts over the years, but he trounces me in golf. Roger Uffington-Leigh, Flight Lieutenant. We called him Ruffles at Cambridge. Now that his squadron's based at Biggin Hill, where Sara works, and he realizes that she's no longer a gangly child, they've become an item. He's a good sort, so I'm happy for her."

As it was early for London nightlife, there were still tables available around the dance floor. But Sara and Roger were seated in a far corner.

"It's more private and not too close to the band, so that we can easily talk," Sara explained when introductions had been made.

She radiated the amiable, vivacious nature of someone fully engaged with life and its possibilities.

"Welcome to adulthood," Theo toasted her with champagne. "By the by, you look beautiful, Sis."

She shimmered in a dusty rose lamé gown with a silver lace overdress. "I feel like Cinderella, released from drudgery for an evening at the ball. As I'm staying with Dad tonight, I promised I'd be back by midnight, unless we get stuck here in a raid. I'm on duty tomorrow as well, so I'll have to catch the early milk train."

"I've brought you a small birthday present," Elyse said, handing Sara a thin parcel.

"How kind!" Her face lit with a smile when she opened it. "Silk stockings and American nylons! Oh, how delightful! I must be depriving you."

"Not at all. My family sent me plenty for Christmas."

"I only have a few silk ones left. But I don't begrudge you your parachutes," she bantered, silk now being used for them and other war-related items.

"I'll try not to use mine," Roger joked.

"Look what Roger gave me." Sara beamed as she showed them the stunning sapphire and diamond bracelet on her wrist.

"He has excellent taste," Theo said, handing her a small box.

Inside were sapphire and diamond earrings. "Was this planned?" she asked in amazement.

"We just know you too well, Sis."

Elated, Sara exchanged her pearl earrings for the new ones. "Now we have to find occasions when I can wear all these treasures."

"Theo told me that you're a Met forecaster," Elyse said.

"I've always been fascinated by weather and clouds. Clear, sunny days like today are a terrible bore. Give me a rousing thunderstorm any time."

"Perhaps you could conjure one up for tomorrow, so that we're grounded and can enjoy a lazy day," Theo suggested.

"Not a chance, I'm afraid. Besides, Diana Barnato's doing her test flight for the ATA tomorrow, so I'm hoping for good weather. She said she might join us here tonight. You know her, don't you, Roger?"

"Of course. You'd have to be from another planet not to know Diana."

"I've never heard of her," Elyse said with a grin.

"Or from the Colonies, where they don't care about the frivolities of British society girls," Roger added smoothly, as if finishing his previous sentence.

Amid chuckles, Elyse said, "But I have heard of Woolf Barnato, the race car champion. Any relation?"

"Diana's father," Theo explained. "He's now a Wing Commander. And he's an old friend of Sid's."

"Of course he is." Backed by an inheritance from South African diamond mines, he was a wealthy playboy – just Sid's type, Elyse thought.

"Diana did a bit of flying before the war, and is tired of driving ambulances, so she's really hoping to be accepted. She has connections, of course," Sara said. "It certainly seems glamorous to be flying in the war."

"Believe me, it definitely isn't! Delivering slow, open cockpit planes to Scotland in the middle of winter is beastly. Even when I wear my fur coat over my fleece-lined overalls, I'm so frozen after a three-hour flight that I can barely climb out of the plane."

"I hadn't thought about that."

"But I do like the freedom of being in a civilian organization," Elyse admitted. "No drills, few rules, no barracks. We get billeted or have a living allowance for our own lodgings."

"*And* you have very smart uniforms," Sara added with a grin. "But I don't have the courage to actually pilot a plane."

"Thank God! You're enough of a menace in Dad's Bentley," Theo teased.

"One of our senior women pilots delivered a Hawker Hurricane today," Elyse related nonchalantly. "So, I expect it won't be long before we get our hands on Spitfires. Then it really will be fun!"

"Wow!" Sara's blue eyes grew large.

"It's incredible to think of lovely ladies flying combat planes," Roger said.

"And rather frightening, don't you think, Roger? They might do a better job of it than we do," Theo quipped.

"They invariably do," Roger admitted with a resigned sigh.

As they were finishing their delectable dinner, the braying of air raid sirens filtered down the two stories, followed by the ominous crump crump of bombs close by.

"I had hoped that this wretched Blitz was coming to an end," Sara said. "I worry about Dad."

"He was complaining that he spends more time kipping in the basement of his hotel than in his rooms," Theo said.

"We're twenty feet underground, so we're safe here," Roger reassured Sara with a tender smile as he clasped her hand. "And we can dance, as long as you don't lose one of your glass slippers trying to get home by midnight. Shall we?"

They joined the other young couples on the dance floor - the men mostly officers in uniform - as popular Snakehips Johnson and his band took over the entertainment.

"I know that Sara is two months older than you, but she seems younger somehow," Theo confessed, watching his sister who was laughing delightedly as she and Roger inexpertly tried to dance to swing.

"That's because she so sweet and guileless." Elyse tilted her head back and blew out a long stream of smoke with the provocative elegance of a Hollywood vamp.

"And you're a jaded woman of the world?"

She raised her Garbo eyebrow.

The band launched into "Oh Johnny, Oh Johnny, Oh!" so he rose and held out his hand. "May I have this dance?"

As she started to get up there was a blinding blue flash, and she felt herself being crushed to the floor in the ensuing darkness.

There were sounds of things crashing and then utter silence. The blackness was thick, suffocating. Like a tomb.

It was a relief to hear groans, to see a pinprick of light as someone flicked a cigarette lighter.

Frantically Elyse called, "Theo?" as she groped on the floor around her.

A woman cried, "I'm bleeding to death. Dear God, help me!"

A few lights from torches began to scan the room, foggy with dust and stinking of cordite.

She was terrified when she spotted Theo lying just a few feet from her, and scrambled to his side, willing him to be alive. Blood was oozing from a wound on his head, but he opened his eyes as she used the hem of her dress to stifle the bleeding.

"Elyse…"

"I'm fine. Let me bandage your cut." She remembered the clean new stockings. They lay beside the champagne bottle that bizarrely stood, unharmed, on the table. She tore open the package and wrapped one around his head.

"Are you hurt anywhere else?" she asked.

"Don't think so." He struggled to sit up as he said, "Sara?" Woozy, he couldn't manage to stand.

"I'll find her."

In the dim light, Elyse grabbed the other stockings, and picked her way through the smashed and upended furniture, the chunks of plaster, the shattered glass, the injured, the dead, and the dying as if in some horrific nightmare. She hardly stopped to think when she saw blood gushing from a girl's nearly severed leg, and tied a nylon tourniquet around it before moving hastily on, realizing later that the victim was almost naked. A pilot examined his hand in awe, wondering where his fingers had gone.

Equally macabre was a table of four startled people, still seated but looking like they were made of wax. Unmarked, they were, however, dead. Elyse learned later that the blast had sucked the air out of their lungs, killing them instantly.

The emergency lights came on, brutally illuminating the carnage. Already, rescue workers were arriving. "For those who can walk, there's medical help in the hotel across the street. Ambulances are on their way," someone assured them.

One of the two curved staircases was twisted and unusable, the bomb obviously having landed there. On the dais below it, among the broken instruments and scattered sheet music, a few of the orchestra members were stirring, while others never would again. Snakehips Johnson was missing his head.

Elyse became more distraught as she searched for Sara, but finally spotted her, covered in dust, blackened by cordite, her gown shredded beyond recognition or usefulness. Muddy tears coursing down her cheeks, Sara was on her knees beside Roger, clutching his hand, shaking his shoulder gently. "Please wake up, my darling. Please, Roger!"

His soft brown eyes were wide open, but unseeing. A large pool of blood was spreading out beneath him. Elyse felt for a pulse – in vain.

Blood was trickling from a cut on Sara's now-bare arm. Elyse bandaged it before taking off her bolero and helping Sara into it. She seemed oblivious to everything but her dead beau.

Elyse noticed that Sara had other lacerations – a slice across her cheek, narrowly missing her eye, a gash on her exposed thigh, but with all the blood on her, it was hard to tell how much of it was hers. Sara was icy to the touch.

Theo staggered over to them. "Dear God!"

"She's in shock and needs medical attention," Elyse said.

He tried to help Sara up, but she resisted. "No! I can't leave Roger! Let go of me, Theo!" She struggled out of his grasp.

A Special Constable came over and said, "There now, Miss, let us deal with this. He'll be in good hands. You wait across the street now, how about that? Get yourself fixed up, eh?"

As if suddenly realizing she must comport herself with dignity, no matter the circumstances, Sara rose.

Theo put his arm about her gratefully, reassuringly, and picked her up in his arms as she collapsed.

"Can you manage?" Elyse asked with concern.

"Yes," he replied with determination.

They joined the stream of dazed people helping each other navigate the debris cluttering the undamaged stairs to the mangled balcony, and then up the long flights to the street.

Theo was wobbly by the time he gently laid the limp body of his sister into a chair in the lobby of the Mapleton Hotel. An employee draped a blanket over her. There appeared to be nurses tending wounds, but they couldn't cope with the countless victims. Ambulances arriving outside the Café were taking the most critically injured.

"I'm going to find a cab to take us to a hospital," Elyse told Theo.

"Yes... yes. A good idea." He put his hand to his head, feeling dizzy, but then looked at her curiously. "Where's your coat? It's freezing outside. Here." He removed his bloodied uniform jacket and handed it to her. Shivering, she slipped into it gratefully. "There's money in the pocket."

Elyse realized that she had left her evening bag behind, as well as her fur coat.

"*I* should be the one to go. The raid's not over," he said. They could hear the drone of planes and shrieking bombs.

She pushed him into a chair next to Sara. "No. You're needed here. Keep her warm. I'll be right back." She kissed him and darted out before he could protest further.

The doorman shook his head and said, "Heavy raid tonight, Miss. Worst in months. Won't be easy to get a taxicab."

"You seem like a resourceful chap. Surely this will help?" She handed him a five-pound note. "My sister is in need of a doctor. The cabbie can have triple the fare. And a generous tip if he hurries."

"I'll see what I can do, Miss." He went out into the bomb-splintered night. A few minutes later, he had procured the taxi.

"The nearest hospital, please," Elyse said when they had settled into the cab, Sara now awake but dazed.

"Charing Cross, Miss, but there's a wicked lot of ambulances going there now. How be I take you to Westminster Hospital?"

"As quickly as you can then."

"Jerry's busy 'round 'ere tonight."

Elyse felt strangely unafraid now as bombs screamed and exploded everywhere as they detoured around burning streets and avoided emergency vehicles.

While Elyse waited for brother and sister to be stitched up, she put an urgent call through to Sir Algernon, and briefly explained to him what had happened.

"How terribly tragic!" She heard the catch in his voice. "So... grateful that the rest of you are... alright. We'd just heard about the Café from patrons who arrived, 'bloodied but not beaten' they said as they ordered drinks. I was about to go over myself to see if... Thank you, dear girl. I will come to the hospital."

"There's no need, Sir Algernon. We'll come by when Theo and Sara are patched up. I'll let you know if anything changes."

"Bless you."

As well as his cut head and mild concussion, Theo had a wrenched elbow, but was otherwise fine. Sara had plenty of stitches, and needed warmth and rest, the doctor ordered.

She collapsed into her father's arms, weeping, when they arrived at the Dorchester Hotel at midnight. The "all clear" wailed.

•   •   •

"You're limping," Theo said with concern as he and Elyse reached their room at the Ritz.

"I seem to have twisted my ankle." She hadn't noticed the pain until now. Her shoulder was throbbing as well.

"I've been terribly remiss, while you've been looking after us splendidly," he said. "But I feel as if I'm just emerging from a fog."

"Bed rest for you. And no flying for at least a week, the doctor said."

They were both still bloodied and dirty, but he pulled her into his arms. "Thank God I can hold you," he whispered against her cheek, not releasing her for a long time. "I'll order some drinks, and ice for that foot while you get first dibs in the bathroom. And I'll telephone Roz, so she can ensure that you're on sick leave for a few days."

Elyse discarded her gown, stiff with dried blood. It wasn't until she saw the water run pink as she washed that she burst into tears, the full horror of the night and their lucky escape suddenly assailing her.

And she realized how much she loved Theo, and that she wanted to spend every moment she could with him. Before their luck ran out.

So, when she cuddled in his arms later, she said, "Early May would be a nice time to get married. If you still want to."

He hugged her tightly. "I never want to let you go."

They had a late breakfast in bed, and Theo insisted Elyse rest while he returned to the Café to try to retrieve their things.

Elyse was just out of her bath and dressed in her uniform when a maid delivered a large parcel for her. She opened the accompanying note.

Darling Elyse,

Algernon told me what happened. Shocking and terribly sad. I am so grateful that the three of you are fine.

He mentioned that you were wearing Theo's tunic, so I'm assuming you lost your coat. I thought you could use this Russian sable. Keep it or give it away as you wish. I have plenty.

Do come to visit some time, darling. You and Theo are always welcome to stay here, as you know, and we needn't be prim about sleeping arrangements.

Affectionately, Sid

Elyse unwrapped the coat reluctantly. It was exquisite, of course, and smelled faintly of Chanel N⁰ 5, which instantly conjured up poignant childhood memories - glimpsing her beautiful mother preparing for a party. The surprised hug and laughter when Elyse had thrown her arms around her. So when she slipped the sable on, it was almost as if her mother were embracing her.

Theo looked quizzically at her when he walked in.

"Sid sent it over."

"It looks tailor-made for you."

"I suppose I shall have to keep it then. I see you didn't manage to find mine."

"Or Sara's. The Constable said that there were looters. They even cut fingers off the bodies to steal rings, for God's sake! It's disgusting!"

She shuddered. "What happened to the 'Blitz spirit'?"

"Propaganda. We can't have Hitler thinking that he's succeeding in creating chaos. You won't see much in the newspapers about the Café either, I'm sure. It seems that by a fluke, a bomb was perfectly positioned to come down the ventilation shaft. The club's manager, who was always touting how safe it was, didn't live to see how wrong he'd been. They say that over thirty died at the scene and another eighty or so were seriously injured. So we were damned lucky."

And thank God that Roz and Charlie hadn't come along

•   •   •

Dear Sid,

How kind of you to send me your lovely coat. Theo told me that you're always generous to your friends.

We're going to be married at Priory Manor on Saturday, May 3rd, if you wish to keep that day free. Invitations will be forthcoming. It will be a small affair with mostly family.

Elyse had agonized about including Sid, but Roz had pointed out that her mother seemed to be making an effort.

"Are you trying to punish her, or are you just hurting yourself more by excluding her from your world? And you can't harangue Charlie about his antipathy to Chas and then do the same with your mother," Roz had pointed out.

"I don't *harangue* Charlie. Do I?"

"No... But that did get your attention," Roz had replied with big grin.

England: May 1941
Chapter 10

"I don't know how I can be so excited about the wedding, and nervous as hell at the same time," Elyse confessed to Roz as they were driving down to Priory Manor. It was her 21st birthday, and the wedding was in two days.

"Because it's too late to back out and you've suddenly realized that you'll lose your fiercely protected independence," Roz replied blithely.

"Hell's bells, I think you've nailed it! Is that what's keeping you from accepting Charlie's proposal?"

"Not exactly. Charlie has a career with the RAF, so after the war, we wouldn't be going home. I'm not sure I can live in this God-forsaken country. Lousy weather, illogical money, a pathological resistance to modern comforts, like central heating and bathroom showers. No drug stores with soda fountains. Names that aren't pronounced the way they're written. You look like an idiot or a spy if you don't know that Worcester is 'Wussta'. I mean, just look at you, about to become Mrs. *Beecham*-spelled-Beauchamp. You should have considered that before spending your life having to explain it."

Elyse laughed. "I like being odd. But staying in Britain hadn't actually occurred to me."

"You have family here. That makes a difference."

"But I'd miss home, especially summers at the lake. I'm already pining for that. I think I've been expecting that Theo would be seduced by Canada."

"For Charlie's sake, I could put up with most of it. But I really can't tolerate the snobbery, and those who look down their long noses at Americans."

"Like Lettice," Elyse said, referring to one of their ATA colleagues.

"You're OK because your mother is an aristocrat, even if you are a Colonial. But whenever Lettice sees me, she grimaces like someone just shoved a cow patty under her nose."

"You brash Americans aren't going to be intimidated by toffee-nosed Brits, are you?" Elyse teased.

"Actually... I noticed a small green worm on her salad the other day in the mess. I didn't tell her. Just watched with childish satisfaction as she ate it."

Elyse burst into laughter. "I would have too! But if staying in Britain is all that's holding you back from becoming my cousin, then you should discuss your concerns with Charlie," Elyse pointed out. "I'll bet he'd be willing to return to Canada, join the RCAF. Or better yet, you two could start your own airline business."

"Now there's a thought!"

"Getting through this war is enough to worry about. We can deal with the aftermath later." If there is one, Elyse almost added. Since the Café de Paris bombing, she'd been haunted by how life could change - or end - in an instant. And Charlie was back on ops with his fighter squadrons.

"I expect you're right," Roz admitted, looking thoughtful. "Now I'm going to give you some sage advice. Make sure you have plenty of condoms, or you'll find yourself firmly grounded, and changing diapers for the duration."

Elyse laughed. "Righty-ho! And they're called 'nappies' here, not diapers."

"Jolly good, old bean," Roz quipped.

"You see, you're catching onto the lingo."

Roz snorted. Consulting a map, she said, "Take the next right. I think. Britain's hard enough to navigate by air, but almost impossible by road, especially with the signs removed."

"I don't know why we have to stop at Farnborough. We're going to meet Jim on Saturday anyway." He was Best Man.

Roz shrugged and Elyse didn't catch her suppressed smirk. "It's on the way. Interesting to see where the latest aviation innovations are happening, don't you think?"

"Of course."

They were expected at the checkpoint and directed to the airfield.

A couple of Supermarine Spitfire Mark Vs were parked, and both Charlie and Theo were there, talking to another chap, who turned out to be Cousin Jim. His was a civilian aviation job, so he wasn't in uniform. There was an obvious family resemblance between the handsome cousins.

"Happy birthday, my darling," Theo said, giving her a quick kiss, his eyes gleaming. "We have a treat for you."

"A special birthday deserves something unique. So, you are about to become the first woman to fly a Spitfire," Charlie said.

She stared at him, flabbergasted.

"You can borrow mine and Theo will fly beside you in his."

"Oh my God! That's super!"

"Jim got us clearance for some *test* flights. You'll have to keep it under your hat, of course. At least for now. And if you break the kite, we'll both be up the creek," Charlie warned.

"And the ATA women would disown me," Elyse admitted.

"Or burn you at the stake," Roz jested. The women pilots knew that they couldn't afford to make mistakes, which would reflect badly on them all.

"You've already been ferrying Hurricanes, so this will be a piece of cake," Theo assured her.

The ATA pilots were trained on classes of aircraft and then expected to fly anything in that class with only the help of their "Blue Bible", which listed the critical information for each plane. Elyse and Roz had recently been given extra training at the RAF Central Flying School to explain hydraulics and other refinements of the more advanced aircraft. That had earned them promotion to First Officers, and another gold stripe on their epaulettes.

"We'll stay under 8000 feet," Theo said. "Less chance of encountering the enemy. But if we do, dive down and high-tail it back here."

"Can we do aerobatics?"

"If you insist," he conceded with a grin. "So, change into your trousers and we'll head out." She was in uniform and only needed to ditch her skirt.

"But I don't have my flying gear!"

"Yes you do," Roz assured her. "I snuck it into the trunk. I mean 'boot'. Along with mine."

"Roz will be Spitfire Lady #2," Charlie said, giving her a loving glance.

"And I will capture it all on film, since you're not allowed to have cameras on the airfield," Jim said.

He snapped Elyse donning her leather helmet, climbing onto the wing, and stepping into the cockpit. Then he handed her a copy of *The Times*. "Hold it so we can see the date, and I'll take a picture to prove you're the first."

"It fits like a glove," she said in awe to Charlie after her photo shoot.

"She'll respond to your slightest touch," he said. He was standing on the wing, giving her instructions, while Roz looked on from the other wing. "Forward visibility isn't good until you're airborne. And you can't dawdle on the ground or she'll overheat. She has a narrow landing gear, so be careful of ground looping when you land. Enjoy, little cousin."

"You're a brick, Wing Commander! Contact!"

The Merlin engine throbbed powerfully, a thoroughbred quivering to be given its head. Heart pounding with excitement, she pulled down her goggles and waved to Theo.

They taxied down the runway and lifted effortlessly into the air. Then they were rocketing heavenward, dipping and soaring among shredded clouds. Elyse felt as if she had just sprouted wings herself, as if she needed only to think of a manoeuvre and the plane would do it. For twenty minutes they played with joyful abandon.

"It's an absolute dream!" Elyse announced when she descended from the plane. "Made for women, I'd say."

"There you go, Jim. A successful *test* flight," Theo jested.

"I don't know how some of our big chaps actually fit themselves into the cockpit," Charlie admitted. He and Roz now clambered into the planes.

"My first Hurricane was a thrill, but this was even more exhilarating!" Elyse enthused, wrapping her arm happily around Theo's as they watched the others take off. "Definitely not the sort of flying we're supposed to do on our deliveries, either. Far too much fun."

"I'll bet the male ATA pilots throw the planes about. Fly under bridges and generally beat-up places," he said.

"Aren't we aviators all daredevils?" she asked with a grin.

"Now you have me worried," Theo retorted.

"I can already tell Elyse is a good match for you, Theo." Jim chortled.

They chatted with Jim while they waited for Charlie and Roz to return, but he couldn't discuss his work, which was highly confidential.

"I have to admit that I'm looking forward to finishing my tour of duty tomorrow," Theo said as they lit cigarettes. "They've got us on the offensive now, flying 'Rhubarbs' over the coast of France. That's what we call low-level strafing attacks. We all hate them. Such a waste of men and machines. At least if we're shot down over England, we're on home turf. And over there, we have to avoid the flak as well as Me109s."

"Then be extra cautious tomorrow," Elyse urged. "Don't become complacent because it's your last day and your thoughts are elsewhere."

"Quite so," Jim said. "Save that for the honeymoon. Where *are* you going?"

"The Lake District for two glorious weeks. It's the closest I can come to giving Elyse a taste of home. And it might be the only place in Britain where we can escape from the war for a while."

"Don't count on it! There are probably secret training manoeuvres going on in the hills."

"A good excuse to stay indoors then," Theo quipped. "Afterwards I'm off to teach at the Heston OTU."

Elyse was thankful that he would be out of battle for six months, but suddenly spooked about tomorrow.

Jim snapped pictures of the two couples kissing goodbye before the men climbed into their planes. It would become a poignant reminder of a special and perfect day.

•   •   •

Elyse and Roz chatted excitedly on the short drive to Priory Manor. "I'm just bursting to tell someone!" Elyse admitted. "At least we can show Sophie the photos." Jim had promised to bring them on Saturday.

Priory Manor was ablaze with spring flowers and blossoming trees. Sophie, an enthusiastic horticulturalist, had designed breathtaking perennial gardens that seemed to flow from the house. She had also turned vast stretches of lawns into vegetable plots, which promised a bountiful harvest.

"We have an unexpected guest for the wedding," Sophie confided as she led them into the sunroom. Beyond the walls of windows, rose vines clambered over the tumbled stone walls amid colourful tulips. The ceremony would be held there, weather permitting.

Elyse was puzzled at the idea of an uninvited guest, but astonished when she saw him rise from the armchair, looking dapper in his RCAF uniform.

"Uncle Chas! What on earth are you doing here?"

He chuckled as she joyfully threw herself into his embrace. "I wrangled a BCATP meeting in London, so I flew over on one of the transatlantic ferry planes yesterday. I cabled Sophie that I was coming, but wanted to surprise you. We couldn't *all* miss your wedding."

"This is the best present!"

"Your father was disappointed that I couldn't manage a seat for him as well, and Ria almost climbed into my bag. But they all send their love, and I've been ordered to bring back dozens of photos and a movie of the wedding. Drew made sure that I know how to handle the cine-camera."

Turning to Roz with a disarming smile, he said, "Do forgive me for prattling on. You must be Roz. Elyse has been singing your praises in her letters."

"I'm delighted to meet you, Air Marshal Thornton! From Elyse's tales, I feel I already know you. And I must say, I'm looking forward to staying in your crackerjack boathouse some time, if I may."

Chas chuckled. "Absolutely! That's something for us all to look forward to. So, let's begin by dispensing with titles, shall we?"

Chas handed Elyse a fat envelope. "This is from your father. The original is in the bank at home."

Inside was a copy of the deed to Blackthorn Island, made out in her name, along with several photographs and a letter. At her astonished look, Chas said, "He wanted to ensure you come home sometimes, and also that your step-mother can never claim it. Entice your husband with the photos."

"I shall indeed! How smashing! Look at these, Roz," she said, handing her the photos.

"Lucky you! I will definitely come to visit."

"Are things not good between Dad and Babs?" Elyse asked Chas.

"She's got him on a tight rein, as you know, and he's chomping at the bit. He knows horses, but not women, I'm afraid. I do think that another divorce is imminent…. Anyway, to make getting to your cottage more fun, Ria and I are giving you a floatplane as our gift."

"Oh, Uncle Chas, how fabulous! And generous!" She gave him a big hug.

"And Sandy sent this so that the groom knows how talented his new wife is." He handed her a copy of the scary movie that she had helped Sandy make.

"*Shadows*! I haven't seen this in ages!"

"Neither have I!" Sophie said. "That will be such fun to watch. See something of home."

"Grandpa, Grandpa!" four-year-old Alayna shouted as she and six-year-old Jason dashed into the room. She threw herself into his arms.

"Grandpa, we've finished supper so we can have story time in the summerhouse, like you promised!" Jason said, offering a book for Chas to read – *The Mystery of Spirit Bay*, by Merilee's parents. "My favouritest."

"Mine too," Chas agreed.

"I think these will go perfectly with it," Elyse said, handing the children each a maple sugar lollipop. "Merilee sent them."

They squealed with delight. "Grandpa brought banas!" Alayna announced excitedly.

"Yummy! I haven't tasted bananas since I left Canada," Elyse replied.

"I've brought you these," Roz said as she pulled two parcels out of her bag and handed them to the children.

They tore open the paper to unveil colouring books and boxes of brand-new Crayola crayons. "Thank you, Miss Fenwick!" Jason said gleefully, while Alayna gave her a hug.

"I don't know how I'll get them to bed tonight," Sophie lamented with an indulgent smile.

But Chas managed to do that before the adults settled down to a relaxing dinner. Elyse suddenly felt nostalgic for home as he caught them up on news.

"The Wyndwood Convalescent Home will be opening soon," he told them. "Ria's done wonders organizing everything, and the RCAF has agreed to staff it. They're adding a few temporary buildings for staff and offices."

"I expect it will be strange having all those airmen on the island," Sophie said.

"I managed to persuade Drew to put off joining the RCAF until after the summer, because he's needed to take the chaps out for boat rides and teach water-skiing to those well enough."

"That couldn't have been easy," Elyse said.

"He's a lot like Ria, so I appealed to his better nature." Chas grinned. "I said that he'd be doing a great service to those fellows, and that he could pick up valuable tips from them. In the meantime, he can get a head start on his aviation studies. Of course, it won't delay the inevitable for long."

"Surely he'd make a good teacher," Elyse suggested slyly.

"I expect you're right, but I won't interfere. He'd never forgive me for that."

Chas looked momentarily downcast as he refilled his wineglass, and Elyse realized he was thinking of his rocky relationship with Charlie.

"I hear that Sandy's really in his element at the NFB. And hopefully stays safely in Ottawa," she said.

"Yes indeed! We're all proud when we see the films he's been working on at the cinema. He's directing one based on his latest script about the contributions of scientists to the war effort. These short *Canada Carries On* films are partly propaganda, of course, but also important so that Canadians realize what *is* going on. In this case, that technology and scientific innovations could be more important in winning this war than brute force."

"And that those who aren't in the forces also make vital contributions to the war effort."

"Precisely!"

"Although I have to confess that there's something irresistibly sexy about a man in uniform," Elyse said with a grin.

"I hope Theo passes muster without one," Sophie quipped.

"Oh yes," Elyse murmured, raising a seductive eyebrow.

The others laughed.

Last minute wedding preparations the next day included gathering flowers for the arrangements that Sophie expertly created. She had grown up in her mother's flower shop in Calais, and had learned that skill young.

Although Sidonie had offered to provide a wedding dress, Elyse was happy to borrow Sophie's beautiful white satin and lace gown designed by Parisian couturier Madeleine Vionnet eight years ago. The few alterations were completed, so Elyse tried it on. She stared at herself in the cheval glass as if seeing a stranger there.

"You look gorgeous," Sophie said.

"As did you. And it feels so glamorous."

There was a knock. "I have something for the bride," Chas mumbled through the door.

"Come in if you can keep a secret," Elyse replied with a grin.

"You look radiant, Elyse," Chas said with deep admiration. "If a little apprehensive," he added with a twinkle in his eyes.

"I swore I wouldn't get married in wartime, just do my job and not make any romantic commitments."

"You take enormous risks with your life every day, so why not one that can bring you so much pleasure and happiness?"

"Why not, indeed? Although it's easier to be brave in the skies."

He chuckled. "Granny sent you a gift. She hoped you might wear it tomorrow so that she can feel like part of the proceedings," Chas said, handing her a box.

Nestled on a plush velvet bed was an exquisite, but not ostentatious, Victorian emerald and diamond necklace.

"Zowie! It's Granny's favourite! This is for me to keep?"

"It is indeed. Your grandfather gave it to her on their wedding day…. Kate got her pearls," he added with a grin.

"Ah, the second-best necklace." Elyse laughed. "I'm so touched and honoured."

It looked stunning on the gown.

"Emphasizes your green eyes," Sophie said approvingly.

As if she were momentarily a child again, Elyse went to Chas for a reassuring hug. "I'm so glad you're here, Uncle Chas. You won't mind that Charlie gives me away, though?"

"Of course not. I'm glad that he can…. Sophie tells me that your mother's coming tomorrow, which rather surprises me."

"I suppose we have something of a truce. At least an end to outright hostility on my part and complete indifference on hers."

"I'm glad, for both your sakes…. Now, how about a game of tennis?"

Chas and Sophie trounced Elyse and Roz on the court. Sophie's husband, Philip Chadwick, arrived while they were having tea with the children at the summerhouse. He had an intelligence job at RAF Medmanham, but couldn't reveal any details.

Charlie arrived just as the adults were sitting down to predinner sherry in the sunroom. Sophie had already warned him about Chas's visit.

"So good to see you, Charlie," Chas said, stretching out his hand.

Elyse could sense the tension between them as their eyes locked. She sighed with relief when Charlie shook his hand firmly.

"The uniform suits you, Dad. I know that you've been doing important work. We'd be floundering without the BCATP."

"And you've done well for yourself, Wing Commander."

"It's more a matter of attrition, being one of the few experienced veterans. I'm flying almost as much, but with responsibility for four squadrons now. A bit daunting at times."

"As you're not expected to do more than two combat tours, you should be out of the firing line within the year. Relegated to a desk job." Chas beamed, and Elyse hoped he was right.

"Technically, yes. But that would leave novices under the leadership of less experienced pilots," Charlie stated. "I wouldn't want that for Drew, if he gets here before the war ends. Would you?"

Chas fiddled with his pipe. "We're always looking for pilots with combat experience to teach in Canada. The RAF offers that opportunity first to Canadians. Gives them a chance to come home for a while."

"I've been asked but declined. I thought *you* had orchestrated that." Charlie stared challengingly at his father.

Chas winced at the implied criticism. "I didn't, actually. Although Mum urged me to. She misses you all terribly. It's actually a good thing that we have evacuees for her to fuss over."

A maid came into the room. "Pardon me, Miss Thornton, but there's a telephone call for you."

Elyse felt an intense rush of fear that threatened to unbalance her as she hurried to the phone in the library. *Dear God, don't let anything have happened to Theo.* She trembled as she lifted the receiver.

"Darling, I'm safely back on terra firma," Theo said jauntily on the other end of the line.

"Thank God!" She leaned against the desk for support.

"We were bounced by a few dozen ME 109s over Calais, but my squadron all made it back this time. So it was a good day. I knew you were worried, darling, but I told you that Thornton Bear would keep me safe."

•   •   •

After dinner, Roz asked Charlie to take a stroll with her in the garden.

"I sense a romance blooming," Chas said, sipping his cognac in the dying light of day in the sunroom. The lovers were ambling arm-in-arm through the Gothic arch of the ruins, heads tilted toward one another.

"Very observant, Dad," Sophie teased.

Chas smirked. "Your mother would have picked up on it right away."

"I haven't seen Charlie this happy for a long time."

"I know how critical that can be to survival," Chas said, gazing into some distant past.

"Roz would be a good Thornton," Elyse said.

"Agreed! She's certainly won me over." Chas regained his cheerfulness.

Elyse was suddenly hopeful that Roz could reconcile father and son as she exchanged knowing glances with Sophie.

When they returned, Roz took Elyse aside and said, "I told Charlie I'd accept his proposal on the condition that he wouldn't try for another tour of combat duty."

"Brilliant! How did he react?"

"Told me he loved me unconditionally, but that if he was expected to play it safe, then so must I. By giving up my ATA job."

"Ah…. Checkmate."

"I said I would as long as he took a training job in Canada. Told him I couldn't stay in Britain if I can't fly. He promised that he wouldn't *volunteer* for another tour, but does have to follow orders. So… we're getting married!" Roz grinned happily.

"How wonderful!" Elyse enthused, hugging Roz. "Will you tell the others now?"

"Should we?"

"Of course! We've already discussed what a good wife you'll make."

"Cheeky!"

It was a happy group that toasted the engaged couple with champagne. Charlie seemed more at ease.

"Let's go and light the stars!" Elyse suggested.

"Oh yes! I haven't done that for ages," Sophie agreed eagerly.

At Roz's puzzled expression, Elyse said, "Wait and see."

It was a chilly night, so they grabbed coats and wandered out to the Gothic garden.

"It only works when there's a dark sky, like at the lake or here in the blackout," Elyse said. "Charlie started it, so he can explain."

"I got lost among the islands once, when I was out in the boat in the morning mist…"

"He was running away from home," Elyse interjected.

"*I'm* telling the story, brat!"

Elyse grinned at him while Roz looked intrigued.

"The motor conked out and I sprained my wrist trying to fix it, so I couldn't row far. I fetched up in a large secluded bay, with no signs of civilization anywhere. I was ten, and becoming increasingly scared as it got dark. There was no moon or even ripples of light from distant cottages. Just me and the lake and the nighttime creatures under an endless black sky. I'd never felt so alone and vulnerable. I lay down in the boat and tried to make myself as small as possible, hoping there weren't any bears around.

"I noticed that stars were lighting up, first a few and then thousands, millions, growing ever bigger, creating a bright cloud that was reflected in the water. I suddenly felt cradled by the glow. No longer afraid, and actually filled with awe and joy at the wonder of the universe, and my infinitesimally tiny place in it."

They looked up. There was only a sliver of moon. Pinpricks of stars began to grow.

"I see what you mean!" Roz exclaimed as she clung to Charlie's arm. "You don't see the darkness anymore, just the light."

"We lie on the boathouse deck to light the stars. Or float on our backs if we're in for a late swim," Elyse said. "A perfect end to a beautiful day, or a lift for your spirits if needed."

"Now I want to know the rest of this intriguing tale. How did you get home?" Roz asked.

"Dad figured out where I might have been, after everyone had searched the lakes for me that day. It was too dangerous to be out in the dark, among the myriad islands and shoals, so he showed up at dawn."

Under the emerging stars, father and son exchanged a glance. Surely there was a softening in Charlie's face, reflecting some of the deep love in Chas's, Elyse thought. Lighting the stars could sometimes work wonders.

Muskoka: Summer 1941

Chapter 11

Surely there were more stars here, Erich Leitner thought as he gazed out from the veranda of his room, regretting that the searchlights that illuminated the grounds and the lake detracted from the celestial lightshow.

He relished sleeping out here on warm nights. A breeze wafted into the deep bay through the screened walls of windows on two sides, the third being a partition between the other half of the balcony, which served the room next door. One of his roommates usually joined him on blistering hot days, but tonight they were allowing him privacy.

The fact that the two letters arrived in the same envelope had already alerted him. They were nested together: hers inside, in the embrace of the other.

Dear Erich,

My heart breaks as I write this, for I never meant to hurt you. Neither of us did. Although we do things with the best and purest of intentions, we can never predict how our lives and loves might be hijacked.

Being together almost daily for the past year, Gustav and I have fallen deeply in love. We tried to deny it, but how can you deny your heart?

Gustav said he would never betray you, but I assured him that I would break off with you in any case. Since we haven't seen each other for almost two years, I'm not certain I still know you. We are children no longer, and our experiences in this war will surely change us even more.

You and your dreams always were beyond what I wanted, which is a quiet country life raising a big family. Not flying airplanes or building things or adventures in new places.

I know that you will eventually find a girl who will love you as you deserve, and as I never truly did. I only realize that now by comparison with my profound feelings for Gustav.

Although he was at first devastated when Irmgard dumped him last year, he quickly realized that marrying her would have been a terrible mistake. She found herself a high-ranking Nazi and married him within two months, and now swans around like the lady she has always wanted to be. Little wonder that during their three-year courtship she would never commit to Gustav. A lucky escape for him. You may think the same of me some day.

For now, I hope you don't hate me, that we can be brother and sister without rancour. I would despair if your relationship with Gustav was torn apart by this unexpected turn of events. Neither of us wanted it to happen, but if you must find fault, it is all mine.

We are to be wed in August.

I leave you with warmest best wishes and sisterly love. Angelika

Dear Erich,

I am ashamed to write this, and guilty that I must. I can only reiterate what Angelika has already told you – that we never intended this to happen, never courted, never even flirted. Just quietly fell in love, and woke up one day to realize that we both felt the same and could no longer pretend otherwise.

Forgive me, dear brother. I am ecstatic for myself, but shattered for you. Is there any way I can ever make this up to you?

Your devoted brother, Gustav

Erich was seized with helpless anger and misery, wanting to punch something or someone to release the pressure of his boiling emotions. Being so far away, he couldn't even try to fight for Angelika. And since Hitler had turned his attentions on Russia in the spring, he was no longer confident that the war would end soon. What if he were stuck here for two, or three, or even more years? Could he blame either of them for seizing happiness while they could?

Watching the twinkling stars through teary eyes, he realized that it was useless to crave something that no longer existed. He might as well wish he could fly to the moon. What good would it do to confront Angelika and Gustav now?

He tried to imagine himself back home, watching them go about their daily chores, spying on them in bed together. But the pictures were broken, like jigsaw puzzles with missing pieces.

He was no longer part of their world.

•   •   •

"You want me to play for Anna Neagle? The famous British actress?" Peggy Wilding squeaked.

"You don't mind, do you, Peggy?" Ria Thornton asked with a grin. "She'll want someone to accompany her. I'm sure you can easily manage her music."

"Like 'Tea for Two'," Merilee suggested.

"Oh, I loved her in *No No Nanette!*" Peggy recalled how she had felt infused with the bubbly, bouncy spirit of Neagle's 'Nanette', her carefree exuberance and lithe grace.

"Good! Then I'll tell Billy that Miss Neagle can choose a time," Ria said.

Anna Neagle and her producer-director, Herbert Wilcox - now working in Hollywood - were staying with Billy Bishop and his family at their cottage across the lake at Windermere. Bishop was on a fund-raising tour with them and other celebrities. Miss Neagle had graciously agreed to give a short concert to the airmen at the Wyndwood Convalescent Home.

Peggy and Merilee were ensconced in the boathouse at The Point for the first three weeks of August, while Peggy continued treatments at the Spirit Bay Retreat. Finally freed from the prison of the leg brace and crutches, she was ecstatic. Although she hobbled with a cane, she felt light and energetic. Swimming was now possible and helping her regain even more strength and function.

Merilee had already spent much of July helping Ria with her evacuees, and was delighted to have Peggy with her now.

On the appointed day, Peggy was nervous as Merilee and Drew helped her out of the launch at Westwynd. There were well over a hundred people milling about the terrace and grounds. As well as the convalescents, there were RCAF officers and staff who ran the facility, and the Wyndwood islanders and their friends, like the Carringtons and Rolands, who had been invited.

A few minutes later, a Grumman Goose roared over the treetops, circled, and swooped down to land on the lake. The seaplane pulled up to the dock, where Chas and Ria greeted the guests as they stepped out. There was tremendous applause when the expectant audience recognized Anna Neagle.

"She's just as beautiful in real life!" Peggy whispered to Merilee in awe.

"You certainly know how to make an entrance, Bish," Chas said to Billy.

"Would you expect anything less?" Bishop countered with a broad grin.

His wife, Margaret, and their two teenaged children also stepped out of the plane, along with a spectacled older man who was undoubtedly the prolific producer.

As introductions were made, Ria said to Anna, "Our British guests are particularly keen to meet you, Miss Neagle."

Fourteen-year-old William Baxter, who had sprouted another four inches in the past year, hung back, but the younger ones pressed close to Ria.

"I expect you miss England, my dears – as do I - but what an adventure you're having here!" the actress said cheerfully.

"Yes indeed, Miss!" twelve-year-old Vera Carmichael enthused. "We've even learned to waterski!" Thanks to Merilee and Drew's tireless efforts this summer.

"How exciting! Perhaps you could show me later?" They were all to go to The Point for drinks after the concert.

"Oh yes! Could we?" Vera asked Ria.

"Of course. We won't be able to do it much longer with the new gas rationing."

The tuned piano had been wheeled out to the far end of the terrace, with rows of chairs stretching back into the conservatory. The island teens perched on the wide balustrade.

Anna Neagle captivated the audience when she began with a light-hearted ditty from *No No Nanette*. "I want to be happy, But I won't be happy, Till I make you happy, too."

Which she proceeded to do by encouraging them to sing along to tunes like "The White Cliffs of Dover" and "Wish Me Luck as You Wave Me Goodbye".

Although still star-struck, Peggy relaxed and enjoyed the artistic bond with the charismatic singer.

Anna introduced her final song, saying, "This is dedicated to all the British guests here, especially the little ones," as she acknowledged the delighted evacuees. There were cheers as she launched into "There'll Always Be an England".

She thanked Peggy by giving her a dazzling smile and applauding her. Peggy was thrilled.

Anna wandered about, talking to the convalescents, some of whom had been wounded in action. Others were recovering from flying accidents in training, or from illness. All agreed with her when she said with a grin, "What a delightful place to recuperate. I wouldn't be in much of a hurry to leave."

Back at The Point, the family and guests gathered on the boathouse deck, where Grayson was mixing cocktails, and cakes and canapés beckoned. The younger children gobbled down scones and lemonade, and scooted off to change into their swimsuits.

The teenagers were lolling on the wide dock that edged the boathouse, sipping Cokes and dangling their feet in the water.

"I hear your dad's gone all Hollywood," Anthea Carrington said to Arthur Bishop and his younger sister, Jackie. "Making a movie about the Air Training Plan."

"Yeah, he was in L.A. consulting with Warner Brothers about it. *Captains of the Clouds*. He's going to have a small part in it, as himself," Arthur replied.

"Next week we get to meet the stars, like James Cagney!" Jackie said excitedly.

"We're flying to some lake up north where they're filming the bush pilot scenes," Arthur explained.

"Lucky you!"

The children came running. "We're all ready, Drew!" Vera announced.

"OK, then why don't you go first, Vera?"

"I'll spot for you," Arthur offered.

While Merilee and Anthea helped the children into life jackets and prepared the skis, Drew and Arthur went into the boathouse to select a runabout.

"You joining soon?" Drew asked Arthur, who was the same age.

"Damn right! Didn't pass some of my finals so I thought I'd have to do another frigging year in school. But the old man just told me that they've relaxed the requirements, so I'm outta here as soon as I round up references. What about you?"

"I was coerced into helping out at the Convalescent Home. My folks are trying to keep me from enlisting for as long as possible."

"My old man's just afraid I won't do well enough to become an officer. Can't let the side down, of course."

"Bloody hard being a Bishop, eh?"

"Or a Thornton."

"Especially since my brother's already won a bunch of medals. He's a Battle of Britain hero."

Arthur snorted. "So you're doubly screwed!"

"You know what worries me more than facing the enemy? Being so damned scared that I can't fight. Some of the stories I've heard from the chaps at the Home…" Drew shook his head.

"Nothing worse than being labelled as 'Lacking Moral Fibre', and being assigned some crap job like towing targets for students to fire at."

"Better to be shot down by Jerry," Drew said thoughtfully.

"Go down in glory… But bail if you can," Arthur added with a grin.

"If I even have the chance to get into action. I'm afraid Dad will wrangle it so that I end up being an instructor, like Alastair Grayson. He graduated top of his class from university and from pilot training, and now he can't even get posted overseas."

"That sucks! I bet my old man makes sure I get into a fighter squadron as soon as possible."

"I do have a consolation for being stuck here this summer," Drew confided with a grin as he backed out of the slip.

"Let me guess.... Anthea."

"That obvious, is it?"

"I noticed the goo-goo eyes. Beats me what a peachy chick like her sees in an ugly devil like you," Arthur teased.

Drew accelerated hard into the bay, making Arthur fall into his seat as they both burst into laughter.

•   •   •

"Oh, well played!" Merilee said to Deanna Tremayne, who had just knocked her croquet ball through two wickets. They were on the lawn at the Spirit Bay Retreat, where Deanna and Peggy were poised to win their match.

Newly out of her braces, Deanna walked tentatively, and Merilee stayed close to her, holding her canes when Deanna made her shots, prepared to steady her if she lost her balance.

There was loud applause when Deanna's ball hit the stake, ending the game. They looked over to see Ross approaching them.

Deanna squealed with delight. "You didn't say you were coming!" she accused when he took her into his arms.

"I told Mum I wanted to surprise you. I have some leave, so I'm staying at Pineridge, and Dad's coming to join us... But just look at you! Winning at croquet. Walking again."

Deanna stood proudly, happily. "And I'm swimming... a bit. Like Peggy."

"You've both made amazing strides," he said, turning to Peggy with obvious admiration. "I applaud your fortitude and courage."

His intense look sent shivers of delight through Peggy, making her momentarily weak-kneed. Now seventeen, she had blossomed. Her amber-green eyes were bright and determined now that pain and frustration were no longer her constant companions.

"How long can you stay?" Deanna asked Ross eagerly.

"An entire week! What luxury."

"Oh, Ross, you have to hear the music that Peggy wrote about Faith the fairy! It's just magical. Will you play it for him, Peggy?"

"What, now?"

"If you're finished here," Ross suggested.

As they shuffled to the rambling building, Deanna revealed, "Dr. Roland said I could start riding again soon. She thinks it will be good exercise for me. I can hardly wait, Ross! Of course, I've been visiting Rebel, but it's just not the same."

"I expect he's missed you as well… That's terrific, Deedee!"

Peggy's spirits soared to see him so happy.

Others gathered around the piano when Peggy began playing. The tune had suddenly come to her, dancing in her head when she had regained the lightness of being unencumbered. It began with a turbulent storm in a minor key, but became gay and whimsical.

It was already popular among the patients, who never tired of hearing it. They clapped delightedly, but none more so than Ross.

"Couldn't you picture Faith flitting about the woodlands after the storm, frolicking in her waterfall under a rainbow?" Deanna asked him.

"I certainly could! You're exceptionally talented, Peggy. A composer as well."

Peggy blushed.

"I made her play it for Uncle Max," Merilee said. "And he was most impressed. Told her he would help her get it published as sheet music. Mum and Dad are thrilled to think that their character has a tune."

"I should think so!"

Peggy was playing "Faith's Fairy Dance" on the grand piano in the Old Cottage that afternoon, stopping every now and then to write down changes to the score, which she was still perfecting.

Merilee and Ria were at the Country Club with the children, teaching them tennis. Even staid William had been persuaded to learn when he discovered that his idol, Troy Roland, was an accomplished player.

Grayson and his wife were busy in the far-off kitchen wing, so the cottage was eerily quiet except for the ticking of the clock on the mantelpiece and the strains of her music.

So Peggy jumped when a voice behind her said, "What mysterious and mystical melody is this? I've never heard it, and yet… it speaks to me."

Peggy turned to see mad Cousin Phoebe, still looking like a relic from the 1920s.

"Grandmother approves," Phoebe stated, glancing over at the rocking chair in front of the fireplace.

Peggy couldn't resist following her gaze, and felt a shiver of fear as the chair moved ever so slightly. Surely it was only the breezes wafting in through the open French windows that disturbed it, but the vivid images from Sandy's movie assailed her. It was too easy to believe in ghosts here. She hoped they were as benign as in the film.

"My Gloria. NO! I mean my Sylvia would like your music. She paints the essence of things. The souls. Few understand, because they don't SEE. It's right there in front of them, but they only see the forest."

Phoebe frowned. "Can you hear the whispers?" She turned abruptly to stare probingly at Peggy. "Can you hear the secrets struggling to break the silence?"

She crashed her hands onto the piano in a diabolical chord. "Too many secrets!"

Peggy slid off the piano bench hurriedly as Phoebe plunked down and began playing wildly, lost in her raging as if ridding herself of demons. Peggy recognized it as Liszt's "Totentanz" – The Dance of Death – and was surprised at how skillfully Phoebe played the difficult piece.

Phoebe stopped suddenly, her contorted face relaxing into a satisfied smile. "There! That will keep them away a while longer. Beastly things!"

She cocked her head, listening. "They're back, and I'm not supposed to be here. Ria says I scare the children. Fiddlesticks!... and stones may break my bones, but words, words... voices... haunt me.... Sometimes I still hear her crying," Phoebe added in a tiny, aching voice.

"Who?"

"Gloria."

Before Peggy could ask, Phoebe spun away, the diaphanous chiffon floating mist-like behind her as she disappeared onto the east stretch of the veranda.

The children clattered in from the other side.

"Are you coming for a swim, Peggy?" Vera asked. "Merilee's already getting changed."

"You bet!"

"Last one in's a rotten egg!" nine-year-old George yelled as he bounded up the stairs.

"That's a childish thing to say, George!" William chided as he and Ria walked in. "And don't go tearing about like that!"

But George just stuck out his tongue and kept running.

"I think the children are getting out of hand, Mrs. Thornton. Forgetting their manners," William opined. "I don't think my parents would approve."

Peggy flashed Ria a sympathetic look as she limped out of the room.

"You needn't worry about them, William. They're perfectly well mannered, and just enjoying being young and carefree. I keep your parents well informed."

Ria wrote to both sets of parents weekly, detailing their kids' activities, achievements, ailments, and the minutiae of daily life, accompanied by photos, so that they didn't completely miss their children's joys and milestones during these crucial years.

Sadly and ironically, she was missing that with her own precious grandchildren in England.

Because Ria rarely saw William during the school year, Troy kept William's father apprised of his progress. He was certainly well placed with Ellie's parents, and excelled at the University of Toronto Schools. But Ria was not surprised that his siblings, Jane and George, didn't seem to miss him.

"May I go to Ouhu now?" William asked.

"After your swimming practice."

"But I know how to swim!"

"Not well enough. The others have been practicing all winter in our pool, so you have a lot of catching up to do." He had only been willing to learn so that he could take the skiff out by himself.

William looked surly as he muttered, "Professor Roland is expecting me."

"Troy knows your routine, and you'll have plenty of time to spend with him. Besides, it's only proper that you have a refreshing dip after a hot game." He didn't seem to be aware that his adolescent body was odorous when sweaty. She would ask Troy to speak to him about hygiene, as well as the facts of life. And, dear God, she'd have to talk to Vera and Jane about menstruation and sex soon as well.

"When you've done three laps of the bay, you'll be free to go," Ria declared.

William stomped off, and she was grateful that, come September, he would once again become the responsibility of the Carlyles, with whom he behaved completely differently.

Down at the boathouse, Peggy asked Merilee, "Who is Gloria? Your cousin Phoebe mentioned her just now. I had the impression she might have been a child who died."

"Not one I've ever heard about. Phoebe's daughter, Sylvia, is nineteen and rather odd, as if she's a bit... otherworldly. If that makes any sense."

"Oh, I think so." Peggy wondered if Gloria was one of the secrets. She told Merilee about the encounter. "Do you think that Phoebe might have had a baby out of wedlock? That would have been scandalous."

"Gosh, I would never have thought Phoebe capable of that! And the baby died?"

"Or was given away. Maybe that's why Phoebe went mad!"

"That makes sense. I'll have to ask Mum, although I doubt if she knows."

"And skeletons don't creep out of the closet easily."

•   •   •

Finished with her treatments for the day, Peggy was resting on the veranda at Spirit Bay waiting for Merilee to pick her up. Deanna had just gone for her physiotherapy, so Peggy was surprised when Ross joined her. She had longed for and relished every brief moment that she seen him this week.

"I wish I could stay longer," he said as he gazed wistfully out over the lake. "But as I'm leaving tomorrow, I wondered if you would care to join me at Pineridge for the dance tonight?"

"But... I can't..."

"I can't jitterbug either," he interrupted with a smile. "We'll just enjoy the band and perhaps shuffle to slow tunes."

Peggy thought she might faint at the thought of being held in his arms, especially since he looked at her with such tenderness.

"Bring Merilee and anyone else you'd like. Deanna will be there." He picked her up every afternoon so that she could dine with her family at the inn.

"That sounds like fun." Which seemed too lame, so she added happily, "I'd love to!"

"Wonderful!... I haven't told Deanna yet, but this is my embarkation leave."

"You're going overseas?" Peggy's heart plummeted.

"Yes. Our troops need engineering support... But let's not allow that to spoil this wondrous time here. Shall I row over to fetch you at about 8:00?"

"Drew and his crowd are going to the dance at the Country Club." Which was flanked by Spirit Bay and the Pineridge Inn. "So Merilee and I can come with him. She was planning to stay at the cottage with me, despite my protests, so I'm glad that she has a chance to attend a dance."

"Perfect! Then I shall meet you ladies at the dock."

"It's not like a date," Peggy declared later to Merilee, more to convince herself not to become too excited, expect too much. "It's just a farewell party with friends."

"Uh huh," Merilee said with a grin. "Then why are you flustered about what to wear?"

"Because I don't have anything suitable!"

"It's not formal, like the Country Club. Your mother's made you some lovely dresses."

"Wholesome cotton. Nothing silky or sexy."

Merilee giggled. "Are you planning to seduce him?"

"Merilee! I just don't want to look like a little girl, or a frump."

"Well, you don't. And Ross obviously likes you just as you are. Cotton and all... But you're welcome to borrow something of mine."

"You're inches taller. I'd look ridiculous."

Merilee went to fetch something from her room. "Here, try this over your white frock."

Peggy's best dress was flatteringly cut, with narrow black piping and prim bows defining the square neckline, waist, and hems. But Merilee's short black lace jacket edged with jet sequins transformed it.

"Oh, it's gorgeous! But what will you wear?"

"My blue chiffon." Which had a sheer, elbow-length cape drooping from the spangled shoulders.

Peggy was happy that Drew drove *Windrunner IX* sedately this time. They stopped at Red Rock Island to pick up Anthea Carrington, and by her side was a chap in RCAF uniform. Merilee's insides clenched when she realized it was Bryce.

"Look who's on leave after his Initial Training," Anthea enthused, hugging her brother's arm gleefully. "Leading Aircraftsman Carrington!"

Merilee had to admit that the uniform suited him. But she didn't care for the scraggly moustache that attempted to proclaim his manhood.

She couldn't fail to see his admiration when he eyed her as if assessing – with approval and anticipation - a prize racehorse. Damn him if he thought he could just pick up where they'd left off last summer!

"Welcome aboard, LAC Carrington. Judging by the propeller badge you're flaunting on your sleeve, the Air Force must have decided you could handle flying," Drew quipped. "Now you'll actually have to learn how."

"Piece of cake, Thornton, if you can do it... Ladies, you're looking luscious... I mean lovely... as ever."

Anthea punched him playfully. "And you're as cheeky as usual. I expect that will land you in hot water with the military."

"I do try."

They laughed as they resumed the short journey to the mainland.

Ross was awaiting them on the Pineridge dock, also in uniform.

"You're not coming to the Country Club?" Bryce asked in surprise as Merilee took Ross's hand and stepped out of the launch.

"Peggy and I are partying with other friends tonight," Merilee replied, and then introduced Ross. She was glad that Bryce looked peeved, but chided herself for even caring. She noticed him watching Ross offer his arm to Peggy as the boat pulled away.

Drew waved to the driver of a yacht coming in, and Merilee realized it was the Thornton's *Lady Ria*. Chas had loaned the sixty-foot day cruiser to the Wyndwood Convalescent Home for the duration so that the RCAF could transport people and supplies to and from the island. But it was strange to see it pull up to the dock at Pineridge and disgorge dozens of uniformed men.

Merilee was quickly surrounded by aircrew eager to invite her to dance.

"I saw her first!" one declared.

"But she's my dream girl," another protested.

"I'm a senior officer, so back off," a Flight Lieutenant ordered jovially.

Merilee giggled and accepted Ross's other arm, much to the disappointment of the new arrivals. She was aware that Bryce was still watching as *Windrunner IX* docked a hundred yards away at the Club.

Merilee did dance with the airmen and was so much in demand that she rarely sat down. She was on her third round with an enamoured Flight Cadet when Bryce cut in. He held her tightly as she tried to pull away from him.

"That was rude!" she accused. "Let me go!"

"Not until you tell me what I did to earn a cold shoulder. I thought we were more than just old friends."

"Seems I am only a *summer girl* after all," she accused snidely. "You didn't even bother to write!"

"I had a busy year."

"So I heard."

"Anthea telling tales, is she?"

He regarded her with amusement, which irked her even more.

"Bryce, you have a girlfriend, so just leave me alone."

"I don't, actually, but I did date other girls. Did you think I wouldn't? It's how I know that I like you best."

"Baloney!"

"Let's get a breath of air and talk."

Although she was reluctant to go with him, she clung to the faint hope that he was being sincere, that her girlish dreams still had possibilities.

The night air was refreshing after the bottled-up heat indoors, and others wandered about under the stars.

"There are girls it's fun to spend time with, but some lose their attraction pretty quickly," Bryce said.

"And you have to test them all."

He chuckled at the sarcasm. "I know that the more time I spend with you, the more I *want* to spend with you." He stopped and turned to her. "I really did miss you, Merilee. Will you let me make it up to you? I have two weeks here."

"I only have one more."

"But you don't have to go home. Surely Aunt Ria will let you stay, if you choose."

"We'll see."

"Good! Now I fancy dipping my feet in the lake. I haven't even had a chance to swim since I arrived. Are you game?"

"I just have to kick off my shoes. It was too hot for stockings."

He laughed. "That's my girl!"

Joy bubbled through her like giddy champagne.

When he'd taken off his shoes and socks and rolled up his trousers, Bryce took her hand possessively as they waded into the warm water. Pineridge had one of the best beaches on the lake, with a long stretch of shallow water, and Merilee loved the feel of the firm, wave-ridged sand underfoot.

"Is there anything that beats wriggling your toes in the sand after you've been confined to suffocating footwear?" Bryce asked, doing just that.

"It's one of the first things I do as soon as the ice is out of the lake."

"That's plucky."

"It's ruddy cold. But it's a rite of spring."

"OK, so let's start a summer tradition! May I have this dance, milady?" he asked, giving her a mock bow.

Glenn Miller's seductive *Moonlight Serenade* drifted down from the dancehall. They were ankle-deep in the water.

"It's certainly cooler here. But let's not fall in."

"I'll hold you," he promised as he drew her close. As they swayed to the music, he kissed her tenderly, and then more deeply. She drew back in surprise at the intimacy, almost overbalancing.

"I keep forgetting you're only sixteen… That's not a bad thing," he added hastily as she stiffened. "In fact, I love your innocence."

His cheek caressed her hair and encouraged her to lay her head on his shoulder.

"Seventeen in October," she corrected him. "Can I just mention that your moustache tickles, and doesn't really suit you?"

He burst into laughter. "You're priceless, Merilee! The offending fuzz shall be dealt with forthwith!"

In the crowded, stuffy dancehall, Peggy and Ross were also shuffling to the popular tune. She delighted in his strong embrace, which made her feel so light on her feet that she momentarily forgot she was crippled. Although he was careful to keep a respectable distance between them at the outset, they were irresistibly drawn to each other. She shivered with delight when their bodies touched.

"I'm going to miss this," Ross confided. "You will write?"

"Of course!"

"I expect to hear great things about your evolving career."

The look in his eyes seemed to belie the lightness of his sentiments. But she would feel a fool if she told him she would wait for him, if he wanted only to be a casual friend. He was, after all, six years older, and probably drawn to more mature girls.

"I'm thrilled that Deanna will be back next summer," Peggy said.

Dr. Ellie Roland had told them both that they were making tremendous strides, and that she couldn't be of any more help. But this evening, Mr. Tremayne had announced that he had already booked Deanna and her mother into Pineridge for three weeks next summer. And Ria had told Peggy that she was welcome to stay in the boathouse with Merilee any time.

"Dr. Roland has given Deanna back her life. We're so grateful to you as well, Peggy. And what could be better than spending time in this wonderland?"

"Just having more friends to share it."

"I'll be here in spirit."

He gave her a brief hug, but Peggy revelled in it.

Back in the boathouse later, Peggy felt generous in her own euphoria, and didn't want to deflate Merilee's elation at her reconciliation with Bryce. After all, how could she judge Bryce's character and motivations when Merilee had known him all her life? She would repress her suspicion that he was a too charming, entitled playboy who would probably break Merilee's heart again.

Merilee did stay the extra week, her excuse being that she had hardly seen Amy this summer. Because the Seaford twins were away at school for ten months, Esme had wanted her children home at Seawynd after work every evening. But the twins had been released from their duties for this last week of August, and were excited to be back with their grandparents at Silver Bay.

As usual, the island friends played tennis at the Country Club, water-skied, tanned on the docks between swims, and gathered for games and dances in the evenings, so Merilee and Bryce spent plenty of time together. The upper deck of the boathouse at The

Point was a popular spot for the older teens, especially as it was out of sight of the main house. And there was something exotically romantic about dancing over the water and under the moon.

"It's just an excuse for smooching," fifteen-year-old Amy, who had no boyfriend yet, accused. "That's why Drew mostly puts on slow records."

Merilee had to agree. Bryce was assiduous in teaching her how to kiss, but she always reigned in his straying hands.

By the time they both had to leave, she was madly in love.

"I'm going to miss you like crazy, Merilee," Bryce whispered against her cheek as they danced on the last night. "*I got my girl, who could ask for anything more?*" he crooned along with the Gershwin hit *I Got Rhythm*.

Muskoka: Autumn 1941
Chapter 12

Merilee was relieved to round the peninsula and paddle towards home. In the September silence on the lake, she had suddenly been spooked by something floating toward her canoe, fearing for a bizarre moment that it might be the body of one of the pilots who had crashed into the lake last winter. Two of the bodies had been recovered, but the other two and their plane were still missing. The lake felt sinister when it could swallow them without a trace, secreting them in its murky depths.

It had just been the white belly of a dead fish, not an arm.

With the lake relinquishing its summer-infused heat, she was surprised to see a number of Germans playing a vigorous game of water polo.

She started to give the prickly boom fence a wide berth, as usual, but saw the ball suddenly sail over the barrier, accompanied by German expletives and groans. It settled calmly on the water in front of her. A few prisoners swam up to the fence.

Erich couldn't believe it was his dream forest girl in the canoe. Just the sight of her sent a warm thrill through him.

"Please, Miss. You give ball?" he asked.

Merilee hesitated. The ball mocked her. Dare she aid the enemy? Would she be in trouble if she did? Surely her father's job was to help them, so why shouldn't *she*? It seemed harmless enough, and the guards on shore made no move to deter her.

She paddled over and scooped it up. Startled by the admiration in the German's bewitching aquamarine eyes, she hastily tossed the ball back.

"Thank you, kind lady," Erich said.

She smiled tentatively and nodded before quickly paddling away, heart pounding at this strange encounter with the enemy.

"Merilee, how could you?" Peggy accused later. "You traitor!"

"I am not!"

"I wouldn't have done it! You know those girls who were fraternizing with POWs up in Espanola have been charged under the Defence of Canada regulations."

"They were writing love letters and smuggled a camera to them. That's not the same thing at all!"

"Well they could go to prison… And maybe they should!"

Merilee thought that harsh, but didn't argue with her friend.

"What I did wasn't wrong, was it, Dad?" Merilee asked at dinner that evening.

"It was actually a good thing, sweetheart. Keeping our prisoners happily occupied keeps them out of trouble as well. And showing them Canadian hospitality gets us good credits to ensure that our POWs in Germany are treated well. I've mentioned that many of the Germans are decent chaps, and I believe we're influencing others into understanding and appreciating democracy."

"What will happen to those girls in Espanola?"

"One of them was mailing letters to the States for the prisoners, which is a serious breach. But as they're only your age, I expect the judge will give them a severe reprimand and a suspended sentence."

"I don't understand how the girls could even have met the Germans."

"You did," her mother pointed out with a grin.

"Yes, but…"

"Officers aren't required to work, but the enlisted men sent to lumber camps, like Espanola, actually get out into the community. I believe they met at a hockey game."

"How Canadian!" Claire chuckled. "And love always finds a way, doesn't it?" she added with a sly grin at Colin.

•   •   •

"It's a crazy idea," Erich said to Axel. "You'll be a sitting duck, and they'll shoot you."

"Nah, the Canadians are too nice. If they recapture me, what will I have lost? A month of living with you farters. I'll get my own private room, daily exercise outside, books to read…"

"You don't read," Christoph von Altenberg pointed out, relighting his pipe and returning to his book.

"Magazines…. Sometimes. It's so damn boring here, what else should I do but plan my escape?"

"Take courses," Erich suggested. "Learn an instrument."

"The only instrument I want to strum is one that makes a girl squeal with delight." Axel demonstrated by rubbing his breasts.

Erich shook his head. "So, you're not planning to return to the Fatherland. Just meet some girls?"

"Why not? Papa Christoph keeps telling us how futile it is to imagine getting home. A few days enjoying the sins of a city will suit me just fine." He grinned broadly. "Anyone want to come along?"

Erich considered it for a moment. He longed for freedom with such an intense ache that he feared he might break apart. But he'd be a hunted man, his face splashed across newspapers. Not free at all.

Wolf Sturm said, "Why not? This place is driving me crazy!"

"Your English isn't good enough," Christoph stated without looking up from his book. "You'll just jeopardize Axel's plan. Easier for one to get away than two, if this harebrained scheme works at all."

"True," Axel admitted.

"Assholes!" Wolf hissed before storming out of the room.

None of them wondered about Wolf's anger and frustration. He had just learned that his mother was gravely ill, and felt helpless being stranded so far away. His father had been killed in the last war, so his mother had no one but him and a few kind neighbours to look after her. "She's probably already gone, and I don't even know!" he'd lamented, since it often took two months for mail to arrive.

"Well, I think your plan is suicidal," Rudi Bachmeier said to Axel. "Remember that two of those escapees from the Lake Superior camp were killed."

"Out of twenty-eight that got away!"

"For a few weeks at most. Even reaching Alberta didn't help them."

"I'll surrender honourably when I have to. The Lagerführer approved the plan, because we're obviously never getting out of here by tunnelling, like the guys up north," Axel said. "The scouts keep finding our tunnels, or we hit rock. How else will we escape if not boldly in the middle of the day?"

"It's in the Lagerführer's best interests to ensure that we're seen to put up resistance, and not just accept our imprisonment," Christoph said. "He doesn't give a shit what happens to you, unless you actually manage to get home. In which case you'll be a hero, and he'll be in Hitler's good books. If you get shot, well... he has a few hundred more pawns willing to attempt an escape."

"You'd better not let anyone hear you talking like that, Christoph," Rudi advised. "The Nazis don't like defeatist talk. Sometimes I worry that the walls have ears."

"You can bet that there are spies among us. I'm damn glad that Major Drechsler no longer shares our room."

"No one can accuse us of shirking our duties, if you'll all help," Axel said.

"Of course!" Erich assured him. "Best soccer game ever to keep the guards entertained."

Erich knew it had taken weeks of preparation for Axel to get to this stage. Registration card and identity papers had been forged, a civilian outfit created by the drama society from fabrics they bought through the Eaton's Catalogue for their costumes, copies made of the maps that had been smuggled in, Canadian money collected from those who had managed to acquire it, usually while being transported from other camps. At least a hundred prisoners would help in the escape. So even Erich was nervous on the designated day.

He and Wolf were on opposing teams and would engage in a mock fight during the well-orchestrated soccer match, which would rivet the attention of the Canadian guards in the watch towers and elsewhere.

Axel was dressed in civvies overlaid with his prison garb, which had been unstitched and loosely sewn so that it could easily be ripped off as soon as he was out of the main enclosure. His roommates wished him luck.

There were plenty of spectators for the exciting match, some lounging close to the chain-link fence – close enough to hide the efforts of an escape committee member who had mysteriously procured wire cutters, which were scything a small doorway through the fence.

At his signal that it was done, Erich tripped Wolf and they exchanged heated words. They pretended to become increasingly incensed with one another. Wolf shoved Erich, who lashed back, and they were quickly involved in a scuffle, during which Axel scooted through the opening in the fence, which was immediately replaced. Heart pounding, not daring to look up at the guards in the two sentry towers that would have him in full sight in the catwalk between the fences, he carefully opened the loose rolls of barbed wire and slunk through. Stripping off his telltale prison garb and shoving it under a bush, he walked nonchalantly across the dirt road that lead to the beach, toward the distant and final perimeter fence with merely two strands of barbed wire stretched over the rocky landscape. He didn't dare glance back, although he heard the uproar of the fight. He feared a bullet might suddenly rip through him, so he barely breathed until he was through, and heading into the woods. Free at last!

Meanwhile, Erich was fending off vicious blows, realizing that this was no longer playacting. That Wolf had lost control and was pummelling him in earnest.

"Jesus Christ, Wolf, lay off!"

Wolf gave Erich a shattering blow to the face.

Rudi, who was one of the referees, realized something was wrong, and intervened, pulling Wolf away. Wolf turned on him, but Rudi, anticipating the punch, dodged and landed a knockout one to Wolf.

Rubbing his aching chin, Erich recalled that Rudi was a champion boxer at university.

As long as no one's life was endangered, the Veteran Guards didn't intervene, since the Lagerführer and a military tribunal of senior German officers dealt with internal squabbles and breaches. But their attention was certainly focussed on the soccer field.

The spectators milled about curiously, wondering what had happened. Although fights among the officers weren't uncommon, issues were usually resolved in the boxing ring. There were a couple of doctors among the prisoners, and one went to examine Wolf, who was regaining consciousness.

"Get away!" Wolf swatted at those who were trying to help him up. But he staggered and fell.

"You have a concussion," the doctor pronounced. "Let's get you into the infirmary."

His roommates visited him there later, Rudi apologizing for the knockout punch.

"It was my fault," Wolf muttered. "Shouldn't have taken my rage out on Erich. Sorry, pal."

Erich's jaw was bruised and swollen, the inside of his cheek cut. But at least his teeth were intact.

"I feel like I'll lose my mind if I don't get out of here soon. It's just going to get worse as winter closes in and we're stuck in here like caged animals!" Wolf exploded.

"You need to change your attitude if want to retain your sanity," Christoph advised. "Don't look at this as a period of just waiting for your life to resume. Consider it an opportunity to broaden your mind and horizons. Take up a craft, if you don't want to do courses. I've observed that you have a bit of talent with a pencil."

Wolf looked forlorn.

Erich said, "Our ruse worked, by the way. The Canucks won't know that Axel is missing until the next roll call. By that time he could already be in Toronto, if he gets lucky."

Wolf grinned. "He's going to owe us big time when he's back."

It was three days before Axel was apprehended on a train bound for Niagara Falls. They were worth every one of the twenty-eight days in solitary, he admitted to his friends later. His only regret was that he hadn't seen the famous Falls.

"You accomplished one thing," Rudi told Axel. "Thanks to you, we now have a proper big football field outside the gate. But we have to give our parole to play or watch."

Axel chortled. "So, they figured out how I escaped."

"And decided that it wasn't good to have so many spectators crammed into a small area next to the fence."

They celebrated Axel's safe return with peach brandy that Erich secretly concocted, the scouts not yet having discovered his still.

"Here's to the brave and crazy *Dutchman*, 'Alex Zeegers'," Erich said as he clinked his glass to Axel's.

Axel grinned. "It worked, for a while. Now let me tell you about the sexy girl I met in Toronto who was so generous to poor, displaced Alex Zeegers...."

•　　　•　　　•

Merilee felt awkward walking up the drive to Peggy's house now that the prisoners had a new sports field between it and the camp administration office where her father worked. The soccer game paused as dozens of admiring eyes watched her. She didn't dare look at the Germans, and breathed a sigh of relief as she entered the kitchen.

"Ned!" Merilee cried with delight. "Peggy didn't tell me you were coming home!"

She gave him a sisterly hug. Peggy could sense him struggling with his emotions as he held Merilee a moment too long.

"Last minute leave. I figured someone would be here," Ned replied with a grin.

They had seen each other briefly at Christmas, and she had written him the occasional chatty letter. Now almost seventeen, she was no longer a child, and Ned tried to hide his admiration and longing. "I noticed you've been looking after Big Red splendidly. How's he been behaving?"

"Splendidly!"

"Merilee drives splendidly, too," Peggy added, and they burst into laughter.

"I hope this isn't an embarkation leave," Merilee said, snatching up a warm oatmeal cookie while eyeing Ned suspiciously.

"Nope! I was accepted for remustering. As a pilot."

"Zowie!"

Peggy was stricken.

"Now, Corporal Sutcliffe, I'd like to see how splendidly you do ride the bike, just in case I can offer some tips. Since you're already in slacks, you can take me for a spin right now."

"You're going to sit in the sidecar?" Merilee asked with trepidation.

"Don't worry, I'll be a model passenger."

When they went out to the barn to get the bike, Ned said, "Crazy, isn't it? Having the Huns so close you could throw a stick at them."

"At least you won't be fighting against these guys. And if they had any sense, they wouldn't even try to escape."

"Yup, people pay a good penny to spend time at our Muskoka resorts," Ned joked.

It didn't take Merilee long to adjust to the difference in weight from slight Peggy, but they stayed on the perimeter roads of the town, where there were few houses and no traffic. When they neared one of their favourite blueberry-picking spots, they noticed a plume of smoke over the treetops.

"A forest fire?" Merilee asked, slowing down.

"Or the Jones farm! Hurry!"

Merilee opened the throttle and zoomed ahead. Smoke was billowing out of a rear window in the old farmhouse occupied by widow Jones. Ned jumped out of the sidecar almost before Merilee skidded to a halt, and bounded towards the house.

"Ned, you can't go in there!"

He waved her away, yelling, "Check the barn!"

Terrified for him, she nevertheless obeyed. The acrid burning smell was wafting into the barn, where the wild-eyed cow was mooing frantically in her stall.

"Mrs. Jones! Are you in here?"

A voice in pain breathed, "I've fallen... Broken my hip, I think."

Merilee found her lying in a pile of hay, where the octogenarian seemed to have dragged herself.

"Tripped over one of the hens." The squawking chickens were scurrying about crazily.

"I'll fetch help."

"Is the house on fire? I left the bacon frying while I came to fetch eggs."

Merilee felt impatient to find Ned, but said gently, "I'm afraid so, but you should be safe here. I must dash!"

There was no sign of Ned, and the house was now crackling like a voracious bonfire. Merilee raced toward it, screaming his name.

"Ned! I've found her! Come out!... Oh, dear God! NED!"

She almost collapsed with relief when he staggered out, handkerchief over his face, coughing. She ran to his side and pulled him away as flames suddenly shot through the roof sending hot embers skyward like fireworks.

"Stay with Mrs. Jones in the barn while I get help," she ordered.

It was too late to save the house, and the barn was hopefully too far away to catch fire, but she sped to the nearest neighbours, half a mile away, and asked them to call the fire department as well as a doctor.

Back at the farm, Merilee pumped some well water into the ever-present bucket and took it into the barn. Mrs. Jones accepted a ladleful gratefully. Ned had thoughtfully draped his sooty uniform jacket over her, since she had only a tattered shawl to keep out the October chill.

"Thank you, my dears. And thank God you came. No one does these days."

The thought that the frail old lady could have been lying here in agony for days, or have succumbed to the cold and her injury, had the fire not alerted them, sent a shiver of dread through Merilee.

"My daughter keeps insisting that I move in with her... But I'm not one for the city," Mrs. Jones admitted. "Been here nigh on sixty years... Suppose I shall have to leave now."

The roar of the conflagration was frightening, but Merilee thought it must be completely devastating for Mrs. Jones, who was not only losing her beloved home, but also most of her past. Photographs and letters, mementoes and prized gifts.

Between bouts of coughing, Ned managed a few welcome sips of water.

"Are you alright?" Merilee asked in concern as she patted his back lightly.

"They say smoking's not good for you," he jested.

"That was kind but foolish of you to go searching for me, young man."

"Heroic, I'd say," Merilee added.

"Yes, indeed."

Merilee pulled out her lace-edged handkerchief, tipped water onto it, and started to wipe soot from Ned's face. Surprised, he grabbed her hand and held it at bay as he said, "Don't muck that up."

His intense gaze riveted hers for a moment. Confused, she retorted, "Nonsense!" as she pulled away and resumed her task.

The firemen could do little but ensure that the blaze didn't spread to the barn and nearby woods. Dr. Lumsden wasn't far behind.

"Well, Nellie, have you been jumping from the hayloft again?" he jested as he examined her.

The old lady cackled. "Would that I could, Ernie."

"We'll have to fix this hip first. I'll give you something for the pain, and then we'll be off to the hospital." The closest one was in Bracebridge, eleven miles away.

Ned was still coughing, so Dr. Lumsden, who was also his and Merilee's physician, examined him quickly. "Rest and fresh air for you, my boy. But if you're short of breath or the coughing continues over the next couple of days, come to see me right away. So, no smoking or dancing this week, in case you two were planning a night out," he added with a twinkle in his eye.

Merilee blushed.

•   •   •

"You're becoming a pilot because of Merilee, aren't you?" Peggy accused Ned when they were alone that evening. "You think that if you can become an officer, then you can try to win her over."

"Flying has always been a dream – an unobtainable one until now. Don't you see how this war is bringing us opportunities we would never have had otherwise, Peg? I'm doing this for myself."

"Don't tell me you're not in love with Merilee."

He shrugged. "If wishes were horses…. Besides, you said she has a boyfriend."

"One of those privileged summer boys. You know the type. He'll break her heart."

"Then maybe I can pick up the pieces."

"If you don't get yourself killed."

England: Autumn 1941

Chapter 13

Oh hell! Elyse thought, as the clouds ahead seemed to coalesce with malicious intent. True to the Met report, the weather on her outward journey to deliver a brand-new Spitfire to a maintenance unit in the Midlands had been manageable, but no major front was forecast for this flight to an RAF squadron on the south coast.

She had been cruising along, delighting in the multi-hued and layered autumn clouds that tangoed with shafts of sunlight, enjoying the power and grace of another Spit, this one outfitted with guns and a radio, almost ready for battle. And she was already anticipating seeing Theo in only a few hours. He was coming to spend his two days off with her. It wasn't always easy to coordinate their leaves.

She dove down to skim under the thickening grey canopy and was pleased that she was able to level off at 800 feet, their minimum ceiling for flying. But the heavy pall of impending rain pressed down on her... 600 feet... 500.

Needing to fly contact, being able to see the ground, and follow the rivers, roads, and railroad tracks for her planned route was crucial, but flying any lower was too bloody risky as she was passing over the Chiltern Hills. She checked her map for altitudes and dangerous barrage balloons.

When she looked up, she was shocked to find herself completely engulfed, as if swallowed by a dirty snowbank. Instinctively she pulled up. *Watch it, you're banking. Straighten up. For God's sake, don't go into a spin.*

Flying blind at 250 miles an hour was terrifying, so she slowed the plane.

Elyse knew she should turn around. She had recently passed Oxford and was familiar with the RAF aerodrome there. But it was possible that the unexpected cloudbank had already enveloped it as well. And if she did manage to get down, she might be stuck there for days until the weather cleared, pilots being in charge of their aircraft until safely delivered. She would hate to miss her time with Theo.

Surely these clouds will thin soon. Concentrate on your instruments. You know the drill. She had some basic instrument training, but Theo had made sure she knew how to blind-fly onto a reciprocal course, a shallow 180 degree turn, which could be a lifesaver. Hills had already claimed a few of her male colleagues.

Instead, she decided to break the cardinal ATA rule and go "over the top". It was what Amy Johnson had done and had lost the gamble of trying to crack through the smothering blanket.

Making sure she was still on her original compass heading, Elyse opened the throttles and climbed ever higher. At 8000 feet, she burst into dazzling sunshine, but was appalled to find herself above a boundless sea of clouds. Surely this didn't cover all of southern England.

She glanced with futile anger at the newly fitted radio. Since she had no helmet attachment, it would remain tauntingly silent for her. There was no way to know which aerodromes were still open, or to get a homing signal from one of them.

Concentrate!

She had checked her watch, and would try to fly by dead reckoning to at least get close to her destination.

Up here she was safe, and able to breathe more easily. The clouds might break apart by the time she neared Tangmere. But if she overshot, she would be above the Channel. A few minutes more and she could be over occupied France. If she was shot down there, it would be her own fault. "Pilot error" would be her epitaph.

Of course, she could choose to jump, hoping to land on solid ground, unlike Amy. The ATA mantra was "if in doubt, bail out". Pilots were too valuable. But it would still be a black mark on her record. She should never have gone over the cloud base.

She spared a thought for Roz, who was in charge of one of the Anson taxis today, dropping off and picking up pilots from their various destinations. She was to fetch Elyse at Tangmere, but Roz would already have aborted that pickup, and was surely either back at home base or had put down somewhere. A planeload of eight or ten pilots was a precious cargo.

At her current speed, it was now only minutes before Elyse should be nearing the fighter base – if her calculations were correct. It was where Charlie commanded a Wing, and she'd been looking forward to surprising him. But not by crashing.

Damn! There was no hole in the clouds. She would have to start her descent and hope that her navigation had been spot-on. But the Downs undulated to over 900 feet, and Tangmere lay just below them. Too close. She needed to overshoot and then head back in from the sea. There wasn't enough petrol to return to Oxford.

Don't panic! Focus! Calculate when to turn. Another part of her said, *Bail out.*

She spent a few more grateful minutes in the sunshine, hoping these wouldn't be her last.

Now trust yourself. As she re-entered the clouds she felt as if they were condensing on her face, but realized it was perspiration. It was frightening to watch the altimeter falling and yet see nothing. At 950 feet she thought of breaking off, and going back up to jump. With any luck, the Spitfire would crash harmlessly into an empty field.

But she was surely past the highest points.

At a nerve-wracking 300 feet, she saw something glimmering through the gloom. A strip of beach. And just beyond it, the ugly, rusty, but oh-so-welcome gasometer at Bognor Regis. Tangmere was just moments to the north. She almost wept with relief.

Elyse flew slowly, flaps down, peering through the roiling cloud and sea mist that sometimes obscured the ground but then thinned to finally reveal the blessed runway lights, which were all on, while green and white Very flares were being fired up.

Damn! That probably meant that they were expecting the return of a squadron. She would have to wait her turn, and keep a sharp lookout for other aircraft suddenly zooming out of the soup.

She stayed close in the circuit over the aerodrome, and seeing nothing else, decided it was safe to land. She was so relieved that she just sat in the cockpit and breathed deeply, touching the necklace that Theo had given her for good luck.

One of the ground crew greeted her. "Nice daisy-cutter, Miss," he said referring to her perfect landing. "We've been expecting you, but weren't sure you'd be getting through in this. Came down awful sudden, it did."

Feeling a bit wobbly in the knees, she allowed him to carry her heavy parachute. A moment later, she was confronted by a pale Charlie.

"Thank God!" he said, pulling her into a hug. "Roz phoned to tell me that Ops hadn't heard from you, so we were still to expect you. We sent a barrage of Very lights up for you. But how did you manage in this muck? Our chaps had to be radioed in."

She grinned at him and cocked an eyebrow. "Woman's intuition, I suppose."

"You went over the top and then took a bloody great risk coming down blind," he said knowingly.

"Don't rat on me."

"As it happens, most of the airfields in the south are closed in, so it wouldn't have been any use turning back – this time. As soon as you've finished your paperwork, I'm driving you home. Giving myself the rest of the day off, as there's no more flying anyway."

There was torrential rain by the time they set off for Hamble, just forty miles west.

A seaside village near Southampton, Hamble was the location of a recently established all-female ferry pool, whose primary job was to move planes from the nearby Supermarine Spitfire and other factories, including twin-engine Blenheim bombers. It was the women pilots' dream job.

Elyse and Roz had found a delightful bungalow to rent along the Hamble River, where their husbands joined them whenever possible. Charlie often flew into the ATA airfield and spent the night. Still teaching near London, Theo would take the train to nearby Eastleigh, where he'd catch a lift. Elyse hardly used her car and thus, saved up her gas rations. She and Roz biked or walked to work every day. One side of the long, grass airfield was virtually behind their house.

It was ideal, and almost too good to be true. Elyse sometimes felt guilty that she was enjoying the war so much.

As if the sky had purged itself, the rain stopped and late afternoon sun broke through the exhausted clouds as they drove through Hamble, a leafy canopy of dripping autumn leaves glowing above them.

Built in the 1920s, "Riverbreeze" was roomy and comfortably modern, with neat, unassuming gardens.

Theo met them in the foyer and took Elyse into a fierce embrace. "I spent the worst hour of my life today, until I knew that you were safe." He kissed her tenderly. "A couple of your colleagues weren't so lucky."

"Martinis, I think," Roz said briskly, emerging from the kitchen with glasses on a tray, and leading them into the sitting room. It overlooked a shaded flagstone terrace and long stretch of lawn down to a winding inlet of the river, where a tiny boathouse sheltered a skiff, which they were allowed to use. To Elyse, she whispered, "Over the top, no doubt. Well done!"

"Here's to lady pilots and their intuition," Charlie toasted.

"And to their notoriety," Theo added, picking up a magazine from the table beside him. "Have you seen this?"

On the cover was a photo of Elyse in front of a Spitfire that she had just delivered. It had been a warm September day, so she had removed her jacket, rolled up her sleeves, and had just taken off her helmet. The photographer had caught her smiling as she swept a hand through her hair, her head cocked to one side as if glorying in the sunshine, the parachute dangling over her left shoulder. She looked professional yet sexy, and seemingly unaware of the camera.

"Hell's bells! I saw the photographer, of course, but didn't realize he'd use a picture of me," Elyse said.

"Well, you're famous now, and so are we. Margot says it all helps our reputation," Roz said of their Commanding Officer. "Although some of the women are appalled at the publicity. They don't want to be thought of as just pretty girls trying to do a man's job. They want to be taken seriously."

"And you obviously can't be beautiful and capable at the same time," Charlie teased.

"It's precisely to dispel that idea that Margot encourages us to look feminine, even glamorous," Roz said. "You wouldn't believe how many men at the receiving end of a Spitfire are knocked sideways when they see a woman step out of the cockpit."

"Audrey always powders her face and applies lipstick before she lands," Elyse said.

"She's jealous as hell that you're a cover girl on the prestigious *Picture Post*," Roz said. "But proud of you as well."

Audrey herself was no stranger to the camera, being one of the socialites often featured in *The Tatler*.

"This is bound to become a classic," Theo said. "But I'm not sure I like having my wife drooled over by other men."

"You'd better get used to it," Charlie advised.

'Sir Felix' wandered into the room and rubbed against Elyse's leg. He was a handsome tuxedo cat with intelligent, amber-rimmed green eyes, and a distinguished black chin that made him look as if he were perpetually smiling. The young stray had decided that he approved of Riverbreeze and its new occupants, so he had moved in, much to their delight.

"I think Felix is announcing dinner," Roz jested as he went over to her.

They dined on a delicious tuna and noodle casserole, with fruit salad for dessert. Roz was an excellent cook and had inventive ways of combining their rations with the canned goods regularly shipped to them from home. Elyse had already learned a lot from her, and relished the ability to be self-sufficient.

The men helped with the washing up. After a lively game of bridge, they danced to the gramophone, and then retired to their rooms.

When Elyse was lying in Theo's arms after their lovemaking, he asked, "Why didn't you bail out?"

"I was too scared," she admitted. "So I had to trust my instincts."

"I'm tempted to make you pregnant so that you'll be safely grounded."

She stiffened.

"But I suspect you might hate me for that."

Carefully she responded, "Thank you for not being deceitful. And I appreciate your concern. But safe is boring. And war is no time to have babies."

"I love you too much to prevent you from doing what you want, my darling. Just be careful."

"I promise to jump next time."

His laughter was interrupted by wailing sirens and the thundering boom of ack-ack guns at the far end of the airfield. The faint whistle of a nearby factory declared enemy aircraft overhead before explosions shattered the night.

Southampton was a popular target, although stray bombs could happen anywhere, including sleepy Hamble. But after their first few alarms, Elyse and Roz had begun to ignore them, even sleeping through them when they were exhausted enough. In any case, there was nowhere for them to shelter.

Elyse snuggled contentedly into Theo's protective embrace.

Muskoka: Summer 1942
Chapter 14

"You will be my girlfriend, Miss Merilee?" Lars Pedersen asked.

She stifled a giggle as she replied, "How sweet of you. But I have a boyfriend." At his deflated expression, she added. "We can be still be friends, though."

"That is good!" Lars raised mischievous eyebrows and added with a disarming grin, "Perhaps you will like me better than your boyfriend one day."

He was an athletic, fresh-faced Norwegian with a broad smile and an untamed mop of curly blonde hair – one of the many men now stationed at the Royal Norwegian Air Force training base at the Muskoka Airport.

Gravenhurst had thronged with over two thousand excited spectators last month when Norway's Crown Prince Olav and his wife stopped by to address the citizens before going on to officially open the nearby base, known as 'Little Norway'. The handsome, charming Norsemen had already won the hearts of the locals, especially the girls.

Merilee and Peggy had just given them a concert, stirring their souls with superb renditions of Grieg's *Morning Prelude* from *Peer Gynt,* and a modified First Movement of his *Piano Concerto in A Minor.*

"Do not worry about Lars," Ole Knutsen advised Merilee. "He finds girlfriends wherever he goes. I have only one, back home."

"May I know if *you* have a boyfriend, Miss Peggy?" Gunnar Svensen asked, admiration lighting his crystal blue eyes.

She blushed. She couldn't honestly answer that Ross Tremayne was anything but a good friend, although he did write to her often. "Not really."

"Then I may visit you?"

"Yes... if you like," she stammered.

"I like very much!" He grinned

Merilee's mother overheard and said, "Would you boys like to come to dinner at our house on Sunday? I'm sure Peggy will join us."

The three young men beamed.

Sunday dinner at Hope Cottage was usually a roast with all the trimmings, and was served at midday, except in the heat of the summer. Lois Wilding provided a delectable maple spice cake. With sugar rationing about to begin, the Wildings' homemade maple syrup was more important than ever.

"Why am I so nervous?" Peggy muttered as she and Merilee sat on the screened porch awaiting the guests. It was early June and the lake was quiet, since even the big steamers hadn't started sailing yet.

"Because a Norse god is interested in you," Merilee quipped. "Peggy Svensen has a nice ring to it."

"Ha! He'll run a mile when he realizes I can't dance." Or know anything about dating, she thought. She had never even been kissed.

"I'm sure you can manage to sway a little. That way you can enjoy being held in his strong arms. And he has the most sensitive, kissable lips."

"You hussy!"

They burst into laughter.

Saxon jumped up and barked. Merilee stroked him reassuringly, saying, "Just friends, Saxon."

The Norwegian trio appeared moments later.

"You live in paradise!" Lars exclaimed as he gave Saxon a friendly head rub.

"Reminds me of home," Gunnar added with a nostalgic look in his eyes.

"Even with the Germans here," Ole stated bitterly. "We bomb them with potatoes when we fly over the camp."

"Gosh, you'd better not let my father hear that," Merilee warned. "It's his job to ensure that the prisoners are safe and happy."

"A bad job to have."

"It ensures that *our* prisoners in Germany are well treated."

"Ole's brother was killed when the Nazis invaded our homeland," Lars explained.

"How tragic! I'm so sorry!" Merilee said.

"Enough sadness! Now we will enjoy ourselves," Gunnar stated, smiling at Peggy. "There was a beautiful photo of you girls in the newspaper. Now it is next to my heart," he added, tapping his breast pocket.

It was a flattering picture of them giving their concert at Little Norway.

They dined on the wide screened porch, the boys enchanted by everything from the view to the food, but especially by the company. Claire and Colin gathered them into the warm embrace of the family.

Lars and Ole, good friends since childhood, were coaxed into relating their escape across the mountains to Sweden, and the long, arduous trek through Russia and India. Norwegian ships took them via South Africa to Brazil, and then on to New York. They had heard about 'Little Norway', which had begun in Toronto, and were excited when, after nine months, they finally arrived.

Gunnar had taken the much shorter but more dangerous route via a small fishing boat across the treacherous North Sea to the Shetland Islands.

"You are so young to have experienced such hardships," Claire said sympathetically. Lars and Ole were only nineteen, and Gunnar, twenty.

"Those were adventures, Mrs. Sutcliffe. Soon the hard part begins. The fight to free our country," Ole stated.

"We worry about our families. That is the worst. Not knowing what is happening to them," Lars admitted.

"I can only imagine," Claire said.

"I write to my family every week, but because I cannot send letters, I put them into my box. So, when the war is over, whatever happens, they will know about my life."

"What a wonderful idea! And now you must think of this as your home away from home. Come by whenever you can. Especially for Sunday dinners."

They accepted gleefully.

"May we swim next time?" Gunnar asked.

"Of course!"

"As long as you don't go near the camp," Colin advised.

"We will not cause trouble for our generous hosts," Gunnar assured him.

They were impressed with Claire's paintings, which adorned the walls, and delighted to be offered copies of *The Mystery of Spirit Bay* as souvenirs.

"So beautiful! And I can practice my English reading," Lars enthused. "Tusen takk! Thank you very much!"

"I hope your children can enjoy it," Claire said wistfully.

"I will read in bed," Gunnar said happily. "Be a boy again."

When the guests had gone, Claire fumed, "They *are* still boys! I detest this war!" and stormed off to her studio.

"She's going to create something special," Colin surmised.

Claire returned a short time later saying, "I have an idea for a story. A dark cloud spreads across the countryside, trapping everyone beneath in a perpetual and sinister twilight. Only a few young people manage to dodge the lightning bolts at its perimeter, and find sanctuary with Faith in fairyland. But the cloud creeps closer and they know that only they can stop it. Faith gives them the power to transform into birds and animals, and they somehow have to destroy the damned thing. That's your job to figure out, Colin."

He and Merilee exchanged knowing grins.

"Sounds like fun, Mum. May I help?"

"You're a talented writer, Merilee, so I think you and Mum should do this. I have enough on my plate as it is," Colin suggested.

Merilee was astonished. "Could I? I mean…"

"I will advise, and edit the story, so I doubt that the publisher will object. It's been a few years since we produced a new book, so he'll be happy. And I'm getting too old to know what appeals to kids."

"Baloney, Dad!"

Merilee was so excited she could hardly sleep that night, as ideas tumbled through her mind. She jotted them down, but was frustrated that the writing would have to wait until she finished studying for her exams. She discussed the plot with her parents at meals, and was thrilled that the bones of the tale were in place by the end of the week. Snatched moments of writing were bliss.

Unlike the picture books with their elaborate colour plates, this novel would be aimed at teens, and thus, sparsely illustrated with line drawings. They hoped to have it out by Christmas.

Claire painted small watercolours for each of the boys, depicting dragonflies heading skyward and seeming to transform into airplanes over an exquisite Muskoka landscape. They were elated and touched when she presented them with these gifts the following Sunday.

"They are a triptych," she said, showing them how the pictures lined up to make one compete scene. "A good luck charm for three friends."

"Your three adopted sons," Lars said, giving her a hug.

"Well, you've inspired a new story, which Merilee and I are working on. We'll dedicate it to the three of you."

The boys preened.

They often hitched rides into town after work and showed up at Hope Cottage. Colin decided that it wouldn't be wise for them to visit Peggy's house, where they would be uncomfortably close to their sworn enemies. So Peggy hung out at Merilee's after school, and Sunday dinner became a tradition. By the time summer holidays began, they were all fast friends.

Especially Gunnar and Peggy. Thinking herself in love with Ross Tremayne, she hadn't expected to fall for anyone else. But Gunnar wooed her, sometimes bringing her a scraggly bouquet of wildflowers or a single, perfect rose. He wrapped his arm supportively around her when they strolled to the lake and stayed protectively close to her when they swam. He stared at her with such joy and admiration when she played piano that she didn't dare look at him or she would lose her concentration. Their first kiss was surprisingly natural, putting Peggy more at ease in his company. Now she could hardly wait to see him.

She was even persuaded to attend dances in town. Gunnar held Peggy so rapturously close that her feet barely touched the floor.

While Ole made the rounds of available partners, Lars never left Merilee's side.

"You don't have to stay with me, Lars. You should find yourself a girlfriend," she suggested with a grin.

"I am most happy in your company, Merilee."

He was so easily lovable, with his perennial cheerfulness and singsong accent, and such fun to be with. She just didn't want to break his heart. "I hope we will always be the best of friends."

"Of course!... But you are leaving us to be with your boyfriend."

"My cousins as well. Only for three weeks."

"We will soon be finished here. Then we go far away to Moose Jaw, Saskatchewan for advanced training. I will miss this." He gazed wistfully into her eyes for a long moment. "But a place with such a name I must see!" he added with a chuckle. "So... now we will dance?"

"Gladly!"

"I don't mean to seem ungrateful," Peggy said to Merilee a few days later. "But would you mind if I only spend one week at Wyndwood with you, so that I can at least see Deanna?"

Although she had an awkward gait, Deanna was able to ride again, and in her glory. The girls had kept up their correspondence and were looking forward to spending time together at the lake.

"Of course I don't mind. You're truly smitten, aren't you? About as much as Gunnar, I'd say."

"I never expected that to happen."

"Is he a good kisser?"

"Mind your own business!" Peggy said with mock annoyance, and then grinned. "Oh yes."

Gunnar promised Colin that he would ignore the Germans if could visit Peggy's house. "I will not even spit on them."

So Gunnar was as eager for Peggy to come home as she. And he swore he would fly over Wyndwood every day to drop love letters for her.

Just before the girls left, the Wildings heard that Ned was coming home for his embarkation leave. So Peggy had another reason to cut her stay short.

It had become normal to see a variety of military aircraft flying over the lakes, but the girls were easily able to identify the Norwegians' Fairchild Cornells.

They waved enthusiastically when the boys zoomed over the treetops at Wyndwood. The first letter taunted as it fluttered down towards Peggy, but it was snatched by a breeze and sailed into the lake. Merilee jumped into a canoe to rescue it, but the ink had run, so Peggy struggled to make out the message. "Miss you and long to kiss you" and "Love, your Gunnar" were legible enough to quicken her pulse.

The next one was weighted with a stone and plopped onto the shore beside the boathouse. The following ones became an enjoyable game for the evacuees, to see who could catch them before they landed.

The three planes always circled around to see the outcome, tipping their wings in greeting. On Peggy's last day, four bags filled with packages of Wrigley's gum and sticks of candy, obviously intended for the kids, joined the letter. They squealed with delight, and jumped up and down, waving, when the trio passed back over.

"I think I'll become a pilot and drop bags of goodies instead of bombs," eleven-year-old Bertie stated. "When people are happy, they won't want to fight."

"That's a lovely thought, Bertie," Ria said. They were sitting on the cottage veranda, the children examining their treats.

William, now fifteen, was reading in the band-shell corner. He looked up with disgust as he said, "You really shouldn't encourage such childishness, Mrs. Thornton. We have to be prepared to face the harsh reality of what the war is doing to our homeland."

"Not until you return. That's why you're here." Ria tried not to let her anger show, but she was heartily sick of his arrogance and know-it-all disdain. "But you're right that the war effort is something we must all contribute to. So, I'm going to recommend that you be sent to a farm for the rest of the summer to assist with the chores."

Merilee threw Ria a congratulatory glance. William looked shocked, and the younger ones smirked.

"You can't mean that!" William blustered. "I have my studies. My times with Professor Roland!"

"I expect you'll have plenty of opportunity to study in the evenings. And the physical, outdoor work will build up your strength. *Healthy body, healthy mind*, as they say. Besides, with so many young men in the forces, our farmers desperately need workers. Surely you're planning to do your bit for King and

Country?" Ria fixed William with a challenging stare. Peggy almost cheered out loud.

He threw down his book and muttered, "We'll see what Professor Roland has to say about this!" as he marched off.

"William shouldn't talk to you like that, Aunt Ria," his sister, Jane, said.

"He has a lot of growing up to do," Ria replied. "Although he doesn't realize it."

Forewarned by a quick phone call from Ria, Troy thought it an excellent idea, and praised William for stepping up to do his bit.

William was thunderous when he returned to The Point, but could hardly disappoint his idol by persisting that it was unfair and unworthy of his genius to become a farm hand.

"Well played," Ria said to Troy later.

"Likewise!"

•   •   •

"Thank God I wasn't considered instructor material," Bryce said, when Drew lamented that he'd been assigned to advanced flight training at Camp Borden.

"That's hardly surprising," Anthea quipped. "I expect your final report stated *insubordinate smart aleck*."

They, along with Merilee, were enjoying a private dinner on the boathouse deck at The Point. The Carrington parents were in the city for an important social engagement, so Anthea and Bryce had taken up Ria's offer to stay over for a few days.

Bryce was being sent to Britain soon, and Drew had two weeks' leave. The boys had the boathouse to themselves, since Merilee had moved into the big cottage when Peggy left.

"I'd rather teach than tow targets for the gunnery students," Drew said, since that was what Bryce had been doing for the past six months.

"Just raise a little hell and they'll ship you out," Bryce suggested with a grin. "The CO called me a few names I can't repeat in present company, and said I'd make a good fighter pilot."

"Sounds like he just wanted to be rid of you," Anthea opined.

"It worked. Man, I can hardly wait to get my hands on a Spitfire! Before the rest of you guys."

"Elyse says it flies like a dream," Merilee informed him with a smirk.

The others laughed at Bryce's miffed expression.

"So you *should* be able to fly it. Eventually," Anthea added wickedly.

"Drew will never fly anything faster than a lumbering Harvard if he doesn't get posted overseas," Bryce crowed.

"That's fine by me," Anthea replied, squeezing Drew's hand.

"But that means he won't have a shot at being a hero," Bryce said, topping up their glasses of wine, although Merilee had hardly touched hers.

"Horse feathers! Teaching cowboys like you how *not* to kill themselves probably deserves a medal. Anyway, I'm going to see if I can get posted to Camp Borden when I join the Women's Division," Anthea declared.

"The hell you will!" Bryce exploded. "Do you know what kind of reputation they have?"

"Being patriotic," Anthea shot back.

"Being of easy virtue. Some of them are away from home for the first time, and they turn into drunken party animals. Trust me, I know."

"So, you take advantage of these naïve girls?" Merilee couldn't help asking.

He blushed slightly.

"Well?" his sister demanded.

"No coercion is needed."

"You'd better shut up before you put your other foot in your mouth as well," Drew advised, looking disgusted. "It doesn't help if people like you are spreading the filthy rumours. Dad's not at all pleased by these lies that are making it all the harder for the WDs."

"I was just trying to dissuade Anthea," Bryce said, shamefacedly. "I don't want her to be tainted by the scuttlebutt. It doesn't matter what really happens, does it? It's what people choose to believe. That the women are there to please the men."

"Which is good enough reason to show the public that they're wrong!" Anthea declared. "Don't be a jerk, Bryce. And you'd better not be taking advantage of girls."

"Mum and Dad won't let you enlist anyway," Bryce said.

"I reminded Mum that what she and Aunt Ria did in the last war was much more scandalous and dangerous. So, I plan to become either a wireless operator or a motor transport driver."

The RCAF Women's Division had been formed the previous year, and was so successful that more positions were opening up for the women, thus releasing men for operational training. Ironically, Hugh Carrington, who hated flying and had begun as a wireless operator on the ground, had been reassigned to be part of a bomber air crew, thanks to young women stepping up to do their bit. He would be going to Britain soon as well.

"You won't like the military discipline. And *they'll* tell you what to do, where you'll be posted," Bryce said. "So, you could end up as a cook on a frozen prairie base, fending off love-starved men, and wishing you were toasting your tootsies in front of home fires while waiting for Drew to be on leave."

Anthea chuckled. "It would be a military blunder to make me a cook. And I have no intention of lolling about just waiting for you fellows to come home. We girls are quite capable of doing important war work, and even marching." She gave him an exaggerated salute.

Bryce shook his head in exasperation.

"She'll be a Wing Commander before you know it," Drew jested.

Anthea graced him with her dazzling, infectious smile.

Smudged, charcoal wisps of clouds unravelled above the glowing embers of sunset. Only a couple of candle lanterns lit the deck when Drew put Glenn Miller's seductive *Moonlight Serenade* on the gramophone.

It had been another blistering hot day, and the boys were happy to be in shorts. The girls had changed into their light summer frocks after their pre-dinner swim.

Bryce drew Merilee close as they began dancing, whispering, "I've been longing to do this."

She reveled in his touch, but said warily, "It sounds as if you had plenty of female company at your aerodrome."

"The WDs do make it more fun. We had dances in the mess." Looking down at her with mock suspicion, he added, "Should I be jealous that you're entertaining Norwegian pilots?"

"My parents have taken a few boys under their wing. We're trying to be welcoming hosts."

"They're all tall, strapping Vikings, from what I hear."

"And sweet and funny. Guileless. Charming. Dedicated and heroic…"

"Enough! Or I *will* be jealous."

He stopped her laugh with a kiss.

As the horizon bled to indigo and stars blossomed, Bryce said, "Let's cool down with our traditional beach dance."

"Traditional?"

"It could be." He grinned roguishly.

Drew and Anthea were deeply engaged in a kiss and didn't notice them sneaking away. Zorro, who was lying alongside the railing, eyed them curiously, but settled his head back down on his paws.

A waxing moon and lights from distant cottages spooled golden threads across the water. The discreet lights at the end of the docks didn't reach into the darkness of the bay.

It felt delicious to be held tightly as they swayed to the music in the soothing shallows. Merilee responded to his hungry kisses and didn't stop him this time as he unbuttoned her blouse. She groaned when his hand cupped her bare breast. He trailed butterfly kisses down her neck and she felt weak-kneed when his mouth found her nipple, igniting fires in her groin. His hand moved up under her skirt to stoke the flames, which died on a sudden burst of panic.

"No, Bryce!" she said, pushing him away. Losing his balance, he grabbed for her and they both toppled into the water.

"Bloody hell, Merilee!" he swore as they sat up, dripping wet. She giggled and he burst into laughter.

Merilee hastily buttoned her sopping blouse as they heard footsteps descending the stairs from the boathouse deck.

"That's not how you skinny-dip," Anthea teased, coming up to the shore with Drew and Zorro at her side.

"Now there's a tempting thought! We were actually doing our beach dance, but lost our footing," Bryce explained, helping Merilee up.

"Uh huh."

"You should try it. The falling-in part is optional but refreshing." He suddenly pushed Anthea in. "See?"

She shrieked and splashed the others amid laughter. Drew plunged in beside her while Zorro barked and bounded excitedly into the water.

Bryce looked at Merilee and said, "Shall we?"

"Why not?"

The four of them sat waist-deep in the water, lighting the stars.

•   •   •

"Impressive!" Drew said when he and his friends walked into the new Dunn's Pavilion in Bala.

"For Muskoka," Bryce chimed in.

"Don't be a snob, Bryce!" Anthea said. "I think it's enchanting!"

A large fountain spraying coloured lights was the centerpiece of the expansive room. Tables and chairs were set up on the second-floor gallery and the area beneath it. The façade of a cottage at one end was the backdrop for the stage. Cedar boughs dripped from the ceiling, while hanging baskets of flowers and scattered palm trees looked exotic. Two floors of windows overlooked Bala Bay and invited in the night air, while French doors led to an outside deck suspended over the water.

"And living up to its claim of being 'Where All Muskoka Dances'," Merilee added, noting the hundreds of couples jostling one another on the dance floor.

"Let's have some fun then. I brought a *pocketful of rye*," Bryce said, patting the hip flask in his jacket. He and Drew sported their uniforms – appropriately enough, since the RCAF Dance Band was playing tonight, raising money for the Rotary War Fund. The girls were glamorous in cocktail dresses.

They had booked a table on the main floor, and Bryce went to fetch glasses of iced Coke so that he could mix in the whiskey.

"Not for me, thanks," Merilee protested as he began pouring.

"Don't be a wet blanket, Merilee. It will loosen you up a bit."

"Just one will do me. I figure it's important to learn how to drink properly before I enlist so that I don't become a drunken party animal." Anthea jested.

Bryce took plenty of breaks from dancing so that he could down more *refreshments*. The heat of the night and the many bodies mingled with cigarette smoke, so Merilee suggested they step out onto the deck.

"I'm going to miss all this," Bryce said, leaning against the railing and gazing over the lake. "The way the war's going, it could be *another* three years before it's over."

"At least you have relatives in England."

"Lord, yes. Too many! Grandmother will undoubtedly try to marry me off to some titled Lady who rides to hounds and resembles her horse."

Merilee giggled. "I hope you resist the temptation."

He pulled her into his arms. "You're the only one I can't resist. Let me show you."

As he kissed her, he squeezed her breast.

"Not here!" she whispered, trying to pull away. Dozens of other couples were cooling off outside.

He chuckled. "Later then. Let's dance."

As Bryce and Merilee threaded their way back to the dance floor, a girl grabbed his arm. "Bryce!"

"Caroline! What are you doing here?" he asked in happy surprise.

"Staying at the Grand Muskoka Hotel with a couple of girlfriends. We're all joining up soon."

She was a pretty girl with an air of sophistication and self-confidence that made her even more attractive. The admiring sparkle in Bryce's eyes said much, and Merilee felt a stab of jealousy. Caroline was still touching him in that propriety, intimate manner of lovers.

"Not the RCAF as well? Anthea is."

"No, the new WRENS. You know that Jonathon joined the navy. Besides, the uniform is smarter," she quipped.

Realizing that the two girls were eyeing each other, Bryce said, "Do let me introduce Merilee. We're old cottage friends."

Not his *girlfriend* then, Merilee thought with a pang.

"Caroline's brother Jonathon was one of my pals at school," he added to Merilee. "We're here with Anthea and Drew. You and your friends should join us, Caroline."

"Thanks, but we're hoping to meet some fellas," she replied with a suggestive smirk. "The uniform suits you, by the way."

"I'm shipping out soon."

They stared at one another probingly, and then she said, "We're staying for another two weeks. Drop over some time."

"Sure thing!"

Merilee's spirits plummeted at his eagerness. As they danced, she noticed his eyes scanning the crowd as if searching for Caroline.

It was only 11:00 when Bryce said, "It's still too damned hot here. How be we go back and have a midnight swim?"

"Now that you've drained your flask," Anthea accused.

"Tsk, tsk. Are you jealous or judgmental? I'm on holiday, dear girl, and planning to revel in every last minute of it."

They were silent on the twelve-mile drive back to the Spirit Bay Retreat, where the Thorntons and friends kept their cars and boats. Drew drove cautiously to avoid deer and even moose that might dash across the road.

"Are you two smooching back there?" Anthea asked, craning around to look at Merilee and Bryce in the back seat. "You're too quiet."

"Bryce fell asleep," Merilee explained. She liked having his head resting against her shoulder, and laid her cheek on his Brylcreemed hair.

"Passed out, more likely!"

"He'll be pulling his weight soon, when he has to row us back to the island," Drew said with a chuckle. "I won't let him off the hook."

With gas rationing now intensified, motorboats were used only when necessary, so they all paddled and rowed these days. Bryce grumbled when he was awakened, but rolled up his sleeves and set to the task of rowing the half-mile back to Wyndwood.

"Now I really do need a swim," he said.

"I'm bushed and would probably drown," Anthea said.

Drew offered to walk her up to the house, giving both couples a few moments of privacy.

"I'll have to go up in minute," Merilee said to Bryce as he took her into his arms.

"I don't have much time left, Merilee, and I want to make love to you properly," he said running his fingers down her neck. "Meet me in the other boathouse in an hour. Everyone should be asleep by then." The upper room of the old two-slip boathouse at the other end of the bay was used as a party and playroom, and was furnished with sofas and chairs.

"I can't."

"If you really cared for me, you would."

"I do love you, Bryce! But it's not right."

"You're obviously not frigid," he said, stroking her breast sensually. "And you needn't be worried. I have government-issue protection. They realize that plenty of us won't be coming back, and need to enjoy every day we have. Are you really going to send me off to war without knowing what it's like to make love to you?"

She pushed his hand away. "You've never actually said that you love me. Making love isn't the same thing."

"It'll bring us closer." He pulled her hard against him, so that she could feel his arousal. "Me, inside you. It's ecstasy. Admit you want it as much as I do, but you're just being coy. I don't have time for that."

"So you just want to get laid."

"Whoa, watch that vulgar language! Very unladylike."

Merilee was just as surprised at what had come unbidden to her tongue. "But it's the *vulgar* truth."

"There are plenty of willing girls around," he snapped as he released her abruptly.

This was exactly what Elyse had warned her about. Merilee was hurt and angry, but even more disappointed. "Well I'm not one of your toys!"

"Oh, grow up, Merilee!"

"I just did." She glared at him fiercely and flounced away.

In the darkest hours of the night, her heart bleeding, Merilee was tormented, wondering if she was right to reject him. He had been somewhat drunk, so she fantasized that he would be remorseful and realize he couldn't live without her. Declare his undying love. If he proposed, she might change her mind.

She sought that glimmer of hope at breakfast the next morning. While she was knotted inside, Bryce was his usual carefree self. At the end of the meal he said, "Thank you for a delightful stay, Aunt Ria, but I'm going home now. I have plenty to do before I head over to Blighty. I'm sure Drew won't mind paddling Anthea back to Red Rock tomorrow."

Anthea looked at him curiously. "I didn't know you had plans."

"You know me. Always full of surprises."

There was regret but also disdain in his eyes when he finally looked at Merilee, who almost gasped with the pain. She was certain he would seek out Caroline.

"Did you two have a tiff?" Anthea asked when they were alone.

Merilee hesitated. "He expects too much."

"Meaning?"

When Merilee looked away, Anthea said, "Oh... Sex."

"He said plenty of girls do it. So he's not wasting any more time with me."

"The jerk! I'd like to blame it on the war, because I hate to think that my brother is a womanizer. Beneath all that bravado, I think he's scared of going into battle."

"And I'm terrified for him! But maybe he's right that I don't love him enough."

"Don't fall for that line!"

"Do you and Drew..."

"We don't go all the way. And he respects that. But you can have exquisite fun without that final bit," Anthea added with a sly grin.

Merilee didn't even know what that involved, so she probably *was* too naïve and inexperienced for Bryce's tastes, she thought dejectedly.

She went for a long, tearful paddle, avoiding Red Rock and the nearby "Stepping Stone" islands. Having promised Elyse to check on her cottage occasionally, she stopped on Blackthorn Island, north of Wyndwood and Uncle Jack's Thorncliff.

Adorned by nooks and bays, the long, white bungalow ambled around a point to capture both the morning and the evening light. Wide, shallow steps led from capacious verandas onto manicured lawns that sloped gently to the granite shore. Someone was obviously maintaining the grounds, although Rafe spent little time here, especially now that he had given the island to Elyse.

Merilee imagined owning a fabulous place like this with Bryce, which just brought more heartache. Perched on a veranda railing, she suddenly spied him paddling past in his canoe.

She shrank against a post, but he didn't glance over. Should she call to him? Should she take this one last chance to win his affection? Should she allow him to do everything but 'go all the way'? But he probably wouldn't be satisfied with that anyway.

And he looked eager as he was – undoubtedly - heading for The Grand Muskoka Hotel. And Caroline.

He's a selfish cad, she told herself to stop tears from spilling again.

With Drew and Anthea spending most of every day together, Merilee now felt superfluous. She helped Amy with activities at Pineridge Inn, and spent the rest of her time with the British children, swimming, blueberry picking, playing tennis at the Country Club. Until she ran into Bryce and Caroline there.

Merilee was surprised and confused that he behaved as if nothing had happened between them. Just old friends, but with an undertone of sexual attraction. Was he playing her off against Caroline, who wrapped her arm possessively around his? Was he keeping his options open?

"I thought he was *your* boyfriend," thirteen-year-old Vera said, puzzled.

Merilee realized that she just wanted to go home.

•   •   •

It was several days before Merilee even let Peggy know she was back. She escaped into her writing and didn't want to talk to anyone. Nor could she face the sympathetic 'I'm not surprised look' that Peggy would undoubtedly give her. But Ned was leaving soon, and she wanted to say goodbye to him. She hadn't to Bryce, but had told Anthea to wish him luck.

Peggy was shocked at how disconsolate her usually cheerful friend seemed, and cursed Bryce under her breath. Merilee wouldn't want to be told that she was better off without that bastard.

She and Ned exchanged meaningful glances.

"You know what I'd like to do before I leave?" Ned said. "Have our end of summer swim and cook-out, like we used to before the Germans took over our beach."

It had been their last act of freedom before returning to school.

"Great idea!" Peggy said enthusiastically. "But where?"

"At our place!" Merilee offered, brightening. "We could build the bonfire on the rock beside our little beach."

"Wizard! We'll bring the hotdogs."

They were a merry trio that evening, although Peggy missed Gunnar desperately. He and the others were at Vesle Skaugum, the Norwegian recreation and training camp on a lake forty miles to the north.

Peggy was glad that Ned could make Merilee laugh. If only she would realize that he was a better man than Bryce. And truly in love with her.

On Ned's last day, Merilee was persuaded to go along to the Rotary Club's Annual Street Fair downtown. There was a midway behind the Opera House, so the three of them went on the Ferris wheel, and the girls cheered Ned on at the shooting gallery. He managed to win them each a teddy bear.

"I'm calling mine Neddy," Merilee said with a grin. "And I'll sew him a little pilot's tunic with wings on his chest."

Ned chortled. "I'm honoured."

Merilee thought how distinguished he looked in his officer's uniform and felt inordinately proud of him.

They munched on burgers and licked ice cream cones as they watched the many entertainers at the Lowney Chocolates Caravan.

They ran into Gail and Gord, proudly sporting *his* new Pilot Officer's insignia and keen to talk to Ned about going overseas.

Merilee was sad to see another of her friends heading off to war. She wondered why boys seemed so eager to fly into battle.

By the time the street dance began, Peggy was flagging. She hated using her cane, so Ned had been supporting her.

"I think we should go now," Merilee said.

"Oh no!" Peggy protested. "I'll just sit and watch. Why don't you two dance for a while?"

Merilee went reluctantly, not wanting to be reminded of dancing with Bryce. But Ned was nimble on his feet and they managed to swing to *In the Mood*, creating plenty of hilarity, especially when Ned twirled her about wildly. Merilee was giddy and breathless by the time they rejoined Peggy, several dances later.

"Gosh that was fun!" she said as she collapsed onto the bench beside Peggy. "Where did you learn to dance like that?"

"One of the WDs at our base gave lessons," Ned admitted. "She charged us handsomely."

"Clever girl," Peggy said.

They were suddenly swarmed by their Norwegian friends.

"You're back!" Peggy cried happily as Gunnar gathered her into a bear hug.

"I could not wait! Vesle Skaugum is a special and wonderful place, but it does not have you."

"This is your boyfriend?" Lars asked Merilee.

"No, this is my good friend, Peggy's brother Ned."

Lars smiled and shook Ned's hand vigorously. "Then I do not need your permission to dance with Merilee."

"I did not expect to see you so soon," Lars said when she was in his arms.

She didn't want to talk about Bryce, so she said lightly, "I wanted to see Ned before he left for England."

"And your boyfriend, he is gone?"

She avoided his probing gaze. "Yes."

"We must go now to Moose Jaw for four months."

"I'll be terribly sad when all my favourite *boy* friends have left."

He laughed.

Dancing with both him and Ned all evening, Merilee was exhausted by the time they set off for home.

Peggy stayed in the truck when Ned walked Merilee to her front door. In the soft glow of the porch light, she said with a smile, "I'll look forward to your letters."

"Likewise."

She reached up to kiss his cheek at the same moment that he turned towards her. Their lips met unexpectedly. It was a gentle kiss, which he managed to prolong, releasing her reluctantly. But the passion behind it had been conveyed, surprising and confusing her. Ned was a best friend, not a lover.

"I'm sorry," he said.

"Don't be… Please look after yourself."

"And you."

She suddenly panicked at the devastating thought that he might never return. Gripping his arm, she said, "Saxon and Neddy will look after me. And we'll all be rooting for you, wherever you are."

She almost wept at the love and tenderness in his eyes.

•   •   •

There was an air of melancholy at Hope Cottage when the Norwegians came for their last Sunday lunch. With Merilee dispirited since her return from Wyndwood, Claire tried to be extra cheerful.

"We might be back by Christmas," Lars said hopefully.

"Then you can help us decorate the tree," Claire replied with a smile.

They brightened as they discussed the traditional turkey feast and the possibility of skating on the lake, if December was cold enough, with a bonfire blazing on the shore.

After the meal of cold ham, salads, biscuits and tarts baked by Lois Wilding, Merilee had the boys pose for formal portraits. She had already taken plenty of photos of them over the past months, and delighted each with a set of prints.

"You are a very fine photographer!" Lars said. "Look how she caught the three of us diving off the dock! And even in our planes flying over the island! Ah, but this is my favourite." It was a snapshot of all five of them lounging on the lakeside rock after a swim, chatting gaily. Claire had taken that.

"I'll take another one of the five of you," she offered.

After their usual swim and teatime refreshments on the dock, the boys prepared to leave. Gunnar asked Peggy to stroll back down to the lake with him.

"I have bought you this to remember me," he said when they found some privacy beneath the pines at the edge of the woodland.

She opened the box he handed her to find a heart-shaped silver locket. "It's beautiful!"

"See the back."

To Peggy, Love always, Gunnar was engraved on it.

"I would like to be more than your boyfriend, Peggy. You do not have to answer me now, but I hope that after the war I will come back to marry you."

She was astounded. "I... But I'm a cripple..."

"Phut! What does that matter? You are beautiful here and here," he explained, putting his hand gently on her face and then above her heart. Looking searchingly into her moist eyes he said, "I think you are not... what is the word?... *Appreciated.* Or you would have already a boyfriend. So, I am lucky, no?"

She wept as she went into his arms and laid her head on his shoulder.

"You must not cry, *kjærlighet.*"

"But I love you, too, and you're leaving."

"Then may I come back to you one day?"

"Promise you will!"

"I will try with all my heart and soul because I am now the happiest man alive!"

Muskoka: Summer and Autumn 1942
Chapter 15

Merilee stopped her bicycle at the edge of the woodland by her favourite blueberry patch. Now that the Germans had taken over Mrs. Jones's farm, they were uncomfortably close. Dare she go and pick berries?

It was her father who had suggested to the camp commandant that the POWs could lease and farm the land – using profits from their canteen - giving them not only healthy outdoor exercise, but also providing them with the satisfaction of home-grown food and a whiff of freedom. Colonel Winterbourne had been as enthusiastic about the idea as the new, and more amenable, Lagerführer, Oberstleutnant Benedikt Richter, who had been a commander with Rommel's Afrika Korps. Colin had earned a promotion to Major for his ceaseless efforts to keep the prisoners happily occupied and out of trouble.

The Germans had built themselves a house for daytime use, a piggery, and a hen house, while the barn now contained two cows and three horses. They had also constructed a shelter and an observation tower for the guards. The extensive sports field and a fishing hole attracted parolees who weren't interested in farming, so it wasn't unusual to see a hundred men, accompanied by a few unarmed guards, marching the two miles to and from the farm singing sentimental songs.

So the parolees would be busy with their crops or games and surely not wandering about this far away. Merilee ventured into the woods.

Below a granite ridge and above a meandering stream, the blueberry patch was somewhat sheltered, but also from the wind. It was a sweltering August day, so she opened another button on her blouse, which she pulled outwards so that she could blow a breeze down her damp chest. "Blast!" she swore, when she realized that her berry-stained fingers had left a mark on her lilac shirt.

Erich Leitner, leaning against an oak, grinned with amusement. He should have warned her of his presence, but he enjoyed watching her as she hummed happily to herself. He could hardly believe that his ravishing dream girl was only a few feet away.

Merilee grabbed her lustrous, shoulder-length hair and twisted it with annoyance into a ponytail, which she knotted loosely at the back of her neck, but already the silken tresses threatened to escape. But for a few moments, Erich could see the long, dark lashes, and the luscious curve of her lips. Everything about her was sensuous - her bare, unblemished arms and shapely legs, the way she moved and popped the odd berry into her mouth. He found himself immensely aroused by her.

They both became aware of the rustling of underbrush and snapping of twigs moments before hearing snuffling grunts. Merilee straightened up with a scream as a bear cub came galloping over the ridge towards her. She turned to flee and shrieked as she crashed into Erich. She knew instantly that he was one of the prisoners, but before she could scream again, he covered her mouth with his hand, saying, "You are in no danger, Miss."

She struggled in his arms, terrified that even if he wasn't a threat, there was still the bear.

"Brunhild also will not hurt you," Erich reassured her. "Come, I will show you," he added, loosening his restraining grip.

The cub had stopped at Merilee's cries and stood several yards away, seeming perplexed.

"No!" Merilee protested as Erich tried to draw her towards the animal. "When her mother comes, she'll tear us to pieces!"

"There is no mother. That is why she is our... how do you say?... *pet*. At the farm." Turning towards the bear, he pointed and said, "Brunhild, setz Dich hin."

The cub tilted her head back and forth as if she understood, but didn't want to obey. Erich took a handful of berries from Merilee's basket, and repeated his order as he held out the offering to the bear. She sat down as directed, gobbled the berries, and licked Erich's hand.

Merilee watched in astonishment.

"She loves blueberries, but she also likes to be with me," Erich explained, scratching the cub's head. "You can touch her if you please."

Merilee shook her head.

"She makes a good guard at the farm. Nothing comes to steal the chickens or the little pigs anymore."

"Have you escaped?" Merilee asked in a small voice, almost afraid to know the answer.

He chuckled. "No, we do not escape when we are on parole. We have given our word of honour as officers. It would not be good to break that. And if we did, we could be hanged when we return to Germany."

Merilee was shocked.

"It is... verrückt... *crazy*, is it not? When we are behind the barbed wire, it is our *duty* to try to escape... But you wonder why I am away from the farm?"

She nodded.

"The guards permit us to wander in the woods a little. They know we need time to be alone. But Brunhild, she did escape, and followed my smell."

The bear rubbed her head against Erich's leg. "Ja, Du kannst jetzt aufstehen. Aber nicht weglaufen." The cub stood up and sauntered over to Merilee's basket. "Nein! Nicht stehlen!" he admonished. With a shake of her shaggy head, she went over to the blueberry shrubs and began feasting.

Merilee couldn't help giggling at the well-trained animal. "She understands German!"

Erich smiled at her amusement, glad that she hadn't run away yet. He wanted to keep her here a while longer. "You had a shock. You permit me to offer you a cigarette?"

Merilee hesitated. She shouldn't, of course. "Thank you."

"There is a pretty rock to sit down," he said, pointing to a large granite boulder overlooking the river.

Merilee was suddenly acutely aware of him as he lit her cigarette and then perched beside her. He was disarmingly handsome, with refined features, a lithe, toned body, and stunning turquoise eyes – not unlike Drew. So she realized that she had seen him before.

"Your English is very good," she said.

"I learned a little in school, but now I have much time to study. When the war is over, it will be good to know more languages. I speak French already."

"J'ai aussi." She told him in French that her Aunt Lizzie's first husband had been a French Comte, with a Chateau and vineyard estate in Provence.

"My family has also a vineyard, in the south of Germany. It is very beautiful there, with many hills. But we do not have a castle," he added with a grin. "We have much land at home, and some animals, like here. That is why I like to work on the farm."

Sensing his nostalgia, Merilee thought how terrible to be so far from home for so long. But having heard what her Norwegian friends had endured, she certainly didn't want to feel sorry for the Germans. They had brought this upon themselves.

"When I must do my duty to my country, I wanted only to fly, not be a warrior." Looking at her intently, he stated, "I am not Nazi. I will tell only you, because I will be in trouble if others know. In Germany, if you criticize the Nazis, you disappear or die. The brother of my father was a history professor at Heidelberg University. He spoke out against the Third Reich and was sent to a camp in '38. We do not know what happened to him."

"But surely here...."

"There are Nazis in our camp who will not change, cause trouble even here, and threaten our families at home. They are dangerous men."

"But how can they know that in Germany?"

He had often cursed himself for helping to build that radio transmitter hidden in the attic, never conceiving that it could be used against him.

"They have ways." His frown disappeared as he said, "But we should not talk of bad things on such a... *glorious* – yes? - day."

She nodded at his choice of word.

"I have seen you before. Do you not live in the white house next to the Fussball... soccer field?"

"That's my friend's house. I visit her often."

"And drive a Motorad... motor..."

"Motorcycle. Yes. It belongs to her brother."

"Ach so!" He seemed impressed. "I hear beautiful music from the house."

"I'm glad you think so!" Merilee said with a grin. "We practice together. Peggy plays piano and I play the flute."

"But I play the flute also! I bring it into the woods with me." He jumped up to retrieve his instrument, which he'd discarded beside the oak when he'd gone to reassure Merilee. "When I play here, it is like there is no more war, only the miracle of nature and music."

"Will you play now?"

"If you wish."

Merilee was awestruck from the first poignant notes of Debussy's *Prélude à l'après-midi d'un faune.* The trembling melody drifted on the soft breeze, curling up through the branches and dispersing into the fabric of leaves and sky.

How could a man who felt music so deeply and played so sensitively be evil?

"I've never heard it performed so well," she conceded when he'd finished. "And I see why Brunhild is your friend." She laughed as the bear came closer and cocked her head at the German.

"She likes me to play."

They smiled at each other and their eyes held for a pregnant moment before Merilee looked away. Even if he wasn't about to rape and kill her, she knew it was wrong to be here alone with him. And to be friendly with him. But he suddenly looked so young and vulnerable, not much different from Drew or Lars.

"Now you will play?" he asked.

"I... should be going."

"Yes. Of course. We are still enemies."

"I hope not. Perhaps another time."

He brightened. "I am permitted to come to the woods one or two days each week, about this time. You will hear me playing."

"Why this spot?" Merilee couldn't help wondering.

"I like the river and rocks and seeing the railroad bridge over there. It makes me think of… possibilities." He seemed wistful for a moment, and she could imagine how much he must long for freedom and home.

Then he picked up her basket and handed it to her. "May I introduce myself? I am Oberleutnant Erich Leitner. Am I permitted to know your name?" He knew, since he had also cut out the photo of her and Peggy from the local newspaper - one of the many papers they were allowed at the camp - but he would never tell her that.

She hesitated but couldn't see any harm in it. "Merilee Sutcliffe."

"You are the daughter of Major Sutcliffe from the camp?"

"Yes."

He grinned broadly. "An excellent man! A good friend to us."

She smiled.

Erich bowed slightly as he said, "It has been a great pleasure to make your acquaintance, Miss Sutcliffe with the musical name."

She tried not to giggle at his formality. "Do you know the song then? *Row row row your boat, gently down the stream, Merrily, merrily, merrily, merrily, life is but a dream.*"

He laughed appreciatively. "I will not forget that. Or the singer."

She blushed.

As she walked away, he played Rimsky-Korsakov's difficult, frenetic *Flight of the Bumblebee* so lightly and effortlessly that she was once again spellbound.

She stopped and turned back. "I won't be able to compete with you!" she called.

"You forget that I have already heard your talent, Miss Sutcliffe."

She waved off the compliment as she hastened away. Riding her bicycle home along the deserted road, she thought that of course she wouldn't see him again. That was ludicrous. A betrayal of her friends fighting the Nazis, and treasonous even to consider it. But the realization made her inordinately sad. She had felt such an instant connection with him that it seemed their souls had met before.

"Perhaps she was just a wood nymph conjured up by my flute," Erich said to the bear, who nudged him for another head scratch. "*Merrily, merrily, merrily, merrily, life is but a dream….* Come, Brunhild, we will go for a swim."

They walked along the stream to a small waterfall at the edge of the farm. The prisoners had mounted a platform across the brink to divert the water a bit further out, thereby creating a shower beneath. A dozen of the others were drying themselves off as Erich and Brunhild arrived. The bear bounded down the bank and plopped into the pool, intent on finding herself one of the plentiful trout.

"Here's Erich back from playing by himself in the woods again," Rudi teased.

"Or playing *with* himself," Axel chimed in.

They laughed, but he said nothing of his encounter with a beautiful young woman. They would have been hungry for details, and envious, but she was his delicious secret. He stripped naked and plunged quickly into the cool water before his sudden vision of Merilee aroused a powerful and obvious desire.

•   •   •

A week later, Merilee returned to the blueberry patch. She had agonized over the decision, lying awake at night thinking that it was morally wrong as well as unpatriotic to be friends with the enemy. But then why was she so drawn to him? Was he a Pied Piper, leading her astray?

Didn't he say that the prisoners considered her father to be a good friend? Then surely there was no harm in speaking with him. For her own peace of mind, she had to see him once more. Berrying would be her excuse. And if he wasn't there, then she would never go back.

Her pulse quickened when she heard the soft trill of music in the distance, and was amused that he was playing a selection from Mozart's *The Magic Flute*. Perhaps he was like the character Tamino in the opera – a handsome prince lost in a distant land.

"*Die Zauberflöte* works after all," he said with a grin when she appeared.

"Ah, but perhaps I will transform into the wicked Queen of the Night."

"Never!"

"A feathery Papagena then."

He laughed delightedly. "So, now you will play for me?" He wiped the mouthpiece with his handkerchief and held the flute out to her.

She took it and said, "This is very fine. Where did you get it?"

"The Eaton's Catalogue."

It was Merilee's turn to laugh. "How very Canadian to order from there!" She wasn't about to tell him that the Eaton family was part of her relatives' circle of friends.

"We buy excellent things from there."

"So do we, but I'm surprised that you're allowed to."

"No tools to help us escape, but things to keep us busy and out of trouble." He looked at her expectantly.

Merilee put the flute to her lips. She knew this piece well, but felt nervous until the haunting magic of Debussy's *Syrinx* possessed her.

When Erich didn't respond immediately, she felt fragile. But then he looked searchingly into her eyes and said, "You have touched my soul. Perhaps you will bring your flute and we can play together."

She realized he was trying to extract a promise from her to meet again. "Don't you think it might arouse suspicion if someone hears two flutes?"

"You are right, of course." He looked at her regretfully, but knew that it was dangerous for them to be together. She could possibly go to prison and he was breaking his parole by speaking to her.

He helped her as she began picking blueberries, although that would only hasten her departure. "So, you will be musician?"

"No. I'm going to university next year to study literature."

"I like books also."

He was impressed when Merilee told him about her parents' books. "So, I think you write and paint also."

She mentioned the story she was working on.

"You are most talented!"

"We'll see. I like to paint as well, but I'll never be as good as my mother."

"There is a tree I see from my room, which I like very much. It is a pine - tall, proud, and turned to hold the moon or catch falling stars." Erich cupped a hand upward to demonstrate. "I try to draw it."

"I know which one you mean! It *is* interesting, and I've sketched it, too."

"You live by the camp?"

Merilee couldn't see any harm in telling him. "Just south of it. My friends and I used to jump from the rocks."

"Ach so! And we have taken over your paradise."

"Some of it," she admitted with a grin. "So, what do you do besides make wine and music?"

"I build my first radio when I was a small boy. I studied to be electrical engineer when the war started. I have luck that one prisoner is engineer, and teaching courses. Another is doctor of physics. I study also chemistry."

"As well as English! You *are* busy."

"It is good to be busy. Not to think too much of other things."

"Or plan to escape."

"That also!" he said with a chuckle.

Their hands touched accidently as they reached for the same branch. They looked at each other in wonder, as if something profound had transpired between them. Erich took her hand reverently in his and raised it to his lips.

The gentle kiss almost unbalanced her. Merilee found it difficult to tear her gaze away from his intense, mesmerizing eyes.

"Thank you for your help," she stammered, reluctantly drawing her hand away.

"My greatest pleasure." He reveled in the taste and softness of her skin, the subtle scent of lavender.

"I mustn't linger," she said, heart pounding.

"Of course.... But may I show you something?" He led her to a large maple, where he pointed out an almost undetectable hollow in a crook. "If you wish to leave me a message."

"Goodbye, Oberleutnant."

"Erich, please."

"Erich."

"You say it so well! It is not easy for the English."

"We were in Berlin for a couple of months when I was six, as my father was doing research for a book. His translator was also my tutor. He was an Oxford educated German, and taught me some of the language as well. *Nur ein bisschen.* But I managed to say *Ich* and words with umlauts, like *knödel*, which I love," she said, referring to German dumplings.

He laughed joyously. "I love knödel also!"

"My mother had to learn how to make them. So we have them with *schweinebraten.*"

"My favourite! Did you like Berlin?" he asked, buying time.

"It seemed nice enough to a kid, but I really enjoyed the house we rented on the Wannsee." It was a lake in southwest Berlin with a popular beach and an exclusive enclave of houses.

"Ach! A villa, you mean. Very nice!"

"I really must go." She glanced around nervously, suddenly worried that someone might chance upon them, and sense the attraction between them. Surely the very air was heavy with that secret.

"I hope very much to see you again, Merilee."

He serenaded her with the playful 1st movement of Jules Mouquet's *La Flute de Pan* as she left. Was Erich the seductive Greek god, Pan, to her virginal wood nymph Syrinx? She hurried away.

How could she be falling for the enemy, Merilee wondered as she peddled furiously down the road. And why was she so excited about it?

She had promised Mrs. Wilding that she would bring blueberries, and wanted to ensure she didn't arouse any suspicions, so she stopped at another spot to add berries to her basket. She didn't want to lie completely about where she had found them, if asked. She was calmer by the time she reached Peggy's house.

Merilee sensed something terribly amiss as soon as she entered the fragrant kitchen. Lois turned from the stove with reddened eyes, while Peggy, sitting stricken at the table, brushed away tears.

"What's happened?" Merilee asked in distress.

"We had a cablegram. Barry was wounded in France. We don't know how badly," Peggy managed to say.

"Dear God!" Merilee went over and hugged her.

"More news will be forthcoming, they say," Lois added. "Surely he'll be fine. We must stay positive!"

But she was fidgeting with her apron, and Merilee could only imagine how terrified they must be.

"Some place called Dieppe," Peggy said.

The telephone rang, and Lois answered. "Yes, she is." Frowning, she held the phone out to Peggy, who took it in puzzlement. No one but Merilee ever called her.

Merilee watched her face crumple from a surprised smile to horrified shock. "Oh no!... I'm so terribly sorry, Deanna.... Please let us know as soon as you hear anything.... Thank you for calling."

When she had fumbled the phone back into its cradle, Peggy hugged her stomach and doubled over as if in pain.

Lois cried, "What's happened to Ross?"

"Missing in Action. At Dieppe."

A dreadful silence hung like a shroud over the room, hearts breaking as each remembered Ross sitting among them delighting in the food and company.

He can't be dead! Peggy kept telling herself, realizing that she did love Ross, despite her feelings for Gunnar. She was confused as well as devastated.

"He could be a prisoner," Merilee muttered in hope. "Dad says it can take months before we hear." She didn't add "one way or the other", but of course they knew from the local paper that it had been four months before the Brydens discovered that their pilot son had been killed over France. "Missing in Action" too often meant the worst.

There was cheering from the prisoners playing soccer in the field next to the house. Peggy glanced out the window, her face thunderous as she swore, "I could kill them all! Bloody murderous bastards!"

Lois didn't reprimand her for swearing.

Merilee felt guilt stain her cheeks. With Erich's kiss still upon her hand, she was surely a traitor.

•   •   •

Merilee was relieved to be spending the last week of summer holidays at Wyndwood again, staying with Amy and Adam at Silver Bay. The distractions of being with a dozen friends and cousins, playing with the British children, writing, and just doing beloved summer activities that predated the war kept some of the anguish at bay.

Anthea had enlisted with the RCAF Women's Division, so her parents had already closed the cottage for the season. Drew was teaching at nearby Camp Borden, but was able to come home on weekends. He always filled their lives with light and laughter, but Merilee could hardly look at him without thinking about Erich.

Tormented by her attraction to Erich, she attempted to absolve him of guilt for Germany's atrocities, his own involvement already curtailed.

It was a tremendous relief to hear from Peggy that Barry would recover from his wounds. She tried not to think about Ross Tremayne, except in her prayers.

She figured that when school started, she would have little time to think about Erich or concoct ways to meet him. But she couldn't get him out of her mind, especially at night. It was as if she could sense him across the few hundred rocky yards that separated them.

She was walking back from her music lesson late one September afternoon when she heard the distant tramping of feet and the strains of *Lili Marleen*. She should have quickened her pace to turn down her laneway and avoid encountering the dozens of prisoners returning from the farm, but slowed down so that she could watch them pass. As they approached, she moved off to the side, but didn't hide. The guards nodded to her in friendly greeting.

Erich's face lit with glee when he spotted her, but then he regarded her with such infinite sadness that she wanted to run up and hug him. She flashed him a tentative smile. Their eyes held for a moment – yearning, promising. She felt bereft when he was gone.

How could she be so foolish? She recalled her mother saying, "Love always finds a way." Is that what this was? After such short acquaintance?

It seemed that some madness possessed her, because she was determined to meet him again. Damn the torpedoes! If no one knew, was it wrong? She wasn't helping him escape. They weren't plotting sabotage. She wasn't passing him secrets. They weren't harming anyone. She merely wanted to show him Canadian hospitality, which was so much a part of her father's job, she thought ironically.

Was she being disloyal to family and friends by caring so deeply about a vanquished enemy? Damn, damn, damn! But he seemed a kind, sensitive person, not a monster.

In case he wasn't there, she wrote a note in prim block letters so that no one could identify her handwriting: "Only Sundays." More subterfuge!

Fortunately, Sunday was a lovely autumn day and she required no excuse for a bicycle ride. It was too cold now to canoe, and she needed to get outdoors.

Merilee was nervous and excited, and terrified of being caught. But she didn't see anyone in the last half mile, and made sure that her bicycle was well hidden in the shrubbery, much of which was evergreen.

Although she knew it was a slim chance, she was hugely disappointed when Erich wasn't there. Before putting her note into the hollow of the maple, she reached in to discover a small bouquet of wild asters, wilted now. She held them to her breast for a moment and then scattered them among the fallen leaves.

Turning to go, she heard a faint, "*Merrily, merrily, merrily, merrily, life is but a dream.*" She spun about with joy to discover him hurrying over the ridge.

Erich restrained himself from enfolding her in his arms, but took both of her hands in his as he said simply, "Thank you for coming." His expressive eyes said so much more.

"I'm busy with school and writing, so I can only get away on Sundays."

"I have classes again also, and cannot come so often. But I wish to see Brunhild and the other animals. Sunday is good for me." He grinned broadly. "Saturday you are also busy?" he asked as they sauntered over to the boulder to sit down.

"I spend the afternoons with my friends. We usually go to the movies."

"We have many movies also. In English."

"Do you have a favourite?"

"*Gone with the Wind.*"

"It's one of mine, too!"

"We like musicals very much. Fred Astaire and Ginger Rogers. Jeanette MacDonald and Nelson Eddy. We even see one in beautiful Canada, with Mounties police."

"Oh yes, *Rose-Marie!*" Her heart quickened when she thought of the echoing, signature tune, "Indian Love Call". "You'll belong to me, I'll belong to you," the stars sing just before kissing. She daren't look into his eyes or there would be no going back.

"Do you have brothers and sisters?" she asked.

He told her about his family, how lucky they were that they had a farm to run and weren't required to do other war work.

"It must be difficult for to you to have been away from them for so long." Merilee took his hand and squeezed it sympathetically.

He smiled gratefully. "And your family?"

"Dozens of cousins."

He marvelled as she described summers on Wyndwood. "Their own islands! Summer homes on such lakes! I like that very much!... I did not think I would be happy to come to Canada. But we cannot know our destiny."

He touched her cheek lovingly and looked deeply into her eyes, reaching for her soul. Their kiss was tentative, as if they were afraid of unleashing an unquenchable passion.

"I must get back," Merilee said reluctantly.

"And I also. Until next Sunday?"

"If I can."

Merilee could hardly concentrate on school or the final edit of the novel. Eager to see Erich again, she was still torn by her duplicity. But she almost wept when she awoke to drenching rain on Sunday. It was one of those days when the bay was darkly wild and the rain, relentless. Was this a sign or a judgment?

She caught up with her correspondence, which distracted her somewhat. Lars wrote weekly from Moose Jaw, his letters lighthearted and filled with humorous anecdotes and observations. He always ended by saying how much he missed her family and signing it "from your future boyfriend, I hope and dream". It would have been much more sensible to fall in love with him.

Ned wrote from England, telling her he'd met up with one of her Wyndwood friends, Alastair Grayson, in Bournemouth, where the Canadians were awaiting their postings. He had been to visit Barry at the Canadian Red Cross Hospital in Taplow. Barry was recovering well from wounds to his chest, and would be sent home as soon as he could travel. His fighting days were over.

She was able to tell Ned that she had been at Taplow some years ago when her father was doing research. Jack and Chas had been treated in that hospital during the last war, Zoë had nursed there, and Ria used to visit the patients. *Dad says that they've now replaced the old buildings, which grew out of an indoor tennis court.*

She didn't tell him that her family knew the Astors, who had donated that space to the Canadians in 1914 and again this time. Nor that she and her parents had dined with Lord and Lady Astor at their magnificent estate, Cliveden.

Merilee wished she could pour her heart out about Erich in her journal, but didn't dare. So, what good was the diary if she didn't record her true thoughts and experiences?

She was frustrated that the following weekend was Thanksgiving and her family was spending Sunday at the Seafords' in Port Darling. Not that she wasn't happy to see Amy and Adam, but how many more Sundays would she get to meet Erich?

It was crazy to try to continue this relationship anyway, she told herself in rational moments. At other times she felt she would risk anything to see him.

So, when they met again in mid-October, she went into his arms and laid her head on his shoulder.

"I could see only your beautiful face in my mind, and not the words on the page. Not good for my studies," he quipped.

"I can't come much longer, if at all. Once it gets colder, I'll have no reason to go out on my bicycle."

"And spring is far away. How will I live through the long months without seeing you? Touching you." He stroked her cheek. "We cannot play soccer in the field by the white house when snow comes. So not even our eyes can meet."

"I can see the very top of your favourite pine tree from my bedroom. We also see the same stars." She told him about the Wyndwood tradition of "lighting the stars".

"Then I will light the stars for you each night! All will be a wish or a kiss. Like this."

It was a tender, lingering kiss. A declaration of love rather than passion, although neither of them felt able to state that. The word was too powerful. Too soon.

"I hope they do not transfer me to another camp. Some come and go. But perhaps they will not take me away from my classes and orchestra. But if you do not see me next year, you must know that it is not my choosing."

She was stabbed by the realization that she might never see him again.

"Do not be sad, Liebling. The war will be over one day."

"And then you'll go home."

"Ah, but I can come back, if I am permitted."

There was such adoration in his eyes that she believed he would.

"My house is called Hope Cottage."

"But that is perfect! How does it have such a name?"

She told him about how her parents had met as patients in the Sanatorium, and wanted to marry, but her father had a relapse. Her Uncle Jack gave his sister the house when she was released, and she named it with optimism when she married Colin, and nursed him back to health in their home.

"So, it is a happy place. Then I will hope also!"

Their parting kiss was bittersweet. "I'll try to be here next week," Merilee promised.

But the weather turned foul.

England: Autumn 1942
Chapter 16

"So, Uncle Chas is managing to keep Drew in Canada for a while?" Elyse asked Alastair Grayson.

They were sitting on the patio at Riverbreeze having drinks with Roz and Charlie. It was a warm and gentle evening for October.

When Elyse had heard that Alastair had finally been posted to Britain, she'd insisted he visit at the first opportunity.

"I was instructed to impress upon Drew how helpful teaching is for racking up hours and experience. But two years' worth was more than enough for me," Alastair replied.

"I should think so!" Charlie snorted. "I chose a desk job instead of training this time." He had just finished his second operational tour of duty, and was being "rested", starting with another week of complete freedom. Roz had taken her holidays to be with him, but they hadn't travelled far – a couple of days with Sophie, and a night in London. They just wanted to do simple things together. Roz was even teaching him to cook.

"It will be strange to be a student again," Alastair said. He would be posted to an Advanced Flying Unit for a few weeks, and then an OTU where he'd be trained on operational aircraft. "I'm eager to get started, but enjoying Bournemouth at the moment. I'm billeted at a very posh former hotel with palm trees and a sea view. But it's sad to see the coastline barricaded with barbed wire and mined with explosives."

Bournemouth, west of Hamble, was the Personnel Reception centre for the RCAF and BCAPT graduates awaiting their postings.

"Do you know who was just leaving Bournemouth when I arrived? Arthur Bishop, going off to AFU," Alastair said.

"Roz's aunt and uncle in Montreal know the Bishops," Elyse explained to Alastair.

"Small world! Drew was miffed when he heard that Arthur was coming over, while he's stuck in Canada, especially as Bryce is here as well."

"I can imagine…. It's so good to have you here, Alastair. You've brought a bit of home with you," Elyse said joyfully.

"You must miss it," he replied.

"Terribly, at times. Mostly I can forget about it when I'm busy with work, but thoughts ambush me once in a while. I long for the vistas of lake, paddling the canoe in the early morning solitude, swimming at any time of the day or night. I can't imagine how you could have stayed away so long, Charlie."

"He's promised to take me to Muskoka as soon as the war's over," Roz confided.

"I was promised that as well," Theo said as he walked out through the open French doors.

Elyse rose to greet him with a loving smile and quick kiss, and then introduced Alastair.

"Grayson," Theo mused as he accepted a whiskey from Charlie. "Isn't that the name of the lady who produces those delectable jams and cakes?"

"My mother."

"I see."

Elyse didn't miss the disdainful edge to those two, simple words, and shot Theo a look that he chose to ignore. "Alastair grew up with us. Chas and Ria are his godparents."

"How fortunate for you."

"Alastair has a degree in aeronautical engineering, so I expect he and your cousin Jim would have much to discuss," Elyse persisted.

"Jim is sworn to secrecy, as you know. Did you manage to get your hands on the new Mark IX Spit before your exile, Charlie?"

"No, but I've certainly heard about it. Two-stage supercharged Merlin engine. Climbs easily to 38,000."

"It's a huge improvement over the Mark V," Elyse interjected.

"Don't be smug, darling," Theo chided.

"Why not? I've flown more types of aircraft than you have. Over sixty now," she added with a grin.

"That's remarkable!" Alastair said.

"The only ones Roz and I haven't been cleared to fly are four-engine bombers, like the Lancaster. Only the men get those... So far."

"Impressive! So, which one's your favourite, Elyse?" Alastair asked.

Without hesitation she replied, "The photo reconnaissance Spits. They're not armour-plated or fitted with guns, so they're wonderfully light and even more maneuverable. They tempt you to ignore the ATA cruising speed and dance among the wispy clouds for a few minutes. And they're the loveliest sky-blue colour."

The others chuckled.

"So the poor bugger who flies that over enemy territory can't even defend himself if he's attacked," Theo observed.

"Just has to rely on his flying skills," Elyse agreed.

"Sounds interesting," Alastair said.

"I've heard that quite a few chaps are volunteering for PR work," Charlie said.

"Probably suits the loners," Theo speculated.

"Apparently the PRU is not fond of fighter pilots. Wrong temperament."

"Exactly! My instinct is to turn and fight. Not flee."

"I certainly wouldn't fancy flying alone over occupied Europe day after day," Charlie said. The fighter pilots always flew in squadron or wing strength, and thus, were able to watch each other's backs.

"What are you destined for, Alastair?" Elyse asked.

"I've heard I'll probably be sent to Coastal Command after OTU."

Theo snorted. "I expect that's boring as hell."

"But so important to protect our shipping," Elyse countered.

"Think of that next time you tuck into Canadian ham," Charlie teased Theo.

"Which will be shortly," Roz said, getting up to go to the kitchen.

They all relished another of Roz's gourmet meals, and Alastair was eager to hear about everyone's exploits, which took them well into the evening.

He had a train to catch, so Charlie and Roz offered to drive him to the station.

"We have a spare bedroom, so do come to stay whenever you're on leave," Elyse offered, giving him a hug.

"I'd certainly appreciate that. Home doesn't feel so far away now," he said with a grin. "And thank you for a delightful evening. A pleasure to have met you, Theo."

"Yes, indeed. Best of luck." Theo sounded gracious, but patronizingly so, Elyse thought.

It was the same subtle prejudice that was endemic among some of the older ATA women pilots. They shuddered at the fact that their once-elite club had been invaded by foreigners, especially a large contingent of American women who had recently come over, and further diluted by ordinary girls - who could never afford to take flying lessons - now being trained from scratch.

"Is it necessary to be so... demonstrative with your *friends?*" Theo asked when the others had gone. "And really... inviting him to stay here?"

"I value my friends. But you obviously don't. Why were you rude to Alastair?" Elyse challenged.

"I wasn't."

"You were being superior. Hardly including him in the conversation. Brushing him off."

"Don't be dramatic, Elyse."

"I detest snobbery."

"His mother's a cook. His father is what... a butler?" he shot back.

"Estate Manager."

"Euphemism."

"Alastair's an officer."

"Yes, well, you Canadians are overly... *generous* in assigning that status. It used to mean something."

"We grant it on merit, rather than who or how wealthy your family is. Alastair is brilliant and well spoken, and infinitely more admirable than some of the privileged *gentlemen* I've met."

"Good for him! So, I really don't understand your problem, Elyse," he snapped in annoyance.

"That *is* the problem! That you don't even realize how supercilious you're being!"

"Don't be ridiculous!"

"I'm not!"

"Where does *your* loyalty lie? With your husband or a jumped-up servant?"

They glared at each other.

Elyse was seething. "You expect me to *choose*?"

Theo walked away. "I'm going back. There doesn't seem to be any point in staying."

"If you only came for sex, then no. I'm definitely *not* in the mood."

With a look of angry disgust, he stormed out.

•   •   •

"What are you dicing with today?" Elyse asked Roz when they had collected their delivery chits from Ops the next morning.

"Blenheim, Spit, Hurricane, and Typhoon. Yummy! The Spit's going to an American Squadron, so I should be able to cadge a slap-up lunch." The Americans weren't rationed, supplying their own food from home, and the ATA pilots liked to eat in the Officers' Mess, where steaks, ice cream, real coffee with sugar, and myriad other treats were available.

"Boxed lunch for me. I'm on taxi duty," Elyse said. "Last pick-up at White Waltham."

"I'll be there."

After being grounded for several days because of foul weather, the pilots were eager to get back to work and clear up the backlog. There was a flurry of activity as the women checked in with the Met and the Map and Signals offices to plan their routes, and collected things from their lockers, including parachutes and overnight bags, in case they were stranded out because of weather or mechanical problems.

Elyse settled into the task of moving pilots from any of the sixteen ATA pools between pickups when Ops couldn't always schedule connecting delivery jobs, and then to collect Hamble pilots at the end of the day.

Delightful to fly and never temperamental, the Anson did offer a relaxing day. Much as she enjoyed the challenge of flying different aircraft, Elyse considered her taxi duties a welcome respite. And today, she was glad that she had passengers and wasn't alone with her thoughts. She was still angry and hurt by the scene with Theo yesterday. But she longed to hear his voice, to sort things out. Now that he was back on ops, she was constantly worried about him.

On her leg to White Waltham in the late afternoon, her only passenger, Johnny Barton, sat in the co-pilot seat. In his late thirties, Johnny was too old to fly in combat, so he'd joined the ATA and was stationed at HQ, which was also the #1 Ferry Pool. As all pilots took their training at White Waltham, he was a well-known and popular colleague, dispensing sage advice to nervous recruits and often, a much-needed pat on the back. A dashingly handsome Canadian, he also set many hearts aflutter.

"If you weren't married, Elyse, I would propose to you right now," Johnny said languidly. "Beauty, brains, spunk. Even blue blood. What more could a man ask for?"

She liked Johnny, and was used to his jesting.

"Your wife wouldn't object?"

"Alas, we are about to become unhitched. She never understood about flying. Thought I should hunker down to the tiresome, if lucrative, family business. Would you ever choose a desk, even if it *is* of the finest rosewood, in a stuffy office in Ottawa rather than the freedom of the skies? The poetry of flight?"

"Never."

"Precisely! Theo's a ruddy lucky chap." Theo had often flown in to White Waltham to visit Elyse when she was stationed there, so Johnny knew him.

A plane suddenly shot out of the shape-shifting clouds and headed straight towards them.

"What's that bloody ass doing? Doesn't he see us?" Johnny muttered as Elyse took evasive action.

Tracer bullets whizzed past them as the fighter closed in. They saw the large black cross on the fuselage at the same time.

"Jeez! Fucking Jerry!" Johnny swore as Elyse banked sharply and pulled the Anson up into the clouds, for once immensely grateful for their presence. But she wondered if the Hun would chase them, or if there was a whole flock of Messerschmitts in their path. They wouldn't have a chance.

After several silent and tense moments, Johnny, with obvious relief, said, "Must have been a lone wolf. Come over to drop a few bombs and skedaddle back before he's detected. Well flown, dear girl."

As she eased back down into a shaft of mellow sunlight, they saw black smoke billowing up from a railway yard.

"Bingo," Johnny said.

"If we don't have at least one bullet hole, everyone will think we're line-shooting when we report this."

"You are my heroine, Elyse. I won't allow anyone to accuse you of exaggerating that skillful escape... By the way, we all know, through the grapevine, that you were the first woman to fly a Spit, although that rankles with some, as you can imagine. But there were *unofficial* flights of Hurricanes as well, before women were deemed capable. So, keep up the good work. And let me know if you ever tire of your debonair husband."

She forced a chuckle.

Most of the Hamble pilots were having tea in the White Waltham Mess while they waited for Roz. Elyse perched on the wall outside Ops, soaking in the welcome sunshine as she lit a cigarette. Johnny sat down beside her.

He passed her a hip flask, saying, "You shouldn't until you're back at Hamble, but one little tipple won't hurt. Courvoisier. Haven't much of it left."

"Then I'm honoured." She took a grateful sip as a Typhoon came roaring low overhead, much too fast.

"Surely that isn't Roz," Elyse said with concern, but feared it was, as the other pilots had already checked in.

"Seems to be going full throttle."

"Bloody hell! There must be a problem with the Tiffy!"

They stood up, watching in mounting alarm as the Typhoon did two more circuits, but wasn't losing speed. The male C.O. joined them, muttering, "What the hell...?"

The powerful engine suddenly stopped, but the plane was still going too fast to put the landing gear down. Roz didn't have enough room to attempt a forced landing and pulled up to avoid the church steeple at the end of the long runway. Then she disappeared from sight.

There was a gasp among other pilots who had gathered to watch. Ground crew had already alerted the "blood wagon".

"Let's go!" the C.O. shouted as he dashed towards his car, Elyse and Johnny hard on his heels. They sped to the meadows beyond the aerodrome, where Johnny spotted scythed grass leading to a line of trees and part of a wing perched drunkenly between two massive oaks, splintered branches drooping.

Jumping out of the car, they raced through the second field, past startled cows and bits of propeller. The ground dipped toward a stand of saplings, bent and felled as if a tornado had whipped through. The other wing and sections of the tail lay tangled in the mess.

Elyse's blood ran cold.

When they reached a clearing, they saw what little was left of the Typhoon, its battered fuselage resting calmly amid the ground-sweeping branches of a sprawling copper beech glowing brilliant red in the autumn sunshine.

Elyse almost wept with relief when she spotted Roz grabbing onto an overhanging branch to haul herself out of the cockpit. Johnny charged over to help her down.

There was a pungent smell of hot engine and spilled fuel.

"Hurry!" the C.O. urged. "It could go up!"

Johnny pulled Roz into a run.

They were just clear when there was a tremendous whooshing noise as the remains of the Tiffy burst into flames.

The ambulance crew arrived and were happy that they weren't needed.

"Damn! I forgot the donuts I brought from the American Mess," Roz complained as she and Johnny reached the others.

They hooted with laughter.

Johnny said, "Here, have a big gulp of this. It'll do you more good."

Her hands shook when she handed the flask of cognac back to him. "Thanks, Johnny."

"Are you hurt?" Elyse asked, giving Roz a grateful hug.

"No. Just shaken up."

"We'll have Doc check you out just to be sure," the C.O. said. "So, what happened?"

"The throttle and boost controls jammed at take-off. I tried everything, but..."

"You should have bailed," Johnny chided.

"I was going to, but was trying to figure out where the plane could come down so that it didn't take out a neighbourhood. But at full speed, I was already approaching White Waltham and the engine was dangerously overheating, so I thought I'd better switch off and bring her down. At least I know this area well."

"You did a damned fine job, Roz," the C.O. said. "Heroic. And lucky as hell."

As Roz turned to look back at the burning Tiffy and the tree that was now ablaze, she said, "What a shame about that magnificent beech."

•   •   •

Despite being delayed, there was a sense of gaiety when Elyse's taxi-load of nine pilots reported back to Ops at Hamble. It had been a fabulous day for flying, with no serious injuries despite close shaves. As usual, there were a few amusing tales.

"When I delivered my Spit to a squadron this afternoon, I spotted aircrew sunbathing nude. You should have seen how they *scrambled* when I pulled off my helmet and shook out my hair," Jackie from South Africa reported to their Operations Officer, Alison King.

"Line-shoot!" Nicole from California accused her.

"Just because *you've* never seen a naked man," Grace teased.

"No, because it's too darned chilly to be naked," Nicole retorted.

There was laughter.

"You should have seen Roz zipping over HQ at 400 miles an hour, Alison," Nicole said. "It was fricking terrifying. We thought she was a goner. And all she's upset about is not bringing us donuts."

"I heard that we have a couple of heroines today. Well done, ladies!" Alison replied, but with less enthusiasm than they expected. The Ops staff didn't fly, and had the often nerve-wracking job of accounting for all their chicks at the end of the day.

Elyse suddenly felt faint as Alison eyed her sympathetically, grimly, saying, "This just arrived for you."

Elyse took the telegram reluctantly, as if by not touching it she could deny whatever life-changing message it held.

The room fell silent.

"I'll... open it at home," Elyse said, stuffing it into her pocket.

Alison exchanged glances with Roz. "Let me know."

Elyse and Roz ambled home as sunset inflamed the smattering of clouds.

"I wish to God we hadn't parted like that last night. I couldn't bear it if... he doesn't know how much I love him," Elyse said on a strangled sob.

"Of course he knows, Elyse. It was just a lover's tiff. Deep down it's insignificant."

Elyse looked at her with brimming eyes. "What if I can never tell him that?"

Roz put her arm reassuringly around Elyse's shoulder.

"I'm going down to the river," Elyse said when they reached their gate.

"Should I come?"

"I'd rather you made us some stiff drinks."

Elyse stood on the bank, recalling how delightful and relaxing it had been when Theo had rowed her up the river on warm summer evenings. Those snatched moments had always seemed idyllic.

Sir Felix clambered down from the bough of an apple tree and joined her, rubbing happily against her legs.

"We'd know, wouldn't we, Felix? Surely I'd feel it."

Heart pounding, Elyse tore open the telegram.

Regret to inform you… Missing in Action.

Charlie joined her and took her into his arms as she burst into tears.

"*Missing* is hopeful, isn't it?"

"Of course it ruddy well is! We have plenty of crew who are now POWs, and some who were successful evaders. We all carry escape kits and have been briefed on survival strategies. He speaks French, doesn't he?"

"Yes."

"That's an enormous help. I'll make enquiries, but don't expect to hear much yet. It can take months either way."

Charlie offered her his handkerchief.

"Months when I can still hope. But right now, I hope he's not injured, not being tortured." She hastily brushed away more tears.

"We have it on good authority that aircrew become Luftwaffe prisoners. They are still chivalrous, and don't allow the Gestapo to interrogate their POWs." He stroked her cheek tenderly. "Be positive. It doesn't help him or you if you dwell on the worst scenario."

She nodded as she drew a deep breath. "You're right, Charlie. I will light the stars for him tonight. I showed him on our honeymoon. Perhaps he will, too."

Roz overheard as she arrived with a tray of drinks. "We all will!"

•   •   •

After two days of trying to distract herself, Elyse couldn't bear to be alone with her tormenting thoughts, and went back to work. Roz was nursing a wrenched shoulder, and had been ordered by the doc at HQ to rest that and her nerves for at least a week. Even Elyse still felt shaken at Roz's close call and was thankful that Charlie was there to look after her.

It was difficult for Elyse to accept the sympathetic murmurings from her colleagues without breaking down, but once done, everyone was expected to *buck up* and *press on regardless*. No long faces in the Mess, if you please.

Elyse was actually grateful for that British stoicism that sometimes seemed like coldness. It certainly helped her to deal with Theo's parents and Sara. There were no tears or broken spirits. Just fatalistic optimism and gritty determination to carry on as usual. "Let's meet up in London some time," Sara suggested.

Charlie discovered that Theo had been shot down west of Amiens in northern France. His wingman had noticed Theo's plane spiralling earthward, and thought he might have seen a parachute, but he'd been too busy trying to stay alive himself.

Had Theo been distracted because of their argument?

"This is strictly between us, OK?" Charlie said. "There are underground networks that help aircrew evade capture. The main escape route is across the Pyrenees and through Spain, which means a dangerous trek down to unoccupied Vichy. And when winter sets in, travel across the mountains could be treacherous. So, if Theo is being aided by the underground, it could be springtime before you have any word of him."

"There's no way to find out now if he's alive?"

"No. Anyone discovered helping evaders is shot."

She could only imagine how harrowing life must be for those in the occupied countries.

A letter arrived from Sid:

My darling Elyse,

I had hoped you would be spared this. I lost too many people I loved in the last war. It breaks your heart and your spirit.

I know you will stay hopeful. But realize that, whatever the outcome, we are forever changed by these experiences. Haunted.

This is one of the reasons I never wanted children.

Do come to stay with me for a break, darling. It could do us both good.

With love, Sid.

Elyse had a note from Johnny as well:

I'm terribly sad and sorry for you, Elyse. Life and love shouldn't be so difficult at your age. But I do believe that Theo will return soon with a harrowing tale of survival. After all, you are the best incentive for swimming across the English Channel. Be strong, dear girl. But you have a shoulder if ever you need it.

Your Canuck pal, Johnny

She could almost hear his chuckle as he alluded to Johnny Canuck, the Canadian comic book hero who was successfully battling Hitler.

A week later, Johnny was killed when his engine caught fire shortly after takeoff.

Muskoka: Winter 1942

Chapter 17

It had been a bitterly cold December week, with temperatures dropping to –40 degrees. Howling winds had swept the snow off the lake into shoreline drifts, leaving an enticing sheet of ice. It didn't take long for the locals to don their skates and head out onto the bay. Some of the prisoners asked to do the same.

Erich couldn't believe that their request was granted. They had less than an hour before dark when they needed to be back. Sections of the boom fence had trapped the snow as well, creating a bank that could easily be clambered over. No one had specifically told them that they shouldn't, so they all did, leaving worried guards behind on the shore.

What freedom to skate far across the bay as if they owned the lake! When Wolf and Axel headed toward the harbour, Erich was eager to seek Merilee's house, and hoped that he would at least catch a glimpse of her.

Merilee was skating in her own cove, wary about venturing out too far in case of thin ice. Perched on the dock, Saxon jumped up and barked as Erich skated up behind her.

"Erich!... Quiet, Saxon!"

They stared at each other longingly, Erich saying, "I know we must not be seen together, so I will not come closer. But I wish with all my heart to hold you in my arms, to taste your sweet lips. I miss you so much I hurt."

"Oh, Erich! So do I!" It took all her willpower not to skate toward him and throw herself into his arms.

He grinned. "Good! Then I have hope and happiness until I see you again. You have a charming – yes? – house. I can now imagine you here, so close to me."

"Yes, I think it *charming* as well. Your English is improving."

"I have a new reason... incentive... to study hard now."

"I'm glad. Aren't you freezing in just your thin jacket?"

He was wearing his prisoner garb with the large red target on the back of his denim jacket.

"I have my hockey sweater under. And we are not foolish enough to try to escape dressed like this in winter."

"I'm glad to hear that!"

"I saw in the paper that you finished your book. Congratulations! I think it will be successful." He had managed to cut out the photos of Merilee and her mother with their new book, *The Curse of the Thunder King,* from the local paper as well as from the Toronto Star. The Star article called it "an exciting adventure for young people, but also a clever allegory about the current conflict, which can be appreciated by the mature reader."

"We're delighted that it's being so well received. I would love to have a career as a writer!"

"I am certain you will. And I hope to read all your books one day."

She didn't tell him that he was the inspiration for one of the characters – a good person caught up in the dark forces through no fault of his own, who finds a way to redeem himself.

In the fading light, he almost reached out to stroke her cheek. She could sense it and her heart quickened. She glanced toward her house, knowing it would be disastrous if they were caught in an intimate embrace.

He took the cue. "I must leave you with your handsome other German admirer now. Saxon is a good name for him." He smiled. "My beloved Merilee, you are forever in my mind, and keep me from losing it."

She hardly knew what to say. "I'll be picking wildflowers in May."

"So will I!" Erich glided away backwards, feeling that if he didn't keep digging his blades in sharply to push away, he would be drawn back to her side, as if driven toward her by the rising wind. So he didn't notice the bump in the ice and fell.

Merilee gasped and then laughed as he scrambled to his feet and bowed with a theatrical flourish, as if he had performed a clownish stunt for her benefit. She discreetly blew him a kiss before turning to head for the dock, where Saxon awaited her with tail wagging.

Erich saw Axel and Wolf returning from the harbour, skating for their lives as angry teenage boys chased them with hockey sticks. "Stay away from our girls, you fuckin' Nazis!" one of the pursuers yelled, swinging his stick menacingly as he stopped. More of the POWs were congregating just outside the snow-bound barrier, and the half dozen locals realized they were outnumbered by "the enemy" and hightailed it back to their shore. An inviting bonfire blazed there, and the parolees looked regretfully down the bay before returning to camp.

"I met my dream girl," Axel said to Erich. "Apple cheeks and ruby lips. Breasts like Hedy Lamarr's. She smiled at me." He was momentarily lost in happy remembrance. "Where the hell did *you* go?"

"Just checking out what lies beyond our little kingdom."

Axel snorted. "Boring! Aren't you *interested* in girls?" He shot Erich a suspicious look.

"Of course I am! Just not interested in getting into trouble with the locals. We're not supposed to make contact with them, you know." He felt such a fraud.

"Yeah, yeah! What are the Canucks going to do? Lock us all up?"

The Canadian Adjutant was waiting for them. "I'm pleased to see that you've all returned. But we've had calls from irate citizens," he told them through the interpreter. "They're complaining that some of you were harassing girls. You were *not* given permission to go beyond the fence. So this will be the one and only time you will have had the privilege of skating on the lake."

"It was worth it," Axel said later to his roommates. "To see real, live girls. Anyway, the ice is usually covered in snow, so it's not likely we would ever be able to skate like that again."

Seeing Merilee unexpectedly, knowing that she hadn't been seduced away from him by handsome Norwegians, buoyed his spirits and gave Erich hope. He dreamt that one day, when peace came, they would make a life together.

Over dinner that evening, Merilee's father said, "We foolishly allowed prisoners to skate on the lake, and there were some unfortunate encounters with the locals. Did you see any of them?"

"I was in my studio," Claire said. "But Merilee was skating."

Merilee hated lying, and knew she did it badly, so she said, "One chap did skate by. He said, in quite good English, that we had a charming house. Saxon was with me, so I wasn't afraid. He seemed quite a pleasant fellow."

"Many of them are," Colin agreed. "I have a lot of sympathy for the chaps who've already been imprisoned for over two years. I'm surprised you didn't mention it right away." He looked curiously at Merilee, who tried not to blush guiltily.

"I know they're not supposed to talk to us, but it seemed so innocent. I didn't want to get anyone into trouble."

"Well, there was no real harm done. I expect the locals had some thrills seeing the Germans so close." He grinned.

"Yes, and I can tell my cousins. Won't they be impressed!" It did excite her that she could mention the handsome and courteous German to them. "He actually looks a little like Drew," she said in her joy, and instantly regretted it. Stupid, stupid, stupid!

"Hmm. Interesting."

Merilee pretended not to care as she said, "They did seem to have fun skating. Do they have a rink, Dad?"

"The tennis court is flooded in winter, but it really is too small. Many of them have enthusiastically embraced hockey. One of the POWs was on the Olympic team, so he's encouraged them."

"Gosh! What about the field they used for soccer, beside Peggy's? Wouldn't that make a big rink?" And she might see Erich more often, even if they couldn't talk.

"That's a good idea, sweetheart. The Germans do take their parole honour seriously, so I don't think we have to worry on that score."

"How far would they get on skates anyway?" she asked with a giggle.

The telephone rang, and Merilee went to answer it.

"You were right, Merilee!" Peggy said excitedly on the other end of the line. "I just heard from Deanna that Ross is a prisoner. It's terrible, of course, but he survived! He *will* come back!"

They were both teary with joy.

"Of course, he won't be treated anything like as well as the bloody Germans are here! But we'll be able to write to him."

Merilee's elation at seeing Erich was once again tainted by the burden of hostilities. She feared that Peggy was probably right.

Colin had almost forgotten Merilee's comment until he saw Erich one day, and instantly realized that he must be the one. He went up to him and said, "I have yet to become acquainted with all of you. Your name?"

"Oberleutnant Erich Leitner, Sir."

"I believe you met my daughter."

Erich felt as if his blood were draining away. "Sir?"

"When you chaps were skating on the lake."

Erich answered cautiously, "I spoke briefly with a young lady."

"My daughter."

"That is your house, Sir? Very fine! But how does she know me?" He tried to still his fear.

"She mentioned that you resembled her cousin. As indeed you do. Good day, Oberleutnant Leitner."

Erich almost collapsed with relief. So their secret was safe, and he would see Merilee again in the spring.

•   •   •

Colin had a few days off over Christmas, so the Sutcliffes managed their usual celebrations with family and friends in the city. But Merilee was also happy to be home again, and preparing for their Norwegian friends to arrive. Finished with their training, the boys were back at Vesle Skaugum while they awaited passage to Britain, and received permission to stay at Hope Cottage for a few days, much to everyone's delight.

Extra camp beds were set up in the guest room for the boys, and one in Merilee's room so that the Peggy could stay over. She didn't want to miss a minute with Gunnar.

Lars turned out to be a gifted wood carver, and presented Claire and Colin with an exquisite Faith the fairy, and the girls each a loon, which he'd modeled after the illustrations in the "Enchanted Waterfall" books.

"Ole and Gunnar painted them, so these are from all," Lars explained.

Merilee and Peggy had knitted the boys scarves and socks, and they were thrilled with their copies of the new book.

"These boys look like us!" Ole exclaimed.

"Yes, indeed," Claire said with a grin.

"You do us a great honour, Mamma Sutcliffe," Lars declared, hugging her.

"Look at the girls," Merilee urged.

"But they are like you and Peggy!" Gunnar said with glee. "Even more special!"

His present for Peggy was an elegant rose brooch made of rhinestones, which made her feel very sophisticated.

They were already a merry group when Peggy's parents and Barry, who was now convalescing at home, joined them for a traditional turkey feast, Lois supplying cakes and other goodies.

Afterwards, they gathered around Peggy at the piano and sang "Deck the Halls" and "The Twelve Days of Christmas", "Winter Wonderland" and Bing Crosby's new hit, "White Christmas". The boys treated them to a traditional Norwegian carol, "Jeg er så glad hver julekveld" with such poignant nostalgia that it brought tears to Claire's eyes.

The young people enjoyed lively games of racing demons while the parents played euchre. After Peggy's family went home, the others sat companionably by the fire sipping hot cocoa.

Peggy and Gunnar managed to sneak a few kisses after Claire and Colin retired. When she and Merilee were in bed, she confessed, "I'm too excited to sleep, and I wish the night were already over! We only have two more days together."

As the next day was New Year's Eve, the boys chopped wood and built a bonfire on the shore, ready for lighting that evening. They shoveled the freshly fallen snow off the ice in preparation for skating. The girls helped them build such an enormous snowman that Merilee had to sit on Lars' shoulders to put stone eyes and a felt hat on him. There was the inevitable snowball fight, with Saxon determined to catch the missiles headed for Merilee.

They were in high spirits as they stomped into the house. Damp jackets and mittens balled with snow were put by the fire to dry.

Lars surprised Merilee under the mistletoe and planted a big kiss on her lips. She pushed him away gently when he attempted another. "I have a boyfriend, remember?"

"Still? You break my heart, Merilee." He grinned and added, "But I have patience."

"You'll be leaving in a few days to find new girlfriends in England."

"If I must," he sighed with exaggerated disappointment. And then grinned.

Merilee later came upon Ole sitting by the fire staring dejectedly at a small photo in his hand. He shoved it into his breast pocket when he saw her.

"Is that your girlfriend back home?"

"Yes, Karina." He showed her the picture, bent and ragged from frequent handling. "She is my good luck."

"She's lovely. And spunky, I think."

He looked at her quizzically. "Spunky?"

"Brave. Spirited."

"Ah, yes! You are so right. That is why I also worry about her. She would be one to be in the Resistance. I wish so much to know if she is safe! And I hope she waits for me. She also does not know what has happened to me."

"I'm so sorry for you all."

"Will you do something for me if... I do not contact you after the war? Will you write to Karina and tell her that I did all I could to free our country? Will you see that she gets your book?"

"Of course! But I hope I won't have to," she said with an encouraging smile.

After dinner they skated under snow-bound clouds that absorbed the lights of the town and those beaming onto the bay from the POW camp. Merilee loved winter nights when it was never completely dark, but she was sorry that there were no stars to light for Erich tonight.

The boys had earlier cleared off the Muskoka chairs, and placed them around the crackling bonfire. Because there were only six, Gunnar insisted that Peggy sit on his lap. She glowed with happiness as they snuggled up.

Wolves howled in the distant, deep woods. Lars chuckled and said, "Ah, that is me," referring to his character in the novel who transforms into a daring wolf. "You are a most excellent writer, Merilee. I will lose sleep again to find out what happens to me and my friends."

Merilee's character becomes a stealthy cat, Peggy's, a swift hummingbird, Gunnar's, a watchful owl, and Ole's, a soaring eagle.

"We can sleep when we're back at Vesle Skaugum," Gunnar said. "But perhaps we will be snowed in here and have to stay longer," he added hopefully as the first soft snowflakes fell.

Merilee heard a faint sound that made her heart sing. The haunting strains of Debussy's *Syrinx* quivered between the snowflakes. Surely that was Erich playing for her.

From the open-sided third-floor sunroom, Erich could see the smoke curling from the chimney of Hope Cottage and the bonfire's glow trapped in the low clouds. He hoped that Merilee was outside, and hearing Pan's lament for his lost love.

Then he heard something that made him want to shout for joy. Merilee must be answering him with Mouquet's lighthearted *La Flute de Pan,* the piece that he had once played for her.

Merilee had excused herself, saying, "I have a fancy to try something." It had felt crazy, even dangerous to bring out her flute and begin playing. Someone, especially Peggy, might realize that she was echoing the other flautist with another piece about the amorous God, Pan. But Peggy was so engrossed with Gunnar that she probably hadn't even heard Erich.

Merilee played boldly, passionately, despite the cold. The others clapped when she finished.

Colin said with a grin, "I expect all the woodland creatures to come out and frolic around the fire with us now."

"It does seem like that kind of magical night," Merilee agreed, as the snowflakes grew larger.

"Tusen takk for this celebration," Lars said.

They fetched a couple of bottles of champagne and glasses, and toasted the midnight hour in the thickening snowstorm.

"Godt Nyttår," the Norwegians said as they shook hands with Colin and embraced the women.

"Takk for det gamle året," Gunnar added, unabashedly kissing Peggy. "It means thank you for the old year, which is now very special to me. My wish for the future is to marry Peggy and buy a big property on a lake with a beach. Build a... what do you call it... resort? In the winter, the guests can ski through the woods, like we do at Vesle Skaugum. Peggy can play the piano and bake the delicious cakes of her mother. And you will all come and stay with us for free when you like."

Merilee held her tongue about Peggy's ambitions to be a concert pianist, but was surprised when Peggy gushed gleefully, "That sounds wonderful, Gunnar! I can already imagine it!"

"You could buy Vesle Skaugum," Lars suggested. "We won't need it after the war."

"Excellent idea! I will tell Lieutenant Colonel Reistad to keep it just for me," Gunnar jested, referring to the commander of Little Norway.

Later in bed Merilee asked Peggy, "Do you no longer want to be a concert pianist?"

"When I wanted to escape from here and be something other than a cripple, it was my dream. But now I can't imagine anything better than sharing my life with Gunnar and *his* dreams. I think it would be lonely, travelling about from one concert to the next, don't you? Anyway, I can entertain people at our lodge. Does it matter if I play for fifty or five hundred? Oh, doesn't it sound just perfect, Merilee?"

Thinking of the possibility of living with Erich, Merilee instantly imagined them in a place like Hope Cottage, but far from others, who would judge and condemn them. Even Peggy would undoubtedly disown her. It would be unrealistic to expect that Gunnar and Erich could ever be friends.

Perhaps a cozy cabin on its own island, like the heroine had in Merilee's favourite L.M. Montgomery novel, *The Blue Castle.* Or a remote cottage on the Nova Scotia cliffs above the restless, battering sea. A place where they had no past.

They woke to a sparkling wonderland. Inches of soft snow perched on even the tiniest branch. The boys offered to clear the laneway. Merilee pointed out that the long slope from the road made a terrific toboggan run. "I always go down it before we shovel."

Amid much gaiety and hijinks, they took turns, Merilee with Lars and then Ole, Gunnar with Peggy, whom he insisted on pulling back up the hill as well. He was struggling manfully up the slope for the third time when the three at the top heard voices singing "O Tannenbaum", and the muffled steps of a dozen prisoners on their way to the farm.

Merilee's heart soared when she spotted Erich among them. But her joy curdled to dismay as Lars put his arm protectively around her and drew her close. She could see the shock on Erich's face, and looked at him beseechingly as she tried to pull away from Lars. But he held her firmly.

She hoped to God the Norwegians wouldn't say or do anything, and breathed a sigh of relief when the two men just stared at their enemies in challenging, hostile silence.

"Jævla Krauts! Dra til helvete!" Ole swore under his breath when they had passed.

"You seem sad," Lars said later to Merilee. "Since we saw the Germans this morning. I think you wanted to run away from them, but you must not let them upset you."

"I'm not afraid of them. I'm just unhappy that you young men are so far from home."

"You do not waste tears on the Huns!"

"I'm worried about the three of you having to go into battle now." But she was also worried about what Erich might wrongly think. How could she assure him that she had not abandoned him? Spring was far away.

The surprising scene tormented Erich all day. He had recognized the RNAF uniforms from the photos in the papers, and was hurt to see the pilot embracing Merilee possessively.

He didn't dare play his flute in the sunroom again because the guards in the watchtowers might become suspicious, thinking he could be passing on information in code, especially if Merilee responded again. But she had last night, so surely it meant that she still cared for him and hadn't fallen for the dashing Norwegian.

But he knew that their tenuous relationship was unfair to her and virtually impossible to keep up. Loving her was a wonderful but unrealistic and surely mad dream.

Muskoka: Winter and Spring 1943
Chapter 18

Riverbreeze,
January 5, 1943
Dear Merilee,
Thank you for your kind thoughts and wishes. Of course I haven't given up believing that Theo is alive, and safe. But I do have dark moments when hope seems futile. So many are dying that it feels as if the war will go on until none of us is left.

My other black doubt - and fear - is that Theo and I seem to have a fundamental and profound difference in our values. My Thornton grandfather was a clerk who shrewdly built a financial empire, as you know, and was applauded for that success in his lifetime. Here, clever and resourceful people are still looked down upon if they dare to invade the upper classes from humble beginnings. Sometimes I even wonder if Theo would have married me if my mother weren't an aristocrat. But could I respect him and stay with him if he thinks my friends are beneath him?

Then I chide myself for my treachery. I do love him and miss him terribly.

So, it's good that I'm able to keep busy, concentrating on flying. The weather is our constant foe, so each day we say we're "dicing with death". Charming, isn't it? Yes, we've developed black humour and a sort of fatalism.

Golly, I'm sounding so bleak! On a happy note, we all loved the presents you sent. I've never appreciated how delectable and exquisite maple syrup really is. Your photos of family and friends – dishy Norwegians! - and my fabulous Blackthorn are divine! They lifted my spirits enormously.

Please do send me a copy of your book! How talented of you, and how exciting to be a published author at your age! Bravo!

I spent a couple of days at Priory Manor over Christmas. Roz and Charlie stayed on longer, but I ~~wanted~~ needed to get back to work as soon as possible. Imagine my surprise when my mother came to visit me at Riverbreeze! I had ignored her invitation to come to London over the holidays, so she drove down and booked into a hotel in Southampton. She thought that I shouldn't be alone with my worries and fears. Kind of her, I suppose.

Because we have to be on the ground before dark, our flying days are short now, which left me too much time trying to make conversation with her. With Southampton often under bombardment, I probably should have offered Sid our spare room, but cocktails here and then dinner at our local pub were enough of a challenge.

I showed her your photos, and she seemed wistful when she saw Blackthorn. Did you know that Uncle Freddie designed it to her specifications?

On the third day she announced that she was going to stay with Theo's family in Salisbury, and wouldn't I like to come along to see in the New Year with them. I had rejected their invitations as well, although I had sent them a Christmas parcel with a few Canadian goodies included.

What I wanted most of all was to be home in Toronto, enjoying the annual gala at Wyndholme. Yes, I'm homesick!

But I felt so much better when Charlie and Roz were back. Then Alastair came to stay with us over New Year, so we had a jolly good time, and regaled Roz with so many happy childhood memories that she feels she knows the Wyndham and Thornton clans intimately.

I was particularly happy to see Charlie speak so fondly of those innocent times. I know what caused the rift between him and Uncle Chas, but I do believe – and desperately hope for both their sakes - that it can be healed with time. Roz, who also knows, is unwittingly helping by corresponding regularly with Chas and Ria, and reading their chatty replies to Charlie. They seem to have grown very fond of her, and I doubt they could have asked for a better daughter-in-law!

It rather puts me to shame, as I could so easily visit mine, and yet don't. Can't, because I'm a coward. Stoicism takes too much energy. I fancy that if we even touched each other in sympathy, I would crack apart and crumble.

Dear, sweet Hugh Carrington dropped by to see me a few weeks ago, and we had a delightful visit. The poor chap confided that he often struggles with nausea and headaches when he's aloft, but is now destined to be part of a bomber crew. Of course he's accepted his lot with courage and determination, but I do fear for him. He quipped that he should have joined the navy, since he's more comfortable on the water. He has plenty of regatta sailing trophies to attest to that.

Brother Bryce, however, got his wish to be a fighter pilot, and is doing his operational training on Spitfires. I saw him briefly when I delivered a Spit to his airfield, much to his astonishment. He's even a cockier than I recall, so I think you're well rid of him. He appears to have already smitten a few WAAFs, so I expect there will be plenty of broken hearts in his wake. I hope that yours is mending.

Do tell Peggy's brother to visit me if he would like. For those who have no family in Britain, it's helpful to have some connection to home. *I already like him for having entrusted you with his prized motorcycle and teaching you how to ride it. At least I've met Peggy, and since Ned and I have known you all your life, we'll have plenty to discuss.*

With a big grin, I am your loving cousin-in-spirit, Elyse

•   •   •

England, March 19, 1943
Dear Merilee,
You and Peggy spoil me with your letters and parcels. I sure will consider the picture you painted of Big Red against the rocky shoreline as a good luck charm. It's small enough that I can carry it in my breast pocket. Thank you for that thoughtful gift!

I also appreciate that you dedicated your crackerjack book to all your family and friends involved in the war. I always figured you'd be a writer, and I'm so proud of you, my friend! I fancy I see a little of myself in one of the characters, although he looks like your Norse admirer in the drawings.

I'm at an Operational Training Unit now, and have "crewed up" with the six others who'll be flying with me. All are Canadian except for the Flight Engineer, who hails from Yorkshire. You might be surprised that my WAG - Wireless Operator and back-up Air Gunner – is your friend Hugh Carrington!

Crewing up was done by letting us mingle and chat and choose one another, so what a coincidence it was to see him there! We'd had a few good laughs at the Manning Depot in Toronto 3 years ago, and although neither of us ever expected to become aircrew, it seemed only natural to join forces now. He and I are the only officers, so we'll spend more time together in the officers' Mess and quarters. The others, all sergeants, are also reliable, dedicated guys, so I got lucky with my crew.

Hugh has invited us all to his grandparents' castle when we're on leave! I won't set my expectations too high after what Anthea told you, but expect it might be more of a shabby palace than a crumbling pile to my eyes. I do find the ancient buildings here quaint, even though they're often draughty and damp, with cranky, inadequate plumbing, and temperamental electricity. An adventure in any case!

And I really enjoy having this extra connection to you and to home.

Flying bombers would not have been my choice for several reasons, including having the direct responsibility for six other lives.

*At least my Flight Engineer, who calls himself a washed-out pilot,
can take over in a pinch.*

*Hugh said that Anthea is in her element as a wireless operator
in the WD. Certainly the equivalent WAAF here are competent and
professional in their duties. But I hope you won't join up, as some
WDs are also being sent overseas.*

*We'll be here training for a few months, and once we're actually
flying ops and complete 30 sorties over enemy territory, we'll have
done our tour of duty. With that happy thought, I will close now.*

Affectionately, your pal Ned

•   •   •

Merilee was tormented by her desire to see Erich and the voice
of reason that urged her to forget him. That became easier as her
winter days were busy with studies and corresponding with friends.

But when she caught glimpses of him skating, her heart
betrayed her conscience.

The dining room at Peggy's house overlooked the prisoners'
sports field, which had become an extensive ice rink. Since the
Wildings usually ate in the kitchen, this was where Peggy did her
homework, and the girls hung out after school.

Although Peggy was a year and two days older than Merilee,
they were both graduating with their Senior Matriculation this
spring, because Peggy had missed a year when she was desperately
ill with polio.

Merilee was helping Peggy with French one day, trying not to
glance out the window too often, although her gaze was drawn to
Erich.

"What's so interesting out there?" Peggy demanded.

"Just daydreaming," Merilee lied. "Wondering what it will be
like to live in the city."

She would be attending the University of Toronto in the fall, and
Peggy had won the Wyndham Scholarship to the Toronto
Conservatory of Music, which was part of the university. Uncle
Jack owned several substantial late-Victorian homes in the
"Annex" at the north edge of the university. Most had been divided
into flats, and the girls would have the ground floor rent-free in his
favourite, where Merilee's mother and grandmother had lived
during the last war. Her cousin, Maxine, who was already studying
for a music degree, would share it with them. They would be just
around the corner from Dr. Ellie Roland and her family, and an

easy streetcar ride from relatives in Rosedale, like Amy and Adam who were living with their Wyndham grandparents while attending school, and Ria, who had already invited them to stay for weekends whenever they wished.

"I'll miss this," Merilee added, trying to hide her sadness. She would no longer be able to see Erich come September.

"Not that view!" Peggy snorted. "I'll be glad not to see the prisoners all the time. It's like they're taunting me. *We're going to survive this war. Will your men?* They make my blood boil!"

Merilee couldn't prevent a gasp as Erich was viciously body-checked and suddenly crashed to the ice.

"What?"

"Nothing... Someone just fell hard, that's all." Erich got up slowly and limped to the sidelines.

"Good! I hope they all break their necks. Why do you care anyway?"

"It just surprised me, that's all."

Peggy eyed her suspiciously and Merilee was more careful after that.

As the days lengthened, she became restless, impatient for the day when the last of the snow in the shadows and crevices of the woods finally melted away.

•   •   •

"Don't take up so much space, Altenberg! You think you're still a God-damn lord?"

"It's *von* Altenberg to you, Geisler," Christoph said. They had just finished dinner, and Helmut Geisler had deliberately jostled Christoph's chair as he was passing.

"You Junkers are worthless!" Geisler spat in disdain at the aristocracy. "There is no room for you in Hitler's Germany."

"Nor for any thinking, reasonable man," Rudi Bachmeier mumbled.

"What did you say?" Geisler demanded thunderously.

"Germany needs to change to survive," Erich interceded, seeing his friend shrivel as Geisler loomed over him threateningly. "Our victory is no longer certain, now that we lost Stalingrad." He almost said *now that the German army had suffered a bloody and humiliating defeat by the Russians*, but knew that would provoke even more ire.

"The Fatherland needs to rid itself of defeatists like you, Leitner! We will see to that, you can be sure," Geisler snarled before marching away.

"I would have preferred that snobs like Drechsler had been kept here instead of making room for more rabid dogs like Geisler and his cronies," Christoph said quietly to his pals.

Geisler and his cohorts had been picking on Erich and his friends almost since they'd arrived, Lothar Krause being responsible for brutally knocking Erich to the ice in a hockey game weeks earlier. It had taken a while for his bruised hip to heal.

"I expect that no camp wants many of those fanatics," Erich said. "Imagine if one of them became Lagerführer! Fortunately, Richter has a high rank and won't easily be deposed."

"We do need to be careful," Christoph advised. "Don't speculate about your future should we lose, Erich."

"You shouldn't be thinking that way at all," Wolf admonished. "They're right that it's defeatist!" He got up and walked away in disgust.

"What's got his goat?" Erich wondered.

"He's a career pilot, and afraid that he'll be out of a job *if* we lose and the Luftwaffe is disbanded, like it was after the last war," Axel explained. "I don't blame him. I'm hoping to stay in it. Better than fixing machines, and a hell of a lot more sexy. Girls love pilots."

•   •   •

Trilliums would be her excuse, Merilee decided. They were carpeting the woodlands, and she wanted to take photographs. Fortunately, that May Sunday was warm and dry.

She hadn't seen Erich since his fall on the ice, and had fretted about him, even wondering if he'd been transferred to another camp. So the joy on her face mirrored his when they saw each other.

Their kiss released the pent-up passion of a long, lonely winter of hopes and dreams. But the reality of holding and tasting each other was more powerful. When they took a breath, he stared deeply and nakedly into her eyes saying, "There can be no such love between others as I feel for you."

She trembled in his arms, wanting and yet fearing the kind of intimacy that had blossomed between her and Bryce.

Erich had to restrain himself from making love to her, realizing that it would be a terrible mistake on so many levels. He respected her too much to get her into such potential trouble. Surely that would be her ultimate treachery. She would end up hating him for that.

"I hope you didn't think that there was anything between me and my Norwegian friends, that day…"

"I heard the message in your playing the night before. Now I have composed a melody just for you, Liebling. I call it 'Muskoka Moonlight'. To me it is also 'Merilee's Song'," he added with a grin.

It was both haunting and glorious, wrapping her in a poignant embrace and flowing into her soul.

"It's… sublime!" she said, dashing away a tear.

He took her tenderly in his arms. "I want nothing more than to stay here with you. Build a life together. With luck the war will end this year, and we will lose, because I detest Hitler. Since I have been in Canada and reading your newspapers, I have found a country and way of life I admire."

"Wouldn't you miss your family?"

"Not as much as I would miss you." He stroked her cheek. "Is it not crazy that I have never felt happier than at this moment?"

She chuckled as she swatted mosquitoes. "I'm glad because you may not be thinking this much longer. We won't even be able to come into the woods now that the mosquitoes are emerging. How would I explain dozens of bites while I'm just bicycling? We have to hope for hot, dry days to kill them off."

Between plagues of mosquitoes and drenched Sundays, it wasn't until the end of June that she was able to meet him again.

She detected his anguish as soon as she saw him.

"Erich! What is it?"

"My mother and my sister Klara were killed in a bombing raid. With my aunt and a cousin."

"Oh, Erich, I'm so terribly sorry!" Wrapping him in a sympathetic embrace, she felt his sorrow course through her.

"Gustav's wife is having a baby, so they were looking for baby things in Mannheim. Staying with my aunt's family."

He had raged when he'd received the news, already many weeks old. His friends had nervously tried to calm him as he'd shouted that the goddamned war should have been over by now. Why didn't Hitler admit he'd never win, and save their families and country from annihilation?

Helmut Geisler had gloated, saying smugly, "So… now we have unassailable evidence that you are a traitor, Leitner. You will hang for that when we're back in Germany."

"Christ, you're in for it now, Erich!" Rudi had said worriedly after Geisler and his bullies had swaggered away.

Erich was somewhat unsettled that the Nazis seemed to be constantly watching him now and whispering to each other. His friends stayed close by his side, but fortunately, the Nazis didn't come to the farm.

Merilee stroked his hair, since there were no words of comfort she could offer. The spectre of their being enemies once again loomed over them. She hoped it hadn't been Ned's plane, and absolutely hated that he and Hugh Carrington were part of Bomber Command. How must they feel dropping death on innocents? It was unfair to expect decent guys like them to live with such horrendous deeds.

"Thank God for you, Merilee. I feel so lost." He looked at her beseechingly. "You are my new world, my life."

"Oh Erich, I can't always be here...."

"You will be at the university, I know. But I hope we will have the summer."

"Next week, Peggy and I are leaving for Wyndwood for two weeks." She didn't want to be away for so long, but what excuse had she? They'd already committed to playing a concert at the Wyndwood Convalescent Home, and one at Pineridge Inn, where they would also meet up with Deanna Tremayne.

"I will be there with you if you describe me the details."

The mood lightened as she took him on a verbal tour of the island and its inhabitants, including mad cousin Phoebe. It suddenly seemed important that she keep nothing from him, as if he were about to become part of the family.

He marvelled that she was related by marriage to the legendary British Ace, Chas Thornton, and longed to know Merilee's world intimately when she talked of canoeing and waterskiing, picnics and regattas, costume balls and midnight swims.

"I will think of you as a princess in your castle on the water," he said, after learning that King Edward VIII had stayed in the boathouse when he was still a prince.

"And I will light the stars for you every night," she promised.

England: Spring 1943
Chapter 19

"Now the damn sun breaks through," Elyse spat as she and Roz reached the gates of Riverbreeze. Cheerful spring blooms embroidered the lawn and gardens beneath ancient trees, as if to defy her mood.

Charlie greeted them at the door, wearing Roz's apron. He was on leave and due to go back on operations at Tangmere at the end of the week. Roz was just starting her leave to be with him. "One of your favourites tonight," he announced. "Boston Bean Roast. I used up the last of the cheddar, so I hope you both get shipments from home soon."

"It smells delicious, Charlie," Roz murmured, going into his arms for a reassuring hug.

"What's happened?"

"The bloody clouds came down and Grace flew into a hill in the Cotswolds!" Elyse cursed. Grace had been kind and light-hearted, with an ironic wit that always brightened the Mess.

"She of the dimples and bright eyes?" Charlie asked. They invariably saw some of their colleagues when they went to the Yacht Club or The Bugle pub in Hamble harbour for dinner or drinks. "How terribly tragic."

"I almost put down at Little Rissington, but just managed to scoot around the incoming front. Grace was only ten minutes behind me. This bloody war!"

Charlie put an arm around her and hugged both women to him. It made Elyse instantly aware how much she missed Theo's embraces. With no word about him for eight months, was there any chance now that he was still alive? Tears suddenly threatening, she turned away, muttering," Must freshen up."

She had a cathartic cry, washed and powdered her face before joining the others in the sitting room for a much-needed whiskey. Sir Felix curled up on the sofa beside her, as if he knew she needed a cuddle. Although he never sought a lap, he wasn't averse to being petted and fussed over.

"Diana Barnato had an amusing incident today," Elyse told Charlie, feeling the need to dispel the gloom. Sara's friend had recently been posted to Hamble. "She was ferrying a PR Spit, and just couldn't resist trying to do a roll. She managed to flip it over, but got stuck upside down, at which point her powder compact fell out of her unbuttoned breast pocket and spilled open. By the time she was upright again, she and the entire cockpit were covered in face powder! She said the worst thing was that a handsome RAF officer greeted her as soon as she'd landed. His jaw dropped when he saw her, and he blubbered something about having been told that a pretty girl was delivering the plane, and all he could see was a ghastly clown. Whereupon he scarpered. She lamented that it could have been the start of a beautiful romance."

They laughed.

"I expect the ground crew weren't impressed with the mess either," Charlie observed.

"It certainly wasn't a high point for women pilots," Roz admitted. "But Diana can get away with those things. She's immensely popular, with a zest for life, and game for anything. Of course, she knows pretty well everyone who's important. But she's refreshingly unpretentious."

"That must come from her American mother's side," Elyse said with a grin. "But I don't know how she keeps up the pace. She goes up to London several times a week after work, parties all night at the 400 Club – often with Sara - and snatches a few hours of sleep on the morning milk train back to Eastleigh, ready for work. And impressively competent."

Diana's pilot fiancé had been killed last year, as well as several friends and former beaux, which had brought her and Sara even closer as they suppressed their heartache beneath gay chatter and flirtations.

"Diana told me that Sara has a new boyfriend," Elyse said. "Very serious. An American pilot, no less."

"Is he Sir-Algernon-approved?" Charlie asked.

"I doubt it. You know what they say about the Americans… 'Overpaid, oversexed, overfed, and over here'," Elyse teased.

Roz guffawed. "Don't remind me! One of our American gals swore she's going to sleep with every officer she meets. I suggested she might not want to broadcast that to the Brits, who are already wary of us."

"There are a surprising number of British girls who are only too willing to trade sex for American nylon stockings and chocolate. It's got our lads riled up, I can tell you," Charlie said.

The telephone jingled in the front hall. "I'll get it," Elyse offered.

"We'll put dinner on the table," Roz replied.

Elyse hoped it wasn't more bad news as she picked up the receiver.

"Elyse?"

Her heart skipped a beat. "Yes, Sir Algernon."

"I've just had a communication from our Spanish Embassy. Theo is in Spain, my dear. It could be weeks yet, but he *will* be coming home."

Elyse clutched the phone tightly and leaned against the wall for support.

•   •   •

"Have you forgiven me for being an arrogant ass, my darling?" a familiar voice asked at the other end of the line.

"Oh, Theo! You've come back to me."

"I'll be home as soon as I've finished my debriefing. I've missed you desperately."

"I've been so scared."

She heard the catch in his voice as he replied, "I love you, Elyse. Nothing and no one is more important to me."

"I want to hold you in my arms. Make sure you're real."

"You hadn't given up on me? Wives do, I've been warned."

"Never!"

"Mum is in London with Dad, so I'm seeing them tonight. I should be able to make it down there late tomorrow."

"I have some leave coming to me."

"Splendid! I can't talk any longer. Till tomorrow, my darling."

When she met him at the Eastleigh train station, she was stuck by how gaunt he looked. They clung to each other for a long time.

With the aid of a cane, he limped to the car, explaining that a ligament in his knee had been partially torn when he'd bailed out, and was reinjured on his trek through the Pyrenees. "I have a brace, but am to stay off my leg as much as possible for a few weeks at least."

"I think that can be arranged," Elyse quipped.

He laughed fulsomely. "I've been looking forward to that as well, my sexy darling."

But they resisted the urge to fall into bed when they reached Riverbreeze. Roz had prepared a welcome home dinner of baked Canadian ham, potatoes au gratin, and sherry trifle.

"I dreamt about feasts like this," Theo admitted.

"Can you tell us about your French escapades?" Elyse asked.

"I'm not allowed to mention names or specifics that could endanger people or organizations. And I'd rather just put it all behind me... I'm off ops. Seems I know too much about the

Underground to risk being shot down again. So, I'll be teaching for now."

"Thank God!" Elyse said.

She tried to draw him out that week, when they were rowing on the river or sitting on the patio sipping cocktails, but he clammed up and looked haunted.

"It's better to talk about it," Elyse suggested one night when he awakened yet again in a cold sweat.

He began reluctantly as she snuggled into his arms. "I had just shot down a Focke-Wulf, and didn't see the other one on my tail. It was a terrifying moment when he blasted away my control cables. I had to bail out quickly, but the canopy wouldn't open. I thought I was done for as I struggled with the release, then pummelled the Perspex as if I could break the ruddy thing. But I must have unjammed something because it suddenly flew off, and out I popped.

"What a relief when I felt the jerk of the chute opening, elated that I might still be able to tell you what a blasted fool I'd been. But as I neared the ground, I noticed a few German troops driving down a road. I tried to steer the chute away, far into a field, hoping they hadn't spotted me.

"I landed hard, twisting my knee, but knew I had to get the hell away as fast as possible. I bundled up the chute and shoved it into a dense hedgerow. Then I dashed into a woodland beyond, and promptly tumbled into a ditch that I hadn't seen because it was filled with autumn leaves. I realized I might evade capture if I burrowed into a deeper part of the trench. But I was terrified when I heard the Germans searching the woods, cringing at the thought of a bayonet stabbing into the leaves. Into me. I stayed motionless until I grew stiff and cold. Long after there was silence, I finally dared to peek out. It was dark.

"I didn't know exactly where I was, and just wanted to get as far away as possible under cover of night, in case the Germans resumed a more intensive search. Thankfully, there was enough of a moon to light my way. But my knee was throbbing, and eventually refused to carry me further. I found a haystack and burrowed into it. Not having had anything to drink for most of the day, I was parched, but the bit of chocolate in my escape pack helped to ease some of the hunger pangs."

That pack also contained a silk map, a compass, and plenty of French francs. He decided to head west, not towards Paris, so he spent the next two days creeping through the bucolic countryside, avoiding main roads and villages, hiding in culverts, shaking every time anyone passed close by. He was overjoyed to find some windfall apples.

"But my knee was now so swollen and painful that I had to slit my trousers open. I'd never felt so alone and miserable and vulnerable in my life. I was growing weak from hunger and thirst, and ready to give myself up.

"I remembered about lighting the stars, and strangely, it brought me comfort. I was able to rein in my panic, think more clearly. And I realized I had to seek help, trust someone, if I wanted to escape. I also remembered that my lucky Thornton Bear was in my breast pocket, so I felt as if you were looking out for me."

"I certainly was."

"Early the next morning, I approached a farmhouse and knocked on the door, scared as hell, I can tell you. A middle-aged woman opened cautiously and looked me over. I was a terrible sight… dirty, unshaven, wild-eyed with fear, no doubt… but she smiled and said, 'Anglais?' She seemed pleased that I answered her in French when I told her I was a downed pilot. She invited me in, gave me a jug of water, and served me the most delicious breakfast I've ever had… a cheese omelette, crusty bread and butter, and coffee with real cream and sugar.

"She was a widow, and worked the farm with her two teenaged sons. They were excited and eager to help me, although they didn't know what to do other than buy me cigarettes, and show me how to smoke them like a Frenchman."

"Which is different?"

"A sure giveaway if I hadn't learned to pinch them between my thumb and forefinger. Madame outfitted me in her husband's clothes. He'd been wider and shorter, but I soon realized that ill-fitting clothes made me look like I belonged."

"No tailored Savile Row suits there," Elyse teased.

"Being out of battle dress certainly helped me to get into the role. I was so well looked after that I grew a bit complacent in the weeks that it took my knee to mend. The boys wanted to learn English, and had me tell them stories about my adventures in both languages. They were amazed that my wife flew Spitfires.

"It was too risky for me to be outdoors for long, but I spent time in the barn, and had a hidey-hole prepared in the hay in case someone came by. So, I learned how to milk cows." He grinned at Elyse. "And I did offer to peel the vegetables."

"A man of many talents! I hope she accepted."

"She did after I insisted I needed the practice to impress my wife."

"You have."

"I could never repay them, Elyse. It worried me that they could be sent to a concentration camp or be executed if they were discovered helping me. And I was aching to get home to you. It was also my duty to return, of course. I told them that if they pointed me in the right direction, I would make my way to Paris, and surely find help there.

"But then Madame's brother, who lives in the nearby village, came by with another man, who questioned me about my plane and where I had landed. A Spitfire that matched my description had crashed into a field about ten miles away, so my story checked out. He said they'd been on the lookout for the pilot. He took a photo, and a week later I was issued with a new name and identity papers.

"I have to admit I was reluctant to leave the tranquility and safety of the farm, and once again face the fear and uncertainty. Madame refused to accept any money, other than what I had insisted on contributing to the household for food, but I had several thousand francs, and left some of it in my room.

"Since my RAF flying boots would have given me away, she gave me well-worn but sturdy boots. A size too large, but thick socks helped. She also insisted that I accept a warm wool coat. Surely a sacrifice, since one of the boys could have used it, but she was adamant.

"It was too risky for me to carry Thornton Bear any farther, so I asked the boys if they would put him in a tin can and bury him. I promised that you and I would come to fetch him after the war. And that we would take them flying."

Elyse hugged him as he lapsed into an emotional silence.

Following directions, he boarded a train to Paris from the tiny village station, nervous to be travelling so publicly, then petrified when a couple of German soldiers entered his compartment for the last leg of the trip. But he remembered his evasion training – don't make eye contact, act nonchalantly. There were millions of French going about their daily business, so just blend in. When the Germans paid him no attention, he realized that his new persona might get him through. He was surreptitiously met by an escort outside the train station in Paris, and conducted to a "safe house" in Paris. From then on he was in the hands of the Underground.

But because the Allies had invaded North Africa in early November, the Germans had secured Vichy – the formerly unoccupied south of France - so it was no longer free. Thousands of Europeans who had sought refuge there were now desperate to get away as well. The Spanish beefed up their border security and threw illegal aliens into jails and concentration camps. The route home had become more difficult.

"I was despondent at first, being shuffled from place to place, often confined to my room, staying away from windows, happy when there were at least books to read. But when I finally arrived at a safe house in Toulouse, I found several RAF evaders already there, including Moggy, an old friend from another fighter squadron. That was a tremendous boost to my spirits. I was no longer alone."

But there was chaos in the organization, as a few of the key people had been betrayed and arrested. By then they had a group of a dozen aircrew, itching to return to England.

"Things were getting a bit too hot with the Germans swarming all over Vichy, so we couldn't wait any longer to try crossing into Spain. We travelled separately by train to a village near the foothills, with instructions to jump off as the train slowed down. There were obviously Germans checking passengers at the station.

"We met up again and walked south into the rugged hills, joined by a couple of guides, thankfully carrying food, as we had been given none to take along. The snow-covered Pyrenees loomed ahead of us.

"We were a motley crew. I had the warmest clothes and boots. Some had nothing more than a suit jacket, thin shoes that were often too small, or their flying boots cut down to look like shoes, but tending to fall off or get stuck in the snow that we soon encountered.

"The climb became steeper, and one of the chaps fell, injuring his leg. His friend opted to help him back down to the French village, as he himself was shivering from the cold, and aching from the unaccustomed exercise. We bade them farewell and kept climbing until we were all too sore and tired to go on. We found an outcropping of rocks that provided a cave-like shelter. I shared my coat like a blanket with Moggy, who was infinitely grateful, since he had only a thin jacket. We slept fitfully and were grateful to see the sun. But not to discover that our two guides had gone and taken all the food with them.

"Bloody hell! How did you manage?"

"We just kept walking south, hoping that we wouldn't encounter any impossible terrain or deep snow. We climbed until late afternoon, when we discovered a goat herder's hut, which provided some shelter from the cold. There was snow to appease our thirst, but we were all starving by then. After a rest, Moggy and I and a couple of others decided we should keep going, as we must surely be close to the border, but the others swore they couldn't go on and decided to stay for the night. One chap feared his numb feet were frostbitten.

"Four of us pressed on, and at dusk, we narrowly escaped being caught by a Spanish patrol. We were thrilled to realize that we'd crossed the border, and managed to find another route around the guards. We were now heading downhill. But as it grew darker, we knew it would be dangerous to continue. In any case, the injury to my knee had flared up, so it was becoming painful to walk. There was no obvious shelter, so we huddled against the bitter cold in a thicket of scrubby trees.

"We walked all the next day without any food, and drank from a mountain stream, but the night wasn't as cold. I dreamt of roast beef and Yorkshire pudding."

"My poor darling."

"By noon the next day, we were in the sun-washed foothills, where we managed to buy milk and a hunk of bread from a farmer. It wasn't much, but it kept us going. Later, we came to a town. We'd been supplied with plenty of money, so the others wanted to go and find some real food. But Moggy and I elected to skirt the place because, scruffy as we were by then, we would stand out too easily in a small community. We never saw them again either.

"Before dusk, we found another farmer who was willing to part with a large sausage, a loaf of bread, and remarkably good wine for an exorbitant sum. But what a meal it was! We settled into a copse of trees sheltering under a cliff and ate ravenously. By the time we finished the wine, we were optimistic, and already tasting our freedom, certain we would reach the British Consulate in Barcelona within a day or two.

"Walking was becoming increasingly difficult, so we shuffled along the roads rather than trek across the rugged countryside. I found a sturdy stick to use as a cane, and told Moggy to go on without me, but he wouldn't hear a word of it.

"We had to avoid police checkpoints, since we had no documents, and neither of us speaks Spanish. We were about fifty miles south of the border when our luck finally ran out.

"The police hauled us off to their station, punched us about, and threw us into a cell. We told them we were RAF, tried to show them our identity disks, but they ignored us. We were fed slop, but at least it provided sustenance. A week later we were transported to Barcelona, where we were thrown into an even smaller cell with a dozen other illegal refugees. There wasn't even enough room for us all to lie down."

Elyse realized he wasn't telling her how horrible it had really been, for he went tensely silent. She stroked his cheek.

"Eventually, we were taken from the cell and interrogated. They finally believed us, since two British officials arrived the next day with proper food and clean clothes, and promised that we would soon be released.

"What luxury it was to be freed two days later and taken to a smart hotel where we indulged in long baths and feasted on delectable food, lubricated by several bottles of fine wine. We were told to lie low, in case we jeopardized our release, the Spanish still not being entirely cooperative. That was no hardship, since we spent most of the time sleeping and eating, but we were anxious to get away before any of the authorities changed their minds. Finally, we were given bus tickets for the long journey to Gibraltar and freedom."

"What an ordeal," Elyse said, kissing him tenderly. "I'm so thankful that you're here."

"Thinking of you gave me hope." He drew her closer. "And you were right. Talking about it has lightened the load."

"Good! I'd like to meet Moggy some time. Is he cat-like?" she jested, Moggy being a British term for cats.

"Montgomery Catterick. What else could we nickname him? Yes, absolutely. We'd already promised to meet up in London soon."

"Super!"

Theo fell into a deep sleep. It was Elyse who lay awake with disturbing thoughts.

Muskoka: Summer 1943
Chapter 20

"I think it's best not to tell Deanna about Gunnar and me," Peggy said to Merilee when they had settled into the boathouse at The Point. "In case Ross has any feelings for me. Which I don't think he does. Not in that way. But I don't want him to find out while he's stuck in a prison far away."

"I think you love him and have for years."

"In a different way from Gunnar.... I mean, I'm sure I love Gunnar more."

"But now that neither one is here, you're confused," Merilee concluded astutely.

"No!... Yes.... I don't know... But Ross never said he wanted to marry me."

"And Gunnar swept you off your feet. That's like being Cinderella. I felt that way about Bryce once."

"Did you ever... you know... do it?"

"No, which is why he dumped me, the jerk! You never had the opportunity, did you?"

"Probably a good thing because I wanted to."

"So did I, but I was scared. And now I'm glad I didn't."

"Aren't we just such *good* girls?" Peggy drawled.

"Even though we don't really want to be."

They looked at each other and giggled.

"Anyway, I think it's significant that Ross sends *you* one of the three letters he's allowed to write every month, the other two going to his parents and Deanna. Don't you?"

"I guess."

"Of course it is, silly! So, what are you giving Deanna to include in his next care package?" Only the prisoner's closest family was allowed to send parcels.

"Some of our maple syrup, Mum's blueberry jam and brandy-soaked fruitcake, a vest and socks that I knitted for him, and your book, which he really wants to read."

"Cool!"

"Do you think we could go past Mazengah Island some time? I don't want to stop in or bother anyone. Just see it for myself. So I can describe it to Ross."

"Sure! I can take a photo if you want."

They'd been surprised to discover that a fellow officer, Arthur Patterson, captured with Ross at Dieppe, was from the Blachford family that had first settled the nearby island in the 1870s. Ross said that he and Arthur had much in common, and enjoyed regular chess games. Merilee often met the Mazengah islanders at Regattas and events, although they were not close friends with the Wyndwood crowd.

"That would be super!"

The British children were delighted that the girls were there for two weeks, and Ria appreciated that they spent so much time with the kids, giving her a break, especially with Drew convalescing at the cottage.

Merilee had been worried when she'd heard that he'd been injured in a crash, but even more scared when he explained what had happened.

They were all having tea on the veranda. His right arm was in a sling.

"I was with one of my new sprogs who was practicing forced landings in the Harvard, which is much more powerful and tricky to fly than what the students are trained on initially. He had the controls and was doing well, skimming low across a field as if about to land and then going up again. We were just rising over a line of trees when another Harvard suddenly came towards us at right angles. I don't know if my student would have reacted quickly enough, but I grabbed the controls and banked away and upwards. The other pilot did as well, but our wings clipped each other, and ours was half sheared off. I fought to keep her level as I put her down, but the other wing caught the dirt and we flipped over. Fortunately, we weren't going that fast anymore. My student just had some bruises and I dislocated my shoulder. The other guy was shaken, but fine. He was lost and out of fuel, so he had to do a real forced landing."

"You were lucky," Chas said. "But you also made the right split-second decision, including burning off the fuel in the engines and cutting the switches, or the plane might have caught fire. You've developed good instincts from those extra 1600 flying hours you've accumulated."

"Then I should be ready to become a fighter pilot. I've got an A1 rating now."

"Yes, and your CO says that you're too valuable an instructor to risk in battle."

"That's not fair!"

"You have to trust the powers-that-be to know where everyone's talents are best deployed." Chas looked at his frustrated son with compassion. "You've trained several dozen pilots exceptionally well. They'll have a better chance of survival because of you, and you'll have more influence on winning the war than a single fighter pilot could ever have."

"I'll be sneered at by the combat pilots, and probably called a coward. They'll say you wrangled me a safe job at home."

"It doesn't sound that safe to me," Merilee said.

"It isn't," Chas agreed. "Last year alone we lost 170 students and instructors, to say nothing of the many prangs that injured others."

"We won't get any gongs for bravery, though, will we," Drew lamented.

"Neither do the ground crews, but the pilots' lives depend on them doing their jobs well. Neither do the decoders, or the men and women building aeroplanes, or everyone else in unglamorous jobs helping to win this war," Chas replied. "In any case, the RAF needs bomber pilots more than fighters now."

"So you mean I'll never get into a Spitfire?"

"We'll see. Maybe HQ will relent if you can train other instructors well enough in your methods. And the more you practice your aerobatic skills, the more likely you are to be deemed suitable for Fighter Command."

Ria looked at him askance, hoping that Chas would use his influence to keep Drew in Canada rather than helping him get to the front lines.

"I don't understand what the big deal is. I just teach them a love of flying, and make sure that they know their aircraft intimately, upside down and every which way, so that getting out of trouble becomes second nature."

"You instill confidence as well as the necessary skills, and I'm told that you do so with maturity and grace. Some instructors are begrudging or indifferent or impatient with their students. I'm really proud of you, Drew."

"We certainly are," Ria chimed in.

"And for now, you'll at least have lots of different types of planes to fly at Trenton, which should make it more fun for you," Chas added.

"That's another consolation for the transfer. The best is that Anthea's there, of course." Drew grinned happily. Once healed and rested, he would be teaching at the Central Flying School. Anthea had been posted there after her wireless training.

"I think you're a hero, Drew," twelve-year-old Bertie Carmichael said, taking another scone. "When will you take me flying?"

"When the war's over. Before you go home again."

"Not sure I want to go home. I like it here." Bertie looked at Ria hopefully.

His fourteen-year-old sister Vera said, "Bertie! Mummy and Daddy will be waiting for us."

"Can't they come here? It's ever so much nicer."

"They certainly can," Ria assured him. "And you can come back to visit us any time. I promise."

"All of us?" eleven-year-old George Baxter asked.

"Of course! You're my little war puppies, aren't you?" It was a term of affection that amused the children, and made them feel special.

William Baxter, sitting in the band-shell at the corner with his head in a book, snorted. He got up and slouched away, announcing, "I'm taking the skiff out."

"He's really starting university this fall?" Merilee asked when he was out of hearing.

"Oh yes," Ria acknowledged. "Troy says he's a brilliant student. But he's immature, even for sixteen, and socially inept. It will be interesting to see how he copes. In the meantime, August spent helping with the harvest again will be good for him."

"At least I won't have any classes with him."

"I'm so glad you'll be able to visit us in the city!" Vera enthused. "My friends all loved your book and would be so excited to meet you."

"Gosh, I'm honoured!"

"Perhaps you can give me some tips on writing. I have ideas for stories," Vera admitted shyly.

"I'd be happy to! My Dad suggested I keep a diary."

"Oh, but I do!"

"Good, because I expect your own adventures will make an interesting story as well."

Vera beamed.

Merilee was amazed at how the children had blossomed, and seemed so happy, despite being away from their parents for three years now. If the war lasted much longer, would they even know their homes and families anymore?

As Drew opened a packet of cigarettes, Bertie and George both shouted, "May I have it?"

Children across Canada had been tasked with collecting the foil cigarette papers for the war effort.

Drew gave them each a piece.

"Do you know what this is for?" Bertie asked.

"Not a clue," Drew admitted. "Dad says it's for a secret weapon."

The boys looked at Chas to elaborate, but he just grinned and said, "It's top secret, and very important."

"Wizard!" Bertie said.

"Time for a swim. Who's going to be first down the waterslide?" Merilee asked, much to their delight.

•   •   •

Erich was unhappy that the Nazis had started coming to the farm, but other than watching him and sneering, they left him alone. But they were surely up to something, since they would usually needle him at every opportunity, and preferred to stay at the camp, plotting escapes. And planning the glorious future of the Third Reich after the war.

He found it difficult to sneak away, but Merilee would be back from Wyndwood and coming today. He longed to see her.

She was already waiting for him and rushed into his arms. He held her tightly, afraid that these trysts would have to stop if he was being monitored by the Nazis. He kissed her passionately and said, "Merilee, if I cannot come back here, I want you to know that I love you with my heart and soul. I don't know what will happen after the war, but…"

"Well, well, well, if it isn't the traitor and his whore."

Erich's blood ran cold. He had been too intent to realize that Geisler and his two cohorts had followed him. One carried a coiled rope.

Erich held Merilee protectively close and whispered, "Run! Do not stop for anything."

He pushed her away and attacked the trio to give her time to escape. But Geisler evaded him and chased after Merilee while his two goons grappled with Erich. Merilee heard the sickening sounds of punches and grunts, and the heavy breathing of her pursuer closing in on her. He tackled her and they fell among the ferns.

Geisler laughed triumphantly, and said nastily, "So I will enjoy myself a Canadian whore. It has been too long since I have a woman."

Merilee screamed as she struggled, but he pinned her down, her face pressed into prickly pine needles and rough stones, her left arm bent viciously behind her back. "Silence! Or I will break your arm."

Merilee moaned in agony.

"But I have a better idea," he said, suddenly releasing his cruel grip. He hauled her up roughly and warned, "Scream again and we will hang him."

Merilee was shocked to see Erich with a rope around his neck, the other end slung over the sturdy branch of an oak, his hands bound behind his back, his face bloodied.

"Oh dear God!" she said.

"You still believe in God?" Geisler spat contemptuously and dragged her over to the others.

Erich stared regretfully, helplessly at her.

"So, we will have some sport," Geisler announced. "You will remove your clothes, and the traitor can watch as you entertain each in turn."

"NO!" Erich cried. And received another excruciating punch to his damaged ribs, causing him to double over and the rope to cut into his neck.

"You will do as you are told, whore, or you will watch him hang!"

"You'll hang me anyway," Erich managed to splutter.

"Perhaps not if she satisfies me."

Erich raged inside, knowing that Geisler would take Merilee by force if necessary. Making him watch was just another knife thrust for Erich. "Let her go, Geisler. You have me. She has no experience of men."

"Then it will be more exciting for me to be her first."

Merilee was terrified. Geisler eyed her so rapaciously that she felt weak-kneed. She didn't know what to do, how she could possibly outwit these violent men. Needing to play for time, she managed to say, "Take that rope off his neck or I won't do anything."

Geisler laughed wickedly. "You cannot make the terms, whore! Do you think I can't easily take you?" He grabbed her arm and pulled her against him.

"That's called rape and you will hang for it," she stated defiantly, taking strength from her fear and anger. "My mother's family is one of the most powerful in Canada, and they will demand justice for me and Erich."

"And what will they say about you collaborating with the enemy? Does that not make you a traitor?" he challenged. "We execute people like you in Germany."

"And we execute murderers like you in Canada."

"There will be no murder. Only a guilty, disturbed prisoner who committed suicide."

"After beating himself up?" she challenged.

"Enough talk! Take off your clothes."

"Remove the rope!" she shot back.

He snorted, but looked at her appreciatively. "I like a girl with fire." He motioned the others to comply.

But Erich was still trussed up and held firmly between his captors. He gazed at her with infinite sadness.

She realized that even if she did manage to kick Geisler in the groin and run, Erich couldn't defend himself. With tears trickling down her face, she slowly began to undo her blouse, praying fervently for divine intervention.

Their eyes locked and for a moment there was only the silent communication between them – the poignant love and regret, sharing the strength and courage to endure whatever was to come.

Trembling, Merilee took off her top, felling ashamed and vulnerable in her lacy bra.

"Faster! We have not all day!"

She glared contemptuously at Geisler as she began to unzip her shorts, but stopped when she heard something rustling through the undergrowth. Brunhild came bounding towards Erich. Now a grown bear, she was a formidable sight, and the Nazis, who had not known her as a cub, fell back in fright. Then all hell seemed to break loose as four other prisoners appeared and, with shouts of alarm, raced over to free Erich.

Merilee hastily grabbed her blouse, and Erich rushed to her side as the others brawled.

"Oh, my love, I am so sorry!" he said enfolding her tenderly in his arms. "You were very brave and saved my life. But now you must go before the guards come and find you here."

"You're hurt..."

"I shall mend. But I will have to leave this camp, or these Nazis will get me another time. And you must never come here again."

He stroked her cheek as she looked at him in anguish. "I have put you in great danger, with your own people as well. You must forget me, Merilee."

"But, I..."

He put his finger on her lips to silence her as his eyes held hers. "I know. But it cannot be, my love. Not now. Perhaps never. Go! Quickly! For both our sakes."

The rescuers were winning, although all of them were tiring. Merilee glanced back several times, feeling like her heart was breaking as Erich stood gazing forlornly after her, patting Brunhild, who would also soon lose her best friend.

Merilee needed a cathartic cry before going home, but her mother noticed that she had been weeping, and had scratches and scrapes.

"What happened, my sweet?"

She tried not to burst into fresh tears. Of course she could never tell her parents or anyone what had happened. That nasty Nazi had been right that she would seem like a traitor. She hated all this deception, but said, "I fell off my bike. Just a few scrapes, and I wrenched my shoulder." It ached terribly from the vicious arm-lock. "I think I'll have a dip in the lake." A cleansing swim.

Back at the farm the Nazis went to lick their wounds, while Erich and his friends, along with Brunhild, went down to the waterfall to clean themselves up. They would have to have some explanation for their injuries, but it wasn't the first time that officers had fought amongst themselves.

Erich felt murderous towards Geisler, but knew it would be stupid to tackle him. He was sure he had a broken rib or two, and wouldn't have managed in a fight, fair or otherwise. But Axel had given Geisler a drubbing.

"They would have hanged you, Erich, like the Nazis did to one of our own out in the Medicine Hat camp," Rudi Bachmeier said worriedly. They'd just heard through their internal grapevine about the murder, and of another prisoner who had run for his life with a mob at his heels, surrendering to the Veteran Guards who protected and helped him over the barbed wire. "We must report this to the Lagerführer. He's a good guy, a moderate. He won't sanction murder."

"And we'll get you transferred," Christoph said. "And not leave you alone until you're safe."

"Thank you, my friends. How did you know to look for me?"

"We realized that you had left, and that the damned Nazis had also disappeared. But we knew that Brunhild would be able to find you!" Rudi explained.

"She's worth her weight in gold," Erich said. "As are all of you. I don't know how I can ever thank you. If you had come even five minutes later..." He tried hard not to break down.

"So, tell us about that beautiful goddess, you sly fox, or I will dunk you!" Axel teased.

"She's just a girl who got lost in the woods," Erich said dejectedly, feeling as if he'd been gutted.

"Well, well, what have you boys been up to?" the Guard asked as he came down to the river. "I must say the others look just as bad. Fair fight was it?"

"Erich started it," Christoph stated, momentarily surprising his friends. "He said that Germany might lose the war. The Nazis didn't like that. I think you should lock Erich up, Sergeant, just to be safe." He stared at the Guard and made a cutthroat gesture with his hand. "I think you'll find a rope is missing from the barn."

"Christ Almighty!"

•   •   •

"Would you like to see Hitler defeated?" Colin asked Erich in the lock-up. When Erich looked around the small room as if expecting spies to be listening, Colin reassured him. "This is between us, so feel free to speak your mind. I'm here to help you, Erich."

If Erich had his way, Colin would one day be his father-in-law, despite what he had said to Merilee. He almost burst into laughter at this absurd and wonderful thought. It was time to bare his soul if he wanted to win Colin's support.

"Hitler, yes! Nazis, yes! Germany... not so much. It is never good to lose. Life was hard after the last war."

"Yes, which is how Hitler managed to rise to power."

"He was good for our people at first. He brought stability, prosperity, pride. But he also brought darkness and fear. Distrust. Neighbours reported those they did not like, who spoke out against the Nazis. We heard stories about the brutality of the Gestapo. Hitler had too much power before we realized what was happening.

"I must tell you that I was in the Hitler Youth. We must be if we want to play sports or belong to a band or club. It was where I learned to fly. My dream! But we did not realize they were also preparing us for war. Most Germans did not want another war."

"Thank you for your honesty. We believe that it wouldn't be safe for you to go into any camp." Colin and his colleagues had been shocked by the murder of a prisoner in the Medicine Hat camp. "Word spreads, so even sending you to another camp wouldn't help. We have a few options, if you're willing to work. As an officer you are not required to, of course, but you may choose to do so. You could work on a farm or in a lumber camp."

Erich was pleasantly surprised. "But my family has a farm! And we make fine wine."

"Excellent! I'll find a farmer who's willing to take you on. Most are desperate for help."

"I will not be locked up?"

"No. It helps that you've never tried to escape, but you must now give your word that you never will."

"You have it!" Erich grinned broadly, then asked boldly, "If Germany wins or loses, may I stay in Canada?"

"We'll see... Now, since you're not being punished, you may have your belongings while you're waiting in here. And I've brought you a book. One of mine, actually, if you're interested in learning some Canadian history."

Erich accepted it gratefully. "Oh yes! Thank you! Very impressive."

"You may keep it."

"You are most kind, Major Sutcliffe. I look forward to not being your enemy."

"As do I, Erich. Is there anything else that would help your stay here?"

"You permit me to have the Gravenhurst newspaper? I like it here very much." And he wanted to know if there were any photos or news of Merilee. The picture of her playing for the Norwegians was falling apart from all the handling.

"Certainly."

"And my friends? Are they not also in danger for being on my side?"

"Not as much, but we *are* transferring them to another camp."

"Will you tell them good luck for me?" Erich asked, suddenly feeling forlorn.

As he stood up to leave, Colin patted Erich on the shoulder. "I'll give you a chance to tell them yourself."

•   •   •

Merilee could hardly contain her anxiety for Erich. How would she ever find out what happened to him, if he was safe from renewed attacks by the Nazis? She couldn't sleep for thinking about ways to interrogate her father.

So, at dinner two days later she finally blurted out, "Dad, you've said that some of the Germans are nice fellows, but lots of them must be nasty or the war would be over by now."

"Unfortunately, the nasty ones still have control. And they're ruthless."

"Then it must be very hard for decent people. I do remember how friendly people were during our stay in Berlin, like Otto, who would tuck a blossom into my hair when I saw him in the garden, and Frau Beutel, who always insisted she needed help eating the Apfelstrudel and Schwarzwälder Kirschtorte."

Her parents chuckled.

Colin said, "You're quite right. Even here we have issues. There was a fight a few days ago between moderates and 'blacks' – that's how we classify the hard-core Nazis. We're getting more of those zealots coming into camp now. It's changing the atmosphere, and I'm afraid we might have more unpleasant incidents."

"What were they fighting about?" Merilee tried to sound casually curious, while attempting to keep her hands from shaking.

"One chap suggested that Hitler admit defeat to save Germany."

"Gosh! So the others tried to kill him?" She realized her mistake instantly.

Her father eyed her quizzically. "I didn't say that. But they see him as a traitor, so we've locked him up for his own safety until we can transfer him. I believe that he's 'white', although few admit to being completely opposed to Hitler and his regime. Most of the chaps are what we call 'grey'. They're doing their military duty by making things difficult for us by trying to escape or complaining about treatment. But I think that many are happy to be out of the war and just eager to get home to their families – whichever side wins."

He paused and added, "It just occurred to me that you actually met this Luftwaffe pilot last winter, when he was skating on the bay. You said he looked a bit like Drew."

Merilee felt the colour drain from her face as her heart pounded in her ears. "Oh, that fellow! Gosh! He certainly seemed nice enough." She tried to appear indifferent as she buttered her bread and changed the subject.

Knowing that Erich was safe was a tremendous relief, but Merilee was heartbroken thinking she would never see him again. She clung to the faint hope of his words "Not now". In the tearful, sleepless hours of the night, she also felt overwhelming guilt for loving an enemy, lying to her parents, betraying her friends.

She had to bottle up her anguish because no one would understand or sympathize. If she were ever found out, she would be vilified.

So the full-page newspaper advertisement of beaming girls proudly in uniform seemed to mock her daily. "We serve that men may fly" the ad stated, and RCAF recruiters would be in Gravenhurst this week to sign up volunteers for the Women's Division.

It would be one way to assuage her guilt, and perhaps help end the war.

•   •   •

"What about university?" Colin asked.

"Gail is postponing going as well. The RCAF needs dispensers, and she's had plenty of experience in her dad's drugstore." Gail was planning to become a pharmacist, much to her father's surprise. But as he had no sons, he was cautiously optimistic that she might one day take over the business. "I expect we'll have important experiences as well as helping the war effort. And at least I won't be going off alone."

"You might have thought to discuss it with us first," Claire snapped.

"I made a decision, Mum. There was nothing to discuss."

Her parents exchanged glances. Colin said, "It's all very well to be caught up in patriotism and want to help out, but you're still young and have much to learn about life. Working on air force bases will expose you to lots of cocky chaps looking for a good time."

"I'm not that naïve, Dad! I'm almost nineteen and can look after myself." She looked at her parents imploringly. "Dad, you told me that I should keep a diary, but these are life-changing times and I don't just want to observe. I want to participate in the history that will eventually be in one of your books. Like so many of my family and friends."

Colin regarded her wryly. "I do understand. And of course we'll support you. But you can also expect a few lectures before you leave."

She laughed and gave him a grateful hug.

Peggy didn't take the news so calmly. "You signed up? And you didn't even let me talk you out of it? Some friend you are!"

"Peggy! You'll be fine in Toronto. Most of Maxine's classes are at the Conservatory as well, so she'll help you get acquainted with the city and using the streetcars."

"I wasn't thinking about needing help! I was looking forward to our adventure together in the city. Instead, you're going off with Gail."

"I don't suppose we'll be together long. I'm hoping to become a photographer. Anyway, you and Maxine will be chums before you know it. She might even take you home to Guelph some weekends, and you'll surely get extra help from Uncle Max if you want."

"I'll be out of my depth."

"Baloney! You already know the family from Wyndwood. They won't behave any differently at home."

Peggy harrumphed. "You mentioned that they had a *country estate.*"

Merilee grinned slyly and said, "Wait until you see Aunt Ria's place. It looks like a Gothic castle, with grand rooms, including a fabulous conservatory with an indoor swimming pool, sprawling grounds overlooking a ravine, complete with tennis court, a gatehouse where the Graysons live..."

"Stop already! Witch!"

"With a 'b'."

"I didn't say that." Peggy grinned. "But I really will miss you, Merilee. I'm a bit scared."

"Me too."

"Can you still change your mind?"

"Nope. I've taken the Oath and accepted the King's Shilling – which is really just a quarter, but of course, he's on it. Gail and I have to report to the Manning Depot in Ottawa at the beginning of September."

"I think I'd go with you if it weren't for this bum leg. I like the uniform."

They laughed.

As Merilee walked home past the detention block just inside the outer perimeter fence, where she knew Erich was safely housed, she began to sing loudly, "*Row, row, row your boat gently down the stream. Merrily, merrily, merrily, merrily, life is but a dream.*"

Erich felt a rush of love and longing as he heard her, and grabbed his flute. Tears pricked her eyes as "Merilee's Song" drifted out to her.

The next edition of the local newspaper had a flattering if grainy photo of Merilee and an article about her joining up, which impressed and concerned Erich. An accompanying ad listed some of the many jobs women could do, ranging from cooks and clerks to aeroplane mechanics and photographers, which would be just the thing for Merilee. But he hoped to hell she would never be posted overseas. There were whispers that Hitler was developing a new "vengeance weapon" against Britain.

Ottawa: Autumn 1943
Chapter 21

Merilee leaned her head against the top bunk and tried to choke back tears. Gail put her arm around Merilee's shoulders as one of the other girls in the dorm mocked, "Homesick already, Sutcliffe? We've only been here two days."

Amid the chuckles, Gail turned angrily and said, "Merilee just lost a couple of friends."

The bustling dorm fell silent.

"Sorry! I didn't realize..."

It was Colin who had called her, since Claire, too, was devastated.

Peggy had received a cable from Ole Knutsen. Gunnar and Lars had been shot down. No chance they had survived. Details to follow.

"I should be with Peggy," Merilee sobbed to Gail.

"My heart bleeds for her. Gunnar was such a dreamboat." Gail was scared now that Gord McLaughlin was in Britain, and she was determined to snag an overseas posting to be near him.

All Merilee's excitement at this new life in the Air Force was numbed. Somehow, she got through the day – the inspection, the marching and drills, the lectures on etiquette and morals, the aptitude tests, being kitted out for her uniform. She didn't even flinch at the five inoculations that made a couple of the girls faint, although her arm became stiff and painful later.

After dinner, she mustered the courage to call Peggy, who was still at home.

"Saying sorry isn't good enough," Merilee said. "That can't even begin to convey the anguish that I feel for you. They were dear to me as well, but I had no hopes and dreams of a future with them.... I wish I could hug you."

"Me too."

"Is there anything I *can* do?"

There was a long pause at the other end of the crackly line. "No... Even if you were here nothing would change... Just be careful."

"Of course I will."

"I have to go now. Pack for Toronto. I'm moving down on Sunday.... I guess."

Peggy seemed so disconsolate that Merilee hated to break the connection.

"You look after yourself as well."

"Sure."

"He really loved you, Peggy. That's something to treasure."

"We never had a chance!" Peggy howled in pain. "I feel as if my heart's been ripped out!"

Merilee held the phone so tightly that her fingers grew numb. "Oh, Peggy, I can only imagine." As if all her energy were flowing through the line to comfort Peggy, Merilee felt limp. "I'll see you as soon as I have leave."

"Sure."

"Gail says to remember that you have friends who love you.... Especially me."

Another emotional pause. "I can't talk anymore.... Thank you for calling."

Like the other girls in the top bunks, Merilee struggled to get into bed that night, the effects of the injections making them weak and sore. Gail, who was shorter, had the lower bunk, since there were no ladders, and gave Merilee a much needed boost up.

There were forty girls from across the country in the room, most away from home for the first time. A few sobbed in their sleep, one babbled, some snored.

Merilee lay awake thinking about the fun times with the Norwegians, tears trickling down her cheeks. It was almost impossible to believe that Lars and Gunnar were gone forever, their vital, cheerful souls no longer part of this world.

She was gripped with icy dread when she thought of her other friends who were still in danger. Even Bryce was back in her prayers tonight.

She also wept for Erich, who seemed just as lost to her as the Norwegians.

Merilee felt drained as well as ill the next morning as she rolled out of her bunk and almost collapsed. There were plenty of groans and some cursing as the girls did their morning ablutions with swollen and aching arms. Some could barely crawl out of bed.

Merilee wondered if she would ever get used to the lack of privacy, which left no room for modesty.

There were almost three hundred of them in this squadron of new recruits, and their parading this morning was awkward and laughable, had it not been so uncomfortable. But it seemed somehow appropriate to be in physical pain when her spirit was so wounded.

"Don't fluff the interview," Gail advised before they went off to face the Selection Board. "Sounds like lots of girls are hoping to get into photography."

But Merilee's training by a professional photographer – her Aunt Lizzie - on several cameras, including the Speed Graphic used by the military photographers, and the fact that she had her own darkroom at home impressed the Board. She would have liked to bring one of her cameras along, but they were forbidden at the Station.

She *had* brought a portfolio of relevant photos. One was of the Norwegian trio, clad in their summer khaki, frozen forever during a moment of light-hearted camaraderie by the lake. A photo of Anna Neagle entertaining a sea of appreciative convalescent RCAF officers also raised interested eyebrows. One of her favourites was of Chas and Drew, both in uniform, sharing a laugh on the veranda at The Point.

"If I'm not mistaken, that's Air Marshal Thornton," one of the four interviewing officers said.

"Yes, and his son. My cousin."

"You certainly have an eye for composition, Sutcliffe, as well as obvious technical expertise. A good addition to the photography unit, I'd say."

The Board had probably also noticed Billy Bishop in one of the shots. Merilee was worldly enough to realize that her social standing and connections would open doors, and thus, could be a benefit in her role as a WD.

Gail felt somewhat disgruntled with her placement. She told the Board she would do any job that got her posted to Britain, but they said that her experience dispensing drugs was vital, and would keep her in Canada. In any case, girls under 21 were not sent abroad.

On Merilee's first Saturday afternoon off, Sandy invited her to his Rockcliffe Park home. The village to the west of the capital was about halfway to downtown Ottawa, and only a couple of miles from RCAF Station Rockcliffe.

"Gosh, I'm so happy to see you!" Merilee said when he picked her up. "It's been ages!"

"Look at you! In uniform. All grown up."

She giggled. "And feeling homesick already. But this helps!"

"I mostly pine for the cottage."

"I kept missing you in Muskoka."

"I can't get away for more than a week or two. We're really busy. But no one complains," he added with a grin.

"I imagine you're having a ball. I would be!"

"We have a Still Photography unit documenting life across Canada. You could come work for us after the war. In fact, we might be using some of your RCAF photos in our documentaries. We get footage from military film units overseas, and even propaganda films captured from enemy ships."

"I noticed that in the one you did about the ferry pilots. With that classic photo of Elyse and the Spitfire. We were so excited when we saw that at the movies!" The short NFB films were shown before the main picture at cinemas across Canada.

He chuckled. "She was certainly a hit. Fortunately, we also got footage of her flying, because everyone thought she was just a pin-up girl posing as a pilot."

"I'm excited to be playing a more active role in this war now, like the rest of you."

"Did you see *Wings on Her Shoulder*, the doc about the RCAF Women's Division?"

"I didn't, but some of the other girls said it inspired them to join. Were you involved with that?"

"No, but a close friend was on the production team. She'll be glad to know that it's doing its job."

"To recruit us. But also, I hope, to show that it's respectable to be in the air force, and that we're doing important work. Uncle Chas is particularly annoyed about the backlash against women in uniform."

"That's why we made the film. But I think you'll find that's still an issue. You can handle it, Merilee. And don't let men try to pull rank for *favours*."

"Is this my big cousin lecture? I got one from Elyse, too."

He laughed.

"I am so glad you're in Ottawa, because my photography training is at Rockcliffe, so I'll be here until Christmas."

"Then come to visit whenever you choose."

They turned off the main road into a leafy enclave of narrow winding lanes with no curbs or sidewalks. Picturesque houses were tucked into treed lots, and mansions sprawled amidst park-like grounds or were glimpsed behind drystone walls.

"This is surprising!" Merilee said. "It doesn't feel like we're in the city at all."

"We're not really. Rockcliffe Park is actually a separate village."

Between pillars announcing "Wyndcrest", he turned down a long drive beneath an archway of sugar maples to a stone and stucco house with leaded and oriel windows, and a hip roof reminiscent of thatch.

"Oh Sandy, this is... *so* charming!"

"You're surprised it isn't more ostentatious, knowing Dad."

She laughed. "It's certainly more *my* style."

"Country house Tudor Revival, Uncle Freddie calls it. Built in the '20s."

"With a real lake!" Beyond the building she could see lush, terraced gardens and a flagstone path leading down to a dock with an upended canoe lying beside it. "Your dad said there was a pond in the backyard."

Sandy guffawed. "Compared to our Muskoka lake, I suppose. But great for swimming and big enough for a paddle. Which is why he was determined to have this place. Made the widow an offer she couldn't refuse. *He* named it Wyndcrest, of course."

"Does he swim when he's here?"

"Every morning before breakfast, from May to November. It invigorates him."

"Good! I do think your dad takes pleasure from what he has, but I also wonder if he actually has time to truly enjoy it all."

"Is that your mother speaking?" Sandy asked with a wry grin.

She chuckled. "Mum worries that Uncle Jack works too hard. She's never forgotten the hardships of their childhood, and is eternally grateful to him for what he's done for the family. But he could have stopped working so much years ago."

Sandy snorted. "A business deal for Dad is a battle of wits. And he gets more thrills from winning than from anything else. So, don't worry about him."

"OK, then I'll worry about you living with his expectations."

"Ha! You are astute, little cousin, but I feel like I'm finally breaking free from all that. Mum and Granny do help."

"Well, I think you're very strong to resist the pressure, and follow your dreams."

"I detect there's a rebel in you as well. I could hardly believe your parents would let you join up!"

"I presented them with a fait accompli."

He laughed. "A true Wyndham! Come, I'll show you around."

The five-bedroom house was equally delightful inside. A kitchen and office overlooked the front gardens, while the sitting and dining rooms commanded stunning views of the lake, its shoreline already aglow with the changing colours. A deep veranda beckoned. Merilee was delighted to see several of her mother's paintings adorning the walls.

"And this is my magic place," Sandy said, leading her up to the attic.

It was one long room with eyebrow dormer windows piercing the sloping ceilings, the one overlooking the lake much larger than the front one, but both letting in plenty of light. Cameras, projectors, editing and other filmmaking equipment dominated, as this was obviously Sandy's studio.

"Cool! Are you working on your own films as well?"

"Whenever I have a few minutes. I might eventually want to start a production company."

"Didn't your film about the Battle of Britain win Best Short Documentary at the Oscar's last year?"

"I only had a small role in helping to edit that one."

"Good start to your career, though."

"Getting paid for having this much fun is like a bonus." He grinned. "Anyway, I'm assuming your swimsuit is in the bag you brought, so, are you ready for a dip?"

"Sure! I already miss my daily lake swim."

Merilee was surprised that most of the shoreline was wooded, with only a few waterfront homes and docks, and not a single person in sight. Their strokes were all that ruffled the serene water.

"This is amazingly secluded. Almost like your own lake," she said when they sat on the dock basking in the fleeting remnants of summer heat.

"It's some consolation for not being able to spend entire summers at the cottage anymore."

"The price of growing up," she lamented. "Although many of us aren't there now, so it's not the same anyway."

"Joe can hardly wait until this school year ends so he can join up," Sandy said of his younger brother. "He's peeved that he couldn't start flying earlier, like Elyse and Drew did, because of the war."

"Unlike Adam, who figures he'd never have the chance to learn if it *weren't* for the war."

"Well, I certainly wasn't bitten by the flying bug."

"Good thing, so I don't have to worry about you as well!" She told him about Drew's accident.

"We actually filmed a crashed plane in the documentary I did about the rigours of pilot training. Fortunately, the pilot was able to walk away from it. I'm afraid that Joe's rather foolhardy."

"Maybe it's better to be fearless for that kind of job."

"You're probably right…. Alain stopped by to see me a few weeks ago, on his way to his new posting. He's quite content to be based at Gander, Newfoundland, and hunting for U-boats."

Alain de Sauveterre was their Aunt Lizzie's eldest son by her first husband, who was killed in a race car accident a decade ago. Which made Alain the Comte, who owned a chateau and vineyards near Avignon, France, and which Jack had been managing on his behalf. Although who knew what was happening there now.

They heard a rustle along the shore, and turned to see a red fox emerge from the bushes. He glanced around and seemed to notice them, but loped off casually as if unafraid.

"What a handsome animal!" Merilee enthused.

"Mr. Tod is a regular visitor."

"He's missing his jacket and walking stick, though," Merilee joked. She loved Beatrix Potter's tales.

"I expect that some naughty badger or, more likely, groundhog has stolen them."

She laughed. "Saxon keeps most of our wildlife at bay. Strangely, he doesn't mind the squirrels, but seems fascinated by them. It's as if he wishes he could soar through the treetops too, when he watches them. Gosh, I suddenly realize how much I already miss him! My parents I can talk to, but Saxon won't understand why I've deserted him."

"Don't tell them that," he quipped.

She giggled.

"So… we could go downtown for dinner, or I can offer you a tasty tourtière… if you'll help peel potatoes."

"Yummy! Are you baking pies now as well?"

"My cleaning lady, Mme. Fournier, bakes them for me. She's almost as good a cook as Mémé." As well as ensuring that their French was up to scratch, their Wyndham grandmother always provided some traditional French-Canadian cuisine when she visited.

"I haven't had a tourtière since Christmas."

"Meat pie it is then!"

As they walked up the path to the house, Sandy hesitantly said, "There is someone I'd really like you to meet. Would you mind if she joins us this evening?"

"Your fiancé?" Merilee guessed.

"If I'm lucky," he replied with a grin.

"Oh Sandy! Of course I'd love to meet her! Why doesn't she join us for dinner?"

"Are you sure?"

"Absolutely! But I want to know more about her before she arrives."

"I'll meet you on the veranda when we've changed."

He brought a tray of tea and croissants with blueberry jam when he joined her.

"Tasty treats and Muskoka chairs to lounge in remind me of home," Merilee sighed contentedly as she accepted a cup. "And you seem to have a splendid statue on the dock."

He looked to see a Great Blue Heron perched there.

"He often drops by. I call him Herry."

She giggled.

"So... I met Rosemary Whitaker at the Rockcliffe Lawn Tennis Club, up the lake from here, soon after I moved in. I was smitten, but she had a steady boyfriend, so we just became friends. She was fascinated by my work, and anxious to do something useful rather than stay at university, so she applied to the NFB – after a little coaching from me – and got a job doing research. She soon added screenwriting and editing to her resume. Working together, we've become even closer. And then one day she realized that she liked me much better than the other guy, who she discovered is something of a playboy."

"Smart girl!"

"And talented. We make mostly 'non-theatrical' documentaries that end up in schools and libraries and such. But the people who can edit miles of raw footage to produce an electrifying film with a compelling script are the ones whose films end up at the cinema, rather than just in the classroom. Rosemary has that theatrical flair."

"Along with you, I should think!"

"Well, yes," he admitted with a grin. "We make a good team."

"She sounds like a catch. You'd better pop the question soon."

"I will if you approve of her," he jested.

"Hell's bells! What do your parents think?"

"They met Rosemary and her family at the Tennis Club in the spring, where, in fact, Mrs. Whitaker introduced them to Crown Princess Juliana of the Netherlands. She and her children are living nearby for the duration."

"And summer on Lake of Bays, we heard. More royalty in Muskoka."

"Rosemary hails from generations of civil servants dating back to Confederation. Her father's a Deputy Minister and her older brother is with the Wartime Information Board. Her mother is involved in numerous charities and fundraising committees, like Mum."

"They sound like well-entrenched Ottawa elite, so your parents can hardly complain about her pedigree."

He laughed. "They certainly liked Rosemary. I haven't mentioned marriage yet. Might follow your example and present them with a fait accompli," he confided with a grin.

Merilee was a little nervous about meeting Rosemary, afraid that she might be a sophisticated socialite and not the sort of person Merilee would envision for Sandy. Not that he really wanted her approval, of course. So, she was pleasantly surprised when an athletic girl in slacks and sweater arrived on her bicycle. She had fresh good looks unadorned by make-up, her blonde tresses restrained by a floral kerchief tied like a hairband with long ends draping flatteringly down one shoulder.

"I'm delighted to meet you, Merilee! I loved your novel, so I feel privileged to meet the author."

"Gosh! Thanks," Merilee replied, feeling a bit flustered.

Rosemary took a bunch of carrots from her basket and handed them to Sandy, saying, "Fresh from the garden." Then she wrapped her arm about Merilee's and steered her towards the kitchen saying, "We can talk while we prepare the veggies. Sandy can provide drinks and add footnotes as we chatter."

Merilee allowed herself to be embraced by Rosemary's natural charm. By the time they sat down to eat, they were fast friends.

"You said your novel was inspired by the Norwegian pilots, which got me thinking that there must be a story in that," Rosemary pondered. "Don't you agree, Sandy? These young men from a far-off land training in Muskoka so that they can free their homeland. A bit different from the naïve boys who just want to fly."

"Definitely!"

Merilee tried not to break down when she said, "Three of them became good friends. Mum based her illustrations on them. Two have just been killed in action."

"Oh, how tragic!" Rosemary put her hand sympathetically on Merilee's. Looking at Sandy, she said, "We need to pitch this idea."

"I'll help anyway I can," Merilee offered. "I want them to be honoured and remembered."

She could feel their excitement building when she told them about the boys' perilous escapes from occupied Norway, and their long journeys to Muskoka. About Crown Prince Olav and his family occasionally visiting Little Norway, and the camp at Vesle Skaugum. About how fun loving the boys were, yet focussed on their training, and how popular with the love-struck local girls.

"All the elements of a riveting tale! I'll contact the Commander of Little Norway on Monday, and see if we can get this project rolling," Rosemary offered. "Thank you, Merilee. I expect you have some photos we might be able to use."

"Yes, I do! I even have a few here with me. I can give them to Sandy when he drops me off."

"Perfect!" Smiling at Sandy, Rosemary added, "We'll be filming in your favourite summer place, and I'll finally see the inspiration for these enchanting paintings of Muskoka."

"You could stay at Hope Cottage!" Merilee offered. "My parents would love to have you there."

"That would be delightful! I'm a big fan of theirs."

"And you'll be interested to see the POW camp right next door! Not that you'd ever be able to do a film about that. People would be angry to know that the Germans swim in the lake and have a farm miles away from the camp that they manage with little supervision. Not how our prisoners are treated in Germany, I fear. But Dad says it actually helps our guys if we treat the Germans well. And they're not all Nazis." She needed to add that for Erich's sake, and felt a sharp pang of sorrow. Where was he now? Was he safe? Would she ever see him again?

Sandy looked awkward as he said, "We sometimes make films that aren't for general distribution, but help the war effort. Can't say any more, but don't even pass that tidbit along."

Rosemary insisted on riding her bicycle home despite Sandy's protest, so he and Merilee followed her in the car for the few blocks to be sure she arrived safely. She waved them goodbye at the gates of her family's estate.

"I approve," Merilee said when they were on their way to her barracks. "Wholeheartedly! I hope she says yes."

Sandy laughed.

Two days later he called her and said, "Save the date. October 30th. Rosemary doesn't want a big production that takes a year to organize, which is another reason I love her."

•   •   •

Rockcliffe,
Friday, Sept. 17, 1943
Dear Peggy,

I'm so glad that Aunt Ria has taken you under her wing, and feel a little less guilty for deserting you. It's also sweet of Vera and the other kids to make you feel at home in "the castle", as you call it, and ensure you don't get lost. And yes, you are welcome to claim my relatives as your own! After all, I think of you as a sister.

I'm not surprised that Uncle Max provided you and Maxine with a baby grand for your flat. You both need to practice, and just any old piano obviously won't do.

I so agree that there is much solace in music.

I had a letter from Ned as well about his weekend at Quincy Castle with Hugh's grandparents. His description of the ancient plumbing and trying to wash amid alternate bursts of steam and ice slayed me. Gail went into gales (haha, sorry) of laughter as well when I read that to her. I'm so glad that Ned and Hugh have become friends. I heard from Elyse that they've also visited her. She finds Ned "refreshingly down-to-earth – a real peach of a chap." I'm not surprised.

He said he was proud of me, but sorry that I was in the Forces now, as Big Red would be idle, and Saxon would be pining for me. But of course, that would also be the case if I were at university, so I know it's his way of expressing concern. I'll reassure him that I'm safe and happy and stuck in Canada, and that Neddy the teddy managed to stow away in my suitcase. Should I mention Gail's advice that in order to avoid "trouble" we should keep our legs crossed? Yes, she's a riot!

We're halfway through our Basic Training, and actually starting to look like "Airwomen" (AWs). We can march in unison now, although our Warrant Officer – a bear of a fellow with a wry sense of humour – despaired of our mincing steps at the beginning, which he blamed on "high-heel syndrome". Our shoes are now sensible Oxfords, perfect for authoritative strides.

A new batch of recruits comes in every week, and we seasoned girls laugh as we watch their squadron stumble about for those first days. Some girls really don't know their left foot from their right!

It's been impressed upon us that we're subject to the same military discipline, rules, and regulations as the men, and that we shouldn't expect any special treatment. But since we only get two-thirds of the men's pay, Gail thinks that allows us leeway for complaints, if nothing else. But of course, we daren't seem like wimps, although some of the girls are struggling to keep their hair the required inch above the collar <u>and</u> look good. So, we've had lessons on sausage-roll hairdos.

I have to say that we're well treated. Our officers are crackerjacks, and the food is surprisingly good and plentiful – no rationing here!

Our uniforms are expertly tailored so that they fit beautifully, and we feel chuffed to wear our "Air Force Blues". I have finally mastered the art of tying a tie and polishing brass buttons. We have regulation shorts and tee-shirts for sports, "Teddy bear" suits – overalls – for cleaning, greatcoats and raincoats, and "glamour boots" which are anything but.

Now that we feel like AWs, it's great fun to go into Ottawa and practice our saluting, there being so many officers about. And gosh, I never realized the complexities of saluting – to whom, where, when, how! Gail joked that maybe we should salute the doorman at the Chateau Laurier since he has "scrambled eggs" (gold braid) on his hat!

It's really beautiful here now that autumn has painted the countryside in cheerful colours. Our Station sprawls on a bluff above the airfield, which is beside the Ottawa River, with its stunning backdrop of the Gatineau Hills rolling away to a distant purple haze.

We have plenty of time off - every weekday evening, and weekends from noon on, unless we're on fatigues - so a bunch of us are going hiking in the hills tomorrow if the weather holds.

Gail and I do get homesick, but at least we're still together for another couple of weeks. Then she's being sent to Toronto for a short course on dispensing drugs – since she already has experience – after which she'll be posted to a Station hospital somewhere in Canada.

Fortunately, we have made a new friend who will be in my photography course. Stella Talbot is from Orillia. Practically neighbours! She was so excited to connect with us, as she's rather shy. Her father has a small photo shop and studio, so she has more experience with cameras and processing than I do.

Since – ironically – we're not allowed to take photos, I've enclosed a sketch of our barracks. Notice the thin mattresses on our rows of iron bunk beds, but also how precisely tidy everything is. We have to constantly clean and polish, because we'll be on the carpet if we can't discipline our things as well as ourselves. One girl figured no one would notice her un-ironed blouse since it's under her tunic, so she only pressed the collar. Darned if the inspecting officer didn't ask her – and only her – to remove her jacket. She's confined to barracks for three days and has to scrub our room from top to bottom every evening while we play ping-pong or watch movies. The military doesn't mess around.

Merilee related her visit to Sandy and mentioned that he and his fiancé would be producing an NFB documentary about the Norwegians.

Uncle Chas is in Ottawa so much with his BCATP work that he keeps a suite at the Chateau Laurier Hotel. He invited the three of us and Sandy and Rosemary out to a posh dinner there yesterday. The surprise was that Drew was there as well! He's in Trenton now, and flew his dad up just to get some time in the air. Gail and Stella were knocked sideways by my handsome cousins. I thought Stella would hardly get through her meal. Billy Bishop stopped by our table to say hello, which only added to her wide-eyed awe.

Uncle Chas has offered to do the inspection for our Graduation Parade, which I'm sure must delight our officers as well. The press will be good for our reputation, since some civilians still don't approve of women in the forces, even though the Governor General's wife, Princess Alice, is our Honorary Air Commandant. Can you *believe that there are stores in Ottawa where they either serve us last or ignore us completely? A middle-aged woman jostled Stella in a coffee shop the other day, and muttered "Slut!" Poor Stella turned beet red and almost wept.*

Anyway, it was wonderful to see Drew and Uncle Chas and feel another connection to home. They thought we looked very smart and professional in our uniforms. They, of course, are incredibly debonair in theirs – as Gail didn't fail to mention afterwards. She was so sweet on Drew that I had to remind her that she and Gord are practically engaged. Haha!

We'll be getting three more inoculations – ouch! - at the end of Basic Training and then a "48", which means two whole days off! So, my parents and Saxon will meet me in Toronto on that Friday evening, and I can spend time with you at Wyndholme!

Because he's going to be here anyway, Uncle Chas has offered to fly the three of us down to Toronto to save us spending most of that weekend on the train. He said that we newly minted Airwomen with wings on our shoulders should fly at least once in our military careers. He has staff pilots and planes at his disposal, since he travels to the various training bases across the country. What a thrill that will be!

I'll be winging your way soon, my dearest friend!

●   ●   ●

"Their squadron does anti-submarine patrols and attacks on German ships along the coast and in the fjords of Norway," Peggy told Merilee when they were lying in their beds at Wyndholme. "Ole said that they did a lot of damage to the German fleet on this sortie, but Lars's Mosquito suffered a direct hit from anti-aircraft guns…. And exploded."

Peggy gasped on a sob and Merilee's body clenched in pain.

"Gunnar's plane was hit as well, but didn't seem to be badly damaged. His navigator signalled that their communications were out, but that they were OK and heading back to base."

There was anguished silence. "But it's a long way to Scotland. Almost 500 miles. Ole stayed close as Gunnar's plane slowly lost altitude. Then his engines stopped. Before Gunnar and his navigator could bail out, they fell into a deadly spin. As Ole followed them down, he prayed that Gunnar could pull out of it, but they plunged into the treacherous North Sea. Ole's navigator radioed in the position. It was a wild day with mountainous waves. Ships in the vicinity found nothing."

"It sounds like a nightmare," Merilee managed to say between sniffles. Saxon rose from his bed on the floor and whimpered as he put his head inquisitively beside hers. She gave him a thankful rub.

"If only I could wake up and find it so.... Do you know what I wish? That we'd made love," Peggy whispered into the darkness. "So that we could have had that one ecstatic moment together. So that he didn't die a virgin."

"Do you think he was? Aren't guys expected to 'sow their wild oats' before settling down? Isn't that why it's bad to be the girls they practice on?"

"I expect that Bryce is no slouch in that area!... Anyway, it's not the same if you're practically engaged." After a long pause, Peggy added, "And what does it really matter these days? Moments are perhaps all we have."

Merilee was concerned that Peggy, already slight, had lost weight and was listless, so she made sure to find enjoyable distractions on Saturday. Maxine, who was staying with her grandparents around the corner, came over to Wyndholme along with Amy and Adam. They had a pool party in the fabulous conservatory that housed the indoor pool. After a wiener roast and ice cream floats on the sunny terrace, they played a riotous game of croquet in the sunken garden. The evacuees were excited when Merilee suggested hide-and-seek among the many nooks and crannies of the old mansion as darkness descended. Mrs. Grayson provided the usual feast – despite rationing – which was followed by music and cards.

When they lay in bed that night, Merilee steered the conversation to Ned, so they ended up laughing as they shared tidbits from his letters.

There were tearful farewells after lunch on Sunday, since Merilee wouldn't be home again until her course ended at Christmas. She met up with Stella at Union Station for the long train ride back to Ottawa. Back to a new life.

•   •   •

"It's a glorious afternoon for a photo shoot," Stella said eagerly as she entered their room.

Once their Basic Training was over, the girls had moved to barracks at the other end of the Upper Station, along with those who were staying on for courses in various trades. Merilee and Stella had snapped up a small corner room with two windows and only one bunk bed. They welcomed the privacy.

Neither had expected how technical some of the subjects in their photography course would be. After the first lecture, which was on "Light and Colour", one of the girls had immediately decided to become a clerk. The rest realized they had plenty of hard work ahead of them. Of the thirty students in the class, only seven were men.

The huge F-24 aerial camera weighed 45 pounds, and they had to know everything about it, including how to install it in planes and teach the airmen how to use it, and how to fix it if something went wrong. They would also need to process the miles of film collected by it and "camera guns".

More fun were the assignments on the Speed Graphic. This latest was to take five photos that were representative of life at the Rockcliffe Station. Merilee had risen early and surprised the bugler when she took a picture of him playing reveille in the misty autumn dawn. Later she captured the station mascot, "Sergeant Pawter", using his sheep-dog instincts to encourage the raw WD recruits to march in unison during morning parade.

"I'm ready!" Merilee said, collecting her gear.

It was a pleasant walk across a meadow and through the fragrant woods edging the top of the rocky cliff that separated the Upper and Lower Station. The last few spicy leaves fluttered from the trees.

As Stella took a shot of planes taking off, Merilee caught one of Stella intent with her camera, against the backdrop of the busy airfield. Of course, they ran into classmates scrambling about, jokingly telling each other not to bother snapping certain subjects since they already had the perfect picture.

Because there weren't enough dark rooms in the school for all the students, Merilee and Stella waited until after supper to process their films, not interested in attending the weekly dance in the drill hall. Merilee was not in the mood, and Stella, who was self-conscious about her dancing, was usually a wallflower.

Merilee was back in her room and assembling her project when Stella returned, looking pale and stricken.

"What's happened?"

"Nothing... I... just got spooked walking back."

"Sorry I didn't wait for you."

"I didn't expect you to."

Although the Photo School was at the other end of the Upper Station, the paths were well lit.

"How did your pics turn out?" Merilee asked, eyeing Stella worriedly. She wasn't carrying anything.

"Um... OK... I guess." She tried to suppress a moan as she sank onto her lower bunk and hugged herself tightly.

"Please tell me what's wrong, Stella."

Tears trickled down her cheeks as Stella sobbed, "I was just coming out of the darkroom when he grabbed me and pushed me back inside!"

"Oh my God! Who?" Merilee sat down and put her arm about Stella, who was now shaking uncontrollably.

"Corporal Bottomley." He was one of their older classmates, who had remustered from Transport. Merilee found him a belligerent know-it-all, who scoffed at women being in the forces.

"What did he do to you?"

Stella hung her head.

"Tell me!"

"He... touched my... private parts."

"Bloody hell!"

"I told him to stop, but he just laughed and said I had to obey orders since he was my superior."

"Not those kinds of orders! How did you get away from him?"

"I screamed and scratched his face. He called me a stupid bitch, and warned me not to say anything, since it would be my word against his. That I'd get chucked out when he told everyone I was a whore."

Merilee was livid as she tried to comfort her weeping friend. "No one would believe that! Let's go tell our C.O."

"I feel so... dirty!"

"It's not your fault."

"I just want to go home."

"You mustn't let him get away with this, Stella, or he'll keep doing it to you or other girls. It could be even worse next time."

After a cascade of tears, Stella nodded listlessly. And then panicked. "Oh no, I left my photos behind!"

"I'll fetch them in the morning."

Fortunately, the barracks was quiet, as most of the other girls were at the dance or in town, it being Saturday, when curfew was extended until 12:30 AM. The WD officers had their own accommodations nearby, fondly known as the "henhouse", and Merilee was thankful that one of them was in.

A university graduate and former high school teacher, Flying Officer Mary Glendenning was only in her late twenties, but carried a heavy responsibility for all her "chicks" at the Station. She welcomed them into the small sitting room.

"We're sorry to disturb you, Ma'am, but something terrible has happened to Stella," Merilee began. "I thought it best to come directly to you."

F/O Glendenning was appalled as the story unfolded. "I don't know how to put this delicately... Was there any... penetration... by his fingers or... otherwise?"

Stella blushed furiously. "No, Ma'am. Just... groping," she mumbled on an anguished gasp.

"That's a relief! Not acceptable behaviour, of course, but it could have been worse. Thank you for your courage, Talbot. I will ensure that this is appropriately and swiftly handled. Would you like a few days of sick leave at the hospital? To regain your composure?"

"Thank you, Ma'am, but I'd rather carry on."

"Well done! Try not to let this discourage you. You're an exemplary member of the Air Force. And don't feel blame or shame."

"Will others have to know?"

"Just the relevant officers. Although we all want to see fitting punishment for this type of behaviour, it's generally not easy to prove. Not that I doubt your word, Talbot, but testifying at a court martial will undoubtedly be even more difficult than trying to put all this behind you."

"Yes, Ma'am."

Corporal Bottomley was not in class on Monday morning, and his colleagues heard that he had returned to Transport to be posted overseas.

A couple of other girls seemed to step more gaily, and there was generally a more congenial atmosphere in the class. They pulled together to help each other through the increasingly difficult bi-weekly tests and celebrated when all succeeded.

But Stella was haunted. Merilee could understand, since the Nazi Geisler terrorized her in heart-pounding nightmares. That's when she hugged Neddy closer to her.

England: Autumn 1943
Chapter 22

"Terrific! Our thirteenth op and they're sending us to Happy Valley," rear gunner "Dicey" Dyson grumbled as Ned's crew left squadron briefing.

"Thirteen's my lucky number," Ned assured them. As pilot, he was the "Skipper", the one ultimately responsible for ensuring that his men worked efficiently and happily as a team. Since he was just twenty-one, that often felt weird, considering that half his crew were older.

In the relaxed and equitable Canadian manner, Ned and Hugh Carrington, although officers, socialized with their five NCO mates – a practice not allowed by the RAF. But luckily, they were with RCAF Bomber Group #6 in Yorkshire. So they bonded over beers at local pubs, even if they couldn't dine together in the Mess, and had adopted the motto "All for one and one for all".

"Yeah? Give me an example," Dicey demanded.

"Well, when I asked WAAF Hobson to dance for the thirteenth time, she finally agreed."

The others chuckled.

"Oh, and my birthday is April 13."

"I'm counting on that to keep the gremlins at bay."

"We've already made sure they're not coming with us," Ned said, for they had done the detailed pre-flight check of their Halifax bomber earlier. It was always comforting to be in their own, familiar aircraft, lovingly maintained by their loyal ground crew.

Despite his happy-go-lucky attitude, Ned was feeling apprehensive about flying into the jaws of hell tonight, along with over 600 other aircraft. The industrial Ruhr Valley was notorious.

As he settled into the cockpit, he patted the small painting of Big Red that Merilee had sent him as a good-luck charm. There was also a photo of her next to his heart.

The aerial armada formed up over the North Sea, which was always an impressive sight. It was reassuring to be part of such an enormous gaggle, yet not without its dangers. From their Perspex bubbles, the gunners kept a close watch for potential collisions, as well as the inevitable German fighters that would prey on them once they neared the Dutch coast. Eyes straining, they scanned the starry night for a darker shape that might suddenly plummet towards them.

As usual, flaming aircraft fell out of the sky as flak soared up and "bandits" picked off other targets. Fragile puffs of parachutes blossomed from at least some dying planes.

"Navigator, note time of collision to starboard," Ned instructed over the intercom. It was particularly sad when they inadvertently knocked each other out of the sky.

One of Hugh's jobs was to drop "window" through a chute. This was packets of hundreds of strips of tinfoil – much of it collected by children - that would burst in the slipstream and confuse the German radar.

The barrage of flak became intense as they neared the Ruhr, which was reputedly protected by 10,000 anti-aircraft guns. Hundreds of frantic searchlights stabbed at them as the air crackled and scorched with continuous fireworks, and the Halifax shuddered and bucked from nearby explosions. Hell seemed to be bubbling red and hot and smoky below them.

Ned had to fly straight and level for the bombing run. "Bomb doors open," he said.

"Left... steady... steady," replied the bomb-aimer. "On target... Bombs away!"

The plane seemed to jump for joy at the release of the two 1,000 pound high explosive bombs. Several more nerve-wracking seconds to drop hundreds of incendiary bombs and take the photograph showing they were on target. Now they could hightail it for home.

Like a bolt of lightning, the dreaded radar-controlled master searchlight suddenly speared them, and dozens of others then latched on to "cone" their plane, spotlighting it for every German gunner for miles around, which spelled almost certain destruction.

"Hang on, boys, we're going on a roller-coaster!" Ned said as he threw the plane into a stomach-churning, corkscrewing dive. His worst nightmare had finally become reality.

Flak banged against the aircraft like angry demons demanding entry, and banshee shells screamed around them, while their own Hercules engines roared defiantly. There was nothing for the others to do, except pray. They had seen too many coned aircraft blown to smithereens.

The plane juddered from the wild ride as the flight engineer, "Yorkie", calmly read out their altitude. "Fourteen... thirteen... twelve... six... five."

At 4000 feet they finally escaped the blinding lights into welcome darkness. Levelling out, Ned breathed a tremendous sigh of relief and asked, "Everyone OK?" as Yorkie went to check the fuselage for damage.

"That was one helluva ride, Skipper. Thanks! Wet my pants, though," rear gunner Dicey replied.

"Upper-mid gunner OK, Skipper."

"Bomb-aimer OK."

"Navigator here. Picked up some shrapnel in the arm."

"How bad is it?" Ned asked.

"Just a scratch, I think."

"WAG reporting a leg injury. Not gushing blood, though, Skipper," Hugh Carrington assured Ned.

Yorkie went to check on him, as the navigator instructed, "Turn onto heading three-one-two."

"OK. Three-one-two... For home," Ned responded. "Stay alert, boys. We're not out of the woods yet." The German night fighters were still out there waiting to pounce.

Yorkie clambered back into the cockpit to report, "The kite's riddled with holes, but it doesn't look like anything vital's been hit. Other than our WAG. Broken leg, I'd say, as well as some shrapnel wounds. I've patched him up as best I can."

"Skipper to WAG. Can you manage, Hugh?"

"AOK, Ned. I'll race you on our bikes when we get back." They all had bicycles for getting around the base and escaping from it when they had time.

"You're on!"

As Ned started to climb, the outer starboard engine suddenly caught fire. He told Yorkie to extinguish the flames and feather the motor, which would now be useless. He hoped to hell that they didn't have to do any more drastic evasive manoeuvres.

And then the outer port engine quit.

"Feather outer port," he ordered, his stomach sinking. "Well, guys, I'm going to try to get back to England on two engines, but you can choose to bail." He figured that Hugh couldn't jump in his state, so there was no choice for the two of them.

"Not leaving my cozy turret to be greeted by angry Krauts," Dicey stated.

"I'll take my chances in our kite, Skipper," the other gunner added.

"I'm not giving up my egg!" the bomb-aimer said. The crews looked forward to their welcome home meal of bacon and egg.

"I'll give you a fix on the closest airfield," the navigator offered.

"Thanks, team. But have your parachutes at the ready."

The tension in the aircraft was palpable as they limped like an arthritic old lady toward the Belgian coast, Yorkie watching for signs of the engines overheating, the gunners keeping a sharp eye out for bandits, Hugh scanning his "fishpond" radar for ominous blips. Flying so low and in a different direction from most of the returning bomber stream, they must have surprised the ack-ack guns, since they didn't encounter much flak.

Ned cursed as an engine coughed. They'd never make it back on one. But it settled down as Yorkie made some adjustments. The straining motors had been gulping fuel, but they should make it to England, he assured Ned.

"Skipper to crew. Make sure your Mae Wests are on properly," Ned ordered, referring to their inflatable life jackets. "Just have to hop over the puddle now. No dozing off," he jested.

Once they were over the Channel, and no longer had to maintain radio silence, Hugh was able to contact the emergency airfield at Manston, north of Dover, to get permission to land.

They had to wait their turn as other damaged aircraft were also eager to touch down, one with an engine ablaze, some with critically injured crew. Despite everything, Ned made a perfect landing. It had been over nine hours since they had left their Yorkshire base, and dawn was creeping in with rosy promise. "Well, that was a shaky-do," he said into the welcome silence.

"Shaky? It was fucking terrifying!" Dicey piped up.

"You saved our skin, Skipper," the navigator applauded. "My mother, my future wife and unborn children will be eternally grateful."

"Brilliant flying, Ned," Hugh agreed, his voice tight with pain. "Now if someone could help me out of here, I could sure use my tot of rum." That was the custom for returning bomber crews, and never more welcome than this time.

Ned stepped out into the fresh new day, exhaustion and aching muscles overshadowed by the sheer joy of being alive, of seeing another sunrise. What he wouldn't give right now to be savouring that again over the lake in Gravenhurst. In his mind's eye, Merilee was at his side.

It was sobering and tragic to discover that 34 aircraft had been lost on that mission – 238 men who didn't get to enjoy their victory breakfast. His crew could so easily have been added to the carnage.

Hugh's ankle and shin were fractured. It would be months before he would heal, and his mates, especially Ned, were sad to lose him. Crews felt superstitious when they had to take on a "spare bod", often a sprog with little experience.

Ned was immediately awarded a DFC - Distinguished Flying Cross – for his superb flying skills, which had saved his men.

"Well deserved!" Hugh said when Ned visited him in hospital. "I wrote a glowing letter to Merilee describing your heroics," he added with a grin.

Hugh had guessed his secret, and had urged Ned to romance her, admitting that his lothario brother, Bryce, certainly didn't deserve her.

"Not heroic at all. Just the instinct to survive."

"I'm forever indebted to you, my friend."

Ned shuffled awkwardly at the sentiment. "We're converting to Lancasters, so we'll be off ops for a while."

"Thank God for that! So, you'll have a chance to properly train a new WAG. I was feeling guilty leaving you all in the lurch with a spare bod. The doc said I might be grounded when I do get back on my feet. The ankle could be tricky."

"I'd be happy for you! One less friend to worry about," Ned admitted with a smile. "We're starting a week's leave. The others are spending it in London, but I just want to be somewhere quiet, so I'm going for a seaside retreat to Cornwall. Merilee's been captivated by it since she read Daphne du Maurier's books, so I thought... well, I can tell her about it. Send her postcards."

"Great idea! Pick up a souvenir for her and I'll take it back with me. They're shipping me home soon. So, I'm going to ask Ginnie to marry me. I'm not wasting any more time." Hugh and Ginnie Roland – eldest daughter of Drs. Ellie and Troy – had been dating before he left, and had grown closer through their many letters.

Ned thought it strange that he had actually met Ginnie a few times when he'd visited Peggy at the Children's Retreat, where Dr. Ellie's three daughters helped out. "Good for you!"

"Take note."

"I will... if I get the chance."

Ottawa Valley: Fall and Winter 1943
Chapter 23

Erich held the newspaper gingerly, afraid it might tear if he allowed his joy and sorrow to grasp it too tightly. It was a photo of Merilee being congratulated by Air Marshal Thornton at her Graduation Parade. How smart and grown-up she looked in her uniform. How beautiful she was.

His heart broke to think that he might never see her again.

He was in the Valley outside of Ottawa. And so close to Merilee. The article mentioned that she would be doing her photography training there. He fantasized visiting Canada's capital and running into her. He wanted to gaze into her eyes once again and assure her of his love.

Stoneridge Farm, where he worked, overlooked fields and thickets sloping to a distant plain bisected by a river and a railroad. Erich delighted in the echoing train whistles, and the locomotives puffing along, so small they appeared to be mere toys. The eastbound ones stopped in the nearby village of Todmorden before heading to the city. A thought that taunted him.

As if guarding its back, the land behind the farm reared up, rocky and bristly with dense scrub yielding to scraggly woodland. An old logging road twisted uphill just beyond the farm. A shallow, tree-lined creek wended its way from the ridge through the farm and fields down to the river, also beckoning him to follow.

RCAF Harvards regularly flew overhead, so there was obviously a training airfield nearby, which made him long to fly again, and see this vast country from the air.

Erich relished his relative freedom, for the fences only kept in the livestock, but the farmer had advised him not to wander beyond the hundred acres alone because locals might think he was an escaped prisoner, and possibly even take a pot shot at him. "There's a couple of troublemakers 'round here," Mr. McKellar had warned.

It hadn't taken long for Erich to encounter them. He and the black-and-white collie, Patch, had been mending a roadside fence in one of the pastures when two teens rode past on bicycles. Noticing his POW-marked denims, they'd skidded to a halt on the gravel and picked up stones, which they hurled at him, shouting obscenities.

Erich had ducked, but a few had hit him on the arm and shoulder. Patch had raced up to the fence, barking madly.

"Shut the fuck up, you Nazi-loving mutt, or I'll brain you!" one of louts yelled.

"My war ended three years ago. You will be in trouble if you hurt the dog or me," Erich had said as calmly and authoritatively as he could. He reached down to reassure Patch, narrowly avoiding a dangerous missile that sailed over his head.

Erich picked up a small branch that Patch had brought him earlier, and was poised to use it like a baseball bat.

"Who'd believe a fuckin' Kraut? Eh? Eh?" the lout had demanded, coming closer to the fence, weighing a hefty rock as he grinned maliciously. "They'll make me a hero if I kill an escaped prisoner."

"They'll string you up if you kill anybody," Lloyd McKellar pronounced as he came up behind the boys. He'd been working in the next field and had heard the shouting. "And I'll have your guts for garters if you hurt my dog or any of my animals."

"Jeez, Mr. McKellar, you scared the shit outa me!"

"Good, because you're too full of it, Wes Skuce."

"Just tryin' to do my bit to win the war."

"Then go work in a munitions factory. Or join the merchant marine. You're sixteen now, aren't you? Old enough. Now clear off, and don't come threatening my farmhand or my dog again. Next time I'll call the cops."

"Asshole!" Skuce had shouted over his shoulder as he and his younger brother had raced away.

"You OK, lad?" Lloyd McKellar had asked Erich.

"Thank you, yes."

"The Skuce family are a bad lot. Live just down the road."

"They are the kind that make good Nazis."

Lloyd snorted. "Well that's scary as hell."

Erich had bolted his door that night.

He'd been given a decaying log cabin to live in – the original dwelling for the McKellar family who had settled the land over a century earlier. It had taken a lot of work to reclaim it from encroaching nature, but it was now serviceable, with salvaged windows, a bed and dresser in one corner, table and chair in another, a washstand that he'd cobbled together, and a fireplace that was finally drawing properly, with enough firewood stacked up to ward off the cool, autumn nights. There was a kettle to heat water, and a zinc tub he could fill for baths and to wash his clothes. He sure as hell wasn't looking forward to winter, despite having stuffed newspaper and straw into the gaps between the logs where chinking had long ago disappeared. He read by oil lamps in the evenings, and used the outhouse perched close to the barn.

He didn't mind the long days dealing with the horses, cattle, and sheep, working in the fields, gathering apples from the small orchard, chopping wood, and myriad other tasks. He felt stronger and healthier for the physical labour. But he desperately missed his pals, the orchestra, the classes, and indeed, the company of others, especially those with whom he had interests and customs in common.

The amiable farmer had explained why Erich had been relegated to the long-abandoned cabin.

"Winnie had a newborn to look after as well as helping my folks out on the farm when I went off to war. Luckily, I was wounded out before long. Still have bits of shrapnel coming out of my arms," he'd chortled. "Our brothers were best friends, and both were killed at Passchendaele. It's why Winnie doesn't trust you yet, lad. But she'll come round. She's fair-minded. Then she'll spoil you."

"She does already. The food is excellent."

"She doesn't stint. But it's no fun eating alone."

Erich arrived at the kitchen door for meals, where Mrs. McKellar silently handed him a tray to take back to his cabin. She always avoided eye contact.

"Do you have sons in the war?"

"Our boy, the third-born, died of pneumonia when he was two. So, we have three daughters, with a big gap between the first two and Sally," Lloyd McKellar had explained. "Our eldest, Marlene, quit nursing when she landed a doctor, and she's too good to come back to the farm now. Anyways, they live in Vancouver. We've never seen our grandkids, 'cept in pictures." He'd tapped the ash vigorously out of his pipe.

"Aileen's a city girl. Went to secretarial college and landed a dandy job in the government. Said her job would be waiting for her and went off to join the RCAF to do her bit. She's a sergeant now, stationed in Halifax. The notions girls have these days!" he'd snorted, shaking his head. "So we're hoping Sally will marry a farm boy, and eventually take over from Winnie and me."

"She loves the farm, I think," Erich had observed. The eleven-year-old cheerfully performed her chores before and after school, feeding the dozens of hens and collecting their eggs, slopping the pigs, singing as she milked Bluebell the cow, weeding and harvesting the extensive kitchen garden. With Patch proudly at her side, she drove the horse and buggy the two miles into Todmorden every Saturday morning to deliver eggs and surplus vegetables to the general store and individual customers.

"Yup! She has a way with the animals. The hens lay better when she's around."

"She talks with love, and they understand, I believe."

Lloyd McKellar had chuckled. "Yup, she's quite the gal."

A knock on the door interrupted Erich's thoughts. Hastily, he hid the clipping of Merilee in the bureau.

He opened the door a crack to find Sally standing there, glancing warily behind her. "Hurry and let me in before Ma spots me!" She slipped in like an eel, saying, "Phew!"

"You are breaking the rules again."

"Hello to you, too!" she retorted. "Nice greeting for someone who's risked her freedom to bring you this!" She handed him a book and waited eagerly for his reaction. She wasn't disappointed.

"The Curse of the Thunder King!" Erich was thrilled. He had already devoured the *Enchanted Waterfall* series, which the McKellars owned. Sally had been surprised at his interest in the kids' books, but he'd explained how grateful he was to the author, Major Sutcliffe, for helping him. And that he actually *did* enjoy the books and the gorgeous illustrations.

"It was finally in the library, but I have to return it in two weeks. And I should read it, too, so I can say how good or crappy it is. So, I need it back in a week. I'm *still* on the waiting list for the latest Nancy Drew mystery," she grumbled.

"This is wonderful! Thank you, Miss Sally!"

"Why won't you call me Scamp?! I like my nickname better than *Sally,* which sounds so silly!!"

"What means Scamp?"

"What does Scamp mean?" she said automatically. He'd asked her to correct his English.

"What does Scamp mean?" he repeated dutifully.

"It means a mischievous person." At his puzzled look she added, "Not bad, but a bit naughty."

"You have knots?"

She burst into laughter. "A different naughty." She spelled it for him. "Like me coming here when I'm not supposed to." She grinned broadly.

"Ach so!"

"I see."

"I see…. But not with my eyes." He frowned.

"It means 'I understand'. Or you can say 'I get it'."

"OK, I get it!"

"Bang on!" she giggled, and explained, "Correct."

He laughed and shook his head.

Scamp had a pixie cut because she hated having hair dangling in her face when she was working. It suited her slender features and large, intelligent brown eyes, as well as her impish personality.

For a skinny kid, she was surprisingly strong, and managed to hold her own with the Herefords.

"Why are you looking at me like that?" she challenged. "Like you're examining a weird bug."

He snorted. "You do not treat yourself with kindness."

"*Treat yourself kindly*," she corrected. "I realize I'm kinda strange. The other girls want to win the baking and sewing competitions at the fair, but I just want to collect ribbons for the best calves in show." She shrugged.

"I like you as you are. You're about the age of my sister Trudi, the last time I saw her. So I feel homesick," Erich admitted.

"I've always wanted a big brother! Mine died a long time before I was born. May I think of you as my brother?"

"I would be honoured, Miss... Scamp. I promise to look after you, as I would Trudi."

She giggled. "Best not tell Ma or Pa yet. Ma's worried that if I'm friendly to you I might be 'consorting with the enemy'."

"She thinks that I am perhaps a dangerous man."

"I've watched you with the animals. You truly care about them. Patch is a good judge of character and he likes you, so you can't be evil."

"He is also a *loyal* – yes? - friend."

"He sure is!"

A knock on the door startled them both. They looked at each other in panic.

Erich went to answer.

"May I come in?" Lloyd McKellar asked. "I know Scamp's here."

She stepped out from behind the door.

"I was just bringing Erich a book."

"I'm not going to punish you. It was Ma's order that you weren't supposed to talk to Erich, which is tommyrot, but don't tell her I said so." He grinned lopsidedly. "And that doesn't matter now, since she's decided to invite Erich to supper tonight. He's been working like a champion, without complaints, and Ma finally realizes that he's not going to kill us in our beds. I told her that Nazis at Erich's camp almost hanged him for criticizing Hitler, and she turned on me in a snit and demanded why didn't I mention that in the first place."

"They did?" Scamp shrieked in alarm.

"I said that Germany was losing the war so why not surrender before more of our families were killed. But I was rescued by a bear and my friends." He related bits of the story, without mentioning Merilee, of course.

"A smart pet bear! That's so cool! Wait till I tell my friends!"

"This is just between us," her father cautioned. "We don't want to bring Erich to people's attention unnecessarily. And the government doesn't want that sort of information out there."

"Then don't make Erich wear these stupid clothes with a target on his back!"

"I've been thinking the same thing. I have full responsibility for the *prisoner*. So, if I decide to dress him like an ordinary farmhand, I can't see the harm in that. But if he escapes, I'll have some explaining to do."

"I would never do that to you, Mr. McKellar. I like and appreciate being here."

"Oh, well said, Erich!" Scamp beamed as if she were his mentor.

"Then it's time to start calling me Lloyd. See you in half an hour in the kitchen. And you, young lady, go and do your homework."

The delectable meal *en famille*, complete with beer for the men, was a treat. There was never a lull in the conversation with Scamp present. She, in particular, managed to sound him out about his home life.

"You said something about wanting Hitler to stop the war before more of your family were killed," Scamp observed. "Were any of them?"

He didn't want to dampen the mood and tried to prevaricate. "There is much bombing of cities."

"And they live on the land. So they're all safe, right?"

"You would think yes."

"Erich! Tell us the truth."

"Scamp, don't be rude!" Winnie scolded.

"But Ma, Erich obviously doesn't want to complain about our side killing his people. Shouldn't we know?"

They all looked at him curiously.

So he told them briefly about his mother, sister, aunt, and cousin being killed. "I do not want to think about it and spoil this pleasant evening," he concluded.

"Oh, you poor boy!" Winnie commiserated.

"War stinks!" Scamp said. "I hate it! I hate that Erich is an enemy when he's one of the nicest people I've ever met!"

"You won't get any arguments from me," Lloyd agreed. "So, let's do what we can to muddle through these terrible times together."

"Erich, there's a large bedroom behind the kitchen, which Lloyd's parents added for themselves as our family grew," Winnie stated. "We've been using it for storage, but we'll fix it up for you. It's plenty big enough for an easy chair and writing table as well, so you'll have a private place out of the cold. And somewhere Scamp can't talk your ear off."

"Ma!"

"That is most generous, Mrs. McKellar! And I do not fear for my ears," he said with a grin.

"*That's* and *don't*," Scamp pointed out. "We need to work on those contractions to make you sound more Canadian. *It's, I'm, we'll, let's, Scamp's a pain in the butt.*"

They laughed.

"And by the way, there's a warm bathroom and flush toilet upstairs," she added.

"We were lucky to get those, and electricity, just before the war, because the farms on the next concession still don't have them," Winnie confided.

At Erich's surprised expression, Lloyd added, "It's a big country, lad, and it takes a heck of a lot of effort and money to run electricity down every dirt road and to every remote farm."

"It sure makes life easier," Winnie said with a contented smile.

"I'll teach you how to play cribbage, and you can listen to the radio with us in the evenings!" Scamp enthused. "Except that it's acting up a bit."

"Perhaps I may help? I built a radio before the war."

"Would you?" Winnie asked hopefully. "We don't like to miss the news, or the music and dramas."

"And hockey on Saturday nights," Lloyd added as he lit his pipe. "Like hockey, lad?"

"I played it at the camp. Our coach was on the Olympic team."

"So you're already part Canadian," Scamp giggled.

Erich quickly found and fixed the problem, and was just as quickly drawn into family life within the house.

Thanksgiving dinner was special because it also happened to be Scamp's twelfth birthday. Erich was paid fifty cents a day as well as his officer's salary, but only in credit. So with Winnie's help, he bought her the latest Nancy Drew mystery novel that she'd been itching to get her hands on - *The Quest of the Missing Map.*

She was overjoyed. "You'll have to read it when I'm finished, Erich. Nancy is so cool!"

"Maybe he'd prefer Sherlock Holmes," Lloyd opined through the pipe clenched between his teeth.

"I will – I'll try both," Erich declared. "I want to know the English culture also."

"*I also want to know English culture,*" Scamp said automatically.

Provided with all his necessities and a generous ration of cigarettes and beer, Erich had few needs to spend money on. He did pay for the Gravenhurst newspaper to be sent to him, and bought some clothes, including a smart navy-blue suit from the Eaton's catalogue, since he could hardly wear his uniform for more formal occasions.

The McKellars gave him new work clothes, which instantly made him feel less like a criminal. Lloyd said that he could start going places with them, and promised a trip to Ottawa once all the crops were in. It was only thirty-nine minutes by train. Erich was thrilled.

They wore their Sunday best on the appointed day, Erich feeling thankfully inconspicuous in his new suit, because military personnel seemed to dominate the downtown. Eagerly he scanned the RCAF women, but Merilee wasn't among them.

He was surprised at how small this capital city seemed on the inbound journey, but was captivated by its setting along the broad, cascading river, backed by the Gatineau Hills.

"That side's Quebec. Where they speak French," Scamp informed him. "Ma says I'll have to learn it when I get to high school. I don't see why."

"It's good to know more languages. My area of Germany is close to France, and has sometimes been under French control over the past many hundreds of years. Even after the last war, for a little time. So I speak French."

She beamed. "So you can help me with my studies!"

"Mais oui!" He chuckled at her expression. "Of course."

She pulled a wry face at him, and then giggled.

The train station was across the street from the opulent Chateau Laurier hotel, and Erich was surprised that they went inside.

"We'll eat here," Lloyd said. "It's Winnie's yearly treat. Makes her feel like a princess."

"Queen," she corrected him with a grin.

"Even better! Worth the king's ransom it costs," he joked.

But they dined in the cafeteria, not the elegant Canadian Grill.

Chefs with tall hats served them generous slices of tender beef, ham, and turkey, and a variety of vegetables filled their plates to overflowing. Washed down with beer, it was a feast fit for royalty, Erich agreed.

Afterwards they strolled around nearby Parliament Hill, and then went to a matinee at the movies. *Lassie Come Home* was a heart-warming tale about a collie dog who found her way back to her family in Yorkshire, from new owners in Scotland.

They were home in time to milk the cows, and all agreed it had been a special day. Profoundly moved by the film, Scamp gave Patch an extra big hug. Erich felt a little closer to Merilee now that he had seen where she lived and worked.

Letters from home were forwarded to him, but unsettled him, with news of Gustav having been drafted into the army, but luckily – so far – just as a guard at a railway station. But Karl, at thirteen, was already having to man anti-aircraft guns at a nearby town. His father's youngest sister, now a widow, and her three children had moved in. Having grown up on the farm, she was used to the work, and a big help. Even the youngsters were quick to learn the chores, and happy to be in countryside.

So, they were able to manage the farm, with additional help from Hitler Youth girls at harvest time.

Erich tried not to worry about them. In some ways, that old life seemed an increasingly remote part of another, forever-lost world.

Erich counted his blessings every night – lighting the stars when he could - and wished only that Merilee wasn't lost to him as well. Surely he had seen himself in one of the sympathetic characters in her novel. Surely she cared.

•　　　•　　　•

Dear Major Sutcliffe,

I wish to thank you again for arranging my release from the camp, and finding such a kind family to take me in. They have also taken me into their hearts, and I'm happy to work on the land and with the animals.

I've been reading more of your books, which Mrs. McKellar brings me from the library. You are a fine writer and historian, but I also enjoyed your children's books. Mrs. Sutcliffe is a magnificent artist!

Please give my regards to your daughter. I will never forget that magical day of skating on the lake, and meeting a beautiful young woman whose warm smile lifted the heart of a homesick prisoner. I think of her as my Christmas angel. I enjoyed her book very much, and I'm most impressed by her talent.

I hope that one day, when the war is over, I may come to visit you, and see again the wonderful lake that lingers fondly in my dreams.

Respectfully yours, Oberleutnant Erich Leitner

Colin was pleased to receive the letter, but by the time he saw Merilee at Christmas, he'd forgotten to pass on Erich's message.

•　　　•　　　•

Rockcliffe
January 5, 1944
Dear Ned,

I was so excited, as well as envious, when I received your daily postcards from Cornwall. It looks just as ruggedly beautiful as I had imagined! Thank you especially for your gift of the Cornish serpentine cabochon, duly delivered by Hugh. I adore the polished red and green veined rock, which seems to hold earth's mysteries within it. Yes, I can easily slip it into my pocket as a good luck charm. Peggy loves hers too and wants to visit Cornwall some time as well.

My leave, which coincided with Christmas, was a whirlwind, but I managed to see family and friends in Toronto before savouring the rest of the time at home. You must miss it!

Peggy seems to be managing alright, although her spirit is crushed. It had been so wonderful to see her glowing when she dispensed with the leg brace and especially when Gunnar came into her life. But I do think it helps her to be corresponding with Ross Tremayne, although she worries about him.

I guess these days we can't take any relationships for granted, as life seems so tenuous. My cousin Kate's pilot husband was recently killed in action.

I was so happy to see Hugh and hear more about your heroic – surely terrifying - adventures. He undoubtedly spared us all the horrific details. He and Ginnie Roland are getting married at the lake this summer, as long as he can walk by then. Aunt Ria has offered The Point for the festivities, since it's the largest cottage and also has the covered dance pavilion next to it. Did I tell you that she and Uncle Chas are Godparents to both Hugh and Ginnie?

Hugh wishes you could be there as Best Man. If the war is over before summer, that might actually be a possibility! I do hope so!!!

I was chuffed to have graduated top of my class, because I get to work at the Photographic Establishment HQ in Ottawa! As students, we were all in awe of "The White House", as it's known, which is in the Lower Rockcliffe Station, and where the latest innovations are happening. One of my instructors said that my photos "not only capture the moment, but also the essence of it", which I guess is why I'll be working with RCAF Public Relations, "shooting" all the bigwigs who come to Ottawa! And patriotic parades, and WDs looking glamorous while doing "men's work", and so on. I have to admit that's more exciting than being on a remote base dealing with that big aerial camera. Poor Stella got posted to the navigation school in Rivers, Manitoba. I had to look that up on a map. I'll really miss her, and Gail, who's now in Summerside,

P.E.I., which she's excited about since it's close to the action, with threats of submarines and plenty of operational aircraft about.

I'm lucky that Cousin Sandy and his new wife live nearby, in that enchanting lakeside house I told you about, which Uncle Jack gave them as a wedding present. They've rather taken me under their wing, so I don't feel lonely here. Their work for the NFB fascinates me, so I'm seriously thinking I might try for a career there after the war. They've already been using my photos!

I'm also thrilled to be an Air Woman First Class, with a camera badge on my sleeve. And can you believe that we actually got a raise in pay because a female MP made a stink in Parliament about men getting 33% more than we do for the same job? As it turns out, two WDs are NOT necessary to replace one man, and we've proven that two can sometimes do the job of three men! Huh! So we now get 80% of the men's pay, which means I earn $1.55 a day!

Hugh's sister, Anthea, just turned 21 and finally got her wish to be posted overseas. But not at all where she expected. She's going to Gander, Newfoundland! She's only consoled by the fact that she gets to wear the "Canada" flash on her shoulder, since it is "foreign" soil, and that Gander is a busy and crucial base, and the jumping off point for aircraft heading for Britain. American flyboys are stationed there as well, so apparently there are 15 men to every WD. I told her that your brother Ken is there with the army, on coastal defence. And she was happy to hear that my cousin, Alain – the Comte with the winery – is there, flying anti-submarine patrol, since she's known him most of her life.

Drew is miffed that he's not yet flying a Spitfire, but he's now CO of a "Visiting Flight", which means that he and a few other top instructors tour the flying schools to make sure that the teaching is top-notch.

Which reminds me... Hugh told me that his brother Bryce had to bail out over the Channel and spent several hours freezing in his dinghy before being rescued. Now he's suffering from battle fatigue, so he's been taken off ops. Uncle Chas said that he hopes Bryce isn't labelled as "Lacking Moral Fibre". They called it shell-shock in the last war, and he's disturbed that the military brass still hasn't realized the strain of unrelenting battle, but that a good CO will handle it discreetly. Perhaps Bryce will be given a desk or teaching job, so he won't lose his commission and his dignity. Drew said that sort of stigma would hardly be fair, since Bryce is most of the way through his first tour of duty, so surely he's proven he's not a coward.

That has made Drew a bit less eager to go into battle now. A good thing, I'd say!

I know that there are no safe flying jobs, but yours sounds exceptionally dangerous, which terrifies me! I do hope that your tour is over soon!

Take good care, my friend.
Affectionately, Merilee

England: Spring 1944
Chapter 24

Having spent the latter part of the day in the darkroom, Merilee welcomed the brilliant sunshine as she stepped out of the RCAF HQ. The green expanse of Lincoln's Inn Fields across the street was a balm to her soul. After almost two weeks, she was still intimidated by busy and bomb-shattered London.

Her photographer's eye was drawn to a dashing young pilot leaning pensively against a tree smoking a cigarette.

"Ned!" she cried in surprise as she rushed across the narrow road.

Having been waiting for an hour, he'd been momentarily distracted and not seen her emerge. "Watch your back!" he warned, shifting his gaze to HQ where others were also leaving. "Hugs later."

Merilee pulled up short. WDs were not allowed to date airmen above or below them in rank, although that was mostly ignored. But being intimate with Ned in front of HQ was too risky. "Oh gosh! Of course. But I'm so happy to see you!... Sir," she added with a cheeky grin as she saluted him.

He returned the salutation, saying, "You do that exceptionally well."

"Why thank you, Sir." As they ambled away, careful not to touch, she said, "I can't believe it's been eighteen months since you left."

"A lot's happened since then. Look at you - already twenty-one," he teased. But he was amazed at how grown up and sophisticated she looked.

"I didn't lie to them, honestly! I just didn't remind them that I'm only nineteen," she added quietly. "I didn't expect you until dinner. Not that I'm allowed to change into glamorous evening dress anyway. Have to be on at least a 48 in order to wear civvies. But I am proud of my Canada flash," she said, referring to the badge on her arm.

"I think you look snazzy in your uniform. All the guys will envy me."

She giggled.

"Anyway, I hitched a lift in an aeroplane, so I've had plenty of time to check into my hotel. We could take a taxi to your place, or just wander back."

"Let's walk. It's only a couple of miles and it's a glorious day. Isn't March marvellous here? Tulips and primroses and rivers of daffodils in bloom!"

Merilee was staying at the well-fortified Dorchester — a concession to her worried parents, since the Germans had been bombing London more often again, although this "Little Blitz" was nothing like the first one. The booming anti-aircraft guns in Hyde Park were even more terrifying than the air raid siren, but she felt safe when she joined the unruffled guests in the comfortably equipped basement, especially when Theo's father, Sir Algernon, took her under his wing. Lady Sidonie had alerted him to her presence, having herself visited Merilee.

"Jack asked me to keep an eye on you," Sid had said when she'd introduced herself. "I see you've inherited more than your share of the Wyndham good looks, so I'm not surprised he's concerned. And you *are* terribly young."

Merilee had been surprised by Elyse's notorious, glamorous mother, and felt like an awkward schoolgirl as they dined at the Dorchester. But Sid soon charmed her as she amused Merilee with memories of her seven-year sojourn in Canada as a fish out of water. Merilee could almost understand Sidonie leaving, if not abandoning Elyse.

"You must come and visit me whenever you feel lonely or have anything you wish to discuss. Jack's brilliant financial advice keeps me in luxury, and he and Chas are among my favourite people," Sid said with a smile and cocked eyebrow, reminding Merilee instantly of Elyse. "And I do hope you'll be free to attend dinner parties that I host. There are plenty of eligible young men who would be delighted to meet you."

Merilee had thanked her and was actually grateful to have a family friend nearby, even if she still found Lady Sidonie a bit intimidating.

She told Ned about her as they strolled through Covent Garden.

"I'm glad to hear that. I do worry about you being in London, especially with this new bombing campaign. But as to potential swains, I think you need to guard yourself against these suave, upper-crust Brits."

"I'm immune to idle flattery," she assured him.

But he worried for her sake as well as his own.

As they passed Canada House at Trafalgar Square, Ned said, "If you stand here long enough admiring Nelson's Column, you're bound to run into someone you know. Everyone seems to gravitate to the Beaver Club or the Canadian Officers' Club nearby. The meals they serve are about as Canadian as you can get with the rationing. I met up with Gord McLaughlin once. He's in an air-sea rescue squadron with Coastal Command. Right up his alley, as he's inclined toward saving lives rather than taking them."

Merilee looked at Ned astutely as she asked, "Does your job bother you?"

"At times. I don't mind knocking out military targets, like munitions factories and airfields, because that makes it harder for the Jerries to attack us. But this carpet bombing that we're doing on cities like Berlin is killing thousands of innocent people, and that doesn't sit well with me. But... I've just finished my tour of duty."

"That's fabulous! Oh, Ned, I'm so happy for you! I'll have to give you an extra big hug. What will you do now?"

"I'll be instructing at a Heavy Conversion Unit. And I've just been promoted to Squadron Leader."

"I should have noticed the extra stripe! That's crackerjack! So, I owe you three hugs."

He laughed and said, "I'm looking forward to them! Now I'm on a week's leave, which means I *leave* all that behind. So, I'm happy to do whatever you want. Dancing, for one, I hope."

"Oh yes! But what else are you planning to do?"

"Spend time with you, if that's OK?"

"Gosh, yes! But I'm only free in the evenings."

"I'll carry your camera equipment when you go on assignments."

"That would hardly be appropriate for an officer... Sir. And you already have your medal, so I'm not sure you'll be allowed into Buckingham Palace. I have an investiture there tomorrow."

"I'll play the tourist outside the gates."

They strolled around Hyde Park, past a crater from a bomb that had fallen just before Merilee arrived, and along The Serpentine.

"It's nice to have this lake and greenery so close. I realize that I'm not a city person," Merilee confided.

"I usually only last a couple of days in London, if I come here at all, and then I'm itching to get out fishing or clambering hills. I think you'd really enjoy where I'm based in Yorkshire. Rambling moors and rolling dales."

"And brooding Wuthering Heights? I'd love to see that countryside! Maybe I could on one of my leaves."

"Sure thing! We could try to co-ordinate ours."

"But you mustn't stay in London this week because of me, Ned."

"Are you kidding? Seeing you is almost like being home!"

"I know what you mean," she said with a grateful smile. "The other girls I came over with want to be posted to London, but I wish I could be in a quaint village on the sea, like Elyse. Isn't her place divine?"

Although Merilee had been at RCAF Personnel Reception at Bournemouth only a few days, she had managed to spend an evening at nearby Riverbreeze. It had been wonderful to see Elyse and Charlie again, and to meet Roz. Theo hadn't been there, but Elyse had told her she must come to stay for her leaves or 48s. Even for a day off - which Merilee had every three weeks - it was manageable to go down to Hamble and back by train.

"Sure is! Almost as impressive as the lady pilots. The planes they've flown! Man!" He shook his head in disbelief. "Anyway, I had a swell time visiting them. Hugh and I only dropped in for an evening, but Elyse said we should come back, and take the rowboat up the river. Maybe we can co-ordinate that too."

"Oh yes, let's try!"

She told him about her trip over on the *Queen Elizabeth,* along with about 15,000 other troops, 50 of them fellow WDs. "I've crossed the Atlantic a few times, so I wasn't seasick, but half of my roommates hardly got out of bed. There were six of us crammed into a first-class cabin in triple bunks, so it wasn't all that pleasant. And we crossed without a convoy, which was pretty scary, although we were assured that the *Queen* was too fast for subs to catch. That's what Aunt Ria had been told during her crossing on the doomed *Lusitania.* Did I ever tell you that Hugh's aunt was on that voyage with Ria? Tragically, she didn't survive."

Although she didn't smoke much, Merilee took the cigarette he offered as they sat down on a bench by the lake.

"So I spent a lot of time on deck scanning the waves looking for periscopes. I can understand why my parents were unhappy about my coming over. I'm sure I wouldn't have allowed me to if I were them."

He laughed. "Lucky for you that you aren't them."

She laughed.

"You could have declined the offer."

"Yes. But most of the girls are dying to get here, so how could I turn down such a unique opportunity? I already have plenty more to add to the diary Dad suggested I write."

"How about adding dinner at the Ritz tonight? A celebration. Then I can tell the folks back home that we were 'Puttin' on the Ritz'," he quipped.

Merilee laughed with delight. She was already feeling so much happier with Ned around.

The Dorchester was across Park Lane from Hyde Park, so Merilee wanted to freshen up first.

"You can't afford this on your military pay," he said when they entered the lounge of the posh hotel.

"I'm earning more since I'm now a Leading Air Woman," she said, pointing out the propeller badge on her sleeve. "But I have some income from the book, and a generous allowance from my parents."

At the Ritz, they joined the many other military personnel in the subterranean restaurant. The government had put a cap on all restaurant meals at five shillings for three courses, but extra – and costly – items on the menu included non-rationed food like lobster and pheasant.

"Do you fancy caviar or... escargot?"

"Snails," she explained with a shudder. "Never!"

"I don't remember that from French class."

"Not relevant for most of us in high school, especially in Gravenhurst."

"Don't see the attraction of slugs myself."

Because supplies couldn't be replenished for the past four years, champagne was prohibitively expensive, so Merilee had a cocktail and Ned, a whiskey.

"I'm so proud of you, Squadron Leader Wilding," she said, clinking her glass to his. He had matured into a ruggedly handsome man who wore his uniform as if born to it.

"Likewise, LAW Sutcliffe. I suspect the brass knew very well that you're underage, but chose to ignore that because of your talent."

"Thank you, kind Sir."

"I suppose you now have to find decent digs."

The WDs in London got a living allowance, but it was odd not to have barracks and a Mess, and have to fend for oneself, although that offered unusual freedom.

"Well... Uncle Jack owns houses in London, and keeps a furnished flat for himself or friends who need a temporary place to kip. That's coming free in a few days, so I'm to have it. A couple of the girls I bunked with on the ship have been posted to London, so they'll share with me. My parents and I stayed there for two months when I was ten and dad was doing research at the Imperial War Museum, so it will seem a bit like home."

"Wizard!"

"So, tell me what happens after you finish your teaching stint."

"Probably another tour," he said dismissively. "I love flying and want to make a career of it, so the more experience I have on the big planes, the better my chances of landing an airline pilot's job after the war."

"I thought you'd be safer now!"

"Maybe the war will be over before my teaching is. Something big is going down soon," he added quietly.

"Let's hope so!"

"One of the things that war teaches you is to enjoy every day. Which is exactly what we'll do!"

They danced until they were exhausted. The slow tunes gave them a chance to hold each other close, and Merilee was surprised that she felt a stirring of passion. Was it the seductiveness of songs like *Blue Moon*, or the infectious mood of other couples striving to make the most of stolen moments together?

So that became their routine, Ned tagging along on her assignments whenever he could, and then the two of them spending the rest of the day together.

They discovered the Maison Lyonses at Hyde Park Corner, close to the Dorchester and part of the national chain of Lyons teashops and restaurants, which had decent, plain food at reasonable prices, with a choice of different menus on its five levels.

Ned seemed happier tucking into his steak and kidney pie with mashed potatoes and a pint of ale than he had at the Ritz, where cold potato soup was embellished with the moniker *vichyssoise*, and waiters were discreetly condescending to those who didn't inflate their bills with extras and big tips. There was no tipping at Lyons, and the smartly uniformed waitresses flitted about cheerfully and efficiently, serving hundreds.

They went on to dance at the Royal Opera House, which had been transformed into an enormous nightclub at the beginning of the war, and now overflowed with American GIs and girls eager to make their acquaintance.

One evening they enjoyed the darkly comic play *Arsenic and Old Lace* at the Strand Theatre, and then dropped into a pub for a plate of fries, which the Brits called "chips".

"The girls at HQ have taken me out to pubs a few times and told me I need to learn how to drink beer. I've managed half a pint so far."

Ned laughed. "I'll drink the other half."

A couple of Australian airmen came up to them saying, "Hey, Canada, what part of that beautiful country are you from?"

"The Muskoka Lakes, a hundred miles north of Toronto," Ned replied.

"Bonzer! We did our advanced flight training in Gimli, on Lake Winnipeg. Such friendly folks there. And you RCAF gals gave the station real class," the Aussie added to Merilee. "My mate here lost his heart, but she said she'd wait for him. Say, can we stand you two a drink?"

Merilee thought the boys - for they were hardly older than she - were probably homesick and having spent time in Canada, felt a connection with them.

"I'd like to hear about your experiences in Manitoba. I have WD friends stationed out there," she said.

They talked eagerly, sharing amusing tales. "In fine weather, the WDs took to sunbathing on the roof of HQ... in the buff! Course we couldn't resist swooping down to take a squizz. When the C.O. became aware of why we were beating up the station, he told the gals they were endangering the men, and declared the roof out of bounds. One of the sassy ones said that the new WD motto should be 'We Serve That Men May Fly... Low'."

They all laughed. "I'll be sure to pass that gem along to my friends," Merilee declared.

"We'll push off now and leave you two lovebirds alone. You have yourselves a good war."

Merilee blushed at the suggestion that she and Ned were a couple.

"How about a game of darts?" he asked when the Aussies had left.

"Sure!"

On his second last day, Ned helped Merilee move into her new lodgings after work. He whistled when he saw the terraced Victorian townhouse at Lancaster Gate, across from Kensington Gardens. "And you expect me to believe that Jack and your mother and their sisters grew up hungry in the slums of Toronto?"

"Oh, but they did! And if it hadn't been for Uncle Jack's cleverness, and boldness confronting his tyrannical grandmother..."

"He wouldn't now be the richest man in Canada," Ned interrupted.

"Well... one of them."

Ned hooted with laughter.

"This place belonged to my great-grandmother's cousin, Lady Beatrice Kirkland, and Jack, Ria, and Chas used it during the last war. Uncle Jack bought it from her when she was in her eighties and no longer inclined to come to London from her country estate. It's been divided into flats, and mine is the one with the balcony." Which sat atop the deep Doric portico.

"Wow! Let's get you settled in then, princess!"

"Hey, I'm just a small-town girl."

"Baloney!"

Six apartments each occupied an entire floor, every successive level having lower ceilings and smaller windows. The basement –

which also had access from a stairwell on the outside - was where the elderly caretakers lived, and where Merilee picked up her keys.

"Bless me, Miss Sutcliffe, when your uncle sent me the telegram, I could hardly believe you're old enough to be here on your own!" Mrs. Travers greeted her. "My goodness, don't you look chic in your uniform!"

"It's delightful to see you again, Mrs. Travers. This is Squadron Leader Wilding, a friend from home who's helping me move in."

"Bless you young people for coming to help us fight the Huns. There are a couple of Canadian Intelligence officers right above you. Dandy chaps…. Now… I'll be doing your flat, so don't you worry none about that. And I can fetch your shopping, if you leave me a list and your ration coupons. You'll be having enough to do without lining up at the greengrocers. I've left a few things to get you started. Tea and such."

"That's so kind of you, Mrs. Travers."

"Nonsense! Your uncle asked us to look after you specially well, Miss Sutcliffe – as if he had to! Now… be sure to dash down here smartly when you hear the air raid siren. The old wine cellar is set up as a bomb shelter for the tenants. But stop in for a cup of tea and chat anytime it takes your fancy."

"Thank you, I will. And I must say, it's reassuring to have you here," Merilee added with a sincere smile. Mrs. Travers preened.

"Very nice," Ned said as they stepped into the tastefully modern, second-floor apartment. "Thankfully not as swanky as I'd expected, or I'd be afraid to visit," he jested as he went over to the glossy baby grand piano, which sprouted a vase of welcoming spring violets, and checked to see if it was in tune.

"This floor used to be just the double drawing room. Or ballroom as the occasion demanded."

"And the family had five other floors to live on as well."

"Only three. The basement and attic were for the servants."

He chuckled. "Of course. And those poor beggars had to haul stuff up and down the blasted stairs all day long… But I wonder how warm this place will be in winter, with these high ceilings and huge windows," Ned observed.

Tall French doors topped by fanlight windows opened onto the balcony from the artistically combined sitting and dining rooms. Light seeped into the kitchen via the pass-through. The claw-footed tub in the bathroom had the required line painted around it to mark the four inches of allowable bathwater, but also had a separate shower stall, for which Merilee was thankful. The two bedrooms at the back had Juliet balconies overlooking Kensington Gardens.

"This certainly beats barracks," Ned said. "We - and the girls at our base - live in tin cans called Nissen huts. Those *are* ruddy freezing in winter."

"It's going to be strange to have so much freedom. And privacy." Merilee said as she claimed the room with a double bed; the other one had two singles. Stella had written that there were ten girls in her bunk-bedded room in the barracks. They had drills, parades, inspections, curfews, and all the usual military discipline and rigmarole.

"But you won't be dining on gourmet Spam in the Mess," Ned jested.

"I think I'll be relying on care packages from home and make do with peanut butter sandwiches."

"In that case, how be we feast at Lyons again tonight?"

"Perfect! I'll just go and put a few things away."

"Take your time." Ned sat down at the piano and started playing *Blue Moon*. Merilee had always marvelled that he could hear any tune and play it on his fiddle or the piano. He wasn't as good as Peggy, of course, but music came naturally to him.

It felt comfortable and reassuring to have him here with her, and she dreaded that he would soon be leaving.

On Ned's last day, he accompanied her to Brookwood Cemetery in the Surrey countryside. She had to take photos of several RCAF graves to be sent to the parents.

At Waterloo Station, she picked up a bouquet of daffodils. "Just to show that someone cares," she explained.

"Nice touch."

Once they were out of London, it was a pleasant train ride through the English countryside. Clouds chased their shadows across green fields sprinkled with early April wildflowers. Blossoming trees reminded Merilee of the popular song "Don't sit under the apple tree with anyone else but me", which they'd heard at every dance this week. And would forever remind her of these poignant days.

"Brookwood is the London Necropolis, but there's also a military section," Merilee explained. "Irene says they've been burying Londoners there for almost a century, so it's really creepy and she's glad she doesn't have to go," Merilee said of a colleague. "She gets to shoot a wedding today instead."

"So, you pulled the short straw."

"This part isn't at all bad," she replied with a grin. "Almost like a holiday. But I'm relieved that you could come with me. It sounds so vast I could get lost!"

The enormous cemetery overshadowed the village of the same name. There was an entrance right across from the railway station, but they didn't have to go far into the main Necropolis to arrive at the Military Cemetery. Here, they wandered past graves from the last war, including rows of stark crosses reaching ghostly arms towards each other in the American sector; past acres of white slabs marking British and Commonwealth graves, to the surprisingly extensive Canadian section. A Cross of Sacrifice punctuated the long sweep of headstones, surrounded by trees on three sides.

"Already so many," Merilee sighed, knowing that these were just the men who died in England, buried close to where they fell. "I'm glad that there are trees. It makes it seem more peaceful... Even if there are planes zooming overhead."

The new graves had no spring flowers blooming, so Merilee was glad she had brought the daffodils. She arranged them artistically at the base of each raw new stone to soften the line where it plunged into the earth. When she'd finished, she left a single flower on each of the graves.

"They're all so young. Like the thousands of fallen from the last war I saw when Dad was doing research in France. It makes me infinitely sad."

Ned put his arm about her and gave her a reassuring hug. She leaned her head against him and thought, *Please don't ever be one of them, Ned.*

"Irene said if we go out this gate, there's a quaint pub in a village just down the road. And afterwards we can likely hitch a lift back to the station from passing military vehicles, although it's only a mile or so if we want to walk."

"Sounds good to me! I think we could both use a drink."

The medieval Fiddler's Green pub had low, beamed ceilings and a deep fireplace that could probably roast an ox, but where, alas, no fire burned because of fuel restrictions. In any case, it was a mild day.

Ned ordered two pints of ale as they perused the menu.

"Rabbit stew. I think not," Merilee declared.

"It's quite tasty, I've found."

"But it could be the Easter bunny," Merilee quipped, since Good Friday was only a few days away.

"Softie!"

"I want him to bring me eggs! Gosh, I already miss them." Rationing was tight in Britain, and eggs were mostly powdered.

"I can understand that," Ned said, telling her about the bacon and egg reward the aircrews got before and after their missions. "Just one egg each, though."

They both ordered shepherd's pie, which seemed to contain real meat as well as ample vegetables under a duvet of fluffy potatoes, and turned out to be remarkably tasty.

"This is a lovely spot. So tranquil," Merilee said, gazing out the mullioned windows to the village green and its pond, where a couple of ducks paddled. It was as if the wavy glass distorted time as well, and she was peering into a simpler past. "But I suppose we'd better head back so I can process the photos."

Ned went to see a movie while she finished work.

"Where would you like to dine this evening, milady?" he asked when they headed back to her flat afterwards.

"At home! I can't keep up this pace." She'd just gotten her period, which was especially crampy and heavy, so she had no desire to dance. "How be we take some fish and chips back with us? Have a relaxing evening?"

"Wizard!"

They washed the greasy, tasty meal down with bottles of ale on the balcony.

"The only thing that's missing is the lake," Merilee said wistfully.

"We could walk along The Serpentine."

Once they crossed the Bayswater Road into Kensington Gardens, they sauntered past the Italian Water Gardens that led to The Long Water, the northern extension of The Serpentine from Hyde Park. There were plenty of GIs about, some with their arms around British girlfriends or stealing kisses behind trees. Some couples sprawled on the grass in blushingly amorous embraces.

Merilee wished she had her camera when she saw a perfect photo opportunity of a strolling couple lit by misty evening light that streamed through the trees and highlighted the grazing sheep around them. With no one else in that frame, it was tantalizingly bucolic.

They stopped at Peter Pan's statue where a group of Canadian flyboys were laughingly climbing onto various levels of the gnarled tree-trunk base to have their photo taken. Merilee found it heartbreakingly poignant to think that they, like Peter Pan, might never grow old.

"Let's go back," she suggested wearily.

Ned sensed her sadness and knew exactly what she was thinking, so he took her hand reassuringly in his.

Back in the flat, she made tea, and they curled up together on the sofa. He put his arm about her, and she sank into his embrace.

"I'm really going to miss you, Ned. This has been such fun, and I feel so alone. I expect it will be better once I get to know my flat mates, but right now I'm terribly homesick."

When he kissed her, she was surprised at her own reaction. No longer tentative, they were both breathless with desire.

He stroked her cheek when he released her. "Would it help if you had something to look forward to? How about a honeymoon in Cornwall?"

She was stunned.

"I love you, Merilee. And I want to spend the rest of my life with you. You don't have to say anything now, but will you at least consider marrying me?"

"Oh, Ned... I'm touched... Honoured!... But I haven't thought about getting married yet."

"We don't know how much time we'll have, but every moment I spend with you is precious to me. I promise we'll have plenty of fun adventures. And you'll adore Cornwall."

There was such love and devotion in his tender gaze that she almost relented. She had never thought about how beautiful his dark-rimmed green eyes were. "I will seriously think about it."

When he kissed her again, a few tears trickled down her cheeks. She felt torn, and guilty about her lingering desire for Erich.

"What's wrong, Merilee?"

"I'm not sure I deserve you."

"I don't care if you've had an affair..."

"I haven't! I just think you should marry a girl who's crazy about you."

"I'm over the moon whenever I'm with you! I would do anything to make you as ecstatically happy as you make me. If you gave me the chance."

She laid her head on his shoulder as more tears escaped.

"Is there another guy? Still Bryce?"

"Gosh no!" she snuffled. "I'm just... confused... You're one of my best friends!"

He took that as a good sign. She had obviously never considered him as a potential suitor.

"Surely that's a good beginning for a life together. But that won't change, even if you can't accept my offer. I will always be here for you."

She wept even more.

He held her tenderly. "You're tired and it's not fair of me to make any demands right now."

His presence was so reassuring that she wished she could ask him to stay. But of course that wouldn't do.

"I have an early start. Come and see me as soon as you have a 48. And call me anytime." He hated leaving her when she seemed so young and vulnerable.

"I will. Thank you, Ned. This has been a truly wonderful week." She hesitated, but remembering the cemetery and the uncertainly of his dangerous work, added, "I do love you." It was true, of course, but not in the same way that he felt.

He grinned broadly. "That's all I need to get me through!"

Her flat mates were due to arrive tomorrow, but when he left, the apartment felt too large, too empty. Turning off the lights, Merilee stepped out through the blackout curtains to the balcony. Since negotiating the streets was like stumbling about blindfolded, it was silly to think she might glimpse Ned walking through the dark, waiting city. But she heard someone whistling *Don't Sit Under the Apple Tree* cheerfully, and knew it was Ned. It filled her with joy.

She spent a tormented night wondering what to do. Ned represented home and security and treasured memories. Kind and thoughtful, he had always been good to her, and invariably made her laugh. Why couldn't she feel the overwhelming urge to abandon herself to him as she had with Erich?

Had that been a reaction to being dumped by Bryce, the excitement of being admired and desired after cruel rejection? Would she still feel the same about Erich now? Was she willing to give up potential happiness for an uncertain, probably impossible future with a virtual stranger? Was it any wonder he seemed in love with her when she was undoubtedly the only girl he had talked to since his capture? Would she even see him again?

Hadn't she once felt completely besotted by Bryce, and then almost immediately afterwards fallen in love with Erich? She was so confused.

Maybe she could atone for her sins by making Ned happy. Maybe she would fall deeply in love with him given the chance. She hugged Neddy the teddy tightly.

She and Peggy really would be sisters.

Three soul-searching days later when she had missed Ned more than she would have imagined, Merilee sent a cable to her parents: *Ned asked me to marry him. Any objections? Young, yes, but time not on our side.*

She waited impatiently for the reply. *Ned is good man. Important to consider if you share goals after war. Hoped to be at wedding. But you must follow your heart.*

Then she had a phone call.

•   •   •

Merilee fought hard to contain her tears as six sombre RAF pilots carried the flag-draped coffin to the gravesite. She had hoped never to have a personal connection to the Brookwood Military Cemetery.

"Oh! I have slipped the surly bonds of Earth, And danced the skies on laughter-silvered wings," Wing Commander Nelson Winthrop began reading the poem "High Flight".

As if on cue, a Spitfire squadron flew low overhead and peeled away in the Missing Man formation into the high, mournful clouds. It was a fitting tribute to their beloved Commanding Officer.

Merilee stood rigidly between Alastair Grayson and Bryce as the bugler played The Last Post. Theo put his arm about Elyse. Sophie leaned against her husband, Philip. Chas took Roz's hand in his.

It was impossible to believe that Charlie was dead.

He'd been critically wounded on a strafing sortie over Calais. His number two, Bob Brookes, had shepherded him back, hopeful that Charlie could land his plane. Bob had radioed that an ambulance should be at the ready at RAF Hawkinge, which was the closest base. But Charlie lost altitude, and when they had barely skimmed over the chalky cliffs west of Dover, Bob had seen Charlie slump over. Moments later, he crashed.

Chas had taken the first transport plane from Ottawa, which regularly carried mail and important passengers across the Atlantic.

When the casket had been lowered into the grave, Roz threw in a single red rose and whispered, "Goodbye, my love."

Tears were hastily brushed away. Despite her heart bleeding for Roz and Chas as well as herself, Elyse knew it wouldn't do to break down amidst this sea of uniforms. Every one of them knew death too intimately. There was no time for grieving. There was a war yet to be won.

But the tension of keeping emotional control was palpable within the crowd.

Their own CO from Hamble, Margot Gore, was here with Pauline Gower, who was commander of the ATA women. None of their other colleagues could come, since there was a big push to move hundreds of new planes to operational airfields. They all knew that something big was about to happen.

Elyse and Roz had been told to take a few days off.

Merilee placed her own bouquet of flowers among the many wreaths as people offered condolences and began to disperse.

Elyse had been only slightly surprised to see her mother, along with Sir Algernon and Lady Marguerite, among them.

Nelson Winthrop, who had been Best Man at her wedding, hugged Roz, saying, "I'm devastated by this, and so sorry for you, Roz. We all thought Charlie invincible. Let me know if there is ever anything I can do for you."

"Thank you, Nelson. You've been a good friend to us. Let me introduce Charlie's father."

"A great honour to meet you, Air Marshall Thornton. Charlie never wanted to ride on the wings of your success, but he was quietly proud to be your son."

"Thank you, Wing Commander. That means a great deal to me."

More than most could ever realize, Elyse thought. It obviously took all of Chas's willpower to hold himself together.

Drained, the family retreated to Priory Manor, which was just twelve miles away.

Merilee had been given the day off and would take a train back later.

They all took the proffered whiskey and drank a toast to Charlie. Roz excused herself and went out into the garden, among the stone ruins, and wandered off toward the summerhouse by the lake.

Elyse wanted to support her, but realized that Roz needed time to herself to grieve. She wished she could as well.

She said, "I hope you can keep Drew at home, Uncle Chas."

"I've never influenced his postings, even if I could have. He's even more determined to get over here now, since he's always looked up to his older brother and feels he has a score to settle."

"Dear God!" Sophie lamented.

Chas faltered, and the others retreated into their own aching souls to give him time to recover.

"This is just between us, but we've been talking with the Brits about winding down the BCATP," Chas admitted.

"So you think the war really will end soon?" Elyse asked.

"It takes the best part of a year to train aircrew. We're anticipating that we won't need many new recruits. So, we'll start sending over the instructors who've been itching to go on ops. But I'm hoping that by the time Drew is trained on Spitfires or whatever, he may not have much of a chance to participate."

"Or get shot down," Sophie added morosely.

Chas reached over and squeezed her hand. "When Charlie first came to us, here, in this house, he wasn't quite three and you – all of eight years old - instantly took him under your wing, proclaiming you were now his older sister…"

"And promised I would always be there for him," Sophie concluded, tears spilling down her cheeks.

"You have been, my darling. And he's still with you. With us."

"He was a big brother to me," Alastair declared.

"And me," Elyse added. She snuggled gratefully into Theo's embrace. Although back on ops as a Wing Commander, he was confined to Home Defence, which he would never admit was a relief. Still flying honourably in battle, he was nonetheless spared the fear of being shot down over enemy territory again. Only Elyse knew how much he still suffered from his previous experience, revealed in recurring nightmares. She noticed how rigidly he held himself at times, as if afraid to break apart. Only when she cuddled him in her arms at night did he truly relax. But it was hard to snatch time together, other than during leaves.

"It used to annoy Charlie when I took so many films of him with my cine-camera, but I'm glad I have those now," Elyse said. "Remember when…"

There were smiles as they recounted stories about Charlie.

"We'll light the stars for him tonight," Elyse promised.

They had an early, light supper for those who had to get back. Roz excused herself and accepted a tray to be sent to her room, but Elyse suspected it would be untouched. They would return to Hamble tomorrow, after a private visit to the cemetery.

Before Philip drove Alastair, Bryce, and Merilee to the train station, Chas said to her, "I have business at HQ on Thursday, so let's plan to have dinner together, if you're free. They have me booked into the Savoy."

"That would be wonderful, Uncle Chas!"

"London's a bit overwhelming, isn't it?" he said, giving her a reassuring hug.

Merilee was relieved that Alastair was also on the train to London, from whence he and Bryce would go off in different directions to their bases. Alastair was teaching at an OTU, since his tour with the RAF Photo Reconnaissance Unit had ended, and Bryce was back on ops at Biggin Hill, south of London.

Bryce seemed more subdued than his usual brash self, and Merilee wondered if he reluctantly went back to fighting, having had a safe desk job for three months.

When the two men had traded a few hair-raising tales, Bryce said, "What you've done is truly heroic, Alastair. Jeez, I couldn't imagine flying over Germany with no guns. And coasting back on fumes sometimes." He shook his head.

"I'm relieved to be teaching for now. And I never had to bail. You've certainly earned your Goldfish membership," Alastair said, and added for Merilee's benefit, "That's a club for airmen who've survived ditching in the drink."

"Something I could have done without.... I thought I was a goner. I was engulfed by mountainous waves, so the search planes had trouble locating me. The wind was fierce. Biting. The water was icy, and I was wet and frozen from my dunking. Couldn't feel my toes or my fingers, although I daren't let go of the ropes or the waves might have washed me overboard. I had a lot of time to think about things. My sins. Regrets." He looked at Merilee.

"When you're high overhead, the Channel seems like a placid silver ribbon barely separating the white-cliffed coasts of England and France. But when you're immersed in it on a rough day, it becomes an endless, voracious sea." Bryce looked haunted.

"I could hardly believe it when a seaplane finally spotted me. It was too rough to land on the water, but they flashed me a message that help was on the way. They kept circling until a navy destroyer approached. Never had a chance to thank those airmen."

"Your guardian angels," Alastair said.

"Damn right!"

Merilee wondered if Gord McLaughlin had been one of them.

When they arrived at Waterloo station, the boys needed to get to different trains. Alastair would be leaving from Paddington, which was just half a mile from Merilee's place, so he said he would see her home. Although it was out of his way, Bryce insisted on coming as well, much to her dismay. What did he want from her?

He got out of the taxi with her when they arrived at Lancaster Gate.

"Come and see me whenever you're in London," Merilee said to Alastair.

"Sure thing. Take care, both of you."

"I can't invite you in, Bryce. My flat mates might not be prepared for visitors. In any case, there's nothing for us to discuss."

"Nice pad. Can we stroll in the Gardens for a few minutes? I do have something to say."

She hesitated.

"Please?" He offered his hand, but she didn't take it.

"Just a short walk then."

Because it was double summer time, it was still light at 8:30, but Merilee had no intention of wandering far. She stopped by the first tree in the park and turned to him with an unspoken *"Well?"*

"I owe you an apology, Merilee. I behaved like an arrogant ass the last time we were together. *I* was the one who needed to grow up. And I have." He looked at her beseechingly. "Can you forgive me?"

She was convinced that his experiences had changed him, and they had a shared history well beyond that summer fling. "As an old friend... yes."

He grinned. "Thank you. I don't suppose there's any chance we might pick up where we left off."

"None at all," she said decisively.

He looked crestfallen. "May I also visit you when I'm in London?"

"As an old friend... yes."

"Biggin Hill is only a half hour train ride, so I could be here most evenings," he said hopefully.

"There wouldn't be any point, Bryce."

"Is there another guy?"

"Even if there weren't, I have no interest in you romantically. That chapter is closed."

"No second chances?" he persisted as she headed back.

She turned to him in exasperation. "Definitely not. Now if you don't knock it off, then I won't meet with you at all!"

"I'm sorry, Merilee. For everything. Just know that you can rely on me if ever you need anything. A shoulder to cry on. Someone to waterski with."

"In the Serpentine?" she couldn't resist asking with a smirk.

"Would that we could!... Whoever he is, he's a dashed lucky fellow."

She wasn't about to enlighten him.

Outside the townhouse, she said, "Good luck, Bryce."

"Stay safe, Merilee." He looked at her longingly and then turned away.

As soon as she was inside, she telephoned Ned.

•   •   •

"This must be very hard for you, Uncle Chas. Having to keep working right now," Merilee said to Chas when they were aboard the Anson airplane.

"It was my excuse for coming over. In any case, it's better to keep busy. We're going to be meeting - and you'll be photographing – other boys who are dicing with death daily. There will undoubtedly be a few who received their wings from me. And there'll be too many who won't be going home again." He fell into contemplative silence and turned to gaze, unseeing, out the window.

Merilee was excited to be with Chas as they were being ferried to RCAF Bomber Command in Yorkshire. At dinner the previous evening, he told her that he was checking up on BCATP graduates, and doing a morale-boosting visit to Canadian squadrons. He had arranged for her to be the official photographer, so she was to prepare for a few days of travel.

When her colleagues discovered that Chas was a relative, they forgave her this plum assignment.

Ned had already been alerted that they were coming and would meet her for dinner. She could hardly wait!

A WD driver collected them at the Linton-on-Ouse airfield and was to chauffer them around for the next two days. They began at nearby Bomber HQ, which had taken over Allerton Park, a Victorian Gothic castle near York.

Beyond the imposing mansion's parkland and tiny lake, the pastoral vista stretched invitingly to distant hills. This was where they would be staying – Chas in the castle itself, and Merilee in one of the women's Nissen huts.

"Just drop your kitbag over there," her WD escort instructed when they had entered the semicircular metal tube that served as lodgings for more than a dozen girls, a couple of whom were attempting to sleep. A pot-bellied stove in the middle provided a little heat. "Flo is on the graveyard shift, so you can have her bed later."

"No cold cream on my pillow, if you please," Flo grumbled as she pulled the blanket over her head.

Although the castle had been transformed into a busy workplace, the magnificent carvings of the Great Hall and other spaces attested to its underlying grandeur.

While Chas dined in the Officers' Mess, Merilee joined a friendly group of WDs for lunch. She was delighted to see Bev, one of the girls who had come over on the *Queen Elizabeth* with her. Bev and the others were keen to hear about life in London.

Her lunch mates agreed to pose in front of the Nissen huts, and a couple grabbed bicycles to illustrate how they explored the countryside in their time off.

Merilee noted names and jobs, and other crucial info, as usual. She had to be careful that there were no features or signs revealing locations, since her photos could be used for national newspapers and magazines. She was thrilled that she would be bringing aspects of the war "somewhere in Britain" to people at home.

Chas suggested Merilee change into her slacks, since they would have a flight in a Lancaster bomber at their first stop. The other girls envied her those, because they weren't part of the WD uniform, except for special trades. The photographers handling aerial cameras were constantly in and out of airplanes. Others might have to clamber onto rooftops to capture the perfect photo. But she was only allowed to wear them as necessary for the job – a pity, since they were comfortable, warm, and rather sexy.

When they arrived at nearby Topcliffe, Merilee was astonished that Ned greeted her. She had to resist throwing herself into his arms.

Ned offered his condolences to Chas, who responded with his congratulations on their engagement.

"Hugh sings your praises, Ned, and Peggy is already part of the family. So, you'd better start calling me Uncle Chas. I've cabled Ria, and she's thrilled for you both. We've decided that since your mother's side of the Wyndhams doesn't have a cottage on the ancestral isle, Merilee, we'll give you and Ned one as a wedding gift. There's plenty of land between Silver Bay and Westwynd, and even more on the north and east sides, so you can choose, and we'll have Freddie draw up plans according to your suggestions. And don't forget a boathouse."

"Oh my gosh, Uncle Chas, that's super! Thank you!"

"Holy mackerel, that's generous!" Ned added, shaking Chas's hand.

"It's only right, since Merilee's grandfather was cheated out of his share. Besides, we all want to have the benefit of your company at the lake. I expect you may not be living in Gravenhurst after the war."

"If I can't get a job as an airline pilot, then I'm hoping to stay in the Air Force," Ned admitted.

"Flying's gotten into your blood, has it?"

"Definitely."

"So, are you ready to entrust yourself to Ned's skills as a pilot?" Chas asked Merilee.

"Oh yes!"

"That's a good start to your impending marriage. I'll look away so you can kiss the future bride, Ned."

Chas wandered off as Ned took her into his arms. "This is a dream come true!"

Merilee suppressed a niggling qualm at her momentous decision, which was already setting events into motion that she couldn't easily stop. But she had never seen Ned so happy, which allayed her own doubts. She was determined that they would have fun together, and what more could she want? Erich belonged to an unreal world, along with Pan and other mythical creatures.

She and Chas were kitted up with parachutes before the three of them were transported to a Lancaster on the airfield, where a trainee crew was waiting nervously. Chas was a legend, after all. But the fact that he had been severely wounded in battle endeared him even more to the men, Merilee discovered.

Amid the roar and oily smells of other planes taking off and landing, Merilee snapped candid photos of the novice crew in front of their bomber, with and without Chas and Ned.

When they clambered into the belly of the long plane, she was surprised at how confining it was inside. The gunners in particular barely seemed to have room in their turrets. They explained that they had to wear electrically heated suits under all their other gear because it was freezing in those Perspex bubbles when they flew at fifteen or twenty thousand feet, so that made them even bulkier.

"But none of us has enough space to wear a parachute," Ned added. "So, we store them close to hand."

They had to crouch in places, and crawl over the main spar to reach the cockpit. Merilee found it rather terrifying, wondering how anyone could readily escape when necessary.

She managed to get photos of the crew in their various positions, although the Wireless Operator had to keep his secret equipment covered.

Ned took over the pilot's seat for this flight. "We'll be cruising under 8000 feet, so we won't need oxygen, and we won't be flying over the coast. But make sure you have the IFF on, WAG."

"IFF on, Skipper."

"That identifies us as *friend* instead of *foe* to our own gunners," Ned explained.

Merilee was amazed that this big metal monster could actually get off the ground. She was awed by the many dials and controls in the cockpit, and impressed that it all seemed so easy and natural to Ned and the flight engineer.

A woman's voice from the control tower gave them clearance to take off.

"Our WDs seem to be professional and cheerful," Chas observed.

"Calmly competent, even when all hell breaks loose," Ned agreed. "They inspire us. And we all appreciate hearing Canadian voices."

They thundered down the runway and, being unencumbered by heavy bombs, rose effortlessly, the glorious Yorkshire countryside opening beneath them. Patchwork fields and tufty woodlands gave way to undulating dales and barren fells. The land dropped into the vast North Sea on their starboard.

Merilee took a photo of Ned at the controls, and several of nearby planes in flight. These were also crews training on the aircraft they would eventually be flying, and Ned told the gunners to keep a sharp lookout for potential collisions.

They skimmed over the Lake District where cloud shadows chased each other across craggy mountains and bright ribbons of water. "I'd like to see that up close," Merilee confided to Ned.

"Oh, you will," he said with a smile.

Chas insisted on taking a photo of Merilee standing behind Ned. The flight was exhilarating.

"I have even more admiration now for you bomber crews," Chas said as he, Merilee, and Ned watched the plane take off again after they had been dropped off. "It's one thing to fly a fighter that you can toss around with the flick of a wrist, but quite another to do evasive manoeuvres with a lumbering beast like this, especially at night and amid a flock of others."

"The Lanc's a good plane," Ned assured him. "We're particularly happy with the Mark Xs built in Canada. And proud."

"Rightfully so," Chas said. "I toured the factory, and the people building the aircraft are equally proud that Canadian crews are flying them."

Chas had forewarned the Station Commanders that he wanted no formal parades and inspections. He was there to observe the men and women at their daily jobs. So, Ned had been given the responsibility of taking him and Merilee on a tour of the Training Base.

She took plenty of photos, including one of the WD with the pleasant voice in the control tower.

At the end of the day, Chas was invited to dine with the officers, who were billeted at Skellfield House, a stately but rundown manor along the River Swale. Ned said it was a big improvement over the Nissen huts at his previous location. Merilee snapped a photo of them beside it, against a backdrop of dramatic clouds.

When she had changed into her regulation skirt, she and Ned strolled to a pub in the village. Among the many other air force personnel - and after several introductions - they managed to find a table in a secluded corner. Over their pints of ale, Ned handed her a velvet jewellery box, saying, "I bought this in London. Just in case."

Inside was a stunning ring of seven small sapphires alternating with six diamonds, set in white gold. "Oh, Ned! It's exquisite!"

"Matches your eyes."

It was a trifle large, so she put in on her middle finger.

"You can have it properly sized when you're back in London. So... now it's official." He took both her hands in his across the table and looked at her with such adoration and desire that she suddenly wished they could just fall into bed together.

"Peggy sent me a cable saying 'Overjoyed. Real sisters.'"

"Mine said 'About time'," Ned confided with a chuckle. "So... let's make plans. We'll obviously have to wait until the *big event* is over, since all leaves have been cancelled for the time being. In any case, the entire south coast is out of bounds right now."

"I still have to get permission from my CO to get married. My parents approve, of course."

"That's a relief! I'm not exactly in your league."

"Don't be silly! We've been neighbours and friends forever!"

"I won't be able to provide you with the luxuries your relatives are used to. Peggy told me about Wyndwood and Wyndholme. Man!"

"I have a confession to make," Merilee said, slightly embarrassed. "Uncle Jack set up a trust fund for me when I was born, and I'll have control of it when I'm twenty-one. It's grown... Substantially."

"So I'm marrying an heiress?"

"Well... it will ensure that we're comfortable."

He looked at her suspiciously. "How comfortable?"

She blushed. "It's up to 120."

His puzzlement turned to shock. "$120,000?"

"Yes."

"Holy mackerel! I thought I was doing well to earn $9.75 a day!"

"I hope it doesn't upset you."

"I'm thunderstruck! And a fortune hunter, I guess."

"Hardly, when you didn't even know about it! And no one else needs to either."

"I love you even if you are wealthy beyond my wildest dreams." She giggled.

More seriously he added, "I'll try to make you proud, Merilee."

"You already have, Ned. But more importantly, you make me happy," she said, squeezing his hand.

His heart took wing.

"I thought we could be married in St. Martin-in-the-Fields," Merilee suggested. "It's such a lovely church, and easy for my friends and probably yours to attend." It was situated at Trafalgar Square.

"Great idea."

"I'll find a hotel for the reception. My parents are footing the bill for that and our honeymoon. We're to spare no expense."

"Wizard! I'll make the arrangements for Cornwall.... Merilee Wilding." He kissed her hand chivalrously.

It sounded so right, she thought.

"Ned, we should talk about kids," she said warily over dinner.

"You don't want any just yet, do you? We should have plenty of fun first. And I need to establish my career before the little tykes come along." He also didn't want her to be a young widow with a child if something happened to him. She needed the opportunity to make a new life for herself, unencumbered. "We'll take precautions."

She breathed a sigh of relief. She wanted the romance and companionship of marriage – and sex, to be honest with herself - but wasn't ready for motherhood and domesticity.

They eagerly discussed their future cottage, Merilee suggesting that the northwest corner of Wyndwood offered spectacular sunsets.

"We can see Uncle Jack's island from there," Merilee added. "I think the cottage should be an L-shaped bungalow, to take in the vistas from both sides. With long verandas, of course. Just like Elyse's cottage, actually, only not as large."

"And no ballrooms or conservatories," Ned pleaded.

She laughed. "No. But a boathouse like Chas and Ria's, which Uncle Freddie also designed. The very tip is a granite slab, but just down from that on the west side is a sandy cove – perfect for a boathouse and a beach.... Gosh, I'm so excited to show you the island and introduce you to my relatives and friends!"

"You'll have to draw me a family tree and tell me about everyone first. Like who Freddie is."

"Freddie Spencer. He's an architect, and married to my Mum's cousin, Zoë, who is Max's twin sister. Zoë's first husband was a doctor who was killed in France, and he was Dr. Ellie Roland's brother."

"My head is already reeling. Is there going to be an exam at the end of this genealogy lesson?"

"I've hardly begun," she said with a chuckle.

They ambled back to Skellfield House in the lingering twilight, stopping in a grove of trees by the river to kiss. They were interrupted by the roar of airplanes, and looked up to see the sky filled with bombers turning toward the coast.

"Zowie!" Merilee exclaimed in awe.

"They'll be joining more aircraft from the RAF. Up to a thousand at a time on a raid."

"That must be terrifying..." she began.

"For the crews as well as the people being bombed. Sometimes we even knock each other out of the sky. We always wonder how many names will be erased from the operations board in the morning."

"Thank God you've finished your tour!"

Ned nodded, but looked grim. "I had a friend I wanted you to meet. Jack Stephen, a fellow pilot. Nicest guy! He was always trying to lighten the mood, and we had some good laughs over a few pints. His grandparents were original settlers with lots of land in and around Port Darling, but his father ended up working in Toronto. The family still spends summers at the cottage that his father had cobbled together, so we had lots to talk about. Remember who owned Big Red?"

"A young guy who was killed when he crashed his floatplane."

"Right. Well, Jack and his brothers went into Port to see the wreckage. Said it was gruesome, and they shouldn't have allowed their little sister, Helen, to tag along. But that didn't deter them from wanting to become pilots.... His younger brother, Andy, was killed when his Hurricane crashed in Wales in '41."

Merilee braced herself.

"We were on a raid over Leipzig in February. Over seven hundred planes. Seventy-nine didn't come back. That's 553 men. Jack and his crew included."

"Oh, Ned!" she hugged him tightly. "I'm so sorry! And that poor family!"

"I'll visit them when we're home. Jack was really protective of Helen. She'll be especially devastated to have lost two brothers."

"So tragic!.... And I can't imagine what hell you've been through."

"That's behind me for now. And you've given me the best remedy of all. I can hardly wait to show you Cornwall. And a few other delights as well, Mrs. Wilding," he added before kissing her seductively.

•   •   •

Merilee was floating in a warm, shallow lake, luxuriating in her nakedness. No matter how far out she swam, the water was never more than waist deep.

The early morning sun sizzled on the calm surface, almost blinding her. Suddenly, someone emerged from the river of light.

He rose to his feet and walked up to her, holding out his arms. She was overjoyed when she realized it was Erich.

"I've been waiting for you, my love," he said.

She went into his arms with complete abandon. "I never left."

The silence was shattered by the scream of engines as bombs and people plummeted from the sky.

Merilee woke with a pounding heart. Overhead, the tired bombers were returning.

She was thankful that she and Chas had a busy day touring operational squadrons scattered about this part of Yorkshire. She photographed aircrew at their daily briefing, ground crews preparing the planes for the nightly forays, including loading the bomb bays, and women in their various tasks. It left her little time to contemplate the disturbing dream.

And she was glad that Ned was taking her out for dinner again that evening. She needed to expunge Erich from her thoughts.

Ned cruised in on a BSA motorcycle.

"Is that yours?" Merilee asked.

"It belongs to one of my British pals. When he saw your painting of Big Red, he figured I could be entrusted with this old thing."

He hopped off and enfolded her in his arms.

"Introductions, if you please," Bev said, as she and other girls joined them.

Claiming him as her fiancé, Merilee heard plenty of disappointed groans as well as congratulations. While Ned was parking the bike in a secluded spot, Bev whispered to her, "Fast work, landing a dishy fella like that."

"We've been friends since we were kids."

"Even better. At least you know he won't turn into a jerk. Mavis just discovered that her hot boyfriend has a wife back home."

Bev was right, of course. So how could she even compare Erich to Ned? It was time to close that chapter of her life as well. Perhaps now she could shed the guilt.

England: Spring and Summer 1944
Chapter 25

"So, it's finally happening," Roz said as she and Elyse strolled down the lane towards Riverbreeze on a gentle June evening.

Tension had been mounting for weeks as convoys of troops, tanks, and trucks blocked the roads around Southampton. Encampments of sombre soldiers had sprouted among the bluebells in the woods around Hamble, and Red Cross ambulances congregated nearby. Military vehicles and ammunition dumps were camouflaged with netting and greenery in fields and car parks and anywhere there was space. Almost overnight, the Americans had built a sturdy pier by the Yacht Club.

From the air, the girls had seen the Solent choked with ships that would have been sitting ducks for enemy aircraft. But surprisingly, none had come.

Delivering Spitfires to Hullavington airfield today, they were astounded that it was crammed with aircraft sporting newly painted black and white stripes on their wings.

Now they stopped for a moment to watch landing craft bristling with soldiers sailing off, the river disgorging its secret horde in a seemingly never-ending stream.

"You can almost feel it, can't you?" Elyse said. "The air seems to be quivering with excitement and fear and the sheer energy of all those men."

"Poor beggars."

Wondering how many of them would see another sunset, Elyse blew them a good-luck kiss. Terror for all her relatives and friends in the forces gripped her.

At least Theo was safe. He was now a Staff Officer with the 2nd Tactical Air Force because he still wasn't allowed to fly over enemy-held territory. He had mixed feelings about being out of the front-line action, and had quipped, "At least I have my own private Spit, so I get to float around the airfields here. Keep my bed warm, darling, as I'm sure I'll drop in often."

Without speaking, Elyse and Roz turned for home. Stiff whiskeys were most welcome.

The past two months had kept them so busy that they hadn't had much chance to grieve for Charlie. Suddenly drained of energy, they threw together Spam sandwiches for supper, which they ate desultorily on the terrace.

From the creek at the bottom of their garden, they couldn't see the activity on the Hamble River beyond, but they could hear the constant thrumming.

"Here's to witnessing history being made," Elyse toasted as she raised her glass.

"Do you think we'll be delivering aircraft to the Continent soon?"

"I expect the men will. The war will likely be over by the time they decide that women are capable of flying across the Channel as well."

"Much as I hate this war, I'll miss this job. We'll never get to fly those exhilarating kites again."

"I rather fancy taking a Spit home with me."

Roz chuckled. "It wouldn't surprise me if your Uncle Chas or Jack could actually pull that off."

"I'll put in my dibs... And take Sir Felix along as well, don't you think?" The cat settled down contentedly between them.

"That might be a bit trickier."

"Have you thought about what you'll do?"

"Become a recluse who just reminisces about her glory days," Roz replied, half in jest.

Elyse knew that here, Roz felt close to Charlie, but he'd left no footprints in her American life. Even his grave would be too far away to visit often.

"You'll have to spend lots of time at Wyndwood. Charlie will be there in spirit."

After an emotional moment of silence, Roz said, "Ah, but will you be there, or stuck here in Blighty?"

"I'm working on Theo. Reminding him of all the riches promised by relatives when we *come home*."

"Bribery!"

"He mumbles about the family estate he'll inherit, but he doesn't seem keen on it. Wants to stay in finance in the city."

"And you?"

Elyse shrugged. "Not a clue. I could take up horse breeding, like my father, if I'm stuck at the Dorset estate. And I could give riding lessons, since I did show jumping when I was a kid. But I used to fancy becoming a film star."

"So it's a choice between Hollywood and horse shit?"

Elyse burst into laughter. "Wherever I am, I'll miss you terribly, Roz. So I'll definitely fly down to Duxbury for tea and fetch you to the cottage if or when we're in Canada."

"I *will* end up a recluse if I move back in with my parents! For a while, sure. It's a picturesquely historic and serene little town, and I love the sea. But it's a place for families or holidays. I also can't see myself living alone in Boston, though. Maybe I should go to college, as I'd planned. But I don't know what I'd want to study anymore. Everything seems so irrelevant."

"We're just spoiled by this adventurous life. And antsy. But Charlie left you well off, so you could do anything, even start your own airline."

Roz snorted. "I didn't realize I was marrying a Canadian Vanderbilt! But what good is all that money if he's not here to share it with me? I would have been happy to settle into domestic bliss with Charlie. Raise a few kids. Live in a place like Duxbury and summer in Muskoka. Or even stay in Britain if necessary." Roz hastily wiped away tears. "Sometimes I wish I'd gotten pregnant. Our child might have helped to fill the aching, gaping hole in my soul."

Elyse didn't know what to say, so she gripped Roz's arm in support.

There was a roar from the heavens as if in sympathetic anguish. Against the darkening sky they could see hundreds of aircraft passing over. D-Day had truly begun.

Elyse woke at 5:30 the next morning to the steady thunder of American B-17 bombers, which were still streaming overhead when she and Roz walked to work three hours later.

Shortly after they arrived at the aerodrome, A BBC bulletin blared out, "Under the command of General Eisenhower, Allied naval forces, supported by strong air forces, began landing Allied armies this morning on the northern coast of France."

Excitement was tempered with trepidation as Elyse exchanged a grim smile with Roz.

In the lull after the long days of working into the late evenings of double summer time, the ATA women were restless as they awaited their chits for the day. They tried to stay busy with their usual activities in the mess – knitting, writing letters, playing bridge – but were tense and unfocussed.

When General Eisenhower's speech was broadcast on the 10:00 AM BBC news announcing the invasion and advising the besieged nations of Europe to hold steadfast as "the hour of your liberation is approaching", it was finally real.

Elyse and Roz went to play a cathartic game of tennis on the court by the hangar.

Not long after, an invasion-striped Spitfire bearing battle scars careened onto the runway and bounced along, with the crash wagon in hot pursuit. They, along with the girls from the mess, rushed over, feeling like they were truly part of this momentous day. Fortunately, the pilot wasn't badly injured.

As Hamble had been designated one of the emergency airfields, several other wounded aircraft landed in the ensuing days. Theo dropped in occasionally in his shiny Spitfire to spend the night. And the girls became happily busy again as replacement aircraft were needed.

Elyse was enjoying a powerful Hawker Tempest fighter on a perfect summer day that suddenly reminded her of home. Tomorrow was Dominion Day, July 1st, an occasion celebrated with the traditional "Stepping Stone" swimming race and costume ball at Wyndwood since long before she was born. Her family and friends were likely there now. The youngest always had the task of helping to decorate the pavilion with fairy lights and fresh flowers sent up to the island from the greenhouses at Wyndholme, thus earning the privilege of dressing up and staying up for the festivities. Chiding herself for being sentimental, Elyse realized what a wondrous childhood she'd had, despite her mother's desertion.

Nearing RAF Newchurch in Kent, she revelled in the view of the sun-sparkled Channel, which she could almost imagine was a placid lake. The chalky coast of France shimmered like a mirage, tauntingly close.

Gripped by poignant thoughts of home, she didn't take much notice of the growing black speck shooting towards her across the twenty miles of water. Idly assuming it was an RAF plane, she ignored it until it was uncomfortably close and making no alteration to its course, finally dodging out of the way as the mindless black rocket zipped past her. Tossed about in its soulless wake, she angrily turned to follow the deadly "buzz bomb" that had been terrorizing Britain these past weeks.

But what could she do to stop its heinous path of destruction? Theo had told her that pilots had been tipping the wings of these missiles, upsetting the gyroscope and causing them to plummet, thus keeping them from reaching London.

Not many planes were fast enough to catch them. But the Tempest was. Did she have the courage to try to unbalance it? If not done expertly, she might collide with the bomb, or if it exploded mid-air, she would be engulfed in the conflagration.

Damn the torpedoes, she chuckled as she opened full throttle. First woman to topple a V1?

She felt vibrantly alive as she gained on it, ready for battle. But like a huffy dragon, it suddenly belched black smoke and, dropping its nose, began to glide to earth.

Elyse watched in fascinated horror as it seemed to pinpoint a sleepy hamlet amidst the empty fields and vast marshlands. She held her breath as it plunged into the churchyard and exploded, reducing nearby buildings to piles of rubble.

Sickened and shaken, she turned back on course.

•   •   •

Having finished photographing an investiture at Buckingham palace, Merilee had decided to walk back to HQ via The Savoy to firm up plans for the wedding reception, which was only two weeks away. The elegant private dining room overlooking the Thames would be perfect for their party of thirty. She was excited, but also apprehensive to think of this big step she was taking. Elyse, who was to be her Matron of Honour, had assured her that she'd experienced similar doubts, but didn't regret her decision.

This last day of June was invitingly warm and sunny. Office workers on lunch breaks lingered on the streets as Merilee also stretched out her fifteen-minute walk back to Lincoln's Inn Fields. She spotted a couple of RCAF officers standing outside The Strand Theatre, pondering whether they should attend that evening's performance of *Arsenic and Old Lace*.

"Would you mind if I took your photo?" she asked them. The ornate theatre was one of two that flanked the equally luxurious Waldorf Hotel, and would provide a terrific backdrop to "personnel exploring London".

"Sure, if you'll come to the play with me tonight," one the pilots retorted with a grin.

"Thanks for the offer, but I'm getting married next week."

"Damn! Just my luck. Aircrew, is he?"

"Squadron Leader, with Bomber Command. Tour expired, so he's teaching."

"Lucky devil... on several accounts."

"If you'd just ignore me and chat gaily about something, I won't keep you more than a couple of minutes," Merilee promised.

"I'd rather be admiring the photographer than the building, I must admit. But I shall behave, and look like I'm having a jolly good time."

"Perfect!"

After taking a few candid snaps, she asked them for their names and other pertinent information that she could record.

"Only if you tell me yours," the jokester said.

"LAW Sutcliffe."

"Soon to be...?"

"Wilding," she revealed, rather annoyed at his probing.

"Wilding? It's not Ned, is it?"

"Yes, it is!"

"Well I'll be damned! We were at Elementary Flying School together! I ended up in fighter training, so we lost track of each other. I'm glad the old boy's doing so well. Tell him that Sam Oldershaw sends his regards. And that he's a damn lucky devil. Well deserved, of course, even if he did find you first."

"We've known each other forever."

"So, you're the girl next door he was sweet on! Wouldn't show us your photo in case we all fell in love with you. I can see why."

Merilee blushed.

They gave her their details, Sam also asking for Ned's current location.

"I'll give him a buzz some time. Good luck to you both."

"And to you!... It's a crackerjack play, by the way – *Arsenic and Old Lace*."

Merilee sauntered away feeling uplifted by the encounter. It was helpful to have connections to home and friends, even if tenuous. But she'd only gone a dozen yards when the air raid siren ripped the beautiful day apart.

She heard the stuttering drone of Hitler's new vengeance weapon, which had begun attacking only a fortnight ago. Up to a hundred a day were devastating various parts of the city. The V1 rockets were so fast that there was little warning or defence.

Merilee looked skyward, momentarily bewildered when the noise stopped. Apparently, those who were hit by a buzz bomb never heard it coming, because the engine shut off before it dove silently to earth.

Suddenly realizing her danger, she sprinted back to the entrance of the Waldorf Hotel, just as Sam and his colleague, Don, dashed over from the opposite direction. Sam grabbed her arm and pulled her inside. They kept running away from the tall plate-glass windows, and up the shallow steps to the reception area, ducking behind the long desk, to the surprise of the staff.

"Down!" Sam ordered everyone as he pushed Merilee to the floor and hovered over her protectively.

A moment later the building shuddered in protest to a tremendous, deafening explosion outside.

When the tinkling of glass had subsided, they got to their feet. Staff and guests rushed outside. With only a few windows gone, the hotel had suffered minimal damage.

Smoke and dust obscured the sun, but not the scene of devastation emerging along the street to the east. They hurried over to see what help they could offer.

Several dazed and bloodied people staggered toward them, so staff accompanied them into the hotel.

The rocket had hit the middle of the Aldwych road, between Adastral House - the Air Ministry building - and the BBC's Bush House opposite.

A couple of double-decker buses had been ripped open like tins of sardines. Bodies, some naked from the blast, lay among the debris. Others had been scythed by glass shards. Several WAAFs had been sucked out of their offices and smashed onto the pavement below. Bleeding, battered victims were crying for help.

Merilee thought she would be sick. Sam and Don steadied her as she tripped over debris.

Civil defence teams and ambulances were already arriving, covering the dead and removing the injured. Those with minor wounds were steered to a First Aid post in the basement of Bush House. While Sam and Don helped them, Merilee snapped pictures.

But not of the dead or dying. Of dust-shrouded, dishevelled people supporting one another. Of stretcher-bearers carrying those fortunate enough to have survived. Of the mess of twisted metal and broken masonry. Of stark trees stripped of leaves, bizarrely draped with shreds of clothing, while the bruised buildings around them stood defiantly.

She didn't realize she was weeping until Sam offered her a handkerchief.

"We've done what we can," he said. "Let's go back to the hotel. We all need a stiff drink."

"I have to get back to work," Merilee protested half-heartedly as he and Don steered her away.

"Not in this condition! We'll escort you back later."

She went along with them, too distraught to attempt that last half-mile to HQ.

Sam ordered three brandies when they'd settled into the bar at the Waldorf.

Merilee took a fiery gulp before saying, "If we hadn't chatted in front of the theatre, I would have been right where the bomb hit." She shuddered and took another sip as she relaxed into the plush leather chair.

"That's because I'm a terrible flirt," Sam admitted.

"I think Ned will forgive you," Merilee replied with a wan smile.

"It's good to see some colour back in your cheeks, Miss Sutcliffe," Don said.

"Do call me Merilee."

Don crinkled his brow. "Say, you're not the one who wrote that book about the kids saving the world from a sinister black cloud, are you?"

"Well... actually..."

"Holy cow! And your parents wrote the *Enchanted Waterfall* series?"

"Yes."

"My little sister raved about your book! Told me I had to read it. I sure as heck will now!"

Merilee loved hearing that she had fans, but was always a bit embarrassed to be in the limelight.

"Clever and talented as well as beautiful," Sam mused. "Do you have a sister?"

She laughed. "No, but lots of cousins and friends." Impulsively, she added. "If you're free two weeks tomorrow, would you come to the wedding?" There was room for a few more guests.

The men looked at each other. "If we can manage it, sure!" Sam said.

"Wonderful! Now I really must get back or they'll think I've gone AWOL."

"We'll accompany you."

"I'm sure I can manage now, but thank you. You can't be wasting so much time with me on your 48."

"We're not just here to pick up girls, Merilee. We value good conversation." Under his ginger mop, Sam's face seemed to hold a perpetual, mischievous grin.

She was actually grateful for their company, spooked by the thought that another "doodlebug" might appear out of nowhere.

Irene Larkin was just coming out of HQ when they arrived. "Merilee! We were wondering what happened to you. Worried you might have been in that explosion by the Air Ministry. We heard it and saw the smoke! They're saying that plenty were killed, including some WAAFs!"

"I *was* there, but my new friends came to my rescue." Merilee introduced them and told her what had happened.

"Thank God for that!"

"Miss Larkin, would you do me the honour of accompanying me to the theatre this evening?" Sam asked. "You look as if you're itching for a night on the town with a devoted admirer."

Irene's delightful laughter was always infectious. "A bunch of us were planning to dance at the Royal Opera House tonight."

"The play's at 6:30. We could dine afterwards and still join your friends. Dance the night away."

"In that case, how could I refuse? As long as I may bring a friend."

"Of course. Don will be a most attentive companion."

"Right on!" Don assured her.

Shortly after Merilee arrived at the flat, Ned called. "Imagine my surprise when my old buddy Sam rang to tell me that I had not only won the hand of the fairest maiden in the land, but also that he's been invited to our wedding."

"I didn't think you'd mind."

"Of course not! That's swell. But I was terrified when I heard the circumstances. It's no good wishing you were safely home in Canada, or I wouldn't be as deliriously happy as I am."

"I worry about you, too. Even your teaching job isn't all that safe, is it? We just have to hope that our luck holds."

•   •   •

With only ten days until the wedding, Merilee began to fret about the arrival of her wedding dress. Her grandmother, Marie, had insisted on creating it, and Merilee had cabled her measurements three months ago.

Marie had kept her children fed with her skills as a seamstress until Jack had begun earning enough money to allow her to enjoy the status of a Wyndham widow. She had then turned her talents to clothing her three daughters – and eventually granddaughters - in her own Parisian-inspired designs, to the envy of other society girls. So, a unique outfit from Mémé had always been a cherished Christmas gift.

With limited space for civvies in her overseas luggage, Merilee had brought only one cocktail dress, and decided that it might have to suffice. But that spangled, sky-blue chiffon – so easy to pack - also reminded her of the evening at the Pineridge Inn three years ago when Bryce had once again won her over, and they had danced in the shallows. With him being among the guests, her uniform would perhaps be the better choice. Ned would be wearing his.

She had been hesitant to invite Bryce, but there were so few family and friends who could attend the wedding, so she had – after consulting Ned.

He'd said, "I should thank Bryce for not realizing what a treasure he gave up."

"Don't tease!"

"OK, I won't rub it in when I meet him." Merilee had heard his grin over the telephone. "If Hugh were here, he'd be my Best Man, so Bryce would have been invited anyway."

"He tried to win me back when we met at Charlie's funeral. But I told him that would never happen. I just want you to know that I'm well and truly over him."

"Lucky me!"

Merilee briefly considered taking up Sophie's offer of her wedding gown, but there probably wasn't time to alter it now. She wasn't as voluptuous as either Sophie or Elyse, who had worn it three years ago, so the basic design wasn't right for her anyway.

The parcel from home arrived just five days before the ceremony. The dress fit perfectly, and Mémé had designed it so that it could also be worn as an evening gown, either alone or with Merilee's sequined black lace jacket, which her mother had included in the parcel.

The white satin was draped to flatter her slender figure. Glittering bands rose from a point at the waist to flare at the shoulders, and then plunge to another V in mid-back. For the wedding, this simple but sexy gown was topped by a sheer, lace-embroidered bolero that swooped away under the arms to cover the exposed back, and ended in beaded points at the wrists, making it appear as if her skin were appliqued with swirls of foliage.

"Oh, how gorgeous! I need to borrow that some time!" Connie Fulton announced.

"I'm willing to share lots of things with friends, but not this," Merilee declared to her flat mate.

"That's hardly the wartime spirit, Mare," Connie snapped.

Merilee disliked how cavalierly Connie had shortened her name. And laid claim to privileges.

"It wouldn't fit you anyway," Eva Nilsson observed drily.

"You mean because I have boobs," Connie said, bouncing them boastfully.

"Don't be flippant, Connie," Eva warned. "We're living almost rent-free. Merilee might decide to kick us out once she's married."

Merilee insisted they pay a generous salary to Mrs. Travers for cleaning and shopping – and often cooking for them - although Uncle Jack had assured her that all expenses were included. But that was so little compared to what others were paying for minimal accommodations, which sometimes included cockroaches.

Connie lay back on the sofa and lit a cigarette. "Hubby's not likely to be here much, so Mare would die of boredom without us. Let's go to the Embassy Club tonight! There's a hot flyboy who's caught my eye. He promised he'd be back."

"Don't count on me," Merilee said. "I still have lots to prepare."

"I have to wash my hair. Or stockings. Or something," Eva said to laughter.

"You two are annoyingly dull!" Connie grumbled. "I guess I'll write to my boyfriend then."

"Which one is it this week?" Eva teased.

Connie threw a pillow at her.

Merilee was pleased that the three of them got along well, most of the time. She had felt an instant connection with Eva, who hailed from Sault Ste. Marie. They shared a love of the rugged Canadian Shield with its myriad lakes, which consoled them when they were homesick. Eva's Scandinavian heritage was evident in her crystal-blue eyes and pale, ethereal beauty. She'd worked as a librarian for a couple of years before joining up.

City-bred socialite Connie was vivacious and popular. Her mother was on the Board of the Art Gallery with Aunt Fliss - Jack's wife and Chas's sister – so there was a tenuous family connection. But Connie's high-handedness sometimes grated on Merilee. Fortunately, they didn't work together.

Being in the records and accounts section of the RCAF, Eva and Connie worked in a converted warehouse of the Harrod's department store just south of Hyde Park – a half-hour walk across that green expanse.

Connie poured herself a large whiskey and sat down at the dining table with a writing pad. Merilee was just about to remove her wedding gown when the air raid sirens began screaming. She fumbled with the zipper as she rushed out of her bedroom. The others were already at the door, but Merilee ran back to grab the rest of the parcel.

"Hurry!" Eva cried.

When they huddled in the old wine cellar, Connie realized that she still had the whiskey in her hand and took a big gulp.

"You can see what Connie considers important to save," Eva jested.

"Looks good to me," Mike, one of the officers from the flat above theirs, said as he joined them.

"Have a sip if you like," Connie offered flirtatiously.

"Don't mind if I do." He was a friendly chap in his early thirties, but with secretive depths, Merilee thought. He was in Intelligence, after all.

"Perhaps I should toast the beautiful bride," Mike said, raising the glass to Merilee.

The ground suddenly trembled with the thunder of a nearby explosion.

"Well, let's hope that's it for the night," he said as they all breathed a sigh of relief. These doodlebug attacks were sporadic and usually solitary, unlike the hordes of bombers that had pummelled the city for hours during the Blitzes. But this was more frightening in some ways, because the stealthy, deadly rockets zoomed in at any time of the day or night.

Merilee was still traumatized by her close call the previous week. Her photographs had captured the haunting scenes with such emotion and artistry that her boss had congratulated her.

The "all clear" didn't sound, so they waited. They later discovered that the rocket had landed in Hyde Park, and, thankfully, injured no one.

"I was just thinking how tragic it would be if we were hit, and they pulled our bodies out of the rubble to discover Mare in her wedding gown."

"Connie!" Eva chided. "What a horrible thought!"

"Well let's hope that the Jerries don't interrupt the wedding on Saturday. And especially the honeymoon," Connie added with a suggestive smirk.

Mike chortled. "Definitely not that!"

Merilee blushed. She was already nervous about that.

She rooted through the rest of her package and found a brandy-soaked wedding cake baked by Lois.

"Smells divine," Connie declared.

Lady Sidonie had offered to help with the wedding preparations, and since she had connections, Merilee had accepted. The reception included a decorated cake, so Merilee said, "Ned's mum's a fabulous baker, so I think we'll be doling this out sparingly. Let's sample it." She broke off pieces of the moist cake for each of them.

"Raisins and almonds and marzipan and lashings of cognac," Connie sighed. "I think I'm in heaven!"

"God, yes!" Mike agreed.

"This was worth going back for," Eva added with a grin.

Later in their flat, Merilee unwrapped the rest of the parcel, which included her white summer pumps, and treasured nylon stockings from Peggy, which she'd been saving for a special occasion.

The note from her mother read, "Maman came to stay for a week while we created your dress to her inspired design. What fun we had, even though we were terribly sad to be missing the wedding. You'll have to wear it again for a party when you're finally home. Maman – always practical - wanted it to be useful for more than just one occasion.

"I've sent you the headdress I wore at my wedding and would be happy if you chose to wear this. It will make me feel just a little bit that I am there with you, my darling child. Be happy."

The jewelled '20s hairband – appropriately enough - resembled two fairy wings fanning out and touching over the forehead. It looked splendid, and Merilee shed a few tears to think that her parents wouldn't be at the wedding.

•   •   •

Ned's CO arranged for one of the trainee crews to do a cross-country flight with a stop at an aerodrome near London, and Ned was to hitch a ride with them. So, he arrived at The Savoy in the late afternoon.

Merilee had booked rooms there for the wedding party, including a river-view suite for them, which Ned would already use that night.

"What a room! Even has its own marble bathroom. I guess I'll have to get used to living in luxury now," he quipped when he embraced her.

"The Savoy has its own farm, so they serve real eggs for breakfast. *That's* luxury. I can hardly wait!"

He laughed.

"Before the others arrive, I have something to show you," Merilee said eagerly.

She led him outside and over to a silver Triumph motorcycle parked in the entrance court. She handed him a key. "My wedding gift to you."

He was astounded. "A Tiger 100! With a dual seat! Holy mackerel, Merilee, this is extravagant!"

"Not as expensive as my ring, I bet. Elyse and Roz found it for me and have filled it up with gas. We can take it with us on the train and use it in Cornwall."

He hugged her tightly. "What a magnificent gift! I'm deeply touched. Hop on and we'll take it for a spin."

"Right now? If I get caught by the Snoops astride a motorcycle in my uniform, with an officer, I'll be on the carpet!" she said of the Service Police, who were diligent in enforcing regulations.

"They'd never catch us," he assured her with a grin.

She giggled. "You'll have to sit on the hem of my skirt so that it doesn't fly up."

Ned revelled in the feel of Merilee at this back as she clung tightly to him. With so few private cars on the roads, it was an exhilarating ride along The Embankment, past Buckingham Palace, and back via Trafalgar Square.

"Gosh that was fun!" she exclaimed as they dismounted.

"We'll have a ball exploring Cornwall on this! I'll even let you drive sometimes."

•   •   •

Alastair Grayson smiled at Merilee as he offered his arm to help her out of the car. Lady Sidonie had provided her Rolls Royce and ancient French chauffeur.

Alastair stepped aside as he said, "Look who wandered into London late last night."

"Hey, little cuz, you look dazzling!"

"Drew! Oh my gosh! What a wonderful surprise!" She hugged him gleefully. "I wasn't expecting you yet!"

"We arrived in Bournemouth two days ago, and I had to use connections to get here in time. Couldn't miss this!"

"Since Drew's you're closest relative in Britain, he should walk you down the aisle," Alastair said. Before Merilee could protest, he added, "But I'm honoured to have been asked. And anyway, I'm not good at making speeches."

Drew offered her his arm and said, "Ready?"

She breathed deeply and nodded.

Elyse squeezed her other hand encouragingly and stepped behind the bride as they entered the church.

Merilee was amazed to see so many who hadn't been invited to the reception, including Mike from upstairs and people from HQ. Mrs. Travers wiped happy tears from her eyes as Merilee passed.

Sam Oldershaw stood beaming next to Irene Larkin. They had hit it off on the first date and were daily writing or phoning each other.

Merilee was delighted to spot Ole Knutsen, and then saddened to be reminded about Lars and Gunnar. Gord McLaughlin gave her a cheerful thumbs-up.

Because Drew reminded her of Erich, a flood of memories suddenly overwhelmed her. Tender moments. Bared souls touching one another as if rekindling old acquaintance.

Dear God, what was she doing getting married to Ned?

But the bridegroom stood proudly awaiting her at the altar, admiration and love gleaming in his eyes.

Erich was in the past, and they never had a future. Even *he* had advised her to forget him at their last meeting. But *Merilee's Song* echoed through her mind, as if she could hear him playing it longingly, far away over the sea.

Perhaps it was symbolic and fitting that Drew was giving her into Ned's care.

She smiled at Ned and went through the ritual that bound her to him, slightly dazed. When his soft lips touched hers, she was jolted back to reality. Of course she loved him. It was time for girlish fantasies to be discarded.

Patsy, the official photographer as well as one of the invited guests, took pictures on the steps of the church, and of the celebrants surrounding the bridal couple in front of the fountains in Trafalgar Square. Colleagues spelled Patsy so that she, too, could be in the photos.

When it was time for congratulations, Sam Oldershaw, with Irene at his side, gave Ned a vigorous handshake and manly slap on the back.

"I always knew you'd get your girl in the end, old chum." To Merilee, he added, without meeting her eyes, "Don couldn't make it, unfortunately. He sends his sincerest regrets."

She feared he was sparing her an unpleasant truth, but no one wanted to mention death on a day like this.

At the reception, Merilee had deliberately not assigned places other than the wedding party. There was plenty of time to mingle over drinks before the meal, allowing people to select those with whom they wished to sit.

Ole gave her a warm hug, saying, "I am so happy to see you again, Merilee! It is a big help to have such good memories of Muskoka, thanks to you and your family. And I am glad that Peggy's brother was the right man, after all."

He was also delighted to see Gord again, and be reminded of the day they had met at the Rotary Street Fair in Gravenhurst. Ole had been permitted a dance with Gail, and now asked after her.

"We're officially engaged," Gord announced with a grin.

"Excellent! I suspected you had a great romance," Ole said.

"And I wondered when you'd finally reveal that," Merilee added.

Gord shrugged. "Being apart, we've realized more than ever that we were always meant for each other. So now we can make plans for our future." He beamed. "And I'm almost as happy for you and Ned."

Bryce and Connie connected as if drawn together by magnets. He had been gracious but cool in his congratulations, and had lost no time downing his first whiskey. Now he was animated in his tales about shooting down V1 rockets, since his squadron was doing interception. It meant that he was staying in Britain on Home Defence for now, and Merilee felt happy for him on that account.

Alastair and Roz were engaged in companionable conversation. Drew was overjoyed to be with Elyse and Sophie and her children – whom he hadn't seen for five years - and completely oblivious to Merilee's colleagues who eyed him with swooning awe.

Theo gravitated to Sidonie's side. "You look strangely lonely and wistful."

"Drew looks so much like his father that I feel like I've suddenly plummeted into the past."

Theo lit her cigarette as he said, "Mum claims that you were in love with Chas."

"Who wasn't? Even your mother was doe-eyed around him."

"Would you have stayed in Canada if you'd married him?"

After her initial shock, Sid chuckled. "Oh yes. His brother was never the man of my dreams... So where is this conversation leading?"

"Elyse is subtly brainwashing me into moving to Canada after the war. Not sure I can live there."

"Too egalitarian for you?" Sid mocked.

"That's rich, coming from you!"

"Au contraire, cher ami. I've never avoided people – or liaisons – based on their pedigree. Jack was just an upstart when we became *friends*. Penniless. Look at him now – a financial genius whose assets are solidly anchored in property. In fact, you could do worse than go into business with him."

"I have to think about my family estate as well."

"I can't see you two being content in remote Dorset. And don't expect Elyse to be lady of the manor while you're off in London and just home at weekends. I know your mother hated that."

"She spent time in London often enough. And we wouldn't have to be in Dorset at all until I inherit."

"But is that really what you want? Elyse is homesick after being away for four years. She has a rich life with her relatives and summer community of friends. It will be interesting to see if love prevails."

"You mean which one of us will give in and possibly be miserable."

"It shouldn't be a sacrifice. That's bound to cause resentment, as I know all too well." She patted his arm reassuringly. "Canada is a young country. Everyone who is ambitious and resourceful has a chance to succeed. It's also a place where you can breathe. I felt suffocated in England after the last war and am feeling that again. This time I shall return to the Riviera. But you, dear boy, have the opportunity for a fresh start, to really make a name for yourself without having to unearth centuries of dubious ancestors."

He laughed.

"You can always compromise. June to October are fabulous there. The rest of the year here, and a few winter weeks in Antibes with me, don't you think?"

"Sounds delightful, but when do I actually work?"

"You two seem to be plotting something," Elyse said, joining them.

"Just contemplating the joys of life after war," Sid admitted.

"So were we! Starting with a big party on Wyndwood."

"Why am I not surprised," Theo drawled, exchanging a glance with an amused Sid.

Taking him by the arm, Elyse said, "You'll love it there, and at *our* cottage on Blackthorn Island. Sid did a marvellous job designing it." She gave her mother a generous smile. "Excuse us, Sid. Theo's opinion is required. But do join us later at the table."

"That was kind of you," Theo whispered to Elyse as they ambled back to the Wyndwood crowd.

"Don't seem so surprised! I'm not heartless."

"No indeed." He gave her a discreet kiss on the temple.

Most of Ned's original crew had been able to come, so Merilee was happy to meet them. They eventually sat with her WD friends.

The tender and ample roast beef and Yorkshire pudding dinner with all the trimmings was a treat for everyone. Magnums of champagne – provided by Uncle Jack – were opened for the toasts.

Drew's speech had people laughing as well as brushing away the odd tear. He concluded by saying, "Merilee has always been a treasured cousin and a good sport, ready for any challenge. She's as talented on water skis and tennis courts as she is with camera and pen, and obviously a force to be reckoned with. So be prepared, Ned!... Let's raise our glasses to wish the newlyweds abiding love, a lifetime of joy and adventure, and success in fulfilling their *Wilding-est* dreams."

After they did, Drew said, "I'm sure no one will object to drinking another toast, so fill your glasses to celebrate our dear friends Hugh Carrington and Ginnie Roland who are tying the knot today on Wyndwood Island. Hugh wanted to invite all his former crewmates, but Ned beat him to it."

They cheered as glasses clinked.

"And now we have a special treat. I'll let Elyse explain."

Staff trundled in a 16 mm movie projector and a portable screen, which they set up at the end of the room while she addressed the guests. "Our cousin Alexander Wyndham is a filmmaker in Canada, along with his wife Rosemary. So they've sent this present for the newlyweds."

Merilee and Ned looked at her in astonishment as she grinned and raised a sassy eyebrow. Merilee expected that Elyse had something to do with this.

A waiter dimmed the lights and the film sprang to life.

Faith's Fairy Dance was the soundtrack as the screen lit up. "Wyndcrest Films Presents: A Love Letter to Merilee and Ned Wilding, July 15, 1944." The words hovered for a moment and then dissolved into the bay at Hope Cottage. Merilee gasped with joy as the camera leisurely panned that beloved lake in full Kodachrome colour, and turned towards the house. Inside, Peggy was playing her tune at the grand piano, grinning happily.

As the music mellowed into the background, Merilee's parents and Saxon appeared. Her mother said, "We all miss you, sweetheart, and wish we could be there for your special day. But we *are* with you in spirit and send our deepest love to you both. What do you say, Saxon?" He yipped eagerly, eliciting laughter from the guests, and lightening the mood.

Her father added, "Welcome to the family, Ned! We wish the two of you every happiness and look forward to having you safely home again."

A teary Merilee gratefully accepted the handkerchief that Elyse passed her.

There were chuckles as the next shot opened in the Wildings' driveway, focussed on Chipper, the Lab, seated in the sidecar of Big Red with his paw draped nonchalantly over the side. A flower-studded banner reading "Just Married" decorated the bike. The camera pulled back to reveal Ned's family against the majestic backdrop of granite, pines, and unfurling maples. When they took turns congratulating the newlyweds, Ned squeezed Merilee's hand, and she knew that he was overwhelmed.

Good wishes and advice from relatives and friends followed. Even Cousin Phoebe was featured, saying simply, "Carpe diem," with that enigmatic smile that suggested she was privy to the secrets of the universe. It sent a shiver down Merilee's spine.

The film was spiced with humour, with cleverly inserted photos and vintage film clips of Merilee and Ned at different stages of their lives, sometimes in ironic contrast to the comments. Hilarity ensued when Adam said, "You'll have your work cut out trying to keep up with Merilee on water skis, Ned," followed by a dozen snappy clips of a very young Merilee falling in myriad awkward ways as she was learning to ski. Amy chimed in, "Adam always exaggerates!" with more recent footage of Merilee expertly cutting in and out of the wake on one ski.

Hugh Carrington, in uniform, his arm around Ginnie Roland, said, "I'm thrilled that two of my favourite people are getting hitched. And that we'll share the same anniversary. Good luck *over there*, you two." He saluted them.

Faith's Fairy Dance ended, and Peggy rose from the piano bench. "We all love you, Ned and *Merilee Wilding*." Merilee knew that Peggy's wink was to remind her of their old game, and how perfect her new name sounded. "And we're going to have a whopping great party when you get home!" She blew them a kiss as the picture faded into the lake and then transitioned into a view of the waterfront at Wyndcrest, with Sandy and Rosemary holding cameras and waving cheerfully. The lens then focussed on the great blue heron standing on the end of the dock as he transformed into a logo for Wyndcrest Films.

There was tremendous applause, and Merilee hastily brushed away tears before the lights came back on. To Elyse, who sat beside her, she said, "Thank you. I'm sure you instigated that."

"It only took a suggestion to get Sandy excited about the idea."

"It's helped to make me – both of us – feel like our families are truly part of this day."

"I'm impressed with how slick and professional it is considering how little time they actually had to produce it. And in colour! But I should expect no less from Sandy. I may have to rethink my career goals. Looks like glamorous gals can be behind the camera as well as in front of it."

"You'll like Rosemary."

"I have no doubt, since she got your approval. You can never be sure that men aren't just so bewitched that they can't think with the appropriate organ," Elyse said mischievously.

Merilee burst into laughter. "You can't possibly stay behind in England after the war, Elyse. We'd all miss you too much!" Since D-Day, everyone had been thinking that the war would soon be over.

As people mingled once more, Bryce said to Drew, "That was swell of you to toast Hugh and Ginnie. I'm pissed off to be missing their wedding. In fact, I've had enough of this bloody country! I hope that Anthea managed to get leave to attend."

"I don't hear from her often. After she arrived in Gander, she claimed it was unreasonable not to date other people when we're so far away from each other."

"Makes sense, I guess."

"I agree! She said we'll discover whether we're really meant for each other or just remain good friends. I'm thinking the latter."

"She's had her head turned by all those damned American flyboys on her base!"

"Sounds more like she and Alain are hitting it off."

"Then she must be desperate, since she always thought him a bore."

"He's just thoughtful and a bit reserved," Drew defended his second cousin.

"Well, don't give up on her, Drew. I fucked up with Merilee."

"*She* seems happy enough," Drew said wryly.

Bryce snorted. When Connie sidled up to him and wrapped her arm provocatively around his, he said sardonically to Drew, "On the other hand, relish your freedom."

"Oh, I do!"

Ole sought out Merilee and said, "Now I must catch a train back to Scotland. It made my heart happy to see your home and families again. This is the cousin who made the film about Little Norway, with pictures of us?"

"Yes!"

"Most excellent! I hope to see it one day."

"You'll have to come back to Canada," she said with a warm smile.

"I will, yes! Tusen takk for inviting me today."

"I'm so glad you could come, Ole! Please visit whenever you're in London... And stay safe."

"You also!"

"I feel so terribly sad for him," Eva said when Ole had departed. "He told me about his time in Muskoka. With his friends."

"I'm heartbroken whenever I think about them."

Drew joined them saying, "Why so glum, Merilee?"

"Thinking of lost friends."

"They would be celebrating with you today, so take heart, and enjoy this special moment."

"Carpe diem, as Cousin Phoebe said," she managed to quip.

"Yes indeed." He looked interestedly at Eva, so Merilee said, "Drew, this is my friend and flat mate, Eva Nilsson."

Blue eyes met and held.

Patsy swooped down on Merilee, saying, "What about a photo of you and Ned on his new motorcycle. Which I just heard about! It would be a lark to have you sitting astride in your wedding gown."

"I'm not missing this!" Eva said.

"Nor me," Drew agreed.

Many of the guests followed them outside.

Merilee perched elegantly sidesaddle behind Ned, her arms wrapped about him and her head laid against his back. He looked lovingly at her over his shoulder, while a dreamy expression and contented smile lit her face.

"I want a copy of that one," Eva declared.

"A classic, I'd say," Drew murmured.

Eva blushed when she realized how intently he was assessing her. As if his words somehow applied to her rather than the photo.

"So, tell me how you ended up over here, and living with Merilee," he said, taking her arm and leading her back inside.

Merilee was glad that people lingered to talk. It would seem almost anticlimactic when everyone had gone, and she was suddenly nervous about being alone with her husband. And his expectations.

Ned sensed her trepidation when he escorted her to their suite. A bottle of iced champagne awaited them. He shed his uniform jacket and tie, and popped the cork as he said, "Kick off your shoes and come over to the sofa."

He handed her a glass. "This stuff's a bit fizzy for my taste, but here's my toast to the most beautiful, intelligent, kind, and inspiring person I know. I will always cherish and protect you, my love.... So don't be afraid," he added gently, gazing into her eyes.

Their kiss became breathlessly passionate.

He unwrapped her slowly, kissing her neck, her shoulder, her breast. He led her over to the bed and helped her out of the gown. Between kisses, he stripped down to his shorts, so that his tumescent nakedness didn't frighten her, and slid into bed beside her.

His caresses aroused such gasping desire that she trembled. Her body opened up to him of its own volition.

When she lay in his arms afterwards, he said, "You can relax now, princess. The worst is over."

Having been inducted into the secret of womanhood, she felt strangely powerful. "If that's the beginning of our adventures in love, I can hardly wait to see what's next."

Ned laughed fulsomely. "You're priceless, Merilee Wilding! It only gets better."

•   •   •

Merilee and Ned lay side by side, their sweaty bodies fanned by warm sea breezes wafting through the open window. Too hot to cuddle after their lovemaking, they held hands.

"I'm going to miss this so much," Merilee confided. "I hate the thought of going back to London, especially without you."

He rolled onto his side and propped his head on his elbow as he gazed lovingly at her.

"Me too... So, let's plan our next leave." Merilee had a week off every three months, with a 48 either tacked on or taken in between. "The Lake District, I think. It'll be beautiful in the autumn. I'll scout out a romantic inn on the water. In the meantime, we'll make the most of our last two days here."

"Beach time?"

"You bet!"

The crenellated Tregenna Castle Hotel in St. Ives was popular with honeymooners and military personnel on leave, especially those from overseas. It sprawled amid extensive gardens and grounds on a hilltop overlooking the picturesque fishing village. Below it curved a wide stretch of champagne sand lapped by the turquoise sea. Palm trees and exotic vegetation justified the boast of this being the Cornish Riviera.

Their routine was to be up with the dawn, not wasting any precious moments of daylight. They would wade hand-in-hand in the shallows of the deserted beach as if it were exclusively theirs. After breakfast, they would head out on the motorcycle along the narrow, hedged roads that skirted the rugged coastline to Land's End, or across to Penzance and down the Lizard Peninsula.

Alastair and Gord had given them petrol ration cards, which aircrew received for their leaves, so they didn't have to worry about fuel. Sophie and Philip's present was a classy Art Deco Kodak camera, because Merilee hadn't been allowed to bring hers to Britain, and couldn't take her professional Speed Graphic along on leave. Since it was small enough to tuck into pockets and clamshell style, she carried it everywhere.

They hiked along the brow of dramatic cliffs battered by the relentless sea, and strolled the crooked, cobbled alleyways of St. Ives and other villages with quirky names like Mousehole. They lingered over a ploughman's lunch or Cornish pasties in quaint pubs, and when they arrived back at their luxurious hotel, they would fall playfully into bed. A late afternoon dip in the chilly bay revived them for dining and dancing, often in the company of fellow Canadians.

But the war was never far away. Many beaches, including St. Ives' harbour, were fortified with steel spears pointing seaward and entangled with barbed wire, or strewn with concrete blocks to impede amphibious invaders. Some were even mined. Pillboxes dotted the shoreline: the ones on their beach cleverly camouflaged to blend into the rocks at either end. RAF planes patrolled the sea, flying from coastal Cornish airfields.

Merilee was excited the next morning when they set out on the sixty-mile trek to Jamaica Inn in the middle of Bodmin Moor. It was an appropriately gloomy day.

She was not disappointed when they pulled into the walled courtyard of the ancient coaching inn. Made of flint and stone, it seemed to have been chiselled out of the desolate, rugged moorland that heaved unbroken for miles in every direction. Surely the sinister characters of Daphne du Maurier's novel could be lurking inside. Merilee was thrilled.

"It's not as run-down and creepy as in the book – fortunately - but I can see how Daphne was inspired by this place. It feels… deliciously haunted," she said over their fish and chips lunch. "Thank you for bringing me here, Ned."

He smiled. "Thanks for providing the transportation!"

"It *is* fun, isn't it?" she said gleefully.

"Every single minute."

He stared at her with such adoration that she felt a rush of desire. She reached out her hand and he took it firmly in his.

"Fish that good?" the landlord jested as he stopped by.

"Divine!" Merilee replied.

"Honeymooners?"

"Yes, and all the way from Canada to enjoy your ale," Ned riposted.

The landlord chuckled. "Thanks to Daphne, no doubt."

"And the RCAF."

"Mind if you're venturing out on the moor. It can be treacherous, especially on a day like today, when the clouds might suddenly come down and you can't see a hand in front of your face. Easy to get lost and end up in a bog. Daphne was lucky that her horse knew how to get back here when she was ambushed by fog."

"You met her?" Merilee asked eagerly.

"She wasn't famous when she stayed here. Nor were we!"

They took heed and didn't wander far onto the moor, but Merilee managed to capture atmospheric photos that included swirling ground mist and wild moorland ponies. She also snapped Ned straddling the Triumph in front of the inn, shadowed by menacing clouds. They thought it prudent to head back before the skies opened.

Ned drove sedately along the hedged and walled roads that were generally wide enough for only one vehicle, because oncoming traffic couldn't easily be seen on the windy roads, and required one driver to back into strategic widenings called lay-bys that allowed the other to scrape by. But he sped up on the straight stretches when there was no traffic.

Suddenly a military truck pulled out from a laneway right in front of them. Ned reacted instinctively, instantly realizing that there was no time to stop and obviously no shoulders or open fields to escape to. They could both be killed if he hit the truck.

He opened the throttle. Merilee clung to him in terror as they just zipped between the front bumper and the stone wall. They heard the truck squeal to a stop.

Merilee was shaking, and Ned pulled over at the first opportunity. He took her reassuringly into his arms.

"Thank God you're such a good driver!"

"Thank God Tiger is so fast," he said as he laid his cheek against her head.

When they returned to their hotel, their lovemaking was slow and tender as they savoured every moment of being vibrantly alive and together.

•   •   •

Merilee felt her spirits plummet and her anxiety rise as the train neared London. Cornwall had been so relaxing, with never a siren announcing impending doom. At least Ned was able to stay with her tonight, before catching a train north in the morning.

"The lovebirds have returned!" Connie exclaimed as they entered the flat. "How was Cornwall? Oh, lucky *you,* got a tan! We've hardly seen the sun."

Merilee grinned. "It was glorious! Peaceful. Only the squawking of seagulls and the crashing of waves. You should consider taking your leave there."

"I booked at the Tregenna Castle after your tempting postcard arrived. Going with Glennis in August," Eva informed her. Merilee knew their friends from work because they sometimes came over in the evenings or went to the flicks together.

"Not going along?" Merilee asked Connie.

"I have other plans for my precious leave." But she didn't elucidate.

"I've brought you each a lucky serpentine stone," Merilee said as she dug them out of her bag and handed them over. "Mine's always in my purse." She looked at Ned meaningfully.

"How beautiful!" Eva enthused.

"Very pretty. Now *do* bore us with your adventures," Connie drawled as she poured them each a scotch.

"Cornwall is enchanting. It evokes rugged pirates and dreamy poets, fiery dragons and mischievous fairies."

"Does she always talk like that, Ned?" Connie asked.

He chuckled. "She's a writer, after all."

"It's a land of old souls and knightly legends, but I was certainly disappointed that King Arthur's sword is supposed to reside at the bottom of Dozmary Pool. It's an overgrown mud puddle on Bodmin Moor and surely wouldn't be home to the mysterious Lady of the Lake. Although I have to admit that it *was* a bit eerie there."

"Aha! Lake Erie," Connie joked.

They laughed.

When Merilee was getting ready for bed, she was puzzled to find a couple of Connie's fancy hairpins on the dresser. She took them out to the sitting room, where Connie was finishing another drink.

"I found these in my bedroom."

"Did I forget, them? Sorry."

"Why were you in my room?"

Eva, who was tidying away glasses and ashtrays, stopped and looked embarrassed.

"Because it wasn't… appropriate to be in mine," Connie said dismissively.

"What do you mean?"

"Come on, Mare. Don't be so naïve."

Merilee was shocked. "You mean you slept in my room?... With Bryce?"

Connie shrugged nonchalantly. "I changed the sheets afterwards. What's the big deal?"

"You can't just take over my room when I'm not here!" Merilee snapped.

"Don't be such a prima donna. Friends share. And help each other."

Merilee was fuming. Ned felt her rigid tension when he put his arm about her.

"You don't waste any time, do you?" Merilee accused snidely.

"We don't *have* time to waste, do we? We could all be dead tomorrow!" Connie took a deep drag on her cigarette and blew out a long stream of smoke as she eyed Merilee disdainfully. "Bryce said you were a prude." She smirked.

Merilee stomped off to her room.

Ned struggled to keep his temper in check. "You might remember that this is Merilee's flat. I wouldn't push my luck if I were you."

Connie snorted. "Perhaps I'll find myself some place less... priggish. And I expect the brass would be interested to know that they sent over someone who's underage. Bryce mentioned she's not even twenty yet. Obviously immature."

"You wouldn't rat on her!" Eva said.

"Might be for her own good."

"That cattiness seems pretty immature to me. Smacks of jealousy," Ned opined before walking away.

Merilee was angrily wiping away tears when he entered their room.

"How *dare* she!" Merilee swept her hand viciously across the dresser as though trying to brush away any lingering fragments of Connie and Bryce.

Ned took her gently by the shoulders. "It doesn't matter, princess."

"My room feels polluted now! I don't want to think of them making love in our bed! Even before we have!"

"We'll evict their ghosts. They can't possibly be as happy as we are, because we truly love each other. It's not just lust." He pulled her close and she laid her head on his shoulder. "I love you more than I could ever have imagined."

Merilee marvelled at how deeply she had fallen in love with him. "Me too."

He hugged her gratefully.

The nightmare returned, but was even more terrifying than usual.

Merilee stood in the shallows, waiting expectantly, the ridged sand firm underfoot. He came towards her out of the shadows, faceless at first. Not her lover, but the Nazi, Geisler! She tried to run, but the sand became boggy, imprisoning her. She panicked as he came ever closer, chuckling. When he was almost upon her, she finally managed to break free. She dashed to the shore where her rifle lay and turned to fire. It was only when her finger had already pulled the trigger that she realized it was Ned.

Merilee woke, gasping. Ned was holding and soothing her. "It's alright, princess. Just a nightmare."

"A monster was chasing me, but then I accidentally shot you!"

He stroked her hair. "You must be remembering that day when the prisoner escaped. And you didn't shoot me, so relax."

She wished she could tell him the truth, to be able to banish Geisler to hell where he belonged. But she was afraid that Ned would despise her for her treachery. She couldn't bear that.

Muskoka and Ottawa Valley:
Summer 1944
Chapter 26

"Oh dear God, Troy! How am I going to tell them?" Ria cried, looking stricken.

Peggy was sitting on the veranda of the Old Cottage with them, delighted to be invited back for a week, and excited to be attending Hugh and Ginnie's wedding tomorrow – the same day that Ned and Merilee were to be married in London. It made it not *quite* so sad to be missing that, although it still seemed unreal that they *were* actually getting married.

But Troy had just revealed that Vera and Bertie's parents had been killed in a V1 attack on London. Their father had been working at the Air Ministry's Adastral House, and their mother, across the street at the BBC's Bush House. Husband and wife sometimes met for lunch, and on their way back to work that day, a rocket had crashed onto the street, killing them instantly. Identification had taken time.

None of them knew that Merilee had almost been caught in that bombing as well.

"We won't tell them until after the wedding," Troy suggested.

"You're right. They've been so looking forward to it." And, in fact, they were currently decorating the dance pavilion with streamers and flowers sent up from the city. Their cheerful chatter drifted over to them, Peggy noting that they were sounding quite Canadian. Only William clung to his British accent, reinforcing it by listening assiduously to the daily BBC broadcasts from London.

"My heart breaks for them," Ria added despondently, choking down her own grief at losing Charlie. Although he had initially been a reminder of Chas's betrayal, Charlie as well as Sophie had been the only good legacy from the last war, and one of the joys of her life. Poignant memories of him were everywhere.

And now she was terrified for Drew. Chas had encouraged Drew to hone his aerobatic skills, which not only gave him a better chance of survival, but also might get him posted to a fighter squadron rather than the more dangerous bombers.

She rubbed her brow and looked up at Troy. "What will happen to them?"

"They'll be John's responsibility now."

Ria wasn't convinced that the parents of William, Jane, and George were particularly warm or attentive caregivers. "Unless Chas and I adopt them," she stated emphatically.

Troy raised an eyebrow.

"I'm sure that Chas will agree. He'll be here soon, and then you can send John a cable. I want to be able to offer the children a home when we tell them. It might help to soften the blow."

Considering that the evacuees were already so much a part of the family - and had more than once expressed their reluctance to eventually return to England - it seemed a marvellous idea to Peggy. "You're so kind, Aunt Ria. I think the kids would be happy as well as lucky to live with you."

"Agreed!" Troy chimed in.

"It will be their choice, of course. They're old enough to decide." Vera was fifteen, and Bertie, thirteen. "But if they want that, then I won't take 'no' for an answer from John." She fixed Troy with a determined gaze.

He chuckled. "I doubt he has a chance against you, Ria. And he'd be a fool to deny them this opportunity."

"I think we could all use a drink," Ria said, getting up to go inside. "Cocktail, Peggy?"

"Not just now, thanks. I'll go back and help the kids. I'm not sure that William is using all his physics smarts in setting up the tables and chairs effectively."

They laughed. William bitterly resented doing domestic chores and usually made a hash of them.

Ria had finally convinced Grayson, now a sprightly eighty, to take life easier, insisting that his organizational skills were the most vital, when he'd protested. So, he managed the two households from his desk, but no longer fetched and carried. Mrs. Grayson, at sixty-five, still cooked, but everyone pitched in. Ria had made a game of peeling potatoes and doing dishes, and no one minded helping to bake cookies or biscuits. She had at least been able to find a sixteen-year-old maid to clean for them. Allowed to use a canoe when off duty, the girl was able to paddle herself to the dances at the Pineridge Inn, which somewhat compensated for being stuck on an island all summer.

Amy Seaford, finished with her education, was excited to be second-in-command at Pineridge. At the wedding the following day, she confided to Peggy, whom she had occasionally met at Hope Cottage over the years, that although she had to supervise at the dances, "Aunt Jean said I could accept the occasional offer to shake a leg. So, I met this deevie Pilot Officer, Stuart, who's convalescing from battle wounds at Westwynd. I think he's sweet on me, 'cause he's been to every dance since. And he comes over for ice cream in the afternoons. I wrote all about him to Merilee." She sighed. "Gosh, I wish she were getting married here! I miss her!"

"Me too. We could always start planning their welcome home party."

"I thought the war would be over by now," Amy grumbled. "Adam was over the moon to be finished grade 12 so he could finally enlist, and hopping mad now that he's been rejected by the RCAF because his vision isn't good enough to train as a pilot! He blames his near-sightedness on studying too hard trying to qualify. How's that for irony?"

"I sympathize with dashed dreams."

"So do I, but I'm so glad he's not going to fight! I'm sure he doesn't want to anyway, and all that talk of *doing his bit* is just bravado. And trying to outdo Gus, who'll be in the thick of things soon, but as a Navigator," she said about Maxine's younger brother. "Dad's happy, of course, since Adam's working in the boatworks now. Adam's crushed that he'll never wear a uniform, but Uncle Chas pointed out that he's contributing to the war effort anyway, and that Adam should start thinking about how he envisions the future of the business. Made him feel like he wasn't just another employee. That this really is his inheritance."

"I think it's a neat legacy to have popular boats with your name on them. Especially ones that have won races."

"Adam's finally beginning to realize that. I'm chuffed about it, even if I do change my name eventually.... I get to take over the Inn from Aunt Jean one day. Stuart thinks that's cool. He grew up on a farm in Saskatchewan, but likes Muskoka, and said he could be persuaded to settle down here." She giggled.

Peggy excused herself and headed for the washroom, although she didn't need it, except to escape from other people's happiness for a moment. She patted her face with cool water and thought about Gunnar. Imagining this as their wedding day. But his face kept slipping away.

Instead, she had vivid, tender memories of Ross, which seemed somehow a betrayal of Gunnar. How could she think she might find happiness without him? But was losing Gunnar any worse than Merilee being rejected by Bryce, when she was so much in love with him? Yes, because Merilee could hate Bryce for his callousness and fickleness! She couldn't find fault with Gunnar for being killed in action.

Ross's carefully worded letters didn't completely disguise his hardships and misery, but when he wrote things like, "My memories of being with you and Deanna at the lake sustain me.

How I long for more such glorious days," her entire being ached for him to be home safe. And in her arms. She dashed away tears.

Peggy was heading out through the sitting room when Phoebe suddenly appeared, as if from nowhere. At least today she didn't resemble a ghost in her modern dress.

"You're back. The piano girl." Phoebe began humming 'Faith's Fairy Dance' with remarkable accuracy.

"I'm Peggy."

"Sad, sad Peggy."

"Why do you say that?"

"Your purple glow. Can't you see halos?" Phoebe looked at her quizzically and then sighed. "No, you're like the rest of them."

"My fiancé died."

"So did mine. But then I found Silas and he was even better." Phoebe's smile drooped into a frown. "I hope Ginnie realizes she'll be living with all the ghosts that Hugh brought back with him. They got Silas in the end, you know."

With that cryptic statement, Phoebe drifted away, humming Peggy's tune.

•   •   •

Peggy was happy to share the girls' dorm with Vera and Jane, the boathouse being required for other guests. In any case, it would be lonely there without Merilee.

But this morning her heart plummeted as she listened to the girls' planning their day – morning paddle around the island followed by a swim, helping out at the Children's Retreat, playing tennis at the Country Club, ice cream at Pineridge.

How wonderfully joyful and innocent they were. If only Vera and Bertie didn't have to be told about their parents. If only that tragic, life-altering knowledge could be kept from them a little longer. Another week. The summer. Till the war ended.

But it was already Monday, two days after the wedding, and it couldn't be put off any longer. The blissful afterglow from that festive event, which still drifted among the pines and rafters and wilting flowers, would be well and truly extinguished.

Peggy was to help the three Baxters dismantle the decorations, while Ria, Chas, and Troy broke the news to the Carmichaels. Peggy could barely choke down her breakfast.

"What's actually transpiring?" William asked as he yanked at a streamer on the pavilion. Now a gangly six feet tall, he could easily reach the top of the posts. "Why are we being kept in the dark? I can tell you know something, Peggy." He eyed her accusingly.

"It's not for me to say," Peggy replied.

"Rubbish! Their parents want them home now that the war is almost over, and we have to stay. That's it, isn't it?" he demanded angrily.

"You'll be enlightened soon enough."

"Don't be so damned condescending! I'm not a child."

"One wouldn't know that from your manners," Peggy couldn't stop herself from retorting.

George snickered and Jane pressed her lips together to suppress a grin.

"You won't think it's so amusing when we're left behind!" William chided them.

"I wouldn't mind at all," George shot back. "I'll wait until Mother and Father come to fetch us, and maybe we can persuade them to stay. Couldn't Father become a professor at the university in Toronto?"

William scoffed, "It's not anything like prestigious Cambridge! Why would he give that up for some colonial backwater institution?"

"That's disrespectful of Uncle Troy," Jane accused. "And it's where you're getting your education."

Ignoring her first remark, William said, "I don't have any bloody choice, do I?"

They were interrupted by a distant wail and the slam of a screen door.

"What the hell's going on?" William demanded, heading for the house, closely followed by his siblings. Peggy hobbled as quickly as she could behind them.

They stopped short in the sitting room to find Bertie weeping in Ria's arms. Chas and Troy looked painfully solemn.

Troy explained, "There's no easy way to say this. Their parents were killed in an air raid."

Peggy pulled Jane into a hug as she burst into tears. George crumpled onto a chair. William grew rigid.

"Vera?" Peggy asked, looking at Ria.

"Ran off."

"I think I know where," Peggy said, passing Jane to Troy for consolation.

She hobbled down to the playhouse, where she heard anguished sobbing. She patted Zorro, who looked distressed as he perched restlessly outside, and knocked tentatively on the door. "Vera? May Zorro and I come in?"

There was no answer, but the weeping subsided. A few minutes later the door opened.

Zorro rushed in and nuzzled Vera, who wept again. Peggy went over to hug her.

"I should be brave," Vera gulped as she clung to Peggy. "But I can't bear it. I can't believe we'll never see them again. I haven't even touched them for four years!"

"I can hardly imagine what you're going through, Vera. But you don't have to be brave. You're allowed to cry and scream and curse and hate the universe."

Tears flowed more freely.

When Vera finally pulled away, she said between sniffles, "Thank you, Peggy. I'll be up at the cottage soon. I need to pull myself together for Bertie's sake. He's my responsibility now."

Vera shed more tears as she hugged Zorro, who stayed with her.

Peggy re-joined the others reluctantly. Bertie was leaning against Ria, snuffling as he said, "I want to stay here, Aunt Ria."

"We can't go back without you!" Jane cried.

"Why not?" William asked. "There's not even room in our house for two more."

"Then I want to stay, too!"

"And me," George mumbled. "I don't want to go back to our dreary house."

"Don't be ridiculous! You've been brainwashed! Don't you care about our parents?" William accused.

"Of course we do! But the war has changed things. Us. Hasn't it? Why should we pretend to like things we don't?" Jane asked defiantly.

William snorted in disbelief. "Wait until I tell Mother and Father about you traitors!"

"That's enough of that," Troy admonished. "This is a highly emotional time for all of you. Of course you'll be going home to your parents when the war ends."

"But you can visit us every summer, if you wish," Ria chimed in.

"Maybe I could go to the university in Toronto, like William!" George said hopefully.

"That's certainly a possibility," Troy assured him, which raised a smile.

"Me too!" Jane declared.

William shook his head and marched out, slamming the screen door behind him.

"He's always been a bully," Jane confided. "And hates not getting his way."

Ria and Troy exchanged knowing glances. She wished that Jane and George could stay, fearing that their carefree exuberance might be repressed once home again. But perhaps their plan to attend university was a good way to escape.

She would ensure that they had the wherewithal to follow through if that was their choice. She and Chas would set up small trust funds for them – enough to give them an education and a good start in life. Even for William, although that rankled. Perhaps he would learn generosity and gratefulness from that gift. And some humility.

Peggy was reminded of her own anguish when she heard Vera trying to weep silently that night. Jane crawled into her bed to console her.

When they were finally asleep, Peggy got up quietly and went out the screen door to the small balcony. The sliver of moon cast scintillating ripples across the lake. She breathed deeply of the fragrant night air as the haunting call of a loon reverberated through her, like a lost soul seeking solace. As evermore stars emerged through the tall pines, she lit some for Ned and Merilee, Gunnar and Ross.

•   •   •

Merilee Sutcliffe, author and Airwoman First Class, married her childhood sweetheart, RCAF bomber pilot, Squadron Leader Ned Wilding, DFC, at St. Martin in the Field in London on July 15, 1944.

Merilee is the daughter of Major Colin and Claire Sutcliffe, author and illustrator, respectively, of the beloved, classic "Enchanted Waterfall" series. Major Sutcliffe is also a noted historian with many critically acclaimed books to his credit.

Obviously, the apple doesn't fall far from the tree, for Merilee's novel, "The Curse of the Thunder King", illustrated by her mother, is a popular best-seller – a great achievement for this talented young lady. Her artistic eye is now focussed on photography for the RCAF.

Merilee is the niece of Canadian tycoon, Jack Wyndham, a dollar-a-year man advising the government on financial matters, and cousin of Air Marshal Chas Thornton. Both have long family histories of cottaging in Muskoka.

Ned Wilding is the son of Lorne and Lois Wilding. The Wildings are among the founding families of this district.

Erich crushed the edges of the Gravenhurst newspaper. The photo showed Merilee and her new husband smiling lovingly at one another. He tried to suppress a howl of anguish.

Had *his* love been insignificant? So quickly forgotten?

But hadn't he told her to forget him?

Fool! You knew that relationship was impossible! Can you blame her?

He even knew her father-in-law, who had been one of their guards, and a decent man.

But what the hell was she doing in London when he thought her safely in Ottawa? With the V-1 rockets now focused on the city, he feared for her.

Through tears he gazed at her achingly. Because he loved her, he hoped that she was happy.

Now he would have to rethink his own future, which seemed only bleak. He took his flute into the woods behind the farm and played *Merilee's Song* with bitter poignancy.

England: Summer and Autumn 1944
Chapter 27

"Arthur?" Drew asked uncertainly.

Arthur Bishop looked over. "Jeez! Drew! You finally got your ass over here!"

"What happened to you? You look like crap," Drew said as they shook hands. Arthur was gaunt and drawn.

"Nice to see your ugly mug again, too. Just had a tooth yanked out in France, without Novocain. Anyway, I'm on my way home. Did my bit. Flew hundreds of sorties. Had a few prangs and close calls. And was shot down a couple of times."

"In that case, I'd say you look pretty damn good!"

"No gongs, but I survived!"

"You should get a medal for that alone. Glad I ran into you before you ship out."

"Getting fitted for a new uniform? I was just settling my account."

They were in Anderson & Sheppard, tailors on Savile Row. Officers were expected to provide their own uniforms.

"Figured I might as well have a backup. Not much happening at Bournemouth, other than waiting to get into an OTU, so I have a few days off."

"Did your old man wrangle you a posting to Fighter Command?"

"Said he wouldn't interfere. But I sure as hell don't fancy flying bombers."

"The brass wouldn't put an Air Marshal's spawn in such jeopardy. Bad enough being a fighter pilot. My COs were always shitting themselves for worry. 'What would your old man say?' ... 'If you get killed, I'm going to kick your ass!'"

They chuckled.

"And you had to live up to everyone's expectations as the son of the legendary top Ace."

Arthur smirked. "Between us, Dad and I got 73 Jerries."

"Good show!" Everyone knew that Billy Bishop had shot down 72 in the last war.

The air raid siren suddenly shrilled. One of the clerks quickly ushered them to the cellar.

Once settled into a quiet corner of the basement, Arthur said, "I can hardly wait to leave all this behind. I'm not ashamed to admit that I've been scared out of my wits in battle. You'd be a fool not to be. But I'm proud that I was able to handle it and press on regardless."

"So you should be. I'm scared, but more for my parents' sake. If something happened to me, I wouldn't know, but they would have to live with it. I'd hate to leave them with a legacy of grief when they've already lost Charlie."

"Heard about that. Jeez, I'm sorry! I've lost a few good pals." Arthur looked pained as he shook his head. "Couldn't you have kept teaching?"

"I want to avenge my brother."

Drew was still reeling at what Chas told him before he shipped out. They'd been alone on the terrace at Wyndholme, sipping cocktails. "There's something I should have told you before, but didn't have the courage," Chas had confessed, looking stricken. "Charlie was your half-brother."

Drew had been shocked, but not completely surprised. He had noticed a strong family resemblance - too much of a coincidence for an adopted orphan. And he recalled that dramatic day at The Point in '34 when Charlie had stormed off to join the air force, seemingly precipitated by an old photo that had infuriated him so much that he'd confronted Chas.

"I was in France, devastated by the loss of friends. In a deep funk," Chas had revealed. "I met a girl who was lonely and frightened after losing her family in the conflict. We found solace in each other. It didn't seem wrong at the time. Not when you fear that every day you take to the skies could be your last. Unfortunately, she became pregnant.

"Your mother and I weren't yet married, but we were deeply in love and betrothed. So I ensured that Charlie's mother had the means to look after him and herself well. When she died of the Spanish influenza, I had to do the right thing and adopt him. Your mum and I never regretted that decision. Just my stupidity in not telling Charlie the truth sooner." He looked at Drew sadly. "And I'm sorry that you didn't know before... it was too late."

"It wouldn't have changed what I thought of Charlie. He was always my beloved older brother. My hero.... As well as you, Dad. And that hasn't changed either."

Overcome by emotion, Chas had gripped Drew's arm before getting up to pour another drink and collect himself. Turning back with moist eyes, Chas had said, "Look after yourself, Drew. Take precautions in all senses. But also enjoy what life has to offer while you're young and able. And please come back to us."

Drew was jolted back by Arthur asking, "Don't you think Charlie would have told you to stay home?"

"I suppose." Drew harrumphed. "You know what the Flight Lieutenant said to us at the orientation session in Bournemouth? That it was about time we bloody cowards finally came over to actually fight the war, which would likely be over before we could get into action anyway. That we didn't have the guts to take on the enemy."

"Son of a bitch!"

"There were a few hundred of us ex-instructors, and you could hear a pin drop, even as you felt anger seething through the auditorium. I couldn't keep my mouth shut, and told him, as calmly and dismissively as I could, that we've trained thousands of pilots who've been helping to win this war. Wasn't he one of them? Or has he only flown a desk?"

Arthur chortled. "Wizard! And you weren't court-marshalled?"

"When we were both hauled into the CO's office, I pointed out that it behooved me, as former CO of a Visiting Flight, to champion those who were required to pass on their expertise before finally being allowed to fly in battle. That this introduction to the RCAF overseas was an embarrassment to the Force. And that I shouldn't have to put up with such rudeness and contempt from an officer of *equal rank*."

"And it probably didn't hurt that your old man's an Air Marshal."

"*I* didn't mention it."

"You can bet that the CO was warned of your arrival."

"Well, the other guy was kept behind when I was dismissed. I sure as hell hope he got reassigned. Not good for morale, that kind of attitude."

An earth-shattering explosion close by made them cover their heads and cringe.

When the rumbling had subsided, Arthur said, "London's not much fun these days…. Jeez, I was surprised as hell to see Merilee in Blighty! She took photos of our squadron before we moved to France. Crazy that she's living in London and being terrorized by this daily."

"I worry about her."

"No kidding! Jackie joined the WDs and is training to be a wireless operator," Arthur said of his younger sister. "My mother was furious, but I'm sure the old man's proud of her. She doesn't like being left out of the action, but at least she's too young to be sent over."

"So, tell me what it was like being with 401 Squadron," Drew prompted.

Arthur regaled him with adventures and misadventures until the all clear sounded.

"They're the greatest guys I've ever known, Drew. When you're part of a team for a year and a half, when you live and fight together, when you have each other's backs and no one else knows what you've been through, there's a special comradeship that develops. I'll miss that.... Give them my regards if you get posted with them."

"Sure thing!"

Back upstairs, Arthur said, "I have a train to catch, but I'm going to pass along some advice I was given when I first arrived in London. Avoid the *Piccadilly commandos,* sonny boy. Unless you want a dose of the clap. Besides, there are plenty of pretty girls looking to get laid." He grinned.

"Safe journey home, Arthur."

"I expect to see you in Muskoka next summer."

"I'll challenge you to a round of golf."

"You're on!"

They looked at each other meaningfully as they firmly shook hands.

•   •   •

Her flat mates were already home when Merilee came in lugging her camera gear. She'd been busy since her return from Cornwall, travelling throughout southern England photographing squadrons soon to head to the Continent. "Glad I came into Paddington, because I heard that Euston got hit by a doodlebug!" she said as she kicked off her shoes.

"Thank God for that!" Drew replied, getting up from the couch in the sitting room to greet her.

"Drew! Oh my gosh! What a fabulous surprise!" she enthused as they hugged.

"I'm booked into the Ritz tonight, so I'm inviting you ladies to dine with me."

"Super, thanks! As luck would have it, Alastair said he'd be coming to visit today. I photographed his squadron yesterday, and he has a few days leave before they head over to France."

"Wizard! Then we'll wait for him."

"And I'll wait for Bryce, thanks all the same," Connie stated dismissively, blowing on her newly painted fingernails. "We're going to the 400 Club. If he gets here."

"Feel free to join us in either case," Drew offered.

"Kind of you, but I think not."

Drew looked at Eva expectantly.

"Sounds delightful. Thank you," she said with a serene smile.

"I'll freshen up. But first I need a sip. I see the rest of you already have yours," Merilee said as she poured herself a small Scotch and added a squirt of soda.

Drew chuckled as he raised his glass to her. "If your parents could see you now!"

She giggled. "They have their cocktails. Anyway, they'd be more worried about the bombs than the booze."

"True! As am I. You girls shouldn't be endangered like this."

"I appreciate the sentiment, but as I've pointed out to Ned, we're in this war together, so just get used to it."

"I said you were a force to be reckoned with!" Drew laughed.

She winked at him before she went into the bathroom.

"I'll be in my room," Connie snorted as she headed there.

"Something we said?" Drew asked Eva.

"She and Merilee haven't been getting along."

"Because of Bryce? Merilee's obviously not interested in him anymore."

"No, but he still seems to be in love with *her*, so Connie's jealous. And being outrageous. She wants us to leave, or at least stay in our rooms when Bryce visits. Merilee told her that's not acceptable. So, Connie's moving out in a few days. She considers us boring anyway, since we don't want to go out partying every night."

"Is someone else moving in?"

"We decided that we preferred to keep the place to ourselves, extravagant as that may be. I'll be pleased to have my own room, and offered to pay more, but Merilee wouldn't hear of it. She says that her Uncle Jack already covers most of the expenses. I feel very privileged."

"I'm sure that Merilee is happy to have you with her. You seem to be attuned to one another."

"It's as if we've known each other for years."

They stared at one another for a long moment, and then Eva looked away as she said, "We thought we could double up sometimes, so guests can stay overnight."

"Meaning you, whenever you have the chance to come to London," Merilee said, joining them. "And Elyse and the others."

"That would be more fun than staying in a hotel."

"I've already taught Eva how to play Racing Demons."

Drew laughed. "I have to come back next week for a fitting at the tailors."

"Consider yourself booked in!"

When Alastair arrived, the four of them headed to the Ritz. Over a fine repast, they caught up on news.

"I had a letter from Mum," Drew said, looking grim.

When he told them about Vera and Bertie's parents, Eva exclaimed, "Merilee was at Aldwych when the buzz bomb hit! And lucky not to get killed."

"Christ, Merilee!" Drew swore. "And you think we shouldn't worry?"

"I have a guardian angel," she assured him, trying not to show how shaken she was to be reminded. Grizzly scenes haunted her and triggered nightmares where skeletal trees dripped bleeding flesh. "But those poor kids."

"Mum and Dad are adopting them."

"Oh, how wonderful! Don't ever tell them I was there. In fact, promise you won't tell anyone. I send light-hearted letters to my parents, just mentioning trivia and amusing things about our lives and jobs. I don't even tell Peggy much more."

"We all do that," Alastair acknowledged. "No sense worrying them unduly."

"I'm glad I'm finally able to share these experiences with you," Drew said. "Although I'm getting antsy not having been posted for advanced training yet."

"There are usually so many pilots at Bournemouth that it can take months to get into the pipeline," Alastair explained. "Most guys want to fly fighters, but they won't because bomber pilots are needed, yet there aren't enough OTU spaces. What would you think about flying fighter reconnaissance? Our main objective is photo recon, but we're also doing tactical recce with the army. Being their advance eyes, warning them of defences, roadblocks, conditions of bridges, stuff like that. You might even get into my squadron. We're equipped with Spits." Like so many Canadians, Alastair had initially been with the RAF. Now a decorated Squadron Leader, he'd recently been transferred to the RCAF Reconnaissance Wing as a Commanding Officer.

"You think that would speed up the process? That I'd have a chance?"

"You already have thousands of flying hours under your belt, so it might help to remind them of that. The Spitfire training isn't as backlogged. And you'll still be able to shoot at any Jerries that come after you."

"That's an excellent idea," Merilee said, thinking it sounded somewhat safer than being a bomber or fighter pilot. "Surely the intelligence gathered from photos is crucial to winning the war."

"Absolutely!" Alastair agreed. "Discovering what the Germans are up to, locating the V1 launching pads…"

"We certainly want you to find those!" Merilee said.

"There's a great deal of satisfaction in delivering that kind of information, knowing it could save lives as well as speed up progress."

"I like that. And doing something different from Dad and Charlie, since I know I wouldn't measure up," Drew confided.

"So choose your own path," Alastair suggested.

"I'll try! But right now, I fancy a bit of dancing, if everyone's up to that," Drew said.

They changed partners frequently at first, but Drew soon monopolized Eva. They were engaged in lively conversation, smiling and laughing.

"They seem to be hitting it off," Alastair said to Merilee.

"As long as Drew isn't still in love with Anthea. I don't want to see Eva hurt."

"I'd say he's completely smitten."

"Hmm…. And what about you? Any war brides on the horizon?"

Alastair chuckled. "Not yet."

"What are you doing for your leave?"

"Heading down to Hamble to visit Elyse and Roz tomorrow. Staying a couple of nights. Then on to Priory Manor to see Sophie. Our current base is only a dozen miles from there, so I'll have another night of luxury before going back. We're under canvas now, and it will only get worse in France."

"Look after yourself over there."

"I presume they won't be allowing lady photographers on the Continent."

"I doubt it. And I have no wish to go anyway. Next week I get to spend a few days with Bomber Command in Yorkshire, photographing the newly hatched crews, and such. And spending time with Ned." Who had booked them a room at an inn for her brief stay. She could hardly wait.

After their last dance, Drew said to Eva, "I'm heading down to my sister's tomorrow afternoon, but could I take you out for lunch? Claridge's perhaps?"

"Thank you, but I'm afraid I don't have that much time. I often take sandwiches and eat in Hyde Park on fine days. I'll make one for you, if you'd like to join me. I still have some peanut butter and jam from my last care package."

Drew grinned happily. "I can't think of anything better!"

•   •   •

"The Americans won," Merilee said as she plopped down on the sofa. She'd been shooting a baseball game between the Yanks and the Canucks who shared the same airfield. "But it was a close game. How was lunch in the park?" she asked Eva.

"Delightful! I don't need to tell *you* that Drew is immensely charming. He has a way of looking at you as if no one else in the world exists."

"The seductive tactics of a wealthy playboy," Connie scoffed, joining them and refilling her glass with a hefty splash of scotch. "Bryce told me that Drew is practically engaged to his sister."

Eva looked worriedly at Merilee for confirmation.

"They dated for a few years, but have gone their separate ways now." Merilee believed that Drew wouldn't deliberately lead Eva astray. "I can assure you that he's an honourable person."

"With his pick of women," Connie drawled.

"So he's chosen well," Merilee shot back.

"Much as I like you, Eva, you're not exactly in his social sphere. Face reality before he breaks your heart. I say this as a friend."

"Baloney!" Merilee accused. "You're jealous that he's not attracted to you."

"Bullshit! Bryce is quite the catch. His grandparents own a frigging castle, for God's sake! Unlike the little fish you ended up with."

"Don't be so rude, Connie!" Eva scolded. "You're drunk!"

"Oh dear. Is *that* what you call it when someone tells the truth?"

"Don't forget that Bryce is still a friend of mine. We even have cousins in common. Perhaps I should warn him of your true character," Merilee threatened, fuming.

Connie glared at her and tossed back the whiskey. "If you bad-mouth me to anyone, I'll report you as underage! Bitch!" She hurled the crystal glass against the fireplace, shattered fragments flying everywhere, and marched back to her room.

"You can sleep in my room tonight," Merilee offered Eva as they began cleaning up the mess. Eva looked paler than usual.

Connie appeared as they finished, lugging her kit bag. "I'm leaving early. Here's my key." She threw it onto the drinks table, where it clinked against the glasses. "You think you're so special, Merilee. But you're just a spoiled, selfish brat!" She slammed the door behind her.

The girls breathed a sigh of relief.

Merilee poured them each a drink, saying, "I hope Bryce comes to his senses. But as I know only too well, he likes to play the field anyway. So *she* might be the one with a broken heart, if she actually cares about him."

"You don't believe that Drew is toying with me, do you? I'm not interested in just having a fling, the way some of the girls are."

"Drew is a gentleman, in every sense of the word. Get to know him and see how things turn out."

"He asked if I'd write to him."

"And?"

Eva smiled. "Of course!"

"Good! And don't be put off by Connie's nasty comment about not being upper crust enough. She obviously thinks the same about Ned. My relatives treat Peggy like one of their own, and I'm sure Ned will be just as welcome. And so would you be."

Merilee was reassured by Drew's obvious infatuation with Eva when he visited the following week. They all had an early start the next morning – Merilee to Yorkshire for three days, Eva on her leave to Cornwall, and Drew back to Bournemouth – so they decided to bring in fish and chips rather than go out for dinner.

Afterwards, Merilee suggested that the two of them go for a walk in the park, because she just wanted a relaxing bath, having been on her feet all day.

The phone rang while she was packing. It was one of Eva's colleagues, who passed along a message.

When Drew and Eva returned, she was saying, "Merilee and I feel that the park keeps us sane. I miss being in the countryside, so I'm really looking forward to hiking along cliff tops and breathing sea air. Wriggling my toes in the sand and swimming in the ocean. And nine whole days away from sirens and doodlebugs."

"I'm afraid I have some unfortunate news," Merilee said. "Glennis has been sent to hospital with mumps."

"Oh no! She was excited about this trip as well!"

"Is there anyone who would take her place?"

"Everyone's had their leave booked for weeks…. But I don't mind going on my own. I'll have to pay more, of course, but I think I can manage."

"You won't be lonely?" Drew asked with concern.

"I'm fine on my own as long as I have a book and my sketch pad. Merilee said there were plenty of Canadian military personnel there, so I expect I won't lack company when I want it…. And I'll write to you every day," she promised with a smile.

"With the odd sketch, I hope."

"She's very talented," Merilee chimed in. "And much too modest. You can almost feel the breezes off Lake Superior in her watercolours."

"May I see?" Drew asked Eva.

She fetched her sketchbook somewhat reluctantly, and opened it to show a long curve of sandy beach with waves lapping at scattered driftwood, backed by thick evergreens and distant hills. "Batchawana Bay," Eva explained. "One of our favourite places to camp. Before the boys went off to war," she said of her brothers, Mathias and Oskar.

The deft splashes of colour in her sketches conveyed the immediacy of the moment and were surprisingly powerful.

"That looks inviting…. This one is unsettling," Drew said as he flipped to the next page showing huge breakers crashing onto a rocky shoreline and thunderous clouds smothering the horizon. "What did you do when the storm hit?"

"We'd stopped there for a picnic, and managed to hightail it back to the car just in time."

"Impressive! Both the art and the artist. I've never known a girl who's slept in a tent, other than my mother when she first joined the ambulance drivers in France."

"That's because you guys never let us girls come along on your camping trips," Merilee accused.

"My father says it restores the soul to be close to nature," Eva said.

"Which is why we spend summers at the cottage. Although in luxury, I have to admit," Drew said.

"I'm not averse to comfort. We stayed in a lodge once, which was fun."

Drew was still leafing through the book. "Is this it?"

She chuckled. "No, that's home."

"Wizard! It looks like a forest hideaway in a fairy tale." The one-and-a-half storey log house, its veranda framed by tree-trunk posts, seemed to grow among the slender birches, lofty pines, and sturdy maples. Swaths of perennials flowed around it, giving it a whimsical air.

"Dad designed and built it on the St. Marys River in the '20s. With a dock and sauna on the shore. You probably don't know about saunas. My mother's Finnish and grew up with them."

She explained when Drew conceded that he didn't. "And after we're thoroughly steamed and cleansed, we have a cool dip in the river. There's always a hole in the ice in winter."

"Good Lord!"

She laughed.

"Then I expect you won't find the sea too cold. But you'll still need to be careful of tides and currents."

"Merilee already warned me. But I appreciate your concern," Eva said with a warm smile.

•　　　•　　　•

Merilee had been home for a couple of days, still basking in the blissful afterglow of nights with Ned, but now sadly tempered by the news that her colleague, Irene Larkin, had given her. Sam Oldershaw was Missing in Action.

"MIA is still hopeful," Ned said over the phone, although he sounded bleak. "We've heard about quite a few pals who became prisoners. And a couple who managed to escape capture and find their way home. But it takes months for that information to reach us."

"Irene's trying to stay optimistic, but she's heartbroken. She and Sam had been planning to get married on his next leave."

"Hopefully we'll be at their wedding, whenever that is. Don't let it get you down, princess."

"Be careful, Ned."

"And you."

Merilee couldn't stay in the empty flat, so she took a long walk in Hyde Park. When an eager American GI tried to pick her up, she smiled and flashed her rings at him. And wished him luck. It seemed that couples stealing precious time together were everywhere. Young people grasping at a chance of some sort of normal life, no matter how brief it might be. Perhaps she understood Connie a bit better now.

She was happy to hear from Drew when she got home.

"I finally got my posting to an OTU, and have a week's leave before I'm expected. So I managed to book a room at the Tregenna Castle, and am keeping Eva company. By the way, she's a terrific tennis player!" he added with admiration.

"Sounds like you're enjoying yourself." Merilee was surprised at this unexpected turn of events. But she believed in serendipity and synchronicity, as did Eva.

"Absolutely! It's even more beautiful here than I'd expected."

"And romantic."

He chuckled. "That too…. I'm planning to escort Eva home, and was wondering if I could stay the night. Then I'll visit Sophie and Elyse before I go off."

"Of course! In the meantime, carpe diem."

"You bet!"

They rolled in late, four days later, sun-kissed, exuberant, and obviously besotted by one another.

"It was glorious!" Eva enthused as she discarded her uniform tunic. "We rented bicycles and explored the countryside, and Gwithian Beach on St. Ives Bay. Did you go there? Miles of sand spoiled by that intimidating anti-invasion scaffolding, but we found breaks in the defences and were able to stroll in the shallows for hours at low tide."

"And run like hell when the tide was coming in because there was soon no beach left that we could see," Drew added as he handed them each a drink.

"There were caves, and rock pools, and seals sunning themselves! Not many people. A few local kids. It was heavenly! And swimming at the beach below the hotel was divine, like you said, Merilee. It was warmer than Lake Superior."

"You're even hardier than I thought," Drew teased, gazing at her lovingly. "We're spoiled on our warm lake."

She flashed him a pert grin as she unpinned her "Victory roll" and shook out her flaxen tresses. "It was such a treat to be in civvies and feel the hot sun on bare skin and the wind blowing through my hair."

Drew wanted to run his fingers through her hair, recalling how silky and sexy it felt. How even the moonlight had caught her luminous glow when they'd danced barefoot on the beach. She'd quoted the last lines of the poem, "The Owl and the Pussycat":

And hand in hand, on the edge of the sand,
They danced by the light of the moon,
The moon,
The moon,
They danced by the light of the moon

Recalling that poem from his childhood, he'd asked, "Shall we sail away in a pea-green boat?"

Grinning, she'd answered, "Only if you tell me what a runcible spoon is. So we can take it along to eat our mince and slices of quince."

"That's easy! It's an elegant implement that cleverly transforms into a paddle if you know its secret."

He'd joined in her gay laughter as he pulled her into his arms.

"Drew taught me how to light the stars! It was magical, especially as they were reflected in the sea. I'm so glad you found that place, Merilee!"

"Me too!... Did you do any sketching?"

"Oh yes." Eva pulled out her pad.

There was the Tregenna Castle, and a narrow, cobbled street in St. Ives. And then Drew with rolled-up trousers examining a rock pool, gazing out to sea from a deserted beach, stretched out among wildflowers atop a cliff.

"Cool!" Merilee said, thinking that surely Eva went to lie in his arms when she'd finished the sketch. She suddenly felt hopeful for them.

•   •   •

Drew's Operational Training Unit was in Heston, just west of London, so he managed to drop in some evenings for a couple of hours, especially on dud flying days, giving him and Eva a chance to get to know each other better. He always brought a bouquet of flowers, which brightened their flat and spirits.

Merilee left them alone as much as possible, declining invitations to go dancing or for a stroll in the park. Sometimes she would come upon them in the sitting room, holding hands, or Eva snuggled up against Drew, just talking.

One pleasant Friday evening in September, the three of them were on the balcony dining on the shepherd's pie that Mrs. Travers had left them. Drew was extolling the virtues of the Spitfire when there was the sound of a distant explosion followed by an ear-splitting double crack, which rattled the windows. A menacing whoosh passed overhead, like a heavy bomber. They jumped.

"What the hell...?" Drew began.

There was no siren. The press had just announced that the rapid advance of the Allies had neutralized most of the V-1 rocket launch sites, so there was plenty of optimism that the war would soon be over. And that Londoners could relax their vigil.

"Definitely not a thunderclap," Eva said beneath the eggshell-blue sky.

"There's a rumour that Hitler has a new weapon even more destructive than the V-1s," Drew revealed.

"An invisible banshee dropping bombs?" Merilee asked.

"God knows! We'll see what the papers make of this."

But there was only mention of a mysterious explosion in Chiswick, probably due to a faulty gas main. Yet the odd and disturbing sounds had been heard throughout London.

Over the next weeks more civilians were killed by "exploding gas mains", always accompanied by those ominous sounds.

When Drew came again, he said, "I wish you two were safely out of London! This talk about gas mains is bull. We figure it's a new rocket, so fast that it can't even be detected. I have it on good authority that the double crack is a sonic boom, which means that the rocket is going faster than the speed of sound and hits its target before we even hear it. And the last roar is the actual delayed sound of the rocket passing over."

"Good God, is that possible?" Merilee asked.

"Apparently."

"That's terrifying! So we have no warning whatsoever. No time to seek shelter," Merilee said.

"Which is probably why Churchill hasn't told us what's really going on. People would panic."

"I think you'll have a mission to find these damn things when you fly recce," Merilee said.

"Damn right!"

She went to answer a knock on the door. The tall, blonde naval officer extended his hand and said, "You must be Merilee. I'm Oskar."

"Of course! I see the family resemblance. I'm delighted to meet you!"

Hearing her brother's voice, Eva rushed over to greet him. He swung her around in a hug.

"I have four days of shore leave this time, so I thought I could manage a visit."

"You can stay here," Merilee offered.

"Thank you kindly. This is better than the Ritz, I expect. Not that I've ever stayed there." He had a cheeky grin, as if an impish, impetuous spirit lurked just beneath the polished social veneer.

"Definitely better," Drew said, shaking his hand as Eva introduced them.

"I have to tell you how much I admire your father for his boat racing championships. He was my hero when I was growing up."

Drew chuckled. "He'll be chuffed to realize that someone admires him for that more than his medals from the last war."

"Only a little more," Oskar quipped.

"My brother is boat mad," Eva explained, looking at Oskar affectionately as she handed him a drink. He was two years older than she, and had always shared his skills and love of boating with her.

"Not surprising that you ended up in the navy then."

Oskar was a radiotelegraph operator on the HMCS Orillia corvette doing escort duty for convoys crossing between Canada and Britain.

"If I'd known what that entailed, I would have joined the RCAF. Crossing the Atlantic in arctic gales and being tossed about by mountainous waves as well as being targeted by U-boats isn't my idea of boating."

Drew guffawed. "No doubt! But you're getting critical supplies and troops to Britain."

"For which we are eternally grateful, "Merilee added. "We've only lost one parcel from home, so we had to do without peanut butter for a whole month."

They laughed.

Suddenly serious, Oskar said, "The hardest part is watching the ships we're trying to protect being blown apart. When the U-boats sneak through our defences… But we are winning that battle now! Better detection equipment and more air cover from long-range planes have sure helped."

"That's another hopeful sign that the Germans are losing," Eva said.

"Do you have any boat-related plans for after the war?" Drew asked Oskar.

"I'm not sure how to make a career out of boats, which is why I took up telegraphy. I give sailing lessons in my spare time, but can't make a living at that. Especially in the winter," he jested.

"We're silent partners in the Seaford Boatworks, although my dad used to take an active interest in the design of his race boats. I say, you can drive any of the *Windrunners* if you come to visit us after the war. We've kept all ten of them."

Oskar's blue eyes lit up. "Holy cow! That would be out of this world! *Windrunner II* won the Fisher Trophy in Miami, didn't she?"

"She did! Before I was born. Fancy you knowing that!"

Eva laughed. "I warned you!"

"You may not be staying at the Ritz, but I'm going to treat you all to dinner there, if you're game," Drew offered.

They were a merry group and stayed afterwards to dance. When Oskar partnered Merilee he said to her, "If I'm not mistaken, there's a romance blooming between those two."

She chuckled. "No kidding!"

"I'm really happy for Eva. As long as she doesn't get hurt."

"I'm keeping a close eye on things."

He laughed. "If you weren't married, Merilee, I'd be falling in love."

It was her turn to laugh. "I'm flattered. But I can't believe that you don't have a slew of girls crazy about you."

He winked at her.

They had three more delightful days with Oskar, and Drew managed to come up to town for his last evening. They were all good friends by the time Oskar left, and promised post-war visits to Wyndwood and Sault Ste. Marie.

•   •   •

Merilee was surprised to see Connie in the sitting room with Eva when she arrived home on a blustery, late September evening. Eva gave her a meaningful glance as Connie nervously lit a cigarette and took a large swig of whiskey.

"I owe you an apology, Merilee. I loved my time here, and I spoiled everything by being jealous."

It sounded sincere enough, but Merilee waited. There was no way she would invite Connie back. She and Eva were much happier now.

"I've come to ask a favour... I didn't know who else to turn to," Connie said on a sob. "I need an abortion. Could you ask Lady Sidonie? She probably knows reputable doctors. I don't want a back-alley butcher."

Merilee and Eva were stunned.

"Oh, Connie!" Eva exclaimed, putting her arm around Connie's shoulder.

"Is it Bryce's?" Merilee asked.

"Of course it is! Although he's not convinced. Said he used protection so there's no way it could be his." Tears trickled down her cheeks as she added, "I swear I haven't been with anyone else! I love him! But he refuses to marry me. I think he's already cheating on me. What kind of life would that be, anyway?" she wailed. "I don't know what to do! But my parents will kill me if I'm sent home in disgrace!"

"How far along are you?"

"Missed my period twice. I've been throwing up in the mornings. Someone will find out soon enough."

Merilee poured herself a drink. She dreaded Bryce being tied to Connie and having her become part of summers on the lake. She suspected this marriage would be a disaster, but what choice was there? "I'll ask Drew to talk to Bryce. He needs to do the right thing."

"There isn't much time! Bryce's squadron might be heading over to the Continent soon, and I won't see him for months! How can we marry so quickly even if he did agree? Your bans took weeks."

"A civil ceremony."

Connie hung her head and nodded reluctantly. "It's not what I've always dreamt of. I don't want my wedding to be ugly. I don't even have a dress!" She burst into tears.

Drew didn't seem particularly surprised. "I always thought you were lucky to get away from Bryce, Merilee. I'll do what I can. Play on his honour."

Merilee contacted Lady Sidonie as well. Sid said, "His youngest aunt is actually an acquaintance, since I knew her sister in Canada. The Countess of Evesham. I'm sure she'll have a brilliant plan."

The Countess, Lady Alexandra, rushed to London from her country estate in the Cotswolds, and took Connie under her wing. She installed her in the family's London townhouse and summoned her errant nephew. Drew had already convinced Bryce that he should wed Connie. The ceremony was to take place October 16th followed by a luncheon at Claridge's. The Countess provided the bride with a suitable gown from her extensive, pre-war, couturier collection.

Eva agreed to be Maid of Honour, and Drew was Best Man.

Merilee was grateful that she was going on leave with Ned and didn't have to attend.

The last assignment before her holiday was to photograph Drew with a Spitfire at his OTU. She had suggested to her CO that Canadians might be interested in knowing that the Air Marshal's son was going into combat after a distinguished teaching career. There had been a few photos in the press of Arthur Bishop doing his bit with a fighter squadron.

After the photo shoot, Drew said, "I want you to know that I'm crazy about Eva.... And I'm going to ask her to marry me." He grinned broadly.

Merilee was thrilled, but wary. "I'm delighted! But what if Anthea wants you back?"

"Anthea's like a comfortable habit. There's no real depth to our relationship. Just fun and games. And fulfilling our parents' expectations that we get married one day. Eva's so refreshing, and makes me feel vibrantly alive."

Drew snorted. "I'm not naïve. Most of the girls I've met see me as the ticket to an easy life. And one-upmanship with their friends. But Eva sees my soul. Feels like part of it. I can't imagine living without her."

"I'm truly happy for you, Drew!" she said, hugging him. "Both of you! And I know that Oskar will be pleased."

"I have a 36 for the wedding. You don't mind if I stay at the flat, do you?"

"Of course not, if it's alright with Eva. Anyway, you're both older than I am, so don't expect *me* to chaperone," she added with a sly chuckle.

He guffawed.

. . .

"I'm glad that's over with," Drew confessed when he and Eva returned to the flat after the reception. "The groom looked miserable and is well on his way to being plastered, and the bride seemed nauseated and barely touched her wedding feast."

"Not an auspicious beginning."

"I hate to say it, but I wonder how long this marriage will actually last. Hopefully Bryce will settle down."

"The Countess seems to be doing her best to make it work."

Connie had to disclose her pregnancy when she asked her CO for permission to marry, and wondered if she would be sent home after the wedding. She'd been told that she would be once her pregnancy was well established, because several girls in their first trimester had had miscarriages aboard ship.

"I'm glad that Connie managed to get discharged from the RCAF here."

"I'm sure it helped that Lady Alexandra has taken charge of her."

"Luckily for Connie! She's relieved that when she goes home, it will be with a precocious baby who might look a few months older than expected, but that most people wouldn't suspect. And she's looking forward to living in luxury at the Evesham country estate until after the war. Apparently, it's not as ancient as the grandparents' castle, and therefore, much more comfortable."

"Which is still not up to our standards. I'll bet there's no central heating."

Eva laughed. "But plenty of grandiose rooms and ornate fireplaces that haven't enough wood or coal to heat more than a few feet away. I'll knit Connie a shawl for Christmas."

"You're so thoughtful," Drew said with a smile.

"I'll knit a scarf and mittens for you. You'll freeze if you're living under canvas in France or Belgium. And bed socks might help."

"I love you, Eva."

She stared at him in surprise and saw the truth in his eyes.

"I adore you. I want to spend every day, endless days with you, exploring life, savouring love." He pulled a small box out of his pocket and handed it to her.

"Yes, I will," she said before even opening it. "I love you too!"

Drew felt exquisite joy as he took her into his arms and kissed her.

"I wish we could sail away for a year and a day in our pea-green boat, like the owl and the pussycat," he said when he released her. "But we already have the ring. Open it."

A brilliant-cut aquamarine surrounded by sizable diamonds sparkled inside.

"Oh, Drew, it's magnificent!"

"Like you. I'm surprised no one's snapped you up before now."

"I've been waiting for my soul mate."

He grinned. "Who's going to treat you to dinner at the Ritz in celebration of our engagement. Then we'll ring Merilee and tell her."

"And send cables to our families?"

"You bet!"

Over dinner, Drew said, "I've been thinking about our future. What would you say to living in Orillia?"

"Stephen Leacock's *Mariposa*!" Eva said enthusiastically. "I feel like I already know the place from his stories. But why there?"

"I'm planning to take a more active role in the boatworks. So, I'm going to suggest to Adam that we expand, and have a factory in Orillia for the popular Seawind runabouts. Make building them more assembly-line and therefore, affordable. His father can keep the custom-built business in Port Darling. Orillia's on the Trent-Severn Waterway and the rail system between Toronto and Muskoka, so it's ideal in that respect as well…. Anyway, I thought you'd prefer a small town, and we could have a house with a sauna by the lake. We could easily fly our floatplane to the cottage or the Toronto Island Airport or to visit your family in The Soo."

"Sounds ideal!"

"I think the first boat built in our new factory should be a beautiful pea-green one for us."

She laughed delightedly. "Oh yes!"

"Do you think Oskar might be interested in working with us in some capacity?"

"I'm sure he would… This is all so exciting!"

"You've inspired me, my darling."

When they cuddled up on the sofa in the flat later, Eva said, "Will you sleep with me tonight?"

"Are you sure?" Drew asked, stroking her face and staring deep into her eyes. "Especially after what happened to Connie?"

"I wouldn't be ashamed to bear your child. We've committed to each other. Conventions can be followed when there's time. I know you're going off soon."

"A matter of weeks."

"So let's make the most of our time together."

"You really are special," he said, pulling her into his arms as he stood up.

"No. Just madly in love."

•   •   •

Clad in her silk negligee, Merilee stood at the window gazing with delight at the shape-shifting mist over Lake Windermere. Sunrise ignited the folded hills and barren fells beyond into a dazzling blaze of autumn colours.

Ned wrapped his arms around her from behind and nuzzled her neck. "Happy birthday, princess."

"I'd almost forgotten! Isn't this a spectacular present?"

It had rained every day since they'd arrived, so excursions had been short, and they'd occasionally been caught in a downpour. Not that they really minded, since the ever-changing sky continually transformed the magnificent landscape and provided plenty of photo opportunities, even from their suite. Which encouraged other distractions as well.

Their country inn was a former stately mansion on the east shore of Lake Windermere, with a three-storey tower at one corner, which housed their spacious sitting area with tall windows in each angle of the bay. With a private bath as well, it was surely one of the best rooms in the hotel.

"We'll head out after breakfast. But now you're chilled and need to warm up," he said as he scooped her into his arms and carried her back to bed. "Early morning tea is here, but I have a better idea."

She giggled as he removed her nightgown.

When they sat in bed sipping lukewarm tea afterwards, she said, "This is the best present. Just being here with you. And I appreciate that you spent a fortune for this suite, although you needn't have."

"Only the best for my birthday girl. But I did manage to find something else for you, to celebrate that you're no longer a teenager."

It was a silver charm bracelet with two joined hearts dangling from it. One was engraved with an *M* and the other an *N*.

"Oh Ned, it's perfect!"

"We'll fill it with charms from wherever we go, so let's look for something to remind us of this place... And I have some good news to brighten your day."

"You're not going back on ops!" she cried. He'd just finished his six-month teaching stint and was about to be reassigned. Another twenty sorties was the usual sentence, unless he was to be posted home. But they didn't need more instructors in Canada now.

"I asked for a transfer to a Transport Squadron that the RCAF formed last month. They carry supplies and people to the Continent and evacuate the wounded. I just received my posting."

She hugged him tightly. "That's the best news! It's surely safe. Even more than teaching!"

"Definitely that! We don't normally fly behind enemy lines. And I won't have to feel guilty about killing more civilians. The Dakota I'll be piloting is a version of the DC-3 passenger airliner that the Americans use, and should help me land a job after the war."

She wept with joy.

"Hey, it's all good," Ned soothed as he stroked her.

"I know," she sobbed and laughed. "I've been so afraid."

He gathered her into his arms and said, "You can relax now, princess. I'm the one who has to worry about *you* living in London!"

"I always have my lucky serpentine with me. And my guardian angel."

"Good!" He kissed her tenderly. "So... what do you want to do today?"

"Could we start by rowing across to Wray Castle to see where Beatrix Potter spent a summer?" The innkeeper had been most informative about places of interest, and mentioned that the author had eventually bought nearby farms and lands, which she'd bequeathed to the National Trust, and a home where she'd lived for thirty years.

"Sure thing."

"It's not a real castle," the landlord informed them at breakfast. "Just a rich man's idea of a home in the last century. Seems his wife hated it on sight, although her inheritance had paid for it. You can wander the grounds, but the Castle itself is being used as a research station. Mind you keep an eye out for ghosts," he added with a grin and a wink. "Especially the man on the white horse."

It was less than a mile across the lake, and the water was mirror-calm. A few threads of mist lingered, twisting as their boat passed through them.

"Are those the ghosts?" Ned jested.

The lake was silent save for distant birdsong and the dip of their paddles. "It is a bit eerie," Merilee conceded.

As they approached the boathouse, she pulled out her camera, exclaiming with glee, "Gosh, that's wonderfully Gothic! I would be surprised if there *weren't* ghosts here!"

It appeared to have once been crenelated, like the Castle rising on the hillside above, but parts of the parapet had crumbled away. One of the two bays was recessed, and both arched entrances were barred with slatted wooden doors like decaying teeth. The rough, grey stone added to its sinister appearance.

"I sense a story brewing," Ned chuckled as he pulled the skiff up to the stone quay.

She grinned. "You never know."

They strolled hand-in-hand up a grassy slope and skirted the hulking edifice.

"Promise you'll never build me a castle," Merilee quipped. "I can see why the wife didn't want to live here."

He laughed. "Promise."

"But I do like the view," she said, looking across the lake at the fells undulating behind their hotel.

"Better than home?"

"Never!"

They ambled through woodland back down to the lake, disturbing a bunny that hopped into the underbrush.

"Peter Rabbit?" Ned asked.

"Can't be. He's not wearing his blue jacket."

"I thought he lost it at Farmer what's-his-name's."

"McGregor. Well, yes, but his mother would have made him a new one."

Ned chortled.

As they rowed back, a Mosquito appeared through the scattered clouds and zoomed overhead, heading west. They saw it circle a few times over high fells in the distance.

"Are they searching for something?" Merilee asked.

"I'm afraid they might be. Hopefully not one of ours," Ned said grimly. "The trainee crews sometimes get lost, especially on night exercises. There was thick cloud yesterday."

Birthday cablegrams from her parents and the Wildings awaited Merilee at the inn, pushing disturbing thoughts out of mind.

"Thank you for letting them know," she said astutely to Ned. "My letter about this leave probably hasn't reached them yet."

"If we can't be home...."

"I have you."

"We have each other."

She melted into his embrace, grateful to be with him. She felt protected within his arms. Aroused by the scent of him. Still sometimes surprised to realize that she was actually married to him. Grateful for every day they could be together, especially when there were so few of them.

"I never thought I could be so lucky." He kissed her lingeringly. "How be we look for a charm in Ambleside before we have a pub lunch?"

"Wizard!"

Amid the slate grey and whitewashed stucco buildings that hugged the narrow streets of the village at the head of Lake Windermere, they found a shop that carried trinkets, books, jewellery, and artwork.

"Oh, look, it's a Peter Rabbit doll!" Merilee exclaimed. "I'll definitely take a couple of these. One for Connie's baby, along with a book," she added to Ned.

"Designed by Miss Potter herself," the shopkeeper declared proudly, as if the author had been a good friend. "As she did all this." She waved her hand over a table of goods from china figurines to colouring books.

"This is adorable!" Merilee exclaimed, picking up a child's Peter Rabbit tea set. "Alayna will love it. Now I need something for a nine-year-old boy."

"I have just the ticket! Field glasses and a bird spotting book."

"Binoculars! What a great idea."

She picked up *Swallows and Amazons* by Arthur Ransome. "Eva will enjoy this, if she hasn't already read it. Peggy and I did," she told Ned.

"Very popular, that," the hovering shopkeeper preened. "Mostly set on Windermere. Our lakes have inspired a few authors and poets."

"I can understand that," Merilee said. "Perhaps you could package all this and we'll pick it up on our way back to the hotel. We plan to do some fell walking."

"Of course, Madam."

"Do you have any souvenir charms for a bracelet?" Ned asked.

The lady smirked. "Indeed, I do! If you haven't seen it, you must. Bridge House. Just up the road."

She pulled the textured, sterling silver charm out of a glass-topped box. It was a rugged building, perched over an arched bridge.

"How cute!" Merilee said. "Our innkeeper mentioned that we should see it."

"The most photographed and painted building in Ambleside." The lady pointed to prints on the walls. "Built to store apples for the landlord's estate three hundred years ago. Then put to other uses over the centuries, including home to a family of eight, if you can credit it! Just two small, stacked rooms. It's now owned by the National Trust."

When they left the shop, they sauntered over to Bridge House, which straddled a narrow, shallow stream. From the roadside, it hardly looked wide enough for a horse and cart to have crossed over the ancient bridge out of which it grew. Outside, stone steps curved up to the second room.

"A family of eight *what* lived here?" Merilee was incredulous. "Mice?"

Ned laughed.

"Actually, it looks a bit like a shoe from this angle. Do you see that? Maybe they inspired the nursery rhyme 'There was an old woman who lived in a shoe'."

"And she sure didn't know what to do! Maybe stop having kids, for starters."

Merilee giggled. "Stand in front of the door. Nobody will believe this."

She snapped away, posing Ned at various spots, the most picturesque showing the wonderfully quirky relic astride the beck. Then Ned commandeered the camera and took photos of her.

"Promise we'll have a bigger house than this one," she teased.

"Promise!"

In a low-ceilinged pub probably as old as the town itself, they lunched on baked arctic char freshly caught in Lake Windermere, and the ubiquitous chips, which they had grown fond of, washed down with pints of hearty ale.

"If only we could get tasty beer like this at home, even if it is warm," Ned said.

"I can't imagine fish and chips without it."

When the aged publican came to clear their plates, he said, "I see you're both with the RCAF. In Yorkshire?"

For riding on the motorcycle, Merilee's uniform, with slacks, and her greatcoat were her warmest clothes. Ned wore his leather bomber jacket over his regulation sweater, along with wedge cap and flying boots.

"I am, but my wife works mostly in London."

The old man nodded. "Sad business. One of your bombers got lost and hit the top of a fell last night. A search plane spotted them just as they crashed, so they have a good idea of the location. Your chaps came looking for a guide to lead them to the site."

"Dear God!" Merilee cried.

"Any chance of survivors?" Ned asked.

"Not much... You take care now." The publican patted Ned's shoulder. "We appreciate what you Canadians are doing to help."

"Oh, Ned!" Merilee looked at him tearfully. "I can't get over all this death! And not even in battle. I'm glad I'm not the photographer who has to record this crash."

"But you've shot others, haven't you?" He frowned. She had never talked about this aspect of her work.

"At OTUs and airfields in the south. Guys who hadn't even started and those who were almost finished their tours! I hate it!" She gulped back her anguish.

Ned gripped her hand. "I wish I could spare you all this, Merilee. You should be home."

"Not without you."

He kissed her hand, still entwined with his. "Let's go for a walk."

Their innkeeper had given them directions for an easy and relatively short walk up Loughrigg Fell that would reward them with stunning views over the lake.

They started up the path through woodland, which opened up to russet bracken and rocky outcroppings painted by colourful lichens. It wasn't a steep climb, but Merilee was glad she had worn her galoshes – or "glamour boots" as the WDs facetiously called them – to clamber over the rough ground still damp from the rains.

Reaching the top of a rise, they saw the length of Lake Windermere stretching away before them, the orange, gold, and purple hills sliding into the water on both sides.

"Gosh, it's breathtaking! I didn't realize how high we'd come." Ambleside lay far below them to the left. Behind them, the land swooped to treed valleys and fields of grazing sheep, and rose to higher fells beyond.

But joy was marred by the thought that somewhere among the forbidding crags lay the bodies of at least seven young men and perhaps an instructor. The cloud shadows that crawled across the landscape suddenly seemed menacing.

"I'm thankful that Gus and Joe probably won't make it over after all," Merilee said of her younger cousins. Gus had just finished his Navigator training, but had been transferred to the RCAF Reserve.

"There's already such a surplus of aircrew waiting in Bournemouth that it makes sense the new graduates are being kept at home. For now."

"Joe won't be finished his pilot training until next spring, so hopefully the war will be over by then... They're just kids, for God's sake!"

"And you're an ancient twenty," Ned teased, trying to lighten the mood.

"I do feel a lot older than when I arrived."

"That's because this is the Old Country."

She laughed.

They climbed a bit higher for an even better perspective. A wooden stile over a drystone fence made the perfect spot for Ned and then Merilee to perch for photos over Windermere.

"If only we could capture the colours!" Merilee said. "Eva would create terrific sketches. She might even want to come here for her next leave, although I'm not sure November will be all that pleasant. Or colourful anymore."

While it had been mild down in the valley that embraced Ambleside, a biting wind scraped the hilltop, so she pulled up her collar.

"We don't need to ramble any further," Ned declared as he sheltered her against his side. Noticing a plane coming in from the southwest and begin to circle over a distant peak, he quickly led Merilee back down the path. This was supposed to be a happy day.

Their next stop was Grasmere, only a few miles north of Ambleside. The lake was small, but it perfectly reflected the burning hillsides, vibrant green fields, and puffy white clouds.

"Zowie! I can see how this landscape inspired poets like Wordsworth," Merilee said.

"Is he the daffodil guy?"

"Yes, who 'wandered lonely as a cloud' here a century and more ago."

One of Wordsworth's former homes in the area was open to tourists, so they visited Dove Cottage. It was primitive to their eyes, but transformed by its lush gardens and the thick vines softening the harsh outlines of the building to evoke the poetic romanticism of its era.

When they left, Ned remarked, "Just think. One day, tourists will be coming to Hope Cottage to see where you and your folks lived. A heck of a lot nicer than this!"

Merilee laughed. "I doubt that! And I hope not!"

"Why not? Good for tourism in Gravenhurst." He gave her a cheeky grin.

They were happy to return to their luxurious hotel where they fell into bed and relaxed in each other's arms.

There was a phone call for Merilee just as she was about to dress for dinner. "Drew is here with me, and we want to wish you a very happy birthday, Merilee," Eva said. "I also thought you and Ned would like to hear some good news. Irene Larkin asked me to tell you that Sam Oldershaw is a POW."

"What a relief! Thank, you, Eva.... How are things with you?"

"Sublime. We're planning to get married during Drew's next leave, which should be in the spring. A garden wedding at Priory Manor."

"Perfect!" Merilee had been thrilled when they'd called a few days earlier to announce their engagement.

"Sam will be buoying everyone's spirits in the camp." Ned declared cheerfully. "It was always hard to keep him down."

"I can imagine. He won't try to escape, will he?"

"I expect he would, but I hope he's taken a lesson from that disastrous escape in the spring."

They'd been shocked to discover that the Germans had shot fifty of the seventy-three recaptured Allied airmen who had escaped from Stalag Luft III in March, including six Canadians.

"Prisoners aren't duty-bound to escape, are they?" Merilee recalled what Erich had told her about Hitler's expectations. Erich, who belonged to a long-ago time and place. No longer part of her world. She could finally let him go.

"Not that I've been told. You don't make it easy for the captors. But actually escaping seems pretty futile."

"Good! And at least I don't have to worry about you becoming a POW."

They enjoyed pre-dinner drinks in their tower alcove as they savoured the multi-hued blue and pumpkin sunset and indigo hills mirrored in the lake. They saw a bomber's reflection before it appeared in the sky. It seemed majestic as it defied gravity so effortlessly.

"Hopefully we'll be doing this at home next year," Ned said.

"That would be bliss."

Europe and England: Winter and Spring 1945

Chapter 28

Drew was beginning to relax as he and Alastair were descending toward their home base at Eindhoven in the liberated section of The Netherlands. They had been on a sortie into Germany to photograph a dam and reservoir, but flak had been so intense that they had to abandon the mission.

Alastair drilled into his squadron that their job was recce, and that they were more valuable than a photograph, because they lost too many pilots to anti-aircraft guns. Some managed to bail, but often over enemy lines. Others, already friends, would never return.

It was an odd way to spend New Year's Day. He allowed himself a moment to imagine that perhaps next year, he and Eva and all their family and friends would be celebrating together at home, with no more war to tear them apart.

"What the hell?" Alastair cursed over the radio. "Brace yourself for battle, Drew!"

Dozens of ME 109s and Focke-Wulf 190s were swarming over their airfield, bombing and strafing.

Zooming down with the sun behind them, Alastair immediately took out an unsuspecting FW 190, and Drew was surprised that the ME he hit belched black smoke and dove straight into the ground. But then they were in the thick of the melee with the Jerries, who were now shooting at them as well. Four returning Typhoons from the Fighter Bomber Squadrons that shared their airfield joined the battle.

Heart pounding, Drew struggled amid the confusion to focus on one target, and then blasted him until the ME crashed into a Typhoon parked on a runway. The hair on the back of his neck suddenly bristled, as if sensing danger, so he jerked the Spit sharply just as Alastair shouted, "Break starboard!" Bullets slammed into the side of Drew's plane behind the cockpit. Alastair destroyed the pursuing Focke-Wulf.

Gasoline tankers and aircraft had caught fire, and the intense heat ignited ammunition that exploded continually, inciting chaos.

Drew noticed white smoke from the nose of Alastair's plane. "You're spewing glycol, Alastair!" His engine would soon seize without the coolant.

"Roger that."

There was no way Alastair could land on the airfield, but he didn't have much time to find a suitable place to put down. Drew followed him when he noticed an ME 109 hard on the injured Spit's tail. Alastair weaved to avoid the enemy fire, but couldn't risk taxing the overheating Merlin engine to outfly the Messerschmitt.

Drew couldn't get a clear shot without endangering Alastair, so he zoomed down to fire up into the belly of the ME, but his squirt of machine-gun fire didn't deter the Hun.

"Back off, Drew. I'm going to deal with this," Alastair ordered.

Drew did, and watched fearfully as Alastair flew almost to the deck, and veered up and over so abruptly that the ME pulled up too late, catching a wingtip on the edge of a barn roof and cartwheeling into the ground, where it exploded.

But flames began licking the engine cowling on Alastair's Spitfire. He made a wheels-up landing in a snowy field, hopped quickly out of his plane, stumbled, scrambled to his feet, and ran away as fast as possible. When he finally stopped, he waved to Drew, who was circling protectively overhead.

Drew breathed a sigh of relief and returned to their aerodrome, shaken, realizing what a close shave Alastair had had. His plane could easily have caught fire, and he hadn't been high enough to bail out. Thank God the field had been there, with just enough snow to make for a soft landing and gliding stop.

Thankfully, the Luftwaffe had gone. But they had left a big mess and dozens of casualties, who were being brought into the Sick Quarters. Even the walking wounded were disturbingly bloody. One guy on a stretcher was screaming as he gazed at his dangling, mangled hands, which barely seemed attached to his arms. Drew had to choke down his vomit.

He borrowed a staff car to fetch Alastair, who was several miles away, and was concerned when he found him hobbling slowly along the road, not far from where he'd landed.

"Sure am happy to see you, Drew!"

"Jeez, Alastair, are you wounded?"

"Think I just sprained my foot in my haste to exit the kite. She didn't blow up after all. Thanks for watching my back. I think you did actually damage the ME, which is why he didn't have the power to avoid the barn."

"That was your brilliant flying."

Alastair chuckled. "Teamwork."

"Thanks for saving *my* skin."

"You see?"

Drew told him about the carnage at the aerodrome. "Fires were still burning when I left, and ammo keeps exploding, shattering any remaining windows. There are some burnt-out kites on the airfield, including a few of Hitler's."

Alastair refused medical help when they arrived back, saying all he needed was a stiff drink. The central Mess was in shambles, but they managed to find some unbroken bottles and glasses, and were soon joined by others. It turned out that two airmen from their squadron were among the eleven dead, and a couple of their pilots, wounded.

"If I'm not mistaken, wasn't that you, Thornton, who sent an ME crashing into a Tiffy?" one of his colleagues asked.

"Yes."

"Wizard! I was watching from a frigging icy ditch. But you've put up a black with that bunch," he teased, and the others laughed.

The Typhoon Fighter Bombers were the ones called in when the Recce pilots located suitable targets. So it seemed a bit ironic that a Recce pilot had inadvertently written off one of their planes.

"Squadron Leader, why is your boot bleeding?" one of the pilots asked casually as he lit a cigarette.

They noticed a small puddle forming beneath Alastair's foot.

"Damn! Not a sprain after all," he grumbled.

"Off to the sawbones with you!"

Drew offered his shoulder as a crutch for Alastair. Fortunately, the most severe cases had already been transported to hospitals.

"I understand that you're one of today's heroes, Squadron Leader," the Medical Officer said. "And you, Thornton. Well done, the pair of you!"

Pulling off Alastair's bloody flying boot, the doctor predicted, "Looks like you're going to be out of action for a while, Alastair." A bullet had ripped through his foot. "Nice exit wound as well, so at least I don't have to dig out the bullet. It may not have done too much damage, which you can either consider lucky or unlucky," the doctor quipped as he pressed around the wounds.

"We'll get this cleaned up and stitched, and then off to hospital for an x-ray. You can count on a month of R & R at the very least. Longer if you need a cast."

"Surely not! I can hobble around and be of some use here."

The MO snorted. "I don't usually hear complaints about being shipped back to Blighty. You should be happy to miss January here. And you're about due for leave, I expect. You'll be sent to a convalescent home once you're on the mend. There's an excellent one that I've visited near the Welsh border. It overlooks the winding Wye River valley and the distant Black Mountains of Wales. Glorious. Quiet. Undisturbed by the Germans," the MO explained wistfully as he stitched the wounds.

"My mother is from Wales," Alastair revealed as he tried not to wince.

"Then you'll enjoy the place all the more. It's run by the Massey Foundation for Canadian Officers in an estate called 'Garnons', and you'll feel like a privileged country house guest there. Our High Commissioner, Vincent Massey, and his wife, Alice, spend their weekends relaxing there, and socializing with their guests. I was fortunate enough to be invited to Garnons for a weekend through mutual connections back home."

"I've met Mrs. Massey at the Canadian Officer's Club in London," Alastair said. "A charming lady. She actually serves the excellent luncheons there."

"And cooks them! She and Vincent established and fund that Club. And they originally organized the Beaver Club."

Drew didn't mention that his family knew various members of the wealthy Massey dynasty – whose farm machinery dominated the Canadian landscape - including Vincent, especially through their philanthropic work. He thought it fitting that Alastair should recuperate in such style.

"There, patched up for the journey. Not much you can do here anyway, Alastair. We have a massive clean-up to do, and kites to replace. First, we have to bury our dead, including four Germans."

"Make that five," Drew said. "Alastair lured one down to kill himself in a farmer's field a few miles away."

"You do seem to have a talent for that, Squadron Leader. We'll look forward to seeing you in February, since I fear we'll still be at war." He rubbed his creased brow. "It's getting rather wearying, this endless conflict. Enjoy your respite, old chap!"

Before Alastair was shipped out, he said to Drew, "You'd better bloody well look after yourself while I'm gone."

"You've taught me well, Squadron Leader. I'll do you proud."

Surprisingly, Alastair had only a fractured metatarsal. They discovered that his Spitfire was riddled with holes, so it was amazing that he hadn't been more badly wounded or killed.

For their heroic and successful actions that day, Alastair received a bar to his Distinguished Flying Cross, earned the previous year for his superb work with the RAF's Photo Recce Unit, and Drew was awarded the DFC.

•   •   •

"Merilee never ceases to amaze me," Alastair confided to Elyse and Roz. He was spending a few days of his leave at Riverbreeze after four weeks convalescing. "She convinced her CO that there was a photo opportunity of me at Garnons, and then effortlessly charmed the illustrious High Commissioner and his wife. They invited her back whenever she could manage a weekend. With Ned if possible. They're keen to read her novel and have it available for their guests. And her CO was impressed that some of the pics included the Masseys, who also insisted on having their photo taken with Merilee."

"She's definitely a chip off the Wyndham block," Elyse said.

"I guess I have to stop thinking of her as a little kid."

The women chuckled.

"You also have to stop feeling like you're responsible for all of us. Your father taught you too well. Not that we don't appreciate your brotherly concern, but now that we're grown up, you can relax," Elyse advised.

"Easier said than done! Especially when Drew's in my squadron."

"It seems like you picked a good time to be away. He said there hasn't been much action because snow and wind have kept them grounded for more than half the time. He's getting bored with movies and such, which is why he's writing letters to everyone."

"So, I'll have to make sure the guys haven't become complacent."

Looking at Roz with a raised eyebrow, Elyse said, "Don't you think they should make him an Air Marshal?"

"Air *Chief* Marshal, I'd say!" Roz replied with a grin.

Alastair laughed. "I wasn't going to mention it just yet, but apparently I'm going back as Wing Commander."

"Oh, well deserved! Let's drink to that!" Elyse refilled their glasses. "*You* never cease to amaze *me*, Alastair. So we don't just look up to you because you're a few months older."

"Hear hear!" Roz agreed.

He raised his glass to them. "That means a lot to me, coming from two very *amazing* lady pilots!"

"With perks, which you will appreciate. We're having a feast tonight, thanks to Roz."

She explained, "When I delivered a Mustang to a U.S. base yesterday, the CO thought it was just swell that I was American. He figured I needed a taste of home, so he insisted on giving me a slap-up lunch, with real ice cream for dessert! And then he loaded me up with goodies from their PX."

"He was undoubtedly flirting with you," Elyse observed.

"He was a suave Harvard man. Dishy, for sure. But I told him I'm married. It's just easier that way." She looked down at her rings, trying to hide her anguish.

Elyse noticed Alastair's unguarded moment of concern for Roz, and decided she would quietly encourage their friendship.

As they savoured their dinner of baked ham, cheesy scalloped potatoes, and creamed corn, followed by tinned peaches, the girls told him about their adventure ferrying to the Continent, the women now allowed to do that, although the ATA men had been since September.

"They finally trained us on the VHF radio," Elyse said. "They could hardly send us over without that. So, we practiced getting homing signals from airfields. So much easier when they give us the course and we just steer that."

"I expect that might have saved a few lives if the ATA had used it from the outset," Alastair said.

"And a lot of terror when the clouds suddenly come down on us," Roz agreed. "But we're still only allowed to use the R/T in emergencies. And only overseas."

He shook his head.

"You should have seen our training in bailing out," Elyse said. "We went to the Southampton Public Baths and had to jump from the high diving board with all our gear on, including an inflatable dingy dangling from our derrieres. Once the dingy inflated, we had to clamber into the damn thing. No easy task, but it made for much hilarity. We all managed in the end, and then the pool was afloat with girls digging through the survival goodies stored onboard."

"And munching the chocolates," Roz elaborated.

Alastair laughed. "I hope someone took photos."

"*We* hope not!" Elyse countered. "We had our typhoid and other shots just before Christmas, which was a good way to ruin the occasion, but we were ready to go in the new year. Roz and I took a couple of Spits over to Brussels, where Theo spends most of his time now." He was attached to the 2nd Tactical Air Force Headquarters there.

"And as luck would have it, we had four gloriously miserable days of weather delay our return, so I stayed in Theo's digs and Roz luxuriated in a hotel."

"We couldn't believe how cheap everything was. And the food, so yummy," Roz added. "Omelettes with real eggs! Cakes and chocolates and wine. It was heavenly."

"We enjoyed that, too, when we were stationed in Brussels for a couple of weeks," Alastair said. "But in the Netherlands, we've heard of civilians starving to death in the areas we haven't liberated yet."

"I'll be so glad when this damned war is over!" Roz expostulated. They sat in contemplative silence until Elyse picked up the thread to lighten the mood.

"We wish we could have stayed longer, but the weather improved for a day, and we had to bring a couple of tired Tiffies back for repairs. Then it was decided that all pilots ferrying to the Continent would fly from only three 'Invasion Pools', the main one being at White Waltham. But Roz and I feel too much at home here and didn't want to move. So, we've had our great Continental jaunt."

Elyse sympathized that Riverbreeze had been Roz's only home with Charlie, and that she was in no hurry to leave it.

"We're hoping to ferry the new Meteor jets," Roz admitted with a twinkle in her eyes. "As consolation."

"Veronica was the first girl to fly one," Elyse explained. "Now we all want to try one, as we're not likely to have that opportunity once our jobs end."

"I wonder if women will ever be accepted into the air force or commercial aviation as pilots," Roz mused.

"They'll be missing a lot of talent if we aren't. Roz has an instinct about aircraft, so our CO recently assigned her a special task. She was advised to be very careful with the plane and not take it if she didn't feel comfortable with it. Apparently, a couple of Navy pilots had indicated an unknown problem and wouldn't fly it. It was a Grumman Avenger used on aircraft carriers. With folding wings. You finish the story, Roz."

"Golly, I didn't discover anything others shouldn't have picked up on. Anyway, I inspected the kite carefully, ran it up, but couldn't take it to full throttle on the ground so I couldn't check the two-speed supercharger. Up to that point, it seemed perfectly fine to me, so I agreed to take it. When I reached 5000 feet, I switched over to the supercharger. The revs plummeted and so did the Avenger. I powered up, tried it again, and the same thing happened."

"Let me guess," Alastair said. "The supercharger was linked up the wrong way."

"That's what I wrote on my snag sheet when I arrived! And our CO had a call later asking her to commend the pilot for solving the mystery." She beamed.

"When the men couldn't. Well done, Roz! So, what will you do after the war?"

"I'm toying with the idea of starting my own flying school. Focus on encouraging gals to live their dreams of flight. Men might not be eager to be taught by a woman."

"My dad got his basic flight training from the Stinson sisters in Texas in the last war," Elyse explained. "And he's the last person I would have thought who'd allow a woman to teach him anything."

They laughed.

"What about you, Alastair? Are you still planning to stay in the RCAF?" Elyse asked.

"Nope. I've had my fill of the military, so I'll use my engineering degree to design aircraft. And fly just for fun."

"Great idea!" Elyse knew that Chas and Ria had set up a trust fund for him when he was born, and that had undoubtedly grown substantially over the past twenty-five years. Not in the same league as most of the Wyndhams and Thorntons, he was still wealthy by ordinary standards, and could afford to buy himself a plane.

"What about you, Elyse?" he asked.

"Get home first and then decide. Granny says Uncle Jack's frustrated that his boys aren't interested, or capable of taking over his empire. Sandy's dedicated to his filmmaking career, and Joe is too happy-go-lucky to be an astute businessman. So Jack is screening Kate's boyfriends for potential business heirs."

"Oh dear," Roz interjected.

"Granny knows Kate won't brook any interference in her love life. She's as strong-willed and determined as her father. So Granny suggested that Theo might be the perfect solution, and I'm to put it to him."

"She wants you home, too," Roz said with a smile.

"I really miss her. She's always been my champion. Brat though I was. Probably still am."

"It's called being audacious and plucky when you're an adult," Roz said matter-of-factly.

"So you were a brat, too!" Elyse declared, much to their amusement.

The phone intruded, so she went to answer it. Her heart skipped a beat when she recognized her mother-in-law's voice, which sounded strangled by emotion.

"It's not Theo, is it?" she asked in a panic.

"No, dear." Marguerite paused. "I'm terribly sorry to have to tell you that... Sidonie has passed away."

"WHAT? How?" Elyse sank onto a chair.

"Her maid just called to inform us. It was cancer."

"But she never said anything! I saw her at Bryce's wedding in October. She seemed her normal self. A bit thinner, perhaps."

"Apparently she didn't tell anyone.... Which doesn't surprise me. She was never one to show her feelings or complain. A very private person."

"She didn't give me a chance to say goodbye," Elyse sobbed. "Just when I was getting to know her!"

"But that's so like her, my dear. She wouldn't have wanted any fuss or pity. Nor does she now. She arranged a private funeral at the village church near Blackthorn, so we're all to come if we can. Algernon has already sent a telegram to Theo through his channels."

"I'll let my father and the others at home know.... I can't believe this."

"Your mother was vibrant, delightfully outrageous, envied and scorned by society at times, and traumatized by the last war. Which is why I've always loved her and remained loyal when so many didn't."

Her mother. Not just the beautiful and scandalous Lady Sidonie. Elyse couldn't stop the flood of tears.

Roz and Alastair couldn't help overhearing her side of the conversation, and it was easy to fill in the blanks. Roz went over and hugged her. Alastair put his arms around them both.

•   •   •

The icy grip of an exceptionally frosty January was easing, and rain threatened. Although it wasn't anything like as savage as winters in Canada, Elyse shivered in her wool uniform and greatcoat as she stood in the churchyard by the new grave. A Celtic-style cross speared heavenward from a plinth with the inscription:

Quentin Edward James Langton, Viscount Grenville
Captain, Royal Berkshire Regiment, Wounded at Loos,
September 1915
Born at Blackthorn Park, February 17, 1892
Died October 18, 1918
Lying with him in spirit is his brother,
The Honourable Sebastian Charles John Langton
Lieutenant, Royal Berkshire Regiment
Born at Blackthorn Park, August 15, 1896
Killed on The Somme, July 1, 1916
Buried at the Serre Road No. 2 Cemetery, France

Our cherished sons and brothers, forever in our hearts

The weathered, lichen-spotted stone bore a fresh carving, painfully harsh:
Lady Sidonie Elizabeth Charlotte Langton Thornton,
Born at Blackthorn Park, June 7, 1894
Died
Reunited with her beloved brothers

Elyse stared hollow-eyed at the incomplete date, as if she could make it not appear. Not yet. There was still too much to discover about her mother and her ancestors. She hadn't even known Sid's full name.

Tasteful bouquets of flowers from Chas and Ria, Jack and Fliss, and her father, she was happy to see, were among the several that infused colour into what was otherwise a monochrome scene under a steely sky.

Next to the grave was a regal headstone, elaborately displaying the family's coat of arms, presiding over two tomb chests inscribed with the particulars for the Earl and the Countess of Bisham, Elyse's grandparents, whom she had only ever met when she was quite young. She had merely a faint recollection of two rather vacant, frail people. They had died within months of each other in 1928.

Theo hugged Elyse to his side as the vicar intoned a few words over the grave, already filled in when they had arrived, according to Sid's wishes. She had wanted no traditional funeral, and a simple obituary after the fact would be put into the newspapers.

Marguerite, Algernon, and Sara stood rigidly beside them.

Merilee, who was spending her leave at Priory Manor to be near Ned, had come with Sophie, but he hadn't managed to get the day off. Sophie had known Sidonie ever since Ria and Chas had adopted her in 1917, and had been sixteen when Sid had left Canada nine years later.

Roz and Alastair – who had travelled with Elyse and Theo - and a few of Sid's closest friends were in attendance. Her maid, cook, and chauffeur hung back.

"Lady Sidonie wanted no pomp or ceremony," the Reverend Emerson Gilford concluded. "But as an old friend, I wish to pay homage to her, so if you will indulge me for a few minutes, please join me in the church. We'll all relish getting out of the cold."

His flowing cassock somewhat obscured the fact that he had no left arm.

The ancient church was not large, but it was surprisingly resplendent inside. Beautiful stained-glass windows brightened the interior, and would be uplifting when sun streamed through them. Artistic urns of flowers flanked the pulpit.

"I met Lady Sidonie when I was at Oxford with her brother Quentin, and I was fortunate enough to be invited to Blackthorn Park on many delightful occasions," Gilford began. "I needn't extol her virtues to any of you, since you undoubtedly know her better than I. But I do want to make you aware of her unsung generosity.

"I lost my arm at Ypres, but found my faith. Unlike Sidonie and others, who felt abandoned by God. And yet, she has invested enormous sums of money to preserve and beautify this church. I came with a new roof, which ensured my living," he confided with a grin.

The congregation chuckled.

"Look around you. At the masterfully carved pulpit and pews from the 16th century, refurbished or perfectly replicated as necessary. At the stonework, some from the 12th century, the Gothic arches, strong and faultless now, the marble inlays, the gleaming brass, the painstakingly restored gilding. Examine the magnificent Tiffany stained glass window that Sidonie commissioned in the Art Nouveau style to commemorate her family. It tells a tale, and filters the western sun, which she fancied is reflected from Blackthorn Park.

"Be sure to visit the Langton Chapel, behind the choir-stalls to my right. Twenty generations of the family, including seven Earls of Bisham, are interred there in crypts and tombs that are works of art in themselves. Quentin and Sidonie, however, had long ago chosen their resting place beneath the quicksilver sky and just a little closer to Blackthorn Park. She jested that she couldn't possibly spend eternity near her profligate grandfather, who had gambled away the family fortune that would have sustained her home, much as she wanted to give him a sharp tongue-lashing."

Elyse smiled, along with the others. She could just imagine that encounter.

"I feel blessed and privileged to have known her, and to have been given the care of this parish church with an endowment that will preserve it for generations to come. God bless Lady Sidonie. She will be sorely missed."

Elyse was stunned by the elaborate tombs of her ancestors, the earliest with recumbent effigies perched atop, their hands in prayer. They were cast in bronze, or marble, or painted stone, as if they were just resting there in their finery. Gilded artwork decorated the arched canopies held above them by ornate columns.

Others lay beneath the slate tiles in the private chapel, commemorated by plaques and sculptures on walls.

"This is... astonishing!" Elyse exclaimed. "Unbelievable."

"You had no idea of your heritage, did you?" Theo observed.

"None!"

"Would you like me to take photos?" Merilee asked, having her Kodak at the ready.

"Definitely!"

"I always wondered who was related to important people like this," Roz quipped. "Your own church!"

"The Langtons owned many thousands of acres around here, including this village and several others," Theo explained.

"Entire villages? Jeepers!"

"But most of the land, along with family heirlooms and art treasures, had to be sold over the years to pay off debts."

The Reverend Emerson Gilford joined them. "Theo, so delightful to see you again. Congratulations on your successes.... Mrs. Beauchamp, I am heartened to see that Sidonie left another legacy. You have a remarkable resemblance to her." He smiled warmly. "She entrusted me with a mission some years ago. I studied history, and this was just the kind challenge I enjoyed. Which was to chronicle the Langton family history with brutal honesty, no matter how dastardly their deeds. She approved of the results and asked me to give this to you personally."

He handed her a leather-bound book with gold tooling, adding, "Do read the inscription."

In flamboyant script, Sidonie had written, *To my darling daughter, Elyse, and her descendants, Enjoy meeting your ancestors: the heroic, the clever, the scoundrels, and the rascals. Consider me among the latter. Love, Sid*

"She never lost her sense of humour, despite everything," Gilford stated. "I can just see her raising a mischievous eyebrow as she penned that."

"You knew her well," Elyse observed.

"She kept in touch all these years. There were so few of our crowd left after the war." He looked momentarily pensive, as if remembering long-lost friends. "So few with whom we had shared memories. Sid liked to come here whenever she was in England, before the war, and we would sit out in the sunshine... It always shone when she was here.... And we'd reminisce. In the last few years, she's visited frequently.... Well, I mustn't keep you. I do hope we'll see you here on occasion."

"Certainly. And thank you indeed for this," Elyse said, clutching the book to her breast.

He smiled and nodded, and then shuffled away to talk to Theo's parents.

"Is he a family friend?"

"Dad was at Oxford with him and Quentin and Chas."

"Was he in love with Sid as well?" she whispered.

"Undoubtedly."

"I never had a chance to tell Sidonie that I'm engaged to Lawrence," Sara lamented as she joined them. She had met Lawrence at one of Sid's dinner parties when she was staying in London on a 48 last year. The American flyboy who'd previously captured her heart had finished his tour of duty and returned to the States. And to his girlfriend. Sara's parents had breathed a sigh of relief. Lawrence Rickard's family was known to them, and they were delighted with the match. Sara had sworn off pilots, who were either getting killed, or regularly moving to other stations and new relationships, so she was happy that Lawrence had a desk job at RAF Medmanham, along with Sophie's husband, Philip. Sara had managed a transfer to nearby RAF Benson to be close to him, and so their romance had flourished.

Alastair was the only one who knew that this top-secret unit in a country house was where interpreters examined the photos that recce pilots like him had taken, in order to keep an eye on everything the Nazis were doing, and to map occupied Europe. What the men and women at Medmanham discovered was critical to intelligence, and he was proud that he'd been an essential part of that team.

"I think Sid knew how well you two hit it off, Sis, so she wouldn't have been surprised. After all, she introduced Elyse and me."

"And you're living happily ever after," Sara quipped.

"We are indeed," he admitted, giving Elyse a loving glance.

The stained-glass window that Sid had commissioned depicted a grand Elizabethan mansion in the far distance against a sunset sky, half of it intact and the other half crumbling. People strolled on the lawn, clad as knights and courtiers in the various styles of the past four centuries. Flowering vines snaked around their feet and toward the church, which dominated the bottom right corner. Two officers from the last war - much larger than the background figures – leaned casually against the towering Celtic cross that marked their graves, brilliant poppies scattered at their feet. Perched in the other corner and observing it all with regret was a glamorous flapper – obviously Sidonie. Richly coloured, the window was stunning.

"It must have been hard to be the last of such a long and distinguished lineage," Elyse said.

"*You're* actually the last, darling," Theo pointed out.

She was momentarily shocked. "Well I'm damn glad that I wasn't saddled with a decrepit house, or haunted by its loss, like Sid."

"So, your only duty is to keep the illustrious line going," Roz said with a smirk.

"We'll do our best," Theo agreed, drawing Elyse close. She felt momentary panic as the chains of domesticity tightened around her.

"I'm always awed by this window as well as profoundly nostalgic," Marguerite confessed as she and Algernon joined them. "And now..." She bit her quivering lip, and Algernon put his arm comfortingly around her shoulders. "Now it's even more poignant." Gently touching the flapper, she mumbled, "Goodbye, dearest friend. I'm so grateful that you gave us Elyse."

"You'll share grandchildren with Sid someday," Elyse assured her. Of course she wanted to have a family with Theo. Eventually.

Marguerite brightened. "Yes, we will, won't we! I have plenty of stories about our girlhood adventures to entertain them. Did I tell you about the fairies we *discovered* in the lakeside woodland when we were eleven? Sidonie and I made mouse-sized tables and chairs from twigs and twine and hid them in a tree hollow. We decorated with tiny wildflowers and made beds of shredded fern fronds edged with pebbles. No one was fooled, but what fun we had pretending!" She chuckled. "Thank you, dear," she added as she patted Elyse's hand.

This tiny glimpse into her mother's childhood stabbed her heart. How little she knew about Sid! Or had wanted to know, until now.

When his parents had ambled off, Theo leaned over and murmured to Elyse, "Have I told you how much I love you?"

"Not today," she retorted with her arch Garbo look.

He gave her a swift kiss on the cheek. "Let's go have a look at the real Blackthorn."

"Can we?"

"It's been requisitioned for a military hospital, so it won't be out of bounds. No good trying to see the inside, of course, since it will bear little resemblance to what it was."

Only a few miles from the church, "Blackthorn Park" was inscribed in a wrought-iron arch connecting stone pillars at the entrance of a long, snaking drive through woods. When they rounded a bend after the trees thinned into parkland, the massive house suddenly loomed on a rise in the distance.

"It's a bloody great palace!" Elyse exclaimed.

Three tall stories were lit with what appeared to be floor-to-ceiling mullioned windows along an extensive façade undulating with bays. Turrets, statues, and endless chimneys decorated the roof.

"A bit big for one family, isn't it?" Roz drawled.

"No one's really certain how many rooms it has, since it was changed and expanded over the centuries, but Mum and Sid once counted a hundred and twenty-five, although they couldn't thoroughly explore the servants' subterranean domain."

"Is it haunted by the ghosts of people who got lost trying to find their way to dinner?" Roz jested.

"Or playing hide-and-seek and never getting found," Elyse added with a chuckle.

"It's not as grand living here as you might think. We don't know what the new owners managed to do to it, but Mum said that only the main rooms used regularly by the family had any heating, and that was just from fireplaces. There was no electricity. Most of the East Wing had been closed for years because of damp rot, and plaster falling off. It was a bit of a journey to find lavatories and bathrooms, along cold, dark hallways, and hot water was a challenge."

"Then why was Sid so devastated when her parents sold it?"

"Because of her family's history with it. Queen Elizabeth once stayed here. Sid loved it despite all its problems and challenges, and wanted to restore it," Theo replied as he parked. "It's not good weather to explore the gardens, but just step out and see the view."

The sloping lawn to the west of the mansion was dotted with massive oaks and spreading beech trees, and flanked by woodland, with sleeping rhododendrons edging gravel paths. Theo led them to where the vista opened up to a sizable lake with a Palladian bridge arching over the stream flowing into it, and a classical Greek temple on the distant shore.

"Zowie! It must be magnificent when everything's in leaf and bloom," Elyse said.

"That's what Mum said, especially spring and fall. There are – or at least were - several follies and naked statues tucked amongst the trees and perched on hillsides overlooking the lake. You can't see it from here, but there's a summerhouse resembling a Gothic cottage, where Mum and Sid spent a lot of time, pretending it was their home, having picnic lunches and teas, and where they would change when they wanted to swim. Or just leave their clothes." He grinned. "Sid was never one for modesty, I've been told. Mum had a harder time with that. And there's a grotto with sculptures of lusty Greek gods and scantily clad nymphs inside. Apparently, it was a good place to hide if someone came upon the girls skinny-dipping, as you Canadians call it, since it was only accessible by water."

They chuckled.

"I can see not wanting to lose *this*," Elyse admitted. "Did Sid ever come back?"

"She wanted nothing to do with the war profiteers who, she claimed, practically stole the place from her parents. And I think she was afraid of what they might have done to change or even destroy parts of it. Our house is substantial, but vastly smaller, and Mum has enough trouble finding help to manage it. A place like this is impossible without an army of servants, and a sizeable fortune for repairs."

"I expect it will take enormous resources to restore it after the military is done with it," Alastair speculated. "So how do these architectural treasures survive in the modern era?"

"Good question! Some owners have donated their properties, with funds for their upkeep, to the National Trust because that's cheaper than paying the taxes. But too many of them have already been torn down to avoid just that," Theo explained. "Death duties are now up to 65% of the value of the estate."

"That's insane!" Elyse protested.

"It's ruinous for the heirs, which is one of the reasons my parents are now considering selling up after the war," he admitted somewhat sheepishly, the estate no longer anchoring him to Britain. "But they also want to live somewhere smaller and less demanding, which they can enjoy into old age."

"So, you don't need to feel obligated to take on all the ancestral baggage."

"It's barely a couple of centuries old," Theo replied with a wry grin.

"Does *your* family own any villages?" Roz asked.

"Well… Only one hamlet," Theo demurred.

Roz chortled.

•   •   •

My darling Elyse,
I hate goodbyes, so try not to be too angry with me for leaving unannounced.

I am proud of the woman you have become, although I know I had little to do with that, other than endowing you with beauty and a feisty spirit.

Growing up under the loving guidance of Chas and Ria, Jack and Fliss, your father and grandmother, and in the company of dozens of friends and relatives, you've had a much richer and happier life than I could ever have given you. Perhaps one day you will thank me for that.

I have only two regrets in my life. The first was that I didn't snag Chas. We had an exquisitely steamy fling when he was at Oxford with my brother Quentin. I didn't realize how much I loved Chas until he was back in Canada, and then it was too late. But it seems that he and Ria were always meant for each other.

And perhaps our fantasies turn to dust when we actually live with people and their quirks on a daily basis. Would I have lasted longer with Chas than your father? I've always thought so, but who knows? Perhaps I'm just fickle and restless.

When Chas was here for your wedding, we dined together in London afterwards. I invited him to stay with me, but he declined, being ensconced at the Savoy. I asked if he was still in love with Ria, playing my last hand to win him back. Hoping that he was going through what so many men do at his age – an eagerness for change and excitement in a new romance. But he would have none of it. I admire him for that, and am glad in some respect, since I've always liked Ria.

So, you see, my darling, I'm a selfish and greedy person. Don't waste any tears or sentiment on me.

My second regret is that you and I haven't had more time together, now that we've become friends. I'm delighted that you and Theo seem so well suited, and hoped to be at least a little part of your family life. Perhaps even visiting you at Blackthorn Island. I did love that place. Try to think of me kindly there.

It's a jest of the gods that the part of my body that gave me the most pleasure should be my undoing. It still amuses me.

Know that I've always loved you despite my determination never again to lose my heart. You see, my darling, all the people I loved in my youth were taken from me, in one way or another. Even my parents became mere husks after my brothers died.

Enjoy life, live it to the full, and cherish your love with Theo.

I am, what I have foolishly denied for too long, your loving mother, Sidonie

"Why does she always do that?" Elyse demanded, swiping angrily at her tears. "Why does she make me hate her a little every time I feel compassionate towards her?"

She threw the letter to Theo, who scanned it quickly, while Elyse sucked on her cigarette and gulped her whiskey.

"You mean her confession about trying to steal Chas from Ria? I know how much you adore them both."

"Exactly! And she knew that, too! They were more my parents that she and Dad ever were."

"But that's her modus operandi, darling. To make you not feel so bad about her death. No regrets. No lamenting what might have been. And also because she was never one to prevaricate or seek approval. She was just being true to herself."

He took her into his arms. "Before we married, Sid said, 'You admire Chas as a hero, but also take a lesson from him as a devoted husband. I'm going to entrust you with my girl's heart. Don't ever disappoint me.' She glared threateningly to ensure I understood."

"You're fibbing to make me feel better," Elyse accused as she snuggled into his embrace.

"Never!" He kissed her tenderly.

Sid's lawyer had also delivered her will, which left almost everything to Elyse. There were generous sums to Sid's loyal servants and several charities, a pre-wedding present of £5,000 to Sara – more than enough to buy a posh London flat or small country estate - and a Monet painting to Marguerite, who had always admired it.

"I expect that Sid chose such a valuable painting for Mum because she knew my parents would be embarrassed to be left any money. They could sell that if they ever needed to."

"That won't be necessary, since we have a bloody fortune!" As well as the London townhouse and the Antibes villa, Sid had left Elyse priceless family heirlooms saved from Blackthorn Park, an impressive collection of art, and several million pounds. To avoid the crippling death duties, Sid had already transferred her properties to Elyse, and the investments were in trusts in her name – thanks to Jack.

"*You* do, darling."

"Which I will gladly share with you." Elyse crinkled her brow and added, "This windfall is a great responsibility. It offers us endless possibilities. But I don't want to just fritter it away on extravagant things or gamble it away like Dad did. I think personal fulfillment flows from using our talents, from our own achievements, and helping others with theirs."

"So, we could start an airline, but not drift around the Mediterranean on a yacht that could finance a small country, having endless, meaningless parties," he summarized, gazing at her with loving amusement.

"Right!" She chuckled.

"I swear that thought hadn't even crossed my mind," he teased.

"Anyway, your father can move out of the Dorchester and into the townhouse, and everyone can use it when in London. In fact, I hope your parents and Sara will help us to look after both places, since we can't be in more than one at a time."

"Especially since we'll be spending summers at Blackthorn Island," Theo quipped.

"Precisely!"

•   •   •

Elyse took a couple of days of compassionate leave to go to London and sort out a few things with Sid's estate, although there was little to do. Sid had been efficient.

Her maid, Monique, as well as Mme. Berger, the cook, had agreed to stay on for the time being, and look after the house and any guests. The chauffeur, Henri, had offered the Rolls Royce – now his – and his services to the Red Cross, but still lived at the house and helped out as usual. They all planned to return to France as soon as that was possible.

Elyse installed herself in the "Lavender Suite" and regretted never having taken Sid up on her offer of accommodation. But she and Theo had rarely gone to London once they had Riverbreeze. Had they spent more time with Sid, Elyse might have noticed that she was ill.

But it was pointless to beat herself up about that. Sid would have denied being unwell.

Elyse went hesitantly into Sid's lavish, aqua and white bedroom, and was immediately thrust back into her childhood. Most powerful was the scent of Chanel N° 5.

A flattering sketch of Sid, naked, and signed "Picasso", hung over the sumptuous satin bed. Photos of Blackthorn Park, Island, and the Antibes Villa decorated the walls among paintings of Muskoka by Jack and Claire.

Silver-backed brushes were laid out on Sid's dressing table as if waiting for her return. Next to them, surprisingly, was a framed photograph of Elyse with her parents on the inviting veranda of Blackthorn cottage. She had been five then, and had just finished doing a pirouette to entertain them, her arms outstretched in childish triumph. She remembered that moment when they had looked at her lovingly. A frozen moment when they were a happy family.

Beside it stood a polished rosewood box inlaid with mother-of-pearl. A note on top read, "For Elyse".

She opened it.

My last missive.

I never could forget you, my darling daughter, much as I tried. Nor was I allowed to, as you can see. By trying to protect my heart from sorrow, I missed the joys of being part of your life.

Take heed, and never be afraid to love fully and intensely.

This brooch was the only piece of jewellery that I took with me when I left. Your father had it designed especially for me at Tiffany's in New York after our wedding. I wanted one keepsake from those early, happy days. I know you will wear it well.

One last caveat. Please don't name any of your children 'Sidonie'. I might have been less outrageous if I'd gone by my middle name Charlotte.

Love, your mother

Elyse could almost see Sid's amused wink.

The peacock brooch sparkled with sapphires, emeralds, black opals, and diamonds set in yellow and white gold. It was stunning.

Beneath it were dozens of photos of Elyse growing up, sent by Chas and Ria, Jack and Fliss. That they were somewhat thumbed was poignantly reassuring.

Dozens of exquisite, couture gowns hung in Sid's extensive dressing room. Elyse fingered them gingerly.

"They will suit you well," Monique declared, startling her. "She never lost her youthful figure. You look so much like her that it lightens my heavy heart. You should stay in her room. She would like that."

"Did she die here?" Elyse tried to suppress a shudder. Never one to be morbid or fanciful, she did, however, feel a bit spooked.

"Yes. But by her own choosing. She did not wish a long and painful end."

Elyse stared at Monique questioningly.

"Cocaine was sometimes a good friend to her. It eased the pains of life. And death."

"I'm so glad that she didn't suffer... Yes, I will take this room." And perhaps feel enwrapped by her mother's spirit.

Sir Algernon gratefully moved into the "Blue Suite" and joined her for dinner.

"Mme. Berger makes the most delectable coq au vin in London," he stated. "Quite the feast for these days, along with a well-stocked cellar."

"I expect that's partly why Sid was a popular society hostess."

"Renowned, I'd go so far as to say. Indeed, she has an illustrious circle of friends." He hesitated as he gazed into the ruby depths of the wine. Glancing around to make sure they were alone he confided, "I'm going to tell you a secret that must go no further. Not even Theo and Marguerite can know about this for now."

"I'm intrigued! I promise to say nothing, of course."

"Sid had influential acquaintances, especially in France, who were known or suspected Nazi sympathizers. They shall remain nameless." He looked down, suppressing his disgust. "So, when Sid came to London, our Intelligence people were alerted to watch her. My department. I had a long talk with her, although I already knew she wasn't of the same persuasion. She agreed to keep an eye on her peers, and report anything untoward."

"You mean she was a spy of sorts?"

"Indeed."

"Zowie!" Elyse recalled an officer leaving Sid's townhouse on the day she first visited. He'd looked around nonchalantly but carefully before leaving. Had he been one of her Intelligence contacts, and not a lover as Elyse had suspected?

"She was conscientious and thorough. I think it empowered her, realizing she was making a vital contribution to the war. These were not friends, but were in her social circle."

"She keeps astonishing me."

Algernon chuckled. "That defined Sidonie. It was an ongoing adventure, being her friend."

Seeing Elyse's emotional vulnerability, he reached out to squeeze her hand. "She won't be easy for any of us to forget, my dear. Not that we would ever want to."

•   •   •

Merilee was a bit put out that she, along with Irene Larkin and a few others, had to stay late to process film that had just been flown in from the Continent. Of course, only the male photographers were with the advancing military, so the girls at HQ were spending more time in the darkroom these days.

She was to start a 36 tomorrow and hoped to get down to Priory Manor before dinnertime, where Ned would join her, his squadron still being based at nearby Odiham. It was a beautiful April day, and there was an underlying buzz of excitement as the Allies daily made huge strides through Germany. Surely the war was almost won.

Being distracted by thoughts of seeing Ned and helping Sophie finalize plans for Eva and Drew's garden wedding, she couldn't make out what image was actually materializing out of the developing bath. It was a strange jumble of sticks in a large ditch. She looked at the caption the photographer had included. It read "Bergen-Belsen. Terrible stench. Can smell it for miles."

"Oh dear God!" she shrieked as she noticed heads and limbs.

Irene rushed over to her and gazed in horror at the photograph. They could hardly believe it was an immense grave of emaciated, mostly naked bodies, piled haphazardly one atop the other like kindling on a bonfire.

"Jesus Christ! What the hell is that?" Irene asked. "I've got one that shows skinny people lining up for food. It's from a concentration camp that we just liberated."

"Not soon enough," Patsy lamented, joining them. "Look what I got."

One photo showed frail women with blank, hopeless eyes, lying huddled on the ground behind barbed wire. The caption read, "Dying of typhus". Another showed mounds of what looked like clothing piled beneath trees. Until they realized that these were hundreds of emaciated corpses.

"Bloody hell! I hope that the Germans treat our POW better than this!" Irene cried, obviously worried about Sam Oldershaw.

They stared in disbelief at the pictures they processed, fighting down nausea. Holding back tears. How could people be treated so cruelly?

A happier, hopeful picture showed smiling children holding their ration of bread from the Allies.

Merilee felt emotionally wrung out by the time she reached the train station near Priory Manor. Ned was awaiting her, and she hugged him fiercely.

"What's happened, sweetheart?" he asked, sensing her distress.

"A terrible day at work. I'll tell you later. I need a stiff drink or two and some sense of normality."

"Tell me now, while we drive," he suggested as he led her to Sophie's car, which he'd borrowed. "Get it off your chest. Then I have some happy news for you."

"I could certainly use that!"

When she finished describing the photos, he said grimly, "We've been hearing about the camps that have been liberated. It's hard to believe the stories of brutality and inhumanity."

"Until you see the pictures." Merilee had to admit that she felt deep anger against the Germans. How could they have let those atrocities happen? Why couldn't good people have stopped them?

She recalled what Erich had told her about his professor uncle, who had been imprisoned for criticizing the Nazi regime. Had he ended up in one of these barbaric concentration camps? Was the populace terrorized into ignoring what the Nazis perpetrated because they would become victims if they protested?

She felt even more guilt now for having loved Erich. The enemy, whose countrymen could be so evil.

"I wish you didn't have to see those photos, sweetheart."

"I expect they'll be in the press soon anyway."

"Maybe not the most horrific ones."

"Perhaps we do need to see them all. So that we never let this happen again."

It was a short drive to Priory Manor. Ned took her into his arms again for a reassuring hug when they arrived.

"Before we go inside, I'll tell you something to lift your spirits. We've been filling our planes with newly released POWs these past few days, and still have a long way to go to bring them all back. But while we were helping today's group board, someone called me by name."

Merilee's eyes lit up. "Ross?"

"Yup! I hardly recognized him at first. He's pretty thin and drawn. But his handshake was vigorous."

"Oh, thank God!"

"That's what I said. And told him that Peggy will be over the moon. He had a huge grin. I've already sent her a cable, and she's to let his family know that he's safe." Ned brushed away tears from Merilee's cheeks. "Too much emotion for one day, eh?"

She nodded. "I'm so relieved and overjoyed! Do you think I can see him?"

"I hear the Kriegies – that's what the POWs call themselves – are going to be shipped home as soon as possible. First, they're getting medical treatment and plenty of good food to build up their strength. But I told him to stay in touch with us, and said that you'd love for him to visit if he has any leave. I gave him your address and telephone number, so expect a call at least."

Over whiskies in the sunroom, Merilee asked, "Did Ross say anything about his experiences?"

"We didn't have much time to talk, but he introduced me to his friend, Arthur Patterson, and told me how they'd all been forced to leave the camp about ten days ago. They were barely half a mile away when they were strafed by machine guns from an American Mustang, killing more than a dozen British officers and wounding dozens more. We've heard that a few times now, about friendly fire getting our evacuated troops, who are being mistaken for Germans."

"Within sight of freedom! How terribly sad and ironic."

"They and their guards rushed back to the safety of their Oflag, but were forced to leave again a couple of days later, this time at night. They marched for five days to a giant encampment holding tens of thousands of Allied prisoners. The German guards disappeared overnight, and the American army arrived in tanks, tossing them oranges and chewing gum amid the cheering."

"I hope Sam's as lucky. Irene can barely contain her anxiety and excitement."

"I can't see anything stopping him from getting back to her," Ned said with a chuckle.

Merilee gazed out at the lush gardens where sun-kissed daffodils, tulips, and primroses danced among the tumbled stone ruins of the ancient abbey, while roses scrambled up the Gothic arch. Rhododendrons blazed in the background, and a haze of bluebells glowed in the woodland.

"I think we should always spend spring in England. Isn't it glorious? All these flowers when we probably still have snow at home."

"Almost guaranteed. And the ice won't be out of the lake yet."

"And I don't have to do my freezing first plunge."

"You were just showing off anyway," Ned teased.

She smirked. "You're right. I bragged about it to my city cousins and friends." Including Bryce once.

"I hope they were impressed."

"Oh yes. Or thought me loopy. I wonder how cold the ocean is in May."

They would be staying at the Tregenna Castle Hotel in St. Ives again during their week of leave after Drew and Eva's wedding, wanting just to wander the beaches and cliffs. And Merilee had warned Ned that she was going to teach him tennis and golf in preparation for their summers on Wyndwood.

"Hopefully warm enough to get our toes wet."

"I can hardly wait to swim in our lake again! And we'll be able to go skinny-dipping at our cottage when we're alone," she murmured suggestively.

"What a tempting thought!"

She basked in the lovingly amused look in his eyes, and thought how lucky she was. "Is it really possible that the war will be over soon?"

"A couple of weeks at the most, I'd say."

"It can't come soon enough," Sophie declared as she joined them, having just put the children to bed. "This continued resistance by Germany is so futile! How many more lives are going to be senselessly destroyed even in the few remaining days?"

Merilee knew that Sophie feared for Drew and Alastair. As did she. Eva was trying to be calm and positive. Thank God Ned was out of combat.

"On both sides," Ned pointed out. "But Hitler is fanatical about not admitting defeat. I've heard about Luftwaffe pilots who are flying into our aerodromes and surrendering. And weary soldiers defecting. Hitler now has children defending towns, for God's sake! It's lunacy."

"The kids and I will be going home to Canada as soon as the war is over and we can cross the Atlantic again," Sophie declared. "I haven't seen Mum for almost six years, and the kids were too young to really remember her. At least we managed to see Dad." But the unspoken reason for his second visit hung like a pall over them.

"I expect that Philip will be finished his duties before long," Ned said to cheer her up.

"At this point, I don't think I ever want to come back here. Once you've all left, and without Charlie around, it won't seem like home anymore." She looked disconsolate. "Not that it will be easy to leave Charlie behind."

After a heavy moment of silence, Merilee brightened and suggested, "We could erect a memorial for him on Wyndwood, like Lady Sidonie did for her brother who's buried in France. That's where he'll be in spirit anyway."

"That's brilliant! And you're so right. He'll always be there with us. I can't think of an inch of the island or a corner of Wyndholme that doesn't evoke some memory of him. More than ever, Canada seems like a better place to live. For the children to grow up with so many family and friends around. I think I can convince Philip that we should move there. He always enjoyed his visits. And Elyse told me that Uncle Rafe would certainly take him into his stables, with the expectation that we'd buy him out eventually."

Philip, who had trained as a veterinarian specializing in horses, had been running his father's stables, which had produced a couple of champion thoroughbreds. But they had farmed out their racehorses to a breeder in Yorkshire when both men had joined the war effort.

"Gosh, that would be wonderful, Sophie!" Merilee enthused. "I can hardly wait to be home again, too! The first thing I want to do after I hug and kiss everyone a hundred times is to take Ned to Wyndwood, overwhelm him with family..."

He laughed and she grinned.

"And show him where our cottage will be. Aunt Ria said that Uncle Freddie has already drawn up the plans."

"Wizard! But there's still plenty of flying to do to deliver supplies and equipment," Ned said. "I feel a bit guilty taking leave in a few weeks, when we have all these ex-Kriegies waiting to be repatriated from the Continent and supplies to deliver to our troops."

"You've more than done your duty, and maybe the guys who've been waiting in Bournemouth for a chance to fly can take over. Hardly fair on them to get all that training and teaching experience and then be left out of overseas action."

"That's true. And I do want to get back before too many other pilots start lining up for jobs with Trans-Canada Airlines."

"Eva says they're already sending WDs home. Married ones first. But I don't want to go until you do!"

"And I don't want to worry about *you* being left behind if I get shipped home first. Anyway, you don't want to miss another summer on the lake! Peggy will be happier once you're back…. And you might have to help plan a wedding."

"Oh, I do hope so! Let's think of this upcoming holiday as our farewell to England. For now."

•   •   •

"I can't tell you how glorious this is!" Ross exclaimed as he and Merilee were strolling through Hyde Park on their way to dinner at Claridge's. He was indulging himself by staying at that luxurious hotel for a couple of nights. "I spent the day just wandering about. Sitting by the Serpentine. Breathing freedom."

Merilee was glad to see that his three years of imprisonment hadn't erased the sparkle from his eyes.

"I expect you weren't treated as well as the Germans at the old Sanatorium."

He snorted. "No lake to swim in for a start!… But I have no real complaints. Of course, if it hadn't been for our parcels from home and the Red Cross, we probably would have starved on the meagre rations. We were allowed out on escorted parole walks, and sometimes marched down to the cinema in the village to watch German movies and newsreels. It made a nice change, and I did pick up quite a bit of German with those and my studies. Always helpful when you can communicate with your captors. And most of the guards were decent enough. Just doing their duty."

"Hmmm. Sounds like there's more of a story there."

"I just want to put all that behind me! Revel in this moment of having survived. Can you feel the excitement from millions of Londoners as we're approaching the final days?"

"Definitely! Especially since we no longer have to fear the rockets. A V-2 landed at Marble Arch just a few weeks ago. Not far from this spot, actually. Three people were killed."

"And too close to your flat! You must have been terrified."

"I've had several close calls, for sure. Don't ever tell my parents, though!"

He shook his head. "You were what, just fifteen when we first met? And here you are, still so young, but battle hardened... A successful author and photographer.... And married to someone who's long cherished you."

"You noticed that?" she asked in astonishment.

"The first day I met Ned. And I'm really happy for you."

"I hope you're not as blind as I was then," she advised with a smirk.

He laughed. "I virtually proposed to Peggy. Asked her to wait for me. Her letters sustained me. Made me fall even more deeply in love with her."

Merilee entwined her arm in his as she said joyfully, "Then we have even more to celebrate, brother-in-law!"

At their insistence, Eva joined them for dinner, having decided to give them a chance to catch up during their half-hour walk. Excitedly, she said, "The BBC just announced that Hitler's dead! According to German radio!"

"Oh my God! Then surely the war is over!" Merilee exclaimed.

"I expect that negotiations for Germany's surrender can finally begin," Ross said. "Even if the news is a lie. With the Soviets closing in on Berlin, Hitler might well have gone into hiding."

"But we can celebrate in any case."

"Yes, indeed," Ross agreed, raising his glass to them. "Here's to joyful, peaceful days ahead!"

"And to the rest of our boys coming home!" Merilee added, smiling at Eva.

"I'll be happier when the last bullet has been fired," Eva admitted. Now that the nuptials were only a week away, she was feeling superstitiously nervous. All the preparations had gone perhaps too smoothly. Even her mother's 1918 wedding gown had arrived safely and fit perfectly.

The news spread quickly, and there was a heightened sense of euphoria in the elegant dining room. And exuberant clinking of glasses.

"This is the kind of feast we dreamt of for years. Roast beef with all the fixings!" Ross sighed contentedly. "I was lucky that Mrs. Wilding sent me buttery cookies and brandy-soaked Christmas cakes, and I can hardly wait to sit in her kitchen again savouring a big slice of her famous spice cake with rum-and-maple custard."

"Sounds delicious," Eva said.

"I'm so excited that we'll all have such fun experiences to share! We'll have lots of room at our cottage for you and Peggy and Deanna to visit, Ross. And Eva and Drew will be on the island, so we'll see plenty of them."

"Believe me, I can hardly wait!" Ross said.

"Where will you spend the rest of your leave?"

"With relatives near Falmouth. Walking the Cornish cliffs and taking tea in another cousin's seaside shop."

"Sounds perfect! Eva and I loved our trips to Cornwall, which is why Ned and I are going back after the wedding."

"I can see why. I stayed there a couple of times after I arrived. We Tremaynes hail from there, but I'd never met our extended family. They took me under their wings as if they'd known me all my life. Such kindness and generosity."

"I've heard plenty of stories like that. Although one of the girls at work found her great-aunt had too many cautionary tales about men taking advantage, and insisting she always wore warm woollies next to the skin. She wasn't sure if that was to prevent pneumonia or to discourage advances."

They laughed.

The next few days were a whirlwind of activity and mounting excitement. Sam Oldershaw was safely back and coming to London to spend time with Irene. Her fiancé having been a POW, she was put on the priority list to go home. In the meantime, she was the official photographer for Drew and Eva's wedding – there was bound to be a photo of that splashed across Canadian newspapers – and Sam was going to accompany her, so Merilee and Ned would see him before he left Britain.

The Germans surrendered in Denmark, and the Canadian troops were instrumental in liberating the Netherlands. Everyone waited anxiously for the final victory announcement in Europe.

Eva had a cable from her eldest brother, Mathias, informing her that he would be at her wedding and happy to give her away. She was ecstatic.

Connie swanned into the city with baby Jennifer, who was only a few weeks old. Installing herself in the Countess's opulent Belgravia townhouse, she invited Merilee and Eva to visit. She looked glamorous in an outfit that was surely from Lady Alexandra's extensive couture wardrobe.

"I'm not missing the victory celebrations by being stuck in the country. And I'll be closer to Priory Manor for the wedding. Bryce might even get leave in time to come. And he can finally meet his daughter. Isn't she precious?" Connie cooed.

"Very sweet," Merilee agreed. It was a bit bizarre to think of Bryce as a father.

"Lady Alexandra said she has the family lips and chin."

So, there should be no doubt that Jennifer is Bryce's.

Connie handed the fidgeting infant to the nursemaid and waved her away before lighting a cigarette and taking a deep swig of whiskey. "It's so exhausting being a new mother."

"Have you two made any post-war plans?" Merilee asked.

"I'm not in any hurry to go home. In fact, I'd actually prefer to stay in Britain, although I don't think that Bryce would. He seems to have some obsession with summers at the cottage. But he did promise that we'd live in the city, and not in Launston Mills. He says it's a narrow-minded hick-town, so he was glad that he was able to escape and attend private school in Toronto. His father has an apartment there anyway, for when Parliament's in session."

"Hugh and Ginnie are excited about moving to his hometown, once he's finished his law studies this summer."

"Bryce has no intention of going into law."

Which didn't surprise Merilee. But without the massive wealth of the Thorntons and Wyndhams behind him, he would have to do something to earn a living. Joining the family law firm was surely the easiest.

"Anyway, let's plan what we'll do when Germany surrenders!"

"I'll probably have to roam about with my camera to capture the celebrations."

"I hate crowds," Eva said.

"You're such a wet blanket, Eva! You'd better get used to being around lots of people. Bryce says they're all very sociable on the lake. I *do* hope you know what you're getting into."

"That's hardly comparable," Merilee pointed out in annoyance.

"I'm just saying that Eva's going to have a lot of adjustments to make. It's not like being an ordinary wife."

"Like you and me, you mean?"

Connie bristled. "I'm hardly ordinary! I'm related to aristocracy now."

"Claiming kinship might help Bryce land a job in Britain. But don't expect any privileges back home. Bryce's mother doesn't even use her title there. We appreciate merit more than pedigree."

"Which is why you settled for a farm boy who won a medal. Sexy though he is, of course."

There was a stunned silence as Connie blew out a long stream of smoke.

Merilee was fuming. "Ned is more sincere and devoted than Bryce ever was, or perhaps ever can be." She almost added that Bryce would never have married Connie except for the baby, but thought it prudent to avoid an argument. "Remember that you, too, have to fit into our society, Connie. We're pretty easy going, but snobbery won't win you any friends. I think it's time we left."

"You were impressive," Eva said to Merilee as they sauntered home through Hyde Park. "Putting Connie in her place."

"I shouldn't let her irritate me so much. It doesn't bode well for our encounters at the lake."

"She obviously thinks I'm not good enough for Drew."

"Connie seems to enjoy meddling and making trouble. Uncle Chas and Aunt Ria sent you such a lovely, welcoming letter."

"They were very kind, but maybe I *don't* fit into that society. When I stop to think about the Thorntons being one of the most prominent families in Canada, I get paralyzed with fear."

"Is that how you feel when you're in Drew's arms?"

"No, but…"

"No *buts*! I can't think of anyone I'd rather see my dearest cousin marry."

They had no sooner entered their flat when there was a knock on the door. Drew stood there grinning.

Eva threw herself into his arms. "Oh my God, Drew! What are you doing here?"

"Having tea with Mrs. Travers while I was waiting for you."

"But I wasn't expecting you for two more days!"

"Alastair said that the war is virtually over, so I should take a few extra days to enjoy the inevitable festivities in London. I think he just wanted to ensure that I didn't get shot down on the last day of hostilities. Two of our pilots encountered MEs a couple of days ago and, fortunately, won the battle."

"How wonderful to have you safely back!" Merilee declared, giving him a hug as well. "I hope Alastair stays out of trouble."

"The army doesn't need recce anymore, and he's not about to put himself or any of our squadron in danger at this late stage if at all possible. I expect we'll be disbanded soon."

"I can hardly believe this!" Eva said.

Merilee went to pour drinks while they kissed.

The girls had to work the next day, their final one before leaves, and then they all went to The Ritz for dinner.

All of London seemed to be holding its breath, ready to explode into joyous jubilation as soon as the announcement of Germany's ultimate surrender came.

"Everyone at the office was more intent on the BBC than their work today," Eva admitted.

"I noticed that in the shops," Drew said.

"You went shopping?" Merilee asked with amusement.

"What's a chap to do in London before his wedding?"

"I hope you found something special."

"I already have that," Drew said, gazing at Eva and taking her hand in his.

"Touché!" Merilee grinned and Eva blushed.

They were just finishing dessert when the hotel manager came in and crowed, "Ladies and gentlemen, the BBC has announced that tomorrow will be a national holiday so that we can celebrate Victory in Europe Day!"

The room burst into cheers and applause.

"At last!" Merilee said as the three of them clasped hands.

"What a wedding present!" Eva beamed. Drew kissed her hand.

"People won't wait until tomorrow to start celebrating, so I should get some photos. Trafalgar Square, I think. That's where the Canadians will congregate."

"Since we won't be here tomorrow, we can at least share a little of this historic moment in London," Drew agreed.

Even during their short walk to the Square, they encountered exuberant people hugging strangers and singing with abandon. Trafalgar was beginning to fill with a flood of uniforms. The four lions at the base of Nelson's Column had acquired riders waving their caps like rodeo cowboys.

Merilee took a photo of Eva and Drew sitting on the edge of one of the fountains, holding hands, while a couple of sailors splashed about in the water behind them.

Some people jitterbugged, and others joined a Conga line, singing boisterously as they snaked around the Square. There was a wonderful, joyful madness to the evening, which Merilee captured on film.

They saw a few of their fellow WDs, including Irene, with an ebullient Sam. Merilee took photos of them as well, and Irene offered to process them all tomorrow, freeing Merilee up for an early start to Priory Manor.

Which was helpful, because by the time the three of them left the flat, most of London seemed to be pouring into the streets, many of which were already closed to traffic. Their progress in the taxicab to Waterloo station was frustratingly slow, and then they had to negotiate their way through a flood of frenetic revellers descending upon the city.

Safely on the train with just moments to spare, Eva breathed a sigh of relief, and said, "I'm glad we had yesterday evening, before London went completely mad. But a family celebration will be so much more fun."

"And meaningful," Drew added somewhat solemnly. He had asked Sophie if they could be picked up at the Brookwood station, which was only a dozen miles from Priory Manor.

But they were surprised that it was Philip who met them. "I have a fortnight's leave, and my discharge should be effective by the end of it!" he explained cheerfully.

"That's wizard! I hope I won't be far behind," Drew mused. "But I think it's going to take a long time to ship us all back."

"As married women, Eva and I will be repatriated before the other WDs," Merilee said. "We hope it's soon, so that we can have the home fires burning for our boys when they return."

"I'm hoping it will still be summer, so you'll have to make it a bonfire. With marshmallows to roast," Drew quipped.

"Delicious idea!" Eva agreed.

Philip drove them in through the main entrance of the Brookwood Military Cemetery. The extensive Canadian section was the first to their left.

Just before they'd boarded the train, Drew had purchased a bunch of pink and white carnations, which he took to Charlie's grave. Red roses were already blooming amongst the rows of white gravestones, and a jam jar held a bouquet of spring flowers that undoubtedly came from the Priory Manor gardens.

"Sophie brings fresh ones every week," Philip explained.

Drew managed to add his to the jar. "And she's always used carnations to pay tribute to her mother," Drew said. "She says that the petals hold memories. And they last much longer than roses or other flowers."

Merilee took a poignant photo of him by the grave with her Kodak.

"Do you mind if I have a few private moments?" he asked the others.

"Of course not," Eva assured him, touching his arm sympathetically.

When they had moved away, Drew stroked the headstone and said quietly, "I'm so glad you really were my brother, Charlie. I hope you know how much I admired you. Loved you." He fought back tears. "I wish you could have met Eva. I'm sure you'd approve of her…. Goodbye for now, my dearest brother. I know you'll be with us at Wyndwood."

He hugged Eva close when he re-joined her.

There was already a party atmosphere at Priory Manor when they arrived. Alayna and Jason were thrilled to have Philip home, and excited to be in the wedding party. They showed the newcomers the beautiful flower arrangements and decorations they'd helped make.

"Grandma sent *lots* of food," Alayna informed them. "And Mummy says we can have real pancakes with oceans of maple syrup for breakfast tomorrow! And oranges!"

"Oh, yummy! I've missed those," Drew said. "And will we have peanut butter and jam for lunch?"

Alayna giggled. "We're having a wedding feast! And Mummy made the most beautiful cake. With real flowers on it! I picked the violets."

"You're not supposed to tell!" Jason admonished his little sister.

"I didn't hear anything. Did you?" Drew asked Eva as he winked at Alayna.

"I'm still thinking about the pancakes," Eva responded dreamily.

"Jason, I think we should have a bonfire to celebrate the end of our war. Could you organize that? I'll help," Drew said.

"Could we, Daddy?" Jason asked eagerly.

"Splendid idea!"

They amassed an impressive mountain of downed sticks and branches from the woodland that was part of the sixty-acre property.

Then Drew picked Alastair up from a nearby airfield, where he'd flown in. "I'll be in more of a mood to celebrate once I've had a long soak in a hot tub," he jested.

"I think we can allow at least six inches of water today. For our heroes," Sophie replied with a grin.

At 3:00 pm they listened to Winston Churchill announce on the BBC that Germany had surrendered unconditionally the previous day. "We may allow ourselves a brief period of rejoicing… But let us not forget for a moment the toils and efforts that lie ahead."

"Aside from talking about defeating the Japanese, I suspect Churchill was also warning us that rationing and shortages will still be the way of life for a while," Sophie mused.

"Hopefully not in Canada," Alastair said. "I'm looking forward to daily hot showers and real, creamy scrambled eggs for breakfast, with lashings of buttered toast and blueberry jam."

"And swimming in the lake or the pool every day," Drew said. "I've already told Eva that we'll have an indoor pool at our new place."

"And not being in uniform or having to wear these God-awful lisle stockings ever again!" Merilee declared. "But lounging about in cool shorts and breezy dresses with my liberated hair blowing in the wind."

"And engulfing parkas in winter," Philip jested to much laughter.

"What about you, Eva?" Drew asked.

"Early morning paddles in the canoe."

"Hear hear!" Merilee said. "A girl after my own heart."

"And mine," Drew said happily.

Having been to Charlie's grave, Eva was especially grateful to hold Mathias in her arms when he arrived a few minutes later. An architect, he was a Captain in the Royal Canadian Engineers, and had spent most of his war in England building beach defences, air bases, and the Canadian wing of the Queen Elizabeth Hospital in East Grinstead, which was famous for its plastic surgery and it's "Guinea Pig Club" for burned aircrew. Since D-Day, he'd been on the Continent constructing temporary barracks and hospitals.

"I'm so grateful for the invitation to stay here," he said, joining them for drinks on the terrace.

"You're almost family now, so we wouldn't have it any other way," Sophie assured him. "We're so looking forward to meeting your parents and your wife."

Mathias had married his childhood sweetheart before signing up. Although she was a teacher, she had thought of joining the WDs with Eva, but he had dissuaded her, which he hadn't managed to do with his sister.

"They would all love this place. It's magnificent! I've developed a keen interest in Gothic architecture, particularly cathedrals, since I came to Britain. Extraordinary engineering feats considering that the ancient builders had no scientific principles to guide them. But look at that arch still standing solidly after centuries, even if the rest of the priory is in ruins!"

"Destroyed in the time of Henry VIII, and most of the stones scavenged by locals over the centuries," Philip said. "Luckily they left enough for the backbone of an enchanting garden."

"I'm sure the spirits of long-ago monks have protected the remnants for us," Sophie said with a twinkle in her eyes.

"I can't think of a more romantic or memorable place to get married," Mathias declared, smiling at Eva.

"You should see the secret gardens that Sophie's created, in the woodland and by the lake and summerhouse," Eva stated. "It really is magical here."

Sophie smiled rather sadly. "It will be hard to leave, but I'll have different gardening challenges wherever our new home will be."

"So, you really are planning to come home?" Drew asked eagerly.

"Sophie convinced me," Philip admitted. "And the rest of you just reinforced it with all the delightful things you're looking forward to again at home.... We can't live in the past, and I think Britain is going to need a long time to find its new reality. We want to be where the children will have the most cousins and experiences and opportunities. My father's actually looking forward to taking back Priory Manor, now that he's remarried and his military job in London is ending. So, the timing is propitious."

"I'll drink to that!" Drew exclaimed.

They raised their glasses in a joyful toast.

Drew explained to Eva and Mathias that Priory Manor had been the first home Sophie and Charlie had lived in after Ria and Chas adopted them. "Our parents rented it for the last couple of years of the war. And Philip's dad, who was a friend, liked it so much that he bought it when they returned to Canada."

"So, you have a deep connection with this place," Eva said to Sophie.

"Very. But not as much as home! And we'll come back to visit Philip's father anyway. Tragically, his older brother, who was a pilot, was killed in the Battle of Britain. He's resting in Brookwood as well."

There was a sombre silence.

"Here's to all those who sacrificed everything, and aren't here to share the victory," Drew proposed, raising his glass.

Ned arrived in time for the pre-dinner lighting of the bonfire, which was a serious responsibility for the kids. Everyone burst into applause and cheers when sparks flew skyward. With a busy day for them tomorrow, Sophie wanted the children in bed in good time.

The adults sat around the dying fire long into the evening. There were unaccustomed lights on the horizon as twilight deepened, and faint sounds of jubilation from the nearby village.

"Maybe it will still be dark enough to light the stars tonight," Sophie said wistfully.

•   •   •

With lights blazing and church bells ringing again, London was a happier place to live and work, but Merilee and Eva were anxious to get home to Canada after their blissful week with their husbands.

Ole Knutsen telephoned from his base in Scotland to bid Merilee farewell. His squadron was flying home on May 22, and he could hardly contain his excitement, mixed with some trepidation.

"I hope my family survived well. That my home is how I remember it," he said. "And Karina... I no longer expect she waits for me. Five years is a long time to be apart, especially when she does not know if I am alive. And we are not the same children who laughed and danced together.... I have met a Scottish girl, a nurse, who has won my heart. Given me much happiness. I think she would marry me and live in Norway. I do not want to disappoint Karina, but..."

"Listen to your heart, not the past. That's how Ned and I found happiness. As did Drew and Eva. I wish I could give you a big hug, Ole! Please keep in touch! Let me know about your family as soon as you have time to write."

"Be sure of that, Merilee! Your mother still writes to me every week. You cannot know how much that lifts my spirits! Sometimes she sends me sketches. Doodles, she calls them."

"I get those, too. Drawings of Saxon, and the lake, and spring trilliums in the woods."

"I treasure them. And the good memories of Canada."

"We'll expect you to visit us whenever you can. There's always a room ready for you and your wife, whoever she may be."

"Thank you! That is my wish also."

Gord McLaughlin was grateful to stay at the flat for a couple of nights. Over dinner he told them, "Gail and I have decided that we'll both apply for the pharmacy program at the University of Toronto. We'll use our veterans' settlements to fund it." They were all entitled to something from the government to help them earn a living or set up a household, whether education, goods, or cash.

"It makes sense that we take over the drug store from her father one day, and I won't be quite such a black sheep in my family," he added with a wry grin. "I'm now content to settle down in the old hometown, boring as it will be once all the military have left. I'll get myself a pipe and a smoking jacket."

Merilee chuckled, but from the veiled, haunted look in his eyes, she realized that he'd seen enough of the horrors of war to appreciate the simple pleasures of life.

"I'm itching to get home. There's no real work for us now, so we're just playing sports and doing peacetime maneuvers to keep us out of trouble."

"Will you miss flying?" Merilee asked.

"I'm ready for a change, but I do fancy having my own floatplane one day. And I think a lakeside house would be ideal. If we ever manage that, Gail and I will fly up to your cottage for cocktails." He chuckled. "Isn't it wizard that we can truly make plans for a future?"

Merilee was reassured to glimpse her carefree and rebellious pal of olden days behind the roguish grin.

She had a sudden inspiration. "I realize that I haven't taken a photo of you in your uniform. Let's visit Peter Pan in the park."

They were lighthearted as they walked through Kensington Gardens to the statue beside the Long Water.

Gord clambered onto the base joking, "I'll have to be careful not to step on any of the wildlife." Mice and rabbits and squirrels were among the creatures sculpted into the brass monument. "If I rub Peter's foot, will I be granted a wish?"

"Or be forever young," Merilee quipped.

"Wizard!" he exclaimed as he reached up to do just that.

Merilee suggested that Eva be in the next photo, but Gord insisted that he take a picture of them. "The famous photographer needs to be in some shots as well. And you'll fit right in with the fairies that could be straight out of your novel."

She laughed. There were several slender-winged fairies perched on the tree-trunk and communing with the animals.

"So, what's your next book going to be about?" Gord asked.

"I'm not sure I can write kids' books anymore," Merilee admitted sadly. "My inner child grew up."

"But your novel's allegorical anyway. That's why we grown-ups like it as well." Gord winked at her. "And it doesn't have to be a kids' story. Nope, you're not getting off that easily. You have fans who are awaiting the next adventure. And I want to be in it, although I did see elements of myself in one of the heroes of the *Thunder King*."

"You and several others, including Ned and Drew," she said with a grin. "Even though Mum based her drawings on the Norwegians."

"So you see, Eva, you have to be careful what you do and say around Merilee. She might immortalize you, and then you'll have a big legend to live up to."

They all laughed.

Merilee had kept up her diary, sometimes just jotting down interesting particulars of the day, and other times, spilling her heart onto the page. But she had no ideas for another novel. She had become used to living in the moment, and her only daydreams were about being home again with Ned. She had no idea where they were going to live, because that depended upon his job. But she had already mentally furnished their cottage, which would be a constant in their lives.

She and their children could spend summers there, along with the rest of the Wyndwood crowd and their island friends. And Ned could fly up to the lake on his days off in the floatplane that Uncle Jack had promised them as a wedding gift.

Surely once she had kids, she would find inspiration to write stories for them, which others could also enjoy. And the war would be far behind her.

The reality of going home was getting closer in mid-June as both she and Eva were told they'd have a week of leave imminently, and were then to report to the Repatriation Centre in Torquay. Fortunately, Eva, being in the Records section, had managed to get them on the same schedule.

They'd stay at Priory Manor so that Merilee could spend nights with Ned, and Eva, time getting to know her in-laws better.

So they were astonished when Drew arrived at the flat.

"Our Squadron is at Biggin Hill for a couple of weeks to ostensibly practice formation flying, some brass figuring that we haven't done enough of that on our solo and twosome sorties," he explained. "Not that any of us will ever need that. I expect it's really to stop us getting bored doing nothing useful on the Continent, and giving us easy access to London for some well-deserved fun. Being married, I'm allowed to kip here every night!"

Eva was overjoyed.

"Alastair's flying down to Hamble to have dinner with Elyse and Roz today, and plans to visit Sophie before we head back to our airfield in Germany. Where we'll play *more* baseball and watch *more* movies until they realize they really don't need us anymore."

"Hopefully that's soon! Sophie and Philip are packing up their household, so they won't be at Priory Manor much longer," Merilee explained. "They're going to ship their belongings, but are taking a Pan Am Yankee Clipper to New York, so they might get back before we do."

"Wizard! I know how much Sophie misses Mum and Dad."

As it happened, the last photos Merilee took included Drew receiving his Distinguished Flying Cross from the King at Buckingham Palace, along with three of his squadron mates. Eva was elated to attend the ceremony, Alastair at her side, proudly overseeing his flock. He'd received his gong during his convalescence in January.

Drew treated them all to a celebratory lunch at the nearby Ritz afterwards, where deeds of valour were recalled with gleeful excitement, and amusing tales of daily life in makeshift digs also downplayed the hardships, obviously made easier by the camaraderie of newfound friends. And by the euphoria of having survived. Promises were made to visit one another once they were back in Canada.

Merilee was a trifle sad to be leaving the flat that had been home for over a year. Her last meal there was fish and chips with Eva and Drew on the balcony. Mrs. Travers shed a few tears at their farewell.

Eva would meet Merilee at Priory Manor at the end of their leaves, and they would travel to Torquay on the Devon coast together. Since it was also part of the English Riviera, they were looking forward to spending time on the beaches and exploring the cliffs while awaiting transport home. A perfect ending to an extraordinary adventure. And Merilee wasn't yet twenty-one.

•   •   •

Ned was eager to get to Priory Manor and be with Merilee as much as possible before she was shipped home. He had long flying days, but at least he could spend the nights with her. And she would be ecstatic to hear that his tour of duty was almost up, and he'd probably be home by August. Now they could truly start living their life together, not just stolen days or a few precious weeks of leave.

It was a beautiful June evening, and he relished the six-mile jaunt on his motorcycle along winding country lanes and through ancient villages, a warm breeze blowing through his hair. Much as he loved flying, it felt good to be unencumbered by all his gear, and breathing the fresh, blossom-scented air.

He was coming around a bend when a puppy dashed into the road, followed by a little girl with bouncing curls and a distraught mother crying out for them to stop. He swerved to avoid them, but skidded on loose gravel and slammed into a stone wall.

•   •   •

Merilee was swimming towards Hope Cottage from the tiny island in the bay, but never got closer. She was losing strength and looked around for Ned, but couldn't see him. He'd been with her only moments earlier, laughing and teasing as they raced for home. Was he suddenly going to pop up in front of her, grinning? As she began sinking, she thought he would surely be there to pluck her out. But she kept descending ever further into the dark depths of the lake. Not even caring to struggle back to the surface.

She woke with a gasp and reached reassuringly for Ned.

But that blissful moment of waking to oblivion was suddenly awash with a black tidal wave of reality. She howled in pain as she doubled over.

She'd hardly been present at the funeral in the Brookwood Cemetery yesterday. The kind words, the sympathetic hugs, the offers of help barely reached her consciousness. She was in the grip of a never-ending nightmare. She knew only that one didn't weep in public here. The war had taken away the right to grieve openly.

So she did it in the privacy of her lonely room.

The telegrams from home were difficult. They made it too real.

Peggy wrote, "So glad Ned had you to love him, even for short time. He couldn't have been happier."

If only she hadn't given him that damned motorcycle! That had made him happy, too. And then destroyed him.

She spared a thought for Peggy and her family, who had lost a cherished brother and son. But did they also wish that they would never wake up again?

Ottawa Valley: Summer 1945
Chapter 29

Erich was perched on the rocky ridge, gazing at the farm and fields and distant landscape that spread invitingly below him. Unlike the long-tamed meadows and orchards, vineyards and hillsides of home, this had the sense of a vast wilderness barely held at bay.

That was what he loved about Muskoka, too – the tiny pockets of humanity carved out of the lakesides and the endless, wind-sighing forests crowding around them. He had noticed that on his train journeys, often seeing no civilization at all for immense stretches. He marvelled at those who had built the railroads that traversed a country wider than the imagination.

Surely in such a young land he could carve out a unique place for himself. Even if he couldn't have Merilee at his side.

If Canada would have him.

He was appalled at what he had heard and read about the camps. In late April, even before VE Day, CBC war correspondent Matthew Halton was broadcasting his observations from Germany about the POW and concentration camps being liberated by the Allies.

Mrs. McKellar had shrieked and hastily dragged a protesting Scamp from the parlour when Halton mentioned that he had seen "the bodies of boys and girls who have been tortured, defiled, and murdered by the Germans." He called Germany a "country of unspeakable evil" and asked, "Do you wonder that the world hates the Germans?"

During the report, Halton had graphically described the horrors that the Allies had encountered, and Erich was grateful that Scamp wasn't listening. "In Belsen concentration camp we found 30,000 people dying. Great heaps of corpses covered acres and acres of ground...

"The ordinary Germans... don't believe that Germany has created unspeakable crimes. It's plain that the military defeat of Germany is only the first of our problems. The second problem is to make them understand...

"It's well to remember that tens of thousands of the people that the Nazis have tortured and murdered were Germans. German heroes who would not recant and for whom the worst tortures were reserved. They are the proof that not *all* Germans are Nazis," Halton had concluded.

Into the awkward silence, Erich had said, "I am shocked and ashamed. We are not all monsters.... But fear and silence helped the Nazis into power, so we are all responsible in some ways."

He'd gotten up with profound sorrow, thinking also of his uncle who had been one of those German heroes. "I should go to my room."

"We don't blame *you*, lad. But I think it was good for you to become a prisoner and be here in Canada, because you can distance yourself from those atrocities."

"You are kind, Mr. McKellar."

"Fair is fair, lad. And don't get all formal on me! I'm still Lloyd." He'd grinned. "How about a game of chess?"

But Erich wondered if he would forever have to prove that he wasn't one of those brutal Germans. He'd gladly removed and burned the Nazi insignia from his uniform, even though he never wore it.

Now Patch bounded towards him, with Scamp close behind. "I wondered where you'd gone! Patch always knows," she added with a grin as she patted the dog. "What are you doing?"

"Absorbing the view. I want to remember it when I'm home."

"I hope that's not soon! But the war's been over for almost two months so it's weird that you're still considered a prisoner. Pa says there's too much the Allies have to do in Germany before they send you guys back."

"Yes." Like dealing with the ex-military, who were all now prisoners of the Allies. His brother Gustav was probably among them, and possibly Karl, even though he was only fifteen.

"You seem kinda glum."

"Glum?"

"Sad."

"Yes... Sad to leave here, whenever that happens. Sad not to have heard from my family for so long." The hard-fought final months of the conflict had undoubtedly disrupted the postal service, but he feared for them. He didn't mention his own horror at the incredible destruction from the relentless Allied bombing, which they had seen in news reports, and contemplating the suffering of his people and homeland. And he felt guilty for having lived in peace and comfort so far away from the fighting.

"Sad to be the bad German in the movies," he added with a smirk.

"That was Nazis in Norway," she protested, referring to the film they had seen yesterday, *Son of Lassie*. "You're not a Nazi."

"Most people won't know the difference."

Scamp frowned, and then brightened. "Maybe you can stay with us! Not have to go back at all!"

"I would like that very much... But I also want to see my family."
Her shoulders sagged. "Of course. But then can you come back?"
she asked hopefully.

"I will try."

"Promise!"

"Cross my heart and hope to die," he swore.

She giggled. "It's going to be a scorcher today, so Ma's taking me
to the beach after lunch. Pa says you can come along, and he'll
manage here."

"What a treat!" Erich grinned happily. They knew how much he
loved swimming, and trips to nearby Constance Bay on the Ottawa
River were the highlight of the summer, although infrequent,
because of gas rationing.

"Oh, and your Gravenhurst newspaper is here. Why do you still
buy that? It's not like you live there or know anyone."

"To see if there's any news about my old camp. It was home for
three years."

Scamp shrugged and pulled up a fat blade of grass, put it
between her thumbs, and blew through it, making a rude noise.

"We had a note from Aileen that she and her husband are being
discharged and coming back to take up their government jobs.
Could they come for a roast beef dinner one Sunday, she asked. Ma
just about had a conniption fit.... That means she got really upset.
'Not even staying home for a few days! After being away for three
years!'" Scamp mimicked her mother.

Erich recalled how angry Winnie McKellar had been last
summer when they'd received a letter informing them that Aileen
had married her boyfriend. All they knew about him was that he
from Ottawa, and had been her boss in Halifax.

"It's not just that she didn't even tell us that they were getting
married, but that they'd already honeymooned in Quebec City
before telling us anything at all!" Winnie had waggled her wooden
spoon as if scolding Scamp and Erich, who were awaiting supper in
the kitchen. "And why couldn't they have come home for their
leave? It's not that much farther than Quebec City!"

"She wanted to brag that they stayed at the Chateau Frontenac
for a week," Scamp had postulated. "It's like the Chateau Laurier
in Ottawa only grander, Aileen said. And she's an officer now, so
she's probably too good for us."

"Perhaps Aileen doesn't want to be around me," Erich said now
as he lit a cigarette.

"That would be stupid!"

"Would it? She and her husband have just been fighting my
countrymen. Why should they now socialize with me?"

Scamp chewed on the grass. "Well, I don't care if she stays anyway! Aileen wasn't much fun when I was a kid. She's *so* much older."

"You mean my age?" Erik teased. He'd be twenty-five in the fall.

"Yeah, well you don't tell me to get lost because you're expecting a friend to come over. All they talked about was boys and make-up anyway."

"I think it would be uncomfortable for everyone if I'm around when they come. You should all be able to speak freely, so I will take my dinner to the cabin." He kept it clean and usable, except in winter, since he sometimes played his flute there, or enjoyed a different and completely private space to study and write letters home. Letters that may never have arrived.

"That's not fair! You belong here more than she does now."

He smiled. "You're very sweet, but I'll invite Patch to dine with me. What do you say, Patch?"

The dog wagged his tail as Erich rubbed his ears affectionately.

"Wait till I tell Aileen that you prefer Patch's company!" Scamp giggled as she leapt to her feet and started down the ridge with the collie at her side.

"You wouldn't!"

She turned and grinned mischievously at him.

"You *are* a scamp!" he shouted after her.

Her delighted laughter skipped across the rocks. Erich shook his head and chuckled.

Scamp was right that it was strange to still be classified a prisoner when he had been reading about the freed Canadian POWs arriving home. But they weren't returning to a war-ravaged, defeated country whose brutality had horrified the world.

His life had been on hold for so long that Erich hardly knew how to contemplate a desirable future for himself. Much as he enjoyed working here, he had no wish to be tied to his family's farm and winery. He still wanted to become an engineer, preferably in Canada. The YMCA's War Prisoners' Aid had provided him with relevant textbooks, which he struggled with at times, but from which he was happily learning. And speaking only English for the past two years – with Scamp always ready to correct him – he felt comfortably fluent. He even preferred his name being pronounced "Erick". It made him feel more Canadian.

But thoughts of a wife and family were so nebulous now that Merilee couldn't be his. He ached for sex, but had no outlet for his desires. It would be dangerous and even suicidal to encourage any of the girls who eyed him provocatively when he was out in the community with the McKellars. Tempted as he sometimes was.

Because of the long afternoon at the beach and extra chores that evening, it wasn't until the next morning that Erich took the Gravenhurst newspaper into the cabin to peruse over coffee. Scamp was right that it had become pretty well irrelevant to him. He was only looking for anything about Merilee or her parents. So he almost missed reading the article "Local War Hero Dies in Tragic Accident."

Squadron Leader Ned Wilding earned the Distinguished Flying Cross (DFC) when he flew his badly crippled Lancaster bomber back to Britain on two misfiring engines....

Erich was momentarily elated, then devastated for Merilee. He wanted to enfold her in his arms and ease her pain. Reassure her of his love.

Perhaps he had a future here after all.

Muskoka: Summer 1945
Chapter 30

"I'm glad for Gail and Gord that she was able to pull a wedding together so quickly. He's arrived home just in time... They've been accepted at the university in Toronto, and want to be married before they start classes. I asked Uncle Jack if I could rent the apartment that Peggy ended up sharing with Maxine, so that I could give them that as a wedding present. He was keeping it available for me in case I want to go to the university.... But I don't think so.... Of course he agreed. And isn't charging me anything at all... So I think I'll add something that will really be from us. Give me some inspiration, Ned."

Sitting on the grass cradling her tucked-up knees and with Saxon at her side, Merilee stared at the polished red-and-black granite memorial she'd commissioned. The RCAF insignia and motto "Per Ardua Ad Astra" – "through adversity to the stars" – was carved into the centre of the Celtic cross, as it was on Ned's real gravestone. On the plinth below, it read:

RCAF Squadron Leader Ned (Edward) Wilding, DFC
Born April 13, 1922   Died June 18, 1945
Buried at Brookwood Military Cemetery, Canadian Sector, Surrey, England
Cherished son of Lorne and Lois, dearest brother of Ken, Barry, and Peggy
Beloved husband of Merilee (Sutcliffe) Wilding

She had wanted to add her birth date and the "Died" to be filled in whenever, as Lady Sidonie had done. Her parents had tried to dissuade her, to no avail. But Peggy didn't pussyfoot around her like most people did these days, and said, "How do you know you'll end up here when the time comes? And when you remarry, what will your husband think about that?"

"I won't remarry!" Merilee had replied, tears brimming.

Peggy had taken her into a fierce hug. "You're only twenty! You *will* find love again. It might take years and you'll never forget Ned. I won't let you!" she'd said as they both wept. "But you have a lifetime of memories to make beyond Ned. He'd hate to see you so miserable and lonely."

Merilee had clung to Peggy and thought that she would never stop crying.

Now she hugged Saxon as she sobbed, "Oh, Ned... I miss you so much. I feel like a lost soul."

Saxon had been excited when she arrived home, and never left her side unless necessary. She took great comfort in his dedicated companionship, especially since Ned had given her the dog.

It was helpful to have this monument to him, and not think that he lay an ocean away. She had put a few artifacts of his life into a steel box – including a wedding photo, a favourite old cap, one of the airplane models he'd built – and had it buried here. So it seemed that he had at least some physical connection to this plot in the small, quiet cemetery just a quarter of a mile from home.

After much soul-searching, she'd kept Big Red, since he'd loved it so. And because the motorcycle practically ran on fumes. With gas rationing still in effect, it was easier for Merilee to fetch the shopping in the sidecar rather than walking the mile and a half into town with her mother and carrying heavy loads home, or using their precious fuel for the car. And Peggy appreciated lifts.

Merilee had planted begonias in front of the monument that was under the shade of a majestic maple, especially welcome on this already sweltering August morning, but she often brought a few wildflowers and scattered them at the base. Today she'd brought a daisy-chain she'd made, and laid it on the grass in the shape of a heart. Her wedding bouquet had been white daisies and red roses.

"Everyone's trying to find things to distract me. Gail needed help with the flower arrangements and music. Peggy claims that the Matron of Honour pretty well plans the wedding, so I've been consulting with Amy. It's cool that it's going to be at the Pineridge Inn! I wish so much that you could be there, Ned!...

"I'm buying Peggy and Ross a baby grand Steinway piano from you and me, but haven't told them yet. I'm sure Peggy will be thrilled, since she loved playing the one at The Point. Ross is house hunting in Kingston, where he's landed a job. I wish they'd be living closer...

"Maxine asked all the relatives and friends who know Peggy to donate money for a wedding gift that would help the newlyweds set up their household. She's collected $7,000! Isn't that amazing? It might pay for a house, although they're hard to find these days. Mum and Dad contributed, of course, but Mum's also giving them paintings of our bay and other scenes to remind Peggy of home....

"Ross is arriving today to stay with us for the weekend, since he's escorting Peggy to Gail and Gord's wedding. I don't know how I'm going to get through all these happy events without you at my side....

"Amy's now engaged to Stuart, the pilot who was convalescing at Westwynd last year. They're getting married at Thanksgiving, just before they close the Inn for the winter. He's going to help run it. I'm really happy for her...."

Merilee bashed her fist on the ground and cried angrily, "I didn't even get a chance to show you all these places I told you about! To see where our cottage was going to be!... I don't want it now. Not without you, Ned."

Saxon whimpered and nuzzled her as she wept. She wondered that she had any tears left.

She felt a gentle breeze on her neck, as if Ned were about to kiss her. A moment later, an iridescent green and blue dragonfly landed on her hand, beside the charm bracelet Ned had given her and which she always wore. She knew that Ria had a special affinity with dragonflies and considered them messengers from departed loved ones. Or reincarnated souls.

"Is that you, Ned? Are you here with me?" As the insect perched contentedly, she was able to admire the delicacy of its translucent but powerful wings and the shimmer of its vibrant, everchanging colours. "I know you would do everything possible to be here with me, in whatever form."

The thought that Ned might not be completely lost to her was oddly reassuring. "I hope you get to fly forever, my love." But the dragonfly stayed.

"Ole writes to us regularly. He's getting married to his Scottish girlfriend in the fall, and they'll visit us when he finishes his law studies. I'm delighted for him. Karina barely waited a year for news of him before she got hitched. But that's wartime, isn't it? People grasping at happiness when they can. I'm so glad we did."

Merilee recalled how conflicted she had been when he'd proposed. How foolish and surprising in hindsight. The fact that she had fallen so deeply in love with Ned made losing him all the more painful. Carpe diem.

"Eva's coming to stay for a few days next week before she meets Drew's train in Toronto. He and Alastair are already on their homeward journey. There's going to be a celebratory ball for them at The Point on the Labour Day weekend, including Elyse and Theo and Roz, who are flying into New York next week. Roz will go home for a few days first.... I expect the party will be hard for her, too...."

"Hey, I just thought of another present for Gail and Gord! How about a canoe? They'll love that, don't you think?"

The dragonfly lifted off her hand and hovered for a few seconds before landing on the cross, fanning its wings.

She got up and ran her fingers across the sharp-edged carving of Ned's name on the glossy stone. "Goodbye, my love. Until tomorrow."

Since the monument had been erected two weeks ago, Merilee came to the cemetery first thing every morning, before breakfast. She rarely had an appetite anyway. And it helped just a tiny bit with the anguish of waking up forever alone, to talk to Ned.

She had gone only a block towards home when she encountered a group of German POWs, led by a couple of Veteran Guards from the camp, heading to their farm. Because of his limp caused by wounds in the previous war, her father-in-law never provided escort to the farm, but the Guards all knew her anyway, and greeted her warmly.

Many of the prisoners still wore their uniforms, which looked even more shabby stripped of all Nazi insignia. Some seemed cheerful and several smiled at her. But others still had an arrogant swagger and cold stares down Aryan noses. She couldn't help hating them.

And then she saw someone who made her heart leap with fear. Geisler, the vile Nazi who had planned to rape her.

Trembling, she pressed herself hard against a tree to keep from collapsing as he recognized her and smirked. He leered at her and licked his lips suggestively as he passed. As if sensing the implied threat and Merilee's fear, Saxon growled deeply and bared his teeth. She patted his head reassuringly and told him to sit.

Geisler couldn't harm her physically now, but, oh God, what if he said something about her to the Guards? What if he accused her of being Erich's "whore"? What if her father was told, if Peggy and her family found out? They would think her a traitor and despise her. She would have sullied Ned's name. Her name now.

Geisler could destroy her.

What could she say in her defence without lying? Was it acceptable to lie to save other people pain? Or was it just to selfishly preserve her reputation?

When she arrived home, her parents had almost finished breakfast.

"The coffee's still hot. I'll make some eggs and toast," her mother offered.

"I'm not hungry. Just coffee, thanks." Although she wasn't sure she could even gag that down.

"Are you feeling alright, my sweet?"

"It's just the heat. It never got this hot in England. I'll cool down with a swim."

Her parents exchanged concerned glances. Her mother had stopped nagging her to eat more, and they tried to keep up a cheerful front, although she knew they were heartbroken about Ned as well as worried about her.

"When are you going to send the Germans home?" she asked her father suddenly. "I just passed them marching to the farm."

"It will be a while yet, I'm afraid. We have to re-educate them first. Our camp was designated as "black" last December, so the die-hard Nazis were transferred from other camps, while many of our 'greys' were sent elsewhere. We moved the 'whites' out long ago.

"The SS officers are particularly ruthless and fanatical, and still threatening the moderates, so it's often tense." There had been another murder of a German POW in the Medicine Hat camp last autumn. "Some refuse to accept defeat. Although we're making headway with others. We realize that the young men have never known any way of life other than under a dictatorship, so showing them how democracy works and how a fair society treats people and gives them freedom and opportunities to thrive is beginning to make an impact."

"Sandy and Rosemary are contributing to that with their documentary films, which are shown at the camp," Claire added.

"That's super!" Merilee said with interest.

"The rabid Nazis scoff at the films, even the graphic footage we were required to show them of the concentration camps. Some laughed and others jeered that it was Hollywood propaganda." Colin shook his head.

"I had to process some of those photos!" Merilee confessed. "Some too awful even to make it into the press. It was... horrific!"

"Dear God, Merilee!" her mother cried. "You shouldn't have been exposed to that."

"I don't have much respect for the German people at the moment, even though I know that they're not all guilty of such inhumanity."

Colin said. "A couple of the boys who've been with us since the beginning want to stay in Canada. One told me that he feels he's grown up in his time here, and likes what he's seen and read about Canada. His family is gone, and he's unhappy about his homeland. Or what's left of it."

"And you're a good ambassador," Claire pointed out.

"Can they stay?" Merilee asked, hoping to hell that Geisler would never be allowed to.

"According to the Geneva Convention, they have to be repatriated. Then they can eventually apply from Germany."

Merilee had a fleeting thought about Erich, who had wanted to stay, and felt guilty, as if she were betraying Ned. But she realized that she couldn't even face Erich without that visceral revulsion for his people right now. If only that crazy and dangerous romance were truly in her past!

She avoided being out when the Germans were going to and from the farm.

But Geisler once again stalked her nightmares.

•   •   •

"I can't tell you how ecstatic I am to have you all home again," Ria confessed, her heart brimming.

"We're loving every moment, too, Mum," Sophie replied. "And the kids can't get enough of all their new-found family and friends."

They were sitting on the deck of the boathouse, sipping drinks. Watching Jason and Alayna cavorting in the shallows with Vera and Bertie, engaging Drew and Eva as they lounged on the beach. Zorro lay contentedly in the shade nearby. Ria felt that the old dog had hung on to be here when Drew came home again, but she feared that his days were numbered.

"I'm glad the RCAF managed to restore Westwynd to us so quickly. Otherwise, we'd be out of room here for guests," she said. Eva's family and Ross were arriving tomorrow to stay for the weekend.

Westwynd now belonged to Sophie and her family. This boathouse at The Point was going to be expanded to include a kitchen and dining area, making it completely self-sufficient. It would be Drew and Eva's until such time as they had children; then they would take over the Old Cottage while Ria and Chas moved down here.

Merilee and Peggy were in the girls' dorm with Vera, who was excited to have company. She and Bertie were missing Jane and George desperately. The three Baxters had returned to England in June, the two youngest in floods of tears and William looking cheerful. Astonished by Ria and Chas's generous trust funds for him and his siblings, as well as the many thoughtful gifts to take home, he'd thanked them with grace and sincerity. A small victory, Ria had thought.

"I don't think it's fair to Drew that we have Westwynd all to ourselves," Sophie said. "Vera and Bertie would be sharing with his family. But they could come and live with us, since we have more space, and our kids would enjoy their company."

"Absolutely," Philip agreed.

"Mum and I have decided that we'll eventually build them small cottages near Merilee's place, if they plan to stay in Canada," Chas explained.

"That's a lovely idea," Merilee said. "But I really don't think that you should build a cottage for *me*." She bit back tears. "I don't know how much I would use it... now."

"You need a place of your own, Merilee. A place for solitude and creativity. A place to share with friends. I inherited The Point and Wyndholme from my grandmother when I was eighteen, and it was liberating!" Ria gave her a tender smile. "And you have so many people here who love you and want to spend time with you. But that would be on your terms, if you have your own cottage."

Merilee gulped her cocktail and nodded, because she couldn't speak. Peggy, sitting next to her, squeezed her hand.

Needing to make final wedding arrangements at Pineridge, they had arrived a few days ago.

Joyful laughter drifted up to them.

"Well, I'm ready for another swim!" Sophie declared. "I've missed this so much. Swimming in our weedy little lake wasn't all that pleasant, but at least the kids learned how."

Merilee and Peggy joined her, and Ria was glad to see the young people, finally released from the dangers and stress of war, being so lighthearted. She knew all too well that they were scarred, that they mourned friends, that so much of their youth had been stolen from them. But they were resilient, and had learned to appreciate and enjoy every moment.

She had been surprised and disconcerted when Drew had announced his engagement to Eva, despite his contention that he'd found the love of his life. The Carringtons were close friends, and they had all thought that Drew and Anthea would get married. Hearing from Antonia's sister, Lady Alexandra, about Bryce's new bride, the Carringtons were not at all happy with *his* hasty marriage.

But Eva had impressed Sophie's family, and fallen into an easy friendship with them. Sophie had sung Eva's praises to her parents. And Ria had to admit that Eva seemed a loving, genuine young woman. And she liked Roz just as much.

"Our boys chose well," Chas had proclaimed to her yesterday. "I think they found women like you."

"Flatterer! I am reassured that Merilee and Eva are such close friends, as are Elyse and Roz. And that all of them get along so well."

"You know how friendships forged in difficult and dangerous times create unbreakable bonds." Ria and Antonia had become best friends driving ambulances in France.

"And that love can grow even stronger," she'd added, stroking his fire-scarred cheek gently before kissing him.

Down at the beach, a sleek mahogany launch approached and glided perfectly against the boathouse dock, Elyse at the helm.

"She makes it look so easy," Theo said as Drew and Eva tied up the boat. "But I've tried it, and it's damned tricky. So I keep being humbled by talented women. Roz just won at golf, and Elyse bested me as well. At least I tied with Alastair. Although I expect he didn't want to put me to shame, like the ladies gleefully did."

They laughed.

Elyse was glad to see that Theo had become more friendly towards Alastair. He was already realizing that things were done differently here. At the SRA Country Club, Alastair was just another respected, long-time member, along with the Wyndhams and Thorntons and the American millionaire friends and neighbours to whom Elyse had introduced Theo and Roz. The fact that Roz and Alastair had a warm, relaxed friendship also helped.

She had arrived at Elyse's Blackthorn Island several days ago, but they dined with the rest of the family every evening. Ria and Chas wanted to become acquainted with their daughter-in-law. And Elyse tried to include Alastair in as many activities as possible.

"You can take over handling the boats from now on, since we'll have to spend the rest of our time here paddling or rowing," Elyse ribbed Theo. "Not much gas left."

"How thoughtful, darling," he shot back.

"We should be off rationing by next summer, and any one of us can teach you how to dock, Theo," Drew said. "We've all been driving boats since we were kids, so it's second nature to us. Vera and Bertie are just as accomplished now."

"I can show you!" Bertie offered excitedly.

"Thanks, old chap. I'd be honoured," Theo replied.

Fourteen-year-old Bertie beamed.

"I *was* on the Cambridge rowing team," Theo revealed.

"Then you'll have to enter the Regatta next August," Merilee suggested. "And you should be sure to be here for that, Roz. Especially since you're a sailor. It's another one of the highlights of the summer."

Peggy was glad to see Merilee smiling. It was so good for her to return to fun summer life among so many family and friends. To forget her anguish for a few minutes, which would hopefully spread to hours and then days.

She was even eating more here, with the distraction of lively dinner conversations. There was too much mournful silence at Hope Cottage, despite Merilee's parents' attempt to re-establish old routines. There was no going back to that innocent, carefree time.

Peggy was torn between her own profound grief at her brother's death and joy at her upcoming marriage. Having had to focus on her music studies when Gunnar was killed had allowed little time to dwell on her loss. And there had been the ever more ardent letters from Ross, who was her first love.

But Merilee was adrift, not even interested in writing. So Peggy ached for her as well.

They were invited to Thorncliff that evening, giving Mrs. Grayson another night off before the hectic weekend of extra guests and a big ball on Saturday night. Alastair wasn't usually included in family meals, so he was spending a quiet evening in his family's small cottage between the two bays at The Point. But yesterday they had dined and danced at the Grand Muskoka Hotel, and Elyse had insisted that he come along for that.

Twenty-acre Thorncliff Island was just a quarter mile north of Wyndwood. Amid the manicured grounds and gardens, the massive cottage rose from the granite foundation as if carved out of the rock. Like stalagmites, rugged pillars grew higher to support the roof of a deep veranda bracketed by screened and glassed sections.

"Impressive," Roz pronounced.

"That's what I said when I came to be introduced to the family," Theo told her. "And all this luxury in the wilderness, including electricity and telephones, no less!" He grinned at Elyse.

The cottage – the only one on the island - was bigger than any on Wyndwood, including among its many rambling spaces, a ballroom and billiard room, music and morning room, formal and informal reception rooms, and numerous bedrooms, some with en suite bathrooms and private balconies.

This was where Chas, Elyse's father Rafe, and Jack's wife Fliss, had grown up, and which Fliss had inherited. Everyone thought it rather amusing that Thorntons now owned most of Wyndwood, and Wyndhams owned Thorncliff.

At the east end of the veranda they entered through French doors into the airy morning room, where two walls of tall windows overlooked the gardens and croquet lawn to the tennis court and enclosed pavilion beside the lake.

Chas's mother, Marjorie Thornton, greeted them warmly and was particularly interested in meeting Roz, her granddaughter-in-law. Despite being a semi-invalid for the past forty years and widowed for twenty-seven, "Granny" had a cheerful, kind nature and plenty of determination to get important things done through her charitable works.

"Oh, my dear, what a pleasure to meet you," she said, taking Roz's hand firmly in hers. "But what sorrow. How we all miss

Charlie.... And dear, sweet Merilee. You have a terrible burden to bear as well." Marjorie reached for Merilee's hand, and held both women close to her.

Merilee had had plenty of emotional reunions at Wyndwood, especially with Hugh Carrington, who had been such a good friend to Ned. But greeting Sandy and Rosemary after Marjorie's compassionate words elicited more tears.

She thanked them again for the beautiful tribute they filmed for her wedding. "I was so glad that Ned got to meet some of our family through your film. I will always treasure it."

"We enjoyed doing it, and I got to know the family better," Rosemary said. "It even inspired a few ideas that we're planning to develop now."

"So, we'd like you to come and work with us, when you're ready, Merilee," Sandy said. "Rosemary and I are leaving the NFB, although we'll be doing contract work for them. Wyndcrest Films has a big new studio and a few employees already. The best documentaries tell compelling stories. And you're a talented storyteller, with words *and* a camera, so we'd love to have you on our team."

She stared at them in amazement.

"We mean that sincerely."

"Gosh!"

"We'll send you a few old scripts so you can see how that's done. And if you're interested, you can visit us and see the rest of the filmmaking process."

"We have plenty of guest rooms," Rosemary offered.

"And Mr. Tod is still around," Sandy added.

Merilee grinned in remembrance of the fox, who had always made an appearance when she visited Sandy's place. "I would really enjoy that," she said, realizing to her own surprise how true that was.

"Good!" Sandy winked at her.

•   •   •

"We couldn't have timed this better," Elyse said to Roz later that evening as they floated in the lake and gazed up at the moonless sky. "For skinny-dipping and lighting the stars."

"Is there some magic here that suddenly makes me feel close to Charlie?"

"It was a night like this when he ran away and got stranded. And had an existential awakening."

Roz chuckled appreciatively. "Ad astra."

"It's also Muskoka magic. Big skies, long vistas, fresh breezes, lapping waves. Endless fun and adventures. It's become part of us."

"I can understand that. There's such healing peace and beauty here. I feel as if I could swim right up into the stars!"

The dark backs of Thorncliff and a couple of adjacent islands were turned towards them, so there was no ambient light to intrude on the night. Just the soft glow of one shuttered lamp in the cottage behind them. The heavens melded with the lake in a continuous arc.

"Soul food, I call it... So, I'm really glad we're here and didn't stay until the bitter end."

Their Hamble ferry pool was closed now, but some of the girls had moved to HQ at White Waltham, which was still operating. She and Roz had managed to fly the Meteor jet, so there wasn't much more they could accomplish. And since Theo had been in the RAF for five long years, he'd received a speedy discharge.

"And *I'm* glad I bought Riverbreeze. I might never go back, but knowing that I can really helps." Roz was renting it at minimal cost to an elderly couple who had been bombed out in Southampton, with the proviso that they look after it and Sir Felix, and move into a hotel – that Roz would pay for – whenever she wanted to use it.

"You can spend as much time as you like at Blackthorn, even if I'm not here. And Wyndwood, I'm sure. You'd already won over Uncle Chas, and you've charmed Aunt Ria as well."

Roz was silent and Elyse could sense her struggling with emotions. Finally, she lamented, "I can't stop thinking about what a wonderful life Charlie and I could have had."

"You have a new family in any case.... And you're closer to me than any sister could be."

"Or cousin, I suspect. Does Kate always flirt so much, or does she have designs on Theo?"

Elyse snorted. "She's always been jealous of me. Sandy and I are the same age, so I was already his pal when she was born. And once she was a young teen, she hated that boys seemed smitten by me and often ignored her. Although I wasn't even interested in most of them. She would needle me by mentioning my notorious, scandalous mother and dissolute father, who had gambled away our fortune so that her father had to support us. Which wasn't completely true. It was Uncle Chas who financed us, and Jack who invested the money wisely. Anyway, she's obviously enchanted by Theo, and if she's trying to break us up, she's out of luck. He thinks she's just a frivolous, spoiled heiress, but can't be dismissive of her if he's going to be working for her father."

"Has he decided, then?"

"He doesn't *have* to work, of course. But he's excited by the challenge, especially looking after the Wyndham European interests. We'll be able to spend time in London and Antibes. Uncle Jack's hard on himself, so living up to his expectations won't be easy."

"Theo can cope, I'm sure. And what will *you* do?"

"Establish the Lady Sidonie Thornton Foundation and find worthy causes to fund. In the meantime, luxuriate in doing nothing for a while. Except help to design and build our house."

Jack was giving them a five-acre parcel of land in his Wyndbrook Estates development. It was an exclusive enclave, and he had built his mansion in the early '20s on thirty of the five hundred acres of rolling fields and woodland that he owned just north-east of Toronto. He'd only sold a few lots since then, so it still had a pastoral feel to it, although the city was creeping ever closer. He was keeping the prime properties - adjacent to his and backing onto a stream - for family and friends. His sister Lizzie and her family were his closest neighbours, with Zoë and Freddie and their three children living next to them.

"Uncle Freddie is designing it, of course, and wants our input. He said if we're thinking of an English country house look, I should consider seeking antique fireplaces and panelling and such in England, since so many historic estates are being knocked down to avoid death duties.... Hell's bells, I wonder if I might persuade the owner of Blackthorn to part with something!" Elyse was suddenly excited. "Sid would've loved that!"

"What about that summerhouse by the lake that Theo told us about? You could pay a bloody fortune for it and make the present owner happy to part with it. Then use it as a playhouse for your kids."

"Brilliant! I think I'll need your help over there, Roz. I'm definitely going to bring back antiques and art from the townhouse, and scout out any treasures at the Antibes villa. Give you an excuse to go back, and all of us a bit of indulgence time on the Riviera, say in November."

"You're on!"

"Wizard!"

"You realize you'll have *four* homes to look after?"

Elyse laughed. "But this is still my favourite."

"What does Theo think?"

"He's a bit awed. This summer lifestyle is quite unique."

"It's glorious! And so is this. The silky water caressing every inch of skin. It makes me feel so in tune with nature. At home, we never swim in the ocean at night. Too many unfriendly creatures, but at least you can see them in daytime."

"Theo tried skinny-dipping when we first arrived. But he was rather worried about fish attacking his dangly bits, so he put on a swimsuit."

Roz burst into uproarious laughter that rippled across the lake.

•   •   •

"You're seriously moving to Orillia?" Anthea asked Drew and Eva. "I grew up in a small town and could hardly wait to escape!" She had her arm firmly wrapped around Alain's as she added, "I'm so excited that we'll be living in a real French chateau!" And that she was soon to become the Comtesse de Sauveterre, although that meant little in modern France.

"In the bucolic countryside of primitive Provence?" Drew teased. "Aunt Lizzie didn't much like it."

Anthea shrugged dismissively. "Alain and Uncle Jack are going over in a few weeks to see how badly it's been damaged by the Germans' occupation. Apparently, they even stole the wine that was hidden in caves under the vineyards. But if it can be restored, I'll make it a showpiece. With lots of bathrooms and central heating and comfy, modern bedrooms for visitors."

"It was bad enough when I was a kid, so you'll have your work cut out. But if anyone can do it, you will," Alain said with an affectionate smile.

They had spent fun times together when they'd both been stationed in Gander, and had fallen in love. Anthea made sure that everyone noticed her extravagant diamond engagement ring.

Merilee was happy for them, even though she sensed that Anthea was somewhat jealous of Eva. So she was a bit concerned for her cousin Alain being second choice. It was just as well that the de Sauveterres would be living in France, even if back in Muskoka for a few summer weeks.

She was also relieved that Bryce and Connie hadn't returned from Britain. Perhaps because he had a wife and child in England, there was no urgency to send him home. So many men needed to be repatriated.

Merilee was finding this welcome-home party at The Point difficult. Of course everyone was celebrating, exultant to have family and friends safe. Sparing a thought or tear for those who didn't come home, but ready to move on with their lives.

She slunk away discreetly and escaped to the quiet Back Bay. There were no docks here, just a dry canoe house and a Victorian change house, which was rarely used now that people wandered about freely in swimsuits. On the leeward side of The Point, this sandy bay was usually calm, and the best place to swim in the mornings.

She took a deep breath as she gazed over the lake to the darker outline of Mortimer's Island more than a mile away. A few lights shimmered along its extensive shoreline, and the thickly jewelled firmament was perfectly reflected in the still water. One star near the Big Dipper seemed to twinkle blue and white, as if it were winking at her. So that was now Ned's star.

Her heart lurched when the buoyant tune "Don't sit under the apple tree" drifted down to her. She was suddenly back in England with Ned, dancing to the song, hearing him whistle it as he walked through nighttime London after proposing to her. She was gripped with such anguish that for a moment, she considered walking into the water until she became part of it and the night and the stars.

"The only thing that could make this more glorious would be the Northern Lights," Oskar said as he joined her. "Care for a smoke?"

"Thank you." She liked Oskar and was glad of the distraction. As he lit her cigarette, she asked, "Did Eva send you to keep an eye on me?"

"She didn't have to. We're all trying to help, Merilee."

"I appreciate that."

The frenetic music and laughter and gaiety billowed over them from the dance pavilion to dissipate in the far reaches of the lake.

"This is all quite surreal," Oskar said. "I can see why Eva feels overwhelmed."

"Are you going to take up Drew's offer to work with Seaford Boatworks?"

"It's tempting, for sure, making design suggestions, being in charge of sales and marketing. I just hope I'm up to the task."

"Now who's feeling insecure?"

He chuckled.

"You'll both be fine. We're really not so intimidating."

"No indeed. Very welcoming, in fact. And generous. Drew offered to teach me how to fly, so I can borrow his plane and easily get home for visits. That's keen!"

"How do you feel about living in Orillia?"

"I'll be happy anywhere there's water, family, and friends. Matt and his wife prefer to stay up north, so my parents are pleased to have them nearby."

"And Eva will appreciate having you close.... I have a friend. A fellow WD photographer who's from Orillia. We were roommates during our training in Ottawa. I'll introduce you to her."

He laughed. "Now who's looking after who?"

"You don't need my help. Stella is sweet and talented, but rather shy, so I was thinking about her."

But she hadn't forgotten Oskar's quip in London about falling for her if she weren't married. She didn't want him to hold out any hope of them getting together.

•   •   •

"Peggy was such a beautiful bride, Ned. Radiant with happiness. It was a perfect wedding and I tried to stay cheerful, to think about Peggy and not my miserable self. But it felt so wrong that you weren't there!... So painful."

A dragonfly flitted about, so she offered her hand for it to land. "Is that you again, Ned? Peggy loved the story I told her about your last visit. She said you knew how she'd been inspired by Drusilla, and wasn't at all surprised." Drusilla was a crippled character in *The Enchanted Waterfall* series who transformed into a dragonfly.

"The newlyweds are spending their honeymoon at the Pineridge Inn for two weeks. Until after Amy's wedding.... Dear God, another one to get through.

"Peggy was thrilled with the Steinway. She plans to teach once she and Ross are settled in their new home, and maybe start an ensemble with Deanna to play concerts for fun. I'm glad they're such pals. Deanna sure was excited to be a bridesmaid...

"Everyone on the islands, except for Drew and Eva, has gone home because the kids had to return to school. Oskar is back with them now, since the guys are spending their days at the boatworks in Port Darling, talking with Adam and his dad about the new factory in Orillia. So, Eva wants me to come and keep her company. I might as well. It's so strange here without you and Peggy.... You can visit me at Wyndwood," she added to the dragonfly.

Ottawa and Muskoka: Autumn 1945
Chapter 31

"I can't tell you how lovely it is to be here," Merilee said to Sandy and Rosemary as she sipped her coffee. They were breakfasting in the dining room overlooking the small lake, fringed with a few colourful leaves tenaciously clinging to the trees. She had arrived at Wyndcrest yesterday evening.

"But I hate feeling that I don't really want to be home right now. Mum and Dad have been trying so hard to make life normal again. But even the birthday party they threw for my 21st last week only had my friends' parents there. Everyone my age is busy getting on with their lives and relationships."

How different from her birthday celebration with Ned last year at Lake Windermere.

"But I don't want to be pathetic or gloomy, so I relish this change of scene. And I'm intrigued by the scripts you sent me. I do think I could write like that."

"We have no doubt," Rosemary said. "We're looking forward to showing you the ropes this afternoon."

It was a mellow, sunny morning, so after breakfast they went for a stroll to the Canoe Club, less than a mile to the north, on the Ottawa River. Sandy and Rosemary were members, enjoying the water sports, and the dances in the boathouse ballroom.

"This is huge!" Merilee exclaimed as they crossed the bridge that connected the building to the shore. There were beautiful views of the river from the two levels of extensive balconies. "Even a diving tower!"

"My brother and I spent most of our summer days here when we were growing up," Rosemary said.

"And quite a few of the trophies inside have their names on them," Sandy added.

"It's like having a resort almost in your backyard," Merilee said. "I guess you haven't missed the cottage all that much then, Sandy."

"That's a different experience and lifestyle," Rosemary interjected. "On remote lakes, surrounded by forests and granite and solitude. I was fascinated, and think that we should do a film about Muskoka. It seems to have a rich and unique history. And you're the perfect person to research and write that, Merilee. If you're willing."

"Gosh!... Oh, yes!"

"You can write at home, if you like, although you might start your research here in the Public Archives," Sandy suggested. "We'll film next year, but you'll want to be involved in the editing process. I don't expect you'll mind being back and forth. All expenses paid, of course."

"You'll find filmmaking a somewhat chaotic life. Research anywhere and everywhere, filming on location, which could be in Vancouver or the Maritimes, and then weeks of intense work in the studio. I think our kids will learn the business from the cradle," Rosemary said as she rubbed her belly.

"You're expecting?"

Sandy put his arm around Rosemary as they grinned.

"How wonderful!"

"We only had confirmation yesterday. So, the baby will have his or her first visit to Muskoka to meet the relatives next summer anyway."

"That's exciting!" Merilee also delighted in the creative freedom of a somewhat Bohemian life for herself.

As they ambled back, Rosemary said, "So, a few pointers to start the creative process. Archival photos contrast with the rest of the colour film, so they instantly convey antiquity as well as a message. Narration fills in the gaps and elaborates when necessary, but letting the visuals do their job is most effective."

"We have lots of old photos even amongst our families and friends," Merilee said with enthusiasm. "Steamships dropping people at the big dock on The Point at the turn of the century. Edwardian ladies in long gowns and picture hats canoeing."

"And swimming in their voluminous bathing costumes that seem more likely to drown them," Sandy added.

"Famous poets enjoying the Muskoka Chautauqua."

"Canoe jousting at the Regatta."

"Uncle Chas racing his boats."

"Billy Bishop and William Barker with their seaplane service to Toronto."

"The future King Edward VIII dancing at the Thorncliff ball in 1923."

"Which would tie in with the recent royal visit of Crown Princess Juliana of the Netherlands, and the Norwegian royalty," Rosemary said.

"And we have our own old movies that we can cut in, like you learning to waterski, Merilee," Sandy teased.

"I loved how you did that bit in our wedding movie. It got so many laughs."

"It's a good lesson in editing. Rosemary is very clever with irony and juxtaposition."

"Humour can be a terrific way to capture an audience," Rosemary explained.

"Often that doesn't present itself until you're actually editing. So, scriptwriting is an ongoing, everchanging process, for us at least. Some filmmakers shoot only what they've scripted, but we like the flexibility of constant inspiration and serendipity."

"That's how I wrote the novel as well. Vague ideas, but when I actually put pen to paper, the characters took over and dictated the story."

They laughed.

After lunch, they hopped onto the streetcar a couple of short blocks away and headed downtown to the Byward Market. Within sight of the Chateau Laurier, they entered a substantial red brick building under the sign "Wyndcrest Films".

"Wow, I'm already impressed!" Merilee said.

"This was built as a hotel and tavern in the 1880s," Sandy explained. "In the '20s, during Prohibition, they converted the main floor into a restaurant, and the second floor into a dancehall, probably selling illicit booze. The third floor had offices."

"So how did you manage to snag it?" Merilee asked.

"It wasn't deemed safe enough for dances anymore, so the owners moved elsewhere. And we got lucky."

They had partitioned the main level into various rooms – film and sound recording studios, the negative cutting room, the processing lab, chemicals room, and a boardroom. Upstairs were the editing rooms, cubicles with writing desks, a small projection theatre, and a lounge. Offices, music and sound effects libraries, film and stock footage storage rooms occupied the top floor.

Although it was Saturday, a couple of people were editing on the moviolas, so they gave Merilee a demonstration of how the machines worked. This was something that she would eventually be doing.

"We're lucky with our staff," Sandy said afterwards. "We don't expect them to work weekends, although we do occasionally have long days, and then go out for a late meal together. But they're often so keen to finish a project that they choose to come in."

"And most of them are friends from the NFB, where we had brutal schedules, sometimes working nights and weekends," Rosemary said. "The NFB has been trimming its staff since the war ended, so we haven't really poached them."

"They appreciate that we work at a less hectic pace to allow time for more polished products. We shoot primarily in 35 mm for 'theatrical' films, although we can reduce them to 16 mm for distribution to schools and libraries and such. The theatricals need to be artistic, poetic, captivating, not just facts. Let's go into the projection theatre and we'll show you the films that resulted from the scripts we sent you, so you can see what we mean."

Merilee was rather overwhelmed by her introduction to the complexities of filmmaking, but seeing the finished products was stimulating. One was ten minutes long and the other – a "two-reeler" "- was twenty. They took her through them both a second time, constantly pausing to dissect them, explaining techniques that made the combination of words and shots most powerful.

"On Monday, you can spend some time in each department, so that you have a better idea of what the different processes entail," Sandy said. "In the meantime, we can discuss more ideas about what to include in the Muskoka project. I shot some footage at the cottage last year. I wanted to be sure to capture the Westwynd RCAF Convalescent Home and the perimeter of the POW camp in Gravenhurst, including the fenced-off lake, before they disappeared. And I'm sure you can locate photos for each that we can cut in."

"There's a Gravenhurst photographer who's taken lots of photos of the camp, including aerial ones and group shots of the prisoners that they could send home to Germany. And I took photos of Anna Neagle's performance to the convalescents at Westwynd."

"Perfect!"

"Gosh... I just had an idea for a title! How about 'Not Just a Pretty Place'? Because it's more than a playground for rich cottagers. It's the hardscrabble settlers and legendary boatbuilders, the lumbermen and ice harvesters, the TB patients at the Sanatoria and the sick children at the Retreat, the exiled Norwegians preparing to reclaim their homeland and their sworn enemies safely in a camp just a few miles away. And somewhere in the depths of the lake north of Hope Cottage lies a crashed RCAF training plane and two pilots whose bodies haven't been recovered. How creepy is that?"

"I can already picture that shot," Sandy said with a grin. "And I like the title. It draws you in on several levels."

Merilee beamed.

"We should train Merilee on the Eyemo, and give her one to take along," Rosemary said to Sandy. To Merilee she explained, "That's a portable 35 mm film camera that we use in certain situations. Then you can capture anything interesting that you come across – like a thunderstorm over the lake or a closeup of a loon."

"Good idea!" Sandy agreed. "We might not use the shots in this film, but they'll be handy in our stock-shot library. We made a few documentaries at the NFB almost entirely with those, and that's where the brilliance of the editor can transform them."

"Into an Oscar winner," Rosemary said. "We'll have a busy day tomorrow, Merilee."

"Sounds like fun to me!" she replied.

"But now, why don't we enjoy an early dinner at the Chateau Laurier before we head home," Sandy suggested. "A bit of a celebration."

"I thought you'd never offer," Rosemary quipped as she entwined her arm with his.

•   •   •

"Nifty place," Scamp said to her sister Aileen. "Cool that it's so close to the canal."

"Except that the rumble of trains on the other side is relentless," Her husband complained. "We'll be leaving here as soon as we can find something better."

"Yes, well beggars can't be choosers," Aileen reminded him testily. "There's a housing shortage, as you well know."

He harrumphed as he lit his pipe. "We could have stayed with my parents."

Erich thought their flat in an elegant, late Victorian house near the Chateau Laurier and their offices at Parliament Hill was delightful. They could walk to work along the canal.

"Since I'm not a tea person, I'll take Erich down to the river until Ma and Pa are ready to go home," Scamp declared. "We'll meet them outside the train station. Is an hour enough time?"

"Plenty," her father assured her with a wink. "Then we won't have to rush to catch the 5:35."

"Is that wise?" Aileen asked. "Leaving Sally alone with a German prisoner?"

"Erich is a member of the family!" Scamp retaliated. "Which is more than you are these days," she mumbled.

"What *did* you say?!"

"They'll be fine," Lloyd intervened. He handed Erich fifty cents and said, "Get yourselves some ice cream. And whatever else you fancy."

Once outside, Scamp heaved a dramatic sigh of relief.

"It wasn't *that* bad," Erich said with amusement.

"Are you kidding? They wouldn't come to lunch or to the movie with us. Are they ashamed to be seen with us *country bumpkins?* 'Come to afternoon tea.' When did tea become a special event? She's putting on such airs."

They ambled along the west bank of the Rideau Canal, opposite the tracks heading into Union Station.

"So, what were your favourite parts of the movie?" Erich asked, to lighten the mood. They had just seen "State Fair".

"I loved the roller coaster ride! And when the hogs talked to each other. That was a hoot! But the rest of it was kinda silly. Who goes to the fair in such fancy clothes?"

"That's Hollywood."

"And we're all supposed to want to look like the heroines. I'm sure they'd run a mile if they actually saw a cow or a swine. Anyway, I didn't like Margy leaving the farm and her fiancé and running off with some slick dandy to Chicago. She reminded me of Aileen."

Erich chuckled.

They found a café on Sparks Street that served ice cream sundaes, and then wandered back to the canal and down to the broad Ottawa River alongside the eight impressive locks tucked between the Chateau Laurier and Parliament Hill.

From maps at the farm, he had seen how little more than wilderness stretched from here to the North Pole.

An odd place to situate the capital city of Canada, but he did find it beautiful. The majestic, Gothic buildings of Parliament Hill perched above the powerful river and commanded attention from any viewpoint. Shafts of sunlight struck gold and vibrant russets from the brooding Gatineau hills opposite. He found autumn stunning in this country, but too quickly gone. Already most of the colourful leaves had drifted from the trees or been ripped off by October gales.

He hoped that one day he could explore the city and the beckoning hills at his leisure. And maybe even stay at the Chateau Laurier. He chuckled to himself. Wouldn't that be something!

As he and Scamp waited outside Union Station for her parents, he looked at the posh hotel across the wide and busy street. Elegant ladies and gentlemen came and went.

And then he saw her. Surely it was Merilee, engaged in animated conversation with another woman and a man. A streetcar passed in front of him, blocking his view. Heart pounding, he strained to see her again once it passed, and just caught a glimpse of the trio entering the hotel. It took all his willpower not to bolt across the road to meet her.

The McKellars arrived, a bit late, so they hastened into the station. When he hesitated, Scamp grabbed his arm and said, "We can't miss the train!"

Once they were underway, she asked, "What were you gawping at back there?"

Erich figured a version of the truth would be a good answer. "I thought I saw a famous author."

"What!? Who?"

"The lady who wrote *The Curse of the Thunder King*. She looked just like the photo on the book cover."

"You should have said! If I'd known it was her, I would have run over to get her autograph. I *love* that book!"

She had, in fact, given Erich the book for his first Christmas, and then borrowed it to read again.

"We had a train to catch, remember?" *Damn!*

•   •   •

"Erich, you got a letter! From home, I think!" Scamp yelled as she ran into the barn.

Although he'd been writing regularly, he hadn't received any mail from his family for nine months and had become increasingly worried about them. He'd heard reports of famine in Germany, and even though they had a farm, it didn't mean that they could be self-sufficient.

September 1, 1945

Dear Erich,

How glad I am that you are safely in Canada! You cannot imagine what it is like here, in a defeated and hated land. Retribution doesn't discriminate, and all now suffer because of the brutalities that the Nazis inflicted.

Erich knew that his father couldn't explicitly criticize the victors, but he was alarmed by what he was reading between the lines.

Thank God, Gustav is home from the prison camp. When they discovered he had an important job as a farmer, he was released immediately. We certainly need him here!

Karl is recovering well from his wounds. He won't be scrambling up trees for a while, but at least he can walk again. He has grown tall and otherwise strong, and his presence is also a great blessing. Women in households without men have terrible difficulties. Thank God that Ilse and Monika came to us when they did.

Christ! What was he insinuating? Erich could guess, and felt a shiver of fear for Trudi and Angelika as well. Rape and pillage were the spoils of war, and the Russians, in particular, were notorious for that.

His cousin Monika and her two young children had been bombed out of their house in Kaiserslautern last summer, so the farm had also become their refuge. Her husband, Uli, a teacher, had been drafted to work in a munitions factory in '44 when most schools were closed.

We are now under the Occupation of the French, and have just heard that Uli is in a prisoner of war camp under their control. God help him return home quickly.

There is no word of my brother Berndt, so we are heartbroken to think that he perished in a concentration camp. He had, rightly, tried to warn everyone of the Nazis' evil.

With help from a few local women and children, who are happy for the money and produce, we are working hard to keep our gardens and orchards productive. And the demand for wine increases. The French are fond of it, of course.

You are in our prayers daily, and we look forward to seeing you, my dear boy. We wish you a happy 25th birthday and will have a great celebration when you are home.

We all send our love, Papa

Erich felt an overwhelming sense of guilt not being there to help out, and to protect his family.

That evening he wrote home, saying how relieved he was to hear from them. Asking what had happened to Karl, since he'd received no news since January.

Then he penned another letter.

Stoneridge Farm,
R.R. #1, Todmorden, Ontario
November 5, 1945
Dear Major Sutcliffe,

I'm happy to no longer be your enemy, but ashamed of the brutality of my countrymen, which I only learned about in the spring. That will be very difficult to live with.

I believe I might be going home soon, much as I would like to remain in Canada. Of course I want to see my family, and need to help them recover from the war. But my wish is to return as soon as possible.

I've spent over five years here – one-fifth of my life – and I feel more Canadian than German now. The countryside speaks to my soul, I like this democratic society, and the people I've met are generally the kindest I've known. The McKellars have been mentors and family to me, and I was honoured to receive a scarf in the McKellar tartan for my birthday. So I suppose that makes me part Scottish now.

I wonder if you could do me a great kindness. Young Sally McKellar – who prefers to be called Scamp – is a big fan of The Curse of the Thunder King *as well as your* Enchanted Waterfall *series. As I am. Would you, your wife, and daughter send her your autographs? Nothing would make her happier. She's also hoping that there will soon be another book.*

When I'm able return to Canada, I hope I may visit you. I long to see Muskoka again.

Respectfully yours, Erich Leitner

•   •   •

"I missed coming to talk to you, Ned," Merilee said. "And Saxon wasn't happy that I was away for almost a month. But I did enjoy learning about filmmaking, and then spending a whole week with Peggy in her lovely house. I wish you could see her glowing with happiness."

Merilee pulled the collar of her coat up against the biting November wind.

"It's handy that Kingston is on the rail line between Ottawa and Toronto, so I told Peggy I'd be visiting her lots....

"When Sandy and Rosemary and I dined at the Chateau Laurier, it occurred to me that there are plenty of other grand CN and CP railway hotels right across the country, like the Royal York in Toronto and the Banff Springs in the Rockies. I suggested to them that those could make an interesting documentary. They agreed, so that will be my next project.... I'm sorry I'll be deserting you and Saxon again.... But it's so hard being here without you!"

She *had* felt less morose in Ottawa. Sandy and Rosemary had kept her busy learning the trade and doing research. Now she needed to get down to work here as well, scouting out photos and interesting tidbits of local lore. Although the facts needed to be correct, this wasn't going to be a history lesson so much as creating a sense of place. One that could enthrall people around the world.

Sandy told her that the most difficult part of the film business was to get wide and lucrative distribution. So, a couple of their units made films for and sponsored by large corporations. That allowed some money for speculative ones like the Muskoka project, which they hoped to sell to a big American distributor. So, it was good that they could include the Americans cottaging here, even from amongst their friends. Aunt Lizzy's husband and Troy Roland were both from wealthy Pittsburgh families, some of whom had once arrived at the wharf in Gravenhurst for the summer in their own private Pullman train coaches.

"I'm chilled to the bone, so I'm heading home now, my love. I'll put your RCAF tunic on and warm myself by the fire…. And I'll take one of your jackets with me when I travel so that I can always feel as if you have your arms around me…. Oh, Ned!"

She still couldn't accept that she would never hear a response. His voice again. The gentle humour, the indulgent love. How could that disappear from her life so instantly and completely?

Her father found her in the sitting room going through old photo albums when he came home from the camp.

"This arrived at my office a couple of weeks ago," he said, handing her a letter. "Mum and I are happy to oblige."

Merilee almost gasped out loud when she opened it. She could feel herself blanch at the shock. What the hell was Erich doing writing? Why couldn't that mad relationship stay firmly in the past?

"Interesting to have fans, isn't it?" Colin said with a smile.

"Who is this?" she managed to say. "Obviously one of the prisoners, but…"

"We had to send him away for his own safety. I believe I mentioned that a couple of years ago. So, he's been living and working on a farm. In fact, you met him once when you were skating."

"Oh… *That* guy!… Well, yes… I don't mind sending young Sally my autograph."

Merilee was unsettled as she lay in bed that night. Her encounters with Erich kept playing through her mind, much as she wished to shut them down forever. There had been tenderness and passion between them. A soulful bond.

But she had no room in her heart for him or anyone now. How could she get that across to him?

•   •   •

Scamp shrieked with excitement as she rushed into the kitchen waving two envelopes. "Look what we got!" She handed one to Erich saying, "Could it really be *her*? *The* author? Merilee Sutcliffe

Wilding it says in the return address. Did you arrange this? Oh my God!"

She tore it open and read it out loud.

Dear Scamp McKellar,

I was delighted to hear that you enjoyed my novel and my parents' series! It means so much to an author to know that her work is appreciated. Unfortunately, I have no other books planned at the moment, but I do appreciate your support. Perhaps that will inspire me!

Wishing you and your family all the best,
Merilee (Sutcliffe) Wilding

We are also honoured by your interest in our series, dear Scamp. The love of stories gives us all wings.
Claire Sutcliffe & Colin Sutcliffe

Scamp squealed with delight. "I can't believe this! Thank you, Erich! For knowing Mr. Sutcliffe and writing to him. Now read yours!"

"I will later." His heart was pounding with anticipation and unease at Merilee's words.

"Come on! I want to know what she said to you!"

"Scamp, leave the poor boy alone. It's none of your business what's in his letter," Winnie chided.

"Probably the same as yours except that her father might have a message for me," Erich prevaricated. "I'll let you know if it says anything special."

Scamp pulled a sour face.

He took the letter to his room.

Dear Erich Leitner,

Thank you for your interest in my family's books.

My father reminded me that you were the skater from the POW camp with whom I spoke briefly back in 1941. A lifetime ago. I hope that returning to your homeland will not be too devasting. So much has changed irrevocably.

My father sends his regards, and was really pleased to hear that you've been with such a good family. He's sure that Canada would welcome you back some day, but that you represent the best hope for a new and better Germany, especially with your excellent English.

Wishing you the best of luck,
Merilee (Sutcliffe) Wilding

Erich felt heartsick. The letter was so terse. So final. Merilee obviously wanted nothing more to do with him.

But what did he expect? A love letter? Of course there was nothing in it that could incriminate her.

Pulling himself together, he forced a smile as he reported back to Scamp. "She thanked me and wished me luck going home. Her father was happy to hear that I'm with such a good family, and said that my English was excellent."

"You must have said some nice things about us! And you're welcome for your *excellent English*." She giggled as she twirled about joyfully.

When he lay restlessly in bed that night, he tried to rationalize Merilee's rejection. She was still a grieving widow. Her husband had been a childhood pal – brother of her best friend, Peggy – so she must have loved him deeply. It was probably too soon to expect she might still have feelings for a former enemy. Perhaps in a few years. When he could meet her openly, as an equal.

He had to make a good life for himself, finish his studies, establish his career. He needed to have something to offer her other than memories of a dangerous, clandestine relationship that could have ruined her reputation and nearly resulted in her rape.

No wonder she'd wanted to move on.

Canada and England: 1946
Chapter 32

Erich made sure that his copy of *The Curse of the Thunder King* was well tucked into one of his kitbags, along with photos of his life on the farm. He was allowed to take two that weighed no more than fifty pounds each. He had packed as many of his Eaton's purchases as possible, but also needed to fit in the presents he had bought for his family. The McKellars had given him pounds of tea and coffee, chocolate bars, canned tuna, plenty of cigarettes, and a couple of tins of the maple syrup that he'd helped gather and boil down last spring.

He still had substantial money left in his POW account, which he was allowed to transfer to the McKellars to be used to send care packages to his family. They insisted they would anyway, and put his savings into the bank to be available to him whenever he needed the funds. Perhaps he could leave it to grow until he was able to return to Canada.

Erich felt uncomfortable in his old Luftwaffe uniform, even stripped of its Nazi insignia, but the only alternative was his prisoner garb.

He draped the scarf that Trudi had knitted for him over his shoulders and picked up the Leitner family crest that Klara had embroidered and which he'd managed to frame. He went into the kitchen where the McKellars looked glum, the women, teary-eyed.

"I have nothing that I can give you to show how much I've appreciated being taken into your home and your hearts. Except for this. It's my dearest possession," he said as he handed the family crest to Winnie.

"But your sister made this for you!" Winnie protested, knowing she had died in a bombing raid.

"I hope it will remind you of me."

"Don't you even think that we'd ever forget you, Erich!" she said, wiping her eyes on her apron. "We'll treasure this."

"But you don't owe us anything, lad," Lloyd assured him. "You've been such a big help on the farm, and brought us joy as part of the family."

Scamp burst into tears and ran over to hug him. "You have to come back! Promise!"

"Cross my heart and hope to die... And this is for you," he said, wrapping the scarf around her.

"Really? You said Trudi knitted that."

"Ah, yes, but I have my McKellar tartan scarf now."

"Oh, thank you! I'll keep it forever!... Please, please, please can I come to Ottawa with you and Erich, Pa?"

Lloyd McKellar was going to hand Erich off to a military escort who would take him to a camp in Quebec, in preparation for embarkation to Britain. Being classified "white", Erich would be in the first contingent of homeward bound POWs.

Her parents looked at each other.

"Please! I don't want to remember him just driving away from here."

"I can't see the harm in it," Lloyd agreed.

"As long as you don't make me cry at the train station," Erich quipped.

"I promise! I'll stop right now."

Winnie handed him a large paper bag. "Sandwiches, cake, and cookies. To keep you going."

"I'll miss your cooking."

"Be sure to write."

"As often as I can. If you don't hear from me soon, it will be because of the mail service."

"There will always be a room for you here."

"Thank you. For everything."

Winnie hugged him tightly. "Look after yourself. Let us know what we can send you or your family." Forestalling his protest, she assured him, "Yes, we will dip into your account if we're short. Not to worry."

It was a frigid January day, and Erich was glad he had a cozy down parka and his Moosehead boots. It seemed appropriate to cover his German uniform with Canadian clothes.

The train ride through endless white fields punctuated only by black sticks of trees, dusted evergreens, and snow-muffled houses was somewhat surreal. God, he was going to miss this land!

Scamp was uncharacteristically silent, so he finally said, "I'll expect long, chatty letters from you, when you have time to write. I want to hear about Patch and Bluebell and the other animals. And write a sentence in French so that I know you're keeping up your studies."

"Very funny."

"When I come back, we'll go for a walk in the Gatineau Hills and then we'll dine in a little *auberge*, so we'll need to order everything in French."

She giggled. "OK, that's a deal!" She made him shake on that.

"I hope you can find someone to help on the farm, Lloyd."

"It will be hard to replace you, Erich. When it gets busy in the spring, I should be able to hire the youngest McNaughton lad to help out, after school anyways. Fraser's fifteen and been working on his family's farm, but his older brothers are finally back, and I know they'll also lend a hand if I can't find anyone else."

"Do they have a tartan as well?" Erich asked slyly.

Lloyd looked at him quizzically and then understood. Erich was referring to Lloyd's long-ago comment about Scamp marrying a local boy and taking over the farm eventually.

"They sure do!" Lloyd replied with a chuckle. "And a dandy one it is, too."

"What's funny about that?" Scamp demanded.

"Just that Erich realizes there are plenty of Scots about in The Valley. Good thing he's wearing his McKellar scarf, eh?"

They didn't have long to wait at Union Station for Erich's escort to arrive.

Lloyd shook Erich's hand vigorously, saying, "Best of luck to you, lad. I don't expect it will be easy back in Germany, so stay strong. If you ever need anyone to put in a good word for you, just ask! We'll look forward to seeing you again."

Scamp hugged him, fighting back tears.

"Hey, I'll always be your big brother, you know. So, look after yourself, and be sure to read my letters to Patch as well," he told her, raising a bit of a chuckle. "And send me lots of photos." He'd given her a Kodak camera for her fourteenth birthday.

She snuffled as she nodded. Lloyd put his arm about her reassuringly.

Erich waved to them from the train window with profound sadness. He didn't want to go back to a broken and suffering homeland.

•   •   •

The best thing about waiting at Camp 40 in Farnham was a happy reunion with Christoph von Altenberg and Rudi Bachmeier. After the fight with Geisler and his thugs, they had been sent to Camp 30 in Bowmanville. They'd heard through the grapevine of prisoner transfers that Axel Fuchs and Wolf Sturm were out in Alberta, felling trees in the Kananaskis Valley.

The three friends discussed plans for the future over glasses of beer from the canteen, Erich maintaining that his would ultimately be in Canada. He had achieved university credits here for courses he'd done in maths and physics, and was determined to finish his degree in electrical engineering. When they were amazed at his English, he explained, "I haven't spoken anything but that for two and a half years. My German was getting rusty."

"My English is much improved, even if not up to your standards," Rudi said. "I think it helped me when I was being interviewed by the Canadians to determine how to classify me. I told them in English that I didn't need to be de-Nazified, since I'd never had any affiliation with that party, that I had been reading up on the Canadian political system, which made eminent sense to me, that I was planning to finish my law degree and then get into government and help to create a new and democratic Germany. So, I'm as *white* as you can get," he added with a grin.

"And no doubt you'll be the leader of Germany one day," Christoph quipped.

Rudi chuckled. "Why not? And you should become a diplomat, Christoph. You have the Oxford English *and* degree, the aristocratic pedigree, the gift of intelligent persuasion. And respect for the British parliamentary system as well."

"You are too kind, my friend. But let me see what my wife wants. I have abandoned her too long and want to make her happy."

Erich knew how he had feared for his family, since none of them had heard from home for too many months. But Christoph's wife's letters had finally gotten through. Early in the war, her parents had moved in with her. And then her sister with four children had joined them in the relative safety of Christoph's estate in the foothills of the Bavarian Alps. But now they were required to accommodate some German refugees in their home as well, so it was no longer private nor spacious. Christoph was loading his luggage with food, clothes, and toys.

"We'll be returning to a vastly different land," he mused with a frown. "Courage, my friends."

In early February, they travelled to Halifax and boarded the Mauretania, along with three thousand other German POWs, many from Alberta camps.

They expected that their stay in England would be brief, given their "white" status, but the British hadn't started repatriating their prisoners, and there was no indication of when they would. It was frustrating, and their camp of Nissen huts near Sheffield made their former Canadian prisons seem like luxury resorts.

Erich suggested they volunteer to work, although, as officers, they were not required to.

They thought they would be doing menial jobs at an RAF aerodrome nearby, but after their first morning of cleaning hangars and cutting grass, the airmen and crews invited them to share lunch and stories of their experiences in the Battle of Britain, during which the trio had been captured.

They were heartened by the respect and curiosity of fellow aviators, both sides exchanging harrowing stories with great enthusiasm. Afterwards, they were assigned to more interesting tasks around the airfield.

Erich was repairing radios and motors, and was soon friends with a Warrant Officer whose motorcycle required constant tinkering. He was eager to find out more about Canada, since he and his wife were considering emigrating there. Erich was happy to oblige.

Reading the newspapers avidly, the trio had seen numerous complaints from outraged politicians and citizens, who claimed that keeping the Germans captive so long after the war ended was hypocritical and contrary to all the Allies had been fighting for – freedom and democracy.

"I can see that they might not want to send the unrepentant Nazis back until they've been re-educated," Christoph said. "But surely we could already be of use at home, rebuilding."

It was obvious that the government viewed them as a source of cheap labour, but used the weak excuse that Germany's economy couldn't yet handle an influx of thousands of extra people. Why then were the Allies expelling ethnic Germans from countries like Hungary and Czechoslovakia and dumping millions into starving, bombed-out Germany?

"Punishment," Rudi declared.

Much to their surprise and delight, Axel Fuchs and Wolf Sturm showed up in early July when another contingent of Canadian prisoners arrived at their camp. They were cocky with stories of their lumbering in the foothills of the stunning Rocky Mountains.

"We had to clear this entire valley that's going to be flooded by a power dam. Century old trees with trunks you could hide a Messerschmitt behind. And all we had were axes," Axel boasted.

"You guys got the short end of the stick, having to stay in Ontario," Wolf crowed. "We spent days on a free trip across most of Canada, and then got to live at the base of the mountains. Man oh man! And they say British Columbia is even more beautiful. And much warmer, which is a good thing!"

"Wolf was so impressed he actually learned English because he wants to go back."

Wolf shrugged. "What have I got to go to home for? I have no one there."

"He thinks he can become a bush pilot in Canada," Axel teased.

"And maybe I can!"

"You and all the ex-RCAF pilots," Axel snorted.

"It's good to have dreams and goals," Christoph intervened. "You can't know until you try."

Axel and Wolf were also welcomed and put to work at the RAF aerodrome.

But returning home was still frustratingly elusive.

Germany: 1946 -1947
Chapter 33

Among the first to be repatriated, Erich was to be released into the French Zone of a Germany now divided by the victors. He was saddened that after all this time together, Christoph and Rudi would be heading to their homes in the American Zone of Bavaria. As if they didn't live only a few hundred kilometres from each other. Axel wasn't being discharged yet, and Wolf had applied to stay in Britain on the advice from their RAF friends. The Brits needed manpower and were happy to keep those who had no family or who were reluctant to return to a home now under Russian control. Wolf figured it would eventually be easier to get to Canada from here.

They had an emotional parting, promising to keep in touch.

The British had warned Erich that the French might imprison him again. To prevent that, they sent soldiers to accompany his group with instructions to ensure that they were properly and immediately released by the French. He appreciated the British concern for their captives and had a new respect for their integrity.

But on the train trip through Hamburg and Cologne, he'd been shocked and dismayed by the massive destruction from the Allied bombings. The cities virtually flattened, the bizarre skeletons of what remained, apocalyptic. Even worse than he had imagined. And how many innocent people had perished?

Only the twin spires of the battered Gothic Cologne Cathedral stood defiantly.

He sweated when they arrived at the French transit camp Bretzenheim. Thousands of troops who had surrendered waited here to be allowed home, or face being sent to work camps in France. They were deemed "Disarmed Enemy Forces", and so were not protected by the Geneva Convention. The men looked ragged and disheartened, and some were dangerously emaciated.

But Erich's command of French and his family's farm and winery stood him in good stead. He was given his discharge papers, ration cards, and eighty Reichsmarks to tide him over until he had a job.

He thanked his British escort, but could hardly believe that after six long years, he was finally a free man.

At the train station, he phoned his family.

Trudi answered and shrieked with joy when she heard his voice. "Is that really you, Erich? Where are you?"

"Bretzenheim. Leaving on the next train for home," he replied brokenly.

"Ach du Lieber Gott!"

"I should arrive in Edesheim in about three hours. I'd walk, but I have lots of luggage." It was only three kilometres from the station, and a pleasant stroll through a picturesque ancient village and vineyards that sloped towards a wooded hillside crowned by a castle ruin.

"Of course we'll be there! Oh my God, I can hardly believe you're finally back!"

How strange it was to board the train with a few comrades going in his direction, but no guards. How wonderful that the final stretch of the journey took him through the forested and familiar hills that he had often explored on his motorcycle. But how small and insignificant they seemed after passing the magnificent, endless mountains, rivers, and valleys of Eastern Canada on the long train ride to Halifax.

Gustav and Trudi met him at the station with the old farm truck. There were tears and smiles and fierce hugs.

"Everyone wanted to come, but Trudi insisted she could squeeze in between us," Gustav said as they set out.

"I offered to pick you up, but Gustav wouldn't hear of it!" she countered. "I couldn't wait a minute longer!"

"You're quite the grown-up young lady now, so I might not even have recognized you." She'd been ten when he'd last seen her. Now seventeen, she looked more world-weary than a carefree teenager should.

"The others are preparing a celebratory feast for tonight," Gustav revealed. "Papa is raiding the secret cellar for some of our best wines and schnapps from before the war."

"Secret?"

"He had the foresight to wall in a section of the wine cellar, but with a clever, hidden entrance. When the French Moroccan army came through last year, they raided the cellar but only found table wines. They took some of our chickens, too."

Gustav looked momentarily grim, and Erich wondered what else they had done. Those particular soldiers were as feared as the Russians.

"Then I don't expect my motorcycle survived," he quipped to lighten the mood.

"Ach, that went years ago to the army. They took all our bicycles as well. At least they left us the truck, because we insisted we needed it for the farm."

Trudi had her arm wrapped tightly through Erich's and leaned her head against him. "You certainly look like the Canadians treated you well. I can hardly wait to hear your tales! Of course, none of us could write the truth in our letters."

"I have only good things to say about Canada and its people. But it seems unfair that I was away and comfortable for most of the war, while the rest of you suffered."

"But we didn't have to worry about you!" Trudi said.

"And we'll be putting you to work soon enough," Gustav promised. "Harvest time!"

"I'm ready!"

"We just don't have a room for you. Tante Ilse and her daughter have your old one, which had been hers when she was growing up. Her two boys are kipping with Karl. Now that Monika's husband is here, her girls are sharing Trudi's room. Papa's in my old room, so you'll have to sleep with him when we find a mattress for you."

"I'm used to sharing, but I could easily sleep on the sofa. I'm just happy to be home."

There were more hugs and joyful tears when they arrived at the farm. Angelika, heavily pregnant, seemed guiltily tentative with him at first, but he put her at ease when he assured her that he was truly happy that she and Gustav had found their path in life together.

He certainly had no lingering romantic feelings for her. It was as if his life really wasn't meant to be lived here anymore.

The presents and food delighted all. The maple syrup he had raved about in his letters would be served up with pancakes and sausages for breakfast. The Eaton's sweaters and toques, crayons and teddy bears, fancy hair clips and nylon stockings, pipes and tobacco, and the bars of Pears soap he had picked up in England on the advice of his RAF Warrant Officer friend were all a big hit. The hundreds of cigarettes were like gold currency.

The mellow wine was exquisite, especially accompanying Schweinebraten and Knödel – pork roast and potato dumplings – one of his favourites. And Merilee's too, he recalled with sudden longing and poignancy.

None of them wanted to talk about the past years in Germany, so he was required to regale them with stories about his Canadian experiences. The evening was filled with amazement and laughter.

Gustav stayed up with Erich for a nightcap when the others finally sought their beds.

"I hope you've truly forgiven me, Erich. About Angelika."

"Of course I have! You two were surely meant for each other." Erich hesitated, but then plunged in. "I actually think that my destiny is in Canada. Not yet. I'm here to help for a while. And to finish my degree in engineering. I've fallen in love with that country and the possibilities for the life I really want to have."

"That's sad for us... But exciting for you, dear brother."

"You won't need me here. Sounds like Uli is re-thinking his career."

As a science teacher, and thus, a civil servant, Uli had been required to become a member of the Nazi party, even though he had never bought into their ideology. So, he wasn't allowed to teach yet, but he *could* work on the land.

"The science of viticulture enthralls him, and he has some good ideas. Different grape varieties he thinks we could try, particularly reds." Uli wanted to expand the winery by buying a neighbouring vineyard, with a house for his family. "Monika and the girls have taken to country life."

"Sounds ideal!" Erich lit a cigarette and stared at Gustav as he said, "So what really happened when the Moroccans came through?"

"The women and children were hidden in the attic. Karl, still in bandages, and Tante Ilse's two boys stood staunchly beside Papa as a line of defence. The French took what they easily could, but didn't go in search of our women."

Looking stricken, he added. "The next day, Trudi discovered that her best friend, Liesl, had been gang raped. So badly hurt she had to be taken to hospital... And she wasn't the only one.... Thank God the Moroccans had to move on in their conquering push eastward. The regular French army that's occupying us now is more interested in taking our products and resources as revenge."

Erich felt sick. He remembered Liesl as a sunny little girl with long, platinum braids.

"Liesl was so traumatized that she drowned herself. Trudi took it very hard, as you can imagine."

"Jesus Christ! Poor kid! And no wonder Trudi looks so haunted." He cradled his head in his hands. "What can I do to help?"

"Just being here already does.... Encourage Trudi to find what would make her happy. Staying here and becoming a vintner in the family business? It's already second nature to her. Becoming an artist or a horticulturalist? She has a talent for both."

Which shouldn't be wasted on just becoming a Hausfrau, Erich thought. Perhaps she could eventually come to Canada with him and start a new life far from the wreckage of this damned country.

•   •   •

"Verdammt noch mal!"

Erich was amused to hear the attractive young woman swearing as she fiddled with a Tiffany lamp on a reception desk – one that continued the Art Nouveau theme of the ornate exterior. On the opposite wall, a stunning stained-glass panel depicting an exuberant flower garden allowed jeweled light into the hallway from the adjacent dining room.

"May I be of assistance?" he inquired.

"If you can tell me why this damn lamp won't stay on, then yes."

"Probably just a loose connection. May I examine it?"

She finally looked at him, her blue eyes sparking with interest, and smiled. "By all means."

It took him only a few minutes to find the problem. "Do you have a screwdriver?"

"In the toolbox." She pulled it out from under the desk. "There are always repairs to be made," she explained with amusement at his surprised expression. "And I can certainly wield a screwdriver and hammer when necessary."

He secured a wire in the light socket. "That should work."

"Thank you! Now... what can I do for *you*?" She crossed her arms and leaned against the desk with a confident, direct gaze. As if she owned the place.

"I was told there might be a room available to rent."

"Perhaps. To the right person."

"Eric Leitner, former Luftwaffe pilot. Back to finish my electrical engineering degree at the Technical Institute." Which was just a few blocks away.

He'd completed one year there before the war, and they had accepted his Canadian university credits and allowed him to start in the new year. His family didn't need him on the farm over the winter anyway.

He'd only been in Karlsruhe a month, but was already tired of the onerous daily trek. Crossing from the French to the American Zone and then back required all passengers on the train to disembark so that their documents and bags could be carefully scrutinized. And after all that hassle, he didn't have a private or quiet place to study at home, as he'd once had.

"You seem to have survived the war well, Erich Leitner. Most men are broken in body or spirit."

"I was a prisoner of war in Canada for six years. They were very good to us."

She smiled as she uncoiled her arms. "Ah, that explains it! Then you're fortunate in more ways than one, Mr. Leitner, as I do have a room that just came available. With a balcony. Follow me."

The curving staircase was a masterpiece of Art Nouveau design, the wrought iron of the balustrade resembling vines creeping along the stairs.

"Quite the showpiece, this building," Erich said. "You're fortunate it wasn't damaged in the bombings." So much of the centre of the city had been destroyed, he was sad to see. Including the baroque Palace, which was now a burnt-out shell.

"Thankfully our block was lucky. My grandfather built this place just before the turn of the century. But it was no use trying to run it as a hotel during the war, so I took in renters. Many had been bombed out. Now I have mostly German-Hungarian refugees. Excellent cooks, some of them, so with their help, I've recently opened the restaurant again."

On the second floor of the five-storey building, she pointed out the bathroom and separate toilet that served the five rooms on this level. "His" room sat above the entrance, which cut diagonally across a corner of two streets, so that angle contained a French door to the balcony, with two tall double windows in the walls slanting away on either side. Furnishings included a large bed, small sofa, writing desk with lamp and chair, and a corner marble sink with hot and cold running water.

"This is perfect!" Erich enthused.

"Good!... Now... this building has a few electrical issues, so I need work done on the wiring. If you're interested in tackling that in your spare time, I'll give you a discount on the rent."

"That works for me, Fraulein...?"

"Frau Simona Forst. Widow." She turned away and led him back downstairs. Handing him keys, she said, "You can move in tomorrow if you wish. And have a meal on the house now as your reward for fixing the lamp," she added as she led him into the elegant dining room, redolent with tantalizing smells.

Aware of sexual undercurrents, he was excited by the prospects of living here.

•   •   •

"You're insatiable!" Simona cooed with delight as she settled into Erich's arms after their lovemaking. "Are you trying to make up for six years without a woman to warm your bed?"

He kissed the top of her head, relishing the feel of her silky blonde hair slithering across his bare chest. "It's because you're irresistible."

"Flatterer! I need my sleep. And you have to be up early for classes."

Shortly after he'd moved in, she invited him for a drink in her flat on the ground floor of the hotel, and then into her bed. He'd slept with her most nights since.

She was four years his senior, and a tough businesswoman who could hold her own against men who tried to cheat or bamboozle her. He had great admiration for her on so many levels.

Her restaurant was popular with the Americans now that they were allowed to fraternize with the natives, and Erich had noticed a particular Captain who was a frequent visitor and always engaged Simona in conversation, sometimes over a glass of wine.

"I think he's sweet on you," Erich said to her one day.

"He probably has a wife at home and is looking for a mistress while he's here. There are plenty of girls willing to sell themselves for trinkets or cigarettes. But he's a good customer and generous tipper, and interesting to talk to. It's also important and useful to have a friendly relationship with those in charge. We all dabble in the black market, as you know, so maybe the Americans turn a blind eye to those of us who aren't being profiteers, just trying to run a restaurant." She grinned. "No need to be jealous, Erich."

He chuckled. "Just looking out for you."

"Appreciated," she said as she stroked his cheek. "But I have lots of experience looking after myself."

He wondered how she had fared under the Nazi regime and then the French Army, including a brigade of Moroccans, who had captured Karlsruhe. But knew he couldn't pry.

He'd had good intentions of going home most weekends, but the restaurant was closed on Sundays and Simona took the day off. So, they'd head out for a day or an afternoon just to ramble about in picturesque places.

Their favourite outing was to nearby Baden-Baden at the edge of the Black Forest. The beautiful historic core of this renowned spa town had survived Allied bombing unscathed, although the residential areas on the periphery had suffered.

There were plenty of French military around, since it was the Headquarters for their occupation of Germany, this area along their border down to Switzerland being part of their Zone. Erich thought how somewhat arbitrary the division of Germany seemed. Karlsruhe was only a couple of dozen kilometres from here and the French border, but prized and carved out like a slice of pie by the Americans for their Zone.

Simona spoke fluent French, and asked Erich to converse with her in English so that she could improve her schoolbook command of the language. Few Americans spoke German, of course.

And when the German-Hungarians discovered he spoke perfect English, they entreated him to teach them as well. Ousted from their homeland, having lost their businesses, homes, and all belongings except what could be crammed into a suitcase for each person, they felt they had no future here. They were resented by most Germans in these times of housing and food shortages. Some had relatives in Canada or the States who would sponsor their immigration.

So communal breakfasts were conducted in English, and Erich was prevailed upon to tell them what he could about Canada. He assured them that the country was vast and wild, young and exciting, but there was no gold lying on the streets ready to be pocketed, as some claimed. "It just means that people have opportunities for success there." That was enough for them.

On one of his infrequent Saturday visits home, Gustav said to him, "If it's a woman who's keeping you away, why not bring her to meet the family?"

"I have lots of studying to do. Not easy here, as you can imagine."

When Erich, somewhat reluctantly, suggested the idea to Simona, she replied, "That would mean we're considering marriage. I don't think we're ready for that. Do you?" She challenged him with a probing stare. "After all, you want to go back to Canada. Nothing's going to take me away from here."

He didn't deny it, and wondered if she expected he would eventually give in and stay with her. He certainly loved her in many ways, but didn't feel the connection he'd had with Merilee. Perhaps that had just been conjured up from loneliness, but he wasn't willing to commit to anything permanent yet.

Simona's husband, also a pilot, had been killed in '44, and she wasn't ready for that either. So, they settled into a comfortable and enjoyable relationship with no illusions.

•   •   •

Feeling guilty for not spending more time at home, and having an idea of how he could help Trudi, Erich invited her to visit him for a long weekend in early May, close to her eighteenth birthday. When he told Simona that he'd give Trudi his bed and sleep on the floor, she chuckled and said, "We certainly mustn't scandalize your family. But I look forward to meeting your sister, and she's welcome to the tiny spare room in my flat."

For Christmas, the McKellars had sent a much-appreciated care package of food, clothes, and the first in the *Enchanted Waterfall* series. The fabulous colour illustrations required no explanation. Erich translated the story, but Trudi was determined to learn to read it herself. And they were all impressed that the author had been the kind officer in Erich's camp who had sent him to the McKellar farm.

But Erich had also noticed how mesmerized Trudi was by the fanciful illustrations, so he wanted to encourage her artistic bent. She would be captivated by the dazzling stained glass, the decorative elements that mimicked nature in the inlaid marble entrance hall, the tree-shaped pillars, the flowery wall sconces, the painted vines growing up walls and along the edges of ceilings in the reception rooms of his hotel. Paintings that were fading, since they had last been refurbished in the late '20s. But one of the Hungarians was an artist, and happy to be working on the restoration.

Trudi was agog when she arrived on Friday afternoon. "This is amazing! No wonder you don't come home much." She glowed as she added, "But I'm excited that only *I* was invited."

"You're going to be spoiled. I'm taking you shopping for a special birthday present. Anything you fancy."

"How can you afford that?"

"I've been earning money doing translations for people. Word gets around." He'd also earned money at home in the fall, fixing radios and such.

"I'm surprised you have time to study."

"He's brilliant and knows his stuff," Simona said, joining them. She shook Trudi's hand warmly as she introduced herself.

"I'm so grateful to be able to stay here, Frau Forst. I have a present for you." Trudi opened her small suitcase and unwound a couple of rolled-up sweaters to reveal a bottle of one of their finest wines.

"A 1937 vintage! How marvellous! And what a handsome label. Thank you, Trudi. You took a risk smuggling it in, since Erich says that the French are keeping tight control of your wines. Not that they need them. They just don't want to share anything with the Americans or British."

Trudi giggled. "I was going to plead ignorance and say that it was a birthday present for my brother, securely wrapped to prevent breakage, if the border guards found it."

"A girl after my own heart! And please call me Simona. Come along and see your room. Then you and Erich can have dinner. You'll find that our other residents here are eager to meet you. They think the world of your brother."

Simona joined them for a glass of wine and conversation as they were enjoying their schnitzel and spätzle.

After dinner, when Erich and Trudi went for a stroll, she confessed to him that she was awed and a bit intimidated by Simona. "She's so self-assured. So strong… But I do like your girlfriend," she added with a sly grin.

He laughed. "Is it so obvious?"

"You two seem like an old married couple when you're together. The way you communicate with your eyes."

"Just old," he quipped. "But you're very observant."

"I'm happy for you. And I won't tell if you don't want the others to know yet."

"I think I can persuade Simona to visit some time, since she's interested in our winery, if not me," he jested. "One day, when things open up again, she's keen to buy from us. Pfalz wines are highly prized."

They had reached the Technology Institute, and Erich said, "So, here's the school that helps me fulfil my goals. What are your dreams for the future?"

"Be safe. Happy… But I don't know what I can do."

"Become a gourmet chef? Opera star? Race car driver?"

She laughed. "You're silly!"

"OK then, what makes you happy?"

"Sketching…. Flowers…. Reading…. Eating Schwarzwälder Kirschtorte."

"That last one I can help with. That will be your birthday cake on Sunday. In the Schwarzwald."

"How exciting! Oh, how I wish I had a camera!"

"Aha! So that will be your birthday present. We'll buy one tomorrow, and you can take it on our excursion."

Trudi wrapped her arm around his in glee. "This is such fun!"

So was the lively and often hilarious English-language breakfast with Simona and the refugees the next morning. There were plenty of German and a few Hungarian words mixed into the "English" sentences.

"I'm amazed that the Hungarians are so cheerful, after having lost everything," Trudi said as she and Erich set out for their shopping expedition.

"I know that when you can't change something, you have to accept the present and make the best of it. It was like that in the camp. Longing for home and the way things used to be just make you miserable."

"You didn't let on in your letters. But I tried to imagine what it was like to be locked away, so far from home, and it scared me."

"But I was lucky! And actually had plenty of freedom, especially when I lived with the McKellars."

"Your Canadian family," Trudi said, taking his hand.

"Yes. And I want you to meet them one day."

Erich helped Trudi become acquainted with her new camera that evening in Simona's flat.

After he'd he left, Simona said, "You're lucky to have a brother like him. I never had siblings. But be sure to create a life for yourself, Trudi. A career that you enjoy and can sustain you. We women can't rely on men to look after us. That's something the war has certainly taught us…. Erich told me about your best friend. So tragic."

Trudi nodded, unable to speak.

"They came through here too. The French bastards! The Americans have done their share of rapes, but not usually in gangs. We were so lucky that we didn't get the Russians here. Stories we've heard about them from our Hungarians are horrific."

"How did you manage?"

"I realized that even when you're terrified, you mustn't show fear. You have to be bold. Aggressive. We were a houseful of women and children. When the Moroccans barged in, I surprised them by speaking in French, and demanded to talk to their commanding officer. When they laughed, I said that my family had known their General before the war, that he had stayed at our hotel. I spoke with such conviction that they looked concerned, and left to find easier prey. That's how we survive, much as I might despair that others suffered."

"They would have anyway. At least you spared your household… As my father and brother Karl did."

Simona took Trudi's hand in hers. "Yes. And there should be no guilt for us in that, dear girl. So, we need to live as best we can to honour our friends and their sacrifices."

Trudi hastily brushed away tears.

"And that begins with a carefree day in the Schwarzwald tomorrow!"

Trudi loved it all – strolling the postcard-pretty streets in Baden-Baden's Old Town and especially the Lichtentaler Allee along the banks of a shallow river through a blossoming park. Trudi took dozens of photos, and Erich snapped a few of her savouring an enormous slice of Black Forest cake at a café overlooking the stream.

Back at the hotel afterwards, she said, "That was the best birthday present and treat ever! I'll send you photos."

"I'm glad," Erich said. "So, think about what you want to do, and how I can help. I'm planning to emigrate to Canada eventually. It'll be a few years before I'm allowed," he added hastily, forestalling her protest. "And I think that you might want to join me once I have a job and can offer you a home. You can start a new life. It's an amazing country, Trudi."

"Oh Erich! I don't want you to go away again! Will you take Simona?"

"She has no interest in leaving here."

"And you don't love her enough to stay? Or any of us?"

"That's why I'm asking you to think about coming with me. This won't happen tomorrow or next year. But sometime." He smiled reassuringly. "In the meantime, why don't you and Scamp write to each other. You have lots in common. Love of animals. Nature. Country living. Then you'll have a friend waiting for you."

"I could try in English," Trudi said eagerly. "If you think she would."

"Of course! She already knows all about you." He grinned. "I'll help get you started."

Trudi hugged his arm. "Can we really leave all this and start a new life?"

"Oh yes."

Muskoka: Summer 1948

Chapter 34

Wrapped in a cozy robe, Merilee was sipping coffee on the wide veranda of her cottage, gazing across the calm lake to the far shore flushed pink by the sunrise. She'd had her morning swim, while Saxon played in the shallows. She loved her L-shaped bungalow - named "Wildwynd" - which was just as she and Ned had planned it. Not too large, but with plenty of room for family and friends to stay. Her parents had just been here for the Regatta weekend, while Gail and Gord had come for several days before that. Peggy, Ross, baby Robert, and Deanna were arriving on Saturday for a week's holiday.

Ria had been so right when she'd said that Merilee needed a place of her own. She travelled so much for research and filming, spent long periods in Ottawa where she took a suite at the Chateau Laurier, and months at Hope Cottage writing scripts.

So this was the only place that was truly hers. It was glorious! And inspirational. She finally had an idea for a new novel.

She wasn't a full-time employee of Wyndcrest Films because she wanted the freedom to choose projects or take time off, especially spending as much of the summer here as possible. And it was the perfect place to write. She and Saxon could easily stay from mid-May to mid-October.

Lying beside her, he twitched his ears and leapt to his feet. Merilee heard the dip of a canoe paddle before she saw the visitor round the short peninsula of her cove. Her heart sank.

"Permission to land?" Bryce called out to her.

"Sure.... You're up early."

"It's the only time I get any peace and quiet. You wouldn't happen to have a pot of coffee on by any chance?"

"I can spare you a cup."

"You look temptingly dishabille," he said with a grin, coming up the four long and shallow steps to the veranda as she returned with a mug.

"I actually have my swimsuit on underneath. So don't get any ideas."

"I won't give up. One of these days you'll realize that I'm a reformed man."

"Who's ready to cheat on his wife," she snorted.

"Ready to divorce her, as I've mentioned. She manipulated me into a marriage I never wanted."

"Seems to me you had something to do with the reason. You have a beautiful daughter, Bryce, whether you wanted her or not. Think about Jenny."

"I'm sure it would be better for her not to hear us bickering all the time. Turns out I'm not anything like as rich as Connie thought, despite my ancestry. We don't have our own cottage like the rest of you, but have to be guests at my parents' place. And we could only afford a modest house in the city, and not in the best neighbourhood. So she's jealous as hell of you and Eva. Calls her a scheming gold-digger, and rants about her having a mansion on the lake in Orillia as well as a swank boathouse cottage and one day owning The Point. She hates it when I point out that Eva and Drew are devotedly happy, and that Eva's a sweet and classy lady. Unlike my wife. So, there you have it. A wartime fling gone wrong."

He looked suddenly serious and dejected. "I might joke about it, but I feel trapped, Merilee. I know it's partly my fault! Jeez, you don't know how much I regret that! But show me one guy who wasn't laying every willing woman when he didn't know if he'd ever get another chance."

Merilee didn't know what to say. Bryce was a lifelong friend, and knowing Connie, she did feel sorry for him.

"But I didn't come here to whine... Or to seduce you. Well, not that I don't want to." He gazed at her intently. "I realize that I really do love you."

She looked away.

"And I know that I blew my chances long ago," he added flippantly before he drained his cup. "But if you ever think of marrying again... If you can forgive my adolescent arrogance and stupidity.... I'm here for you."

He got up, saying, "Thanks for the coffee. I hope we'll always be pals."

She felt incredibly sad for him. "Of course we will, Bryce!"

He turned and looked at her from the bottom of the stairs. "I envy you this, Merilee. Your freedom. I've never had that. From home to the military to matrimonial hell."

Hugh had mentioned his concern about Bryce's excessive drinking. They knew that too many men traumatized by the war tried to cope with alcohol. But being in an unhappy marriage only made things worse.

She felt unsettled after he left, trying not to dwell on the hollows in her own life. It seemed that all her family and friends were having babies. Peggy's Robert was four months old. Eva, Elyse, Anthea, and Amy were in various stages of pregnancy.

And Roz had just married Alastair.

Merilee hadn't really been surprised, because they'd become such good friends. But she wondered how Roz had moved on.

"Charlie will always be a part of me," Roz had told her. "But I realize that I can open my heart to another as well. And when you find the right man, Merilee, you'll know that you can honour Ned and still have a new love. A different life from what you had imagined together, which is also a good thing. I know that Charlie would approve, especially since he was so fond of Alastair."

Merilee was excited that Roz and Alastair were going to be her closest neighbours. Ria and Chas had wholeheartedly approved of the match and were building the newlyweds a cottage between Wildwynd and Sophie's Westwynd. With Thorncliff Island a quarter mile away, and Elyse's Blackthorn just beyond that, they would have quite a close community at the north end of the island.

Merilee went inside to get ready for the day. Part of her routine was to commune with Ned. Photos of him, some with her, were displayed on every surface that could hold one. Wedding pics, of course. Others from their trips to Cornwall and Lake Windermere, at the London flat and Priory Manor, in Hyde Park and Yorkshire, and anywhere else she had managed to capture him. It felt as if he were there with her, just not physically present at the moment. Stepped out to get wood for the fireplace or to pick up supplies or to have a swim. It was soothing and yet heart-wrenching.

She'd hesitated about putting out the honeymoon photo of Ned astride his Triumph motorcycle in front of Jamaica Inn. But with the brooding clouds and ground mist swirling, it was a powerful photo that also depicted who Ned was. The quiet hero who had skillfully avoided them being killed by a military vehicle that day. *Oh, Ned!*

Her new novel would pay homage to him. He would be the main character of a group of teenaged cousins who solved mysteries, but without Faith the Fairy and the fantasy elements of the previous book. This would be uniquely hers.

This first in perhaps a series would be set in the English Lake District, where the Canadian teens have an eccentric aunt – a bit like Cousin Phoebe - who lives in a bizarre castle with a reputed ghost. Like the place she and Ned had visited on Lake Windermere. He would love the tale. Hadn't he predicted she would set one there?

So she was eager to get to work on it. She would forgo tennis at the Country Club today, but was looking forward to dinner at The Point to welcome Roz and Alastair back from their honeymoon. Drew and Eva were there, as were Oskar and his wife.

Merilee had been surprised that Oskar and her friend Stella had actually hit it off when she'd introduced them. Stella had gained enormous confidence as a WD photographer, and had expanded her father's studio in Orillia. Oskar had settled happily into his job with Seawind Boats, and they had a lovely lakeside house near Drew and Eva. Merilee was delighted for them, even if she had a slight nagging thought that if she ever married again, Oskar might have been the one man she could see herself with.

So now there was no one she was even remotely interested in. Which was for the best, as she was still completely invested in Ned.

It was time to devote herself to her writing and let everything else fall by the wayside. She could be with Ned on their fictional travels together.

"The Adventures of the Wildwynd Island Cousins. Book 1: The Haunting of Castle Windermere." Or something like that. What fun!

Muskoka: 1951

Chapter 35

Erich couldn't quite believe he was back at his former prison, but enjoying the freedom of the beautiful setting as a guest of the Gateway Hotel. The owners had done a good job of renovating it into an attractive summer resort, which ironically catered mostly to Jewish clientele. He was nonetheless welcomed as a former internee here.

It was strange yet heartwarming to see "his" pine tree still reaching up to capture the stars. The one that had also connected him to Merilee. And to have no barbed wire barrier in the lake to prevent him from swimming to a tiny, uninhabited island in the middle of the bay, or around the rocky promontory to spy on Hope Cottage.

It was foolish to think that he might glimpse Merilee there, sunbathing or swimming or heading out in a canoe. At least he knew that the Sutcliffes still lived there, having mentioned to the hotel manager how kind the Major had been to the prisoners. What a positive influence he had been to frustrated and homesick young men.

Erich had arrived in Halifax as an immigrant in early April. He'd been surprised at how easy it was to be accepted by the Canadians now that they allowed Germans in, especially since the McKellars had sponsored him.

What a reunion that had been at Stoneridge Farm! He truly felt like a son coming home. His bank account had even grown, since the McKellars had never used any of it to pay for the care packages.

Scamp, now twenty, had said, "I'm so glad to have my big brother back! Even Patch is happy to see you."

Trudi and Scamp had developed a close friendship, comparing farm jobs, school, and boyfriends, much of that illustrated by photos.

Encouraged by Erich, Trudi had attended the Agricultural College south of Stuttgart to study horticulture. Not to be outdone, Scamp had spent two years at the Kemptville Agricultural College, only thirty miles from home, to learn the science and methods of modern farming.

"I hope Trudi's going to immigrate as well," Scamp had said. "She seems keen to. Dad says she and her husband could probably get jobs at the government Experimental Farm in Ottawa. Wouldn't that be cool?"

Trudi had met him at college, and both had ambitions to breed new cultivars – she, for flowers, and he, for crops.

"I think she'll convince him. She's very determined. Like someone else I know," Erich had replied with a grin. "So, when can I meet your special guy? As an older brother, I have to approve of him, you know."

Scamp had laughed. "Well, he's like you and Pa. Always coming up with good ideas. Able to put his hand to most anything."

Erich already knew a lot about Fraser McNaughton, who'd helped out at Stoneridge after Erich had left. His eldest brother would inherit the family farm, which was a couple of concession roads away, and his second brother was already working as a veterinarian in the area.

Erich *had* approved of Fraser when they met, and was happy to see that the boy was devoted to Scamp and respected her opinions. He'd attended the Kemptville College and inspired her to, so they had overlapped by a year and begun dating there.

Erich had been amused that Fraser called her Sally, and that she hadn't objected. When he'd teased her about it later, she said, "Scamp is kinda childish now that I'm grown up."

"I approve. But I think that Sally will always be a bit of a scamp. Which is a good thing."

She'd responded with her cheeky grin.

While he was applying for engineering jobs, Erich had helped out at the farm. But it didn't take long for him to find one in Toronto, in telecommunications research, which excited him. He'd managed to find a room in a Victorian boarding house, which was not as nice as what he'd had in Karlsruhe.

Once he'd finished his degree there, he'd found a decent job in Ludwigshafen on the Rhine, commuting the forty kilometres from home on the motorcycle he'd managed to buy. Simona hadn't been satisfied with weekend trysts, so she'd taken an American officer as a lover. Erich had had fleeting thoughts of settling down with her, and didn't know if she had deliberately set him free or if she was completely enamoured with her new paramour. But he'd realized that he was actually relieved, and began happily dreaming of Canada again.

So, here he was and determined to meet Merilee. But how? Of course, he wanted to see Major Sutcliffe, but if he knocked on the door at Hope Cottage and she wasn't there, how could he find out where she was? How to get in touch with her without revealing their past connection?

He took his flute to the boundary of the resort, where he could glimpse Hope Cottage among the trees, and played "Merilee's Song" with passion. But there was no answering music this time.

After dinner he took a canoe out and explored the bay in the lingering sunset. There were no lights at Hope Cottage or Saxon barking at a potential intruder. The family was obviously away.

He needed to rethink his strategy.

Erich laboured over the letter the next morning.

Dear Merilee Wilding,

You might remember having met me long ago, skating on the lake when I was a prisoner at Camp 20. What a unique experience that was! At my request, you once sent a note to Sally (Scamp) McKellar, a big fan of your first book, whose family was so kind to me. How thrilled she was to receive it!

I'd mentioned in my letter to your father that I hoped to return to Canada one day, to a land and people I fell in love with, and where I envisioned my future. So, I'm fortunate to now be an immigrant here. The McKellars sponsored me, and as a small favour to them in return, I would be so grateful if I could give Sally an autographed copy of your new novel, which was another hit with us both.

I have a job as an engineer at a company in Toronto, and am excited to be back in Muskoka for a long weekend, staying at the place that once imprisoned me. I love the landscape, the same trees that had become so familiar to me, and have nothing but good memories of my time here.

I would also be most pleased to see your father again to express my gratitude in person for his help.

Would there be a convenient time when I could come by with the book for you to sign? I have weekends free and could easily come to Gravenhurst or wherever is most convenient.

Thank you for your consideration. Of course, I understand if it's too much of an imposition.

Sincerely and respectfully yours, Erich Leitner.

The letter to her father was easy to write. He took them to Hope Cottage, wished them good luck, and left them in the mailbox. Then he decided to revisit the old farm.

•   •   •

The letter fluttered from Merilee's hands. Damn! Why was Erich trying to connect with her again? Why wouldn't he let her forget the past? Had he not found someone else after all these years?

Damn, damn, damn!

But poignant memories of him suddenly assailed her. How they had seemed to be soulmates from the moment they met. How their eyes had locked in love and strength that day in the woods when there had seemed no way to escape the brutality of the Nazis. How she had cried for him afterwards, and dreamt that one day they could be together in a different world.

She had to admit that she was lonely. It was hard to see most of her friends happily married and now having their second round of kids. She felt left out. On the outside looking in on the life she should have had with Ned. But which could never be.

Yesterday had been the annual Summer's End Ball at Thorncliff, but Bryce, now divorced from Connie, had kept pestering her to dance and she hadn't stayed long. She was increasingly restless these days, especially since she'd just finished another novel, which she was in the final stages of editing.

Most of the islanders were leaving for home tomorrow, some returning for a few more weekends before closing up for the season, others, eking out a few more September days. Her parents were on a month-long excursion to British Columbia by train, her father gathering ideas for a new book. So, she came to check on Hope Cottage occasionally. Lois and Lorne Wilding looked after the place regularly, but they were in Kingston to meet their new granddaughter.

Gravenhurst had settled into hibernation after its bustling wartime heydays. With gas rationing and tires virtually unavailable then, the steamships had thrived. But tourists and cottagers now drove up congested highways, mostly bypassing the town, so there were few trains coming into the wharf station and only two steamships still in service. But for how much longer? She had grown up to the whistles of so many of them that she already missed their distinctive voices. Cars and affordable powerboats would surely be their death knell. Drew had mentioned that sales of the popular Seawind runabout had soared in the past few years.

Thankfully, Gail and Gord lived in town, but they were busy with the pharmacy and their new daughter, so she didn't see them often.

Merilee didn't have any projects planned with Wyndcrest Films at the moment, although they were busy and popular, having won several Canadian and international film awards, hers among them. She had been mulling over an idea for a script – a journey along the

Trent-Severn Waterway which stretched over two hundred scenic miles from Georgian Bay to Lake Ontario. They could highlight the communities and their history along the waterway, including Orillia, which is where the thought occurred when she was visiting Eva and Drew. She wasn't ready to start another solitary journey writing a new novel, and craved the stimulation of travelling and working with a creative team.

She should talk to Ned about it.

She and Saxon were just entering the road from their long laneway when she spotted Erich walking towards her. She felt faint as her heart pounded crazily.

His astonishment turned into a searching tenderness as he approached her. "I've dreamt of this moment since we last met. When you saved my life, Merilee."

She hardly knew what to say. "I'm glad that things worked out for you, Erich. And your English in impeccable. I just read your letter."

"Do you have time for a chat? Perhaps we could become reacquainted." His intense gaze delved into her soul.

"We're not the same people who met nine years ago."

"I believe we are, in the core of our beings. We've had joys and sorrows we haven't shared, so we have much to discover about each other."

She looked away. "I... yes... Well, I suppose we could sit on the veranda."

"I subscribed to the Gravenhurst newspaper when I was at Stoneridge Farm," he said as they walked down to the house. "And I was very sorry to read about the tragic death of your husband. It's hard enough to lose a childhood friend, but even more when he's also your partner."

"Thank you. I still feel lost without him." She wanted to make sure that Erich didn't have any expectations.

"I understand."

When they had settled on the veranda, she said, "I was going to offer you tea, but I think we both need a stiff drink. Scotch?"

He grinned. "Sure, thanks! It was a special occasion at Stoneridge Farm when Lloyd McKellar and I had a wee dram."

Merilee laughed.

"We serve it on the rocks in the summer. OK?" At his puzzled expression, she explained, "Over ice."

"I thought you meant we'd be sitting on the rocks."

"We could do that too. A new Muskoka experience - scotch on the rocks on the rocks."

His smile was disarming. "I've missed these rocks. Long ago, I carved my initials on one of them. Very small, but they're still noticeable. It was a declaration that I belonged here." He looked at her with such love and longing.

And she remembered the touch of his lips, the passion of their embraces.

Merilee suddenly felt hopeful.

Watch for more novels by Gabriele Wills at
Mindshadows.com

Online support for the author is greatly appreciated. If you enjoy
Gabriele's novels, visit theMuskokaNovels.com or
Mindshadows.com for links to "Like" her on Facebook, GoodReads,
and other social media.

Comments and questions are always welcome by email at
info@mindshadows.com

Author's Notes

The following notes might answer some readers' questions:

- Life in the German Prisoner of War (POW) camp in Gravenhurst was as described, surprising as it may seem. Prisoners "on parole" were allowed to swim in a fenced off section of the lake and run their own farm several miles away. Photos show that they had a pet bear.
- There was a civilian house within the POW camp enclosure, which eventually had a large soccer field/ skating rink right beside it for the prisoners.
- As mentioned in the book, 2 German POWs were murdered in the Medicine Hat camp by Nazis fanatics. 5 Nazis were tried and hanged in 1946 for the murders. In the Gravenhurst camp, one former POW recalled how he and his friends, who had spoken out against Nazism, had to escape through a window when SS officers broke into their room. They placed themselves into protective custody with the Canadian guards, and were given jobs outside the camp.
- Quite a few German POWs in Canada ended up working on farms, some living with the farm family who took responsibility for them. Many warm, lifelong friendships were formed, and the Canadians often sponsored those who wished to immigrate later.
- Over 35,000 German troops were sent to POW camps in Canada, and 6000 asked to remain there after the war. They had to be repatriated, but many immigrated once the Canadian government allowed that in 1951.
- The former sanatorium turned POW camp in Gravenhurst did indeed become a resort mostly catering to Jewish clientele after WWII. A few former prisoners returned, often with their wives, to see the place again. Most had very fond memories of their time in Muskoka and Canada.
- There is a plaque and illustrated info display at the site of the former POW camp in Gravenhurst. It's situated in the waterfront Ungerman Park. More information and plenty of photos can be found in Cecil Porter's rich history of the camp – *The Gilded Cage: Gravenhurst German Prisoner-of-War Camp 20 1940-1946*.
- The British Commonwealth Air Training Plan (BCATP) was one of Canada's major contributions to the Allied cause. It graduated over 131,000 aircrew, almost 73,000 of them Canadians. Many came from affluent families.

- 151 BCATP schools were established across Canada, with more than 100 airfields constructed, thus becoming the world's largest air training centre. U.S. President Franklin D. Roosevelt called Canada the "aerodrome of democracy".
- While many thousands of RCAF airmen served with British RAF squadrons, there were increasingly more dedicated Canadian squadrons overseas. This is especially true with No. 6 Group of Bomber Command, which was made up of 15 Canadian squadrons, like Ned's.
- The RCAF became the 4th largest air force in the world during WWII.
- 13,498 RCAF airmen lost their lives in WWII. 75% of those served with Bomber Command.
- The plane collision that Erich witnessed in Chapter 7 actually occurred. It wasn't until 2011 that the second plane was located at the bottom of Lake Muskoka. The remains of the two pilots – Ted Bates and Peter Campbell - were eventually recovered and received a military burial in Guelph, Ontario in 2013.
- The Wyndwood Convalescent Home for the RCAF was based on one that existed on Lake Muskoka, thanks to a family who donated their cottage for the duration of the war.
- "Little Norway" was established at the Toronto Island Airport in 1940, but elementary flight training transferred to Muskoka in the spring of 1942. There is a memorial to the Royal Norwegian Air Force (RNAF) at the Muskoka Airport, as well as a small museum. For more information, read Andrea Baston's excellent history of the RNAF in Canada - *Exile Air: World War II's "Little Norway" in Toronto and Muskoka.*
- There were 168 women from various nations, including 5 Canadians, in the Air Transport Auxiliary (ATA). Episodes in the novel are primarily based on real incidents. 16 women were killed in flying accidents. There are several fascinating memoirs by remarkable ladies, like Diana Barnato Walker, about their ATA flying adventures.
- More than 17,000 women served in the RCAF,WD (Women's Division). Training and life as a WD was much as described. Hundreds were sent to support the RCAF in Britain, mostly with No. 6 Group Bomber Command in Yorkshire, and some, like the photographers and clerks, with HQ in London.

- Unlike the RCAF,WDs on all the bases, the girls in London had to find their own accommodations, and as such, were not constrained by military routines and curfews. There was at least one WD in Britain who was only 19, despite 21 being the minimum age for overseas postings. Newfoundland did not become part of Canada until 1949, so it was "overseas". My friend Fay Patterson's mother, Isla, was a WD stationed in Gander, Nfld.
- The University of Toronto was one of the many organizations that sponsored child evacuees from Britain. Over 5,550 children came to Canada in 1940, but the overseas evacuation stopped after 77 children died when the *City of Benares* was sunk by a German U-boat in September 1940.
- The description of the Café de Paris bombing was taken from eyewitness accounts, as was the V1 rocket explosion on the Aldwych road between Adastral House and the BBC's Bush House, which Merilee witnessed.
- Dunn's Pavilion was a popular dancehall in Bala, with top bands such as Duke Ellington, Guy Lombardo, Glenn Miller Orchestra, and Louis Armstrong. It became the "Kee to Bala" in the 1960s when rock music dominated, and still attracts famous bands. Some of those include Aerosmith, Lighthouse, the Tragically Hip, and Drake.
- British actress Anna Neagle and her husband, Herbert Wilcox, did visit Air Marshal Billy Bishop's family at the Eaton cottage in Muskoka during a fund-raising tour. Billy's wife, Margaret, was the granddaughter of Timothy Eaton, founder of the famous department store and its catalogue, which is often referred to in the novel.
- Billy Bishop flew to Britain during the war on RCAF business, although he surprised his son, Arthur, when he showed up in London shortly after Arthur arrived in the UK. So, it's quite realistic that fictional Air Marshal Chas Thornton does as well.
- Canadians often ran into friends or connections while in Britain. Arthur Bishop's detailed memoir, *Winged Combat*, is filled with the names of people he came across while he was overseas. Meeting up with his (fictional) acquaintance, Drew, would not have been at all unusual. Trafalgar Square was popular with the Canadians, since several clubs specifically for them were located there, as well as "Canada House", the offices of the High Commission of Canada.

- While the Canadian army spent years in Britain awaiting action on the continent, the troops were building infrastructure and training. But on August 19, 1942, 5000 Canadians were involved in the disastrous raid on Dieppe. Over 900 died, and almost 2,000 became prisoners of war.
- The Muskoka Novels were inspired by visits to my friend Fay Patterson's century-old cottage on Lake Rosseau. Her father, Arthur, a tank regiment lieutenant, was captured at Dieppe and spent the rest of the war in a POW camp in Germany, as mentioned in the novel. His POW "friend" Ross Tremayne is fictional.
- The Canadian army played a significant role in the defeat of Italy from 1943 and then Germany from D-Day in 1944. Canadians are still fondly remembered and feted annually for liberating the Netherlands and bringing supplies to the starving populace.
- The Dutch royal family lived in exile in Canada, as mentioned, and indeed, Princess Margriet was born in Ottawa in 1943. As thanks for this refuge and for the liberation of their homeland, the future Queen Juliana sent Canada 100,000 tulip bulbs. Further donations of 10,000 tulips annually inspired the Tulip Festival in Ottawa in 1953, and continues to this day, with bulbs still arriving yearly from the grateful Netherlands.
- My parents were ethnic Germans born in Hungary. They and their family members who weren't married to true Hungarians were expelled from their homeland post-war – losing their homes, livelihoods, all possessions except what each could carry in a suitcase - and dumped into war-ravaged, starving Germany along with about 13 million other "Displaced Persons" (DPs). Just teenagers, they met and eventually married in old army barracks in Bavaria, where I was born, and we emigrated to Canada when I was three. I'm forever grateful to them for choosing Canada, and Canada, for accepting us!
- Great care was taken to realistically portray the era. For example, although some expressions may sound very modern to our ears, all slang was verified through *The Oxford Dictionary of Slang*. Research materials included hundreds of books and other sources.

For additional information, including reviews, please visit
theMuskokaNovels.com

Other Novels by Gabriele Wills:

The Summer Before the Storm
Book 1 of the Muskoka Novels

Muskoka, 1914. It's the Age of Elegance in the summer playground of the affluent and powerful. Amid the pristine island-dotted lakes of the Canadian wilderness, the young and carefree amuse themselves with glittering balls and courtly romances. When Jack Wyndham, the destitute son of a disowned heir, joins his privileged family at their cottage, sparks fly and life will never be the same. He schemes to better himself through alliances with the Wyndhams' elite social circle, as well as with his beautiful and audacious cousin, Victoria.

But their charmed lives begin to unravel with the onset of the Great War, in which many are destined to become part of the "lost generation".

This richly textured tale takes the reader on an unforgettable journey from romantic moonlight cruises to the horrific sinking of the *Lusitania*, from regattas on the water to combat in the skies over France, from extravagant mansions to deadly trenches - from innocence to nationhood.

The Summer Before The Storm, the first of the epic Muskoka Novels, evokes a gracious, bygone era that still resonates in this legendary land of lakes.

The Summer Before The Storm was selected for the esteemed Muskoka Chautauqua Reading List in 2010.

Elusive Dawn
Book 2 of The Muskoka Novels

Elusive Dawn continues to follow the lives, loves, and fortunes of the privileged Wyndham family and their friends. While some revel in the last resplendent days of the season at their Muskoka cottages, others continue to be drawn inexorably into the Great War, going from a world of misty sunrises across a tranquil lake to deadly moonlight bombing raids, festering trenches, and visceral terror.

For Victoria Wyndham, too many things have happened to hope that life would ever return to normal, that innocence could be regained. Caught in a vortex of turbulent events and emotions, she abandons the safety of the sidelines in Britain for the nightmare of

France. Her fate as an ambulance driver remains entwined with those of her summer friends, all bound by a sense of duty.

Living in the shadows of fear and danger awakens the urgency to grasp life, to live more immediately, more passionately amid the enormity of unprecedented death. Those who survive this cataclysmic time are forever changed, like Canada itself.

Impeccably researched, beautifully written, *Elusive Dawn* will resonate with the reader long after the final page has been turned.

Under the Moon
Book 3 of The Muskoka Novels

The catastrophic Great War is over, but the survivors now face the final battle - to rebuild their shattered lives and protect their secrets. Some find solace amid the rugged beauty and serenity of the Muskoka lakes. Others seek to reinvent themselves among the avant-garde of decadent Paris and the opulence of the blossoming Riviera.

Meanwhile, the inevitable momentum of civilization ushers in a daring new era of scandalous excess and social upheaval that threatens the strictures of Edwardian society. On the forefront of this revolution are two diametrically opposed Wyndham cousins, Lizzie and Esme, who struggle to defy convention in the name of love and ambition. Only time will tell whether their worlds are ready to embrace change.

In this gripping third volume of the acclaimed Muskoka Novels series, Gabriele Wills vividly evokes the triumph and tragedy of the glittering Jazz Age as it seduces a privileged summer community, and we stand witness to its sultry dance on the dock, *Under the Moon*.

A Place to Call Home

Set in the turbulent, formative years of Ontario, this compelling saga spans five decades and two generations. Barely surviving a disastrous journey on a cholera-ridden immigrant ship, Rowena O'Shaughnessy and her family settle in the primitive backwoods of Upper Canada in 1832. Her complex relationship with the wealthy and powerful Launston family leads to tragedy, and eventually to redemption.

Their lives are played out against a rich tapestry of events - devastating plagues, doomed rebellions, mob uprisings, religious conflict, and political unrest.

A Place to Call Home is a novel about Canada, and its less civilized pioneer past.

Moon Hall

Two women who live a century apart. Two stories that interweave to form a rich tapestry of intriguing characters, evocative places, and compelling events.

Escaping from a disintegrating relationship in the city, writer Kit Spencer stumbles upon a quintessential Norman Rockwell village in the Ottawa Valley, where she buys an old stone mansion, "Moon Hall". But her illusions about idyllic country life are soon challenged by reality. Juxtaposed is the tragedy of Violet McAllister, the ghost that reputedly haunts Moon Hall, who comes vividly to life through her long-forgotten diary.

Moon Hall is a gripping tale of relationships in crisis, and touches on the full spectrum of human emotions – from raw violence and dark passions to compassion and love.

About the Author : Gabriele Wills

Born in Germany, Gabriele emigrated to Canada as a young child. With degrees in the social sciences and education, she's had a varied career as an educator, literacy coordinator, and website designer, and has been an active community volunteer, particularly in heritage preservation and the arts. She also produced an award-nominated feature on CBC Radio.

Her real passion, however, is to weave compelling stories around meticulously researched and often quirky or arcane facts in order to bring the past vividly to life.

Gabriele grew up in Lindsay, Ontario, enjoyed several years in the Ottawa area, and currently resides in Guelph. The sublimely beautiful Muskoka lakes provide soul food and inspiration.

Made in the USA
Monee, IL
17 April 2021